Prologue

Innocent of its beauty and the importance of its title, Nitaya lived all of her young life on the planet Mizar. The oldest known and third aligned planet in the far procession of four, Mizar was referred to as the Bright One for its array of Day Circles and the almost seemingly endless supply of light they cast to the neighboring worlds. Mostly dry and uninhabitable, Mizar remained well known for its endless dunes of sand that blanketed without bias over the vast landscape. With only patches of sanctuary scattered through its globe, the water oasis created remote homes for many of its people. Amongst such a treasured haven, hidden quietly at the base of the Quitorta Mountains, young Nitaya lived.

Oasis Nyllo, large, cavernous and richly thick with the growth of greens, easily flourished with minimal assistance from its tenders compared in contrast to its harsh, outer habitat of arid, sandy sea. Its grand waterfall effortlessly offered nutrients to the welcoming ground, bringing forth wonders of flora rarely known to those beyond its sanctuary. The waterfall or Quito Falls as it had been titled for the Mountains that had given it life, soared high into the sky at the heart of Nyllo, providing an endless bounty of nourishment rarely known throughout the dunes of Mizar. Often standing at its base, Nitaya would shield her eyes in a repeated attempt to spy the top, searching eagerly on tip-toe for the answer to its source, only to once again be halted by the blinding light of the second Day Circle.

Mizar was indeed blessed with the gift of light, of three blazing orbs that expectedly danced their fated pattern throughout the sky. Offering their warmth for eighteen hazon of the day, each rotated in and out of the endless blue above. Only

1

then, as the third hunkered low to the east, did the darkness fill their sacred world. As the shadows of the Quitorta Mountains consumed them, the only remaining lights guiding those on the ground were those which were handmade. With the sky giving into that final cycle of complete darkness, the Mizans lit their paths, creating their own way above their heads so they could live amongst the lushness at their feet. Yet as the darkness possessed its array of endless wonders for Nitaya, it was the constant rise of the first Day Circle that she secretly dreaded.

Providing their warmth of life, the trio of orbs circling the globe and their eighteen hazon of heat allowed each lengthy day to be filled with wondrous things to see and experience. Despite all that Nyllo had to offer however, young Nitaya remained ever distracted.

A slender, though strong young girl, with long, dark brown and eyes that could at one glance appear the color of the Quito Falls and at another the shade of the dark sky, Nitaya possessed more than external beauty, for it was her quizzical mind that had all others cringing as they awaited her next whim. Her skin, unlike her temperament however, remained new and pale, regardless of the Day Circle's shine, for her Momar Lydra, ever the doter, saw careful to her tending. That is, she saw to it when she was not as usual laboring over some more *serious matter.*

"Oh, how can anything in Nyllo be so dire?" Nitaya thought, turning from the wall and rolling over to lay flat on her back. Resettling in her high bunk and staring out into the open sky through the ceiling glass above her, Nitaya again lay silent, listening to the expected rain, its droplets playing their soft music upon the glass. The dance they created, seemingly only for her as the first of the Day Circle's rose into the sky, always had her dreaming in awe, curious as to what lay beyond her small world. Yet as the colorful glow of light intensified and the droplets played out their final steps of the dance, Nitaya's thoughts were forced to return to the present.

It was far passed time for Nitaya to be up and prepared for the day that began eons ago for others, yet as always she dreaded placing her bare feet on the cold floor. Instead, shivering off the thought and defiantly pulling her cover up to her chin, Nitaya lay still a moment longer focusing on the sounds of the world about her small room. Rubbing her small feet together as she always did, she wished she could remain in her cozy nest a while longer.

After delaying the inevitable as long as she dared, Nitaya reluctantly tossed her cover aside and rose, grumbling and traipsing across her small room. Her feet soon adjusting to the coolness below, she began changing out of her night garb and into her work clothes of dull grays and blues.

"Oh, how I dread this," she thought, running her hands down the length of her dress. She paused to stare at her reflection in the glass. "There is just so much else I would rather do!"

Sighing, Nitaya turned away from her image, slowly separating and pulling her long brown tresses into the standard three rolled sections as was custom amongst the Nyllo females. With the final pins at last secured at the nape of her heck, she stood back, tilting her head and imagining herself clad in a lengthy gown, dancing with the one that would one day claim her heart. Yet as the image of gray returned to the glass, Nitaya again sighed, returning to the task of tidying her things.

Finishing with the straightening of her cover then turning to see that once again all was as it should be...as it had always been, Nitaya scanned the room, turning lastly to pat her favorite small blanket upon her bunk before heading out into the day. If only she knew what a day it would be.

***

Stepping out onto the rising to the right of the falls, Nitaya looked down to the routine busyness below. All proved the same as each day before, and the day before that and Nitaya could not help but shake her head as the tenders rounded silently to their tasks. As always Jovaar was there, scurrying about with his usual smirk, taking notice of her up above.

"It is passed time, Nitaya," he shouted above the din of the falls, waving to her from below. A tender passed by with several tools, Jovaar easing his load by claiming one for himself. "You must hurry, Nitaya. Your Momar will notice and worry."

3

She knew Jovaar's words to be true and with a rather showy sigh of her shoulders as her answer, Nitaya reluctantly grabbed hold of the smooth pinus railing to descend the spiral staircase into her fated world.

"So good to see you this day, Jovaar," she began as usual, meeting the elder at the mid-level landing where he had risen to meet her. Nodding yet saying nothing, Jovaar gestured with his eyes, taking notice of the day circle above them.

"I know, I know," Nitaya answered his unspoken order, only slightly quickening her pace down the lengthy stairs. "I am on my way."

As Mizans of all ages and races rushed about her '*going nowhere,*' or so she thought as she toyed with a rare jagged sliver of the pinus railing beneath her palms, Nitaya paused to stare as they scurried to gather the day's nourishment or hurried to help those who were. It was once again harvesting time of the cympas, and harvesting time was the busiest time of all at their station.

The cympas, sweet within with the moistest of juices were encased in the hardest of shells and Nitaya knew how true this was by the scar on her right thigh. Rubbing it just once before descending further down to the ground below, she looked back at Jovaar and thought back several onars to yet another time of her learning.

***

When Nitaya had grown to but six, Jovaar had demonstrated to her how to properly skin the cympas, teaching her that it was important to know, understand and most importantly appreciate what those around her labored for nourishment. Patiently, he had gently sat her down, showing her how to properly use the sybar stone to cut through its tough outer shell. Showing her impatience and *great wisdom* however, Nitaya stubbornly sat to show *him* that she could do it without assistance. Perched on a large stone and placing the cympas between her knees, Nitaya struck it forcefully with her sybar, only to miss on her first try, striking her thigh.

Jovaar merely stood shaking his head.

***

"Such a foolish act," Nitaya mumbled, looking out into the busying crowd and unconsciously rubbing at her scar. Shaking the distant thoughts from her mind as she felt Jovaar's stare at her back, Nitaya stretched her arms wide then headed down to ground level and into the world that thrived without her below.

Nitaya reached the final tier of her staircase at the water's edge and breathing deeply, relished the wonderous, moist air. Closing her eyes as the steam from the falls lifted ever so slightly, giving her a slight misting at her ankles, she stood silent allowing the dew to moisten her skin. The smells of the greens dancing in the air proved glorious, creating with the falls their familiar sense of beginnings.

The surrounding vibrant flowers of sydadis and umperti emitted their sweet smell that blended perfectly with the greens of gytmus and riolus. Nitaya, of all things she easily dismissed, never took these wonderful scents for granted, and rather, took great pride in her people for not disrupting their beauty.

Kneeling and opening her eyes to flutter a gytmus bulb amongst her fingers, she enjoyed the creation for just a spell before surrendering to the fact it was indeed time to go below. Sighing with resignation and rising, she brushed her now dew-covered hands on the length of her cover.

"It is time," she thought, rising and facing the gloriousness of the falls. Taking one final peek at its top, Nitaya stopped to rub her eyes at the Day Circle boring down upon her. Reluctantly turning at the approach of another worker, she headed off to the dreaded Lower Levels and her most certainly impatiently awaiting Momar.

Inhaling the simplistic beauty a final time, Nitaya gave in to the inevitable and crossed over the aged Falen Bridge. Passed the people, the smells, and the organized busyness of it all, she at last reached the large Crossing Door. Secretly enjoying her repeated ritual of arriving at the Lower Levels entrance, Nitaya sauntered up to Hylin, who stood stoically at attention, as always.

"He is *truly* handsome," she thought, covering her obvious grin with her hand. Rounding the bend of thick riolus, she allowed its branches to fall away at her back. "If only he was not so old."

Hylin proved a giant to Nitaya's small stature, with reddish blond hair that swept passed his shoulders and the greenest of eyes that resembled the color of gytmus. At the sound of her arrival through the greens to his right, he looked up at the sky as Jovaar had done only moments earlier, and spied the placing of the Day Circle, noting the time to Nitaya with only the squinting of his deep green eyes.

"Yes," she thought, wringing her hands as she neared. "I am late once again. But oh, do you have nothing to say?"

As was his norm, Hylin said nothing at Nitaya's silent protest and only stood, looking slightly amused. She knew her Momar and Palle would be most displeased.

Respectfully, Hylin opened the large door for the young arrival and nodding in turn, Nitaya began to descend the sterile series of stairs. With the dampness settling into her skin with each lowering step, Nitaya at last arrived at the First Sublevel...what her Palle deemed the Life Floor.

She rarely visited the many rooms on this level, at least that is what her Momar and Palle were led to believe. Yet in truth, she often stopped to visit Khyra who spent a few spare moments when she could showing Nitaya what she was studying or what she had built to make the upper world work as efficiently as possible. Khyra had informed her at their first meeting that the entire level had been built for, and remained dedicated to, that purpose alone. She had smiled as she said the Mizans above knew nothing of her work below, living wonderful if not moderate and ignorant lives. Khyra had said it pleased her that she could be of assistance without selfish ideals. Nitaya had immediately taken to her.

The first door to Nitaya's right, she knew, contained a type of home for greenery, a shelter for graftings of nourishment greens creating what could one day be a major source of sustenance if Khyra got her way.

"Oh, how she loved producing the impossible!" Nitaya thought, envying her wise elder and dallying amongst the greens

6

on one of her visits. "If only I was given such an important task."

Khyra was quite tall and only slightly gray for her age and was an endless source of wisdom to Nitaya and an underappreciated soul to the world above who knew nothing of her existence. To Nitaya though, she was simply a second Momar and a great, understanding friend, and oh how she enjoyed the times they had shared for no one listened to her young cares quite as well as she.

Despite her many onars, Khyra above all others seemed to understand Nitaya's true feelings and at most times, instead of offering her age-wise wisdom, she would merely sit and listen as Nitaya spoke of all her troubles. On many occasions they had included Hylin and Khyra had never once showed disapproval. Yes, Nitaya had grown to love Khyra. Unfortunately though on this day, there was no sign of her dear elder, and sighing, Nitaya continued on down the narrow corridor.

The next door to her left contained the oddest of gadgets and whatnots that Nitaya admitted she had never quite understood, Rarely did she visit Khyra while she worked there for she simply preferred to play amongst the greens. Tip-toeing now to peer into the small, high glass of the door, Nitaya shook her head at Khyra's odd notions on the slabs within.

Understanding in her own way how things were produced in the world above, Nitaya could not however, fathom how these so-called *miracle gadgets*...or so her elder had deemed them, could change their lives for the better. Nitaya trusted Khyra however, and was confident that her silly, miracle gadgets that lay untouched in the now darkened room, would someday play a part in their future.

Nitaya hummed, tracing her small fingers down the coolness of the outer wall as she continued on down the pass, clearing the last of the doors without consideration. The last remained locked to all but Khyra and her Palle, and although she was forever curious, often jumping to peek through the small glass each held, this time Nitaya continued reluctantly to the next set of stairs. This next descent led directly to Sublevel Four.

"How odd," Nitaya thought, shaking her head as she reconsidered the most curious of names to a level a mere two levels below ground. "Why would Palle deem the second tier to be titled Sublevel Four?"

Nitaya supposed it was because the stairs below seemed eternal as she wound quickly down their length, often skipping steps two at a time with the coolness growing with each leap. "But why not name it Sublevel Two? And why would Palle never explain?"

Shrugging, Nitaya sighed, shaking off her repeated question from all her previous days and instead hurried to the next level. "Almost there," she thought, rounding the next bend. "Almost there."

At last rounding the final curve of the corridor, Nitaya released the end of the rail, having reached her destination. As usual, the rather large barricade remained guarded by her Palle's regular sentries, X-Dor and X-Dom. Shifting her stance, Nitaya stood shoulders back to greet them.

Amused at the necessity of the pair of orbs for such a hidden and well guarded place, Nitaya could not help but smirk, tipping her head to watch their separation. One orb, transforming into separate shapes of smaller ovals, appeared to blink acceptance of her arrival.

"Good morning, X-D's," she said, chuckling.

"Good morning, Miss Nitaya," they echoed in return, preprogrammed for response to her usual arrival. "Please place your eyes before the lenses."

"Tedious and useless," Nitaya thought repeating her steps as she had on all previous days, following the order. "No one knows what is here, or *why* it is here for that matter, but as Palle has always said 'protocol is protocol,'" she mumbled with a deepened tone, hands on hips and echoing her elder's words.

Nitaya leaned forward, shaking her head before pausing, letting the scan pass over the daily random, required eye. After a brief pause, the green light scanned above the chosen retina, and the announcement of *"all to proceed"* reverberated throughout the corridor, offering their consent of passage. X-Dor and X-Dom appeared to blink their approval, yet as she again stood erect, eyeing the wonders of the devices rejoining into a single orb, Nitaya recalled her Momar's long ago words, assuring her it was merely their program and not humanism. Nitaya however, could not help but wonder. As the green light altered to orange and the double D's with their reflective cover shielded what one would now consider a single eye, their tube-like neck receded back into the wall and the large double doors slowly opened in welcome.

Silent with hope for something new from the tedium, yet knowing she would again be disappointed, Nitaya peered out into the large room. The underground world once again came to life before her.

***

Lights randomly, yet expectantly flashed amongst the enormous panels of the room, their bright colors of green, red and yellow synchronized into a musical rhythm danced seemingly without guidance. Despite their twinkle against the pale grays of the Lower Level walls, Nitaya's full attention was drawn to her Momar, Palle and of course, the ever eager Norell.

"Ah, Norell is at Palle's side I see," Nitaya thought sarcastically, shaking her head and crossing the threshold, the X-D's long forgotten as the doors closed swiftly at her back. As was the norm, no one appeared to take notice or interest of her arrival, reminding her once again of her less than important role amongst her family. The enthusiastic, knowledge-driven child with soft tendrils matching Palle, however, stood both solid and conforming amongst the panels and their dancing lights, proving once again to Nitaya that Norell would remain their Palle's dream.

Nitaya approached the trio hesitantly, their appearance more restrained than typical, choosing to stand just to their right, leaning back against a low bank of panels. Receiving Norell's typical stare of intrusion she returned his disgust with a silent snarl, yet all traces of sibling rivalry were erased as their eyes diverted to the main screen positioned high at the central consol of the room.

"They have arrived," Norell said, unflinching and without turning, instead staring mouth agape at the enormous image on the screen. Assuming she understood what he was referring to, Nitaya crossed around him with casual step to look closer,

9

though soon realized she was undoubtedly wrong. Norell was not toying with her this day.

"Switch to your lo-con panel and scan to penetrating level three," Palle said commandingly, Nitaya's quizzical eyes turning from Norell to her elder. "We must scan to be certain."

The second-level pynars seated before Palle held his absolute attention, following the standard order after gaining what they stated to be additional approval, adding something referred to as 'micro-tech scanners' to their search. Nitaya, intrigued by their urgency yet uncertain of its cause, found she could not look away.

The Lower Level pynars, performing dissimilar tasks to those working alongside the oblivious people above intrigued Nitaya, for as she was able to interact with those below, regardless at a distance. The headshields they bore were made from melted iron, formed to the individual's head, protruding with the oddest of shape which caused her to stare. Her Palle had informed her onars before when she first had come to know of the world beneath the ground, that they were all the same, all holding the same purpose, yet their headshields were sized and appropriated by rank. A younger, or lower-level pynar, received a smaller headshield and lesser tasks, yet they would be recast larger with their growing rank and status.

"How odd," Nitaya often thought, wishing she could reach out to touch one of their prided caps. "What if a younger Pynar simply had a larger head? How would one sleep wearing such a contraption? Surely they would often bumb into one another." Although desperately eager to learn the answers to her questions, Nitaya was rarely one to challenge her Palle and instead, chose to keep these particulars to herself, saving her inquisitions for something that would prove more worthy.

Sensing the urgency of her Palle's pynars, Nitaya turned swiftly, noting them surprisingly panicked at their stations. Panic was a trait she had never before witnessed from the beings. Pivoting to scan the other faces of the room, her hands holding firm to the bank of panels at her back, fear filled her as all concentrated only on their own minimal screens or the large one at the central station.

Even those with tasks of tidying were staring in silence. Aware of someone oddly watching her, Nitaya turned to Norell who remained at their Palle's side and silently grumbled at the demanding look of his eyes. Clearly they gestured, 'I know you do not understand because you never pay attention.' Exasperated with his correct summation, Norell huffed, grandly pointing to the top, right screen panel.

"Patch side-screen five to main," Palle ordered, the pynars quickly following his word. With the main screen altering within mere moments from his order, Nitaya became even more baffled, shaking her head at Norell before turning back to the large screen, the panel baring nothing but endless blankets of sand. The oddness of silenced lights, those that had proven to never cease their dance across the sea of panels however, rippled a stilled chill over her skin.

"They have landed in quadrant four," the elder pynar said, unturning. Palle rounded the being's long shield and lowering his gaze to the individual station, squinted to get a closer look.

"Zoom in," he ordered, the pynar tapping his panel. Momar leaned over his shoulder and Norell's fears became transparent as he too stepped closer to Palle. Nitaya, unable to contain her own fears, released the panels at her back to cross to the main console at the rear of the others, at last understanding what the commotion was about. The image on the screen grew with each step.

The ship that now filled the large panel stood massive, frightening against the glow of sand surrounding its frame, like nothing she had ever seen. Shaped like the large leaf of an artibust tree yet slightly pointed at its front, the craft rounded at its sides, flattening out on its end with what appeared to be stems spanning from its backside.

"They must be the exhausts," Nitaya thought, pride filling her that she may have understood at least part of the craft. Despite her fleeting moment of clarity however, she trembled as her roaming eyes fell upon the ship's base. Mounted atop what appeared to be an enormous foot, Nitaya shivered, considering the actual size and realness of the ship.

"Why, it could stomp out the entire oasis," she thought, her lips parting in awe as she stared at the craft's large support. Frightening as the enormous shaft appeared however, Nitaya's attention was soon drawn toward the front of the craft.

"Four canons," Palle said interrupting her thoughts, crossing round the elder pynar to the panel to direct the attention of the others. "Another four at the belly," he added, surprising Nitaya as if pointing with almost personal knowledge.

Although alarming to Nitaya for both its size and the look of fear it brought to her Momar's eyes, Nitaya could see no noticeable movement on the outside of the craft. Wringing her hands against the anticipation of what could possibly come, she attempted to calm her nerves against the motionless scene. Who, and more importantly what lie in the massive ship, Nitaya could not imagine, yet the tenseness of her Palle, Momar, and even Norell made her realize that this was not just any ordinary visitor.

The pynars stared anxiously with the others, awaiting a sign from the unannounced visitor and soon Nitaya found herself leaning closer to the main station. Staring, she spied a previously hidden small door atop the ship opened, seemingly splitting in two at its center. Startlingly, a foreign being shot out feet first from within.

"How is that possible?" Nitaya asked unintentionally aloud, both Palle and the elder pynar turning to her words. Her Momar, fingers laced, merely closed her eyes in prayer as Norell unable to open his own cowered at her back.

***

"Hurry," Palle shouted, Nitaya instinctively stepping back, returning to the tall bank of stations in an attempt to get out of the way. Her hands once again flush against the coolness of the lower panels she clawed desperately for something to hold.

All but the lone pynar hunching over the main controls began rushing about their emergency duties amongst the resumed colorful lights. In all directions, Nitaya watched pynars changing screens, adjusting controls and sounding out alarms, each performing their own tasks as orders rang out over the com, yet as dutiful as they appeared, Nitaya could clearly see fear in their large eyes.

Palle, although obviously shaken by the strange arrival, continued directing his orders as he had done so many times during testing. His strong voice ringing out for all to hear, Nitaya could not grasp the exact meaning of his words for they proved far from typical. High-pitched and eager, yet firm and organized, Nitaya remained confused by her palle's guidance.

"Open the rear hatch-gate," Palle ordered the lead controller, gesturing to the instant-altering side screen.

"Sir," the pynar questioned, looking from his panel for the first time.

"Send out two transoids to scout the area," he added, nodding to Momar before looking back to the pynar reluctantly following his word. "The rear gate is our only vantage point."

"What is happening?" Nitaya whispered, no one hearing her whimpered cry. Releasing the bank of controls, she dodged two workers, crossing to her Momar's side to cling to the folds of her gown. "I do not understand," she said fearfully, her momar turning to touch her cheek.

"We can never be completely certain, child," Momar said, attempting to bear a brave face. "But no matter what, you must promise me that you will remain at my side at all times. I must know that you are with me, always."

"I will," Nitaya answered, nodding. Momar patted her hand then turned back to Palle and the main panel, Norell gritting his teeth yet refusing to look into her eyes. Continuing her firm grasp of her momar's gown, Nitaya anxiously waited with the others for the first sighting of the rear hatch and Palle's transoids.

***

Nitaya had, as far back as she could remember, been curious about the transoid beings, and although she did not completely understand the specifics of how they operated or even how they were built, she had in time learned enough to appreciate them as almost human. Momar Lydra had told her at a young age that even her GraPalle was a transoid being, and although Nitaya had not known him as his true self prior to the chosen transformation, she dearly loved him for what he was.

GraPalle had over the last several onars given Nitaya simple answers as to how he had come to be, and sitting on his knees amongst the greens below the falls, she eagerly listened to his every word. Nitaya had hung on his every word for she simply accepted each description as it was given, for within her young heart she loved him, and that was all that truly mattered.

"Only a select few are revered and chosen to become a transoid," GraPalle humbly told her so long ago, sitting at their usual spot at the base of the falls. "They must be of some value to the Resistance, perhaps for their knowledge of greens and nourishment for those above or maybe for their advanced understanding of technological systems that are used both below in the Lower Levels and beyond passed the wonderous Day Circles. Yet no matter the reason, my dearest Nitaya, they must possess uniqueness for them to be chosen for life extension."

Nitaya had heard the term *Resistance* several times before yet never proved brave enough to ask the questions she longed to learn answers to. GraPalle had mentioned it quite often as they had walked amongst the greens, vaguely describing the lives of those Nitaya could only imagine, yet when he had attempted to offer more, they had been sternly interrupted by Momar Lydra, informing them both that a child of her age should not worry of such matters.

"But Norell is allowed to be…" Nitaya had stammered, pointing in his direction on one occasion, noting he was encouraged to learn of the outer world. Momar had merely shaken her head at her anger, instead leading Nitaya to the tasks that she had described were more suited to a girl of her stature.

Toiling without a given purpose as expected each day within the Lower Levels, Nitaya grumbled, assisting where needed…tidying stations, sorting aged document files or performing some other meaningless task. Although she knew these assignments made it difficult to learn more about what was truly important to those below, she secretly admitted that the happenings meant little to her and that she longed to spend her onars above learning from GraPalle or playing below the falls with her friend Elari.

Yet as the pynars now scrambled about her for their own understanding, Nitaya somehow knew that this day of all days was different, for surely from the look of her Palle's face this was not a routine test. Instead, at this most anxious time, she stood nervously wringing her hands at the central station waiting to understand, for she was certain that this was a day she would never forget.

**

Staring wide-eyed at the jumble of multiple screens with the center panel bearing the oddly-shaped ship, Nitaya watched anxiously as in succession additional beasts popped from above its hardened shell. Their numbers were rapidly growing. Another screen to her right held the Lower Level's rear hatch-gate where her Palle had ordered the two transoids to emerge, yet though the large ship and strange visitors proved gripping, this remote site is what now held the attention of all below.

Human-like despite their metal exterior and proving extremely agile, the transoids moved free of weapons. At the ready and willing to serve however, on this particular order, Nitaya noticed they were unusually mounted with an array of additional gear. Her skin prickled with a growing fear.

On all previous occasions that Nitaya had been privileged to be in contact with the beings, she had seen that they were gentle, or "defensive-prone," as he palle had said. Consisting solely of their metal-like bodies with a pack secured to their back, that she understood due to the teachings of her GraPalle, carried their *life line* they had been slow moving, obedient and loyal. This day however, the pair was armed with what appeared to be weapons, although Nitaya could not be certain for she was never able to be present...unlike Norell, when they were in use.

Far different from anything she had ever seen, the mere size of their gear had her trembling for Nitaya was certain that whatever would erupt from the large holes at the ends of the shafts would most certainly blow a cympas from its root. Standing frightened at her Momar's side, she leaned closer, unable to turn from the pair, noting that each carried other large,

15

foreign equipment as they exited the hatch. Despite the added baggage, each transoid moved surprisingly with ease.

Not knowing their uses, Nitaya turned to her Palle's shout, his deep voice giving the order to patch side screen to main. As the once defensive-prone beings made their way round the backside of the Lower Levels, her heart raced as they crept their way through the tall, dense brush that served as camouflage for the station. Watching them pick up their pace with the thinning greens, racing through the zone that held the series of air vents specifically placed throughout the area to support the lower ventilation functions, her heart beat faster as if she raced alongside them. Whatever the transoids were about to face, she was certain from the size of the gear they carried, the numbers they were facing, and the tone of her Palle's words that it was evil.

"If this area of the greens was investigated closely it could pose a serious threat," her GraPalle had told her so long ago during one of their walks through the outer quadrant. "We are fortunate that those above do not venture this deep into the vines," he continued, further from Nyllo's center and deep within the brush, pausing to check the airflow amongst the dense brush. "If they were to find out our little secret…" he added, pausing to hold out his hand to assist young Nitaya over one of the many fallen trees. "Who would know for certain how damaging that could be to our cause?"

Although not truly understanding her GraPalle's fears, Nitaya said nothing as they continued their walk through the brush. Instead, merely nodding, she chose to enjoy the time shared, leaving all that nonsense about bad things happening to Norell. Hopping over the next fallen limb, she had grabbed her GraPalle's cool, metallic hand so her elder could lead her further into the dense greens. Oh how she loved listening to his stories.

***

Eyeing the main screen closely, despite Norell's increasing whimpers, Nitaya watched the transoids make their way through the landscape of dark pinus and oarkla, recognizing the undergrowth of gytmus and the rising of the riolus from her

16

long ago walks with her GraPalle. To her amazement, the beings inched closer to the ship. Eyeing the heavily clad pair at last reaching the edge of sand just beyond the craft, Nitaya glanced back to the side screen to grasp the count of the ever increasing numbers of the enemy.

"Please hurry," she thought, wringing her hands loose from her Momar's gown, the two beings at last setting foot onto the bright sand. Yet as she considered their odds, glancing from one screen to the other, Nitaya retracted her plea and rather prayed silently that they would hold at a distance for she was certain that the enemy's numbers, which which were still growing, were far too great for the lonely pair.

Unable to turn away, the Day Circle's light dancing off the flatness of sand, Nitaya stood transfixed, looking out into the openness of the place she was forever forbidden to go. Unable to turn away, she saw the transoids creeping their way closer to the enemy. Amazed to have the remote images of what she considered a sacred place before her, Nitaya squinted at the brightness the sand created all the while the transoids formed their station at the base of the closest mound.

Watching the droids prepare their gear within the small inset of sand to the right of the ship, Nitaya stood unmoving as they began laying out their surveillance. The transoids were however, immediately spotted, and she watched in horror as the strange, darkened metallic beasts took them with little difficulty. The battle, if a mere moment without fire could be described with a single word, was over. Her palle lowered his head, having no words

***

Instead of providing logistical data for her palle, the transoids had obviously encouraged the darkened beasts forward. Several now hovered over the mangled metal remains of their bodies, and Nitaya placed her hands over her eyes in attempt to block out the evil images. Yet hearing her GraPalle's teaching words in the back of her mind, knowing that she could not look away if she was to truly understand, she reluctantly peeked through her delicate fingers, watching with tear-filled eyes as the beasts kicked the transoid bodies, scouring the area for their own information.

Seeming to recognize the technology of the droids, one of the beasts appeared to set out to gathering anything not destroyed, yet it was the remaining four that drew Nitaya's attention. Ceasing their search and returning to the deformed remains, Nitaya stood in horror as one knelt next to the first droid, pulling it forward and turning it over to remove its heart.

The transoid heart was located at the crest of the head just beneath the cap and knowing its location. Standing transfixed, unconsciously lowering her arms to her sides, she eyed the beasts that remained on foot call forth for what appeared to be a non-fighter, or one that at least did not carry a weapon. This sixth being, scampering clumsily up the bank of sand toward them, immediately sat next to the other, beginning without order to remove the metallic outer layers of metallic skin, easily locating the small mound within.

Obviously having performed this task before, the being followed suit with the second droid with little difficulty then when satisfied, placed the two hearts within a small container and rose, nodding to his counterparts before quickly, yet clumsily trudging his way back toward the massive ship. All that transpired took place under the guarded supervision of those four standing, although they had done nothing to interfere as their counterparts scoured the surrounding areas. However, once the heart-seeker had retreated, the largest being gestured for the others to return to the site, simultaneously appearing to be listening to his hand.

"What is he doing?" Nitaya thought, startled by a pynar whisking by, ramming her without care. As if in a daze, Nitaya had forgotten that her palle and the others were busily making preparations for the invasion of the uninvited ones. Sensing no urgency from the arrivals however, Nitaya was confident that even if they gained the location of the oasis, they would never find the entrance to the lower levels. Turning back to the colorful, blinking lights and watching her palle's eyes for a sign, Nitaya's confidence waned as he again lowered his head, the majority of his pynars leaving their stations and retreating from the room.

"We are out of time," palle said at last, slamming his fist at the pynar's station. Nitaya jumped, startled from his words. "Sound out the alarm that all sectors are to rebound to Sector Two, board their assigned miniducts and head to the rendezvous!"

Palle could do nothing more to help those above. Ordering the controller pynar to patch several screens to show various stations throughout the oasis, he stood back silently, leaning on the rear consol and covering his mouth with his hand as chaos erupted in the upper world. Nitaya, Momar Lydra and Norell could do nothing to help.

No one above appeared to understand what they were running from, yet hearing the second sounding of the Roaring Horns, each immediately dropped their tools, racing toward Sector Two. Momars instantaneously released the knots that held the cympas at their backs, grasping at their young while they ran through the thick outer brush toward the transports, leaving behind everything they had ever known without question. Racing passed the oarklas and stamping down the gytmus and riolus, Nitaya knew that those would be nothing more than memories against the outer layers of Nyllo.

Many reached the miniducts, yet many more did not. Women and children and even some men appeared trampled in the chaos, their bodies scattered amongst the crushed greens throughout the debarking sector. Nitaya could not hold back her tears. Looking from one screen to the other, her hands in fists of both rage and fear, she spied another transport appear fired and detached only half full.

Crossing to stand at the image at her lower right, Nitaya muffled her shouts with her hands, watching her closest friend Elari emerge frightened on the lower screen. Wide-eyed and staring within a breath of the familiar face, Nitaya knew she could do nothing as her frightened friend searched for her family. Opening her hand to the screen and lowering her head, she prayed that someday she would learn of her fate and somehow see her again.

Reluctantly looking back to the screen, Nitaya saw that Elari was now gone. Closing her eyes, she quickly reopened them at the first sounds of intruders ringing throughout the lower levels at her back. Stifling her whimpers, she returned to her Momar's side to await the arrival of the evil beasts. Nitaya wished that she too had somewhere to run.

***

Although distant and muffled, Nitaya knew the enemy neared with each passing moment. Flinching at what most surely was weapons sounding against the familiar corridors in the nearing distance, she cringed with fear of what they would bring. Stepping back, Nitaya prayed for both Hylin and Khyra's safety knowing they remained somewhere beyond the safety of the main door. Covering her ears, she mimicked her palle and Norell.

With tears of disbelief in her eyes, momar returned to palle's side, drawing Norell near within their arms, the reality that like those above, they were not going to be saved becoming clear. Nitaya darted the few steps to rejoin her family, momar extending her arms to claim her youngest child.

"What is to become of Hylin?" Nitaya cried, peering up through the folds of momar's gown, terrible thoughts of the handsome boy guarding the entrance above filling her head. "And what of Khyra?"

Unable to answer with the approaching blasts filling her senses, momar merely shook her head. Drawing her children close, the clanging growing nearer, she closed her eyes. Her lips moved silently in prayer.

Nitaya freed herself from momar's grasp, dismissing without thought the safety of both momar and palle she instinctively slunk from the center of Command, stepping backward into the outskirts of the room furthest from the main entrance. Creeping away from the main controls, the pynar stations and her family, something deep within told her she must hide.

Unable to find words, Nitaya never spoke out to warn the others of her thoughts yet instead, kept slowly stepping back, the trio unaware as they held their ground with the lone remaining pynar. With her white-knuckled hands fanned out to guide at her back, Nitaya reached the flat wall of the rear alcove. Turning, she spied a hidden door that oddly she had never seen before. Quickly reaching out to test its opening with her palm, she found it remained firmly locked. Turning again to find an alternative place to hide, she instinctively dropped to the floor at her palle's shouts.

"Where is she?" he screamed, momar clinging to Norell, panicking as she too scanned the room. "Lydra, where could she have gone?" Rather than answering her palle's pleas however, Nitaya again reached back, finding two stacks of what appeared to be old panel screens that were no longer of use. Spying a crevice between the larger models in which she could hide, the sounds of the approaching beasts growing ever loud, she scooted back within the small space. Nitaya heard her momar cry out her name, yet she again said could say nothing. Instead she covered her ears and closed her eyes, praying that all that was happening was just a terrible dream.

The sounds as Nitaya referred to them, grew increasingly louder as she lowered to her knees in the darkend space and she knew without question that they were within mere moments of the door beyond central Command. Peering out of the small crevice of her hiding spot, her whimpers catching in her throat, Nitaya watched palle move to shield momar and Norell, instructing both to flee.

"We cannot leave without Nitaya!" momar shouted, struggling against his arms.

"I swear I will find her," palle answered, firmly shooing the pair away.

"For the sake of us all, please Jovan," momar begged, palle turning to kiss her forehead.

"It is time, Lydra," he answered, claiming her hands. "You know it is time."

Nodding without further argument, momar grasped Norell's hand and although reluctant, began moving away from the center station. The doors at her back simultaneously were forced open, the evil beasts racing inward to Command. Palle stood his ground never flinching from the gaseous blast.

"You have me!" he shouted, raising his arms above the din of dying fire. "Do not hurt those who know not what you seek!" Hidden from direct view, Nitaya watched momar Lydra palle's back, releasing Norell's grip. He at once darted toward Nitaya's general direction.

"No, Jovan, no!" momar shouted, the nearest being claiming her wrist, silencing her with a narrow stare.

"It is not a matter for you, woman, but Jovan Riolle must come," the beast said firmly. Two others claimed palle's arms, quickly escorting him without word from Command. Momar was quickly forced from the room at his back.

The remaining beasts appeared to scan the area with odd handheld devices, passing by Norell and his hiding place, yet quite easily finding Nitaya in the rear nook. Speaking not a word as they approached, the nearest listened into his hand as Nitaya had seen him do before on the main screen, the two others pulling her forth, Carrying her to join a group of pynars, they began to ascend the stairs she had casually descended only a hazon before.

Flung over the back of one of the strange beasts, Nitaya groaned, punching her fists into its sleek outer shell, her pleas ignored. The troop soon reached the Life Level. From her high obscure view, Nitaya was certain between blows against her unflinching captor, that she had spied Khyra through a glass pane of the gadget room door.

"So someone will remain behind to save us," Nitaya thought, groaning as the beast wretched forward, tossing her to her feet. Catching both breath and balance, Nitaya wiped the stain of tears from her eyes just as Norell arrived, thrust forward to join her from the rear of their group. Staring at the backs of the unspeaking beasts, Nitaya knew deep within her heart that all was about to change. With Khyra safe within the Lower Levels however, she also knew that if anyone could, it would be Khyra who would find a way to save them.

***

Except for the images on the screens at Command, Nitaya had never seen the brush that lined the forbidden sand's edge, yet as she was dragged roughly through it now by the silent beasts, she ruefully wished she had just once ventured out to admire its beauty. For even though the brightly colored, greenly dense area sliced at her ankles, she was reminded of her GraPalle, whose whereabouts remained unknown, as she was pushed once again forward through the unforgiving tundrels.

The metallic beasts however, appeared to take no notice of the sharp undergrowth, easily stomping through the greens without care. Although Nitaya was distracted by the endless nuisances as she walked, she studied the silent few, certain that their unfeeling was due to their sleek armor and their obvious disdain of their captures.

The troop journeyed back within more familiar brush as if attempting to leave no trail, and Nitaya immediately spied the vents that fed the Lower Level's air supply. Pushing forward with both Norell and the pynar's steps waning, Nitaya numbed against the slashing at her ankles, counting four of the nine she knew existed amongst the greens.

"We are headed east," she thought, amazed that she could remember so much of her GraPalle's teaching, regardless of what was happening about her. "That could only mean..."

Standing in amazement with parted lips, she stood at the outer edges of the brush, looking out into the breathtaking rise and ebb of endless sand. Brighter than she had ever imagined, Nitaya shielded her eyes with both hands against the light, the ugly, impatient beasts thrusting her forward out from the shade and into the unforgiving glow.

Dragged further into the depth of sand, it ironically sparkled while, laying its hot and unforgiving path at her feet. The beings however, seemingly unaware of the heat just as they had been against the slicing greens, reined Nitaya and the others methodically toward the enormous ship. Regardless of the certain immediate danger however, Nitaya's mind could not help but wander.

"If they come out by a shoot," she thought, stepping quick and light atop the burning sand. She simply could not shake the beast's feet-first entrance from the ship. "How do they ever expect to get us in?"

At long last they reached the large craft. Standing in line to enter amongst her palle's frightened pynars, Nitaya's thoughts returned to the present. Her lips again parted as she looked from her own small feet, forward then up to the enormous, foreign craft before her. Nitaya would not wait long to find her answer.

***

Pulled along to the edge of the ship's massive base, Nitaya's eyes at last looked down, finding the stronghold even larger than she had imagined. Standing transfixed by its grand size, the make of its frame and the twists and bends of the strange metal, she at last took true notice of the others who had attempted to flee Command. Lined up in no particular order both before and and at her back, Nitaya leaned on tiptoe to spy her family. Unable to move far however, she squirmed as the metallic beast oddly claiming Nitaya as his sole interest, once again listened to his hand.

Palle, Momar Lydra and Norell were no where in sight. Nitaya tried desperately to search behind her through the crowd of frightened pynars, yet as one by one those before her were brought to the side of the large base, she found the silent beast's persistent urging too consuming. At last focusing forward, she found herself drawn to the commotion at the root of the ship.

There, a small hatch-like hole had sprung open before them and guided by the beasts, each of the members of Nyllo were pushed toward the bright light emerging from within. As the first pynar approached it appeared to *gleam* him inward. The light, yellow-orange in color and oval in shape, eerily seemed to be breathing as it claimed its first victim.

Turning back and forth, her hair loosening from its binds, Nitaya's fears grew with the continuing thrust of pynars into the oval light. Knowing her turn was soon coming, her heart beat faster as her eyes raced in search of those she loved. Growing anxious and rescanning the group at her back for Palle, Momar Lydra and Norell, she at last spied them off to her right, standing without restraint and waiting amongst several of the rigid, darkened beasts.

"Why are we not bound?" Nitaya thought, staring down at her free hands then to the others at her back, unrestrained. Knowing her Palle and Momar Lydra would not be able to help her, yet uncertain as to why they all had not been secured and more importantly why they had been singled out, Nitaya looked to Norell's tear-stained face then reluctantly turned back to the oval light, the last pynar gleaming forward into the unknown.

Turning one last time for encouragement, Nitaya nodded at Palle thrusting his chin high as if he was silently urging her to do the same. When her time had at last come to endure the unknown, she turned to face the breathing light unafraid, standing tall as she too was gleamed forward.

Unknowing of what lie ahead and although worried for her family who appeared for the moment to be remaining behind, Nitaya knew that regardless of her fears and the uncertainties of those that meant her harm, that with the strength of all that she had been taught she would face the unknown with courage, but alone.

***

At once Nitaya found herself standing in an eerily-lit hallway, framed solely in cool, unforgiving metal. Void of all life but herself, it stood a complete contrast to the sand and heat beyond. Spying none of her palle's pynars that had been brought through before her and more importantly none of her large silent captors, Nitaya searched the open corridor with her eyes, afraid to move. Pivoting slowly in place, her breath danced rhythmically just beyond her face.

"It is just cold like GraPalle has told me it could be," Nitaya thought attempting to calm her nerves. At last Nitaya raised her arms, covering her chest to warm both her skin and fears. "You have seen this many times before within the test reactors. Relax, Nitaya," she continued, vigorously rubbing her arms with her hands. "It is just cold and nerves."

Slowly glancing in each direction of the silent, hollow corridor, Nitaya heart at last calmed, sensing she was truly alone with the exception of the strange screen and scanner before her. Although gray and blank as if asleep, Nitaya shifted slowly toward it with arms wrapped tight about her waist. Leaning close to peer inward, she was startled as it surprisingly sprang to life, jolting her back to the far wall.

"Place your ring finger within the scanner," the machine instructed flatly, the tube-like contraption parting at its center to bear a small, glowing blue lense. Hesitantly looking about for someone, anyone to appear with assistance, Nitaya straightened as the screen simply repeated its order.

"Place your ring finger within the scanner," it said again. Oddly, Nitaya sensed that the machine was somehow showing irritation with her delay.

Wiping her brow which proved damp with sweat despite the coolness of the ship's air, Nitaya reluctantly crossed back to the screen. Placing her right ring finger within the scanner, she was again surprised, this time receiving a negative response from the strange device.

"Input denied, place your fourth finger within the scanner," it said, its tone now obviously annoyed. It did not blink, but left its bright glow upon the screen as it awaited the correct prompt.

"I did as I was told," Nitaya grumbled, withdrawing her finger and staring at the odd machine. Rubbing her fingers together to warm them and consider the annoyed tone of the prompt, Nitaya tilted her head and placed her left fourth finger within the tempered scanner. As if knowing she had solved the machine's riddle, Nitaya stood straight to await the sequence of acceptance. Startled however, by the surprising jolt of the device, she stared transfixed as the screen blinked in coded green, springing to life.

The screen showed nothing more than a garbled array of letters and numbers moving right to left. Attempting to step back to take in the information from a clearer angle, Nitaya proved once again startled as the device held firm to her finger. Certain that because she was merely a child the data it was collecting could be nothing of importance, Nitaya remained startled but unafraid, shaking her head with the amount of time the device was consuming.

"This should not be taking this long," Nitaya whispered, growing only slightly anxious. She craned her neck to scan the length of the empty corridor as the device took its time, holding firm to her finger. Again spying no one in the cold, narrow passage, Nitaya considered prying her finger from the device just as the screen froze, its hundreds of orange letters and numbers stilled across its face.

Leaning inward to the array of nonsense, intrigued by its odd configuration, Nitaya jumped again as the screen instantly sounded as if in reaction to her close proximity. The sudden appearance of the glow above drew her eyes upward. Having no sense to move from the immediate corridor, she stood transfixed by the aweness of bright lights filling the empty space. So intrigued, Nitaya barely took notice of her finger being released, instead almost willingly accepting the new breathing light above. Once again, Nitaya found herself gleamed into an unknown world.

***

Appearing swiftly in a small, circular room, Nitaya shielded her eyes and pivoted slowly in place, staring in awe at the brilliance of white walls. With the exception of an oval-shaped object appearing cut out from its exterior, its covering resembling its naked surroundings, the room proved glaring and void of any other structures.

Having turned full circle, Nitaya returned her gaze to the oval-shaped object at the opposite of the room, uncertain whether to step from her entrance. She could not help but wonder why no beasts had returned. Making no sense as to what to do with no door, no glass and no life but herself, Nitaya lowered to the floor. Shaking upon the cold white, she stared at the eerie oval object and pulling her knees up to her chin, rocked as if a child.

***

Clutching her legs tightly to her chest, uncertain as to how much time had passed, Nitaya looked up to the swift sound, her skin chilling as an unknown door moved upward at her back. Coolness entered from the exterior corridor. Turning to eye the assuming beast, Nitaya peered over her shoulder yet refused to give her full-body attention to the enemy, a glow of green light cascading over the room to shield their arrival. Squinting, however as two beings with faces she could not distinguish stepped abruptly through the unmarked entrance, Nitaya struggled against their grip. Saying nothing and claiming her by each arm, the pair dragged her toward the oval object. Nitaya soon found she was little match for their strength.

Reaching the oval frame, Nitaya watched spellbound as one being reached off to her right, maintaining his hold of her arm while prompting a hidden control. The front of the odd frame slowly opened before her. Its panel however, sprang surprisingly out despite the slow movement, then just as quickly slid to the side for use.

The second being released his firm grip, crossing to the once hidden panel and Nitaya remained in a daze as he began keying into some sort of prompter. Certain the device had not been there before, Nitaya's questions grew with the beasts' order of three hose-like tubes. Appearing from above they simultaneously lowered, connecting to the oval.

"This is a cocoon!" Nitaya screamed, kicking violently from her daze with both legs. The being firmed his grip, his counterpart returning to assist, forcing her forward to its shell. "You will never get me in there!" Nitaya desperately tried to claw herself from the strength of the beasts, shouting for her palle to save her. The pair merely lifted her small body with ease to the mirrored, oval opening.

"Help me! Someone please help me!" Nitaya cried, kicking against the edges of the oval's opening. The beasts ignored her pleas, simply thrusting her forward, forcing her into the cocoon and into a cramped fetal position. Despite her greatest efforts, there was no room to maneuver otherwise.

Arms flailing, with her will to fight strong and unfailing, the small door swiftly moved sideways, closing before her despite her white-knuckled grip on its edges. The beasts simply stepped back as Nitaya's heart raced wildly, continuing her cries into the small cramped space that was consuming her. Clawing in desperation at the outer walls of the now closed shell, she screamed for both her palle and momar Lydra as the water began to rise.

Trickling and toying with her ankles as it seeped into her narrow tomb, Nitaya wretched violently at the outer walls. The water slowly rose unceasing to her waist. The dark liquid, rising ever higher without prejudice, engulfed her chest then soon her shoulders. Panicking, Nitaya screamed, thrashing violently against what she knew was the inevitable. Breathing heavily at the coolness quickly reaching her chin, Nitaya lowered her arms, tipping her head upward to gasp her last breath, frightened that so much could go wrong in such a small period of time. As the beast's watery tomb reached her mouth and at last her nose, she muttered merely 'no,' before her world became dark.

***

Unbeknownst to Nitaya, the beings crossed the small room without feeling, maintaining their silence as they returned to the panel. Instructing the prompt to perform the final retraction controls, they left the white oval room without fanfare. Having not heard, nor cared about the girl's muffled screams, they instead returned to their prompted tier with a new programmed purpose.

Once the door had closed at their backs, the white room and oval object no longer filled their systematic thoughts, the floor simply reverted back within the wall. Despite their lack of knowledge, the gloriousness of the ship and its tube-like halls spanning the height of its hull, filled with endless oval-shaped doorways containing life, stood silent. Nitaya and her cocoon, despite her continued white-knuckled fists, would remain a guest of the vast corridor for some time.

***

Nitaya awoke gasping. Had she been unconscious for mere moments, hazons? Unable to judge the length of her forced slumber, she no longer focused on the duration of her entombment, yet rather concentrated on the fact the she was no longer breathing. It was as if she were merely swimming beneath the Quito Falls, her body completely submerged within the cocoon's bed of water. Her body, remaining in the position the beast-like beings had placed her, remained curled, infant-like, her joints aching with lack of movement.

A soft green glow had replaced the darkness of her shell at some point while she slept. Nitaya, now fully aware waved her fingers before her face within the gentle flow, for the moment enjoying the offered wonders. Wanting desperately to stretch yet adjusting to the space given to accept the moment, she forced herself to calm to consider her newest situtation.

"I can breathe," Nitaya thought, shaking her head in disbelief. "How can this be possible?" As quickly as the incredible thought found her however, the idea of breathing beneath the air brought about a deep sense of fear, the excitement of the possibility immediately gone. At once Nitaya reached out to grab hold of anything that could possibly set her free. Unable to find anything tangible to grasp in the small cramped space, panic quickly claimed her senses.

Frantically pushing outward against the cold hard shell, her heart pounding, Nitaya's arms ached as she attempted to scream, yet nothing but groans escaped her amongst the flow of water. Slowly resigning herself to the hold of the tomb, the sense of awe in breathing completely leaving her, Nitaya settled back to steady her fears. Nervously, yet unrelentingly continuing an endless path of the outer wall with her fingers, she vowed to never give up hope for escape as she awaited her fate.

***

Drifting off in thought with the continuous hum of the cocoon's skin, Nitaya suddenly jolted as the water began to descend from above. In reflex, she quickly cupped her ears, closing her eyes with the ensuing abrupt change in pressure. Peering upward as the top of her head felt the cool sensations of incoming air, Nitaya sat transfixed, unable to move as the water receded further. Releasing her nose and mouth, waves of violent coughing wrenched her throat.

Water spewed from her lungs and her face heated with endless, violent spasms. Nitaya clutched her chest with one arm, reaching out against the outer wall with the other. "I am dying," she thought, straining desperately for air, struggling to find her breath against the ripple-like reactions in her throat.

Coughing out the last droplets of water, Nitaya shivered against the wetness of her tomb, the chills of air shaking her uncontrollably within its shell. At last taking in her first steady, full breath of air, although strained against the roughness of her throat, Nitaya jolted against the curved wall as a loud hum from the unknown sounded beyond her cocoon. Eyes darting for a sign of exit, she shivered to a dull ache, the water continuing its descent to her chest, to her belly, and at last to her ankles. At the last, Nitaya lie soaked, lined with both water and fear, yet again breathing air.

"What is happening to me?" she cried, covering her face. The green glow brightened above, hurting her eyes. "Where is my family? Palle, where are you? Palle!"

Lying chilled and shaken with no new signs of change, Nitaya thought back to only a short time ago when her greatest worry had been if Hylin would take notice of her, and of her treasured joys of spending time with both Khyra in the world below and Elara, ignorant in the bliss of above. Now however, trembling and alone in her cold shell, Nitaya prayed simply for her life.

She held no concept of time. Sitting within the unforgiving oval shell, her back aching, Nitaya gasped, silencing her quivering lips with her fingers as again she heard the strange huming from the outer room. Waiting impatiently for what was to inevitably come next, her ever inquisitive mind wandered back to the moment the beings had first entombed her.

"They had been forceful, yes," she thought rubbing her small feet together, resuming her search of entry along the shell's outer walls. "Yet they had said nothing. Where did they take me?" she whispered, peering closer to find a seam in the sleek cocoon. "Am I still on the ship? Have I been placed in a traveling pod as GraPalle had once described? Where are Palle, Momar Lydra and Norell? How did I ever breathe without air?"

So many questions filled her. Lying motionless, she closed her eyes against her rapidly beating heart, yet just as Nitaya inhaled deeply in an attempt to reclaim her calm, the loud hum beyond her cocoon resounded, startling her oval eyes wide.

Ringing out and muffled as before immediately beyond the shell of her cocoon, Nitaya grasped the outer walls as one

31

beep followed by a second ordered her hidden door to slowly open. Although frightened, Nitaya remained reclined against the arc at her back, refusing to look out. Fear filling, Nitaya begged her mind to relax.

"If they were going to kill me," she thought, wrapping her arms tightly across her chest. "They would have done so already." And yet, remaining clutched as the arm of a being reached within, Nitaya at last gave into the urge and opened her eyes to the brightness of the room, squinting as the beast quickly wrenched her without care of harm from the damp shell.

Exumed only half way from the dew-filled cocoon, Nitaya remained stiff, not of her own volition. With the second being guiding her body forward, placing her weight on a type of inforgiving metal cot, Nitaya shivered to her core against its cold frame. Placed swiftly on her back, the beings released her from their grasp, and Nitaya attempted to stretch out her legs. Only then did she realize she was unable.

"What is wrong with me?" she screamed, her words trickling from her mouth with a mere quivering whisper. The beings ignored her pleas, appearing expectant of her lack of voice. Laying wide-eyed, Nitaya watched the enemy furthest from her turn, holding some sort of foreign device. She hovered on the cot rightened as he crossed to her, slowly passing the odd, red scanning light over her body. Almost instantly however, Nitaya felt the transformation.

With the assistance of the being the glowing red beam rose gradually from her feet toward her thighs and Nitaya could not help but sense the instant warmth flowing through her, her upper body proving able to at last extend her legs. Although straining, the stiffness at last drained from her and Nitaya arched back and slowly straightened, able to at last lie flat on the cold frame.

Confident that the task was complete, Nitaya turned her head slowly toward the enemy, its back to her as it returned the scanner to the rear of the bright room. Turning to the other she shuttered as it crossed in the opposite direction without word. Nitaya followed his lead and said nothing as it prompted the door.

Her captors remained silent as they exited the small room. Nitaya attempted to lift her head slightly to demand what was to become of her, yet felt the jolt of her cot moving before she could attempt to speak, forcing her head back to the cold frame. Floating without assistance, Nitaya stared upward to the bright lights.

Led behind the pair of strange creatures, Nitaya found that for the first time since the invasion she was more curious than afraid. As the trio traveled further into the bowels of whatever held her, rounding the third bend to their left, she focused her attention forward, learning and listening to the sounds of the strange beings.

Their bodies were built of a strange metal that eerily matched their surroundings of sleek gray. Taking in all she could about the pair, Nitaya rubbed her feet together and suddenly realized that these were not those responsible for bringing her to this cold place that held her cocoon. Although similar, these quiet ones were less bulky and carried no visible weapons.

As much of their exteriors resembled the larger intruders, the pair of beings before her held oddly, wide-shaped heads over their narrow shoulders with what appeared lightly colored wires extending down from the nape of the heads to the base of their backs, similar to that of the transoids. What eerily held Nitaya's attention however, was the faint glowing light of a color...a color she oddly could not name, centered at the highest point of their heads.

With the return of the sensations of circulation, Nitaya once again rubbed her feet together, transfixed by the blinking glow of both beings that appeared to respond to her movements. Her GraPalle, although a transoid, had never possessed such a wonder.

"It has to be an eye," Nitaya thought, her feet now reflexively pressing together, the flicker of lights echoing their response. "Even with their backs turned they are watching me."

Struggling with the rawness of her throat, Nitaya attempted to speak out at the glow to force the beings to turn, yet with her mind awhirl with questions of her captors and what was

33

to become of her, she found she remained unable to form the words. The cot continued its flotation around the next bend.

Nitaya at once looked away, tears filling her eyes as she struggled with the weight of her position. Resigned that she was, at least for the moment unable to communicate with the beings, she shook away her tears and instead bravely assumed the position of learning all she could of her surroundings. Perhaps she would gain some useful.

The corridor, although wide enough to allow the pivots of her cot at its endless bends, proved narrow and cold and floating around the next turn, she stared at the repeat of unwielding doors passing from her view all colored the same cold gray. Nitaya could not recount the exact number of those she had passed, yet with the obvious large number available for use, she was startled that they had not encountered any other life. Before she could attempt to question her surroundings aloud however, she was once again jolted, her cot abruptly stopping. Nitaya could only assume that they had reached their destination.

Having not ever heard the strange voices of her captors, Nitaya lay motionless, listening as they began speaking, their tone appearing to echo amongst the corridor. Ringing high and then low with no consistency or reasoning, she grew frustrated, unable to understand their dialogue. As the faint flicker of light at the tip of their heads reclaimed her attention however, she was startled at the sounding of a hidden door sliding upward before them. At once Nitaya's cot resumed its float at the pair's back.

***

Floating into the surprisingly spacious cabin, Nitaya lay still as her captors rounded to her sides. Merely touching the cot ceased its movement at the room's center. Once again attempting to question the pair, she found herself silenced by the slight raise of one captor's hand. As if gliding they turned, leaving her alone in the the silent room.

Sitting up on the base of her forearms, Nitaya took advantage of her time alone to survey her surroundings. Spying the wonderous plantlife, she was unable to contain her smile for it had seemed eons since she had smelled the wonders of greens.

As if for the first time experiencing what she had had each day along her walk below the falls, Nitaya relished the aromas that filled the room, exuding their fragrance from the foreign species.

A towering plant off to her far right grew from floor to ceiling with leaves larger than the head of her palle's highest-ranking pynar, and to her left, the strangest of ground-cover slithered its way strangely across the gray floor. Scattered amongst the dominant growths in the corners stood various smaller species from jagged stems to abundant ovals, all glowing with their own pale colors, yet what most held Nitaya's curiosity was the ever vibrant flower standing oddly alone on a table at the base of her cot.

Leaning forward, Nitaya reached out to inspect it further. Transfixed, her fingers danced over its bright orange petals. Standing alone on what appeared a mere stick, its golden center feeding life to its deep hue, Nitaya marveled at the solitude of its frame as no leaves or stems shared its bed. No leaves, no stems, it was the most beautiful flower she had ever seen.

***

Nitaya remained focused upon the solitary bloom. Ignoring the other sights of the cabin regardless of her aching limbs, she was startled from its trance, turning at the sound of a trill interrupting her thoughts. Releasing the large petals and slowly sitting straight to await the return of the beings, she turned, unable to contain her smile. Looking into the eyes of a beautiful woman, her body eased as the elder entered, crossing the room from a rear hidden door.

Wearing colors that closely resembled the flower before her, Nitaya watched the glorious, floor-length materials flow about the woman's ankles at her approach. Her hair, rich and golden blonde was pulled back from her face and hung long, cascading down the length of her back. Appearing no older than Nitaya's own Momar Lydra, the woman seemed to almost glide across the floor toward the edge of the cot. Although smiling with the deepest of chestnut eyes, Nitaya sat nervously awaiting her words.

"My dearest child," the woman began, folding her hands at her waist. "I know that you must be frightened, but please lend your ear for I have so much to share with you." Nitaya remained silent, the woman hesitant as if questioning her opening line. Resigned however, she sighed before placing one hand to her heart, the other warmly upon Nitaya's arm.

"First though," she paused, claiming another breath. "I realize that you must be tired, hungry and oh so very cold. As anxious as I am to speak with you, you should know that I have made arrangements for you in quarters connecting with my own. You will be escorted there to freshen and soon a meal will be brought for nourishment. When you are sated, we will at last begin."

Turning and forcing herself to be patient, the woman crossed to the center of the cabin, looking down at the delicate flower before continuing with her back to Nitaya. "I have been growing this for you for such a long while," she whispered, her words filled with warmth. She paused in obvious thought, running her fingers down the length of its stem.

"Although chosen, I knew in my heart it would please you. Zyn," she added, lifting the large base, the lone being returning with the summons. "Take this with you to Nitaya's quarters and inform me when the child is properly readied for her return."

Turning with a warm smile and pacing back to Nitaya's side, the woman gently patted her knee before quickly crossing and exiting through the rear door. Nitaya, without another option turned to the being who now held a name, watching without word as he gathered the magnificent flower. Tilting her head at the one titled Zyn, she followed his turn in the opposite direction with her eyes. Attempting to rise from her cot, she stopped as it resumed its floating.

Descending a step at the cabin's center then ascending on the opposite end, Zyn prompted the door, well hidden in the rear alcove and led Nitaya's floating cot within her new quarters. Placing the large urn on a table just inside the cabin, Zyn turned to face her, clicking his heals as if a subordinant. Nitaya once again attempted to rise from her stable cot.

"Please do what you will for all you see is yours," Zyn began, his tone flat and controlled. Nitaya could not help but smile at the sound of his first words. "Your nourishment will be placed here," he added despite her demeanor, pointing to the low table. "And will be at the ready upon your return from freshening. I will then arrive in two hazon to retrieve you unless you send for me prior."

Zyn sharply nodded then retreated toward the exit. Although strained, Nitaya at last found her voice. "Unless I send for you prior?" she asked, uncertain of the being's intentions.

Zyn's answer however was without hesitation, the being quickly turning, reclicking his heals to face her. "Nitayatinus, I am assigned as your servant and will serve when called," he said flatly, abruptly retreating toward the door. Although she had so many questions to ask, Nitaya was allowed not a word for Zyn quickly and quietly left her alone to her tending.

***

"My servant?" Nitaya whispered to the empty cabin. Surprised at finding her voice, she grabbed at her throat.. "What is happening? What did he call me? Nitaya what?"

Dangling her feet over the cot's edge and staring awkwardly at the attempted comforting room, Nitaya replayed in her mind all that had happened. Her body shivering anew with memories of the cocoon, she was at once reminded that she was very wet and very cold. Grasping her arms tight to her chest, she raised her eyes to the foreign wonders of her cabin, yet despite spying the attempted softness of its hues amongst the dimly lit lights, Nitaya found herself surprised at her instant warming.

Cheery, roomy and colorful, a contrast to her small room above the falls, Nitaya warmed at its amazing openness. Drawn to a set of airy drapes cascading down from the ceiling in the corner nook, Nitaya smiled, enjoying the brightly colored greens placed with precision on the small table positioned next to a cozy bench that oddly resembled her old cot. A wooden cabinet, standing just to the right of the alcove stood adorned with the brilliant plantlife as were several other pedestals positioned just so throughout the room. It was as if those who created the space

37

had created it specifically for her. Turning to peer over her shoulder, Nitaya again smiled, spying the plushness of coverlets that adorned the large cot. Its soft folds sent chills over her skin.

Unlike the unforgiving coolness of her floating cot, this heavily-downed trundle exuded warmth, willing Nitaya to lie beneath its heft. Complying, she sprang quickly upon the floor, anxious to dive into its pleats. Although teetering as she landed, Nitaya ignored her unsteadiness, unable to look from its glorious view. Yet stepping away from her floating support, she could not help but stumble to her knees.

"How long was I entombed?" Nitaya whispered rubbing her hands over her thighs, sighing at the wonderous view. Stubbornly rebalancing however, albeit slowly, she stood with the assistance of the old, then taking a step toward the new was surprised as the old began floating at her side. Guiding her slowly to the edge of the soft covers, Nitaya fell effortlessly upon them, the cold metal form ceasing its movements with a simple release of her hand.

"How did *you* get here?" Nitaya asked gleefully, grabbing hold of her favorite blanket folded neatly at her side. Forgetting her worries as she pressed her nose eagerly within its familiar fabric, Nitaya inhaled deeply, smiling as she smelled the warm scents of Nyllo. Nestled warmly atop the abundant covers, sleep quickly claimed her.

***

Nitaya arose with a start not knowing how long she had slept yet was certain she must promptly freshen if she were to be prepared when called. Propping herself up on the base of her arms, she spied a small door hidden behind the bench in the rear alcove. Tossing her legs over the cot's edge however, she paused recalling her lack of strength.

"I have to at least try," she thought, reaching her hand out to the floating cot and placing her feet on the cool floor. Smiling, Nitaya found her strength had almost completely returned. Hesitantly crossing the spacious cabin all the while enjoying the array of greens, she was able to reach the small alcove with a rhythm of slow and steady steps.

Passing the quaint low bench on her right, she rubbed her hands over its intricately detailed cloths as she crossed to the narrow door. Finding the facilites as expected, she stepped within and removed her clothes, hanging each garment on the awaiting hooks on the sidewall then placed the pins from her hair on the shelf below the glass. At last she stepped into the large basin.

Obviously the task of washing was going to prove difficult. Not knowing the specifics on how the device even remotely worked, Nitaya hesitantly prompted the control to her left. A cascading stream of cold water washed over her body.

"Oh my!" she shouted, quickly reprompting the knob. Shivering, she pushed her sopping hair from her eyes. "Alright then," she continued, clutching her body, her eyes turning to the right and spying the adjacent control. "Perhaps it is you that I need."

The second prompt followed by a brief tap of the third, gave Nitaya the temperature her body had ached for and unable to move beneath the spout, she could not contain a slight moan, the warmth of droplets dancing over her face. As steam soon filled the height of the basin, she sighed against its heat, finding the cleansing soap on a small shelf to her left. Lathering it briskly in her hands, she was careful to cover every inch of her skin.

Studying the array of controls beneath the spout as she rinsed herself clean, Nitaya selected what she found to be a cleanser on her right. Heaping a generous amount into her hands, more than she had ever been allowed in Nyllo, she began vigorously scrubbing her hair. Stepping beneath the water and rinsing her long tresses, Nitaya grumbled knowing that the woman was most likely awaiting her return with an air of impatience. Prompting the lower controls to cease the water's flow, she looked back to the knobs below the spout, selecting the one that was simply marked 'air.'

Quickly yet thoroughly warmed from the gusting waves of heat, Nitaya stepped from within the basin, spying a fresh set of clothes folded neatly on the side table. "Were those there before?" she thought, hesitantly walking toward the colorful folds. "Surely I would have noticed."

Shrugging with lack of time to consider the options of the arriving clothes, Nitaya knew she had not dawdle, so quickly she set out to testing their fit. Once certain that all was in its proper place, she turned to the glass to examine the reflextion of her new attire.

"This cannot be!" she shrieked, gasping at the image before her. Her hand quickly darted to cover her mouth. "I do not understand," she whispered, reaching forward and touching the glass. With the image reflecting beneath her fingertips, Nitaya stared at a face that could not be her own. Bringing her hand to her cheek, she ran her fingers slowly over her brow then her chin and neck, standing agape into the eyes of a stranger.

"This cannot be possible," Nitaya repeated, touching her fingers to her lips with her words. "How can I be this old?" Trembling, Nitaya's fear quickly turned to rage. "This cannot be real!" she shouted, pounding her fist on the smaller basin. "How long was I in that cocoon?"

Nitaya had been certain that only a few hazon had passed in the cocoon regardless that her limbs had ached, yet as the image of her older self stood wide-eyed before her, she knew there could be no other explanation. "Onars?" she questioned, shaking her head and closing her eyes, the images of the beast's scanner easing her stiffness filling her thoughts. Forcing herself to breathe deeply and willing her younger image to return, Nitaya slowly looked up to once again look peer the eyes of her aged reflection.

"How long could it have been?" she whispered, tears welling in her squinting eyes, nostrils flaring as the steam cascaded down her cheeks. "How could you have done this?" she shouted, anger filling her. She punched her fist straight at the image, several shards of glass sprinkling to the floor. Wincing, Nitaya wiped the tears from her face, spying the fresh blood dripping from her hand.

"Foolish," she grumbled, snarling at the wound. Three large shards glared at her, embedded within the fist of her hand. Drawing them near for closer inspection, her eyes for the moment diverted from the aged image in the glass. Quickly she pulled them free, hissing at the pain with each yank. The glass had shown her *true* self she knew, and yet as her eyes resettled on the now skewed image before her, so many questions remained.

"How long was I entombed?' she thought, rinsing her hand in the small basin. "What do they want from me? Why am I here? Where is my family?" she pleaded. Gritting her teeth, she knew with certainty that the blood would not stop without proper cover.

Knowing no answers were coming from the glass, Nitaya replayed the questions in her mind as she thought of her impending council with the awaiting woman. Frightened and although injured, she desperately wanted to learn more.

Although relatively minor, Nitaya could not stop the red flow from her hand. Quickly racing back to the main cabin to find something to use as pressure, she paused, spying the large cabinet of drawers. Unwilling to summons Zyn to assist, she paced to the large cabinet and yanked open the top tier, praying she would find something of use. She found only large garments of various shades of gray. Although they were not as appealing as the ones she now wore, Nitaya dared not shred them.

Dismissing the first and slamming the drawer closed, Nitaya reached to the next only to find more of the same. Although the same size however, these consisted of materials she had never seen. Smiling as she ran her unwounded hand through the glorious folds, their colors radiated with the shift of her fingers. Knowing she had no time to enjoy her treasured find however, Nitaya closed the second hoping that maybe later she could return to them before wrenching open the last, finding this held items that might work to her advantage.

"Possibly," Nitaya thought, yanking out a small sash and shredding it in two. Quickly she wrapped her wound. "Such a pity," she thought, tying the last of it and using her teeth to tighten a sturdy knot. "But it had to be done."

With her hand at last in order, Nitaya's mind again shifted, her thoughts immediately turning to the aroma of her meal. Pivoting in place, she found the array of nourishmennt that she had been told would be there.

"Not yet," Nitaya thought, ignoring the scents and her watering mouth, instead turning back toward the facilites to return everything to its place. Crossing into the alcove and reentering the small room, she stooped to gather the small shards from the floor and the basin, yet when she stood to examine the glass on the wall she found it was once again unbroken.

"How can this be?" Nitaya whispered staring in amazement, moving her hand out to touch its surface. Famished and with already too many questions to remember, Nitaya tossed the shards from her hands into a receptacle in the side wall. Picking up the brush from the side shelf, she hastily began running it through her long hair.

"This is truly unimaginable," Nitaya whispered, thinking of the intact glass, yet in that instant realizing the length of her hair. Half turning as she continued her strokes, staring at her new older image, Nitaya remained in utter disbelief of how her tresses now cascaded to her waist, surprised that she had not realized it earlier. Having obviously been too engrossed in the warmth of the basin's water to realize, Nitaya now shook all of the meaningless the thoughts from her mind.

Replacing the brush then reaching her hands up to separate her hair into the custom three sections, she smiled, spying the small pins waiting to be put in place. The extra length of hear took quite a while to tame properly. With the last of them secured however, she looked one last time at the strange though familiar face. Rubbing her throbbing hand as she gave her appearance a final glance head to toe, she at last followed the trail of aroma to her meal.

***

Well sated from a wonderful mixture of greens, meat and breads, Nitaya finished the remnants of her drink, placed her mug on the tray and sat back, crossing her arms over her well mounded belly. "I never believed I could devour so much in one setting," she said to the empty room, moaning and covering her midsection. She could not help but rethink the last slice of bread lathered in its heavy cream.

"But then again, it has been a quite a while since I last nourished," she said as if entertaining a guest. "I wonder what is to come next." Although expecting no response to her open thoughts, Zyn abruptly reappeared through the door. "It is time," he said, simply. "Please follow me."

"How convenient," Nitaya thought, leaning forward to set her lapcloth next to her tray. A slight smile crossed her lips at the return of her steward. Knowing the time had at last come to learn the answers to her many questions however, Nitaya gracefully rose, crossing the cabin and passing her hand over the wonderful petals of the orange flower at its center. Releasing its wonders for answers however, she turned and trailed after Zyn, stepping through the door to the adjoining room to learn of her future.

Walking at the rear of the slow-paced steward, Nitaya glimpsed the small, steady light at the back of his head. Now more familiar and less afraid, she wriggled her nose, smiling as the light blinked at the slight of her movements. Stiffling her giggle of play, she straightened as Zyn turned to face her, stopping at an odd-shaped bench on the opposite side of the cabin. Tilting her head and trying to remember if it had been there earlier, Zyn merely nodded, gesturing with his arm for her to sit.

"This has been exumed as ordered," he said, extending his hand to assist Nitaya. Although uncertain what Zyn had mean by 'exumed,' she merely accepted his gesture, surprised at the warmth of his touch.

"It will be just a moment," he said simply. Silently turning, Zyn left Nitaya once again alone.

***

Waiting for whatever was to come next, Nitaya cast her eyes about the room settling her gaze over at the table at its center, spying yet another potted flower. Identical to her own yet of a different hue, it radiated with the brightest of blues, cascading outward from its wine-colored center, proving just as breathtaking as her own.

Stunned with their similarities, Nitaya was startled from her trance with the opening of the door to her right. Turning quickly to see the newest arrival, she watched as the woman's small stature glided over the floor. As beautiful as Nitaya

43

remembered, her folds danced slowly about her legs as she crossed to the bench, extending her hands in obvious welcome. Politely accepting the gesture, Nitaya waited eagerly, the woman claiming her own seat. Remaining politely silent, Nitaya anxiously awaited the woman's words.

"My dear child," the woman began, her voice a soft lilt as she folded her hands atop her lap. "My name is Selena and I am so very glad that you have joined us. I realize that you must be dearly stressed and afraid, yet rest assured that I am here to take all that you fear from you."

"So much has happened during your short life of which I know that you are unaware," she continued, her tone steady yet obviously strained. "Before we continue further however, I must again reassure you that we did not come to Mizar to harm you. The steps we have taken for you to be among us are great, and although they may have seemed harsh, the Resistance unfortunately had no other choice. I am certain that you have many questions of whys and hows, dearest Nitaya, but if you will allow me to continue, I am confident that you will soon receive the answers that you seek. Will you agree?"

Nitaya, not knowing how to properly answer, merely nodded. The woman titled Selena merely smiled and rose. "If you would, I would like you to lie back so that I may attach the view screen," she said, gesturing. "I assure you it will not harm you, but will rather put you in a trance-like state as if you were asleep and dreaming. I promise, dear child that once you are finished, I will be right here waiting for you, and once the sequence is complete, you will at last understand the importance of who you are."

Uncertain yet comforted with the words of Selena, Nitaya reclined as instructed and lay still, her elder moving the view screen out from its cradle, placing it over her eyes.

"The images you are about to witness are a part of your past," Selena continued warmly, securing the last of the device. "As it may seem impossible, you must know that you have been monitored from the day you were born, each hazon, each onar, and every important step in your life. Although I so much want to share more with you now," Selena added, placing her hand gently on Nitaya's arm. "Our discussions will be much easier once you have finished. I am about to begin the sequence Nitaya, and as the device begins you will hear a slight humming sound in your ears. Do not be afraid," she added, prompting the control on the side of the viewer device. "Just lie still and the images will begin shortly."

As Selena tapped the viewscreen for what she described as only 'a sequence,' Nitaya lifted her arm, brushing the folds of her gown. "Thank you for your kindness," she said, so much in need to understand more. "But I must know before we begin if my family is safe. When the beings arrived they..."

"You must be calm, little one," Selena whispered warmly, Nitaya's seat slowly reclining with prompting. "I promise you that all of your questions will soon be answered."

Accepting Selena's words as true, Nitaya lowered her arm to her side as the bench flattened to a slight angle. Lying with dancing nerves, awaiting her promised answers, she glanced right and left within the viewscreen as the humming sounded, growing loud as if nearing.

Dark for only a moment, the low hum was quickly replaced with the colorful screen as it sprang to life before her eyes. At first bearing nothing but a jumbling of random numbers and shapes, she lay transfixed as the images slowly became clear. Nitaya was an observer, as if floating above while the world below her lived.   And so it began.

PREY FOR REIGN

The Arrival of One

One

Wynin lay draped in a tattered cover on a makeshift cot amid the waste of Manine, Adoni. She shivered in the center of the crumbled room. The walls that served as her shelter stood layered in old paperings, faded with time and war as most of the once beautiful tapestry had been lost with the endless blasts. Random holes, some large enough for a being to pass through, littered the devastated room, while eerily intact with only its shredded cloth blowing amongst the dusty wind, stood the hollow window as a reminder that once Adonians had lived and thrived in the desolate city.

Time-worn parchment along with the many decaying greens, fluttered along the littered floor amongst remnants of what was once a place of nourishment, and as Wynin lay lowly moaning atop where a thriving family had once gathered to take meal, blasts continued their wailing beyond the rocked frame.

Three men sat on a low bench against the rear wall as a forth took watch upon the dusty floor, his weapon aimed out into the night through a gaping hole to the east, yet as Wynin called out, succumbing to her pain, Martus raced from the others to her side, wiping his hands on his dusty, worn cloak.

Motioning to the seated men for assistance, Drider quickly stepped to the opposite end of the table. Holding Wynin's legs and anticipating the onset of birth, Jovaar crossed to her face, placing a small cloth over her mouth. Struggling as she inhaled the ancient scents, Wynin's arms at last rested at her side, yet as Jovaar quickly lifted the mixture-laden fabric, a bolt of light shot through the room, another blast making contact eerily close to their location.

Jarring with the weight of the explosion, Martus and Jovaar quickly covered the length of Wynin's body, Gordal's slender frame at last reappearing through the haze, returning fire. "We must hurry, Jovaar," Martus said, wiping away remnants of dust and stone as he stared at yet another gaping hole. "Give me your blade."

Following the direct order of his elder, Jovaar quickly unclipped the knife from his ankle holster, the enemy fire ringing near, his hands trembling as he handed the blade to Martus. Flinching as another blast sounded just beyond the decayed opening, he spied Gordal amidst the newest cloud of dust, doing all he could to keep the enemy at a distance.

"I cannot hold them much longer, Martus," Gordal shouted, simultaneously coughing and taking aim at the insurgents to his right. "You must move more quickly."

Turning back to Wynin with Jovaar's blade in hand, Martus crossed quickly to her left side as Jovaar claimed her opposite, Drider holding firm at the base of the slab. "Forgive me, my love," he said, slicing at the mound of her womb.

Cursing himself that the first pass produced little at its narrow depth, Martus swung a second stroke, careful to miss what he had learned to cause fatality as yet another flash of light brought the room to a quake.

"Hurry, Martus!" Gordal screamed, taking aim at the nearing beasts. "You must take it now!" With the final slice made as accurately as was able with the constant ringing beyond the thin walls, Martus pushed Wynin's folds to the side, reaching his hand deep within her womb. Weeping, he pulled forth the screaming child.

"It is a girl!" he cried, succumbed with joy as he cradled the small bundle to his chest. "Jovaar," he added, hearing the growls of the nearing blasts. "You must take her as I have instructed. You will not look back and you will not attempt contact. We will find you and my dear child as we are able."

Freeing his hand from beneath her small frame, Martus ran his finger down the length of the child's tiny nose. "Be brave, my little one," he said, yet another flash of light ringing through the sky. Handing the child hurriedly to Jovaar, Martus nodded in assurance, tears welling in his eyes. "You must go!" he shouted, wiping his face with the sleeve of his cloak. "And I will pray to my last dying breath that somehow you will find your way."

***

Accepting the wailing child from his elder's arms, Jovaar snapped the small cover from Wynin's unfeeling hand, covering the wee one's small body. Nodding to Gordal, he made his way hurriedly through the door of the meal room. Creeping through the darkened corridor of the shattered home, Jovaar peered out through the random holes, crouching low and struggling against the rising dust.

The narrow, debris-filled pass proved difficult to cross as only flickering rays of light littered in through the remnants of walls. Regardless of his fear of being spotted through the larger openings, he flitted amongst the aged ruins quickly making his way toward the adjoining home's meal room.

Spying the small opening in the wall just ahead, Jovaar ducked with the oncoming squeal, a stray blast piercing an ancient framed photo hung tilted on the wall at his back, crashing to the floor only moments after he had passed,. Glancing down at its shattered pieces amongst the rubble, Jovaar shook his head and pulled the child near, crawling desperately toward the entrance to his assigned exit.

The adjacent meal room, although having been long since deserted, held the remains of what had once been normalcy. Dismissing the past however, he slithered with minimal difficulty despite the added bulk of the child through its narrow opening, hugging the corner wall and finding broken cooking pots and rotting nourishment. Flinching against the stench as small vermin scurried for their next tasty meal, Jovaar covered his face with a corner of the child's blanket, hunkering low toward the center slab.

Knowing the exact location of the exit having worked the schematics himself and for being forced to traverse the catacombs below at his brother's side to reach the secondary above birthing site, Jovaar flung the center slab that had been returned to its given place, to the side. With his haste, both stools and aged nourishment scattered to the floor. Clutching the child, Jovaar flung the worn tapestry toward the now turned table in his desperate search for the hidden exit, the babe whimpering low in his arms.

"Hush, little one," he whispered, coddling the child as he and grasping for the evasive opening. "We must be brave together. Blasted!" he groaned, seething through his teeth, his hands finding no sign of the indentation. "I know it is here!"

Struggling with his unfathomable lack of results, Jovaar reluctantly laid the child on the floor at his side, the blasts ringing out beyond the thinning walls. On hand and knee, he frantically searched for the small elusive handle in the dark. "At last!" he shouted, taking grip of the form, tugging violently to lift its heft.

Surprised at not having remembered its long-ago weight as it had been Drider who had raced ahead, hefting both door and slab to rise above, Jovaar groaned, the veins of his shoulder wrenching with the lift of the thick barricade. Thankful with the force of gravity, he flexed his aging arm, watching as it slammed against the dusty floor. Quickly he gathered the babe, crouching to descend the rungs.

Difficult as it was to shelter the child and simultaneously lift the weighty lid, Jovaar somehow managed to keep his balance. Descending with the screeching of time-worn latches amongst the melee of sheiks from the approaching fire, he took hold of the rungs with his free hand as the cover slammed closed above. At last he was able to make his descent into the dampened darkness.

***

The ground sloshed beneath his feet as he pivoted, desperately feeling up the side of the rungs for the ancient lantern he had placed there, hidden an onar before. Unless disturbed by another, tt had remained untouched as there had been no time to grasp it earlier upon their assent. Finding it on the second try high up on the left side, Jovaar lowered the aged device to his face. Fumbling with the small knob in the darkness, he hurried to ignite its glow.

"This will not work," he mumbled, struggling with the child at his chest as he lowered the lamp to the ground. "I should have listened to Drider." Kneeling to steady himself, Jovaar shook his head with the thought of his younger, laying the child's blanket on the low rung of the rail. Leaning forward and low to keep her from falling, he shifted the babe carefully to his back. With the child thankfully remaining hushed and at last in place, Jovaar grabbed the corners of the small blanket, wrapping it around her wee body and securing it at his chest.

"This should hold for now," he said, standing to test his balance as he reached back to ensure the blanket in fact covered her. When satisfied the makeshift pack would hold, Jovaar stooped to gather the awaiting lantern. At last with two able hands, he found he could ignite it with ease.

With the flame dancing to life in the musty air, Jovaar held the lantern high to lead the way, warily looking out into the eerie pass. "It is not far, little one," he said, reassuringly patting her tiny foot at his waist as he paced the dampened corridor. "Just hold tight and pray the enemy is not lying in wait ahead."

Having memorized the layout of the narrow passes during the time of their construction amidst rehearsal of programs and at last having been forced down their moistened walls upon discovery, Jovaar knew he must take the first left followed by two rights. As the first bend came into view just ahead, he was pleased his memory remained reliable despite the seemingly endless engagements above. Reaching the first turn however, he remained edgy as the muffled blasts continued their ceaseless tirade, closing in on his kin. Although muted and out of his own reach, Jovaar found himself tense in anticipation of a lower ambush.

Leaning against the side wall and peering out into darkness, lowering the aged lantern to his side, Jovaar heard no sounds other than those muffled above...even the babe remained thankfully hushed. Extending his arm and reaching out with the lantern to shed light on the length of the next pass, he spied no movement in either direction. Lowering the glow back to his side, hesitantly stepping into the open corridor, Jovaar reached the second bend as easily as he had the first, hugging the inner wall and peering silently round its edge.

"All is well, little one," he whispered, bringing the lantern to his side, again stepping into the open pass. "We are almost there."

Jovaar knew from memory that the third passage was longer than the others, narrowing at its end on the opposite side, and as he at last reached the lengthy bend, the walls barely passable with the addition of the child, he found himself panting, beads of sweat streaming from his brow. Wiping the moisture with the back of his hand, he again hugged the inner wall, peering quietly around its corner and praying they would be as fortunate as they had been before. Sucking in his breath he spied the slight of movement ahead.

Immediately extinguishing the lantern's glow, Jovaar did his best to steady his breathing, praying the child would remain hushed at his back. Crouching low, he again peered round the corner, staring into the looming darkness.

"Nothing," he thought, his legs aching with the odd angle, impatiently waiting for further sigms. "Yet I know I saw something."

Choosing for the moment, to wait out whatever lay beyond, Jovaar lowered himself to the ground, intermittently leaning round the bend in search of what was most assuredly lying in wait. Yet as he wiped the endless sweat from his brow with his sleeve, his patience waned as nothing more...no movement, no sounds but the ever present echos of the ensuing war above filled his ears. Rubbing his tired eyes with the back of his hands, the child slumbering peaceably despite his unending movements and heavy breathing, Jovaar prayed Gordal was able to hold the enemy off long enough for all those above to somehow escape.

***

Uncertain as to how much time had passed, Jovaar rubbed his aching muscles and slowly rose to change position, squinting as he spied a flutter in the darkness followed by a faint

51

noise just ahead in the distance, as if someone on the ground appeared to adjust their own stance. "One or two?" he wondered, straining desperately to hear more, the child beginning to stir at his back. "No, little one," he thought, reaching back to steady her quickening movements. "Not now."

Having no choice but to act as the babe would most certainly awaken both hungry and frightened, Jovaar slowly gathered the lantern, creeping as silently as possible amongst the muck of the dampened corridor. Clearly spying two shadows ahead in the arch of what was to serve as his secured exit, Jovaar worried over the escape paths of Drider and the others as the darkened forms flickered against the glow of blasts from the upper lanes. Thankful that his steps were at least shielded by the shreiking muted wails from above, Jovaar inhaled deeply to calm his rapidly beating chest, creeping closer to the unknowing enemy.

With only half of the corridor's length remaining, Jovaar reached within his cloak to retrieve his only weapon, yet leaning against the damp wall to test its readiness, several small vermin crept over his foot, startling him in his shielded darkness. "Who is there?" the beast shouted from the opposite end nearest the exit, speaking in the tongue of the notorious Lyclos. "Come forward or we will be forced to fire!"

"Blasted," Jovaar grumbled, hunkering low to consider his options for retreat, yet as the child again stirred at his back, he knew he had no other choice than to remain. Pointing his weapon high, spitting out his fear, Jovaar secured the knot of the child's blanket and crept slowly toward the enemy.

The pair of Lyclos, obviously flinching at the blasts above remained hidden just within the arch, one standing, foot hidden from sight toward the exit door, the other lying prone in the muck, weapons raised and turned toward the uncertainty at the opposite end of the corridor. Hideous creatures, the Lyclos' beady eyes glared into the darkness, snarling in fear and baring an ugly array of large, disproportioned teeth.

Jovaar remembered the nuisances of these creatures and the air of superiority that they attempted to bear having made several treks to the planet Mizar, overseeing the construction of the underground passages. Despite their attempted dominance and the freedoms they were allowed by their current ruler, he found them to be nothing more than an irritation. In spite of their hideous facial features, the Lyclos' stature were quite human-like which should have proved them an agile opponent upon close contact, yet the Lyclos proved a robust and clumsy race. Although they attempted to instill both dominance and fear in those having to endure their existence, a true human, regardless of his size, would prove quite capable of taking several of them down if properly trained.

With the Lyclos' stand still several paces ahead, Jovaar doubled his steps, sprinting toward the arch in an attempt of surprise. Keeping to the left of the passage then quickly darting right, he used the opposite wall as leverage, taking careful aim, the child crying out from the blast.

The beast positioned beneath the small archway was taken immediately, not even having fired his aged weapon. Although the prone beast would have most assuredly hit him had it not been for Jovaar's trained maneuver, he lay stunned with the ambush as Jovaar landed on his feet, the enemy's fate sealed with a single blow.

As the duo beneath the arch proved no longer a threat, Jovaar secured his weapon, quickly untying the knot at his chest. Pulling the child gently before him, he attempted to soothe her obvious fears. With both gentle rocking and soft, kind words, the child's cries at last waned, and releasing a final coo against the backdrop of muted blasts, Jovaar was certain he spied a slight, fragile smile.

"You have survived so much already, little one," he said, reaching down and taking hold of her tiny hand. "Be brave, and be hushed," he added, wiping the last trace of tears from her small face. "And I promise we will get through this together."

With one last moment of connection, Jovaar returned the child to his back, securing her with the small cover, reknotting the blanket at his chest. Together they continued over the lifeless pair, through the arch, and up the stairs.

***

At last reaching the final segment of their escape from below ground, Jovaar arrived at the top of the stairs, the child creating her small sounds at his back. As he peered out the opening below the arch, glancing from side to side down the eerie pass, Jovaar noted the immediate area was clear regardless of the continuing rumblings in the distance. Confident they would not be spotted he crept against the sheltered left remote wall, and turned his attention south to the buildings from whence their journey had begun. Catching his breath, Jovaar stared shaken at the remnants of stone and wood.

"It is gone," he whispered, reaching within his cloak to kiss the medallion at his neck. "I pray to the stars that they survived."

Tucking the token back beneath the cover of cloth, Jovaar reached behind him to reassuringly brush the child. "I made a vow, little one," he said, wiping his face with the sleeve of his free hand, the babe cooing quietly in response at his back. "I made a vow that I intend to keep, and upon my last breath I *swear* I will see you to the final destination."

As if trusting his words silenced her play, Jovaar remained a moment longer, staring at the dilapidated frame of the home that had been the child's place of birth. "For the sake of us all," he whispered, stepping out into the dark deserted lane. "For the sake of us all, you must survive."

***

With a new sense of urgency of not knowing the fate of Martus and the others he held dear, Jovaar raced down the side of the main lane, hugging the tattered buildings and kneeling beneath their random, open panes, making his way toward the imposing hall. Reaching the last corner thankfully unscathed and leaning against the length of what had once been an immense structure, Jovaar hesitantly peered round its corner. Finding it thankfully void of all signs of Lyclos, he turned back to reconsider his route, staring into the openness of the eerie, wide pass.

"We must go, little one," he said, reassuring the slumbering child, yet more than not his own nerves as he clutched the medallion to his chest with his free hand. Inhaling a final, deep breath, knowing that due to their ultimate misfortune of the unthinkable happening, the time had last come. Jovaar raced out into the barren lane.

Darting furiously down the thankfully deserted pass with the grand doors of the hall in sight, Jovaar darted midstride through the most visible sector when the first blast rang out, barely missing his right heel. "No!" he shouted, maintaining his pace and reaching to his back. Drawing the wailing child to his chest with a single, graceful swoop of cloth, Jovaar glanced awkwardly over his shoulder, spying the enemy numbers growing, both in location and size.

***

The Great Hall had once stood magnificent, its large and imposing arches above the lower field and grand inner circle playing host to the most gut-wrenching of Sporyax wars. Thousands had come to this ancient site to wager against the powerful creatures, pitting their beasts one against another until death claimed the weaker, their lyclos tamers both losing and profiting accordingly.

The Sporyax had been reared for no other purpose than battle. Having been unforgiving and forthcoming with the entertainment they provided, relentlessly stomping the loose soil of the inner circle, they now stood as mere stone replicas, undaunting despite their trailing eyes. As Jovaar raced to the rear of the first solid beast at the foot of the dilapidated hall, he paused hunkering low, acknowledging its significance of battle and using its dominate frame as a shield against the enemy fire. The evil snarl of the beast glared its broken teeth above him, and Jovaar knew he could not linger. Returning fire against the swarming lyclos, knowing he was unable to hold his ground with the child cradled in his arms, Jovaar knew the time had come. Staring down at the frightened, yet surprisingly silent babe, Jovaar urged his feet to move. Racing for the doors of the inner circle, he prayed silently that the ship remained.

Despite the guttering assault of enemy blasts, Jovaar safely reached the lower entrance leading directly to the inner circle. Darting through the door to his left, held ajar in anticipation of his return, four members took aim at the ensuing lyclos. As his comrades handedly dealt with the last of the enemy's initial assault, Jovaar slowed his stride within the outskirts of the massive hall, once again attempting to soothe the child. His fear of capture ever present, he kept his pace even, the back of his fingers caressing the babe's cheek as he crossed the main entrance to the inner circle.

Once a place of boisterous activity, Jovaar and child passed the eerily emptiness of what had been a vital part of the Sporyax wars. The site of where bet takers had claimed their winnings, the main corridor vaguely resembled its past existence, looters and time having tarnished its forgotten glory. Tattered remnants remained where once a glorious candelabrum had emitted its glow upon the initial steps of the arriving bettors, yet at Jovaar's feet, rodents now skittered upon the shards of a mosaic floor. Nothing had been spared from the destitute of Manine. Shielding the child with her blanket against both mustiness and filth, Jovaar dismissed the long-forgotten corridor, as all others had done for some time, and continued through the next set of doors that led directly to the grand, inner circle.

Two

Its high arched frame opening to the darkened skies above, the Great Hall echoed with its history of violent death, yet Jovaar sighed thankfully amongst its ruins, spying the ship unscathed at its rear. Reassuring the child as he trotted, shielding her from the dry dirt twirling at his ankles, Jovaar hurried to its side. Although considered small, the ship held a crew of twelve comfortably. Running his hand over the sleekness of its underbelly, his smile widened as he spotted Phydin waiting at the foot of the plank.

"I had feared the worst," Phydin began, clasping Jovaar's hand welcomingly.

"Forgive me," Jovaar reassured, accepting the gesture and turning to walk the plank at Phydin's side. "I encountered more than I had anticipated. Head to Command and order the crew to prepare for detachment."

"Martus and the others?" Phydin asked, turning in the well lit hull, his hand hesitant on the door prompt.

"I do not know," Jovaar answered, shaking his head and continuing his rock of the slumbering child. "But I fear the worst."

Looking down at the small, ever important bundle and then at last to Jovaar, Phydin, for the first time, read fear in the eyes of his leader. Although desperately wanting to learn more on the fate of the others, yet because of the look of Jovaar's face, Phydin simply reached out to touch the child's arm before reluctantly racing without additional words to Command to give the order. Once again alone with the child, Jovaar sighed, his fears unrelenting as he peered down, pulling the blanket from her small face.

"We have arrived as promised," he whispered, tapping the tip of her nose. "Although our journey has been difficult, I am afraid it is not quite over. For the sake of those who remain filled with faith, little one, we must together be brave."

The child, seeming to understand his words, radiated a slight grin, as babes do, as she slept. Basking in the hopes of what lay in his arms and what was to come Jovaar returned her smile, enjoying a brief moment of calm with his elder's child.

***

Startled, Jovaar lifted his eyes to the door as three of his final four comrades entered midship, dotted with sweat despite the dampness of the nighttime air. "Where is Yanci?" he asked, covering the child with the blanket as blasts rang from the hall's inner circle.

"He did not make it, Sir," the man answered, his chest heaving with every stride to claim his seat. "We attempted to retrieve him but were unfortunately overrun. Forgive me."

Cursing himself for allowing another loss, Jovaar simply nodded, having no words of comfort to offer. Cradling the child in the crook of his arm, he turned, quickening his steps to Command.

His men, having heeded Phydin's order were postioned at the ready, each performing their detachment processes at their assigned posts. Confident of their permormance, Jovaar sealed the rear cabin door and stood silent, overseeing their progress.

The narrow Command consisted of six stations; pilot, navigation, communications, data control, system ops, and the helm. Hurrying to his given post, Jovaar handed the child to the tending steward who impatiently waited nearby. "Take her to Med-deck and check vitals," he said, abruptly claiming his seat. "I will come for her status when we have cleared the atmosphere."

"And Wynin?" she asked fearfully, ignoring Jovaar's sternness. Jovaar simply shook his head without turning and the steward's eyes welled silently at his back. Bundling the child to her breast, she crossed to the rear door, leaving without word.

The members, refusing to return her stare despite their own fears, instead made their final preparations for debarkment.

"All systems report," Phydin ordered, hearing the swoosh of the door at his back, simultaneously tapping his screen.

"Nav go, Comms go, DC go, SO go, Command go," Jovaar added at the last.

"Thrusters on," Phydin continued, expertly piloting the ship's controls. "We have detachment, tri-legs up, flaps down. We will be exto-atmos in twenty."

The ship ascended with only a minor tremor of the thruster's leaving contact with the ground and Jovaar peered out the side glass, glancing down just as hundreds of lyclos swarmed the inner circle. Firing one last fruitless effort to take the rising craft with weapons raised with rage, the lyclos remained unrelenting to the last. Unscathed, Jovaar turned his gaze from the shrinking images below to his station, yet no smile crossed his face. Phydin indeed sailed them swiftly and safely into the sky yet he knew as did they all, that their journey was only beginning.

***

Reaching the outer atmosphere with swift precision and ridding themselves of Adoni within the timeframe and scope Phydin had indicated, the short-lived, relief-washed crew frantically readied their stations for battle, the sight of a new enemy filling their screens.

"Why did our scanners not indicate?" Jovaar groaned, abruptly altering his panel. "We could have possibly avoided this!"

"I am aware of that," Phydin answered, hastily lowering the overhead controls, prompting the ship sharply to the right. "Had I known, I could have flown through an alternate sector!"

"All personnel restrain immediately!" Jovaar added prompting the com, his eyes however, trained on the number of approaching enemy. "And prepare for evasive actions!"

Phydin diverted their course sharply east as two massive Sugin ships lay waiting in ambush and the trained crew monitored their status, preparing for incoming enemy fire. Jovaar however, made their decision for retreat.

"Nav, set course for Yani Substation, hyper drive," he ordered, knowing the setback was unfortunate, but necessary. "There is too much at stake to do otherwise. If we were to sail directly to the rendezvous we would undoubtedly be followed...if we even made it there at all. The substation is a necessary diversion. If we can land there and regroup, then we stand a chance, albeit a small one of saving the child."

"I am counting at least twenty minios approaching from Sector Four," Data Com chimed, downloading stats of count, speed and model to each station.

"Man guns and fire at will," Jovaar ordered prompting the com, DC's information filling his screen. Three gunmen heeding his order, quickly claimed their positions in the firing pit, its bulk situated at the belly of the small ship, its shaft circling its hull. "Disregard the Sugin sisters and concentrate all firepower on the minios," Jovaar ordered. "We need time to set the course for hyper."

The men relied upon to man the sub-level guns, having spent onars behind their formidable controls proved their skills once again. The minios swarmed round the ship like pests, yet easily succumbed to their expert aim. As each shattered the tedious enemy with the aim of their hefty arms, they could not contain their cheers, the remaining shards of debris cascading downward, fading from view.

"We are down to half," Kroy noted, pivoting his station to the top of the ship. "Starboard side, two sailing in, one main, one sub, take the offensive."

"I'm on it," Jax answered, pivoting right, opposite his comrade. "You just take care of yours."

The gunners continued their onslaught on the dwindling hostiles, undaunted as the ship careened against another direct hit. Despite the violent movement, the gunners danced with ease along the archs designed by Jovaar's younger. Fidaldi however, frantically keyed his panel, his brow beading with sweat as he prompted maintenance.

"We have lost the shield on port!" he shouted, struggling to remotely rebond the midship electronic connections.

"Do what you can," Jovaar answered, his eyes trained on his own panel. "We have to elude the Sugins sisters and we must do it at once if we are to survive. Nav, where are you? We need hyper and we need it now!"

The commanding Sugins appeared lying in wait having yet to fire their larger guns, instead allowing the fruitless attempts of their minios to maintain their enemy's attention. Phydin, maneuvering to avoid the last strays of the pesky ships, grumbled as he awaited the coordinates.

"Hyper up, ready, and go," Luvin said, accepting the last information of their path, sighing in relief that he had been able to coordinate in time.

"Restrain for hyper!" Jovaar shouted into the com to those in the rear, trusting he need not wait for a response. With one last stick adjustment as his screen accepted the charted course Luvin provided, Phydin had his comrades and the small child in rear with her steward, sailing swiftly and safely into the shield of awaiting stars.

***

With tear-filled eyes for both the loss of Wynin and the hope of the child in her arms, Selena carried the small bundle down the narrow corridor of sub-level midship. Passing the firing pit with a slight smile to the two visible gunners, she entered Med-deck, nodding at the impatiently awaiting medofficer.

"Hand the child to me," he said firmly, extending his surprisingly shaking arms. Selena reluctantly placed the child in his hands and watched him carry her fragile body to the incubation unit. Lifting its weighty glass cover, the medofficer carefully placed the babe within.

Folding her blanket neatly as the man readied the monitors, Selena held the soft folds to her face, inhaling the child's scent longingly before quickly placing it at the babe's feet. Unmoved by Selena's gestures, the medfficer attached the small nodes to her chest and heart. Swiftly closing the lid and latching its lock, the medofficer crossed the room to his monitoring cart. Guiding the floating device with a single palm toward the incubation unit, he quickly began his series of tests.

Unable to cease the program once it had begun, the medofficer barked his orders as the ship careened about them. "Attach the line in case we lose power due to those minio-nuisances," he said, keying rapidly on his panel without turning. Following his stern instructions, Selena quickly reached behind the incubator, pulling the lifeline free, attaching it to the UPS unit.

"It is done," she said simply, wringing her hands and looking for approval. Seeing there was nothing further she could do to assist him, the medofficer's eyes fully focused on his panel, Selena restrained herself per Jovaar's order to a small bench adjacent to the child. Silently watching the officer frustratingly secure his own restraints, Selena held firm to the base of her seat as the ship once again careened, the machine unwaning, gathering its essential vitals.

The ship sped through the darkness, at last sailing smooth amongst the stars, yet Selena's grip never left the base of her seat as she stared nervously at the thin lines of light dancing upon the medofficer's screen. Having previously been informed of their meaning; green indicating the child's blood flow, yellow her rate of breathing, and red representing heart waves, Selena somewhat eased, along with the slowing ship as all appeared within normal levels.

"You are strong one," the officer said, rising from his seat to cross the room. Placing his hands through the incuzone passage, Selena watched as he rubbed her thigh with the cleansing cloth, allowing a moment to turn and reassure his assistant.

"It will only hurt for a moment," he said, his tone flat despite his reassurances as he turned back to the tearing child, striking her with the needle. Flinching as the babe frighteningly wailed, Selena at last released her restraints, crossing to her side. Clearing her own hands through the zone, she caressed the child's small face.

"Attach the line to the fluid release," the medofficer ordered, shooing her from his work. Following his knowing instruction, Selena freed the lifeline from the UPS, connecting it the incubation unit. "There now, little one," the officer whispered, pulling his hands free of the zone and tipping his face close to the glass. "I promise that what I have done is for the best, not only for you but for us all. Sleep well, small one and let the serum do as it is intended."

"I have followed all given orders," the officer added, his voice booming as he straightened, crossing the cabin and returning the monitoring cart to its station. "Stay with the child and inform me if there are any changes in her condition. Otherwise, I will freshen and return shortly."

Nodding as the man crossed silently to the door, Selena returned her hands within the zone, placing the blanket over the child. The medofficer stopped, turning with curiosity. "Selena," he said, grasping the opened jam as she turned to face him. "Her name?"

Turning to look back upon the face of the sleeping child, Selena smiled at her delicate features then turned with pride to face the officer, confident the child was at last through the worst. "She will be known the world over as Nitayatinus Savius," she said, extending her fingers to the child's face, caressing her fair skin. "Yet we will call her Nitaya."

"It is a good name," he whispered, tilting his head in approval. "I am certain that Wynin and Martus would approve."

Three

Jovaar was anxious. Although pleased that they had been able to use the hyper drive to escape the Sugins sisters and their minios underlings, he remained troubled with the standoff of the massive ships. "Why did they not fire?" he wondered, staring out the glass into the darkness. "Why did they not fire or even follow? Surely their capabilities were sound. Why would they not even…"

"Hyper is stalled," Phydin said, interrupting Jovaar's thoughts as the ship slowed to a more comfortable speed. "If there are no further enagements we should be docking at Yani within two hazon."

"Very well," Jovaar answered, running his fingers through his hair. "That will give me enough time to look in on the child and get some rest. Can you manage the Com?"

"Of course," Phydin answered, nodding over his shoulder.

"DC," Jovaar continued, logging off from his station. He rose, turning to his younger counterpart. "I want you to keep scanning for those Sugin monstrosities. I am not comfortable with their lack of response."

Accepting the order with a silent nod, Orvi keyed his panel, patching his secondary screens for a more thorough scan of the surrounding areas. Jovaar nodded his silent approval. "I will update you with any sign, Sir."

Satisfied that all precautions were in place, Jovaar crossed to the rear door. "If needed," he added, prompting the hatch. "You can reach me in Med-deck."

***

Pacing the narrow corridor through the empty midship, Jovaar rounded the few vacant seats then lowered to the sub-level, reaching the firing pit opening. Pausing, he rounded the rungs, taking a moment to look in on his men. One remained at his post.

"What is the status on gear?" he asked, leaning against the right rear track. The gunner, having not heard his commander's entrance sat facing the aft monitor. Jovaar repeated his inquiry with a bit more zeal and the man quickly turned to his familiar voice.

"Three of the four are operational, Sir," Kroy answered, brushing his long dark locks from his face. "Jax and Uvis are down below attempting to get the fourth up and running."

"Very well, Jovaar answered, crouching to look into the cramped pit. "Have here been any improvements thus far, Jax?"

"Sir," he answered, wincing as he rammed his head into an overhead support. Stewing, he motioned for Uvis to continue the soldering. "One of the minios hit dead on disrupting several of our cables, but it is nothing we can't solve," Jax said, vigorously rubbing his wound. "We should have her operational within a half hazon."

"That is good news," Jovaar answered, chuckling at his subordinate's discomfort and rising to his knees. "Update me as soon as all systems are a go. And Jax," he added leaning low into the pit, seriousness returning to his tone. "When you have finished the repairs, I want the two of you down to quarters. We have less than two hazon until reaching Yani, and I need the three of you rotating down so you remain alert."

"We are in better shape than I had hoped," Jovaar continued, standing as Kroy retracted his monitor, attempting to rise with is superior. "No, Kroy," Jovaar added, halting the man with his hand. "For the moment, remain at your post. I have ordered Uvis and Jax to their quarters once the repairs are complete."

"Of course," Kroy answered, reattaching his restraints. "I will inform you once our status returns to one hundred percent, Sir."

"See to that, Kroy," Jovaar answered, glancing out the glass over Kroy's shoulder. "And if you need me, I will be in Med-deck or my own quarters for the next hazon."

**

Jovaar continued on to the rear in search of the medofficer, yet prompting the door to Med-deck, he instead found the steward softly singing to the sleeping child. Embarrassed at his interruption into the room, she ceased her lilt, crossing to the incubator.

"All vitals are within normal range, Sir," she said, gesturing for her commander to come forward to the far benches. "The medofficer has returned to quarters, yet should return momentarily. He of course will be able to give you the specifics on her condition, however he has assured me that all indications prove she is sound."

"That is excellent news, Selena," Jovaar said ignoring the offered seat, instead crossing to claim her hands. "I had feared the child might have been more seriously hurt in our escape."

"Unscathed and resting peacefully at the moment, Sir," she answered, blushing at his gesture. "Such a strong little girl," she added, holding back her welling tears. "Wynin would have surely been proud."

"Do not weep, Selena," Jovaar whispered, brushing her lonesome tear with the back of his hand. "We are not certain of Martus and Wynin's fate. Although it may seem grim, we must not lose hope for as you can plainly see, hope forever remains within the child. For her we must be strong."

"She has a name, Jovaar," Selena whispered, Jovaar simultaneously lifting her chin to peer into her eyes. "Her given title is Nitayatinus Savius, yet as I, all others dear to her will call her Nitaya."

"It is a strong name, Selena," Jovaar said, looking over to Martus and Wynin's slumbering child. "It is a strong name for a strong Savius. You have done well and you should be proud. I am just sorry that you were not able to give the babe her title in the proper setting." Smiling, Jovaar reached out to caress Selena's cheek, dismissing her obvious discomfort of providing the posible's fated name in haste. Having calmed the elder, he then crossed to the incubator to speak quietly with the child.

"Nitaya," Jovaar whispered, his face a mere breath from the glass. "It is I who will protect you, teach you and guide you in your palle's absence. Grow strong, wee one, for there is so much for you yet to do."

As if understanding his words, Nitaya opened her eyes to his warm tone and smiling, appeared to look back at the man who was to be her protector. With the moment of hope for what was to come proving all too brief however, Jovaar watched the child again close her eyes. Both Jovaar and Selena proved startled with the opening of the rear door at their back. The medofficer had returned.

"I assure you, Sir Savius, the child is sound," he began, grandly entering the cabin. "All vitals are within normal range yet I did however, notice a minor drop in her blood flow. I have there have returned with the pulsar as standard."

Shaken by his previously unknown prognosis, Selena balled her fists, releasing her anger. "You did not tell me of this, officer," she glared, crossing to his side. "Is she truly safe? How bad is her condition?"

"Calm, Selena," he answered, placing his hand on the woman's shoulder. "I assure both of you that it is only minor and more than likely due to the intense trauma she received during the escape. I will scan the pulsar for any blockages in her flow and will give her the serum only if necessary. I assure you this in only a precaution."

Jovaar drew Selena away from the medofficer and the pair stood tense as he placed the machine within the incubator. Keeping watch over the red light scanning above her small body, Jovaar claimed Selena's hands in his. Knowing that the Officer had not been with them long, yet relying on his knowledge alone to see that Nitaya was well, Jovaar remained uneasy despite his outward assurances.

"There," the officer said, gesturing toward Nitaya's heart. "There is in fact a small blockage near the base of the neck. The serum will be able to dissolve it in approximately a hazon… possibly less. I promise you both that she will not feel pain. May I continue, Sir Savius?"

67

"Of course," he answered, patting Selena's hand. "You must do whatever is necessary for with the most probable loss of the others, everything depends on this child."

Nodding and simultaneously crossing to the small cooling box, the medofficer scanned cursiously long over several vials before selecting the antedote. "Here," he said at last, closing the door and returning to the unit. "I will just insert this into her fluid tube and then soon we will know for certain that all is once again well."

As the pink fluid began its long trek down the narrow tube mixing with the clear solution, it slowly entered its combined mass into the child's fragile system, Jovaar and Selena standing anxiously next to the unit, awaiting her reaction. "It will be some time," the medofficer said, pulling forth the now empty tube.

"Then I will be in quarters if there is the slightest of change," Joavaar answered, nodding to Selena and releasing her hands. "Please do not hesitate to notify me."

"Of course, Sir," the officer answered, unturning. "I will remain with the child at all times."

"Very well," Jovaar added crossing to the door, unwilling to divulge that he required rest. "I will return prior to our arrival at Yani."

***

Crossing the narrow corridor, Jovaar spied his gunners at the end of the pass, obviously in full discussion. Turning slightly to the right to palm his entrance, he chose to leave the pair to their seemingly endless arguments and instead, entered his cabin.

"Just as I left it," he said, sighing at the empty space. His cot stood invitingly in the far corner of the room. Rather than accept its obvious invitation however, he stepped to the tall cabinet to change out of his less than appealing attire.

Unfastening his outer cloak and dropping it to the floor without thought, Jovaar paused before the length of the glass, staring at the last eighteen hazon sketched plain on his face. Covered in filth, stubble, and with splattered bits of blood on his cheek, he paused, wondering if the dark remnants were his or that of another. In the chaos he had not noticed being struck.

"Martus, I am sorry I could not do more," he said, staring at his aged reflection. Sighing once again and removing his filthy smock, he crossed to the washroom, placing the tattered garment on a low shelf to the right of the basin. Quickly he took out his familiar supplies to cleanse his face from Adoni's waste. Briskly lathering to cover the stubble, Jovaar made haste with its removal, careful to slow his hand as he passed over the blood.

"Blasted, it is mine," he winced, cursing himself as he mistakingly sliced the wound further. "And I just added to the blasted mess."

Rinsing his face with frustration and a clean cloth, Jovaar reached up to touch the now decent sized gash and grimaced, finding that one small shard remained. Leaning closer to the glass and gently pulling it free, he groaned, grabbing for the cloth to dab at the slow trickle of blood. At last when the oozing had stopped, he exhaled loudly, his image appearing only somewhat improved.

Knowing he had precious little time, Jovaar removed the last stitch of his clothing and opening the door of the wall unit, tossed the bundle into the shoot before stepping into the basin. Remembering the exact sequence of controls, he prompted the two that would give him the temperature he desired and shivered as the hot flow gushed over his body. Lifting his head to drench his face in the glorious warmth, Jovaar stood only a moment to enjoy its heat before quickly gathering the cleanser, covering his skin with the thick lather.

"I should have found a way to do more, Martus," his said, choking on his words, his voice echoing off the walls with the filth of Adoni rinsing away at his feet. "It was not supposed to turn out like this."

Angry with himself for not being able to save them, Jovaar punched at the wall before him then reluctantly turned off the controls. Head down, he opened the stall door. Grabbing a clean cloth from a nearby hook he wiped off his body rather than prompting the basin's dry mode, took special care around his wound before tossing the damp cloth into the shoot. Although disheartened but at last refreshed, he returned to his empty cabin. Pacing to the cabinet, he quickly dressed in the nearest garment.

"There has been no sign of the Sugin ships, Sir," Luvin began, his voice echoing over the portal as Jovaar secured it at his wrist. "We have entered Yani airspace and should be landing in a half hazon."

"So noted," Jovaar answered, selecting a fresh cloak. "I will return to Command as soon as I have looked in on Nitaya."

"I am sorry, Sir?" Luvin quickly questioned, uncertain as to what he was referring. "You will be looking in on what?"

"The child, Luvin," Jovaar answered, clasping his cloak at his neck and stepping back to access his reflection in the glass. "The child has been given her title. She is to be called Nitaya."

"Yes, Sir," he answered, pausing. "Tis a good name."

"That it is, Luvin," Jovaar answered, closing the connection. "So much for a little rest," he grumbled, eyeing the warmth of the cot across the room. Shaking his head as he lowered to grab his gear, his tired image quickly forgotten, Jovaar paced to the rear, reluctantly prompting the door. If all others were indeed lost, he would risk everything to save the one entrusted to him.

Four

Retracing his steps down the narrow corridor, ignoring the vacant firing pit, Jovaar turned, whistling to steady his nerves as he climbed the rungs. Reaching the top however, his tune ceased. Stopping on the last tier, he stared at Selena racing toward him, fear obvious on her face.

"It is Nitaya, Jovi!" she screamed pulling on his cloak, not waiting for him to reach the last rung. "The child is non-reactive to stimuli!"

"What do you mean?" he shouted, grabbing hold of her quivering arms, regaining his footing on the upper floor. "I left her only a half hazon ago and she was…"

"The serum, Jovi!" Selena interrupted, gasping for breath. "I think the serum was a ruse. The medofficer sent me from the room on some tedious errand and when I returned the door would not open at my prompt. I do not know what he is doing to her. He will not let me in!"

Brushing Selena to the side and retracing his steps down the rungs, Jovaar returned to Med-deck, Selena catching up with him just as he prompted his code to the door. He found it remained firmly in place.

"Let me in!" he shouted, banging on the barrier with both fists. "What are you doing? I demand you open this door at once!"

Selena anxiously paced the corridor at his back yet Jovaar knew there was no time to comfort her. If the medofficer meant to do Nitaya harm, he had to somehow get passed the obstruction if he stood any chance of stopping him.

"System Ops!" Jovaar shouted, brushing his sleeve to the side to give the order into his portal. "Open the Med-deck door immediately!"

"Sir," Fidaldi abruptly answered from Command. "What is wrong?"

"I have no time to explain," Jovaar scowled, eyeing Selena mumbling at his back. "Just open the blasted door!"

Leaning against the frame of the jam for what seemed an eternity, Jovaar jumped as Fidaldi's voice rang over the com. "Systems are functioning, Sir," he said, having overrun the system from his station. "Re-key your code." Punching in the sequence to the only door aboard ship that required one, Jovaar stood back as it quickly sprang upward. Racing into the cabin, he found the MO removing Nitaya from her chamber.

"You are too late," he said simply, not turning to face the pair. Ignoring his words, Jovaar ran to his back, yanking his shoulder then standing horrified, shock filled his eyes. "A phymbial," he whispered, grabbing hold of the limp child and staring into the ugly yellow eyes of his enemy. "This is not possible."

"I assure you that it is, you simple man," the medofficer-beast said calmly, shrugging away from Jovaar's grasp. "And as I have been in your presence for quite some time, I find it amusing that you had never once detected me."

"There is nothing you can do," the phymbial continued, the child lying limp in the crook of Jovaar's arm. "The babe is in coma and will soon die. Your efforts have been fruitless and now my task is done. The earlier syrum that Selena all too easily allowed me to inject has blended quite well with the last. You will never have what it is that you seek."

Holding the child, Jovaar was unable to reach out in time to stop the beast as the phymbial withdrew the small needle from the sleeve of his cloak. Forcefully injecting it into the brightness of his left yellow eye, Jovaar stood stunned as the being fell quickly to the floor.

"Selena, take her," he said, gently placing the limp child in her arms. "Get her back into the incubation unit at once. I cannot let him die if we are to have any chance of saving her!"

"What did you give her?" Jovaar screamed, kneeling down to shake the dying creature. "Where is the antidote?"

"As I have told you," the phymbial answered, rolling his head and blinking with the only eye that remained. "You are too late. All praise King Sugin."

As the being gasped his last breath, Jovaar watched without choice, the lone trail of clear blood trickling from the beast's parted lips. Shaking his head and sitting back on his heels, guilt filled him for having been so careless.

"I have not done this myself," Selena panicked, the babe unresponsive in her arms. Opening the incubation unit, Selena's cries startled Jovaar from his trance as she gently placed the child within. "I did watch him closely, Jovi. I know how to reattach the lines but regardless they will be useless without the antedote."

"Do what you can," he answered, leaving the lifeless body of the phymbial on the floor. "There has to be something here to save her." Crossing to the coolant box nestled deep within the rear wall, Jovaar searched frantically for anything that would show him what the child had been given. Pushing the foreign-named vials and odd-shaped containers to the side, he ran his hands through his hair. He could find nothing that resembled the serum.

"He must have stored it in here!" he shouted, tossing a small container to the floor. "Look on the body and see if you can find the vial he used on Nitaya." Kneeling to quickly search through the med-officer's garments, tears of frustration welled in Selena's eyes. She could find no trace of the small evil tube.

"There is nothing here, Jovi," she said, wiping her face with the sleeve of her cloak. "But wait," she added, rocking on her heels to face him. "All discarded materials are placed in the disintegrating hatch! Maybe he placed it there!" The pair darted without words, meeting at the hatch. Jovaar stood nervously as Selena yanked open its door, tilting up on her toes to peer inward.

"It is too late," she cried, covering her face with her hands, the lid slamming firmly back into place. "The phymbial prompted the release sending the contents to disposal."

"Where does it go?" Jovaar asked, taking firm hold of her shoulders.

"To Recycle, Jovaar," she answered, quickly raising her head. "Lowest level, but we cannot possibly…"

"Make sure all lines are secured to the unit," he ordered, Selena's eyes wide as she turned back to the child.

"I think this is right," she said, securing the last of the lines. "Although I cannot be certain, Jovi."

"It will have to do," he answered, quickly claiming her hand.

"But someone should stay with…"

"We must go now," he interrupted, leading Selena to the door. "Come," he added, keying the code for the door to rise. "There is not much time."

***

Selena lagged at Jovaar's back as he took the narrow pass with the fewest of strides, bypassing the rungs and skidding down the outside poles. Pirvoting in the cramped space he at last faced Recycle, housed within the largest foot stomp of R8. Selena simultaneously reached his back with the sounding swoosh of the door at his front and the pair stood silent, staring at the remnants of the ship's waste.

Although appearing as nothing more than a narrow hallow tube extending from the highest point to the lowest of the ship, Recycle held the complexities of its larger compression unit counterparts. As discarded articles were placed in their slender shoots throughout the ship, the waste would travel with the assistance of airflow through the tubes until landing at the base of the compartment. Upon arrival, the machine's thin robotic-like arms, extending double elbowed joints, would spring forth from the rounded walls.

Picking apart the refuse, the machine would place recyclable pieces in small cabinets as specified doors popped open in receive mode. All that remained would then be compacted with the condensed version of the mash. Upon completion, the base of the unit would open, dropping the rubbish to the disintegration chamber.

The Recycle process initiated every half hazon as programmed and as the system did not allow for interruption,

Jovaar calculated that they had mere moments to spare. With the array of stray materials lying in wait at the bottom of the shaft, including the old cables Jax had replaced in the firing pit, Jovaar reached into the machine knowing that once the process began his hands would be fair play for the joints.

"It has to be in here!" he shouted, hastily rifling through the tangled debris.

"Quickly," Selena begged, wringing her hands at his back. "We are running out of time!"

Reaching low between the twisted cables, straining as the rubbish pushed against his neck, Jovaar felt a slight prick on his finger, causing only a slight pause in his search. "What is it?" Selena asked, peering over his shoulder.

"I have it," Jovaar answered, wasting no time with the possibility of penetration. Pulling the syringe free, he leapt as the machine sprang to life. "I will return to Med-deck," he added, prompting the recycle door to close and turning to steady Selena's trembling shoulders. "I need you to head back to Command to inform DC of our situation. Tell Orvi I need information on..." he paused, rotating the vial in his hand. "Tell him I need everything he can give me on JLP4. Have him patch all data to the med-officer's monitor then meet me there. I will need all the help you can give me."

Selena waited impatiently below despite his speed as Jovaar raced up the rungs before her. Once clear, he shouted for her to follow, his hands claiming hers as soon as they were within reach. Although anxious to return to Med-deck, Jovaar assisted her in continuing her ascent up the rungs before returning to rear pass. At last clearing the last of the rungs, Selena turned left, bypassing the vacant stations. Gasping, she prompted the command door, hunkering low as she attempted to speak. "Orvi!" she shouted, trying desperately to catch her breath. "Jovaar needs all the information you can gather on JLP4!"

"We are about to begin our approach, Selena," Orvi said, turning slowly from his station. "Can this not wait until we reach Yani?"

"No," Selena continued, rising, her hands planted firmly on her hips. "Nitaya is laying lifeless in Med-deck! The med-officer was apPymbial. I have no time to explain, Orvi. Just get me the blasted information!"

Pivoting abruptly from her, Orvi immediately altered his screen for search, keying furiously on his panel, the remaining members with the exception of Phydin staring in shock at her words. "JLP4?" he asked, not looking from his station.

"Yes," Selena answered, crossing to peer over his shoulder. "You must hurry, Orvi!"

Selena could feel time fading as she held firm to the back of Orvi's seat, and knowing the child lay limp in the small unit at Med-deck, she struggled with the delay of the search knowing that Jovaar would be feeling the same fear. Gripping, her knuckles white as she stared desperately at Orvi's small screen, its flash of letters passing quickly over its face, Selena shook her head as Phydin began his rhythmic orders for approach knowing there was little time before all would be required to restrain.

"All systems report for final approach," Phydin ordered, expertly adjusting the stick without turning. "Nav go, comms go, SO go," they said routinely, each monitoring their given stations.

"Orvi, status!" Phydin shouted, glancing over his shoulder with gritted teeth.

"I am trying," he answered, wiping the sweat from his brow. "I have almost got it." With the flickering beauty of Yani appearing through the forward glass, Selena released Orvi's seat, wringing her hands as the remaining crew sat tensly waiting his clear.

"Orvi!" Selena screamed, balling her fists and circling in place. "We need the information now!"

"I have it," he answered, keying the response and bringing up the data. "Is Jovaar in Med-deck now?"

"Yes," she cried, reclaiming the seatback. "Forward it to the phymbial's screen."

Abruptly transferring the data, Orvi rang his com with the last of the clearing data. "Jovaar," he said, staring at the endless array of medical jargon. "The transfer should be on your screen now."

"I have got it," he answered, his voice ringing throughout command. "Tell Selena to get down here!" Orvi turned with the order yet found Selena was already prompting the rear door.

Pivoting back to his station as she raced from the cabin, he altered his screen to respond to Phydin and the others who sat impatiently awaiting his response.

"DC go," he said, keying the last of his strokes. Phydin acknowledged the awaited confirmation, having slowed their descent to Yani as required without all approval, and Orvi exhaled loudly as his superior gave the final order.

"Flaps down and prepare for attachment," Phydin said altering to his landing screen, his eyes once again concentrating forward. With Yani growing larger in the glass, all eagerly watched from their given stations as their pilot steadied the ship to began their fateful descent.

***

Selena ran as fast as her legs would carry her toward the rear, lower level of the ship, sensing the craft slow with the onset of landing with each step she took. "How much time has passed while we searched for the answer?" she thought, taking hold of the rungs. "Is there still a chance of saving the child?"

Afraid for Nitaya's life and for the purpose unto which she was born to serve, Selena raced to the Med-deck door knowing they were less than a quarter hazon of reaching Yani. Keying her code to the right of the barricade, she spied Jovaar staring intently at the phymbial's panel, the door receding swiftly at her back.

"JLP4 has a life of a hazon," he began, having disregarded his restraints to peer closer to the screen. "The serum consists of particles that travel through the blood stream, neutralizing the nervous system. Nitaya will permanently lose all mobility if an antidote is not administered by..." he said, hesitating while he scanned the data. "We might have already passed over the time, Selena, yet you know as I do we must try."

Jovaar shifted at the med-officer's station, his tension clear as he altered the panel's various screens. Selena crossed to him, strapping in to the seat at his back. "Phydin has us on approach," he said, not raising his eyes from the data.

"Yes," Selena answered, straining to peer over his shoulder. "We should be arriving momentarily." Ignoring the rumbling of the ship's thrusters, his eyes never leaving the screen bearing Nitaya's vitals, Jovaar multi-patched the data so that he was able to read both her life line and the schematics of the medication.

"She is fading," he whispered, the box to key the sequence urging the necessary equation. "Hurry," Jovaar added, concentrating on the side screen. "Read to me the contents list so I can input them into the program." Straining to view the data as Jovaar inched to his right, Selena named off the five items and their required amounts listed on the side screen.

"That is all there is, Jovaar," she cried, leaning back to look over to the child. "Surely that cannot be all of it."

"It has to be," he answered, frustratedly keying the order. "I have entered the ingredients as listed. If the data is true and if I have performed the correct sequence of functions, the system should create the antidote. Pray, Selena. Pray we have done this right."

Knowing that they would have to stabilize the child prior to debarking the ship, there was no time to consider other options. With the machine behind the small panel beginning its rhythmic hum, the pair sat silent, the program devising the requested dosage.

The slender vial produced itself at the base of the small glass enclosure and as the pin-sized spout rotated, dribbling its array of colored liquids into the narrow tube, the whir ceased, the final arm joint thrusting the vial forward. The spout, withdrawing to the rear of the space so that the glass could be sealed, darted backward allowing for the liquid's blending.

"All systems complete," the mechanical voice said, the glass door quickly rising. Looking over his shoulder to Selena, Jovaar grasped the vial of blue tinted liquid from the clutch of the joint then unclasping his restraints, rose and crossed to the child.

Nitaya had remained as before, attached to the life line within the confines of the unit, yet as Jovaar began opening the side door of the chamber to administer what he prayed would save her, Selena gabbed his arm, stopping him. "You must first attach the needle," she said, reaching down to the side compartment to retrieve it. "Then you must use the incuzone passage," she added, steadying herself against the flutter of the ship using the unit's base for balance. "Here, let me help you."

Guiding Jovaar's hands forward through the pass, Selena watched as he followed her careful movents, tugging everso slightly on the life line. Finding the connection in tact, he inserted what they prayed was the antedote just as the ship slowed into port. "Be strong little one," Jovaar whispered, caressing the crook of her frail arm. "There are so many of us depending on you."

Leaning against the unit to offset the reeling tilt from the ceasing thrusters, the pair's eyes could not look away from the blue liquid mixing with the clear. "How long until we know?" Jovaar asked, his nose mere inches from the glass. Freeing her hands to cross to the panel, Selena claimed the phymbial's seat to find his answer.

"I cannot be certain, Jovi," she said, scanning over the endless information. "But if we have selected the proper elements, it should not be long."

"Well, we have obviously arrived and have no time to wait," he answered, ignoring Selena's flaring eyes as he tossed open the unit's door. "If she is to survive, and I pray that she does, Nitaya must do so without this contraption. DC, we have done all we can from here," Jovaar continued, prompting his portal as he reached in to unfasten the now clear life line. "Update the rest of command then reroute all crew to Med-deck. I will need everyone's assistance transporting the child off the ship."

"Copy that, Sir," Orvi answered, silencing communications.

"Selena," Jovaar added, peering over his shoulder. "Head to quarters and grab all essentials then meet us back here. You must understand that we have to debark immediately."

Knowing Jovaar was right Selena took one last unsteady look at the drifting child. Nodding, she quickly turned to prompt the door.

Five

Having hastily performed their post-flight processes immediately following their uneventful landing on Yani, the members stood surrounding Jovaar and the bundled child at the center of Med-deck. Anxiously awaiting their orders, Orvi dragged the lifeless phymbial to the back of the cabin. Phydin joined them at the last from Command.

"What is our movement plan?" he asked, securing his gear at his back. Warily he peered over his shoulder at the creature and his protruding syringe.

"We have to transport the child through the substation tropolis and make our way unseen to the sublevels," Jovaar answered, tucking the loose ends of the blanket at the small of the child's back. "I have a friend there who can help us if we can reach him without detection. Did you notice anything suspicious upon our arrival, Phydin?"

"Nothing to take notice of, Sir," he answered, looking to the others. They stook in agreement, shaking their heads. "I have secured the ship in loading dock four amongst several other transports. I am not certain as to the cause but there are a number of dignitaries arriving, all of which have been routed to our particular hanger. Due to their numbers we should go unnoticed for some time."

Nodding his approval over Phydin's choice of ports, Jovaar's eyes only diverted from the child as Selena reentered the cabin hefting three large totes over her shoulder. "Take her load," he ordered, two of the men quickly offering their assistance. "Orvi, I need you to help me with the child's line."

With the door to Nitaya's unit standing open, Orvi followed Jovaar to its side. Standing near he watched his superior reach within. Anxious, Selena quickly joined the pair.

"Selena," Jovaar said, fumbling with the slender tube with the child lying silent in his arms. "Take Nitaya's life line and attach it to a transportal. We do possess one, do we not?"

"We do," she answered, nodding with excitement for knowing not only that the ship held one, but that she confidently knew how to use it. She turned, offering the last of her totes before crossing to the storage unit where the device was stored. Turning back to the child, she attached the crucial line with ease. "This should last two hazon if fully charged," she said, securing it firmly in place. "Surely it is enough."

As Selena backed away from the unit, hands in the air before her as if showing she had done all she could, Orvi quickly gathered the remnants of the line to the transportal. Carrying the lifeless child to the Med-deck door with Orvi at his back, all paused as Jovaar turned to face them.

"Wait," he said abruptly, shaking his head. "What was I thinking? This is not just any landing. We cannot all walk out like this. Anyone with half a heart will know we are not dignitaries or dock crew." Gently easing the child into Selena's arms, Jovaar paused to think, looking to the others for suggestions.

"Phydin and Fidaldi," he said at last, confidence returning to his tone. "As will the others, I need you to use your cloaks for cover, but here," he added, retrieving two of the other men's burdens. "Take these as you pass down the landing plank. Phydin," he added, lifting his sleeve. "I need you to key this location."

Mimicking his elder's movements, Phydin adjusted the pack at his back then turned his wrist to bear his own portal com, prompting the side control for entry. The mini panel burst open bearing the map readout of the substation having automatically adjusted upon landing, and he awaited Jovaar's further instructions.

"Head out and down the left side lane," Jovaar continued, pointing out the length of the location, his fingers dancing upon the portal's glow just above its flat screen. "And do not under any circumstances look back."

"Once you have reached the main lane," he continued, all standing anxious to leave the ship, those at the rear peering

81

nervously over the shoulders of those in front. "You must appear to be taking in the merchants, purchasing your wares as ordinary visitors if you will, then you must make your way here," he added, gesturing toward the small glowing screen at Phydin's wrist. "Inform them that you are with me, only using my given name with them, and them alone. I assure you that once you have escaped all prying eyes, they will see you safely to my contact. We will meet you here," he added, pointing at the final location."

"How long?" Fidaldi asked, peering over Phydin's shoulder.

"As long as it takes," Jovaar answered, frustration clear in his voice as he regathered the child from Selena. Disgusted for having asked such a stupid, moot question, Phydin hit Fidaldi in the chest with his elbow, the remaining crew nodding in gritting approval.

"Move on," Phydin ordered, gesturing for his imbecilic Systems Officer to head out to the hatch at mid-ship, several others anxiously stepping into place at his back. Nodding to Jovaar as he passed through the crew, Phydin headed silently from Med-deck to guide their first line into the depths of Yani Substation.

***

"I want the rest of you to appear to be unloading," Jovaar continued, the antsy men shifting in place, shortened merely by two. "Kroy, you will take the final tote and order the crew to carry out several of the supply crates placing them on the docks below, then you will return to the ship commanding the team, overseeing the dispersal of more. I do not care what is in them for you must know as well as I do that we will not be returning. Once you have unloaded enough to buy the rest of us time, I want you to debark along with the other dignitaries. Use two of you as prominents to set the ruse."

"Here," Jovaar added in haste, grabbing Jax's arm and prompting the man's portal. "You will head down the far, right lane and do as the others with the merchants. Rendezvous at this location here, and as I have instructed the first line, inform the contacts that you are with me. You and your so-called servants should then reach the site soon after Phydin and Fidaldi."

Jax nodded his acknowledgement at Kroy's back, seriousness surprisingly filling his eyes as he set out silently to mid-ship to prepare the crates. "Orvi," Jovaar said, stopping him on his way to the rungs to assist Jax above. "I will need you with us. Selena shall carry Nitaya as if her caregiver with you at her side with the life line hidden beneath your cloak. I will continue on just ahead of you to scout out the area."

"Yes, Sir," Orvi answered, shifting the weight of the line on his shoulder.

"I just need to stop at quarters," Jovaar added, handing Kroy the final tote. "We shall meet at the vacant seating above and when Selena, Orvi and I have at last crossed the plank with the child, you can begin the unloading. And Kroy," he added, grasping the man's arm as they reached the top of the rungs, pacing to peer out the open hatch. "Keep your eyes open."

***

Jovaar skirted through the uneasy last few of his crew at mid-ship, leaving them to their task of collecting crates. Pacing the narrow corridor, he at last returned to the rungs. Once again reaching the lower levels, he could not contain a chuckle however, as he spied Orvi clumsily attempting to straighten the child's line.

"Take my hand and be careful," Jovaar said, shaking his head at the nervous man as Selena made her way toward her ascent. "Wait here," he added, halting Orvi with his hand at the rung's base, the firing pit empty at their backs. "I will not be long."

Proceeding to his quarters and leaving the pair anxiously waiting before the empty firing pit with the child, Jovaar entered his cabin for the last time, scanning the room that remained as it had been only moments before. Crossing to his cabinet, he removed three cloaks then paced to his side table, opening the small drawer to withdraw his second eyes. When certain he had gathered all that was needed, he returned to the door, pausing as he held his hand over the prompt, both panting and anxious.

83

"If you are alive, Martus, I swear I will find you," he whispered, lowering his head to the cold wall of his cabin. "And with all that I am, I promise you, as I have since the moment I learned of my task, I *will* make certain Nitaya is safe."

Knowing the others were waiting impatiently for him to lead them to safety, Jovaar prompted the door without looking back, lifting his weary head. Spying Selena and Orvi pacing at the end of the corridor as expected, he straightened his shoulders in an attempt to hide his tired frame and raced eagerly to join them.

"We must hurry," Selena said, nervously wringing her hands at Jovaar's approach.

"I agree," he answered, struggling with his heavy load. "As I said earlier, you must appear as if you were passengers, dignitaries or a small family that merely required passage, it does not matter," he added, shaking his head. "You will follow me, but you must not appear to be following me. You understand," he added matter of factly without waiting for a response, handing over the lightly colored garbs from his cabin. "Take these and cover yourselves. Orvi, rest assured that although it is cumbersome, it should serve nicely as a cover for the life line."

Assisting Orvi with the clasp of the newly weighted cloak at his neck as the man easily shielded the weight of the device, Jovaar smiled, attempting to reassure Orvi's obvious anxiousness. "It will work," he said, patting him on the shoulder when finished. Satisfied that the colorful robes would suffice and that Nitaya would hide securely beneath Selena's oversized cloak, Jovaar assisted the pair up the rungs. Shaking his head, he caught the trail of the line, ascending at the last to mid-ship.

Jovaar joined the last of the crew as they stood panting, sweat-covered with their heavy unloading. Ignoring their anxious eyes, he paced silently to the hatch's edge, scanning the open surrounding areas as the next pair of 'stewards' made their way down the grid-lined plank to the dock.

Two transoid loaders stood questioning Jax and Kroy at the center of the main strip as the final two stewards joined the pair on the dock, mingling with several workers from the adjacent dignitary craft. Nervously returning his gaze to the obviously debated pair from his stance aboard the ship, Jovaar knew he could not risk intervening and instead peering over his shoulder, eyed Selena gasp with worry, wringing her hands. Attempting to resume her pacing, he reached back to claim her arm, gently pulling her forward.

"There is nothing we can do, Selena," he whispered, pleased that for the moment Nitaya slept peacefully beneath her cloak. "Stay with Orvi and appear to be nothing more than I have asked. I will head up the central lane then upon my signal, you will both follow me, yet as I have said...do not trail too close."

Hesitating yet trusting that Jovaar knew what was best, Selena raised her chin, ceasing her anxious hands. Raising her chin, she stepped from within the darkened hull and out onto the plank. With Orvi reaching her side, she nodded to Jovaar over her shoulder and appearing without hesitation, slowly descended the grid. Spying Jax point the droids confidently toward the crates and the seemingly oblivious members, her breathing skipped regardless of the lack of attention received as her feet at last reached the dock.

"I am a dignitary," Selena firmly told herself, raising her chin ever higher in the ruse. Although frightened for the others, the guards continuing their bantering, Selena knew she would do anything including leaving the others behind to secure the safety of the child.

"Only a few steps more," she whispered, nodding grandly at the lowly workers, Orvi reaching out to claim her shaking hand. Accepting his gesture and resting it gently on his free arm, she understood that each of the players, although joined in the just cause, were now ultimately on their own.

***

As Nitaya remained thankfully quiet in Selena's arm, Orvi led both woman and child through the maze of large crates on the dock. Despite struggling with the continued weight of the portal unit on his shoulder, he led her with earnest over the hazardous fuel lines. Finding their way to the center lane, he eyed Jovaar roughly twenty paces before them. Watching his careful movements, Selena halted Orvi as Jovaar stopped,

85

surprisingly lowering to the ground. Sighing as he appeared to be merely lacing up his boot all the while looking right and left for the enemy, Selena slowed her apparent escort, adjusting to Jovaar's movements.

"The area must be clear," she whispered, Jovaar once again standing, making his way casually forward amongst the array of both people and beings. "He would not move on if otherwise."

Bearing the weight of both Nitaya and her vital line, Orvi and Selena continued on as instructed, Jovaar ducking swiftly and silently from view about the seemingly endless crowd. Stopping off at the second merchant stand to their right as Jovaar had instructed, they continued their ruse despite his absence, appearing to marvel at the humble man's display of glass wares.

Riffling through the small tokens and simple crafts, Selena picked up a piece of tall soft-colored glass, then returning it to its small shelf with disinterest, purposefully ran her fingers through the rough cloths hanging from the display to draw attention. Noting Javaar once again off to her left appearing to read a Yani directional on the adjacent lane wall, Selena was surprisingly startled with the intrusion of a hopeful sale.

"A trinket for the child?" the merchant asked, his jarring belly protruding from his tattered cover.

"No," Orvi answered abruptly, scowling at the vile man. "We are just glancing." Yet as Selena pressed Orvi's arm to move toward the dangling wares of cloth, the foul merchant continued his selling push, rounding the dilapidated shelves.

"Surely there must be something," the man said, bearing only a few scattered teeth. Orvi shielded Selena with his body, the stench of the man emanating from his mouth, his hair, his skin. "A deal I will have for you, yes?" he added, opening his heavy, sweating arms.

"No, although I extend you our thanks," Orvi said sternly, raising his hand to halt the latest intrustion. "Come Momar," he added, noting Jovaar had moved on, continuing his way down the lane. "If we are to arrive to prepare for the morrow's ceremony, we must go at once."

"A bobble for the beautiful lady," another merchant cried out from his stand, the pair strolling casually down the lane.

"No, we give you thanks," Orvi answered, tipping his head and anxiously holding firm to Selena's arm, pressing her onward.

"Some cympas?" cried another, Orvi quickening their steps, his eyes never far from Selena's frame. Nervously shaking his head as the merchant bellowed his plea to yet another passerby, Orvi could not contain his panic, the transportal growing heavy at his back as his palms sweated against the transportals thick strap.

"This way, Selena," he said breathlessly, leading her to the opposite side of the lane. "I have again lost site of Jovaar," he added, reaching the shelter of a small alcove. "Yet I do believe we should be able to relocate him from this angle."

Stepping from the slight shelter provided by the shade of the Day Circle, the pair walked casually toward the stand of yet another merchant and his wares. Seemingly admiring the tokens of his mundane trade, Selena secretly watched Orvi's eyes dart right and left for a sign of Jovaar.

"Ah, my lady seeks pampering," the newest merchant began, brushing back his scraggly hair and rounding the slab. "I have just the thing!" he added, pulling out a cloak of red fabric.

"No," Orvi insisted, showing obvious distress as he attempted to position himself between the racks so he could relocate Jovaar.

"It is lovely though, I thank you," Selena added, attempting to placate the scrawny man. Secretly she clenched Nitaya to her breast beneath the light-colored cloak, urging her to keep hushed. "Such elegance, we could not possibly afford it."

"Aye, then something more suitable to your um, standing then, my lady?" the merchant persisted, quizzically admiring her current garb as he gestured toward another hanging garment.

"No, I am sorry," Selena answered, blushing. "It is lovely, but we could not possibly..." she added, interrupted by Orvi's stare.

"We must go now," he said abruptly, pulling her on further through the wares without hesitation, adjusting the weighted strap at his back. Unfettered, the merchant urged her unrelentingly toward his next trinket, yet regardless of his persistance, the pair successfully ignored him, blending once again into the busy lane.

**

Passing several other congested stands, each merchant unrelentingly shouting his various wares for sale, Orvi shoved at those who ventured too close to Selena and the child, gesturing at the last with his head toward several baskets of greens at the next stand to their right.

"There," he said, shaking his head with frustration, once again adjusting the strap of his shoulder. Selena, careening her neck passed an array of colored cloths in the general direction of his nod, sighed in relief as she too spied Jovaar, appearing at the moment to be bartering for something. His eyes were fixed sternly on the robust man before him.

Leading Selena and the babe closer to the shielding display of greens, Orvi held firm to her delicate arm all the while appearing to test the freshness of the products, yet straining to listen to Jovar's conversation. Selena, following his intrusive movements, anxiously leaned forward doing the same.

"As I have told you," Jovaar said, growing anxiously annoyed, glancing nervously over his shoulder. "I am Jovaar Savius, son of Mathius. I must speak with…no," he added, interrupting the merchant's argument before the man could continue his questioning. "He is not expecting me, but I must speak with him at once."

The merchant, obviously sizing up the man before him, refused to turn from the intruder's penetrating eyes, silently tapping a random, small trinket to his lips. Sighing loudly, he tossed the small token into the cart amongst the abundance of repeated, unwanted replicas, his eyes unwavering and filled with questions.

"Sir Gidoran has been quite the desired topic this fine day," he began, his oddly deep voice resonating as he crossed his thick arms at his chest. "I admit my interest is well piqued."

Ignoring the man's attempt at hidden pleas for more information, Jovaar indicated with a slight movement of his head for Orvi and Selena to follow, offering nothing further despite the merchant's persistant stare. Nodding in understanding, Orvi held firm to Selena's arm, gladly leading her from within the folds of cloth remnants.

"Come with me," the merchant said when all were at last assembled, adding nothing further beyond the firm glare of skepticism in his eyes. Yet as the three members followed the man silently through the green-filled baskets toward an unknown tall, rear building, darkness shadowed the substation ground at their feet. Unbeknownst to the anxious trio, the Sugin searcher droid secretly trailed their lead.

.

    ***

Using the small alcove at the face of an adjacent building for cover, just to the right of the suspicious merchant, the SSD stared intently at the bartering men for his invitation, noting the two others who joined them stood obviously waiting without individual purpose.

"What filth these humans create," he mumbled disgustingly to himself, kicking a small piece of waste at his feet. Although he tapped the side of his head to perform yet another scan for his King, he did nothing but grumble about his surroundings, remaining unreactive to the humans' inquiry.

The captured laser-visual or LV flashed before his left eye, storing left then pivoting to the base of the dimensional device. Cataloging along with the images of those he had acquired prior, the SSD noted with his unobstructed eye that after each inquiry and considerable questioning, the merchant had allowed the arrivals to follow him into the building directly at the rear of his station wares.

"Five so far," he stated flatly, raising his portalcom to report his findings. "There could be others, Sir. Shall I maintain my post?"

"No," the commanding voice answered, unconcerned. "We know of their location. Return to the visitor's dock and download your scanners en route."

"As ordered," the droid responded, sealing the scan beneath the angled flap to the side of his eye before turning to make his way quickly through the stands toward his ship. "And none too soon," he thought, shaking his head at the endless array of vulgar wares, their merchant's shouts mingling with the congested voices of eager purchasers. "Humans are the worst of sub-life."

***

Leading the next apprehensive arrivals toward the building at the rear of his cart, the merchant gestured with a slight wave of his hand at the stationed sentry. He merely nodded in their general direction as the group entered one of the many substation's rental quarters for beings who lived and labored upon Yani. Its forefront however, as anxious as the arrivals were to enter, proved appalling and Selena drew Nitaya nearer to her breast in response to the odor that mingled with the view. Tremcling, she reached forward to claim Jovaar's arm, attempting to pass the tattered, rotting furnishings without ill.

An age-old green bench covered with scattered parchments tilted haphazardly against the far wall before several old seats of various hues, obviously someone or something's sad attempt at civility. Void of all signs of green life, for how could something requiring any clear light or careful tending thrive in such a desolate place, the walls merely bore ancient hangings that appearing to have been hastily spattered by an angry child.

"It is not much," the man said with a hearty laugh. Abuptly stopping, he gestured toward the rear of the large room. "But it is a living we make, one better than maybe you believe."

Merely nodding at the man's attempts for casual speech, Jovaar glanced to Selena who now stood uncomfortably at Orvi's side then turned back, gritting his teeth and glaring at the oaf with impatience. "Ah yes, Sir Gidoran," he said as if at last recalling the arrival's request, rubbing his scraggly chin. Standing firm, the merchant slowly crossed his arms before his chest. "Yet I believe a small fee for my trouble is not unreasonable amongst friends." Having known this line would eventually present itself with the reputation of those who served wares upon Yani, Jovaar reached within his cloak for the desired pents.

90

"But of course, my good man," he answered, withdrawing several of the small tokens, producing the sparkling glimmer of interest expected from the merchant. "Surely this will cover your efforts. However," Jovaar added, toying with the wide-eyed man, simultaneously returning all but one to his cloak. "I believe I will give you this now," he said, offering the excited merchant the lone prize. "And you will receive the others once we have actually been greeted by Sir Gidoran."

"Ah, yes," the man said, claiming the token and licking his aged teeth in agreement of his future prospects. "I believe your offer is quite acceptable. Now, if you will follow me."

     ***

Pacing to the rear corridor, its narrow floor littered with dusty, mildew-covered waste, the merchant stalled the anxious trio with his stubby hand, flicking some grim from his obtuse fingers as they at last reached the travel shoot. "Sir Gidoran is stationed on Sublevel Three," he said, gesturing toward the slender portal, his tone both surprisingly educated and light. "We must obviously use the shoot to reach his level, unless of course you would prefer the old fashion way," he added, pointing to the dilapidated elevator.

"Obviously no," Jovaar said, toying the man with his repeated word as he turned to the more modern of devices. "The shoot will be quite suitable. How many are able to travel at once? I am assuming that by the state of your outer layer of quarters this is not the most current model."

"Right you are, my friend," the merchant answered, ignoring the minor slight as he patted the frame of the machine. "We spend far too little pents and time on upgrades, and find our earnings, oh how shall I say," he added, jabbing Orvi in his midsection as he ogled Selena's. "Most suited for our own entertainment and therefore I am afraid only two are able to ride at once. Will you have me travel first?"

"No," Jovaar answered, abruptly shaking his head at the oddly toying man. "Send the pair first then you and I will follow. I want to be certain that all arrive safely. I offer you my apologies up front for my lack of trust, but you must understand my position."

"But of course," the merchant answered, baring his dingy-wide smile yet sincere eyes. "And as you must also understand my position, I am afraid we must get moving. I undoubtedly have customers awaiting my return."

Although doubting the notion of purchasers eagerly pining for the man's withering greens, Jovaar merely shook his head, gesturing for Selena and Orvi to step inside. "Is this truly safe, Jovaar?" she asked, peering over her shoulder at the ancient elevator. "I have never once in all my onars traveled in a shoot quite this small." Before Jovaar or the merchant could respond, Orvi surprisingly interrupted the pair with the halting of his hand.

"If I may," he began, clearing his throat and simultaneously adjusting the weighted tote over his shoulder. "I have ridden the shoots often in my onars as a lad on T-902. Of course they were more modern of models," he added, tipping his head respectfully to the merchant. "No offense meant."

"None felt," the man replied, uncrossing his arms only to stuff them beneath his cloak. "Please though, if you could speed this up I have others waiting."

Orvi nodded to the obvious impatient man, and tipping his head to Selena leading the hidden babe forward, spoke to the awaiting monitor, entering the small frame swiftly at her back. "Sublevel Three," he said with confidence, guiding Selena backward to the crook of his arm. The shoot's glass doors slid from both top and bottom, joining at the center. Watching the pair speed quickly downward without incident, the child thankfully remaining hidden beneath Selena's cloak, Jovaar sighed at the woman's fearful face, knowing that she shared his silent prayer that the jarring would not wake the babe.

"Our turn at last," the merchant said, gesturing for Jovaar to enter first. With the glass again closed before the newest pair, the man prompted the awaiting monitor. "Sublevel Four," the merchant said, glancing warily at Jovaar.

"Four?" Jovaar roared, his voice echoing within the compartment as the machine raced downward.

"Now Sir," the merchant continued, attempting to calm what he knew would be an angry passenger. "You must not fear.

I assure you that your companions will be held quite safe, and if you all are whom you claim to be, then they will join you shortly. Sir Gidoran is quite untrusting of new faces as you too have proven to be. I am certain though that once he sees an *old friend* as you claim you are, he will promptly send for the others."

Although fuming as he listened to the vile man's words, Jovaar completely understood and appreciated Sir Gidoran's position regarding new arrivals. Despite his understanding however, he turned to reorder the panel. Expecting the reaction, the merchant quickly secured his arm.

"They are all under guard," the merchant pressed, boldly smiling as he allowed Jovaar to yank free from his grasp. "Yet I assure you they will remain well tended until summoned." Leaning closer to toy with arrival's obvious anger, the merchant chuckled, smiling his toothless grin. "That is," he added, Jovaar flinching backward from the filthy stench of the man's breath. "That is *if* Sir Gidoran pleases, of course."

The shoot's flat voice indicated their arrival at Sublevel Four and the toying man purposefully ignored Jovaar's glare. Instead stepping lively from the platform, he lead the way down the long, narrow passage passed several unmarked doors. Dimly lit and cramped, the merchant paid no mind to his surroundings, instead scurrying onward and idly whistling.

"Where do these lead?" Jovaar asked, grumbling at the merchant's back and gesturing to the barricades as they passed.

"They are of no importance," the merchant answered, annoyance in his tone as he glanced slightly over his shoulder. "Please follow me."

Anger returning and fists clentched, Jovaar continued on behind the man in gritted silence as the pair reached a T at the end of the corridor. Turning sharply to the left, his angered tempered, his interest turning to the next passage which proved much shorter with only a lone door at its end.

"I will leave you here," the merchant said, gesturing to the solid frame. "And if you are the friend that you claim to be," he added, extending his hand in accord. "I am certain we will meet again. However, if what you have said to me proves false, it is now my pleasure to inform you that you will never again set your eyes above the ground."

Accepting the offer despite his constant irritation with the man, Jovaar grasped his fingers tightly around the man's stubby hand, their eyes meeting equally as firm. Simultaneoulsy reaching within his cloak, Jovaar slowly withdrew the final tokens.

"For your trouble," he said, slamming the three pents into the merchant's palm. "And I assure you that not only will you again set your eyes on mine, there are others not far behind. I will presume that once my name has been confirmed, they will be allowed free passage."

"As you say," the merchant answered, shrugging. Retracting his hand, he appeared untroubled by the arrival's attempt to prove superior. Without further word and retracing his steps down the narrow passage, Jovaar merely shook his head at the departing grotesque figure. Curiously, he found himself smiling at the most surprisingly whistling lilt produced by such an odd man. Turning as the merchant vanished at the now familiar T, Jovaar at last turned to face the lone door.

Six

Void of the usual prompter or any other time-worn entrance device, Jovaar shook his head. Smiling he reached up to actually knock on the darkened frame. "You may enter," the voice answered, the door springing surprisingly upward. Walking into the brightly-lit, well furnished room, Jovaar stood silently stunned. Although knowing Sir Gidoran as he did, he truly should not be surprised with the contrast between the world above and that which now stood before him.

As no one stood at the entrance in proper greeting, Jovaar took the moment alone to admire the wares his old friend had acquired. With both old and new appropriately placed throughout the room, he respected how they blended perfectly with the lightly colored hues of the walls. At once warmed to the displays and Gidoran's obvious careful hand in their care, Jovaar's eyes immediately fell upon an ancient clock hanging on the far wall still displaying its aged, darkened hands. Crossing to its wonderous face, Jovaar could not help but marvel, remembering back to the times of his childhood.

Reluctantly leaving the aged device, for there was so much more to see in such a short time, Jovaar pivoted where he stood, his gaze returning to the center of the room. A beautiful display of white-colored furnishings, more modern in taste yet blending perfectly with the olden relics placed here and there, teased his eye. Combined with the whiter tones were greens scattered throughout the open space, cascading both from ceiling urns and bases upon the floor, made from olden wares that had once been used in daily life yet blended perfectly with the wall hangings that had obviously been created from a much more modern hand.

"My friend has done well," Jovaar thought, turning his eyes to the sounds of a beautiful approaching woman.

"May I be of service, Sir?" the figure asked, slowly tipping her head and folding her hands gracefully at her waist to await order.

"Yes," Jovaar answered, hastily crossing to her side, in the blink of the moment the relics becoming a distant memory. "My name is Jovaar Savius and I am a friend of Sir Gidoran. If I may have a word with him, I am most certain that he would be pleased to greet me."

The woman, appearing both young and confident with long golden- blonde tresses cascading down the length of her back, did not offer a smile against the brightness of her blue eyes. As Jovaar marveled at the unique color, a shade he could not find words to describe, he felt surprisingly at ease in her presence, as if the woman was speaking with her manner, telling him she was calm and unafraid of his arrival.

"If you will wait a moment, Sir," she continued, her words soft and airy. She clasped her hands calmly at her belly. "I will speak with Sir Gidoran to see if he is willing to entertain. I must inform you however, that he is so very consumed, and therefore I am not certain he will be able to give you what it is you seek."

"Please just give him my name," Jovaar whispered, uncertain as to why her presence held his gaze or more importantly why he felt the need to hush his words. "I am confident he will accept my council."

Appearing to glide silently across the floor, her long gown of green flowing gently at her feet, Jovaar watched the woman retreat through an unknown rear door. At last released from her spell, he then turned back to the clock, shaking his head from his trance to admire the olden-aged workmanship. Although suspended against the wall, its length stood much taller than Jovaar, spanning almost from ceiling to floor. Reaching out to touch its fragile surface, he found he could not contain his smile, enjoying the rich, warm colors that oddly found its home amongst the lower levels of Yani.

"You were once magnificent," Jovaar whispered, fondly remembering times long past.

"Yes I was," the man said, coyly smiling at Jovaar's back. "And even in my advanced age I still like to think of myself as so." Quickly turning to the familiar voice, Jovaar crossed to his old friend, his smile both genuine and relieved as he embraced him at the center of the room, the clock all but forgotten.

"So good to see you," Sir Gidoran said, patting Jovaar heartily on the back.

"And you as..." Jovaar began, pausing as he spied the return of the young woman at Gidoran's back. "Who is she?" he asked, stammering at her image altering before his eyes. "I mean...well...I mean *what* is she?"

As the men began their joyous reunion, the young woman crossed the room to retrieve the proper nourishment and again returned carrying a large tray of greens and teeming mugs, her hair fading from golden-blonde to brown then to a surprising black, her gown simultaneously altering from a vibrant green to the palest of blues. Releasing Sir Gidoran's grasp, the woman neared to place the tray upon the low center table. Jovaar stared in disbelief as her eyes faded to the once colored green of her gown.

"No time for pleasantries then?" Sir Gidoran chided, exuding a small laugh as he patted Jovaar's back. "As always you only have a mind for the ladies."

"No," Jovaar replied, unamused. He glared over his shoulder to his friend. "You know all too well that that was not my intention. I merely..."

"Calm yourself, Jovi," Gidoran interrupted, crossing to the low table for his drink. "You will work yourself into one of your fits again if you are not careful."

"Ha!" Jovaar sneered, yet despite his quickened anger to impropriety, he was quite warmed by their old familiar banter. Beginning again to protest the views of his friend however, he found himself silenced by the raise of Gidoran's hand.

"I only asked because she is the newest model of servants," Gidoran continued, walking casually about the cabin. "Servants designed for...well...let us just say that there is not any harm in having someone do menial work that looks quite more than menial. Would you not agree, Jovi?"

"I suppose I am not following you, which proves typical," Jovaar answered, stooping for his own mug and gulping deeply.

"And might I remind you once again that I despise you referring to me in that way."

"Yes Jovaar, I am quite aware," Gidoran answered shaking his head, taking a large swig of the dark, cool liquid for himself. "But come my friend, let me introduce you to my latest purchase. As you can see," Gidoran continued, extending his arm forward and gliding it without thought through the air. "My hand floats right through her. Try for yourself," he added, claiming his friend's arm and guiding it through the servant's image.

"You see," Gidoran said, an air of smug filling his words. "She is a servant yes, and as I said earlier a nice one to admire, yet now that you know of her qualities you understand you can only do so with your eyes. And she will appear seemingly from nowhere when called," he added, obviously pleased with his latest purchase. "She is quite amazing, do you not think?"

Jovaar did not know what to think and said nothing, instead simply stared at what had appeared to be a solid form. "I am rather surprised that young Drider does not possess one of these latest models or for that matter, designed one himself," Gidoran chided, reaching low to grab a morsel from the tray and tossing it quickly into his mouth. "Ah, it does not matter, Jovaar. Let us sit."

Motioning to the plush bench at their backs, Jovaar rounded the low table yet found that he was unable to take his eyes from the marvel of the steward. "And what brings my fine friend Jovi for a visit?" Gidoran asked, casually laying the length of his arm across the back of the low bench. "A friend I have not seen in ages appears at my humble home and not once has he asked how I am fairing. I do believe you have developed Martus' tendencies, Jovaar. Just how are the Savius men these days? Am I asking too much at one time?"

With a mere snap of his fingers, the steward vanished from the room and at last Jovaar felt free to speak, his focus on his friend as he turned to face him. "I believe she is a distraction for you," Gidoran said, interrupting Jovaar's thoughts as he reclaimed his mug. "And I also believe that you have not heard a single word from my mouth. What is it, Jovi?" Gidoran pressed, his face now serious as he noticed the troubled look in his friend's eyes. "Is it…"

"Gidoran," Jovaar interrupted, pivoting in his seat to face his friend, ignoring both the nourishment and the memory of the one who provided it. "I am sorry, G, but we have a situation."

"Of course you have a situation," Gidoran said, sarcasm filling his words. He claimed another morsel without thought from the tray. "The Savius men are always deep within situations, and I am gathering that it is I that you are in need of to break you free of this one, otherwise why else would you have come for a visit? How long has it been, Jovi?" he added, a tinge of annoyance in his tone. "Several onars, I believe. You were quite abrupt the last time."

"And this one will be the same I am afraid," Jovaar said, his voice flat despite Sir Gidoan's bait, combing his fingers through his hair in frustration. "I need to know that you can help me, Gidoran. This has nothing to do with the Stratus."

"My dear, old friend," Gidoran continued, sitting on the bench and reaching out, placing his hand on Jovaar's knee. "Do you truly believe that I still hold that against you? Come now," he added, swatting Jovaar's leg as he returned his attention to the offering of morsels. "What are friends for? Now tell me," he added, intrigued. Settling back onto the bench, he tossed the last bite into his mouth. "What is it that I can do?"

***

At last at ease, Jovaar quickly recapped the latest events of the Resistance plight leaving nothing from his friend, including all information on the birth and naming of Nitaya through their narrow escape from the Lyclos, Sporyax and Sugin ships. He continued with the retelling of the upsetting, almost too-late discovery of the phymbial med-officer and their struggle to save the child, how she was still quite weak, yet that he was pleased with her improvements regardless of how long they were taking. Jovaar finished with their uneventful arrival at Yani which proved oddly absent of enemy tailing ships. He provided the specifics on the location of the docked ship, the status of his crew, and at last how they had crossed the lanes in three separate groups, reaching and donating to the merchant who reluctantly escorted them below.

Gidoran listened, nodding as the events were laid out before him then when certain Jovaar had completed his tale, sat straight with the seriousness of the situation, the tray of nourishment long forgotten as he stretched to give his opinion. "So you are telling me that all this time your comrades have been in holding?" he shouted, shaking his head and slapping his knees as he stood. "For shame, Jovi!"

"Appear," Gidoran ordered the empty cabin, the woman abruptly returning with the echoing summons. Her tresses now the deepest of garnet and her gown the purest of white, Jovaar was once again drawn to her beauty, all thoughts their arrival escaping him as her form elegantly glided across the floor.

"There are several of my friends in holding on Sublevel Three," Gidoran began, crossing the cabin to meet his servant, his tone serious in an attempt to placid Jovaar. "Send for them immediately and have them brought to me. No worries, my friend," he added, assuring Jovaar as he stole a large morsel from the tray. "I am quite certain they would have been held without harm. My transoids are top of the line."

"Of course they are," Jovaar added sarcastically. Gidoran sneered at the back as his rising friend.

"Once they have joined us, I will see what we can do to get you again on your way," Gidoran continued, slowly lowering his head despite Jovaar's snide. "I just cannot believe that the onars have passed so quickly, Jovaar. The time is upon you, my friend...upon us all," he added, all edginess subsiding as the reality of the situation sank in. "The time has at last come after all that has been planned. It truly has arrived as was predicted. If you will," Gidoran added, lifting his gaze as the servant returned, knowingly crossing to refill his mug. "I do believe this calls for a toast."

Jovaar felt the tension again ease with Gidoran's seriousness and understanding of all the elitians had endured to arrive at this moment, and knew that despite their eternal bickering, Sir G would do all that he could to sustain the life of the child. The odd tingling sensation flooding his wrist however, reminded him that despite the aid of those choosing to assist on the path to their fateful future, he could not change the fickleness of the past.

"Thank you, Gidoran," Jovaar answered, attempting to dismiss the interruption of pain as he claimed his half-filled mug. "I do not know what we would have done without you. Had we not been in position to…"

"But of course, Jovi," he interrupted, turning as the servant refilled his friend's drink without urging, her gown of violet flowing soft at her knees. "As I said before," Gidoran added, wiping his mouth on the sleeve of his cloak, obviously pleased with Jovaar's endless spell with his latest purchase despite the seriousness of their circumstance. "What are friends for?"

Seven

Jovaar excused himself to freshen while waiting for the others to arrive and Sir Gidoran used the time to resummons his servant to prepare nourishment for his impending guests. Entering the facilities and crossing directly to the basin, Jovaar rinsed cold water over his tired face then pulled the sleeve of his cloak up high to get a good look at his arm.

"No indication," he said, pleased there was at least to exterior sign. "Even the tingling is gone. Surely I am making too much of this."

Grumbling to himself for worrying, Jovaar used his cloak sleeve to dry his face, then placing both hands on the outskirts of the basin, stared into the eyes of an apparent aged man. "This will work," he whispered, staring intently at his reflection. "This has to work."

Sighing as he glanced at the awaiting, unused dry cloth on the wall to his right, Jovaar lowered his dampened sleeve into place. Flexing his fingers and thankfully feeling no pain, he mussed the unused cloth in frustration and turned, retracing his steps back to the main room to await his members.

     ***

The crew arrived just prior to Jovaar's return from refreshing and Selena rushed to his side openly carrying the child as he entered the room. Jovaar smiled at the obvious, comforting look upon her face.

"Nitaya has begun to stir, Jovi," she whispered, beaming at the child cradled in her arms. "It is truly a good sign."

"It is," Jovaar answered, he too relieved as he softly touched the babe's hand. "It is the most wonderful of news. Sir Gidoran," Jovaar continued, the man eagerly parting from the back of the group, approaching the pair. "This is Selena. She carries the burden of protecting the child that as you know means everything to the Resistance."

"Such formalities yet...I do believe we have met on one earlier occasion," Gidoran chided, jabbing his old friend in the midsection as he downed the last of his drink. "Tis a shame we had not been properly introduced. You may call me G, as this brute has so long ago dubbed me, Selena. Informal is more appropriate, do you not agree?"

"I do, yet I believe I will stick with simply Gidoran," she answered, blushing and accepting his offered hand. "And I thank you not only for your prior assistance at Central Docking but for your hospitality and for the transport you have agreed to attain for us. I must admit though that I was not so certain of your intentions when we were placed in hold, however I offer you my humbleness now that I indeed understand your discretion."

"The others are my crew, and a good crew at that," Jovaar interrupted, uncomfortable with Gidoran's close stare at Selena, his eyes roaming not just her face. "I am afraid we have no further time for pleasantries."

"Pleasantries?" Jax added, crossing to the trio, nourishment messily in hand. "Do you *know* where they have been holding us? They placed us in a small cabin, all of us with no nourishment, no furnishings upon Sublevel Three...the level that you were *supposed* to be stationed. I have not even mentioned how uncomfortable Selena must have been with the babe! Not one word of what was going on. We had no idea if you had even survived, Jovaar! How could you do this?" he grumbled, glaring at Gidoran, the man calm despite the flying accusations, downing another morsel.

"Calm yourself, Jax," Jovaar said, raising his eyes from the child, certain without questioning that Gidoran would have seen to at least the member's minor comforts. "All is now well and we must concentrate all of our energy on our departure plan. G, that of course is where you come in."

"Ah," Gidoran answered laying his arm over Jax's shoulder, regardless of his attempt at shrugging the man off inbetween bites. "So that is my duty. And here I thought I was merely testing the Stratus theory and entertaining guests."

"How can you be so smug?" Jax mumbled, choking on the last of his swallowed food, dismissing Sir Gidoran's arm free of his shoulder. "Do you not understand what's at stake?"

"Relax, my new friend," Gidoran answered, patting Jax wholeheartedly on the back. "I know very well what is at stake and furthermore I promise you I will be able to acquire you suitable arrangements. It is *I* who manages Yani, and it is *I* who knows all of its secrets."

"Please, come and sate yourselves," he added, winking at Jovaar and gesturing the others toward the comfortable bench. Jovaar and Selena joined them at the last. "Attaining your transportation is of little consequence and easy enough, yet it will take much planning to go unnoticed Had I been preinformed..." he added, glancing up to Jovaar yet simultaneously dismissing the motion.

"Regardless," Gidoran continued, shaking his head and returning his eyes to the anxious crew. "Let us sit so we may discuss your exact requirements."

***

Following Jovaar's lead the members sat, however reluctantly around the plentiful nourishment displayed on the low table, feasting on fresh greens, breads and cheeses that the beautiful steward had happily replenished without word. Selena, sitting at Gidoran's right, could not help but stare at the wonderous image, envy filling her as the woman's lustrious, white gown flowed at her ankles as she crossed the room to gather yet another round of drink.

"She is beautiful, yes?" Gidoran asked, interrupting her thoughts and leaning close. Startled, Selena uncomfortably turned to him.

"Why yes, she is," she answered, absently fumbling with the small blanket wrapped about the sleeping child. "I have never seen such an array of vibrant colors. And the most recent white...I dare say I feel quite drab in my present attire."

"Your beauty radiates beyond your oversized cloak," Gidoran said, grinning and patting Selena's knee. He winked openly at Jovaar's incessant stare. "But watch if you will. You have seen nothing yet," he added, smiling and settling back in his seat. "Think of a color...any color. Think of the truest of blues or perhaps the brightness of yellows. Do you have one in mind?"

"A glowing orange, I think," Selena answered describing one of her many favorite hues. The woman transformed with ease to the exact color she envisioned. "But how?" she asked, amazed at the wonderous form. Gidoran simply laughed, explaining to all of his newly acquired friends his most impressive recent purchase.

Selena stared in amazement as Gidoran explained the processes of how his servant was capable of such wonders. Intrigued, she began to offer another color so that she could once again see the awesome transformation. Nitaya stirred in her arms however, and her attention once again drawn to the small bundle.

"Open your eyes, little one," Selena said amongst the din of the others, torn with the struggle the child was forced to endure. "Please open your eyes."

Seated on Selena's opposite, Orvi quickly pulled the life line from within his cloak, shooing Jax's crumb-filled hands from the device to check the contents. "They are almost depleted," he said, flicking the machine with his finger. "And it seems just in time. The transportal's energy is running near empty."

"Come on, little one," Selena said urging the babe on, the others hushing with the possibility of movement. Nitaya's eyes opened for the slightest of moments, yet just as quickly they again closed. Looking fearfully to Jovaar as he reached out his hand, Selena sat silent and unmoving, watching him gently rub his fingers over Nitaya's cheek.

"You can do it," he whispered, drink and nourishment quickly forgotten by all. "Come, Nitaya. It is time."

As the last of the words escaped Jovaar's mouth, the most welcoming of wails filled the room. Cradling Nitaya to her breast, tears welling in her eyes, Selena beamed at the joyous faces about them. "She is alright," she whispered, Sir Gidoran leaning close to spy the babe's quivering lips, warmly touching Selena's knee. "Thank the stars she is alright."

Nitaya's cries were soon overrun with the clanging of mugs and the shouts of elation, the servant in her brilliant shade of orange, returning bearing a smile as well, once again replenishing the abundant dark liquid. For just a few moments the worries of what was to come escaped their thoughts, all gathering close to the child.

"She needs her mother's milk," Selena said, turning quickly to Jovaar. "I did not think that far ahead."

"Not to fear," Gidoran interrupted, shouting above the din and quickly summonsing his servant to his side. After a quick explanation of Selena's dilemma and the child's needs, the servent floated silently from the room then soon returned, balancing a large vessel of milk.

"I thank you," Selena said, accepting the urn, the group once again silenced by the steward's ever changing appearance. Dressed this time in the darkest shade of emerald, her brown hair wound tight at the base of her neck, she merely nodded then turned, leaving to gather yet another tray.

"Now that that is over," Gidoran said, leaning forward onto his knees, the others turning mouths agape to his words. "Where were we?"

***

"I will obviously need a ship that can carry at least ten to allow for comfort," Jovaar began, seriousness returning to his tone as Selena busied herself at his side with the cooing child. "And it is vital that it possess enough energy to carry us around the near side of the system to the planet Kindawa. With our current circumstances and most probable tail, I assume you understand she must also possess hyper drive capabilities. We will also require all the supplies and weapons the craft can hold, yet I understand that with our time constraints we may have to make do with less. Obviously, we will gladly accept any and all that you would be able to acquire."

Gidoran nodded at Jovaar's words, yet when he paused as if waiting for him to respond with the difficulties of short notice, he merely gestured for him to continue. Once again he familiarly patted Selena's knee. "The ship needs to be in fair condition but not so well off to draw notice," Jovaar said, glaring at Gidoran's roaming hand. "The last thing we need is to arouse suspicion, for I am certain there are searcher droids in the area."

Taking notice of Jovaar's discomfort with the placement of his hand and smiling at the fact that he had once again unnerved his old friend, Gidoran refused to budge from the warmth of Selena's knee, instead choosing to rub his chin with his free fingers as he considered Jovaar's request. "Is that all?" he asked, the others looking from Gidoran to Jovaar expectantly.

"This is no time for sarcasm, G," Jovaar groaned, his annoyance evident as he leaned forward to his knees. "Just tell me, can you get us what we need?"

"Of course, Jovi, of course," he answered, nodding with his best attempt at seriousness. Jax, looking from Sir Gidoran to his commander, could not help but mock the pair.

"Jovi?" he asked, the others snickering behind their hands.

"You are not to speak it again," Jovaar stated firmly, glaring at his subordinants, Gidoran reclined back against the plush bench pleased with the annoyance he had stirred in Jovaar and resting his hand this time at Selena's back, the others merely grinned, quickly returning to their nourishment and drink. Despite Selena's reassuring eyes and the chuckles of his men, Jovaar could not take his eyes from Gidoran's hand.

***

Sir Gidoran stepped from the cabin to consult with his staff as Nitaya finished off the last of her milk, seemingly safe from the injection and with no adverse side affects. The others nibbled at their remaining greens, quietly talking in anticipation of what was to come.

"Are you certain we can trust him, Jovaar?" Phydin asked, kneeling before his commander. "I have never once heard of you mentioning his name."

"I am as certain of G as if he was my own brother," he answered, brushing away the stray remnants of his meal. "And I have never mentioned his name for obvious reasons. You never truly know whom you can trust, Phydin, yet Gidoran and I have known each other for most of our lives. Although I have not laid my eyes on him for some time, I trust him entirely with my life and more importantly with the life of the child."

"In our youth," Jovaar continued, the others appearing at ease and talking quietly amongst themselves. "It was I that was forever in the midst of trouble. Of course Gidoran was the one who instigated most of our messes, yet unfortunately it was I who was blessed with the brunt of the fall."

"You see," he explained, folding his hands as the others one by one turned to listen. "G was the good child, the one who shined above the others, and as he proved to be marked with the seal of good, I was quickly dubbed the troublesome boy who lived on down the way. You have to understand though that when it came time, Gidoran would always find a way to make things right...at least with me. I still of course had to serve punishment. He will do right by me...by all of us, Phydin, and I know this because he always has."

Having listened without interruption to Jovaar's words, Selena's insecurity waned knowing that he truly knew what was best for Nitaya. Setting the small urn amongst the remnants of greens on the low table, she rose, gently handing the child to Orvi.

"If you will take her for a moment," she said, wrapping the babe snuggly in her blanket. "I would like to use the facilities to freshen."

Smoothing his cloak before accepting the squirming bundle, Orvi looked to Selena, clumsily adjusting her small cover. "Please hurry," he said, his voice crackling at Selena's toying smile as she straightened. "I am afraid I have not had much practice with little ones."

"I will," Selena answered, looking to Jovaar and chuckling at Orvi's obvious uneasiness. "We will be leaving soon and I am certain I look dreadful." Seeing that Nitaya was once again resting comfortably despite the shaking of Orvi's nervous arms, she smiled broadly at the odd pair then hurriedly left the room.

***

The crew continued their discussion of the day's events and the possibilities of what was to come next with their eyes filled with both anxiousness and awe as the beautiful steward quickly removed all remnants of their meal. Jovaar however grew impatient with each passing moment, his leg bobbing with the delay of Gidoran's return. "I will not be long," he said, standing to face the group. "Use your portalcom if Sir Gidoran returns before I do."

"Sir!" Jax answered, smartly rising and following protocol. Jovaar merely shook his head. Adding nothing further, he followed Selena's path from the room.

Approaching the beautiful woman as she was leaving the facilities, Jovaar smiled at the renewed smoothness of Selena's hair. "Is it not wonderful?" she asked, claiming his hand. "Is it not wonderful that Nitaya has recovered so easily?" Peering into his questioning eyes however, she could not help but straighten her tone. "Will we be leaving soon, Jovaar?"

"Ha!" he answered, shaking his head and tucking a stray tendril behind her ear. "You would not be teasing me, Selena, now would you?"

"Oh no, Jovi," she answered, a sly grin crossing her face, leaning close to brush her lips over his. "How odd that your childhood companion refers to you as I do, but on a more serious note, Jovi, this most certainly is not the place or time."

"I am aware," he answered, drawing her close. "But oh, how I have missed you."

"And I you," she answered, warmed by his embrace. "I remained at my quarters the entire time you were in that hovel within Adoni's Manine so that no one would notice the fear in my eyes. What if you were killed? What if the child did not survive the birth? What if…" she added, Jovaar hushing her worries and gently tipping her chin.

"We cannot think of that now," he whispered, halting her protests with a finger to her lips. "We must concentrate all of our efforts on ridding ourselves of Yani. Gidoran is a good man, Lena. We must trust that he can do what he says."

"I agree Jovi," she answered, lowering her gaze. "Yet I still cannot help but worry."

"I know," he whispered, lightly kissing her brow. "But try not to. I promise I will see all of you safely to the final destination."

"I know you will," she answered, Jax's voice interrupting over his portal.

"Sir Gidoran has returned, Sir," he said, mocking formality.

"We will be right there," Jovaar answered, recovering the device with his sleeve.

"You should not have said *we*, Jovi," Selena added, a coy grin crossing her face.

"As always you are right," he answered, laying his lips upon hers one final time. "It was foolish. Wait a moment or two before you return to the main cabin. We do not need to raise suspicion."

"But of course, Sir," she said, smiling and reaching out to touch his arm. A good bye kiss then?"

"You are such trouble," Jovaar added, leaning in and kissing her nose. "I must go," he added, turning to peer into her warm eyes. "Do not be long." Nodding her answer as Jovaar crossed through the rear door, Selena leaned against the wall at her back to await her turn.

Eight

Jovaar reentered the main room finding his crew as he had left them, yet Gidoran now stood facing the anxious members with a young man at his side he did not recognize. "Ah, Jovi," Gidoran said, gesturing to his approaching friend. "This is Hylin, another merchant if you will. He mans one of the stands above, yet as I was just explaining to the others, he serves me directly and keeps watch for anything out of place. He in fact forewarned me of your arrival," he added with a hearty laugh, patting the boy's back. "As you see, I have eyes everywhere."

"You are telling me that *the boy* is one of your commanding officers?" Jovaar asked, questionably eyeing the lad.

"Ha!" the pair answered as one. "No, Jovi," Gidoran continued, his hand relaxed on the younger's shoulder. "Hylin is no commander, yet he knows this station better than anyone and I trust him like no other. I have been quite fortunate to have had him entrusted to me since his younger onars and in regards to your much needed request, he has proven quite useful. Because of his endless abundance of knowledge of Yani and its capabilities, I have been able to secure a ship, armed and fully loaded as you requested. It will be Hylin's next task to see you there safely."

Jovaar guardedly looked the boy over, yet ruffling the incoming scruff of his chin, he shook his head, his frustration evident with the audacity of Gidoran's judgement. Jovaar was quickly losing his patience with the time they were wasting.

"You are trusting our safety and the safety of the possible to a mere child?" he asked, his temper flaring. He openly struggled with Gidoran's apparent lack of judgement. "Why can you not guide us, G? I assumed all along that it would be you."

111

"Jovaar," Gidoran said, sobering his tone. "You must understand that I am known by all throughout Yani. If I were the one to guide you, I assure you that *everyone* would take notice." Considering Gidoran's words, Jovaar knew his friend's insight was sound.

"But a boy?" he asked, his frustration unrelenting.

"I am no boy!" Hylin roared, unable to contain his anger as he crossed, arms flailing at Jovaar. "I am a man and as Sir Gidoran informed you of earlier, I know this station better than anyone. It will take some time and careful planning to make our way through the lanes to the ship, yet I *guarantee* I will see all of you safely there."

"Guarantee is a bold word, little one," Jovaar said, ignoring the boy's tempered fury, instead turning to face Gidoran. "You are certain he can do what he says?"

"With all that I am, yes," Gidoran answered, nodding. "And do not be too judgmental, Jovaar. Hylin is more of a man than most I know and you and I have been fortunate to know many."

With no other option available, Jovaar placed the fate of the child in the hands of a child with his trusted friend's word. Reluctantly shaking Hylin's hand in annoyed acceptance, he looked up at Selena's return, watching as she reclaimed the babe from Orvi.

"I thank you," she said, bundling Nitaya and accepting the vacant seat next to Jax. Settling comfortably with the child nestled in the crook of her arm, Jovaar watched as she first took notice of their newest arrival. Looking to Jovaar quizzically, her eyes calmed with his nodding approval.

"Alright, G," Jovaar continued, turning back to the awaiting pair, both his old and newest friend's appearing eager to assist in their path. "We are all once again present. Now tell me, what is your plan?'

***

"The ship will be ready within two hazon," Gidoran began, motioning for those remaining standing to claim a seat. "And unfortunately it will eat almost all of that time just to get you there. Hylin has devised a plan that will separate all of you, and only after every detail was thoroughly explained to me, can I assure you that it is the most advantageous path."

"You came to locate me in three groups," Gidoran continued, anxiously looking from one member to another. "Yet your numbers must be smaller this time around. No more than two of you can travel together and unfortunately some will have to go it alone for all beings on Yani are suspicious of anything out of the ordinary, especially large groups of travelers of unknown status."

"Everything is out of the ordinary here," Jax said, shaking his head. Phydin slapped his subordinate's knee, stifling the ill-timed outburt.

"Ah, but perception and what *you* consider out of the ordinary is far different from my people's point of view," Gidoran answered, dismissively waving off Phydin's anger. "Please, let me continue. Large groups of men will undoubtedly be noticed," Gidoran pressed, his tone firm as he turned back to the whole of the group. "I do not have the time to explain why, but please trust me on this. It is that reason alone that Hylin was able to detect something was amiss when you arrived, then as protical, he notified me. Now, I am trusting that most of you are equiped with portals regardless of their model. If you would simply open your side or lower screen maps, you will see that Hylin has already uploaded an additional link, laying out the path that each of you must take to reach the ship."

"Jovaar," Gidoran continued, turning to his friend. "I assumed that you would want to travel with Selena and the child, and therefore I had Hylin place you together. There will be two other groups of two, and lastly three will go alone." Opening their portals, Gidoran continued his explanation of the outlined path, the members grumbling amongst themselves having retrieved their individual assignments.

"Why must I travel alone while Uvis is partnered with Kroy?" Jax groaned, shaking his head with disgust. "Kroy outranks me and as all of you know, he uses that to his advantage whenever possible. Therefore I am turning it against him by saying it should be *he* that travels alone. If nothing else, he is *almost* the marksman that I am and should have no trouble

113

making a clean shot," he added, Kroy sneering in his direction. "Therefore with less rank and experience, I should be paired with Uvis."

"The idea is that none of you should have to take that shot," Gidoran continued, shaking his head. "Yet we can make the adjustments if Kroy, your outranking gunner, agrees."

"I am quite capable of taking care of myself," Kroy answered, glaring at Jax. "Send him with Uvis. They are not as quick minded as I am anyway."

"Now wait one blasted…" Jax snarled, Jovaar halting the ensuing argument with both hands.

"We have no time for this, Jax," Jovaar said firmly, grabbing his shoulder. "Kroy you will be reassigned. G, have Hylin transfer their screens then if we have no other disagreements as to orders, prepare your gear. We must leave at once." Keying into his portal with Sir Gidoran's nod of approval, Hylin made the last minute adjustments then slapped in his side screen, the maps simultaneously altering all necessary screens.

"Are there any other questions?" Gidoran asked, looking to the anxious crew. The members shook their heads and he nodded, turning back to Jovaar. "Then the time has come," he said, placing his hand on his friend's shoulder. "Gather your belongings and I will accompany you above ground, yet you must understand I will leave you at the exit."

With the remaining crew anxiously gathering their gear, Selena stood back, covering Nitaya with her cloak. She turned at the young steward in a dark shade of blue approaching with an urn of liquid for their journey. "We thank you," Selena said, placing the small pot of milk within her heavy cloak. "It seems you have thought of everything."

With the men securing their burdens over their shoulders, making their way one by one toward the door, Selena marveled once again as the steward simply vanished before her eyes. "I could never quite get used to that," she whispered to Jovaar, looking down to the sleeping child, and as the others stepped passed Gidoran's guiding hand through the opened door, she hurried with the bundled babe, smiling at her newest friend and eager to catch up with the others.

***

Walking in silence through the corridor, the group turned at the first bend then continued down the familiar door-lined passage until they at last reached the shoot. "As you noted traveling down and through the sublevels," Gidoran began over his shoulder, leading the members as Selena approached at the rear. "The shoot is designed for no more than two people and two people only. This coincides with Hylin's plan."

"You two," he continued, motioning to Phydin and Fidaldi. "You will go first. Follow the map provided and under no circumstances are you to stray...not even for a moment. The pilot will meet you on the dock just prior to boarding."

"How will he recognize us?" Fidaldi asked, Jax and Kroy parting so Fidaldi could be heard.

"Your arrival is expected," Hylin answered, nodding to Gidoran. "Please, just hurry. Enter the shoot and prompt the Main Level. You will be brought back to the surface then you must immediately set out on your route."

The pair stepped within the shoot as instructed, the others saying nothing as they stood anxiously waiting their turn. With the glass panels now closed before them, Selena smiled at Phydin, watching him and Fidaldi race toward the surface.

"Next a single," Hylin chimed. Kroy stepped forward, eager to begin his path.

"I will go," he said, scowling at Jax. He stepped quickly within the now empty, glass frame. Jovaar nodded to his subordinate and the others watched in silence as Kroy mouthed the order for the Main Level. Their heads tilted upward as one with the racing shoot.

"Jax and Uvis," Hylin continued, turning to the eager pair. Gesturing them in and watching the men race toward the ground, he turned to the five and the child that remained. As the glass again opened, Luvin, assuming he was next and traveling solo, stepped forward and within, yet Hylin joined him upon the platform. He looked surprised at the boy.

"Are you coming with me then?" Luvin asked, lowering his heavy tote to the the floor.

"No," Hylin answered, shaking his head. "I will ride to the surface with you then wait for the others at the top. Jovaar, you and Selena are to obviously take the rear with the child and once you have arrived at the surface, you will see that your given path directly follows mine. As Sir Gidoran has informed me of the child's vital role in the future of the Resistance, I will personally escort you to the ship. You have your map in case we get separated, yet barring any unforeseen difficulties, you should remain several steps at my back. I will see you on the ground. Sir Gidoran," he added, saying good bye with a nod. With the doors closed, Hylin gave the order for the world above.

***

With Hylin and Luvin disappearing above, Jovaar turned to his friend one last time. "I cannot repay you for all that you have done," he said placing his hand on Gidoran's shoulder. "If you had not…"

"It is *I* who should be thanking you," Gidoran interrupted, repeating Jovaar's warm gesture. "I have not had this much excitement in...well, since the last time you needed me at Central Docking. On a more serious note though, I know that you will see Nitaya safely to her rightful title, yet along the way do try to take care of yourself, old friend," he added, tapping his chin with his finger. "And I say farewell easily for as fate will take hold, I am quite certain we will meet again soon."

Giving Gidoran's shoulder a final squeeze, Jovaar stepped into the shoot and waited for Selena to join him, tipping his head as she claimed Gidoran's hands. "I thank you so very much for your kindness," she began, gently bouncing the child in her arms. "Jovi and I are forever in your debt and I promise you that the Resistance will hear of your courage."

"Although I have gladly served the one you carry, I will say that you are quite welcome, my dear Selena," he answered, leaning close to brush the tops of her hands with his lips. "Yet what I have done weighs far too little compared to the difficulties you are about to face. And as I pray for the oaf that guides you, I will also count the moments until I am certain that both you and the child are truly safe."

Snickering behind her hand and boarding the shoot, Selena felt Jovaar's stare and slowly turned to him. "What did he say?" he asked, grimacing. She merely smiled at his obvious jealousy. Before he could ask of her further, Gidoran shouted from beyond the sliding glass.

"Did she call you Jovi?" he asked, standing shocked in the empty corridor. Jovaar, merely smiling, placed his arm around Selena's shoulders and stared at his oldest friend, prompting the shoot abruptly upward.

Nine

Emerging from the shoot into the dingy rear corridor, Jovaar and Selena found Hylin impatiently waiting. "You must act quickly, old man," he said, Selena squeezing Jovaar's arm urging him to remain silent. "We have no time for delays. Now, you will need to follow me. And of course you must keep your distance as I said earlier. Furthermore, I have allowed time for you to appear to be glancing at wares as a distraction, yet only a brief amount of time at that. Come," he added, adjusting his tote. "We must get moving if we are to arrive within two hazon."

The trio made their way back through the filthy, main hall toward the front of the facility and Hylin turned as they reached the entrance, spying the sentry dozing at his post. "I have sent the others out of the building through different exits," he said, halting their approach with his hand. "I am well known here, yet not with the same status as Sir G. It would be out of place for me to leave from any other exit. I will speak briefly to the guard and then will move on. Wait here until you see me leave then emerge and follow."

Hylin stepped with confidence from within the building allowing no time for an argument, jostling the dozing sentry as Jovaar strained to hear what was being discussed. Yet as quickly as their conversation had begun it had ended with Hylin straightening the man in his seat. Shielding Selena at his back, Jovaar ignored the glare of the sentry and instead scanned both directions of the lane spying Hylin turning left, disappearing into the crowded pass.

"It is time," he said nodding, stepping out into the brightness of Yani's merchant row. Taking note of Hylin's repeated shouts, this time in a pleasant salute to one of the tattered merchants, he claimed Selena's hand to follow the boy's quickened steps.

Desperately attempting to appear as casual travelers, Jovaar halted Selena at the third stand on their left. Gesturing for her to play the ruse of purchase, he scanned the surrounding areas with the shift of his eyes.

"And how about this one?" she asked, turning to Jovaar and holding up the brightly colored cloth.

"No," he answered, not turning to face her. "Let us look further down the row." Sighing loudly and shrugging at the disappointed vendor, Selena gently replaced the garment and accepted Jovaar's arm, allowing his lead further down the lane.

***

Jovaar and Selena passed several other clustered merchants, each shouting their wares of greens, trinkets and garments, each competing desperately to get any prospective buyer's attention. Ignoring their incessant pleas however, the pair continued through the thickening crowd until Selena suddenly grabbed his arm, stopping his stride. "I have lost sight of Hylin," she whispered, nervously peering round the nearest cart. "Where has he gone?"

"He turned the corner up and to the left," Jovaar answered, studying the portalmap at his wrist. "According to this we are here," he added, pointing at the small screen. "We are half way to the location and at the moment all appears to be going as planned. Stay calm, Selena. With or without young Hylin, I promise I will see you to that ship."

Stepping back out into the lane, the pair reached the next corner, rounding an ancient building as shouts rang out from within. Passing its open door seemingly unnoticed, Jovaar spied Hylin at the base of the adjacent building, deep in conversation with a station crewmember.

"They actually have lane cleaners in this filthy place?" Selena asked staring down at the rubbish at her feet, Nitaya thankfully shielded from the stench beneath her cloak.

"Obviously not those who take pride in their work," Jovaar answered, kicking at a discarded mug. "Come," he continued, reclaiming her hand. "The boy is moving on."

Continuing down the narrower pass shielded within the shadows of the taller buildings, Jovaar guided Selena amongst the endless maze of buyers, easily spying the SSD just ahead, across the lane in an entrance alcove. "Blasted," he groaned, pulling Selena close. "Do not look, but as I had feared there is a Sugin searcher droid just beyond the lone stand on our right. They know we are here."

"What do we do?" Selena whispered, fear consuming her. For reassurance, she at once peeked at Nitaya within her cloak. "Hylin crossed him easily and is just up ahead," she added, looking over Jovaar's shoulder into the lane. "Use your portalcom."

"Stupid," Jovaar answered, grumbling and running his fingers over the device, using the abundance of purchasers for cover. "We did not synchronize the boy's with ours. I do not know what frequency he is using. Walk slower, Selena. We can not let the droid know we are on to him."

As if knowing the enemy was near, the child instantly cried out in Selena's arms. "Hush, Nitaya," Selena pleaded, attempting to soothe the babe beneath her cloak. "She knows, Jovi," she whispered, rocking her gently side to side. "She knows he is close!"

"Do what you can to calm her," he answered, lifting his sleeve to search his portal. "We have the map. We will just divert down this side lane and make our way back around to here," he added, shielding his arm from prying eyes as he pointed. "We may be able to lose him."

"Hylin said not to stray from the path," Selena added, panic filling her voice. She looked toward the seemingly unknowing droid on briefly before shielding her eyes.

"We have no choice," he answered, slamming his side screen closed. "We will keep walking just a bit more and then the turn should be just beyond those stacks of crates. Appear confident, Selena. It is our only chance."

Trusting Jovaar as always, Selena did not question his judgement yet instead reached within her tote to find the urn the beautiful steward had given her. Nourishing the child as they walked, Selena was thankful that for the moment it appeared to appease the babe's cries. Finding the corner as Jovaar had predicted, they turned, facing the much darker pass.

"Are you certain?" Selena asked, staring into the even narrower passage then turning to peer over her shoulder at the lurking droid.

"As certain as I can be," he answered, placing his arm about her waist. "Now trust me," he added, attempting to shield his uneasiness. "Walk confident, Lena and under no circumstances are you to look back."

    ***

Hylin reached the ship unscathed and with time to spare, meeting the pilot on the main dock just outside boarding. "Have the others arrived?" he asked, peering into the open hatch of midship.

"Yes," the pilot answered, adjusting the final clasp of the flight gear. "Where is the rest of your group?"

"They should be arriving shortly," he answered, patting upward at the man's shoulder. "I lost sight of them a few lanes over but I am certain they are not far behind. I will be heading aboard to check on the rest of the crew. Inform me as soon as they arrive."

"Of course, Hylin," the pilot answered, stepping aside to allow him passage up the plank. Finding the members had arrived safely, relaxing and adjusting to their newest surroundings, Hylin was greeted warmly as the members discussed their various routes to the ship.

"Good to see you have made it safely," Phydin said smiling, parting from the others and crossing to their newest arrival. "Are Jovaar and Selena not with you?"

"They should be arriving shortly," Hylin repeated, standing before the now silent crew. "I just wanted to see for myself that all of you made it safely aboard. Store your gear below then make preparations for detachment. I will wait for Jovaar and Selena on the dock with the pilot."

Anxious to get on their way, the crew began storing their totes and claiming their stations at Hylin's request, Jax and Kroy turning to the rear of the ship to scope the gunnery and Hylin left them, descending the plank to speak with the pilot.

"Any sign?" he asked, skirting a dockhand to look out to the massive opening.

"None," the pilot answered flatly. "And I am afraid we cannot wait much longer. I have noticed an SSD questioning several pilots on the far side of the dock," the pilot added, pointing several stations down and to the right. "I am certain he will make his way here soon."

"Blasted," Hylin groaned, crossing his arms at his chest. "Something must have happened. Per Sir Gidoran's orders, I have no choice but to go after them. Give me your weapon. I could use a spare."

Without hesitation the pilot released the small strap and handed over the hefty piece. "How long should I wait?"

"A half hazon," Hylin answered with confidence, unlocking the device before shielding it beneath his cloak. "And if we have not returned by then, you must debark with the others as instructed."

"But what about you? What about the child and those that carry her burden?" the pilot asked, shouting after Hylin's retreating back.

"I will get them here," he answered, returning the pilot's pleas over the din of the nearby exhausts. "Or will die trying."

***

With his portal open and now visibly guiding their way, Jovaar led Selena through the darkness of the side lane, intermittently peering over his shoulder for any sign of the enemy. The pass, eerily narrow, became moreso with each passing step due to the large crates that were stacked high, leaning against the building's exterior walls on both sides. At times, Jovaar was forced to step before Selena and the child, not knowing what lie in wait in the darkened shadows.

Brimmed with the station's refuse, Jovaar scowled at having no other choice but to lead Selena and the child through the disgusting filth. With several small creatures scurrying passed atop their feet, he grit his teeth at having to turn sideways to clear the most tightest of areas. Jumpy and on edge with Selena's attempted shielding of high-pitched screeches, he grit his teeth to hold down his temper.

"It is alright," he said attempting calm. Fighting his labored breathing, he wiped some fallen shred of cloth from the portal's screen. "Just stay close to the crates. We will use them for cover."

"It seems I have little choice," Selena answered, holding Nitaya close and stumbling through yet another tight crevice. Yet as the smells emanating from the large crates proved unbearable, forcing her to pull the sleeve of her cloak over her face to shield against its vulgar stench, Selena sighed, at last spying the turn up ahead and to their left.

"We are almost there," Jovaar said, peering a final time over his shoulder. "Blasted. Selena run! He is on to us!"

The shouts grew louder. Reaching the corner of the tall building, at last free of the crates rounding its high frame, Jovaar and Selena found themselves staring at the oddest of displays. Beings, horded en masse appeared to be reveling in some sort of strange celebration. Quickly using the dense crowd for cover against the approaching enemy, Jovaar claimed Selena's hand, weaving her through the cramped area until they reached a small alcove on the opposite side of the lane. Jovaar, scanning his portal to again confirm their route, its small screen altering with each step of their journey, remained focused on the approaching enemy. Selena however, could not help but marvel at the colorfully dressed creatures.

Masked, costumed and obviously well sated, it appeared both Yanians and visitors were enjoying the festivities as one, with no sense of order or propriety. "It must be a lane festival," Jovaar said, at last raising his eyes from his screen. "This is good. We will blend easily with the crowd. Keep your eyes out for that droid Selena and come. He will certainly not be far behind."

Struggling to keep pace with Jovaar's long strides through the joyous mob, Selena could not help being startled by their various faces as each displayed colorful masks of widelife that were only outdown by their outlandish covers. Bright, with their facial features exaggerated, they drank from tube-filled mugs, their brilliant cloaks displaying tusks, feathers and protrusions varying in the oddest of shapes and sizes.

Not one appeared the same and neither did one appear unfettered by the presence of the unmasked pair. Each carefree and jovial with another, and proving their ease as Jovaar and Selena labored with the crossing of the dense crowd of beings, both were surprisingly handed masks of their own by a stray lane vendor.

"Put it on," Jovaar said, grumbling as Selena chuckled at his pointed features. "This is not the time, Selena," he continued, adjusting his new outer skin. "Put on your mask and keep moving. The droid cannot be far behind. Do not," he added, peering over her shoulder. "Do not under any circumstances look back. We will go to that stand just ahead to our right where I will purchase a tube 'n' mug, then for the time being we will carry on with the others. According to the portalmap, the loading dock is not far. Just keep moving and do what you can to blend."

Nodding and accepting his lead all the while unable to dissolve her hidden smile, Selena clung to Jovaar's hand as he wove her through the thinning revelers, at last arriving at the mug vendor's stand at the far right end of the lane. Reaching within his cloak, Jovaar withdrew two pents to cover payment for the tube 'n mug.

"Your pents are no good here," the yellow-clad merchant said, shaking his oversized head and tossing a stained rag over his shoulder. Jovaar began to protest that pents were the most common of currency yet te man interrupted his argument, lifting his odd-shaped mask of horns.

"It is the Festival of Swari, my good man," he said, his laugh robust as other creatures joined the makeshift slab. "Although we dwell far from Clooxin, mugs are of no cost this fine day."

"I thank you then," Jovaar said, replacing the tokens within his cloak. The man filled the mug to the brim, thrusting its sloshing, dark liquid into Jovaar's hand. "To Swari," he added, downing a long drink. "Tis a shame we have not been blessed with one so willing to provide."

"Agreed! To Swari," the merchant echoed belching without care, shielding his smiling face with the yellow-feathered mask. "All praise Sir Gidoran."

**

"I see him," Selena said, Jovaar stepping from the slab and offering her drink. A trio of green puffy-faced creatures claimed their nook, yet Selena merely shook her head beneath the yellow-colored mask.

"He is just over and to our right, Jovi," she mumbled. Unable to read her face beyond the brightness of the feathered cover, Jovaar could however clearly read the fear in her eyes.

"He is not looking this way," he answered, spying the enemy in an alcove against a side building, his obvious, non-conforming profile facing them. Come," Jovaar added, turning to pace to the far side of the lane. "We are almost there."

Jovaar did not drink again from his mug for he was in no mood for celebrating, and although he toted the nuisance to further appear as a reveler, he grumbled at the sloshing liquid falling without prejudice against his cloak. The lane, however dense, cleared with each step as the pair reached the outskirts of the main festivities, and Jovaar, spying the massive entrance to the docks, replaced his anger with relief as he raised his yellow mask, smiling.

"There," he said, gesturing with his chin. "A few more steps and we have made it." Yet as the triumphant words escaped his lips, three Sugin searcher droids appeared at their side.

"You will come with us, and you will not struggle," one ordered, mechanically nodding to his fellow guards. Turning to Selena then back to the droids, Jovaar tossed the dark liquid of his mug into their faces.

"Run!" he shouted, thrusting Selena in front of him toward the massive entrance. Turning, he knocked the nearest droid on his back. Grapsing for his weapon, Jovaar trailed after Selena's lead.

Racing as fast as her feet would allow, Selena clung tight to Nitaya as the persistant droids struggled through the melee of beings at her back, yet as the first blasts rang out in the distance, Selena watched in fear as those before her scattered, their revelry ceasing with the intrusion of the Sugin force.

Jovaar urged her forward regardless of the dodging obstacles and keeping pace at her back returned fire, spying the comical costumes at his rear dodging behind merchant stands to avoid the blasts. Fixing his eyes once again on Selena's back, Jovaar lost his step, just missing a man dressed in bright blue, his mask a glowing hue of golden fur. Lurching sideways to avoid the man's hazard path, the droid's blast at his back connected at the reveler's chest before him. Watching the man fall to his death, Jovaar racing to once again catch up with Selena, he grit his teeth at not being able to save the innocent.

With its use no longer necessary, Selena removed her mask midstride, tossing it to the ground as she reached the open intersection at the end of the lane. Nearing the massive entrance however, she cursed her foolishness, spying several more searcher droids closing in from the adjacent direction.

Discouraged that their masks had done little to deter the enemy, Selena slowed her pace, circling away from the approaching numbers. Searching for somewhere to hide, she whirled in place, her fears facing her as she cradled the wailing child to her breast. Her eyes widened at Hylin's nearing.

Panting and racing to Selena's side with several of his guards taking aim at the Sugins to his right, Hylin shielded Selena and the child, rushing her toward the entrance.

"There are three more at our backs," Jovaar shouted, at last catching up with the pair. Hylin turned and took confident aim at the nearest, Jovaar placing his arm about Selena's waist. "Alright, two," Jovaar added, panting and guiding both Selena and the child to the large arch.

"Where did you go?" Hylin asked, aiming at another that attempted escape from his guards. "I told you to stay your path! Forget it," he added, shaking his head as he watched the enemy numbers depleting. "We have no time to discuss it here. Come. We must get you to the ship at once."

Racing into the open port, the shots dissipating at their backs, Hylin remained at Jovaar and Selena's rear to ensure that no droids had been allowed to pass, motioning for the pair to continue on without him. Nodding in response, Jovaar rushed ahead of Selena through the oblivious dockhands, eagerly searching for the awaiting ship.

"Which one?" Selena asked, walking briskly to his side, unable to take her eyes from the vast array of crafts.

"These are not large enough for us all," Jovaar answered, craning his neck to see further down the dock. "Come," he added, reclaiming her hand. "It must be further down."

***

Spying the approach of the frightened pair, the pilot motioned silently for them to come forward. Keeping a hand ready on the active arm at his side however, he awaited acknowledgement as the duo reached the plank. Panting, Jovaar noticed the hesitation, and shielding Selena to his back, spoke immediately.

"Hylin is right at our backs," he said, gasping to catch his breath. "Have all arrived and are we prepared for detachment?"

"We have been prepped and on standby awaiting your arrival," the pilot answered, his voice flat behind the shielding mask.

"And the others?" Jovaar pressed, peering into the open hull.

"They are inside and restrained for detachment," the pilot answered, unwavering. "If you will climb aboard and claim your stations, Sir…"

"Savius," Jovaar interrupted, reassuring the man.

"As I was saying then," the pilot continued, gesturing the newest arrivals within. "If you will climb aboard and claim your stations, we will…"

Blasts erupted throughout loading and the pilot, staying close to the ship's wing gestured for Jovaar and Selena to follow. Racing toward them, dust scattering from the blasts at Hylin's heels as both dockhands and passengers raced to avoid the onslaught.

"Get to Command!" he shouted, turning to take aim at the ensuing droids as they cleared the massive entrance. "We are being overrun and must detach at once!"

Motioning for the trio to board before him, Hylin returned fire, racing up the plank as the remaining guards did what they could to hold the enemy at bay. Sealing the hatch and turning to the frightened faces of the crew at midship, Hylin ordered all to their stations then assisted Selena with the child. Prompting the rear door, Jovaar confirmed his gunners.

"The pilot will require two," Hylin said over his shoulder. Nodding to Phydin and Fidaldi and returning to mid-ship, Jovaar gestured for them to release their restraints then joined them in the narrow corridor.

"I know that you are both anxious to help," he said, prompting the command door. "And I promise you that if at any time the pilot cannot do as he says, it will be you, Phydin who navigates this ship. Until he proves his worth, I will feel more confident knowing that you are prepared to claim the stick."

Entering Command as the colorful lights danced across the wide displays, the men trailed by Hylin quickly claimed their stations surrounding the concentrating pilot whom had thrusters ignited and was without falter, making final preparations for detachment.

"Stay calm," Jovaar said, looking to Phydin who sat anxious before the Navigations screen. "We should be exto-atmos soon."

Phydin merely nodded in disgust for he knew he could handle the ship better than any nameless pilot. Knowing there was no time to argue however, he grit his teeth and turned to the panel of his inferior postion.

"Selena," Jovaar said, prompting the helm's com. "Is Nitaya secure?"

"She is in med-bay with the droids," she answered, her tone attempting calm. "I will be able to return to her when we stabilize."

"I will head to the rear to look in on her as soon as I can," he answered, releasing the com. Turning, he faced the pilot, joining the others to await the sounding of detachment.

"Concentrate all energy to the rear shield," the pilot ordered, Fidaldi keying the ordered data without hesitation. "And get final coordinates for the hyper drive." Prompting his screen and mapping the specified route, Phydin grumbled, the ship gyrating with the adaption of the impending thrust without his assistance.

"Coordinates set," he said flatly, informing the pilot with the ship's release. "We will reach EA in five, four, three, two, one. Hypo in ten, nine…" the pilot continued, lowering both hands to the stick. The ship, having detached with ease regardless of the speckling of fire, leveled as Jovaar secured the last of his restraints.

"Two, one, hypo go…" the pilot said, the pressure from the jolt sailing the members through the stars. Their backs crushed to the rear of their seats with the order.

"We have reached hypo as I have been instructed by Sir Gidoran," the pilot began, speaking through his mouthpiece so that all could hear his words over the pressure of the stabling cabin. "He informed me that you would then give me the coordinates for our destination, which I was assured that you would know in order to continue. Stalling hyper," the pilot added, lifting and removing his face shield with the settling ship.

Completely taken aback with the pilot removing the darkened face guard, Jovaar sat stunned as the short blonde hair emerged from within, trickling down to tease the pilot's slender shoulders. The pilot proved not a man but a woman, and shaking her hair free from the restraints of the headgear, her voice that had been disguised by the mask spoke in a most eloquent tone.

"Our destination?" she asked, smiling at Hylin seated at the back of Command, urging someone to respond to their newest discovery. As the others, Jovaar sat dumbfounded, unable to form words, amazed he had missed all the signs.

Looking the blonde over, of course now he could see the distinctions; sleek long legs, the delicate hands, the slender waist. She was older than he yet handled herself quite well for her age, and in her maternal tone she pressed the gawking man once again. "Jovaar?" she asked, coyly tiling her head. "The coordinates?"

"Um, yes, forgive me," he answered at last, peering over his shoulder to spy Hylin enjoying the ruse. "Kindawa. It is the second in the…"

"I know of its location, Jovaar," she interrupted, placing her hands on her hips. "Why do you not head back to check on

129

the others? It will be some time before we arrive and Hylin is more than capable of assisting me here. Have your crew settled and try to get some rest. There are extra garments in quarters," she added, eying his rather filthy attire. "I will inform you when we are within a hazon of arrival."

Still amazed at the reflexes and stamina the pilot had exuded against the oncoming Sugins, Jovaar could not believe that a woman of her age could have outperformed many men that had worked at his side. "Your name?" he asked, clearing his throat as he at last found movement, unclasping and rising from his restraints.

"My friends call me Khyra," she answered, leaning on the back of her seat and winking playfully at Hylin. "Yet until we become friends...you may refer to me as Ma'am."

   ***

Jovaar exited Command scowling after the slight from the pilot. Grumbling, he returned to midship where he found his crew in various stages of unclasping their restraints and moving about the cabin. As Selena appeared to be struggling with her clasp, he knelt before her to assist.

"Let me get this off you," he said, easily releasing the strap.

"Thank you," she answered, settling her hair. "I was about to head back to look in on Nitaya. Will you be joining me?"

"I will be along in a moment," he answered, rising to take her hand. "I want to get everyone up to speed first." Nodding and turning to leave, Jovaar stopped her, placing his hand on her shoulder. "Which way is Med-deck?" he asked.

"They refer to it as Med-bay, Jovi," she answered, Jovaar giving her the slightest glare. "Forgive me," she added, covering her mouth to clear her throat. "I mean Jovaar. It is just down the corridor, second door on your right."

"I will catch up with you soon," he continued, releasing her. "It will be some time until we arrive, so there is plenty of time to freshen. I have been told that there are extra garments in quarters."

130

"I will get to that eventually," Selena said, looking down at her tattered cloak. "My main concern is of course the child."

"Of course," he answered, repeating her words. Crissing the cabin to head to the rear, Jovaar turned at her exit to update his tired crew.

Ten

Motioning for the others to join him, Jovaar crossed passed the restrained stations and settled onto the large, plush bench in the reclining area. The members whispered amongst themselves, following his lead to claim their their seats. When all were seated, Jovaar began.

"I would like to take a moment to congratulate all of you for a job well done," he said, looking from one to another and clasping his hands between his knees. "Yet I must stress that the word *done* is far from appropriate. The stopover at Yani, although I was aware it could be a possibility, was not a part of our direct route, and since I am certain there will be further attacks from the Sugin army, I feel I have no other choice but to inform all of you now of our final destination."

Having entered and claimed the pair of vacant seats at the rear of the others as Jovaar had begun to speak, Fidaldi and Phydin erupted with the rest of the crew at his startling words. Phydin's voice however, rang high above all others.

"Jovaar," he shouted, the crew quieting to his insistant tone. "You have told us from the beginning that the final destination must be kept secret for fear of capture, for the safety of the child, and for the further cause of the Resistance. We accepted that, and I must say I question your tactics now. If you are certain that others must be made aware, perhaps you should reconsider and inform only a few, perhaps those who have been with you the longest."

"Before this day I would have agreed with you," Jovaar answered, running his fingers through his matted hair. "Yet as the Sugins somehow learned of our whereabouts on Adoni, I am certain it will not be the last time our location is breached. I know now that it is vital that all of us are aware of where we are headed and what must be accomplished in order to see to

Nitaya's safety. If we are attacked or separated, every one of you must know the plan Martus laid out for his child for everything depends on her survival."

"I understand your reasoning," Phydin continued, leaning forward on his knees. "Yet again I must stress my opposition. If we are not to fly directly to the final destination, I feel it would be more appropriate to inform only a few of its exact coordinates, and then perhaps trust the information of the next location with the others. I trust each and every one of you, yet with the life of the child at stake, I must insist, Jovaar that you keep your silence with the majority."

Jovaar listened to Phydin's argument, cafefully considering his friend's words. Sighing and leaning forward however, he was certain of what must be done. "Alright then," he began, rubbing his tired eyes. "As always, I appreciate your advice Phydin, and after careful consideration I will grant you that you have a point. For Nitaya's safety, I will inform all present of our path, exluding only the final destination and for now I will remain completely silent, as will you with regards to the pilot and the boy."

The group's various opinions hushed as one, and although reluctant and simultaneously eager to learn of the secret path Martus Savius had laid out onars before, each felt both pride and fear for with the knowledge of the possible's route. All gathered fully grasped the weight of their individual importance yet the members also felt small against the overall result. Prompting the central holoform on the low round table to better relay his instructions, Jovaar found himself uneasy, yet without options, he looked to his men and relinquished the specifics he had swore never to share.

   ***

Selena eagerly entered Med-bay finding Nitaya in her small cubicle flanked by the pair of droids who had claimed her upon boarding. "Status please," she said, crossing to the babe's side. The nearest droid turned slowly to face her.

"The child is restless yet all vitals are within range," it said, turning back to the high panel.

"Restless?" Selena questioned, her mind flashing back to the med-officer phymbial aboard R8. "Are you certain nothing is wrong?"

"Quite certain," it responded, the second droid unmoved by the dialogue. "She is in need of nourishment however, and I was just to begin to administer when you arrived."

"Ah," Selena said, smiling and turning to the cooing child, her fears waning. Leaning close, she jostled her small toes. "Nitaya tends to get that way when in need. Are you in need of nourishment, my little one? I will take her to quarters and settle her there," she continued, gently tapping her finger to the babe's nose. "If you are needed further, I will send for you."

"Of course," the droids answered in unison, one handing her the urn of white liquid. Unsettling Nitaya's cart, Selena prompted the main door and led the child eagerly from the cabin.

***

"I have been told that we have several hazon before arrival," Jovaar said, completing the last of the specifics. "Take to quarters, freshen and get some rest. As you are well aware by now, you will require every bit of your strength."

The crew sat speechless as Jovaar reclined in his seat, yet looking to one another with the knowledge of what had been laid out before them, each in turn reluctantly rose, leaving him alone with his thoughts. Jovaar added nothing further but a slight nod as Phydin disengaged the holoform and stood, and when at last all had exited the mid-ship cabin, he tipped his head into his hands, running his fingers through his hair.

"So much is at stake," he thought, exhaling loudly. "Did I do the right thing by telling them? Should I have told them the entire plan? There is no going back now," he said aloud, sighing and staring into his hands. Feeling the weight of the day heavily upon him he at last stood, following the path of his tired crew toward quarters.

Heeding Selena's instructions, Jovaar stopped at the second door to his right, commanding it open with a gesture of his hand. Startled as he found only the two med droids in the bay, one seated before a large screen and the other folding Nitaya's blanket, he instantly began to worry.

"Where is she?" he demanded, fearing another secret attack. He stomped into the cabin prepared to take them both on.

"She has been taken to quarters by the woman Selena," one answered, slowly turning to face the newest arrival. "All vitals are well, Sir Savius."

"If all was well that blanket would be with the child," he said, impatiently claiming the small cloth from the being. "Which door leads to her quarters?"

"Next door down on your left, Sir," the droid answered unmoved at anger. Jovaar balled Nitaya's only possession in his fists and grumbled yet said nothing, returning to the corridor.

"Humans," the droid at the panel said, his lone eye blinking to its counterpart. "They are such rude creatures."

       ***

Jovaar reached the door to his left having passed it on his way to med-bay without knowing its purpose. Before prompting the opening device to Selena's quarters however, he turned to the sounds of the cabin opposite the corridor over his shoulder. Finding the door surprisingly open, he strode to the entrance unnoticed. Leaing against the jam of the door, he folded his arms as three of his crew members lazed on their cots, viewing the high show monitor. Jax, Phydin and Fidaldi, obviously finding comfort in their surroundings, laughed at the comical display on the screen.

"Where are the others?" Jovaar asked, his voice booming, startling the trio.

"Calm, Jovaar," Phydin answered, slapping his cot and roaring at the ancient show. "They are in there," he added, pointing. "They are washing the Adoni grime from their bodies and unfortunately for us, Hylin helped them win the bet, so they were priveledged to use the facilities first."

At Phydin's calming words and the camaraderie of the crew, Jovaar lowered his arms in attempt to ease his tension, an act the others appeared so easy at doing. "I suppose I am a bit edgy," he said, hesitating as Phydin turned away from the screen. "Forgive me."

Waving a sign of 'no need' to his commander, Phydin, Jax and Fidaldi once again erupted in a fit of laughter, the familiar three boisterous men across the large screen continuing their ranting of play. Jax assumed Jovaar had left them however, and faded the image from the comic to the beautiful. Staring at the sensuality that now filled the display, Jovaar straightened, his serious tone returning.

"Where are Selena and the child?" he asked, startling Jax and testing the knowledge of his crew.

"Just down the corridor, Sir," he answered, trying desperately to re-alter the image.

"Do not spend too much time watching that nonsense," Jovaar ordered, Jax giving up his fruitless attempts at hiding the image.

"But the women..." he added, hands held high in defense.

"We will request it off soon, Sir," Phydin interrupted, tossing his cover at Jax's pleading hands. "We will then rest as ordered."

"Very well," Jovaar answered, refusing to look at the images as he straightened from the jam. "I am off to see to the child and then get some rest myself. I will return before our arrival."

"See to the child?" Jax chided, turning to Phydin and throwing the cover back in his direction. "Selena is no child," he added, snickering and turning back to the screen. Retossing the cover, followed by Fidaldi pelting Jax with his own, Phydin straightened on his cot, attempting to also prove serious.

"Jovaar has enough on his mind," he said, lowering his feet to the floor. Finding they could not look away, each turning back to the sounds of the high display, all instantly broke out with laughter.

***

Jovaar found Selena sitting with the child in the next cabin, and although he was certain she heard his entrance, she

136

did not turn. Instead she gave her full concentration on the song she was singly softly to Nitaya.

"You have an angel's voice," he said, leaning against the rear wall. Instead of responding to his words, she again chose to finish her lilt.

Reaching the end of her words, Selena placed the now empty urn on the low table next to her seat. Shifting the child to her shoulder, she patted her back lovingly as if the babe were her own. Watching as she performed the task of a knowledgable momar with such ease, gratefully giving unquestionable love, Jovaar simply stood relishing the scene of Selena with Wynin's child.

Selena's cabin proved bare of all but essentials and eyeing the space as she returned to her tune, Jovaar noted the pair of untouched cots lining the left side wall, a small table separating the pair. The facilities room, he assumed, lay just ahead and to his left, and a small workstation equipped with a large panel against the far wall, stood situated to his right. A small cubicle cart sat idled beside the bonding pair, and Jovaar presumed Selena had made arrangements for the child to remain in her quarters. As if confirming his thoughts, she paced the few steps to the trundle's side, at last laying the sleeping babe to her rest.

"I found this with the droids," he said, handing her the bundled blanket.

"Oh, I had thought it lost," Selenea whispered, placing it gently upon the child. "I thank you, Sir," she added, sarcastically.

"Now Lena, you know that…" he began, Selena turning, halting the eternal argument with her hand.

"I know, Jovi, I know," she said, lowering her head. "But it is so very hard to not show my fear for you, my love for you. Why must we keep it to ourselves?"

"It is not proper," he answered, lifting her chin with his fingers. "You knew this onars before and you said then that you understood."

"I know what I have said in the past," she answered, turning to stroke the child's face. "And I do understand. It is just so hard."

"I know it too, Lena," he answered, enveloping her in his arms. "But it will not be much longer. Now go and freshen," he added, kissing the top of her head. "I will watch over the child until you return."

"I suppose you are once again right," she answered, stepping from the warmth of his arms. "You said there were fresh garments?"

"They should be around here somewhere," he answered, crossing to the cabinets on the far wall. "Here," he added, finding suitable attire on the third try. "And take your time. It should be several hazon before we arrive."

Crossing to the open door and selecting a few pieces, Selena turned, attempting a smile. "I will not be long," she said, not waiting for a response. Anxious to freshen, she quickly turned to enter the washroom, leaving Jovaar to question her sadness in silence.

***

The facilities proved small but efficient and Selena easily made do with what little space she had. Prompting the door closed and removing her cloak, she placed it on a lone hook to the the right of the glass. Reaching within the basin to turn on the flow of water but spying the flat barren walls, she stood erect considering the lack of manual prompts.

"Water on," she ordered, assuming it was a command model. With the water springing forth at her words, she decided that it was hot enough without further prompting. Ridding herself of her filthy garb, Selena stepped gratefully within, steam quickly filling the room.

The warmth of the water proved gloriously inviting and although knowing time was a gift she did not possess, Selena stood still, letting its massaging heat cascade over her head and down her tired body. Knowing the child could awaken any moment however, she succumbed to the urge of movement and reached for the wash bar and began lathering, scrubbing her hair and the grime of Yani from her limbs.

Satisfied that she had done all she could, Selena ordered the water's flow to cease and then smiled when she assumed correctly with the request of air mode from the updated unit. Fully dried from the blast of warm air, she squeezed the last remnants of water from her hair, stepped from the basin and stood facing the glass. Staring at the dark circles under her eyes, she rubbed at them with the heel of her palms.

"I need desperately to rest," she sighed, eyeing her aged reflection. Knowing the cot awaited her just beyond the door, she quickly searched within the drawer under the basin, finding a small comb. Preparing her hair, adorning the provided clean garments, and tidying the small facilities, Selena stood pleased that all was once again in place.

"And now I can close my eyes," she said, tucking a fallen tendril behind her ear. Inspecting her reflection a final time in the glass, Selena quickly returned to quarters.

   ***

Finding the pair nestled warmly beneath the down of her cover, Selena walked quietly across the cabin to the edge of the cot, her tired smile beaming at the most wonderful of sights. There they were; Jovaar with his low rumble that labeled his sleep with exhaustion, and Nitaya wrapped tightly in her blanket, cradled and sleeping peacefully within the crook of his arm.

Selena sighed as she noted Jovaar had rearranged the cots so that the two were side by side with Nitaya at their center. With the opposite side standing with its cover's corner slightly open and inviting, she crossed round the foot of the cot, claiming its welcoming invitation.

Covering herself with the heavy blanket, Selena smiled and closed her eyes, laying her hand over Nitaya's small arm, at last finding Jovaar's hand. It seemed sleep would come easy for them all.

Eleven

The chime of the com startled the slumbering trio. Leaning up on one elbow, Jovaar felt the ache of his muscles as he rubbed at his tired eyes.

"What is it?" he asked, his voice cracking above the whimpering cries of the child.

"We will be on approach to Kindawa in less than one hazon," the pilot curtly answered.

"Thank you," Jovaar said, pulling his arm free from beneath Nitaya, sitting up and running his fingers through his hair. "Selena, please do what you can to calm her."

"I am sorry," he added, chiding himself for his rudeness as Selena gathered the child, crossing the room to the cubicle. "How long have I been asleep?" he asked, attempting to start anew.

"It seems we have all rested for quite some time," she answered, her tone bearing her obvious unnerving.

"Selena," Jovaar pleaded, lowering his hands to the cot. "I said I was sorry. Do not be like this. I am just exhausted and there is still so much to do."

"I know, and I forgive you...this time," she answered, a grin creeping across her face as she changed Nitaya's napping. "Go," she added, gesturing toward the door. "Do what you must do. I will stay here and see to Nitaya. She is ready for another feeding anyway."

"I suppose you are right," he answered, standing and stretching his arms. "I will stop off at the crew's quarters and then will work my way to Command. If you need me you can reach me on the com." Crossing to Selena's side, Jovaar leaned down, kissing her brow.

"I will see you both soon," he added. Turning to gather his tote, he could not contain his smile as Selena began singing another of her soft lilts. Meeting her eyes, he winked before clearing the cabin door.

Crossing the narrow corridor, Jovaar rubbed his arms and prompted the crew's door. Shaking his head, he found that all were awake but Jax, who still lay asleep on the corner cot. Crossing to Phydin, he interrupted the man's screen viewing and motioned quizzically toward the sleeping member.

"He would sleep through anything," Phydin said, chuckling at the slumbering sounds that escaped him.

"Not this time," Jovaar said, crossing his arms. "Wake him up, get everything in order and meet me in the main cabin."

"Yes, Sir," Phydin answered, pleased that the time of resting had ended. Pacing the few steps to Jax's side, he awoke the man with a quick blow of his down pillow. As Jax wailed out in startled anger, Jovaar merely laughed at his comical display and turning back toward the open door, left his men to prepare their update.

***

"How long do we have before arrival?" Jax asked anyone who would listen, slowly climbing off his cot.

"Not long," Orvi answered, prepping his gear. "We should be on approach soon."

"You could have let me rest longer," he whined, Phydin shaking his head and tossing his tote over his shoulder.

"You should not have spent so much time watching that blasted show monitor," Phydin scowled, Jax replacing his footgear. "Is everyone ready then?" The crew grumbled and nodded as they made their final preparations then slowly, each paced to the door.

"I will catch up," Jax said to the backs of his friends.

"Do not be long," Phydin answered, prompting the door and gesturing for each member to head to mid-deck. "There is not much time," he added when they were alone.

"I know," Jax answered, slamming his foot to the floor and fumbling with the clasps. "I said I will be right there."

Knowing nothing but Jovaar's words would prompt Jax to move more quickly, Phydin merely nodded at the groggily man. Turning toward the open door, he shrugged his shoulders and trailed after the others to learn of the next step of their journey. Pacing the corridor, Phydin jumped at the sound of the com.

"We are on arrival," the female pilot reported. "We should be landing in less than half hazon."

Grumbling with the com again quiet, Phydin turned back and returned to quarters.

"I know, I know," Jax said, quickly gathering his gear. Bearing his own frustration, he crossed to signal off the show monitor.

"You were delayed for that?" Phydin shouted, pointing at the device.

"But the women..." Jax argued, gesturing toward the blank screen. Crossing the room, Phydin grabbed Jax by the shoulder, dragging him and his gear roughly from the empty cabin.

"I said I was coming!" he shouted, Phydin shoving him through the door.

"You are such a child," Phydin said sternly. Unable to contain his smile as Jax mumbled a spat of incoherent nonsense and stumbled down the corridor, he could not help but grit his teeth, agreeing with the man's disposition. "Women are always getting in the way."

***

Jovaar was in midsentence rehashing the crew's assignments as Phydin and Jax rushed in. "What kept you?" he asked, glaring as they approached the low bench.

"Nothing important," Phydin answered sarcastically, slinging a tote into Jax's midsection and thrusting him into his seat.

"Alright then," Jovaar continued, ignoring the obvious feud between two of his most trusted men. "Everyone knows their tasks, everyone understands their importance. Are there any questions?" No one answered.

"We know what is at risk, Sir," Phydin said, rising and rubbing his hands together. "And we will not let you down."

"I am counting on it," Jovaar answered. Standing and placing his hand on Phydin's shoulder, he reassured him with a slap on the back.

"Wait here until we begin our arrival and then strap yourselves in. I am counting on you to oversee the others. Orvi," he added, glancing to his right. "See to it that the child is secured in Med-bay and that Selena is restrained for attachment. I will be with the pilot in Command if you need me, otherwise I will see you upon arrival."

"Yes, Sir," they answered standing as one as Jovaar left them to prepare for landing. The crew, ignoring Phydin's familiar ramblings about Jax reclaimed their seats on the low bench to review the plan.

***

Jovaar found the annoying pilot where he had left her, seated and making preparations for landing. Hylin worked Phydin's panel with ease at her back.

"Do they not ever sleep?" he thought, choosing to keep the question to himself. Rolling his eyes, he claimed his own station. "How long have I been away, Ma'am?" he asked with obvious sarcasm.

"Nearly four hazon," she answered, without turning. "I found no need to wake you considering I did not pick up any indication of pursuit on our outer path. My system is not as modern as most, but I believe we have traveled unnoticed thus far."

"That is good news," Jovaar said, the woman glaring over her shoulder. "And I thank you," he added, attempting to appease. The arrival on Kindawa and the riddance of this overbearing woman and her lackey could not come quickly enough.

"What sector holds the landing sight?" she asked, scanning the readout of the planet. "You do realize that this planet consists mainly of water."

"Yes, that is the point for us landing here," Jovaar said, adjusting his panel. "It is remote and isolated and was chosen specifically to use that to our advantage."

"If you say so," she said, shrugging and turning back to her screen.

"Sector Two," Jovaar continued, speaking to her back. "There is a landing platform just above the water on a small strip of land and..."

"I need to know who it is you are seeking council," Khyra interrupted. Pretending to ignore his words she secretly scanned her monitor for Sector Two. "There will be questions asked upon our approach."

"I am unable to give you that information for..." he answered, Khyra interrupting yet again.

"There!" she said, abruptly. "There is a small ship approaching from the right."

"We are expected," Jovaar said, curtly. "I am certain it is our welcoming."

"Well, I for one am never certain of anything," she said, altering her panel with her free hand and holding firm to the stick with her other. "Ship G92 on approach to planet Kindawa, Sector Two," she said attempting an air of confidence, speaking into her handheld.

"Ship G92, your cargo?" the deep voice abruptly answered over the com.

"Crew of eleven, no cargo," Khyra answered, peering over her shoulder to Jovaar.

"Your destination?" the booming voice asked, impatience filling his tone from his ever approaching ship.

"He needs an answer, Jovaar," Khyra said, glaring over her shoulder.

"Tell him Mathius Savis is expecting us," he said, leaning forward to get a closer look out the glass.

"Sir Savius is expecting our arrival," she said, repeating Jovaar's instructions and releasing the com to await a response.

"Follow your current path," the voice answered at last. "I will escort you in."

"Responding," Khyra answered, releasing her handheld and pivoting in her seat. "It appears *someone* is welcoming us," she said, looking from Hylin to Jovaar. "Yet, as neither you nor that pilot has given me specifics, I can only hope that you know what you are doing."

144

Tailing the lead ship into final approach, Jovaar watched their guide at last steer left, allowing Khyra to begin their final descent.   Keeping true to her form, the mighty Ma'am confidently stated the necessary procedures, leading them in on her own.

"I never would have known this was here," she said, to no one in particular.

"That is the point," Jovaar answered, the small strip of landing coming into full view.

Khyra glided the G92 with ease, producing a landing with nothing more than a slight jolt as the ship's legs made contact with the ground. "Well done," Jovaar said to her reluctantly.

"Thank you," she replied, prompting the com to inform the others. "Landing is complete.   All are to prepare for debarkment."   Lifting the pilot bar and stalling the controls, she pivoted in her seat to face the men.   "Your crew should be awaiting your orders at the plank," she said, stowing her headgear in the compartment beneath her seat. "I will join you there momentarily."

"Your task here is done," Jovaar said, firmly.   "I thank you for your service, yet I am in no further need of your ship."

"Ah, so I know," she answered, slowly removing her gloves finger by finger.   "But I have been ordered to see you safely to your final destination and I have surmised *all by myself* that this is not it."

"I have a very capable crew," Jovaar continued, his patience waning as he released his restraints.   "Your assistance, although appreciated, is no longer needed."

"Say what you will," Khyra said, rotating to her screen. "I have my orders, Sir Savius and you have yours.   You may either accept me as part of the crew or I will continue to follow you on my own.   You must understand that I never disobey an order, especially one from Sir Gidoran."

Disgusted Jovaar stared at her back, grumbling to himself as he stormed from Command.   Eager to be of use, Hylin kept step at his heels.

"Women!" he groaned once they were alone in the corridor, his hands digging into the sides of his hips. Shaking his head at the grinning boy, Jovaar gestured with a nod for him to follow him to the plank.

Twelve

Throughout all of his travels Jovaar unfortunately had never set foot on Kindawa, yet his Palle had told him endless stories of its glorious sea. Descending now amongst the weight of the wet air to the foot of the plank, he could not help but stare out in amazement, the richness opening before him.

"What blue," he thought, ignoring the advancement of the others as he took in the wonderous view. "Nothing...nothing but glorious blue," he whispered. Yet the sea alone could not claim the beauty from the small landing strip, for the sky proved richer than any he had ever seen, shielding the moment in secret where it joined with its mate of the sea.

The craft's down plank had opened toward the aft of the landing strip, and pausing at its base to look to his feet, Jovaar noted that with just a mere few steps forward he would be engulfed in wet with the coolness of the water. At the moment though, the sea proved calm and inviting with only a slight movement of shallow waves, and looking again to find where the sea wed with the sky, Jovaar at last sensed the moist air upon his skin.

His thoughts were interrupted by the sounds of the others above the low din of the sea, and slowly turning from the endless view of blue, Jovaar followed Selena with the babe at their rear, joining them to walk toward the bow of the ship. Noting the watercraft moored to their right, he dragged his hand against the moisture of G92 as they met the awaiting welcoming at its tip.

"You are delayed," the man said, all standing still, facing him.

"Yes," Jovaar answered, passing the others as they parted like the sea. "We unfortunately required the diversion at Yani. I am afraid it was unavoidable."

"We were beginning to worry," the man continued, folding his arms. "I was about to send out a search team when I got word of your approach. I was most pleased to hear you were safe."

"I am sorry for your worry," Jovaar said, reaching out and clasping the man's offered hand. "Please forgive me, yet as you can see we survived the journey."

"Come," the man answered, motioning to the others, the last member joining them at the rear. "Let us get you inside and settled. Maintenance will refuel the ship so that the crew will be able to detach without delay. We do not get many of the likes of that particular craft way out here, and will want it back on its way as soon as possible to avoid notice."

"I could not agree with you more," Jovaar answered, glaring at Khyra and shaking his head. Lifting his chin, he turned to follow the man's lead.

***

Silence ensued as they paced onward down the path of greens trailing the elder man, but debating what would surely prove to be the inevitable, Jovaar could not help but question speaking of the matter further in the open.

"I have been told that you have camo capabilities," he said, referring to the many conversations he had had with Drider regarding the device. "And that the ship could be hidden until departure."

"Of course Drider is correct," the man answered, unturning and maintaining his pace. "If you will look behind you, I believe you will all be quite pleased."

Jovaar turned at the man's words as did the crew, smiling as all were instantly filled with awe for the ship was nearly indiscernible. Various shades of green foliage had appeared from nowhere, almost completely concealing the ship with various types of native flora.

"Amazing," Hylin whispered, staring at the denseness where the ship had once stood bright against the blue sea. "It is simply amazing."

148

"I thought you would enjoy that," the man said having at last ceased his steps. Chuckling, he motioned for the members to continue. "Now come. We have prepared nourishment and have much to discuss."

Some turned and followed at the elder's order yet most simply stood, unable to take their eyes from the shield of colorful play. "It *is* amazing, Jovi," Selena whispered, cradling the stirring child. "I have never seen anything like it."

"I have," he answered, peering into Selena's deep chestnut eyes. "I am looking at her."

Selena blushed at his kindness. Unable to contain her smile, she lowered her gaze and passed in front of him to follow the others. "Come, Jovaar," she said, pulling her cloak free from the stirring babe. "Nitaya is ravished."

Taking one last deep breath of the moist sea air, Jovaar turned leaving the pair of questions unanswered. Where the location of sky meeting sea joined as one and how his younger could possibly construct such a clever cloaking device, Jovaar could not allow time for understanding. Instead he quickly followed the others up the path.

***

The pass narrowed with each step, the members walking silently at the elder's back. Lined on either side with Kindawan various rock and greens, their guide described the uniqueness of the port to his newest arrivals. Jogging a bit to catch up, Jovaar could not contain his smile as he listened to the words he had often heard in night tales of his youth.

"The ships that you had passed in port, as you crossed the length of your ship, are submersibles," the man said, enjoying the opportunity for newcomers to learn. "These to your left are watercraft, used for patrol and nourishment gathering. You see?" he added, pointing toward the approaching whir. "There is a return patrol coming in now."

The members stood silent to watch the watercraft approach, slowing its way into port. "Anything today?" the man asked, crossing to the edge of the dock.

"Nothing, Sir," the man answered, securing the line. "Quiet as we prefer it be."

"That is good news," the guide continued, assisting the man with the ancient line. "Straighten the ship and report to the Landman as usual."

"Aye, Sir," he answered, keying the odd panel. Their guide simply nodded, motioning for the members to follow.

Hylin noted the trees and greens about them were thickening as the large group traveled further into the landmass. Approaching two guards oddly placed amongst the flora, his eyes only moments before scanning the sleekness of the patrolman's ship, he could not help but chuckle at the stiff and vigilant men before the front of a large hill.

"Sir!" they said as one, clicking their heels together.

"We have guests," the man replied, motioning the group to come close. With all eagerly watching, the two guards turned, marching silently in opposite directions, each stopping at a tree in their path.

"System one, go," the first said, prompting the hidden device.

"System two, go," the second replied, mimicking the first's motion. Surprisingly, the hill slowly opened before them.

"Please follow me," the guide said, grandly gesturing amongst the group's quizzical whispers. Following and stepping within the darkness of the pass, all were once again hushed as the elder continued his tale of their new surroundings.

"You have now entered a place very few have set foot," he said, his voice filled with pride, its tone echoing in the narrow pass. "As I have just allowed you to witness…for my trust in you all is great, our entrance to the compound is made difficult by the systems we have set in place. It takes two, as you have just seen, to open the well hidden door. The trees our guards marched in opposite directions to reach are actually artificial, although I must admit that even for an old man like me it is difficult to tell."

"If one was to gain access to our small strip of land, they would not only have to locate this site, but also the location of the trees and their well-hidden devices," the man added, nodding to Selena and the cooing babe. "One will not operate without the other, and therefore adds to the difficulty."

The guide spoke as he walked, his back to the crew, pacing the short barren passage until they reached yet another large obstacle. All stopped at the appearance of the round metal orb emerged from the wall. Separating into two, it extended on individual slender necks of metal.

"Please place your eye on the reader," the voice said, awaiting acknowledgement in the silent corridor. The man, obviously expecting this order, leaned forward toward the small scanner without question.

"Cleared, you may proceed," the voice said, the scan proving curtly complete. Authorized for clearance, the guide motioned the members forward, disregarding the now retreating device.

"Please," he said, the group walking as one through the newly opened door, the man prompting the next device solely with his words. "Lesslevel Two," the elder said. His smile proved he was pleased.

    ***

The large door closed at their backs with Fidaldi entering at the last. With the compartment's smooth and apparent slow descent, the guide again smiled, folding his hands before him to explain his odd phrasing.

"Lesslevel is a safeguard," the man said, looking to each new face of the crew. "Yet another difficutly for our unfriendly outsiders. In all other places that I have been fortunate to have traveled throughout the systems, I have encountered the standard programming for 'sublevels.' This system does not recognize the familiar term however, leaving the intruders here, locked and contained until they can be properly dealt with."

"Ah, we have arrived," he added, the compartment ceasing with his lesslevel tale. "The crew that will be leaving shortly should step out. Nina, there you are," he added, the slender woman approaching, her hands held open in welcome before her waist. "Please see to our guests and inform me alone if there is anything they require that you cannot provide."

151

The woman nodded at her elder's order and stood patiently waiting, her eyes soon puzzled as no one stepped forward. "Ma'am," Jovaar said, peering over his shoulder to Khyra. "I believe this is your stop."

"I do not think so," she answered, glancing at Hylin. "As I said earlier, I am to continue on with you and the rest of the crew."

"That is not part of the plan," Jovaar answered impatiently, gritting his teeth and urging their guide for assistance.

"It is a part of Sir Gidoran's plan, Jovaar," Khyra added, firmly crossing her arms. "As I informed you earlier, I always follow orders."

The others stood uncomfortably silent, looking to the woman titled Nina standing confused opposite the door. All eyes awaited Jovaar's ultimate decision. At last grunting both displeasure and frustration, he nodded his concession. Jovaar's crew could not contain their whispered laughter at his expense.

"Forgive me for the inconvenience, Nina," the elder man said, the woman turning to leave alone. "Lesslevel five," he ordered, the large door once again closing. "It appears you have difficulties amongst the ranks," he chided, grinning at the scowling man, the others lowering their heads in an attempt to hide their persistent grins. "I must admit that regardless of our most difficult task it is quite amusing."

***

The compartment soon ceased a second time, and anticipating the opening of its massive door, Selena took a stepped forward with the child. "Not yet," the guide said, stifling a slight grin before gently claiming her arm. "I am afraid there is just a bit more."

Selena looked to Jovaar with the sensation of the compartment shift and placing an arm around her shoulder to comfort her fear, all felt the now lateral slide. Although this section of the trip below proved much smoother and longer than the first, Selena looked again to Jovaar for assurance.

Simply nodding, he glanced at their guide, the compartment continuing with ease along its path. With the machine slowing to its stop, the inner and newly outer doors opening before them, the man stretched his arms grandly, his voice filled with obvious pride. "My friends," he said warmly, slowly lowering his head. "Welcome to Kindawa's Neptune."

Selena took a few steps forward then abruptly stopped to stare in awe at her surroundings. "Your open mouth is the most common of facial expressions upon newcomers," the man said, smiling at the inquisitive group. "I take it you approve?" Unanswering, Selena simply stood, enjoying the magical view with the others, glancing in wonder about the large open room.

Grand and completely surrounded by large panes of glass so that one could look directly into the heart of the sea while hundreds of sealife swam by, only Selena could find words to describe their their newest setting. "There are so many colors around us...above us," she said, looking up into the dome of the room.

"Yes," the man said, looking out to admire the familiar beauty. "We made our deep descent and then we were carried laterally through the travel shoot and at last to our world."

"But surely the defenses..." Hylin interrupted, shoving Phydin aside and stepping forward.

"Yes, my young man, it is a fine point you raise," the guide interrupted, claiming the boy's arm. "That is why we have erected the blast shield. When any ship enters our seaspace, the shield closes us in creating an impenetrable tomb. It is quite confining when you are used to the open air traveling above, but please come, my friends," he added, motioning the new arrivals forward. "We will head to dining so that you may nourish and then I will personally see you to your quarters."

Eyes wide, the group traversed the busy Command floor, Hylin snickering at Jax nearly ramming the central post with his distracted walk, his eyes focused on the array of life beyond the glass. "Watch it," he said, slowing to ruffle Hylin's hair. "I am older and wiser than you." Hylin merely laughed at his teasing words. "Well...maybe older."

The members laughed at the jesting of the pair as they too awed at the wonders beyond the glasss, and leaving the main cabin to continue down the next passage, they descended a series of steps to the next room. Again caught by surprise, the world beyond them reappeared with its endless wonders.

Turning to admire the actual setting of the room, Hylin stared at the head table furthest from where they stood, where three additional settings had been added to its perpendicular. "This place would feed an army," he said in amazement, crossing to the slender rail.

"You have said my thoughts," the guide answered, gesturing them round and forward. "This room will soon fill with other members of the Resistance and you will dine amongst the bravest of men. And since the trust has been set in place and it is to be you who will be joining us, I believe I must now introduce myself to our new friends, Jovi." Nodding to the elder man, Jovaar merely smiled.

"I am Mathius Savius, and it is my great honor to welcome you to our cause," he said, motioning for the members to claim their places. The crew however stood stunned at Selena alone crossing to claim Jovaar's arm.

"Is it truly him?" she asked, the child again stirring in her arms. Mathius gave a simple laugh and merely smiled at his son opposite the cabin.

"Not what you expected, I am certain," he said, his smile broad across his aged face. "Yet I believe my grandchild knows it to be true." Selena looked down at the babe and again to Jovaar.

"My Palle," he said nodding, a slight grin creeping across his face. "It is so good to see you again, Sir," he added, turning back to his elder.

"It has been far too long, Jovi," he answered, ignoring the offered hand to whole-heartedly embrace his kin. With the crew snickering at the warm encounter, Jovaar gave them a calling stare over his Palle's shoulder.

"Please join us," Mathius continued, releasing Jovaar and gesturing to the large tables. "I have reserved a place at my table for you and your elder, Jovaar. I am not alarmed, yet I am assuming Martus will be along shortly."

Uncomfortable with the uncertainty of Martus' wherabouts, the crew began whispering amongst themselves yet

Selena stood firm at Jovaar's side. With Nitaya's fingers breaking free of her blanket, seeming to dance in the heavy air, Jovaar gathered his strength, his smile fading as he turned to face his elder.

"I am sorry, Palle," he began, reaching out to claim Nitaya's small hand. "I cannot be certain of Martus's survival." Mathius, abruptly looking from the babe and into Jovaar's eyes, avoided the expected unpleasantries.

"Not here," he said, his gaze returning to the child. "We will of course continue this in private." Restraining himself against news he did not wish to hear, Mathius composed his fears and turned back to the nervous crew.

"Please enjoy our offering," he said, leading the members to their given seats. Although eager to learn of his eldest, Mathius stood strong as his station, instead enjoying the moment of the possible and those that had brought her safely to him.

***

A male steward soon arrived extending his arms for the now obvious hungry child. Looking to the elder Savius for assurances, Selena relinquished Nitaya with his confident nod before claiming her seat with the crew. Her eyes however, never left Jovaar as he walked slowly at his Palle's side, the pair making their way at last to the head table. Sadly, Selena spied the look of fear in Mathius' eyes as Jovaar plainly told him of their journeys. Feeling sorry for them both, she attempted to rise from her seat.

"No," Phydin said, laying his hand upon hers. "Let them be. They obviously need this time alone."

Reluctantly agreeing to Phydin's words and lowering once again to her seat, Selena tipped her head, staring at her empty hands, not raising her glance until Phydin patted her knee. Unable to form words, she watched the members of the Kindawan Resistance begin their entrance into the room.

Entering in stages, some in small groups and others alone, the members of the Resistance sat in their various assigned places amongst the long, narrow tables. All adorning long robes in various hues of green over what Selena knew to be gear of combat, many glanced at the newcomers without addressing them directly. With respect however, each paused for a moment, tipping their heads at Mathius before claiming their seats.

Soon the room was filled, the silence eerie despite their large numbers. With the last claiming of the swarm claiming his station, Mathius at last stood, mug raised in hand.

"A toast to new beginnings," he said, all others simultaneously standing, raising their mugs in unison. "It is this day that my son Jovaar has returned to me, traveling through great hardship and carrying the child of his brother, a possible future to our cause. Be sorrowful, yet be joyous for the next generation lies before us."

Cheers rang throughout the room as members clanged mugs before sitting to nourish. Mathius claimed his seat at the last, the food and drink offered proving plentiful.

As expected, oblivious conversation broke out amongst the tables and as Phydin joined in a casual discussion with his fellow comrades at Selena's side, she kept her thoughts to herself. Enjoying the lull in excitement, the remaining members delved into the aromas aplenty before them.

Her body told her she was ravished, yet Selena held no appetite and ate sparingly with worry for Jovaar and the child. Ever so often, someone would make a small comment to her...Khyra urging her to take drink, Jax mumbling his pleasure of the offered nourishment, yet although she gestured accordingly, Selena otherwise sat quiet amongst the boisterous crew.

"So much is at stake," she thought, looking down at her awaiting greens. "So much is still to be done."

Glancing again to where Jovaar sat next to his Palle, he at last sensed her stare and smiled. He appeared so very confident amongst the eager members at the head table. Oh how Selena wished she felt the same.

***

The meal although enjoyed by all, appeared over just as quickly as it had begun, the members rising and patting each other's shoulders as they made their way from the large room.

Jovaar stood at its front, shaking the hands of those at his table before walking its length and crossing over to where his crew remained seated, anxiously waiting.

"I have been informed that quarters are through that door at the rear," he said, pointing at the back exit, several turning to follow his nod. "Finish up here and then I am ordering you to get some rest. Take the boy and see that he is accounted for. Tomorrow will be a very busy day."

Turning to face Selena rising from her seat, Jovaar could not hide his pride. "Are you nearly finished?" he asked, claiming her hands.

"Yes," she answered, covering her long forgotten nourishment with her cloth, accepting his gesture. Attempting civility the others respectfully turned away from their whispers.

"Then come," Jovaar continued, not noticing her plate and ignoring the prying eyes of the crew. "We will look in on Nitaya together and then I will see you to your quarters."

Taking hold of Jovaar's arm to climb out and over the bench, Selena fell into step at his escort from the room. Pausing as they reached the rear door, Mathius joined the pair, raising his hand to keep them from their exit.

"Jovi," he said familiarly, grasping his younger's arm. "I beg you to introduce me to the woman that you say has taken such great care of my grandchild."

"Of course, Palle, please forgive me. This is Selena," he answered, nodding and turning to face her. Mathius, claiming her hands with kindness in his eyes, warmly smiled.

"It is an honor to know you, my child," he began, tears welling in his eyes as he stroked the back of her hands with his thumbs. "And I thank you for all that you have done. Sir Gowdar is undoubtedly proud."

"No thanks are needed," Selena answered, stiffening yet accepting his obvious kind gesture. "It has been my honor to see to both Nitaya and the cause of the Resistance."

"Well, I thank you regardless," Mathius continued, turning to place his hand on Jovaar's shoulder. "Go, my son. With all that must occur from now until Nitaya at last reaches her fated destination, you must get some rest. I promise I will look in on you soon."

Jovaar nodded to Mathius then led Selena through the door, continuing down the glass tube-like corridor behind the crew. "Do you not find it amazing?" he asked, not looking for an answer as he stared at a large orange lifeform beyond the glass.

"It is, Jovi," she answered, shrugging at the whimsical being, its friends joining in the play as Jovaar tapped lightly on the glass. "Yet I cannot see us concentrating on these little orange fellows when so much remains at stake."

"Do you think I do not know what we face?" he asked, his hand quick from the glass to tilt her chin to his eyes. "I swear on my life that we will reach the final destination and prevail over Sugin's wrath. For the sake of our future, for the sake of all of our futures, we must."

Jovaar's words did little to settle her nerves yet Selena smiled reassuringly just the same. "I know, Jovi," she said, attempting a brave face. "I believe I am just tired."

"Then come, Selena" he said, claiming her hand. "We will look in on Nitaya together and then we will both get some rest. I assure you, it is not only you that needs it."

***

Reaching the door to quarters, Jovaar released Selena's hand to prompt the opening device. Upon entering the room, he found Nitaya sleeping peacefully, the male steward seated at her side.

"All is well, ma'am," he said simply, Selena crossing to the babe's side. With a slight wave, Jovaar excused himself to freshen.

"My name is Selena," she continued, smiling with the swish of the door at her back. "Please refer to me as so." Nodding and crossing to the door, the steward turned as he reached it, remembering the child's blanket he still held in his hands.

"She is well nourished and should rest for some time, Selena," he said, handing her the small cover. "Yet if you need me for anything further, do not hesitate to prompt the com."

"Of course, and I thank you," she answered, absentmindedly wrapping the blanket about her hands. Turning as the steward left the room, she laid its familiar folds gently over the child.

The cabin proved peacefully quiet and as in most other rooms of the undersea world, its exterior walls were made of glass. Regardless of the wonders that played beyond them however, Jovaar reentered the room to find Selena ignoring the outside view, instead singing softly over the sleeping babe.

"There is so much at stake," she said, ceasing her lilt with his approaching steps.

"Yes, but do not fear," he answered, running his fingers through her hair and tucking the loose familiar tendrils behind her ear. "Just stop for one moment and enjoy the life about you, Lena. You waste this day worrying about the next when you should be enjoying exactly what we have, for we can never be certain what that next day will bring."

"I try so desperately not to," she answered, taking a deep breath and turning to face him. "No, I promise to try harder."

"That is good to hear," he answered, leaning to kiss her brow. "I am off to check in on the others and to get some much needed rest myself. You will be all right here alone?"

"With Nitaya I am never alone," she answered, coyly tilting her head. "But yes, *we* will be fine."

"Til the next day then," he said, lowering to kiss her lips. "Until then, enjoy your time with Nitaya but for me please take a moment or two to enjoy the world about you."

"I promise I will," she answered, laying her hand on Nitaya's arm. Turning to leave the pair, Jovaar heard the soft words of song at his back and smiled, knowing the creatures beyond the glass would never, no matter how much he urged, grasp Selena's gaze.

***

Jovaar soon heard the voices of his men. Easily following the sounds of cheers, he reached their quarters to find them as he had left them on R8 with the view screen blaring for their attention, yet all were now seated on two bunks surrounding a low table. Walking toward them unnoticed to see what the commotion was about, he immediately spied the Rodaous Game

159

in play. Smiling and crossing his arms, leaning against the side glass, Jovaar stood back to enjoy the battle.

"You cheat!" Jax shouted, flailing his arms wildly about. "You all cheat!"

"Ha!" Phydin roared, shoving Jax backward into the cot. "You say that every time you lose!"

"Jovaar," Hylin added, having noticed his entrance from his seat at Fidaldi's back. "These so called men know nothing of the game."

"They are but simple men, Hylin," he answered, nodding in agreement. "Surely you can show them how to win properly."

"That I can," he answered, proudly crossing to his elder's side and mimicking his stance. "Only they will not let me play."

"A boy he is," Jax continued, overhearing their conversation, leaning in to rejoin the game. "Although maybe *he* does not cheat so maybe we *should* let him play." Grumbles filled the cabin as Fidaldi threw the game Intels in Jax's direction.

"It seems the game is over," Jovaar said, laughing and kneeling to pick up an Intel off the floor. "How about a good game of rest?" he asked, his tone half ordering.

"Sir," Orvi and Kroy said as one. "I was losing anyway," Kroy added, throwing his Intels on the table and climbing off the central cot before crossing to his own.

"I will return as the day begins," Jovaar added, ruffling Hylin's hair and crossing to the door. "See that you all are prepared. I assume we are in for more of the same." The grumbles of the crew continued, yet calmed as news of the impending journey refilled their thoughts.

"Rest well," Jovaar said prompting the door. Stepping into the corridor in search of his own quarters, Jovaar paused as Phydin picked up another scattered Intel off the floor and trailed after him.

"If you have a moment, Sir?" he asked, joining his superior within the glass tube.

"What is it?" Jovaar asked, Phydin gesturing for him to walk closer for privacy.

"I worry about the woman," he whispered, motioning toward Khyra through the open door, sitting alone in the corner of the cabin.

"Sir Gidoran said we could trust her," Jovaar answered, folding his arms across his chest. "The G92 departed Kindawa some time ago and therefore we have no choice than to allow her and the boy to become one of us. I am afraid we must make do, my friend."

Phydin huffed yet said nothing, instead turning and pacing back to the quieting cabin. With the closing of the door at his back, Jovaar sighed, shaking his head in the empty corridor.

"That one is troubled," he thought, walking the few steps to his quarters. Prompting the door and spying the lone cot in the corner however, Phydin's dilemna quickly left him. Pacing to its welcoming side Jovaar lay down, all thoughts of his crew escaping him. At last he allowed himself that much needed rest.

***

Jovaar awoke some time later, the darkness only broken by the exterior lights cascading from the sation's outer world. The chime of the com had startled him from slumber. "Why does this always happen to me?" he grumbled in disgust, rising and rubbing his tired eyes.

"Yes? What is wrong now?"

"Jovi," Mathius said, his tone filled with concern. "It is unlike you to rest over. Your crew awaits you at Command."

"What do you mean rest over? What time is it?" he asked, sitting up straight beneath the folds, his Palle's words causing worry.

"Past the time of rest," he answered, oddly chuckling. "Get yourself and your gear together and meet us here. Mathius out."

Jovaar sat with his face in his hands yet looked up to spy yet another large orange creature staring at him just beyond the glass. "And what do you want?" he asked, the creature jostling his direction and swimming on.

Grimacing at rising to change and gather his gear, Jovaar chided himself for delaying his crew. When at last all was in

161

order, he turned to spy the orange creature returning with several copies of himself. Without time to toy with the little fellow or his friends, he quickly set out from his cabin in search of his own.

***

All were assembled as Mathius had said. Storming into Command, Jovaar lowered his hefty gear to the floor and crossed to his awaiting crew. "Is the ship ready?" he asked, Mathius rising from the helm to join him.

"Just," he answered, nodding. "It is fueled and fully armed. Data readouts of your course are current and your communications have been expanded. You will be able to reach us at any given moment, yet as you are well aware, you must use it only if necessary."

"Yes, I know. Thank you, Palle," Jovaar answered, turning to the others. "Phydin, take the crew aboard and get everyone into position. I will…"

"The Landman is waiting your arrival on dock," Mathius interrupted his son, turning to Phydin. "He will guide you through the required procedures."

"Sir," Phydin answered, nodding at both Mathius and Jovaar before turning to face the others. "Let us go," he added, his tone once again serious to the task. The crew abruptly rose to follow, eager as always to move on. Jovaar however, could not contain his grin at Hylin following the boisterous men with Khyra, ever the reluctant as always, in tow.

Thirteen

Phydin led the members as instructed yet no one spoke except Hylin who stepped eagerly alongside Khyra at the back. "I have never been in a submersible ship," he said, wishing the men would hurry. "This is going to be exciting."

"Exciting is not the word I would choose," she answered, adjusting the pack over her shoulder. "Keep your eyes open and your mouth closed, little man. I have been on several of these and I will be the first to admit that they are not easy to maneuver. Everyone has a role, Hylin and everyone will need to concentrate on that role."

"I bet I could do it all by myself," he said, rubbing his hands together.

"I would take that bet if so much was not at stake," she answered, attempting to settle him by placing her hand on his arm. "Yet for now, Hylin, for the welfare of the child you must do as I say."

"Let us go," Phydin ordered, the crew reaching the large door leading up to the patch of ground. Gesturing all within, he gave the command for the main level. Aware now of the comparment's route, each member stood silent as the unit slid lateral. Stopping briefly as the systems reengaged, they soon shifted as one to begin their assent. Impatient, Phydin nodded to the others with the unit at last slowing to a stop.

Prompting the door, Phydin led the members passed the familiar guards, retracing their steps down the narrow path to the docks. Overhearing the mumblings of the crew, he looked up at their words to see the area proving once again free of foliage.

"Stay focused and keep it coming," he ordered, motioning for the crew to follow. Turning right, he led them down the familiar narrow path to the side of the strip where the submersibles and the Landman awaited. Taking notice of the man just ahead at the third dock, Phydin nodded, waving them forward.

"I have been instructed to see you aboard and to answer any questions you may have," the man began, gathering all around. His aged hands waving high overhead. "It is my understanding that you have never operated such a vehicle."

"That is correct," Phydin interrupted, peering at the others over his shoulder. "Although I am certain it will not be a concern."

"As you say," the man continued, grinning at the newcomer's unfounded confidence. "Please follow me." Khyra remained silent with her knowledge of the craft, yet as Hylin attempted to speak in her defense, she grabbed his arm, halting his words.

"Let him have his moment," she said, glaring at Phydin's back. "I believe I will quite enjoy watching him bring about his own demise." Grinning secretly at Khyra's deviousness and gesturing to seal his mouth shut with his fingers, Hylin turned back to the others as the Landman gestured them aboard.

"As I said before," he whispered, leaning close to Khyra, Fidaldi stepping aboard before them. "This is going to be exciting."

***

The interior of the ship proved much smaller than Phydin had anticipated. Although there was enough room within for the crew and their gear, it was obvious that all nonessentials would have to be left behind.

"This is clearly a transport ship and not one for comfort," Jax said, grumbling as he searched for the gunner seat. The remainder of the crew said nothing however, choosing to ignore Jax's usual banterings as Phydin adjusted their loads.

Discarding all non-crucial supplies, Phydin cleared their packs and gestured them toward their given stations. As each settled in to their new surroundings, Khyra and Hylin took their seats at the rear to eagerly listen to the Landman's explanation of the elements the craft had to offer to their overconfident superior.

"As you can see," the man began, speaking loudly for all to hear. "The ship is small but what you do not see is that it is well powered. All of the main operations are performed from this cabin, yet there is a smaller one just to your rear for gun power that doubles as storage." Turning at the words of 'gun power,' Jax spied the rear door and elbowed Kroy, who traipsed after him eagerly.

"I will continue on and then will see that they are settled before I debark," the man said to Phydin, nodding at the pair venturing to the rear.

"Please," Phydin said, shaking his head. "You were saying..."

"Yes," the man continued, clearing his throat. "All navigations are manned there," he said, pointing to the station on his right. "Those systems are common knowledge and your SO should have little difficulty, as should your DC whose station is directly at his back. The stick controls are a little tricky though and if you do not mind, I have been ordered to review them."

Phydin grew weary of the man's rambling, his confidence set, yet he humbled the man as he gave an overview of the system. Khyra sat back, crossing her arms and knowing all too well the capabilities of their new ship.

"I am certain I can be of some assistance," she said at last, smiling from the rear of the cabin, Hylin elbowing her arm.

"I will let you know if it comes to that," Phydin answered, then turning, obliged the man with his attention. When finished, the Landman turned to face Phydin then glanced at the remaining crew.

"I think that covers everthing," he said, patting Phydin on the shoulder. "Are there any questions?" When no one spoke, Phydin thanked him for his trouble and escorted him from the main cabin, shaking his hand as Jovaar and Selena made their way onto the ship.

"Sir," the Landman said, Phydin returning to the helm at his back. "I believe all is in order. I have instructed your pilot on the essentials as well as provided a basic overview of the ship's layout per Sir Mathius' order. Is there any way I could be of further service?"

"Yes," Jovaar answered, glancing to the child in Selena's arms. "I need the most secure of places for the babe. I am assuming my Palle has secured me a ship that is equipped for her needs."

"But of course," the Landman answered, pacing the narrow midship corridor. "I have been instructed to accommodate your requirements and although the rear of the ship is mainly for gunners and storage there has since been prepared a small compartment made suitable for the child. If you will follow me," he added, crossing to the rear door. "You will find it this way."

Carrying the sleeping child, Selena followed Jovaar through the narrow pass, finding Jax and Kroy cramped within the shell of gunnery. "Is everything in order," Jovaar asked, Jax lancing up the side of the arc, familiarizing himself with the systems.

"Sir," Kroy answered, pivoting in his seat. "The system is comparable with most. We are performing a final sweep now to avoid any difficulties."

"Very well," Jovaar answered. "Carry on."

Walking through another small corridor, the trio at last reached the rear chamber, its opening nothing more than a large oval hole in the rear wall.

"I was told this would satisfy your needs," the Landman said, gesturing about the small cabin.

"Yes," Jovaar said, moving to the side to allow Selena room to enter. "It will have to do. Selena, do what you will. I apologize for my haste, but I must see to the crew. We are already behind schedule."

"Of course," she answered, stepping within and placing the child into the small prepared bunk. "I will make certain she is secure then will ready myself for the journey."

"Very well," he answered, again leaving her to her own devises. Stepping from within the narrow pass, he turned and ducked his head through its opening a final time. "I will look in on you as soon as I can."

***

"All is in order and I thank you for your assistance," Jovaar said, nodding. Standing atop the lowered plank, he shook the Landman's hand and looked out to the awakening sea below. "We will make way as soon as the ship is secured."

Smiling and returning to the strip, the Landman turned as Jovaar secured the plank. "Sir Mathius is a strong leader," he said proudly, turning to meet Jovaar's eyes. "And I am confident that the son of such a man will lead the Resistance to victory. May the strength of the many be upon you."

"I thank you, my friend," Jovaar said, the side hatch beginning to close without his prompt. "But if all goes as planned, it should only take but a few."

Fourteen

"Systems go?" Jovaar asked into his portalcom.

"Systems go," Phydin answered from the helm. "We are prepared for detachment upon your arrival and will reach depth fifty in five."

"I am on my way to Command now," Jovaar added, the rear hatch at last secured. "See to it that everyone is in place."

"Sir," Phydin answered, sealing his line. Releasing his com, Jovaar paced to the rear of midship to look in on his gunners.

"So what do you make of our defense capabilities?" he asked, the door swiftly closing at his back.

"As Kroy said earlier," Jax answered, looking up from his station. "This system is fairly comparable to our last ship. It is quite small in here but we will of course make do. I have looked over the equipment and am making our last system checks now," he added, placing his headset within his ears.

"The Landman told me there is a quick overview program in the system's database," Jovaar said, leaning upward to scan the circular track. "You may want to take a look."

"I don't need an overview," Jax scowled, Kroy rolling his eyes at his friend's back.

"We will check it out just the same," Kroy said, punching Jax in the arm. "You can count on us."

"Very well," Jovaar said, crossing the small cabin. 'I am heading to Command. If you have any difficulties, do not hesitate to let me know."

"Sir," they chimed as one, grunting their pleasure at the combined response. Clasping their restraints for the impending detachment, they bantered with one another as to who required the overview program more. Leaving them to their seemingly endless fued, Jovaar crossed the empty midship to return to

Command.

Entering the helm, he found Phydin obviously annoyed, heatedly arguing with Khyra.

"I know what I am doing!" he roared over his shoulder, Khyra fuming in her rear seat at Hylin's side. The boy's own temper was obviously moments from eruption.

"No, you do not," she answered, flailing her arms. "You have been sitting there going over systems checks and you do not even know what you are looking at! There," she added pointing toward a blinking yellow light to his left. "What does that do?"

"I do not need to know every minute detail and I do not need some woman telling me how to run my ship!" he screamed, raising the overhead controls and pivoting in his seat.

"Well for your information, it..." she shouted, stopping as she took notice of Jovaar. "Sir, it is quite clear that your pilot is not capable of operating this ship. I however, have piloted very similar ones and feel it would be best if I manned the controls."

Straddling the jam of the door, Jovaar stared at the fuming pair knowing what he must do. Knowing what he should do however, did not mean he looked forward to the conversation he must have.

"Phydin, will you step over here a moment?" he asked, gesturing toward the corridor. Phydin, reluctantly unbuckling his restraining belt, bumped his head on the overhead controls and grumbled. Crossing over the small cabin, he purposefully turned away from Khyra.

"I can do this," he whispered, frustratedly rubbing his minor wound.

"How familiar are you with this type of craft, Phydin?" Jovaar asked, folding his arms commandingly across his chest. "And do not give me some gibberish that they are all the same. I need a confident man at the helm."

"I am more capable than she is," he answered, gesturing in Khyra's direction. "I have never piloted a submersible before but I am quite confident that I will be able to do so now."

"I am sorry, my friend," Jovaar said, placing his hand on Phydin's shoulder. "I need the best..." he paused, holding up his hand with Phydin's protest. "I need the best," he continued, waiting for his subordinate to return his gaze. "And although I am certain you could handle this if necessary, you must understand that if we run into any combat I need to have a man who is confident at the helm."

"But she is a woman," he groaned, gritting his teeth and glaring toward the helm. "There is no way she could do better than I."

"Let me rephrase, I need the best *person* at the helm and be that as it may…and regardless of your arguments, Khyra should pilot," Jovaar said firmly. "You will be right at her side and I am counting on you to be ready if called upon." Phydin said nothing for he knew that the decision was made.

"Khyra," Jovaar ordered, stepping into Command and turning to face her. "Take the helm and ready the ship for detachment."

Standing and pacing the cramped cabin, Khyra smugly strapped herself in before the stick, lowering the overhead controls at the last. Turning to reassure Phydin, Jovaar knew he could not placid him or his huffing gestures and instead allowed him a moment to find his station at the rear at Fidaldi's back. Having maintained his silent disapproval, Jovaar left the decision to lie on its own.

"This is the last thing we need right now," Jovaar thought, shaking his head. Noting Hylin's grin, he grimaced at the boy's obvious pleasure. Knowing there was nothing he could offer to resttle the mood of his crew, he crossed the cabin and claimed the helm to ready for detachment.

***

"All systems report,' Jovaar ordered. Clasps secured, he pivoted to his screen.

"SO go, DC go, Nav go, Helm go," Jovaar said, following the last of the sequence.

"Weapons cramped but go," Jax added over the com.

"Tone it down, Jax," Jovaar ordered his gunner, Selena entering Command at his back. "How is the child?" he asked, glancing over his shoulder to see her claim the now vacant seat at Hylin's side.

"Resting peacefully, Sir," she answered sarcastically, clasping the last of her restraints. "I would have rather sat with her at departure," she added, sighing.

"I am sorry, but not without proper restraints," Jovaar answered, not turning from the controls. "You may return to her once we have safely reached fifty depth."

Shaking her head and glaring at the back of Jovaar's, Selena gave Hylin's leg a small squeeze. "You all set?" she asked, attempting excitement.

"You bet," he answered, rubbing his hands together. "This is the coolest thing ever. I have never taken a ride in one of these before. Have you?" he asked, anxiously.

"Not that I can recall," Selena answered, settling her head on its rest. "And I am hoping this will be my last."

"All systems go," Jovaar said, tapping for the ship's layout on his screen. "Khyra, order ready for detachment."

"Detaching in 5, 4, 3, 2, 1, detach," she ordered. Comfortably adjusting the stick, the woman prompted the release of the main clamp, disconnected the cables and pulled their craft from the dock with skilled ease. "Ready to submerge," she continued, pivoting within the overhead controls and steering the ship away from the small strip. "Nav, patch the readout to my screen."

"She certainly seems to know her way around the stick," Jovaar thought with a slight shrug. Preparing for the impending plunge, the ship jostled about the awakening sea. "I must remember to thank G."

***

"Preparing for compression," Khyra ordered, keying in the proper coded sequence. "You will hear a slight hum in your ears, followed by a pop, yet I assure you it is normal." Prompting the last of the controls, the system's female monotone voice sounded throughout the ship.

"Plunging in 10, 9, 8..." she began, slowly counting down as Khyra tapped her map screen for the below readout.

"Another blasted woman,'" Phydin whispered, rolling his eyes. Hearing his remark, Jovaar turned with a quick look of annoyance, stifling his verbal anger.

"4, 3, 2, 1, plunge is confirmed."

Jovaar and the others stared in awe out the glass, Khyra guiding the ship bow tipped with ease as the members began their descent into the deep. Watching in amazement with the water reaching the top of their view, they were at once immersed in the dark water. Each proved affected by the hum almost instantly.

Several moments passed in the darkened world about them and Jovaar watched as one by one, each member felt the pop that Khyra had warned them of. As all showed minimal signs of discomfort, he too dealt with the minor annoyance. Khyra spied Phydin with his fingers in his ears, struggling at the rear and shook her head.

"Just relax, Phydin," she shouted over her shoulder, rolling her eyes. "The pop will come soon."

"What?" he asked, patting the sides of his head. "I cannot hear you!" Having recognized the muffled words from her mouth, Phydin reluctantly followed her lead, and all watched as the change affected him, the slight pain at last subsiding.

"I said to stop struggling," Khyra continued huffing, folding her arms frustratingly across her chest. "Next time, do as I say and just relax." A mere bystander of the battle between the pair, Jovaar sat back, unable to contain his chuckle.

"Once we reach fifty depth, we will be able to maneuver and will be at last on our way," Khyra said, adjusting the overhead controls. "In the mean time, if you will look to your right you will be able to get a much different view of the Lesslevels."

Eagerly turning as one, each of the members glimpsed the magnificent station as it came fully into view with their smooth sail. "It seems so much larger that I had thought," Selena said, craning her neck to see out the glass. "It felt much smaller when we were inside."

"I agree," Jovaar said, smiling at the surprise in her eyes. "Look there," he continued, pointing out the small frame. "There is the shoot that took us to the main cabin. It is longer than it felt during the ride down, do you not agree?"

"And there," Selena added enjoying the view, pointing out the glass to the brightly lit facility. "There is the main cabin. I can even make out the crew."

The ship continued its calm descent at Khyra's hand, and she slowly pivoted the craft so that the enormous station and its dancing glow could be seen by all. Its elaborate maze of shoots connecting to the larger cabins was indeed an underworld city and each sat in awe of its wonders. Looking back to the main cabin, Jovaar spied what appeared to be his palle waving to them. Reaching up with his hand to wave in return, his smile faded as the station's lights began blinking. Mathius's voice rang urgently over the com.

"We have a ship entering airspace in quadrant three," Mathius said, the metal shield beginning to close about the massive base. In mere moments the entire station became black as the darkest of nights.

"Leave now, my son," Mathius ordered, unwavering behind the shield. "We are not expecting visitors and I fear the worst."

"We can stay and help fight," Jovaar shouted, not wanting to leave his palle to his own defenses.

"No," Mathius answered, abruptly. "You must take Nitaya and go now!"

Looking to Khyra already making the final preparations, Jovaar tightened his restraints and glanced at Selena, the system's voice resounding throughout the cabin with Khyra's prompting. "Fifty depth in 5, 4, 3, 2, 1, fifty depth."

"Punch it," Jovaar ordered reluctantly, staring out the glass. Nodding, Khyra pulled the release lever without question and sped them swiftly away from Mathius and further into the Kindawan deep.

***

"We have found the small island, Sir," the pilot said, honing his screen to better survey the strip of land. "Shall I begin our approach?"

173

"Aye," the Commander answered, pacing to the man's station. "You will land at the rear, here," he added, pointing.

"But, Sir," the pilot interjected, peering at his commander over his shoulder. "It is completely covered with foliage. There is no possible way to..."

"The coverage is false," Carsian interrupted, gritting his teeth. His subordinate turned back to his panel, staring in awe at the massive display of greens. "I am certain of it," he barked. "Make your preparations for descent."

"Aye, Sir," the pilot answered, doubt remaining. However, he prompted the controls to ready for landing.

"There," the Commander continued, pointing to the main screen. "It seems our approach has not gone unnoticed. There are several ships entering airspace and others are dispersing below. Send out the fighters."

"Are you certain this is even the right location, Sir?" the pilot asked, hesitantly eyeing the Nav officer to his right. "This could be a mere colony or..."

"This is *no* colony and do not question my authority again!" the Commander roared at his back. "Send out the fighters and continue our descent. Order all ships to destroy at will!"

"Aye, Sir," the pilot answered, prompting the control for the station's warning system. Blinking red lights and wailing sirens at once filled the ship as battle pilots scurried to their fighters.

"And the ships below, Sir?" the pilot asked, tentatively.

"No," the Commander answered, a smile crossing his face. Crossing his arms before his chest he returning to the glass. "Concentrate all power to the ships in the air. We will deal with the others once we have landed."

"Aye, Sir," the pilot answered, turning back to his station to prompt the com. "All BP's are to fire at will!"

***

Carsian's pilots climbed aboard their ships, the crew members frantically scurring to release their cables before the rising of the side hatch, and one by one the sleek crafts raced from within. Solo-manned, the small fighter S12's proved the Commander's choice, their sleek bodies and small wing spans making them difficult targets. As expected, it took less than one half hazon to destroy the small Kindawan enemy.

Keeping a watchful eye over the melee in the blue sky, the Commander stood pleased with the quick results, hands clasped at his back. "Continue our descent," he ordered, not turning from the glass. "The remaining few are no threat to us now."

"Aye, Sir," the pilot answered, engaging the controls. "But there is a large unidentified craft just arriving port side. Shall we not engage?"

"No," the King answered, without turning. "The enemy is below and we would only be wasting time with what I am certain is a freighter. Order only a warning shot then descend below as instructed."

"Aye, Sir," the pilot answered, ordering the gunnery. Turning to make his own prompts for the drop, he lowered the ship to the small island.

Continuing its descent, the King's ship appeared too large to land, seeming to engulf the tiny strip of land below with its impending shadow. "Thrusters on, flaps open," the pilot ordered, holding firm to the stick. Anticipating contact with the plush greens, and cringing with expectation of the ship ramming against the dense foliage, he sat amazed despite his Commander's assurances. The foliage appeared to dissipate with the ship passing through.

"Any external damage?" he asked Data Control.

"None, Sir," the officer answered, amazed at what he had witnessed. "All systems are surprisingly functional."

"As I have told you," the King said, ruffling his chin. He shifted his weight with the ship's contact with the strip of ground, stiffening his stance at the last.

"A trick it is and I might add not a very good one," he tsked. "Have all fighters return and ready the BP's for ground battle."

"Aye, Sir," the pilot answered, stalling the ship and giving the order.

"Send ten assault rangers to the left hatch and have them wait for me there," the Commander continued, turning to face his crew. "I will deal with Mathius myself."

"Aye, Sir," the pilot answered, prompting the com with his free hand. "Shield down, left hatch open, ten ARs report. It is done, Sir," he added, raising the overhead control. Pivoting for approval, the pilot only caught a glimpse of his Commander's cloak, the King abruptly exiting Command without word.

***

"We should go back, Sir," Jax said into his headset from the gunnery station.

"No," Jovaar sighed, the ship calmly traversing the underworld greens at Khyra's hand. "It is too big of a risk. As much as I would like to return and defend, Nitaya's safety must come above all others. Nav," he continued, loosening his restraints. "Patch into system maps and pull up the TI4B file."

"TI4B, Sir?" he asked, uncertain.

"Its name is trivial, Luvin," Jovaar answered, glaring at his subordinate. "A mere title so that it could not be traced."

"Sir," he answered, pivoting in his seat. Tapping his screen, he quickly brought up the file as ordered.

"Patch it through to Khyra's panel," Jovaar added, eyeing Luvin's questionable stare. "We will obviously be altering our course."

Luvin quickly followed his Commander's order and with a few added taps to his screen, had the data sent to Khyra's station. Leaning forward to better understand the layout, she tilted back and looked to Jovaar over her shoulder.

"Is this accurate, Jovaar?" she asked, turning back to her screen. "We will be traveling through some rather rough terrain."

"Yes, it is accurate, Ma'am," he answered, sarcasm thickening his words. "This map has been carefully developed over the last several onars for this specific voyage. I seriously doubt it would be flawed."

"Of course, Sir," she answered, keying in the alternate coordinates. Turning to pose another question, she paused as Mathius chimed in over the com.

"Our air fleet has been depleted," Mathius said winded, his crew shouting out at his back. "The ship has landed and our scanners indicate assault rangers are heading in our direction. Do not under any circumstances divert from your agenda. You must see to the child's safety. We will do what we can from here. I am downloading all necessary files to a portal unit and will leave as soon as possible. We will rendezvous where previously indicated."

Staring helplessly at the others, Jovaar prompted the com to protest, but Mathius was quicker on the controls. "They are at the hill!" he shouted, obviously turning from his side screen to main. "This is all happening too fast. Make haste my son! I have to see that the remaining crew gets away. Mathius out."

"Palle! Palle!" Jovaar shouted. Panicking he prompted and repromted the controls, yet gained no response.

"We can help!" Jax shouted, having overhead the transmission. "We must go back!"

"No," Jovaar answered, gritting his teeth and tightening his restraints. "Ma'am, is this ship capable of hyper drive?"

"It is not considered hyper drive below the sea but I can speed it up quite a bit until we reach the next sector," she answered sympathetically, turning back to her panel. "I will have to slow down considerably at its edge to maneuver through the terrain."

"Do what you can," Jovaar answered, running his fingers through his hair. "Selena, go see to the child and take Hylin with you. I will look in on you as soon as I can."

Nodding, Selena and Hylin simultaneously unlatched their restraints, leaving Command without word. "Jax, Kroy be ready," Jovaar ordered, the door closing at his back. "Make sure all weapons are fully armed and keep your eyes open. They will surely track us soon."

***

177

The assault rangers traipsed the narrow pass and quickly reached the hill, finding the two guards standing firm at its entrance. As the King approached at the backs of his men, he stood pleased to find the guards had been easily overtaken.

"Open the gate," he ordered, watching them struggle against the clasps. "I said open the blasted gate," he repeated, flailing his arms in frustration.

Knowing he would gain nothing from the men verbally, the King sent his rangers to scour the area for the required control mechanism. "It could be hidden in anything," he said, eyeing the guards for any indication. "A rock, a bush, a tree," he continued, spying the secured men look to each other.

"Ah, a tree then," he continued, unable to control his grin. "Search all trees in the area. I am certain in will not be far." The two guards stood tense as several of the assault rangers searched for the hidden device. Ever confident, the King crossed his arms to patiently wait.

"Here!" a ranger shouted to their right. "I have found it."

"Very well," the King answered, the other AR's doubling back, gathering round. "Now open the gate."

"Aye, Sir," the ranger answered. Ducking behind the slender tree, he maneuvered the secret control. "Nothing is happening Sir," the ranger at his side shouted. "Perhaps…"

"There must be more than one blasted control," the Commander interrupted, waving for his men to continue their search. "Mathius Savius is a sly one. Keep looking!"

Several moments passed with the King's fleeting patience, his eyes glaring at the somber pair of guards. "I have found it," another ranger said, startling the group from their left. Nodding to his counterpart, they simultaneously pulled the controls and the King stood back as the gate slowly opened before him.

"Well done," he said, crossing to the large opening. "We will take the guards with us in case we encounter any other surprises. Let us go!" Entering the narrow pass, the King paced eagerly amongst his men until they arrived at the expected device.

"Please place your eye on the reading card," the mechanical device said, flatly.

"It seems bringing them along has proven quite useful," the King commented, snapping his fingers. "Bring one of them forward."

Dragging the whimpering first through the guards, the two rangers thrust his head down toward the narrow reading card.

"Negative," the orb chimed, blinking its metal lids.

"Bring the other one," the King said, annoyed with the tedium. The first guard was pushed backward as the second was brought forward, his tearing eyes thrust low to the scanner.

"Cleared. All are to proceed," the machine said, quickly rejoining and withdrawing back within the wall.

"Shall we dispose of them now?" a ranger asked, looking to his commander.

"No," the King answered, staring into the empty compartment. "They may well remain useful. Follow me. Which level?" the King asked the bound men, stepping within knowing he would not receive an answer. "Which level?" he repeated, fruitlessly.

"Sublevel One," he ordered, gritting his teeth, the compartment remaining firmly in place. "Sublevel Two," he scowled, his temper flaring, the guards glancing uneasily to one another. "They have obviously coded the system to a specific term," the King said, looking to his men with annoyance. "We do not have time for this." Grabbing hold of the nearest guard, the King yanked at his cloak, pulling him forward.

"What is the term?" he asked baring his teeth, the guard careening his head. "What is the term?" he repeated, roughly shaking the fearful man.

"I will never reveal it!" the guard shouted, his words echoing in the cramped space. The Commander frustratingly tossed him into the wall of his men.

"Get out the serum," he ordered the ranger to his left, watching the fear grow in the guard's eyes. "Inject him quickly. We are losing time."

"Aye, Sir," the ranger answered, tipping his head. Pulling the syringe from his side holster, he turned to the trembling man without hesitation. Reaching for the guard and struggling within the cramped space, the ranger maneuvered between his comrades as they tilted to avoid the needle.

"Hold him down," he ordered, the men regrouping and grabbing at the man's arms, at last restraining him. Lowering the syringe, the ranger injected its slender head into the guard's thigh and watched as the transformation took place in the recesses of his eyes. "He is ready, Sir," he said, replacing the needle at his side.

"Very well," the King answered, turning firmly to the pliable guard. "As I was saying, which level?"

"Lesslevel Five," the man answered, tears welling in his eyes. The compartment at once responded to his spoken words, and the King merely smiled, refolding his arms across his chest as the compartment sped them into the deep.

Slowing to a stop, several of the rangers stepped forward anticipating the exit. "Not just yet," the guard slipped, covering his mouth in anguish. With the compartment beginning its lateral slide, the rangers reclaiming their positions surrounding the King, the man wept silently, begging for forgiveness from his counterpart.

The door at last opened and King Carsian snapped his fingers for his men to proceed. "Find him at once," he said, the guards darting quickly into the main cabin. "For I do believe that it is time I had words with Sir Mathius Savius."

Fifteen

"I am estimating we will reach Quadrant Four in three hazon," Khyra said, pivoting at her station. "That is if we run into zero obstacles."

"Very well," Jovaar answered, unclasping his restraints. "Continue your current path. I am going to look in on Nitaya and will return shortly."

"Yes, Sir," Khyra answered, lowering her glance to her hands. "Jovaar," she added, hesitantly. "I am sorry about Mathius."

Shaking the thoughts of his palle from his mind, Jovaar said nothing and instead turned to his trusted friend. "Phydin," he said, standing and stretching the aches of his lower back. "Take the helm while I am gone."

"Sir?" he questioned from his seat at the rear.

"I am certain you are quite capable, Phydin," Jovaar continued, pacing to the rear door. "And furthermore you are doing me no good sitting there wallowing."

"Sir, yes sir," he answered, briskly removing his restraints and standing.

"No bickering," Jovaar added, pointing his finger in Phydin's face.

"No, Sir," Phydin answered, crossing to the helm. "I will not let you down."

"I know, Phydin," Jovaar answered, prompting the door. "And for that I am grateful."

Pacing quickly through midship, Jovaar hurried passed the gunnery yet turned and retraced his steps to the thick, metal arches. "Did you run the overview program as I had suggested, Jax?" he asked, staring up into the emptiness above.

"Yes, Sir," he answered, reclining in his seat. "And you were right as usual. We could have had some major difficulties

181

had we not studied the schematics. This system is much more complex than I had first anticipated."

"Very well," Jovaar answered, pleased as always with the results of the pair. "I will be in quarters looking in on Selena and the child. Inform me of the first sign of the enemy."

"Sir," they answered as one, Kroy rotating and joining them at the lower docking station. Nodding, Jovaar turned, crouching to enter the rear cabin.

Selena held the child in her arms nourishing and rocking her gently, looking up unstartled at the swish of the door. "Are you comfortable?" Jovaar asked, crossing to Selena's side.

"Yes, thank you, Jovi," she answered, smiling down at the child.

"Have there been any signs of incoming ships?" Hylin excitedly chimed in, rising from his seat before the glass.

"Thankfully none so far," Jovaar answered, ruffling his har. "Yet I am not optimistic."

"I know we will get through this," Selena added, staring at Nitaya's face, her lids fighting to remain open. "I just look at her and know that everything with be alright."

"I pray you are right, Selena," Jovaar added, running his fingers over the child's arm. "I pray you are right. If you have everything in order here, I should head back to Command."

"Can I come with you?" Hylin asked, eager to be with the action.

"I am sorry, but no Hylin," he answered, shaking his head. "I need you here to look after our girls. The situation may change any moment and things could get out of control. I would feel more confident knowing you were here to help with the child."

"But it is so dull here," he stammered, slumping back onto his seat. "There is nothing to do."

"You will think of something," Jovaar said, smiling and crossing to pat the boy's head. "We would not be here without your help and I promise you I will not forget that. Your quick thinking is an asset to me, to all of us, as I am certain it will be to you now. You will think of something," he repeated, chuckling. "Notify me if you need anything, Lena," he added, turning from the sulking boy.

"I will," she answered, lowering Nitaya to her small chamber. "And please be careful, Jovi," she added, smiling and turning to face him.

Nodding in intimate understanding, Jovaar turned to find Hylin grumbling, staring out the glass. Gently touching Selena's cheek, he smiled then quickly turned and set out for the helm.

***

With weapons raised, the assault rangers entered the realm of the underwater main cabin, trailed by their ever confident King. "The room is deserted, Sir," one said, running about the area.

"Search the remainder of the station!" the King ordered. Flipping his arm wide through the air, he stomped to the helm. "They could not have gotten far."

"Aye, Sir," they answered as one, quickly setting out to scour the area.

"You," the King said, pointing to the nearest ranger, the two captives having been secured at its rear. "Get all systems up and running. We should be able to hear the last of their transmissions just prior to their attempted escape."

"Aye, Sir," the ranger answered. Immediately claiming one of the data stations, he frantically began searching the system.

"Clear," another ranger shouted from the rear left of the room. "Clear," another echoed, leaving the main cabin to continue their search.

"They have jammed the frequency, Commander," the seated ranger continued.

"Use this," the King said, reaching within his cloak and pulling out the odd input.

"Aye, Sir," he answered, interpreting the King's forethought and connecting the device to the main drive. "I think I have got it," he added after a only few moments. "It should be coming up on screen now."

The large panel at the center of the room sprang to life filled with static, yet the images soon became clear enough to decipher. Anxious, the King and a few stray rangers stood to

183

watch the scene play out before them. Oddly, the King made no mention of their relaxed state.

"Our air fleet has been depleted. The ship has landed and assault rangers are heading in our direction. Do not under any circumstances divert from your agenda. You must see to the child's safety. We will do what we can from here. I am downloading all necessary files to a portal unit and will leave as soon as possible. We will rendezvous where previously indicated."

Chaos erupted throughout the room behind the aged man and glancing over his shoulder, he turned back quickly to the helm's panel. "They are at the hill! This is all happening too fast. Make haste, my son! I have to see that the remaining…" Static returned to the screen.

"That is it, Sir," the ranger said, silencing the deafening screeches.

"So, it seems the child survived," the King scowled, ruffling his chin. "And Mathius has downloaded their path into a portal unit. Send all rangers to the docks. It seems my old friend is intending to leave in haste. It is a shame, for him mind you, that he will not get far."

***

Mathius quickly boarded the final ship at port, bypassing the massive stature of the newest arrival with the last three of his remaining men. Racing to the smaller Command to ignite its systems, Mathius took his portal unit, injecting it into the intricate mainframe.

"This is our only chance of finding them," he whispered, downloading the vital information. Tapping his fingers impatiently on the screen, it danced in its expected array of colors. Wringing his hands, Mathius stood tense until the program at last confirmed the transfer. Encrypting the file so that he alone would be able to retrieve it, Mathius breathed a sigh of relief as the barrier sealed in place, knowing that if anyone were to attempt to open it, it would immediately destroy itself.

"It is time," Mathius said, turning to his small crew scrambling at their stations.

"Sir," the pilot said, not turning from his controls. "We are not finished fueling. We need more time!"

"There is no time left to have," Mathius answered, claiming the helm. "Disconnect the fueling line and prompt your stations. We are leaving now!"

"Yes, Sir," the three answered in unison, hastily clasping their restraints.

"All systems report," the pilot ordered, ignoring the overhead controls.

"There is no time for that," Mathius shouted, ejecting his array of panels. "Do you not know what is at stake? Just get us out of here!"

"Yes, Sir," he answered, pivoting in his seat to begin the countdown. "Detachment in 5, 4..." the pilot said, falling forward into his panel with the blast from the rear.

"Leaving so soon, Mathius?" the King asked coldly. Mathius sat frozen at the helm. Recognizing the dark voice with his first words, Mathius' hands firmly gripped the rests of his seat, his frightened men looking to him with lowered eyes.

"King Carsian Sugan," he said, slowly rising and turning to face his enemy. "You are too late. The child of Martus Savius has survived and left onars before. The Royal Committee will still have its choice."

"You speak yet gibberish spews from your lips, old man," the King said, smiling broadly and folding his arms at his chest. "I know full well that they left merely a hazon ago, and rest assured it will not be long until we find them."

Mathius stood slack jawed. The King could not possibly know of this information. "Ah, my old friend, do not look so surprised," the King continued, boldly crossing to him and shaking the small device in his hand. "With a son as intuitive as your young Drider, you of all people should understand that technology is a wonderful thing. This small yet powerful device easily countered your security measures and I was able to witness first hand what transpired."

Returning the minute object to the sleeve within his cloak, the King recrossed his arms and nodded over his shoulder to his men. "Secure them and take over Command," he ordered, standing firm. Three quickly claimed their stations as additional rangers dragged the pilot's body and the final two crew members from the cramped quarters. At the last, the King grandly claimed Mathius' helm.

"It will not be long until we have them, Mathius," the King said, additional rangers securing him at the rear. "Then in all my glory, I will see the Sugin reign continue!"

Sixteen

"We have entered Quadrant Four," Khyra said, not turning from her screen. "Systems slowed. The path you have laid out will not be pleasant, Sir. All should prepare for rough terrain."

"Just do what you can, Ma'am," Jovaar answered, realigning the route on his screen. "It is all we can do."

"Yes, Sir," she answered, lowering a side panel. "Luvin, zoom in so I can get a better view. I will have to rely on both the screen and the glass. It is just too murky at this depth for glass alone."

Luvin furiously keyed his panel and with a few additional strokes, honed the image on Khyra's screen. She gasped at the enormous formations.

"I have never seen anything like this," Khyra whispered, shaking her head at the cloudy images. "Look there," she added, pointing toward the glass. "Have you ever seen coral so large?"

"It is not coral," Jovaar answered, raising his overhead monitor to get a closer look out the glass. "They are eggs from a Polatio. You would be wise not to disturb them."

"The what?" Khyra asked, leaning closer toward the glass.

"The Polatio," Jovaar answered, nodding for the others to take a look. "It is a large creature that lives in the deepest recesses of the underworld with young the size of our ship. If they are disturbed in any way, they could break way prior to gestation and regardless of their current stage, they could easily devour us."

"And we must travel through here why?" Khyra asked, fuming. Shaking her head in disgust, she turned to face him.

"Because it is the only way," Jovaar answered flatly. "Trust me, ma'am, it is the *only* way."

The crew sat motionless, their tasks ignored as they gawked out the glass toward the enormous oval shaped eggs. At first glance appearing to be huge coral as Khyra had initially surmised, their thick tubes attached at the top, twisting and turning in the water soon gave the monstrosities away.

"Stay low to miss the feeders," Jovaar ordered, turning back to his lowered panel.

"Alright then," Khyra said turning back to her screen, guiding them toward the opening of the zone. "Here we go. Luvin," she added, the eggs growing larger before them. "Call out any obstacles I may miss."

"Pray that you do miss," Jovaar said, Khyra quickly glaring at him over her shoulder. "Everything we are fighting for depends on it."

***

"Easy now," Jovaar said, attempting an air of calm. Khyra guided them through the first set of eggs as he carefully monitored their route for he knew that the enormous maze, clouded by muck and mire would prove extremely difficult for any pilot. The beast's eggs were beige, with sea life nourishing from their nutrion-filled shells, their feeders, darker in color, flowing with the steady current of the deep.

"Orvi, pull up all data on the Polatia," Jovaar ordered, staring out at the endless population of awaiting births. "It would be prudent for all to have a better understanding of what we are dealing with."

"Here it is," Luvin began, having prompted the system's search program. "The Polatia lay their young in extreme depths," he said, leaning forward to read the small text. "The Polatio, singular of Polatia, exist in the deep of several locations throughout the galaxy, although they have certain characteristics depending on which planet they dwell. This particular Polatian Swarm lives in waters of mild temperatures and lays its young in extreme depths, as I said earlier. The female is pollinated while in a sleep-like state as the male swims above, constantly in a state of defense. The female senses the change in her system, and while not knowing what has transpired, attacks what it assumes is a predator. The male is then devoured over a period of several hazon then the female with belly full begins her cycle, laying the eggs within three days."

"Go female," Khyra said, pumping her fists. Jovaar noted Phydin's grimace.

"Typical," Phydin mumbled, Luvin clearing his throat to continue.

"The eggs double in size each day until reaching maturity in seven," he read. "The mother guards the eggs during that time then eats away at them until they are hatched and then the cycle begins anew. If this is accurate…"

"The mother lies above us," Jovaar interrupted, returning to his overhead panel. "Ma'am, do your best not to disturb her."

"Yes, Sir," Khrya answered, nervously guiding the ship forward, looking through the glass for signs of the angered beast. "I will do my best."

***

Ordering his men to begin detachment, the King lowered the overhead panel and injected the small device into the narrow opening. "I am assuming, Mathius, that you have uploaded your portal," he said, smiling and looking over his shoulder at the enemy. "This program will overstep any encryption that you may have entered and I will momentarily have the information I seek." Mathius squirmed in his restraints yet said nothing, the helm's system springing to life before his eyes.

Entering the information request and tapping the panel eagerly, random numbers filled the small screen. Waiting with overt patience, the King gloated as the data proved easily deciphered.

"So you have tried to out-maneuver me again, Mathius," he said, shaking his head. "No bother. My scanner will soon pick up what I seek."

Slowly opening the data from top to bottom, the King smiled once the route the others had plotted ticked opened before him. "You see old man," he said, pivoting in his seat. "It was useless to resist."

As the machine continued its requested program the system slowed, blaring its warning signal. Carsian turned back to the rapidly blilnking panel. "What is this?" he asked gritting his teeth, whacking the small panel with his palm. When not one of his rangers responded however, he glared at Mathius then turned back to his screen.

"I suppose it will have to do," he said, attempting calm and reclining in his seat. "We have most of the information we need, and I am confident we will find the rest. Pilot!" he shouted, turning back to his crew. "Order our detachment!"

"Aye, Sir," the ranger answered, hastily prompting the program. "Detachment in 5, 4, 3, 2, 1, detach. Commander, we will reach fifty depth momentarily."

"Very well," the King answered, glaring at his captive. "Let us watch together how quickly the gap closes."

***

"It is so murky," Khyra said, guiding the ship through the bending pass. "There, Jovaar?" she asked, pointing toward the glass and the narrowing obstacles. "We are to go in there?"

"Yes, ma'am," he answered, flatly. "Slow more and patch your screen to main. We will do what we can to help guide you."

"Sir," she answered, refusing to remove her hands from the stick instead nodding for Luvin to follow the order. "There must be hundreds of them," she added, wiping her brow with her sleeve. "Nav, increase our depth by tens until I say otherwise."

"Got it," Luvin answered, prompting the alternate screen to Khyra's, simultaneously keying the adjustment at his panel.

"That's it, that's it," Khyra said, staring intensely at her screen. "Good, hold us there. I think we are almost through. Blasted!" she said, the ship slightly jarring, the members looking to her anxiously. "I think I hit one. DC report."

"Nothing, Khyra," Orvi answered, scanning the ship's maintenance data.

"No wait," Luvin chimed in, altering his readout. "We have movement."

"Is it the egg or the mother?" Jovaar asked, leaning closer to his screen. "I do not see anything."

"There," Luvin added, pointing out the glass. "It is the egg. No, it is several eggs. Sir, I see at least three stirring and…"

"And what?" Jovaar interrupted, frantically scanning his own panel.

"The mother, Sir," he answered, prompting his alternate screen. "According to my sonar she is headed our way."

"I cannot see anything through all of this muck," Khyra shouted, lowering the eye screen to better guide the ship through the narrow pass. "Where is she?"

"Port side," Luvan answered, his panel dancing before him. "She is either coming forward to eat open her young or to take care of us."

"Take evasive actions," Jovaar ordered, the mother Polatio entering the main screen. Before anyone could respond however, the cabin jeered violently from the angered beast.

Most remained in their seats, yet the shift flung Orvi against his panel then subsequently to the floor. Fidaldi fell next to him, knocking the pair unconscious.

"Jax, Kroy," Jovaar shouted, prompting the com. "Fire at the beast yet keep an eye out for her eggs. We will not sustain very many hits like that, but we also do not want more of the creatures out there."

"Sir!" Jax responded, rotating up the hollow shell.

"Phydin," Jovaar continued, releasing the com. "Take over DC and give me an update on our stability. Ma'am flank left and concentrate on the path. The rest of you keep an eye out for the momar."

"Stop already with the 'Ma'am,' Jovaar," Khyra shouted anxiously, unable to turn from the eyepiece. "I think Khyra will now do, do you not?"

Jovaar could not help his smile yet said nothing as his attention was once again drawn to the Momar, the beast now swarming parallel to the ship. Not making contact, the creature instead sailed by as if gathering data on her enemy, allowing the crew to get a better look at the weight of her.

"Look at her size," Luvin said, gaping in awe out the glass.

"Just concentrate on our path, Luvin," Jovaar ordered, prompting the com. "Selena, report in." Awaiting her response, the beast swam by once again. With the moments ticking away, Jovaar turned back to his com ready to reprompt, but at last Selena's sweet voice filled his ears.

"We are fine Jovaar," she said, her voice fighting against static. "What is happening?"

"Everything is under control," Jovaar answered, feigning the sarcastic stares of his conscious crew. "If he is not needed, we could use Hylin at Command. If that suits you, send him forward and strap Nitaya and yourself in."

"You are freightening me," she cried, the static distorting her words.

"We will be fine," Jovaar answered, nodding at Phydin's obvious glare. "Just do as I have said. Is Hylin on his way?"

"He darted out of here the moment you said he was needed," she answered. "He should be there any moment now."

"Very well," Jovaar answered, the rear door springing open with Hylin sailing in. "Try not to worry."

"Hylin," Jovaar continued, releasing the com. "You said you wanted more to do so now is your chance. Take over as DC and watch out for the momar. Hold on!" he shouted, the angry beast coming dead at them, the ship rocking with the hit. Hylin careened from the jolt, but somehow used the cramped quarters to his advantage, sustaining the hit remarkably unscathed.

"What about them?" he asked, gesturing to the pair on the floor.

"They will be all right," Jovaar answered, shaking his head and turning back to his screen. "Just let me know if you get sight of her, and keep me updated on our systems."

"What am I looking for?" Hylin asked eagerly, out of breath as he claimed Orvi's seat.

"That," Jovaar said, pointing out the glass, the momar passing to their left.

"What the..." Hylin asked, pausing as the large beast sailed by yet again.

"Exactly," Jovaar answered, scanning through his own eyepiece. "Keep me informed of our damage."

Seventeen

"Fifty depth in 5, 4, 3, 2, 1, fifty depth," the system's female voice rang calmly over the com.

"All systems go," the pilot answered, prompting the controls to rotate the ship in pursuit.

"Do you have the readout on the enemy craft?" the King asked, not turning from his screen.

"Aye, Sir, it is uploading now," he answered, patching his alternate panel. "Their path proved fairly calm throughout the first sector of their voyage. I am confident that we will be able to make up for much of the distance."

"This pleases me," the King answered, peering over his shoulder to Mathius. "Order systems full throttle," he said, an evil grin crossing his face. "They will not get away this time. And meanwhile," he continued, tapping his chin in thought. "I believe it is time for Mathius and I to have our little chat. As you can imagine, there is much to be discussed. You," the King added, pointing to the guard seated next to his enemy. "Bring Savius to the rear cabin."

"Aye, Sir," the ranger answered, releasing his restraints. Abruptly standing, he released the prisoner, the King striding confidently out the rear door before them.

   ***

"You are wasting your time, Carsian," Mathius said, thrown into the cabin at the King's feet and rubbing the spittle from his chin. "You will never catch them!"

"Restrain him and leave us," the King ordered, ignoring Mathius' pleas, waving his hand dismissively toward the door. Nodding, the pair of rangers quickly followed their commander's

194

orders, and shackling the elder man to the large rear bench, hastily exited the rear cabin, heads bowed.

"Your confidence is misplaced, my old friend," the King began, pacing the cabin with his hands folded confidently at his back. "It is a shame, for you mind you, that when my reign is proven to continue due to your so called Royal Committee having no other alternative, I will have to use this little escapade of yours against your kin."

"Your reign has brought nothing but chaos to this galaxy, Carsian," Mathius groaned, breathing heavily and struggling against his restraints. "Have you not seen the destruction on the icy Fourth? Have you not seen the poverty on all sides of Clooxin? Your rangers run rampant and destroy entire villages and yet you do nothing but encourage them! Intimidation is not the answer, Carsian! You have no heir! And furthermore, you give too much attention to one name. There are several other possibles left. Destroying one will not get you what you seek, and I promise you I will do everything in my power to see that all have an equal chance of surviving until given their proper chance at title. The Sugin Reign will come to its end, Carsian! With my last breath…"

"Is your little speech about finished then?" the King interrupted, unfettered and chin raised high, crossing the room to stand before his enemy. "Your trivial insight means nothing to me, Mathius. You sit there beneath me where you belong as your fleet depletes without backing. Your weakness is your faith. My power is in my numbers. You will soon be begging me for leniency, yet I will delight in denying it to you. You speak of the other *possibles* as if I am unaware of their measly existence, yet at this very moment I have the best of my seekers and hidden assets destroying them as well. I chose your name to contend with myself for reasons you are well aware. I will quite enjoy watching you and yours die."

"The Royal Committee will not stand still for this!" Mathius shouted, angrily tugging on the tightening restraints. "It is law that the elite members of the core will produce the possibles of which one will be chosen, and of which you have none! Our age in time is over, Carsian. The law is the law."

"You speak of the law, yet what you do not understand is that *I am* the law," the King shouted, raising his leg and stomping his foot on Mathius's hand, the elder crying out from the blow.

"We have movement up ahead, Sir," a ranger interrupted over the com.

"I will be right there," the King answered, lowering to face his prized prisoner. "It seems we will have to continue this enlightening conversation at a later time," he said, reining his anger and rising, crossing to the door. "As you can see, my friend, I have other pressing matters to attend to. Rest assured though, that I am saving you for the last so that you will be able to watch every last one of them die. Ranger," the King added, prompting the com next to the door. "Retrieve the old man and bring him to the Com. I want him to witness their destruction."

***

"I made contact on the second pass-by," Jax said, pivoting low through the gunnery's hollow shaft.

"As I feared, it appears not to affect her," Jovaar answered, running his fingers through his hair. "Double your efforts and keep her from ramming the bow of the ship. I do not think we will be able to sustain another blow like that last one!"

"Yes, Sir," Jax answered, pivoting high on the opposite side.

"It is like she is circling us now, Jovaar," Khyra said, staring forward through the eyepiece. "Yet we should be through the egg field soon...as long as she keeps at this distance."

"Very well," Jovaar answered, straining to see out the glass. "Maintain your speed and keep your..."

"Sir," Hylin interrupted, pivoting at his borrowed station. "I do not think she is circling. Look to the main screen. She appears to be laying eggs."

Leaning forward and straining to look closer through the murky underworld, Jovaar's eyes widened as he witnessed the beast facing down at her precious young. "She is not laying eggs!" he shouted, turning back to the mapped route on his screen. "She is opening them! Khyra, we must go faster! We will be surrounded in no time!"

"I am going as fast as I can!" Khyra roared, keying the controls with her free hand as she maneuvered the stick. "Luvin, is there a way around the pass up ahead?"

"I cannot be certain," he answered, keying furiously at his station. "Give me a moment."

"That is about all you have," Jovaar added, shaking his head and looking back to main. "You must hurry, Luvin!"

"We could possibly by-pass the field by sailing up and over the gorge rather than through it," Luvin continued, unturning. Tapping his screen, he searched through various paths of the darkened underworld. "I am uncertain of the terrain, yet I *am* confident when I say we will no longer be under radar. I am afraid we could possibly be trading one evil for another."

"Jovaar?" Khyra questioned, unable to turn from the eyepiece. Jovaar ran his hands over his face considering their options. Turning to the glass just as the beast passed, obviously eager to greet her birthing young, he could see no alternative.

"Do it," he said, shaking his head. "We have no other choice. What is the duration of our vulnerabilty within radar, Luvin?"

"I am approximating at less than a hazon, Sir," he answered, prompting the steep route to main. "We should be able to duck back down in the next sector where the route proves clear of Polatia."

"Then let us get moving," Jovaar said, staring at the larger screen, the vertical incline coming into view. "It appears the momar has her pack and I do not particularly want to hang around and become their nourishment. Khyra, punch the stick for climb."

***

Within moments Khyra had the ship climbing at a rapid incline, yet with the beast spying their hasty retreat, she quickly swam after them, ramming the aft of the ship alongside her eager young. "Jax!" Jovaar shouted, prompting the com. "Will you take care of her already?!"

"We're doing the best we can, Sir," he answered, Kroy's blasts echoing in the slender shaft. "At least five remain. The outer cover of the young proves permeable. We have killed off three so far, but they keep coming out of nowhere!"

"Keep on it," Jovaar ordered, grimacing. "They should retreat with the warming temperatures as we reach higher levels."

"Yes, Sir," he answered, returning to his task and opening fire.

"Hylin, give me a read out on systems," Jovaar ordered, turning for assistance from the young boy.

"Both bow and aft shields are down," he answered, tapping his monitor to bring up the requested data. "There is a small pressure leak in the equipment cabin but I have sealed that off until it can be tended to. Another aft hit could possibly depressurize the entire ship. I am not certain how it has held together this...."

"They appear to be retreating," Phydin interrupted, having altered his screen from the gunnery load.

"Reaching thirty depth, Jovaar," Khyra added, the ship's tilt at last leveling.

"Radar range in five," Luvin chimed, the calm of the settling ship proving just as easily lost as it had been found.

"Just get us through, Khyra," Jovaar answered, his eyes returning to the glass with the clearing waters. "I will have Kroy work the centralized panel and get all systems operational once we have reached higher ground. Just get us through."

"Yes, Sir," she answered, Jovaar prompting the com.

"Kroy, get to the CP and give me a full read out," Jovaar ordered, altering his screen to see the damage Hylin had described. "We need all shields functional immediately then check the equipment cabin for..." he said, slamming his fist on his panel.

"Blasted," he continued, wiping the sweat from his brow. "The CP is in the equipment cabin. Hylin, is there another way to reach it?"

"There is," he answered, eagerly prompting yet another screen. "The cable shoot runs the entire length of the ship then

T's down to the necessary components. Let me just bring up the...," he added, tapping his panel, Jovaar waiting impatiently.

"Here," he said at last, pointing. Jovaar released his restraints and crossed the small Command to get a closer look. "I do not see how it can work though, Sir," Hylin added, looking up to his elder. "The shoot can be no more than twelve inches across."

Jovaar rubbed the stubble on his chin, considering the lack of space of their only route. "There is no way that Kroy can get through that," he whispered, prompting Hylin's screen for other possibilites. "What if we..."

"Sir, if I may," Hylin interrupted, pivoting to face his new commander. "I am the perfect size. I know I can do it."

"You know nothing of the intricacies of a submersible," Jovaar said, his frustration evident as he reclaimed his seat. "And furthermore you are only a boy. There must be another way."

"Sir," Hylin pressed, eager to to prove his worth. "Just give me the tools and a chance. I know I can do this."

"We have no choice and you know it," Phydin added, pivoting from his station before Hylin, Khyra glancing warily over her shoulder. "Kroy can give the boy the instructions through the com. It will be just like he were there making the repairs himself."

"But if he fails to make the proper connections, we could instantly depressurize and then..."

"Trust me," Hylin interrupted, crossing from his station and placing his hand on Jovaar's arm. "I know I can do it. And when I do, I will insist that you stop referring to me as a boy."

Sighing, Jovaar knew there was no other way. "Kroy," he said at last, prompting the com. "Disregard and get up here. I need you to prep Hylin for repairs."

"But..." he began, Jovaar cutting off his gunner.

"Just get up here."

"Yes, Sir," he answered, Jovaar releasing the com and turning to face their only chance at fully repaired shields. "I hope you can deliver what you say, for everything depends on it."

"I will not let you down," Hylin answered, anxiously rubbing his hands together. Khyra looked fearfully over her shoulder.

"I pray you are right," Jovaar added, glancing warily at Phydin. "And if so, I promise I will never utter the word 'boy' again."

***

"I have tracked movement up ahead, Sir," the ranger said, zooming his screen. "They have slowed and have begun making an ascent. I am certain that they must be trying to maneuver over the lower pass as a diversion, since the path below appears the least in distance. Shall I follow them, Sir? Their original route had them sailing well below radar. I must admit I am baffled to their…"

"No," the King interrupted, ruffling his chin. "Let us travel below them for a while longer. If we make good time as our pilot has been so easily doing thus far, we should come out just ahead of them. The perfect scenario for a surprise attack," he added, his smile widening as he turned toward his enemy. "Would you not agree, Mathius?"

***

"Fully level and stabilized, at least for the time being," Khyra said, slowly prompting the stick forward. Easing the lower thrusters, she altered their angles in assumption of Jovaar's impending order.

"Very well," Jovaar answered, prompting the com at mid-ship. "Maximum speed over the gorge and get us back below radar as soon as possible, Khyra."

"Yes, Sir'," she answered, smiling with her insight. Jovaar turned to face Kroy and Hylin in the empty cabin.

"Kroy," he began, salvaging through his tote and handing the boy the device he was thankful to have brought from his quarters on R8. "You will be able to see everything Hylin sees from the mid-ship station. Hylin, your head set is dual purpose for both communications and second eyes. It mounts like any headset, yet this lens here…" he added, pointing. "It will make it so Kroy sees all that you do."

"Are you certain you do not want me in there?" Jax shouted through the open door separating mid-ship from the gunnery.

"We need you where you are, you are not the right size, and blasted I do not have time for explanations!" Jovaar shouted, placing the headset on Hylin. Stomping across the vacant cabin, he glared at his gunner hanging high in the arc and prompted the door closed.

"The mechanism will adjust to your head in just a moment," Jovaar continued, shaking his own as he returned to the boy. Prompting the small side button, Hylin stood anxious with his new gear, the headset closing about his small head as expected.

"There," Jovaar said, tilting the boy's face side to side to test the fitting. "It should be fairly comfortable in this position."

"It is fine," Hylin answered a bit uneasy. Sensing the concern in the young boy's voice however, Jovaar chose for the moment to ignore it.

"We will attach this cord to your ankle and then you will have to drag the tools at your back," Jovaar continued, grabbing the rope from the rear open cabinet. "Once you are in place, you will pull them toward you and will then unbind the knot."

"Excuse me, Sir," Hylin interrupted, shaking his head and looking to Kroy. "But I think it would be easier to push the tools in front of me. I just do not see how I will be able to get them around me once I am in there. I think pushing them would prove more logical."

"He is right, it would be easier," Kroy said, shrugging his shoulders in agreement.

"It seems I am mistaken then," he continued, nodding. "We will bypass the cord and do it your way," he added, tossing it to the ground and gathering the tool pouch.

"Are you ready then?" he asked, handing the boy the heavy bundle, Hylin bending forward from its weight.

"Yes, Sir," he answered, struggling to drag the tote to where Kroy stood opening the hatch.

"It should be no more than fifteen paces…or what would be a pace if you were walking," Kroy said, leaning down to gather Hylin's burden. "When you get to the second drop, you will need to detach the panel and remove it. You will then have to decode the second panel and that should get you in. When you reach that point, notify me and I will instruct you on how to proceed."

"Will you not be monitoring my progress?" Hylin asked, staring up to the height of his new friend.

"Of course," Kroy answered, ruffling the boy's hair. "But these systems are dated and I am concerned that with the the possibility of blasts from above, your gyrating in the shoot may cause some interference. If that is the case, I will need to rely on your voice rather than your second eyes."

"It will work, Hylin," Kroy added, once again ruffling the boy's hair. Stooping to take hold of the hefty pouch, he hoisted it up and into the cramped pass of the shoot, shifting it to the right and out of the way of Hylin's entrance.

Claiming his own headset off the side shelf near the mid-ship station, Kroy placed it over his head. Prompting the control, he waited as it closed in easily about him. "It will be like I am right there with you," he said, reassuringly. "Are you ready then?"

"As ready as I can be," Hylin answered, scratching at the tautness of his own device, secretly twinging with the thought of enemy fire.

"Very well," Jovaar said, interrupting the bonding pair. "You need to get going, boy. We are within radar and therefore you must understand how important it is that we get the shields operational. Do not let us down."

"I will not let you down," Hylin answered, placing his foot into Kroy's folded hands, his elder easily hoisting his small frame upward. "I promise," he repeated, his voice echoing in the confines of the hollow tube. "And soon you will stop calling me boy."

Eighteen

"Light on," Hylin said, the brightness instantaneously filling the cramped space. Lying prone on his belly with the tool pouch in front of him and level with his eyes, Hylin rotated slightly to his side, noting the large cables above. "It is tighter than I thought," he whispered, grunting as he returned to his belly. "Are the second eyes working, Kroy? Are you getting this?"

"They would work if you would turn them on," he answered, chuckling and shaking his head. He looked up from his screen to Jovaar, his smile at once erased with his superior's scowl.

"Oh," Hylin answered, feeling foolish. "Sorry about that, Kroy. Second eyes on. Anything now?"

"Got it," Kroy answered, claiming the small mid-ship station, staring with his screen dancing to life. "Now get moving. As Jovaar said, we are within radar and although you are not to the rear yet, I do not like the idea of you being on the outskirts of the ship unprotected."

"I agree and am on my way," Hylin answered, Kroy doubling his screen to show the layout of the ship as well as what Hylin was broadcasting.

"You need to reach the second drop," Kroy continued, having located the proper layout. "You will know when you have passed the first because several of the cables above you will drop down on the outer wall. I will keep watching your progress yet just the same, let me know when you have reached it."

"Yes, Sir," he answered, pushing the pouch forward, slowly trailing after it.

Several anxious moments passed as Jovaar stood waiting at Kroy's back, staring intently at the dual screen. "Should he not be there by now?" he asked, turning to pace the bench-lined cabin.

"Calm, Jovaar," Kroy answered, dismissing all formalities as he tapped the screen for the next sequence of the path. "Hylin does not have much room to maneuver and regardless he is making good time. Why do you not head back to Command? I can update you once we have reached the site."

"No," he answered, turning back to the panel, leaning on the back of Kroy's seat. "Khyra has the controls with Phydin there to assist her and they both know what is at stake so they should be able to contain their bickering for awhile. I will remain here until all systems are operational."

"I think I see the first drop up ahead," Hylin said, startling the pair. "Kroy, are you getting this?"

"I see it," he answered, zooming in to get a closer look. "It does not look good, Jovaar," he added, shaking his head and muffling the com so Hylin could not hear. "The cables dropping down take up more space than I anticipated. I am not so certain he will be able to pass."

"I am almost there," Hylin continued, grunting with every push forward of the pouch. "Kroy, do you see that? I do not know if I can…"

"You have to get through it, Hylin," Kroy interrupted, glancing up to Jovaar. "Everything depends on it and…."

The explosion from above sent them reeling.

***

"Jovaar, we have company." Khyra said, surprisingly calm over the com. "We need you up here now." Turning, Jovaar shouted his orders to Kroy over his shoulder.

"Either get him by the first drop or get him out of there! Jax!" he added, prompting the door to gunnery. "Rotate to top and give us cover fire! I will send Phydin to assist Hylin and will have Kroy backing you as soon as possible!"

"I'm on it," Jax answered, punching the seat controls and gliding upward.

"Phydin," Jovaar said, panting as he entered Command. "Get to mid-ship and assist Hylin so Kroy can back up Jax.

Khyra," he continued, hastily restraining his clasps. Phydin skirted his entrance and fled the helm. "Order maximum speed!" Jovaar demanded. "Get us back below radar now!"

"It is not that easy," Khyra answered, jarring from another hit from above. "There was a reason we were supposed to travel through the gorge, Jovaar. Look out the glass," she added, Jovaar pouring over his several mini-screens for signs of damage.

"Look, Jovaar," Khyra shouted, prompting the manual override and rising from her seat, crossing to him to point out the glass. "Just blasted look!"

Jovaar could see nothing through the denseness of green beyond the glass. "What in the name of…" he asked, his mouth open as he turned to Khyra.

"Spotted Weed," Luvin answered, keying and tapping his screen for the complete text on the strange undergrowth. "I have run an informational and I am afraid it does not look good. The Spotted Weed grows in shallow waters of no more than thirty depth. It is extremely dense and its outer layer consists of a sticky residue. Anything that comes in contact with the weed adheres to it and becomes food for the plant, thus bringing us to our current dilemma."

"What do we do?" Khyra asked, having returned to her seat.

"We have no choice but to continue through it at maximum speed," Jovaar answered, disregarding the newest nuisance as he turned back to his maintenance screen. "And pray we can break through. We do not know how many ships are above and we have no time to circle back. The boy is traversing the pass now and as long as he is on the outskirts of the ship, he is in danger. We can use the weed for cover but ultimately our only hope is that it breaks soon so we can return to the greater depths."

"Yes, Sir," Khyra answered, refusing to show her fears for Hylin's safety and aggressively prompting the stick forward. "I will have to rely on the screens alone. Hold on!" she added, the ship taking a grazing hit from above.

205

"You must go faster, Khyra!" Jovaar shouted, struggling to reclasp the last of his restraints, his eyes full on the green-filled glass. "We are running out of time!"

***

"We have them in our sights, Sir," the ranger said, pivoting in his station at the sound of the King return to Command.

"I am obviously aware of the sighting," the King answered, shooing away the offered restraints. "Give me an update on their damage."

"We have managed several hits," the man answered, hesitantly. "But they are still moving forward, although at a much slower pace, Sir."

"Stay on them and have your gunners maintain their status of fire at will," the King ordered, prompting the external transmission device. "We are closing in on them below," he continued, speaking confidently into the relay to the ship above. "Do you have us on your screens?"

"Aye, Sir," the ranger answered, his voice confident. "We are aware of your location and will cease fire once you are within range."

"Very well," the King answered, grinning. "That should not take much longer. As I have ordered..."

"Sir," the pilot interrupted, not turning from his post, sailing the ship through the deep recesses of the seascape. "There is movement just ahead but it is not a ship. What would you have me do?"

"Through the blasted gorge!" Carsian shouted, irritated as he slammed the relay closed. "We are quite capable of taking care of minor sea creatures!"

"Aye, Sir," the pilot answered, guiding the stick forward. Swerving around yet another large mass, he was startled with the immense images clearing through the murk of the water.

"Sir?" he questioned, hesitantly.

"What is it now?" the King asked, peering over his shoulder at Mathius. His enemy turned defiantly away.

"I am not certain, Sir but they are huge!" the pilot continued, his eyes wide with fear as he turned to face his commander. "There must be at least five of them."

"Forward all guns and destroy whatever swims in our path, ranger!" the King answered, not turning from his enemy. "Nothing, not even a beast the size of this craft will stop me from reaching the Savius possible."

***

Sweat poured from his brow. Panting within the narrow confines of the shoot, Hylin spoke hoarsely into the headset. "Phydin," he began, knowing that Kroy had returned to the gunnery. "I have reached the first drop but I cannot see how I can get through," he added, anxiously holding firm to the outer walls of the pass, preparing for the surety of another enemy hit. Surprisingly receiving no answer, Hylin released his grip, tapping his headset a second time, repeating his words.

"Phydin, can you hear me?" Again, receiving no answer, he shook his head, groaning. Struggling up onto his forearms, he thrust the tool pouch forward toward the cables.

"Phydin!" Hylin shouted, resting his head on the warm metal of the shoot, his arms aching with every inch forward. Not knowing what to do, he stared out at the vertical cables and waited. Surely Phydin could see what he faced and would somehow guide him through.

Hylin took deep breaths in an attempt to calm his nerves, struggling to find another way on his own. Staring out at the oversized cables dropping below at midship however, he felt hope was lost and merely lowered his head into his hands.

"There is no possible way," he said, his voice echoing in the tube. Looking up and thrusting the pouch forward in frustration, it rammed against the first of the cables, jamming firmly in place as expected.

Opening and removing the tools from the pouch, Hylin studied them individually not knowing what was essential. Turning them from side to side, he tried to envision what would be needed. Settling for three of Kroy's devices, he forced the remains down the narrow length of his body, leaving them behind at his feet.

Pushing those he chosen forward into the darkness, Hylin smiled with the rising light at his head as they easily cleared the troublesome cables. Sliding himself the final short distance to the drop, Hylin reached for the large tubes to use as leverage against his frame. Catching his shoulders on the first attempt, he lowered his tired arms, pausing to reconsider his options.

"Phydin?" he said, his voice echoing in his quiet shell. "Phydin," he repeated, lifting his head. "I should just go back, but then what will we do? Maybe if I turned…" he paused, the cabled nuisance mere inches from his face. "Maybe if…" he thought, attempting to lie on his side, yet as the shoot proved wider rather than tall, he was unable to make the full half turn.

Lying slightly turned on his side, the idea immediately struck him. "What if I…yes it might work," he said, his energy revived. Remaining in his tilted position, Hylin attempted to scoot forward, taking hold of the cables and pulling. Despite his efforts however his elbows rammed into the outer walls.

"I will just have to use my feet then," he said, undeterred and wedging them against the outer walls of the shoot, stretching his arms straight above his head. All thoughts of enemy fire left him as he scooted again with the thrust from his feet.

"Yes!" he said, feeling triumphant on the third thrust, his shoulders at last passing the large cables. Lowering his arms he pushed against them with all his strength, cheering as his legs made the pass.

"At last," he said, panting and tilting his head to peer up ahead. Spying what he knew must be the second drop, he eagerly shoved the tools forward. "Phydin, if you can hear me," Hylin said, excited to be once again on the move. "We are almost there."

***

"Can you hear me, Hylin?" Phydin repeated, grasping the sides of his panel, the ship careening from another blast. "We have lost communications, Jovaar," he continued, frustratingly prompting the com. "I am able to see how Hylin is doing, but so far I am not able to guide him. He has successfully passed the first drop."

"All this technology and you cannot speak to the boy?" Jovaar asked, Khyra's anxious voice shouting her orders to the men at command.

"I am working on it, Sir," Phydin answered, sarcastically.

"I know, I know, Phydin," Jovaar continued, running his fingers through his hair. "Just do what you can and keep me updated. Khyra tells me we are almost through the Spotted Weed and should be back below radar soon. I am not certain how many more hits we will be able to sustain. Uvis is doing his best to keep the rudders from getting clogged but we could really use some good news about the shields."

"He has reached the second drop, Sir," Phydin said, closely monitoring Hylin's progress.

"Very well, my friend," Jovaar answered, staring out the glass at the endless green. "Inform me as soon as pressurization can be activated. We need those blasted shields!"

***

"Headset off," Hylin said, waiting while the device expanded. "What is wrong with you?" he continued, removing the mechanism from his head and rotating in his hands, the light flickering against the narrow shoot.

"Light off," he said, testing it quickly, completely shrouding himself in darkness. "Light on," he continued, the slender beam once again filling the cramped space. "Second eyes off, second eyes on," he said, sweat dripping from his brow as both appeared to be in working order. "Voice on. Phydin, can you hear me. Phydin?" Hylin grumbled, frustratingly gaining no answer.

Shaking the device then taking a slow, deep breath to settle his rising anger, Hylin searched the set, again turning it from side to side. About to give up, he rammed the gadget against the outer wall, squinting as he spied the small dial on its side.

"It cannot be that simple," he whispered, slowly turning the knob. "Phydin, can you hear me?" he asked again, hopeful.

"Hylin, I hear you loud and clear," Phydin answered, pleased that the boy was once again within reach. Sitting up straight in his low stool, he sighed with relief.

"I must have turned the knob off shuffling through this blasted thing," Hylin said, looking up into the dim-lit space.

"We have no time for that now," Phydin answered, once again leaning forward toward his screen. "Get your headset back on and get that panel open. We need that cabin pressurized now."

"Yes, Sir," he answered, placing the set back in place, waiting for the device to recompressed. "I am opening the panel," Hylin continued, grabbing the needed tool to begin. "Do you expect anymore fire? Those blasts really shake me around in here, and I cannot begin to describe the..."

"You know I cannot be certain," Phydin interrupted, dismissively waving his hand in the empty mid-ship cabin. "Just remove all six bolts and slide the panel out of the way. Let us hope the damage is not too severe."

***

"Orvi," Jovaar said, turning from the weed-filled glass to prompt the com. "What is our status on the rear rudder?"

"It clogs up the moment I have it cleared," he answered, frustratingly shaking his head, tapping his screen violently fighting the dense greens. "This system is not easy to operate, Sir. The arms get stuck in the blasted weed and it is difficult to even see what I am doing. I have lost one arm already, Sir."

"We should be through it soon enough, Orvi," Jovaar said, prompting his screen to oversee the arm's progress. "Just do what you can. Khyra will..." he stopped, the ship jarring with yet another blow.

"Orvi?" Jovaar screamed, leaning close to his screen to search for damage. "Are you still with us?"

"Yes, Sir," he answered, obviously shaken. "But the blast cost us the second arm. I am afraid I cannot do any more."

"Then get yourself to Jax and Kroy and help them with cover fire until we have full shields," Jovaar ordered, eyeing Phydin warily.

"Yes, Sir," Orvi answered, signing off the fruitless program. "I am sorry, Jovaar, I did my best."

"I know you did," he answered, running his fingers through his hair. "Just get to the guns."

Nineteen

"I am in," Hylin said, wiping the sweat from his brow with his wrist. "What do I do now?"

"Take the scanner and slowly run it over the entire panel so we can locate the problem," Phydin answered, marveling at the clarity of Jovaar's second eyes device as he scanned the clear panel from mid-ship. Hylin, reaching to his left for the needed scanner, groaned with anger, realizing it was not one of the three he chose.

"I do not think I have it," he said, panicking and fumbling the few he brought forward in his hands. "Is there anything else I can use?"

"What do you mean you do not have it?" Phydin shouted, running his hands over his face, his eyes glaring at the small screen. "Jovaar said that Kroy specifically placed it in your tote. It has to be there."

"I am sorry, Phydin," Hylin continued, lowering the tools to the base of the shoot. "I was forced to open the tote when the space tightened at the first drop, and in between blasts, I selected the tools I thought were most important. I am sorry but I did not bring them all. Can I make do with what I have?'

"Hold on," Phydin answered, frustratedly staring at the floor of the shoot through the second eyes, Hylin obviously lowering his head in fear of disappointing his elders. "What tools *do* you have?" Phydin asked at last.

"I brought the driver set," Hylin answered, raising his head and regathering what few items he possessed. "And I have the power joint and the solder. I am sorry, Phydin. I selected based on what I am most familiar with. Can I make do with those?"

Phydin leaned forward against the panel to think. Without the scanning device, Hylin would be working with a live feed not knowing where the problem existed. If he inadvertently touched the wrong cables he would be electrocuted.

"Hylin," he said, slowly reclining in his seat. "You are at risk without the scanner. Secure yourself so my screen is not shaking. That way I can get a better look at the panel."

Shifting as told, Hylin did what he could to steady himself in the cramped space, yet as another small blast jeered the ship, he instinctively covered his head. Phydin's view at once was completely obscured. "Can you still hear me, Phydin?" he asked, reclaiming his footing with the settling ship.

"I am still here," he answered, his screen scrambling back to the image.

"This is the best I can do," Hylin said, holding his arms tight against the outer walls so Phydin could survey the panel.

"You are doing well under the circumstances, Hylin," Phydin answered, leaning closer to the screen. "Keep it there and give me a moment."

Phydin looked the panel over and almost instantly could see a few possible breaches, yet they were mere guesses on his part and he hesitated giving Hylin the 'go-ahead.' "Jovaar," he said, prompting the com to the right of his screen. "The boy has reached the panel. He has it open and is about to repair the cables but there is a problem."

"Of course there is, Phydin," Jovaar answered, his frustration evident. "I have several at the moment. What is it now?"

"Hylin is not in possession of the scanner," Phydin continued, running his hands over his face. "Jovaar, he will have to make the repairs live. How would you like me to proceed?"

"I cannot believe that I am saying this but we have no choice, Phydin," he answered, turning again to peer out the weed-filled glass. "We are soon to drop back below radar but we cannot know what is lying in wait and therefore you know as I do that we must have those shields. Even if we get passed the ship above there is still the possibility that we are being trailed through the gorge. It will be difficult, but I need you to walk the boy through it the best you can."

"Yes, Sir," Phydin answered, releasing the com and wiping the newly formed sweat from his face with his sleeve.

"Alright, Hylin," he continued, reopening the line to the headsets and scooting forward in his seat. "This is what you have to do."

***

"Take evasive actions!" the King shouted, the ship sustaining yet another hit from the beast. "All rangers to guns!" he continued, securing his footing against the side wall and balancing against the nearest panel. "I want this nuisance taken care of now!"

"Sir," the pilot said, settling the stick, his comrades hastily keying prompts at their scrambling, unforgiving screens. "This gorge limits our movement and I have not been able to out maneuver the few beasts that remain. Do you want to order an ascent?"

"No, you imbecile," the King shouted, tossing a subordinate to claim the helm. "Do not assume you understand my intentions! We have to stay unnoticed, so keep your men firing and maintain our course as ordered!"

"Aye, Sir," the pilot answered, lowering his head.

Pivoting to Mathius restrained at the rear, the King scowled at the smugness his enemy obviously gloated. "What are they?" he roared, gritting his teeth with impatience. Mathius merely shook his head. The King at once rose from the helm, crossing and lowering himself before his adversary.

"I said," he whispered, mere inches from Mathius' face. "What are they?"

"A momar and her young," Mathius at last answered, openly smiling at the King's frustrations. "It is unwise to upset a momar."

"So I can tell," Carsian answered, rocking sideways and steadying himself as the beast once again made contact with the ship. "But never fear, my old friend," he added, his evil grin widening with a notion, his length imposing as he rose to his feet. "All momars eventually bow to their King."

***

214

"Use the power tester and slowly touch each individual cable," Phydin continued, monitoring Hylin's progress from his station. "Our biggest problem is that the cable in need of repair could be a live one and without the scanner, we have no way of knowing where the breach may lie. Let us hope we learn enough to maximize our chances."

"Alright, Phydin," Hylin answered, pulling the tool before him. "Here I go." Hylin removed the power tester from its holder, extending its pair of testing rods then slowly reached forward, touching their small tips to the cables one at a time.

"One has power," he said, his tense arms shaking as he removed the connection. "I am moving on to the second."

"I am with you," Phydin answered, tapping his screen to zoom left. "Cable one is at one hundred percent and has zero defect," he added, gaining the readout from his monitor. "Keep going, Hylin. You are doing well."

Touching the slender rods to the second cable, Hylin let out a sigh of relief, safely retracing the tips from the line. "Cable two has power," he continued, using his sleeve to wipe the never ending sweat from his brow.

"I have your reading," Phydin answered, pleased with their progress thus far. "Cable two is at fifty percent. It could possibly cause difficulties and will have to come back to it and find its fault, but for now, continue on to the third."

Moving the rods to the final cable as ordered, Hylin immediately sensed the difference from the others. "No power, Phydin," he said, retracting the tester. "We found the problem."

"Hang on while I gain the readout," Phydin answered, tapping at the data on his screen. "No," he continued, at last. "Cable three is an intermittent cable, Hylin. It is shut down until it is needed. Our problem lies with cable two."

"Alright then," Hylin answered, accepting Phydin's word without hesitation, dropping his weary head to the shoot's floor. "Now what do I do?"

Staring at the frozen image Hylin had created on his screen a moment longer, trying desperately to think of another way, Phydin shook his head at the last knowing there was no other choice. You *should* use the scanner to pinpoint the exact fault," he said, leaning closer to stare at the panel. "Yet without it you will have to do select and repair manually. Open the solder and driver sets and find the smallest units," he added, pausing as Hylin followed the order. "This is going to get tricky."

***

"We have destroyed the last of the young, Sir," the gunner ranger said over the com.

"Well done," the King answered, a pleased grin crossing his face. He reclined comfortably in his seat, displaying overt satisfaction to his enemy. "And the momar?"

"As furious as any momar would be," the ranger answered, the ship sustaining yet another hit to the rear.

"Coming up on the gorge exit," the pilot added, rounding the final bend.

"Very well," the King answered, his attention drawn back from the rear hit to Command. "Ascend to depth forty before that monstrosity does any more damage."

"Aye, Sir," he answered, Carsian peering over his shoulder at his enemy.

"It seems we have survived this little snag," he said, his evil grin once again filling the chiseled features of his face. "I am quite certain this angers you and that only adds to my enjoyment. One hundred percent shields and all gunners to their posts!" Carsian ordered, not taking his eyes from Mathius. "The Sugin reign is about to be extended."

***

Selena sat in the rear cabin uncertain of what to do. She had been frightened by the earlier blasts in the gorge, yet with her minimal understanding of the ship, she had successfully opened the com so that she was aware of all transmissions from Command. Although confident that they were away from the angry momar and her young, she now understood that they were engulfed by the Spotted Weed and trailed by the unknown presence above. She could not help but feel torn with not being able to do more for the others.

Nitaya lay sleeping quietly at her side and with the child at last settled regardless of the intermittent blasts from above, Selena became even more restless. Although they had not sustained another hit for some time, she worried that the enemy was merely luring them toward something far worse.

"I cannot take this anymore," she said, wringing her hands and crossing to the panel at the far end of the room. "There must be service capabilities on this type of craft," she whispered, keying the side panel for the search.

Selena's youthful learnings proved useful, her fingers easily dancing across the panel, tapping out her eager request. Smiling confidently with the system darting to life before her, she felt at ease, as she had within her suite atop Central Docking those long ago onars, controlling a similar program.

"There you are," she added, at last tapping the offered odd-shaped prompt on the screen. The requested holoform flickered to a solid form before her. Reclining, Selena smiled in her seat, hands folded confidently behind her head, awaiting the completed image.

The woman-form wore a long, white flowing gown, her dark hair sleeked low, cascading and flowing down her back as if the cabin held a breeze. Her delicate hands remained folded at her waist. Bowing, the holoform reminded Selena of Sir Gidoran's servant.

"May I be of service?" the image asked, her programmed words both soft and comforting.

"Yes," Selena answered, sitting straight in the station's seat. "The child should rest for some time and I have other matters to attend to. I would like for you to inform me as soon as she wakes."

"Of course," the woman answered, gliding across the room and laying her transparent hand on Nitaya's bedside. "Will you require anything else?"

"That is all for now," Selena answered, rising and crossing to the door. "As soon as she wakes," she repeated, waiting for the form to concur.

"Of course," the woman repeated, smiling down at the sleeping child, turning slowly to face Selena. Although she was reluctant to leave Nitaya with the strange new being, Selena was confident that from her own youth and dealings with the forms that Nitaya would be well tended. Prompting the door as the image turned back as expected, peering down at Nitaya, Selena nodded without word then hurried off to see to the others.

***

Exiting the rear cabin, Selena found Jax alone at the gunnery station, slowly descending the exterior track. "Are we passed the danger?" she asked, leaning on the side wall of the outer runner. He turned, startled by her voice.

"I am hopeful yet I am scanning the area to be certain," he answered. Kroy's seat whirred to a rest at the bottom to their left before returning round the bend toward the top. The aweness of the system held her gaze.

"The others are up front at Command," Jax added, disappearing up the left side of the ship from where Kroy had just traveled.

"Thank you," Selena shouted, uncertain if he had heard, her focus at last returned. Shrugging as she now stood alone in the gunnery, the vacant track blinked its silent response with its endless array of lights. Turning, Selena left the pair to their tasks, passing the familiar midship, Phydin curiously monitoring a station in the corner. Leaving him to his duties without question, Selena headed directly to Command.

***

Jovaar stood leaning over Khyra's station talking low as she entered, and standing back to await his acknowledgement, Selena watched and waited to the sounds of the cabin. The constant whir of the various systems was only interrupted by the occasional blip from one of the controls, the remainder of the crew proving deep in concentration. Selena left them to their tasks, tapping her fingers against the door at her back in time with the dancing lights of the panels.

Looking from one station to the other then back to the rear seat that she had claimed at Hylin's side, Selena tightened her eyes, noting the boy's absence. Instinctively she began to worry. Jovaar, secretly watching her, noticed the transformation of her face, her eyes scanning left to right at the crew, and he crossed to her reassuringly.

"Is the child safe, Selena?" he asked, placing his hand on her shoulder. Startled, she jumped at his touch, having not seen him cross the small cabin.

"She is, yes," Selena answered, wringing her hands and looking over Jovaar's shoulder. "But where is Hylin?"

"At the moment he is in a shoot at the rear of the ship," he answered, calming her hands with his own. "And hopefully he is repairing our damaged shields."

"Is he all right?" Selena asked, grabbing Jovaar's arm with worry. "I was listening to your conversations from Command and knew that someone was overseeing the shield repairs, yet I never guessed it would by Hylin. Should he be doing something so difficult? He is only a boy, Jovaar. Why would you not send Jax or Kroy? Surely they would be better suited."

"We had no other choice," he answered, placing his arm about her shoulder. "He was the only one who could fit in the tiny space. It pleases me that you were able to prompt the system, Lena," he added, attempting to change the subject and calm her fears. "Not everyone has the knowledge to do so. You had long ago said how unuseful you felt. It seems you have skills even you had forgotten."

"Do not coddle me, Jovi," she whispered, shoving free of his arm and placing her hands on her hips. "Hylin is somewhere in this ship doing things a boy should never be forced to do and your attempts at appeasing me are taking the attention away from him."

"I had a point," Jovaar continued, a grin creeping to his face.

"And it was?" she asked, annoyed.

"My point is that you yourself possess skills that not all have abilities to match," he answered, his voice calming. "Hylin is no different. At this moment he is performing a task that Jax or Kroy trained onars to do. I was wrong to call him a boy and I am confident he will be fine. Why do you not return to mid-ship and see for yourself? Phydin is guiding Hylin through the

219

procedures and Khyra has dropped us back below radar which as you can feel has ceased the blasts from above. We should be able to maneuver undetected for the time being so for now you are free to move about the ship, however I am afraid it should not take the Sugin's long to pick up our trail again so you must be prepared to restrain at a moment's notice."

"I have been speaking with Khyra and Luvin about an alternative route, and…" he added, glancing over his shoulder to his pilot. "And I really need to get back to it. Go to Phydin and see for yourself how the boy, forgive me, I mean how Hylin is doing."

"I am sorry I interrupted," she whispered, feeling a bit brushed aside.

"You did not interrupt," he said, reassuring her with his smile. "There is just so much still to do. If I get a spare moment, I will come back and look in on you."

"All right then," Selena answered, knowing he was right. "If I can help in any way…"

"You have the most important job of us all, Lena," Jovaar interrupted, reclaiming her hands. "And I am proud of your strength and how you have handled yourself. But I need to do my part now."

"Jovaar," Khyra said, interrupted the pair.

"I am coming," he answered, turning back briefly to Selena. "Now go," he added, slowly brushing her cheek with the back of his hand. Turning, he left her to return to his pilot.

Watching Jovaar once again lean over Khyra's shoulder, Selena's thoughts quickly returned to Hylin. Turning to prompt the Command door, she set out in search of Phydin to oversee the younger's progress.

***

Sweat streaked annoyingly to his eyes and his legs were beginning to cramp, his muscles tense pushing against the confines of the shoot. "Now what?" Hylin asked, impatiently waiting for Phydin's instructions.

"Take the driver and wedge it between the cable and the panel wall just below where the visable gash is located," he answered, zooming his screen in on the tear. "Yet watch that the metal does not, I repeat does *not* touch the fibers."

Staring at his screen, Hylin carefully wedged the tool as instructed. Phydin did not turn at the sound of the Command door. "How is he doing?" Selena whispered nervously, trying not to interrupt.

"Oh," Phydin answered, attempting surprise. "I thought you were Jovaar. He is uh..." he paused, turning back to his screen. "So far so good."

Jovaar had warned him over the com that Selena was headed his way and that she was overly worried, ordering him not to tell her the dangers of their task. "Hylin is at the damaged site now and he is just beginning the repairs," he added. "However they should not take long and therefore he should be out of there soon."

"That is wonderful news," Selena answered, placing her hand to her chest. "I must admit I began to panic when I heard what you two were up to.

"No need, I assure you," Phydin answered, attempting to prove himself relaxed, crossing his ankle over his knee. "It is a very minor..."

"I am all set, Phydin," Hylin interrupted, having secured the wedge. "Now what do I do?" Phydin motioned to Selena that he had to return to his task. Pivoting back to his darkened screen, he leaned forward to closely look over Hylin's handiwork.

"Well done, Hylin," he said, pleased. Staring at the panel through the bouncing light of the boy's headset, he nodded with growing confidence. "Now open the solder kit and place the eye lenses on."

Adjusting his position within the cramped shoot, Hylin reached low for the kit and opened it, finding the small box that contained the lenses. "Are these supposed to hurt?" he asked frustratingly, placing the small discs onto the surfaces of his eyes.

"No," Phydin answered, shaking his head. "You must have them on backwards. Take them back out and place the rounded side on the curve eye. Hold your lids out and after a moment they will form fit similar to your second eyes."

Doing as told, Hylin withdrew the tiny discs then reinserted them, his elbows growing raw against the metal beneath him. "They closed in just like the headset," he said, blinking rapidly.

"Then they are in correctly, Hylin," Phydin answered, nodding to Selena. "Now take the solder and slowly work your way bottom to top."

"Bottom to top?" he questioned, turning the device in his hands. "Should I not work top to bottom?"

"No, Hylin, you should not work top to bottom," he answered, Selena leaning over his shoulder trying desperately to understand what was happening. "Work bottom to top as the solder possesses its own gravitational force and do not at any time touch the fibers. You will be working on the outer cable only."

"But how will…" he asked.

"Hylin I do not have time to explain this," Phydin interrupted, impatiently gritting his teeth. "Just work bottom to top up one side, then bottom to top up the other. You will repeat the process until the outer gap is sealed."

"What about the damage to the fibers?" Hylin asked, resecuring his footing against the shoot's outer walls.

"I will take care of them on this end once the cable is sealed," Phydin answered, fearful the boy was taking to long. "Just get going."

"Alright," Hylin answered, wiping the never-ending sweat from his brow. "Everything is all green now that I have these lenses on. Here goes."

Phydin sat back and Selena dropped to one knee, the pair watching the teetering light of Hylin's headset side by side as he set to work. "Are there any risks?" she asked, peering up into his eyes.

"There is more risk if we do nothing," Phydin answered, steering clear of the brunt of her question.

"What will happen if we sustatin another hit while he is in there?" Selena pressed, returning her gaze to the screen. "I realize we are once again below radar, but Jovaar said we could be found out at any moment."

"I hate to consider the notion," Phydin said, his gaze at last turning to Selena. "Let us just pray that that does not happen."

Twenty

"We are through the gorge and climbing, Sir," the data station ranger said, turning to his commander.

"What is the younger Savius' position?" he asked, pacing the narrow cabin at his back.

"They have dropped back below radar, Sir," he answered, nervously. "The ship above is unable to track them now."

"That is obvious!" the King roared, grasping his hands at his back. "Those beasts took up too much time! You," he added, pointing to the ranger at the navigation station to his left. "How much map is left?"

"I am afraid not much, Sir," the man answered, watching the trail dwindle on his screen. "And I cannot pinpoint a destination. There is just nothing out there, Sir."

"Well, hone your search and find something you imbecile!" the King shouted, his face reddening in anger. "I have not come half way around the galaxy to fail."

"Aye, Sir," the ranger answered, hesitantly prompting his alternate screen, his comrades hunkering low in their seats.

"You there," the King continued, motioning to the two rangers at the rear. The pair straightened to attention with their leader's prompting. "Restrain the prisoner's legs and bring me my gear."

Waiting impatiently for his men to follow his word, the King watched Mathius' eyes as the rangers briefly left the cabin. Turning to the glass to think, a smile soon filled his face as each of his men returned holding a strap of the large black tote.

"Set it down in front of him and open it," Carsian ordered, without turning from the glass. "Let Savius have a good look at his near future."

Following orders, one ranger restrained Mathius' legs as the other opened the tote at his feet. Spying the device, Mathius instinctively struggled against his restraints.

"I grow weary of your silence," the King said, grimacing and at last turning from the glass. "It is a shame that I carried a mere one vial of my beloved serum, yet I must admit now that I quite relish not having the substance at hand. Instead, you will willingly give me the information I seek or you will suffer greatly for your silence. The choice, my old friend, is ultimately yours."

Continuing his protest and gritting his teeth, Carsian turned from both his nemises and the tote to resume his pacing, choosing to make Mathius wait for his torture without audience. "Continue our path," he calmly ordered, pointing to the pilot. "I want three routes laid out to consider for the next sector. Inform me when the information is available. Once determined, Mathius and I," he added, glaring over his shoulder. "We will *discuss* our options,"

***

"To be prepared, we have to assume they have stolen the portal map and are closing in, Sir," Luvin said, reluctantly. "Despite that, I have been scanning the next sector and I am not so certain we will be able to deviate. There was obviously a reason the path was laid out as it was."

"See here?" he added, pointing at the right of his screen. "The terrain is mainly uncharted territory and regardless of our advances, my systems cannot get specifics on the life that may be out there. We may run into more beasts like the momar or we could sail straight though unnoticed. I just do not know, Sir."

Jovaar, having stared at the route on Luvin's screen, dropped his head to consider their options. Their path had been laid out onars before yet he could not resign himself to consider it, and it alone. "What do you think, Khyra?" he asked, at last raising his head.

"We need the shields at one hundred percent, Jovaar," she answered, not turning from the eyepiece. "Without them I think we have no other choice than to stray from the course. Although

I have piloted a submersible in the past, you saw that I was not so graceful through the egg field. If we end up facing the Sugins, I am not so certain I will be able to out-maneuver them. I say we stray off course and take our chances. But it is up to you of course."

Jovaar exhaled deeply, eyeing the others and raking his fingers through his hair. "Let me see to the shield and Hylin's progress before I make a decision," he said, shaking his head. "Khyra, stay the current course until I return. I will not be long, but let me know if we run into anything else."

***

"This is not that easy, Phydin. On the last pass I burned my blasted hand!" Hylin shouted from the shoot.

"Just concentrate," Phydin answered, looking over at Selena's worried face. "I know you can do this."

"How long has he been in there?" Selena asked, now sitting on a small gray crate that she had pulled near Phydin.

"Quite some time," he answered, sitting back and crossing his arms. "But he has to get this done, no matter how long it takes. Regardless that we are well below radar, our shields have been down for far too long."

"That was good, Hylin," he added in encouragement, sitting straight and leaning toward the mid-ship screen. "One more pass and I believe you have got it."

"I swear I will nourish on everything on this ship once I am through and then I will never volunteer for anything like this again!" he said in frustration. "I would even drink the juice of the blasted cympas, and oh how I loathe those!"

"Easy now," Phydin continued, his grin evident. His eyes never leaving Hylin's panel, he leaned ever closer to his own. "That is it...just a little more...there!" he said, sighing in relief. "Now get yourself out of there."

"Gladly," Hylin said, reaching to regather the tools. "It will take me a moment longer on the way out having to scoot backward."

"I will continue to have you on the headset and will watch your progress," Phydin answered, nodding with

226

encouragement to Selena. "Then I will meet you at the exit to assist you down."

"I am moving out," Hylin said, smiling and shimmying feet first, dragging the tools above his head. Selena, staring at the flickering light of his narrow journey on screen, spied something out of place and grabbed Phydin's shoulder instinctively.

"There," she said, pointing just as the panel left their view. "Is that important?"

"What?" Phydin asked, pivoting back to the darkened panel. "What did you see?"

"I am not certain," she answered, rising from the crate. "But if you would have Hylin move back, I can show you."

"Hylin," Phydin said, sighing as he tapped the side of his headset. "You must go back to the panel."

"Go back?" Hylin groaned, his frustration evident. "You have to be mad, Phydin! I am so very…"

"No, Hylin, go back," Phydin pressed, his tone serious. "Selena believes she saw something we missed."

"Since when does Selena know anything about the wiring of a submersible," he asked rudely, lowering his head to the metal beneath him. "My legs are stiff and my arms are…"

"Just go back," Phydin ordered, the pair staring at the mid-ship screen and the return of the flickering light.

With Hylin once again in position, Selena leaned even closer to Phydin's panel and with her eyes mere inches from the screen, squinted at what appeared to be a slight fracture. "There," she said, pointing to the bottom of the image. "Is that another gash?"

"No," Phydin answered, confidently shaking his head. "All the areas were sealed."

"Are you certain?" Selena pressed, wrinkling her brow. "It is the same cable."

"Then I suppose we will seal it to appease your fears," Phydin added, reluctantly turning to the screen. "Hylin," he added, staring at the slight tear on the cable. "I am afraid Selena has provided a little more work for you to do."

***

Legs bound and arms restrained at his back, Mathius wished so very much that he could take drink, yet he would never show his weakness by making the request. Carsian had been busy giving orders and pacing the narrow aisle of the cabin, ignoring his prisoner, his black robe flowing violently at his ankles. His rangers feared him, anyone could see it in their eyes, and although five remained in command, Mathius could not be certain how many were in the rear. Knowing the schematics of the craft however, he assumed it was fully loaded for twelve. But what did it matter? He could not finish them all off, especially in his current position.

Intently listening to Carsian's orders of their current depth and the guestimated location of his son, Mathius took in every detail of his surroundings, including what weapons were installed, how many Polatia had been destroyed, their current path, and the ever growing irritation of the King and his crew. It seemed it would be of little use to him, yet there was nothing else he could do, for the rangers had confiscated his prime weapon the moment he was taken.

Although certain the King's men would find his only remaining hope with the binding of his legs, they thankfully missed the hidden blade and had not thus far removed it from his calf. Reaching it at this point however proved impossible, and so instead he listened to Carsian's never-ending ramblings while concentrating on unbinding his hands.

It was in his favor that Carsian's cronies had chosen to use simple twine rather than the commonly used metal clamps, and as he continued his desperate attempt to work out the array of knots, he smiled inwardly at the first two giving way with little difficulty. Tedious as it proved to be, it was his only hope of avoiding the device waiting in the black tote at his knees.

"So, my old friend," the King said, turning his attention again to his adversary. "Have you decided to at last speak?"

Gritting his teeth, Mathius merely shook his head, secretly continuing to work at the knots at his back.

"Well then," the King continued, folding his arms confidently at his back. "With your choice of silence, we will have to rely on *other* methods. Ranger!" he grunted, his voice

228

filled with rage as he gestured to the man closest to them. "Begin the electro-process. Let us see how much the old man can endure."

Kneeling before the black tote at Mathius' feet, the ranger reached within and quickly prompted the control to begin the process. With the whir of the device filling their ears, Carsian stood smiling, folding his arms at his chest as Mathius stared wide-eyed at the monstrosity growing slowly from its home.

Robotic and slender, the machine folded out in short lengths, each jointed leg extending and straightening as it rose. Its C-shaped head and evil pair of prongs jutted unforgivingly forward. Although consisting mostly of the strange dark green hued metal, several colorful tubes and wires ran the length of its frame, supporting the menace Mathius knew it provided. The face of the device however held his eyes. When at last the threat stood erect, its height reached Mathius chest then as expected abruptly froze, waiting further prompting.

"Dial in minor," the King ordered, the ranger making the necessary adjustment without question Backing away from the King's prized weapon, all watched as at once the unit's head became surrounded in the reddish glow, electricity flowing violently from one protruding tip to the other. Reaching capacity, the King stared intently as the head inched forward to its prey.

Amazingly powerful for being labeled minor, the first jolt violently gyrated Mathius upon the floor and all watched as the unit pressed inward, receding then pressed inward again. Only moments were allowed for recovering from his spasms in between jolts. Struggling against his restraints, all eyes remained on his pain. As the fourth pass cleared, Carsian ordered the ranger to cease with a simple wave of his hand.

"I would like a moment," he said, leaning around the device to Mathius. "Are you ready then?" he asked, grinning widely and staring into his enemy's eyes. Mathius refused to speak, his glazed eyes refusing to show fear. The King merely laughed, turning his back to his enemy.

"I thought not," he said, crossing to the glass and staring into the darkness of the sea. "Dial in mediate!"

More brutal than the last, the next wave of assaults exuded such power that Mathius was certain he would lose consciousness. As before, the device retreated then stabbed at him again. Finding the effects waning against his tired body, Mathius' inner strength prepared without mindful assistance for each dealing lash.

Struggling within the restraints and jarring against them with each bolt, Mathius grit his teeth, fighting the urge to strain as he fumbled with the neverending series of knots at his back. Unwilling to reveal his pain with shouts, he glared at Carsain, the prongs moving in for the last of their sequence.

"Another moment if you will," the King said calmly, the ranger again kneeling to cease the torture. "Now, Savius?" he asked, allowing his adversary a moment to catch his breath. "Just give me something, my friend, and I can make this stop.

"I will give you nothing!" Mathius shouted, gritting his teeth against the shivering of exhaustion his muscles felt, sweat beading without end on his brow.

"So it continues then," the King said, carelessly shrugging his shoulders as he looked to his faithful servant. "Ranger, dial in maximum strength!"

"Aye, Sir,' the man answered, prompting the controls. As ordered, the unit once again whirred to life, its tone however strengthened with the growing intesity.

"This is your last chance," the King whispered into Mathius's ear. Turning to look straight into the eyes of death, the unit closing in, Mathius lashed out. Taking hold of the powerful device and experiencing the worst pain he had ever felt, Mathius somehow managed to turn the head of the mechanism, ramming it into the King's eyes. Releasing the machine and its unending glow of shocks, he fell lifeless into the back of his seat.

Wailing on excruciating pain the King wretched to the floor, the electricity flowing violently through him. The ranger responsible for the device darted to the tote, at last ceasing the torture but his movements proved too late. As the King dropped prone to the floor, lying on his back with eyes blackened from the intense heat, Mathius breathed his last breath. All thoughts of his nemesis for the moment forgotten, Carsian jolted with uncontrollable spasms.

"King Sugin!" the ranger shouted, scooting toward his Commander's face, his comrades looking on, uncertain what to do. "Can you hear me, Sir?" he asked, helplessly straightening his King's limbs.

"I..." Carsian answered, struggling to open his eyes, his body flitting with aftershock. "It..." he continued, slowly blinking as he attempted to find words.

"It is alright, Sir," the ranger continued, spying no movement from Mathius then motioning for his comrades to assist with their leader. "The prisoner is dead, Sir. We will take you to Med-deck and..." he continued, the King slowly turning his head, at last opening his eyes.

"I..." he repeated, grasping the ranger's arm and forcing him near. "I am blind."

Twenty-One

"That should just about do it, Hylin," Phydin said, arms folded as the boy solder the final strip. "Well done."

"I will regather the equipment together and should be heading back momentarily," he answered, thankful the task was complete. "I will meet you at the drop."

"Selena, if you would not mind," Phydin said, pivoting in his seat to face her. "Could you meet him there? The shaft is just at the near corner of the midship entrance to command. Hylin will need some assistance getting down and I really need to get working on the fibers."

"It is not fixed then?" she questioned, startled and gesturing to the screen. "I thought Hylin…"

"Hylin only sealed the cables," he interrupted, turning back to his panel. "I still need to repair the damaged fibers inside."

"You can do that from here?" she asked, rising to stand at his back.

"I can, yes," he answered, keying furiously on his panel. "We had to repair the outer shell on site though, in order to protect the current flow. If you could just wait for him at the shoot drop…"

"Of course," she answered, patting his shoulder and replacing the small crate to the corner of the cabin. "Shall I bring Hylin back to you to see to the final stage of repairs?"

"No," Phydin answered, tapping his screen. "Just take the boy to the rear to get some rest. I am certain he needs it." Nodding, Selena turned and left Phydin to his final task then eagerly set out to await Hylin at the drop.

***

"Remove the body and get me to quarters," the King ordered, struggling against his agony. The two nearest rangers assisted him to his feet as another released Mathius' leg restraints, dragging him simultaneously from command. With an arm around each of his subordinates and relying completely the burden of his entire weight upon them, Carsian stepped slowly from Command, gingerly making his way down the narrow corridor to the rear cabin.

"Help me lie down and then order the AP to take over the ship," he said, reaching out blindly for the low cot. "I need to have a few words alone with the pilot and navigator. Send for them at once."

"Aye, Sir," they answered in unison, one unclasping the King's black cloak. Placing it on the hook next to the cot, he stood silent as the other assisted their ruler prone.

"Now go!" the King gasped, the strength of his limbs only slightly returning, attempting authority and flickering his hand. Once situated and lying in his enemy's hand-made darkness, Carsian refused to speak further in their presence, yet listened intently as the two left the cabin without a word.

"How foolish of me!" he grumbled, confident he was at last alone, covering his face with his hands. "How blasted foolish! I should have known Mathius would find a way regardless that it cost him his life. I should not have trusted these fools to see to his restraints! See? I *cannot* see! And I have no way of..." he stopped, his remaining senses piqued as he heard the pair enter.

"Sir," one said, the duo rounding to his side, snapping firm to attention. "You requested council?"

"Yes," the King answered, lowering his arms from his face. "I need to know our exact options. How much of the map is left?" The ranger serving as NAV stepped forward.

"We have reached the end of the retrieved route, Sir," he answered, hesitantly eyeing his comrade. "I was hoping we would be successful in gathering more information from the prisoner, Sir, yet..."

"An answer of zero-map would be sufficient ranger," Carsian interrupted, gritting his teeth in frustration. "Pilot!

233

What setting is our course? Has there been any further sightings of the younger Savius' craft?"

"We are sailing blind, Sir," he answered, instantly regretting his choice of words, quivering at the King's side. "I meant we…I mean…" he said, his discomfort evident.

"I know what you meant, ranger! I may be temporarily unable to see but I am not ignorant!" the King roared, flailing his arms, unable to find light in his darkness. "What you are saying is we have zero-map and are sailing with no course. Have our radars either above or below picked up any sign of the enemy ship?"

"No, Sir," the second ranger answered, afraid to anger the King further, stifling his stuttering comrade with his hand.

"Well then," the King continued, angered at having to rely on his obvious incompetent crew. "It seems we have hit yet another setback, but I say this now. In the end we will prevail. Pilot!" he shouted, balling his fists. "We are to return to Mathius' docks and board the airship. We will monitor the skies for as long as it takes. You are to deviate and perform a one-eighty and sail above the gorge. I see no reason to awaken the beast again. Inform the AS of our new coordinates and have them fully fueled and on alert awaiting our arrive. Now leave me!"

"Aye, Sir," they answered as one, yet the pilot although hesitant pressed further. "I will send for you once we dock," he added, bowing.

"That is all!" Carsian roared, bearing his grave annoyance. Laying prone on his cot, he folded his arms as the rangers quickly left to inform the others.

"I promise you, young Savius," he whispered, confident he was once again alone, staring into his temporary darkness. "This is not over yet."

***

"I cannot believe you said we were sailing blind," the NAV ranger chided, the pair walking briskly back to Command.

"Stuff it," the pilot answered, anger filling him for his foolishness. Without further thought, he gave the ranger a harsh backhand to his midsection.

"Touchy," the NAV answered with a slight smile, catching his breath against the blow. Reaching the end of the corridor, he could not contain his smile once he prompted the door to Command.

"All personnel prepare for roundabout," the pilot ordered, ignoring the slight and stomping passed the helm. "We are to head back to the airship per the King's order."

"What about the beast?" a ranger asked to his right.

"We are sailing above the gorge on return," he answered, crossing to the pilot seat, his comrade reclaiming his own station. "Inform the airship commander to meet us for boarding."

"Aye," the rangers answered, the pilot at last restrained, lowering the overhead control and tapping the cease of the manual function.

"DO," he continued, without turning. "Inform me of any obstacles outlined above. We needn't displease the King with further delays."

"Aye," he answered pivoting at his station, the NAV officer relaying his data to the pilot's screen.

"Coming about," the pilot continued, pivoting the stick. "Ascending to thirty depth."

"We should ascend to twenty depth," the NAV added, silencing the crew.

"Reason?" the pilot asked, peering over his shoulder.

"There is an unknown substance above the gorge," he answered, scanning the endless data. "I cannot get a definition but I insist on a greater ascent."

The pilot considered the officer's recommendation in silence. Searching the data on his own side screen and recalling what they had faced earlier, he saw no other option than to agree.

"Twenty depth then," he ordered, having for the time being forgotten the earlier error of his words. "Inform the airship of our coordinates. We do not need any further mistakes."

"Aye," the pilot heard in response. With the ship quickly gaining speed into the shallow of the deep at the instruction of his hand, the crew settled in to carry their commander home.

***

"Phydin, are you still there?" Hylin asked, his voice echoing in the slender shoot. "I am almost to the end of the pass."

"Selena is at the drop to assist you on your climb down," Phydin answered, quickly eyeing the boy's progress on his split screen then returning his focus to the task of repairs.

"Selena!" Hylin shouted, knowing she could not possess a headset. "Can you hear me?"

"I am here," she answered from below. "What can I do?"

"I am going to pass over the drop and hand down the tools," he answered, scooting another length backward. "They are heavy so be ready."

Staring above her at the open hole, Selena watched Hylin's feet come into view, his legs and chest slowly passing by overhead. "Here," he said, lowering the first of the many tools, leaving the tote containing those he had left behind for the last. Thankful to breathe the fresh air of the ship, he could not help but pause for a moment, gasping in his position above, his garb drenched in his own anxious sweat.

With the last of the loose tools accounted for, Hylin retrieved the lightened tote possessing the ever-important scanner he had left at the drop at those blasted cables! Lowering it and creeping forward until his feet once again appeared before Selena, he slowly lowered them, hanging finally at the waist.

"I have got you," Selena said, struggling to grab hold, Hylin releasing his full weight into her hands. At last releasing him unceremoniously to the floor, Selena gathered his soaked frame to her, brushing his sopping hair from his face as he gasped for air.

"You are to head to the rear for rest," she said, her hands squeezing the sides of his face. "And I will bring you all the nourishment and drink you can handle."

"I am all right," Hylin answered, panting and lowering to his knees, his legs weak with exhaustion. "I just need to get to Phydin in case we…"

"Phydin specifically ordered for you to return to the rear," Selena interrupted, rising and extending her hand at Hylin's attempted protest. "You will rest and get freshened and it will give me a chance to look in on Nitaya."

"I will hear no argument, Hylin," she added, waving off his firm hand and assisting him to rise. "Leave the tools where they are and come. You can see that they get to their proper place as soon as you are back to your old self."

In his current state of exhaustion, Hylin had no strength to argue. As Selena put her arm around his waist to help him rise, she led him passed the row of rear seats and Phydin's back, the elder tapping his screen to repair the shield's damage. Hylin's tired limbs proved he had no choice but to let her lead.

***

"We have made very good time, Sir, and should be arriving within the hazon," the ranger said, standing at attention at the foot of the King's bed. The King gave no response to his update, the subordinate staggering, bending to repeat his words.

"Take me to Command," the King said at last, licking his lips. "I will wait out the final moments of our arrival there."

"Aye, Sir," the ranger answered, thankful to gain a response. Quickly he scrambled to reach cotside as the King's attempted to rise.

"I am blind, but I am not useless!" Carsian roared, the ranger fumbling with his his arm, uncertain how to proceed. "Just lead the way," he snorted angrily.

Trying desperately to honor his King's wishes, the ranger did his best to comply. Uttering not another word in fear of upsetting him further, he carefully led him through the cabin door toward Command.

***

"An update!" the King shouted, the rangers rising to his words as Carsian reclaimed the helm.

"We have begun our final approach, Sir," the pilot said, turning back to prompt the ship to manual. "The airship is on

237

standby, is fully fueled and ready to depart as ordered. I have informed the Med-Officer of your…situation. He has the clean room ready for procedure."

"It seems for once all is in order," the King said, his tone calming. Grumbling, he shooed his subordinate away. "Any sign of the younger Savius?"

"No, Sir," the pilot answered, returning to the stick. "Not from below or above. All probabilities suggest they have continued their laid out path."

"As I suspected," the King answered, sensing the pilot's return to his station by the tone of his voice.

"DC update," the pilot ordered, moreso to inform the King than himself, his attention firm to the stick.

"All systems clear," he answered, repeating his earlier words.

"NAV update," the pilot continued, unturning.

"NAV clear," he answered repeating his own, the ship breaching the surface, sailing toward the dock.

"Preparing for attachment to the airship in 5, 4, 3, 2, 1, attach," the pilot ordered, the ship careening only slightly with the joining of the massive ship above. "Systems stalled," he added at the last, the ship's controls claimed by the docking system.

"Sir," he continued, pivoting in his seat. "We are ready for your debarkment. I will remain behind and finish the last of the procedures."

"Very well," Carsian answered, rising from the helm and motioning for assistance. Returning to his tasks, the pilot could not help but peer over his shoulder at his confident King slowly being led from the submersible.

    ***

Reaching the enormous dock and spying the contingency approaching to their right, the King's rangers held him vertical to await the First Officer's approach. Flanked by four of his men, the heavy wet Kindawan air filled their senses.

"I relish the thought of being rid of this planet," the King said, loud enough for the five approaching men to hear.

"Welcome back, my King," the First Officer said, tipping his head in customary respect regardless of his master's current state. The rangers slammed their weapons to the dock in formation, claiming their positions.

"There is no time for pleasantries, Terdoni," he answered firmly, recognizing his subordinate's voice. "We must leave at once to monitor the planet from above."

"Of course, my King," he answered, moving to the side to allow the rangers to lead the King from the ship's dock. Nodding to the others that stood waiting, he quickly followed King Carsian toward the open door.

With the last of the rangers walking the flat catwalk, the final guard entered the main of the ship. As programmed, the plank pulled free, retreating back within the wall. With a flick of his hand at the panel to his right, Terdoni peered over his shoulder through the entrance, smiling as the now useless submersible was sent back to whence it had come.

    ***

"We are coming up on the First Sector and will be beginning approach within less than a half hazon," Khyra said, the Spotted Weed long forgotten at their backs. Prompting the stick forward, she could not be more pleased with her results. "I am pulling all screens to main but I suggest you use the glass. The view is simply unbelievable."

Turning to her suggestion, Jovaar watched tiny specks of light fill his view, and with the nearing ship, the images grew more intense, seeming to multiply before their eyes. As Khyra steered the craft around the monstrous-sized rock, the lights gave way to the gloriness of the city. Displayed calmly before them deep within the cavern, Jovaar's anxiety at last waned.

Appearing in vibrant random colors against the darkened backdrop of the sea, Jovaar and the others peered through the glass at the awaiting city. Distinguishing between compartments, the many brightly lit shoots connecting them, several small ships sailed normally amongst their passes. Three however, headed directly in their direction. Having been informed by Jovaar that they were welcome, Khyra held firm to

239

their course. When the first small jolt hit the ship however, she looked to him in surprise.

"Why are they firing at us?" she asked, not knowing how to respond, attempting to secure the ship's shields.

"No damage sustained," Orvi reported, before Jovaar could respond. "Shields are at one hundred percent."

Smiling simultaneously for being thankful that Phydin and Hylin were able to repair the shields and for their uneventful arrival, Jovaar shook his head. It was unthinkable that the submersive sustained yet another jolt. The slight tremor was so slight with the shield in proper form.

"It is minor fire," he said, prompting his screen. "And with the shields up and at last operational we should be fine. Khyra, keep you current course and Orvi pull up the communications log. Get me the sequence for Polatus."

"Yes, Sir," he answered, Phydin racing into the cabin to see what the commotion was about.

"It seems we got the shield repaired just in time," he said, pacing to Jovaar's side. "The last of the repairs took longer than I anticipated yet regardless, their importance obviously proves justified. Selena and Hylin have returned to the rear quarters with the child. Who is firing on us now?"

"Polatian guards," Jovaar answered, not turning from his panel. "Yet it is only because they do not recognize us. I am confident that once they know who we are we will gain clear passage. Orvi, do you have the sequence?"

"I have just entered it and we should be good to…" he answered, the strange voice interrupting over the com.

"State your purpose and cargo," the foreign voice said, sailing swiftly port side before rounding starboard. Jovaar quickly bypassed Khyra's controls.

"Resistance submersible," Jovaar began, looking to his pilot who merely shook her head and steered toward the docks. "Carrying only passengers and seeking clearance to Polatus Landing Bay Four. Jovaar Savius. I am scheduled for council with Prince Iaco."

The long pause that ensued caused Jovaar to question his own confidence, yet he sat exuding the opposite, turning to stare out at the deep city. "Ease up," Jovaar said, smiling. The members about him collectively held their breath. "I assure you, we are expected and...."

"Resistance ship to Polatus Landing Bay Four, cleared to proceed," the voice answered without fanfare. "Prince Iaco awaits your arrival. Please pardon our indescretion."

"As I told you," Jovaar said, sighing privately in relief and resettling into his seat at the helm. "Luvin," he continued, turning to the obvious engrossed man. "You should find the path to Bay Four in the sub-box attached to the Polatus screen file. Pull it up and patch it through to Khyra's screen."

"Yes, Sir," he answered, turning from the glass and keying his panel. Within a few moments, he transferred the data and Khyra had the coordinates. Smoothly she proceeded passed the station on their left, under and over the many glass shoots.

"Selena," Jovaar continued, prompting the com. "Bring Hylin and the child to Command. We should be arriving shortly. You are missing an amazing view."

"We felt the ship slow earlier and of course the minor blasts," she answered, having returned to Nitaya's side. "We have been watching our arrival from the rear. It really is beautiful, but what is with the fire? Are we in any danger?"

"It is nothing for you to be concerned with," he answered, reassuringly. "Just come to Command for docking."

"We are on our way," she answered, silencing the com.

Khyra continued with confidence on their current path knowing Jovaar had asked the others to the helm. Taking notice of Bay Four as they neared the massive dock, she slowed the stick, readying herself for attachment.

"Up ahead, Jovaar," she said, gesturing toward the large opening.

"Bay Four is clear for landing," the strange voice said into the com. Steering clear of the surrounding shoots for their entrance, Khyra confidently manned the controls much to Phydin's obvious displeasure, guiding them in.

***

Although engulfed within the deep waters of the Kindawan sea, Khyra could clearly see on her screen the images of the two-pronged dock, steering the ship low than upward to their ordered port. Guiding the ship with ease through the endless shoots, avoiding both smaller crafts and transports, she succeeded in attaching to the dock's large prongs somewhat smoothly.

"All systems stalled," she said, tapping the last of the required steps and raising the overhead controls. With the lift transporting the members the final distance of their journey below, all turned to watch the bay doors close at their backs, marveling out the glass at the silent meeting of the seams simultaneous with their landing. Sitting in awe, no one spoke of the water rapidly receding about them.

"If anything or anyone had been in that bay during the drainage," Khyra thought, shaking her head at the amazing image opposite the glass. "They would have most certainly have been sucked out with the sea."

Once the sounding was given 'all clear to proceed,' the blue light of port danced throughout the area. Startled, Khyra's hands jolted from the controls to her face with the surprising opening of the ship's side hatch without prompting.

"Apparently our controls are now being operated by someone or something within Polatus," she said, staring at her panel as Selena entered Command with Hylin and the child. "Are you certain that this Prince Iaco is a friend of the Resistance?"

Nodding to his pilot while reassuringly smiling and patting Selena's hand, Jovaar rose to speak with his crew. "We will not be returning to this ship," he stated, turning to face the eager members, taking firm hold of Hylin's shoulder to turn the boy's anxious eyes from the glass. "Following the plans set forth by my palle, it is to be demolished soon after our arrival on Polatus so that no trace can be set upon it. I am debarking now to present our contigency to Prince Iaco. While I am beyond our walls, I need you to strip the ship of all essentials and be prepared to haul them once directed. I will see that someone is sent for you shortly to assist."

"Yes, Sir," they answered in unison, Selena's grip firm on his arm.

"Are we to wait behind also?" she asked, looking down at the sleeping child then back to Jovaar.

"Of course not, Lena," he whispered, warmly smiling and claiming her hand. "It is Nitaya who we are to present. Now let us go," he added for all to hear, both Jax and Kroy joining the rest of the group at Command. "We do not want to keep Prince Iaco waiting."

***

"King Sugin," the Med-Officer began, crossing the cold cabin to his commander's side. "It is truly an honor."

"Are you ready to begin?" the King asked, annoyed as he lay prone on the cot.

"We are," the officer answered, gesturing to the ranger toward the clean room, guiding the King forward.

"Instruct Terdoni to inform me the moment he finds them," the King whispered, gritting his teeth. He had been foolish to allow Mathius' bravery to divert him from his task.

"Aye Sir," the ranger answered, the Med-Officer halting him at the clean room door.

"I will lead him from here," he continued, not looking to the ranger. "Your services are no longer required." Nodding, the ranger turned and left the corridor without word.

"My King," the Med-Officer continued, laying his gloved hand on his ruler's arm. "If you will allow me to…"

"Just get on with it," Carsian interrupted, shooing the MO's hand.

Choosing to defer from comforting words that were obviously unwelcomed, instead silently guiding Carsian's cot to the center of the room, the Med-Officer hesitantly patted his commander's shoulder. Shaking his head, he at last turned to his screens.

"You may begin the program," he said, nodding to his assistant who sat awaiting the order at the prompter across the room. With the man expertly entering the sequence of data, the Med-Officer turned back to his patient, the lights instantly dimming with the device beginning its descent from above.

Long, box-like and thin, its neck stretched downward, the Med-Officer's impatience evident with his reaching up to help guide it into position. "This will not hurt, Sir," he said, lowering the device. "Yet the program is extensive and will take some time. You will feel some slight pressures on either side of your head as the mechanism closes in to restrict your movement. Once the program begins, we cannot cease it until we have reached completion. If you are satisfied with this, we will begin."

"Just get on with it," Carsian repeated, feeling tense and equally impatient, gritting his teeth as the MO began the program. Laying still at the officer's urging, Carsian knew the sequence and sensed the sounds of the mechanical arms springing forth about his face.

"I am crossing the cabin to the prompter," the MO said, the King lying silent on the cot. "The program will begin momentarily."

***

Jovaar led Selena and the slumbering child down the narrow plank, seawater trickling away at their feet through the system's drains. Moisture clearly hung in the air dampening their skin as they crossed the narrow platform, the trio continuing without assistance toward the large set of doors.

"Is noone to welcome..." Selena whispered, pausing as the far door grandly opened outward, exuding a bright glow at the back of their supposed trio of greeters.

Shielding her eyes, the bright light contrasting with the blinking blue of the landing bay, Selena drew Nitaya nearer her chest. Walking with an air of confidence toward the strangers, Jovaar smiled, arms widening with his lightened step.

"Prince Iaco," Jovaar said with a slight bow of his head. The location of the females embedded in his thoughts, his confidence remained assured despite the wariness of the welcoming party. "May I present my steward Selena and the child Nitaya, one of the surviving possibles."

"Are we through with the niceties then, Sir Savius?" Prince Iaco asked, badly attempting to contain his grin. "They do bore me so."

"Of course you good-for-nothing non-lifer!" he answered, grabbing the man roughly for a boyish embrace.

"It is great to see you too, Jovi!" the Prince said, releasing his friend to look into his eyes. "When your palle informed me that you would be arriving, I spared no expense in preparations. A celebration is in order! Now come, let us get you out of this wet hole," he added, taking Jovaar's arm and leading the trio through the door. "Surely you must be..."

"I have several men aboard and some minimal gear," Jovaar interrupted, his thoughts quickly returning to their task. I will need someone to..."

"Vankailo-dov will see to the needs of your crew and I brought Agye to attend the child," the Prince interrupted, nodding to the silent pair. "Is there anything I have overlooked?"

"It appears that you have thought of everything," Jovaar answered, shaking his head. "At least for the moment, I believe you *do* have all in order, openly displaying your annoying dependability, as usual."

"Very well then," the prince added, smiling despite the obvious snub. "Banquet is set and waiting. Let us get you inside and nourished, my friend. I do believe you need some fattening."

With Prince Iaco claiming Jovaar's ear, leading him grandly through the large passages of Polatus, Selena walked silently with the child at their rear, the steward the Prince had referred to as Agye remaining close at hand. She knew from the Prince's words that the girl was there to tend to Nitaya's needs, and she was pleased that he had thought to offer her assistance, yet peering over her shoulder at the quietly smiling steward she could not help but be hesitant of handing the wee child to a stranger.

Selena smiled as the Prince continued his ramblings of memories only Jovaar and he shared. Although she tried to concentrate on their words, Jovaar obviously relishing the humor of their host, she could not draw her full attention from the beautiful young girl of color that had quickened her steps, now walking at her side. With hair as black as the the darkest of nights and oval bright eyes the shade of brilliant green, Selena could not help but notice that her given qualitites matched perfectly with her rather tight clothing of various shades of the same hues.

The young girl smiled as if aware of Selena's critique. The woman's warmth appearing genuine, she kept her words respectfully soft.

"Shall I carry her for you?" Agye asked, slowly extending her arms.

"No, yet I thank you," Selena answered. Wary, she rocked Nitaya gently in her arms. "There are others behind at our ship," Selena continued, stepping closer to the young girl, Jovaar and Prince Iaco roaring with laughter, rounding the next bend. "Will they be joining us shortly?"

"But of course," Agye answered, anxious to answer any of her questions. "It is not much further and Vankailo-dov will see that they are brought along momentarily. If I may speak freely, I must admit that I was most pleased to learn of your arrival," she added, speaking with ease in words clearly advanced for her age.

Eloquently describing their surroundings as they passed through a sliding glass door and entering into the first of many shoots, Selena calmed to the young girl's words, finding herself enjoying the steward more with each step. "I spend most of my time overseeing the children's activities on Polatus," Agye continued, obviously confident of her responsibilites. "We so rarely have guests of Prince Iaco, especially guests with young ones," she added, folding her hands before her. "I look so very forward to assisting you in any way that I can."

"And I appreciate your kindness," Selena answered, nodding, the Prince's voice echoing before them in the slender shoot.

"It is just through here," Agye said warmly, gesturing with her arm. Looking to the sound of the opening glass door, Selena stopped as the others continued through, enjoying glorious views of the small nourishment hall.

An oasis of endless wonders, a large odd-shaped table encompassed the center of the cabin surrounded by oversized dark chairs and a brilliant waterfall sprang forth from the ceiling above. Cascading down into a pool at its center, hundreds of brightly colored fish swam amongst the trickling drops.

The outer areas were filled with trees and greens in various shapes and sizes and small wildlife chirped their songs along their branches and amongst the array of flowers that poked their petals out haphazardly between their bases. The exterior walls were of the same glass as the shoots they had walked, and as before when they had reached the Less-Levels of the small Kindawan strip, they found themselves surrounded by the wonders of the sea. Leaving nothing undone, Selena spied that Prince Iaco had even prepared a place for Nitaya, a half egg-like shaped trundle to the right of one of the dark chairs.

"If you will kindly take your places," the Prince said, gesturing widely toward the table, his attention at last turned to the others. "I invite you all to enjoy the very best of Polatus."

Twenty-Two

The program was taking longer than expected. With the King suspended in his trance-like state as the machines cleared the damage to his eyes, the Med-Officer felt the weight of the outcome on his shoulders. "We should be at the final layer by now," he said anxiously, not turning from his task. "What is your readout?"

"Hovering in the sub-layer, Sir," the assistant answered, scanning his panel and keying in the next configuration. "There is extensive damage to this area and the cells are reproducing slower than expected. We are on target, Sir. It is just taking longer than we anticipated."

With the lasers continuing their lines deep within the recesses of the layers working simultaneously on each damaged eye, the Med-Officer, sitting to the right of his most prestigious patient, kept constant watch over the delicate process. "The King's vitals?" he asked, making a slight adjustment to the device.

"Well within range, Sir," he answered, hunkering over his station across the cabin. "There, we have entered the inner layer on the left eye."

Tension remained adrift in the air with one eye lingering behind schedule. Reaching to search the machine's database for alternate methods if the program proved unsuccessful, his assistant halted him, spying the breakthrough on his screen.

"We have entered the inner lay on the right eye as well, Sir," he said, exhaling loudly. "It should not be much longer."

"Very well," the MO answered, removing his waiting hand from the machine and wiping his brow. "I will feel much better once the process is complete. One mistake, one tiny slip of the laser and we could do permanent damage. I personally would not want to be the one that cost King Sugin his sight."

***

Having claimed their darkened seats and accepted the welcoming cool drink, the falls played its melodic tune at the center communal. All sat eagerly waiting Prince Iaco's self-described 'glorious feast, and Selenda nodded to Phydin as he at last joined them at the large table. When he too was settled, offering his thanks for his given mug, several servants emerged from within the trees handing them cloths and replenishing their numerous decanturs.

Selena lowered her arm into the tiny cot at her side, watching Nitaya nourish from the bedside arm. Pleased that Jovaar appeared at last at ease, laughing at one of the Prince's endless tales, she lowered her eyes to her hands, saying a prayer of thanks. Sitting back and lowering her guard, she relished the brief moment of calm.

She could not remember the last time Jovaar had appeared so full of joy, seeming to forget for a brief moment all that remained at stake. Truly enjoying the olden tales foretold by their host despite all that lay ahead, she could not contain a chuckle as Prince Iaco reveled in yet another tale. Only appearing exhausted once he reclaimed his seat, the Prince appeared to return to his senses with the serving of the first course.

An individual bowl of a delectable smelling burnt orange soup placed before all, Selena nodded to the others once the last had been served. Only then picking up her spoon to delve in, the sounds of her body exuding its musical hunger.

"If I may," the Prince said again rising, raising his mug and clearing his throat. His gaze tuned both right and left amongst his old and new friends. "It is with great joy that I celebrate your arrival," he began, raising his mug in a toast. "I realize that this journey you partake in is for a much greater cause, and it is my honor to do my part for the Resistance. However, may you find peace during your stay in the deepest of seas, and may you also find what you seek once you have left us. Yet until that fateful time, please raise your drinks in a toast of friendship, of peace, of the child that has survived such turmoil, and of a new beginning for her and for us all."

"Salut," they said in joyous unison. Reclaiming his seat, the Prince appearing at last spent of speech. Anticipating the first course, all enjoyed listening to Jovaar and Phydin boisterously retelling their own versions of the tales of their journey. Taking a small sip from her mug, Selena lowered it to the table, quickly reclaiming her spoon to taste the wonderous aroma of the dark liquid.

Much thicker and hotter than it initially appeared, she burned her tongue on the first spoonful. Quickly reaching forward to claim a bun from the glass bowl before the little falls, Selena lathered it generously with cream and devoured it in an attempt to settle the slight pain of her lips.

Watching Selena's reaction to the bowl of soup, Agye sat stifling a small chuckle, waiting for the woman to glance her way so that she may offer assistance. Once spotted, she placed a small dab of a white cream into her hot liquid. Blending it thoroughly, she smiled as Selena did the same, mimicking her graciously, the pair silently sampling the much more pleasant temperature of nourishment. Knowing she had helped the woman, albeit slightly with her minor dilemma, Agye nodded and took another spoonful yet remained quiet, listening to the Prince and Jovaar's conversation as the pair appeared almost oblivious to the wonderful nourishment before them.

The servants returned several moments later, removing bowls and placing oblong plates in their places, yet Jovaar and Prince Iaco could not be quieted. Selena could not help but smile at the pair roaring with yet another private tale. Thanking the silent steward once served, Selena looked down and squirmed at the thin noodles drenched in a creamy white sauce, spying several types of small sea creatures blended in with the various greens. Staring at her plate, uncertain if she was indeed famished enough to devour the little morsels, Selena gulped, nervously looking to Agye.

"I assure you it is quite delicious," the girl said, taking a bite and leaning toward her. Shaking her head in disagreement however, Selena remained hesitant and instead pushed the little creatures to the side before stirring the noodles and taking her first bite. Surprised by the texture and coolness of the dish, Selena nodded, and although Agye appeared to be enjoying the entire medley, Selena preferred to leave the Kindawan sea creatures alone.

The remainder of the meal was filled with happy conversation and soon Phydin joined in with the Prince and Jovaar, telling his own stories of his adventures with his Commander. Surprisingly the Prince sat silent, at last taking his first bite all the while relishing Phydin's words.

"You and I should continue this conversation another time," he said, jabbing his elbow into Phydin's chest and pointing his spoon at Jovaar. "A man can never have enough useless knowledge of his leader. And knowing Jovi all of my life, you can imagine how much I have to share!"

"That is enough, Iaco," Jovaar ordered, gritting his teeth and returning his mug to the table. "You need not bother with the trivialities of our youth. Gidoran has already fed them enough of that rubbish."

"Ah, G," the Prince continued, amusement filling his face despite wiping his mouth clean of the soup. "How is the man? Still operating that filth-ridden Yani?"

"He is, yes," Jovaar answered, a steward replenishing his drink without prompting. "Although the advancements he has made are quite noticeable. Obviously he sends his love."

"Ha!" the Prince bellowed, rising from his seat. "Now I know you are lying. Gidoran is a good man but sending his love? No, he has no time for love. He just creates beautiful things to look at. Like young Drider yet not quite so technical. Am I right?" he asked, slowly leading Jovaar and Phydin from the table.

"That you are," Jovaar answered, nodding to Phydin. "His latest proved quite stunning."

The three walked slowly away from the waterfall and table through the greens toward the side door and Selena rose alone, feeling forgotten as she gathered the slumbering child. "She was quite stunning," she said, sarcastically repeating Jovaar's words.

"I am sorry. Were you speaking to me?" Agye asked, turning and rising to assist with the child.

251

"No," she answered, embarrassed that she was overheard. "It is nothing. I was just talking to myself as always. If you would show me the way to quarters, I think I would like to rest for awhile."

"Of course," Agye answered, lowering her cloth to the table. "I cannot imagine how tired one would be after a journey such as yours. Please follow me." Crossing the cabin through the tree-lined aisle and passing stewards who busily tidied the cabin, Agye approached the rear door, prompted its opening and gestured for Selena to pass.

"Are we not to follow the others?" she asked, peering over her shoulder at the door the men had cleared.

"I am sorry, but with your request, no," Agye answered, smiling and folding her hands before her. "Quarters are this way. It would seem Prince Iaco and his friends have other plans."

"So it would seem," Selena echoed, annoyed that she was not asked to join them.

"This way," Agye continued, ignoring the woman's obvious stifled anger. Motioning Selena through, she assumed the lead down the corridor, the door closing swiftly at their backs. Knowing that with the child she had no other options, Selena rocked Nitaya gently in her arms and reluctantly trailed after the young girl.

* * *

"There," the Med-Officer said, pleased with the machine coming to a stop, at last retracting into the ceiling. Crossing the cabin with the mini-lenses in hand and reaching the bedside of his Commander, he slowly covered the King's eyes.

"How long will he have to wear them?" the assistant asked, crossing to the other side of the cot, the King remaining unconscious despite their hovering.

"It should not be long," the MO answered, settling the small pieces into place. "The shade dial is set for small adapting intervals and he should be comfortable with his own sight within several hazon. Finalize the program," he ordered, the assistant crossing back to his panel.

"Sir," the MO began softly, leaning over Carsian and patting his shoulder. "Can you hear me, Sir?"

"I can," the King answered groggily, slowly opening his eyes. "The room is very dark and everything appears hazy as if in aged black and white."

"That is exactly how it should appear, Sir," the MO continued confidently, standing tall. "I am proud to say that the program was successful."

"That is good news," the King answered, raising his hand to his brow. "How long until I am again able to see in color?"

"Not long, Sir," the Med-Officer answered, eyeing his commander's reflexive blinking. "The shade dial is in place and will gradually allow more definition into your sight, including color. You will be able to remove them soon, but I had to awaken you for confirmation of sight, Sir. I will need to begin the next phase and put you down again in order to repair the skin damage."

"No," the King answered, struggling to rise to his forearms. "A Savius did this to me. I will not have you repair it until every Savius has paid. It will stand as a reminder of what they have done. Now take me to Command," he continued, slowly turning and lowering his legs to the floor. "It is time for the paying to begin."

                    ***

"Your cabin is just this way," Agye said, gesturing down the corridor to a row of several doors. "I will just take Nitaya to the children's quarters so you will be able to get some rest."

"I would rather she stayed with me," Selena said hesitantly, pulling the child close and entering the offered fourth door on the right.

"I understand," Agye continued, crossing to the bedside table and tapping the softened lamp. "Yet I must insist. I have been informed that you will be here with us for some time and most certainly you agree that you cannot watch over the babe at every moment. It will do both you and the child good to have a moment of peace. Please," she added, extending her arms for the child.

"I suppose you are right," Selena answered, reluctantly wrapping Nitaya tighter within her small blanket before handing her over to the awaiting steward. "I just worry so when she is not with me."

"Of course you do," Agye continued, coddling the child who comfortably continued her slumber in the crook of her arm. "Here," she added, handing Selena the monitor she had retrieved from the low table. "Take this. You will be able to hear everything through it. I carry one with me always so I know how my children are doing and as you will see they continue on quite easily without us."

"Your children?" Selena questioned, tilting her head.

"I think of all the children of Polatus as my own," Agye answered, tapping the light low, graying the room. "This monitor keeps me informed of the condition of them at all times. I am quite comfortable knowing they are all doing well, as will you. Now please, get some rest," she added, crossing with Nitaya to the door. "I will send for you once she is ready for her final slumber."

Selena reluctantly nodded and crossing to the door handed over Nitaya's tote, Agye prompting the open panel of Selena's narrow, private quarters. Staring at the pair walking slowly down the pass, she smiled as the steward began a beautiful tune not so unfamiliar to her own, bringing a longing to her arms.

"She will be fine," Selena whispered, leaning on the narrow jam. Sighing, and turning to her empty room, Selena spied the cot in its corner, prompting the door closed at her back.

Small and inviting with the soft glow of the olden lamp Agye had dimmed, Selena surveyed the rest of her room, turning to the outer glass walls, astounded by the beautiful array of creatures of the underworld. "It is amazing," she began, stifling a small yawn as she warmed to the colorful beings. "It is simply amazing how calm all can be."

Turning away from the creature's dance of play, Selena smiled at the inviting cot in the darkened corner, properly placed away from the low light. Crossing to it, she ran her hands through the white flowing cloths that cascaded at its corners, drawn back by thick golden cords. On the verge of giving in to its welcoming folds however, she spied the enormous bouquet on the center table. Drawn to its beauty siloueted by the exterior light of the glass, she tilted her head for the slightest of moments, admiring the vibrant orange hues.

Turning back to the softness of the down cover, Selena ran her hands over the glorious thick and welcoming material. Moaning as she gave into its pleats, all at once she sensed the weight of her limbs. Muscles aching and stretching them into the lushness of the cot, Selena flitted out of her shoes and curled up, wrapping the blanket tightly about her. With eyelids heavy and stifling another yawn, sleep claimed her all too easily.

***

"Polatus is truly magnificent," Jovaar said, Iaco giving the men a lengthy tour of the main chambers. "It reminds me greatly of Kindawa's Neptune."

"So it does," Prince Iaco answered, gesturing the pair through the enormous door. "Although, I must assume that under Mathius' supervision, his Neptune would prove quite stale compared to this…"

"You assume correctly, my friend," Jovaar interrupted, staring upward into the expanse of the grand hall. Three stories high and greatly resembling the inner sanctuary of Sir Gowdar's Central Docking with a massive golden chandelier at its center, the large room was surrounded in the same glass as the connecting shoots, yet nothing could compare to the view of the deep sea, its walls of glass joining the inner world with the out.

"And for what would one need a room like this, in a place like this?" Jovaar asked, shaking his head at Iaco's extravagances, his feet circling in place to better take in the view.

"For celebrations of course," Iaco answered, quite proud of the structure. "I designed it myself and as you know, I love a good celebration."

"So you do," Jovaar answered grinning, his gaze returning to his friend. "It is amazing that a place like this exists with little outside knowledge of it. You should be proud, Iaco."

"I am," he answered, nodding confidently. "And thank you for the compliment. I am certain it was quite difficult for you."

"Indeed it was," Jovaar said, chuckling in unison with Phydin, their voices echoing in the large room.

"What are your security measures," Phydin interrupted, seriousness quickly returning, the pair appearing startled as if forgetting the weight they all faced.

"I assure you that we have state of the art technology," the Prince answered proudly, nodding to Jovaar. "As with Neptune I assume, the fortress if you should call it so, seals up quite tightly at the slightest hint of an attack. You should rest well knowing you are well protected."

"I am not so certain we will rest well," Jovaar interrupted, patting Phydin's shoulder. "Yet we will rest. I will not feel completely comfortable until we are safely on Mizar."

"Always the doubter he is," Iaco said, grinning and leaning closer to Phydin. "I will lead you to quarters to rest, for a celebration is in order for this evening after you have had a chance to freshen. I think the both of you could use a nice distraction after you have taken your own time, of course."

"Yes," Jovaar said, nodding in agreement. "I feel quite out of sorts in this fine hall wearing this getup," he added, peering down at the current state of his clothing. "I am certain with a chance to freshen and relax, we might be able to spare a few moments to celebrate reaching thus far. My crew, I am certain, would appreciate your kindness."

"As will you, my friend," Iaco said, draping his arm of Jovaar's shoulder. "This way," he added, crossing through the large hall to the next set of double doors. Continuing his incessant rambling, Phydin could not help but replay Jovaar's words in his mind.

"Mizar?" he thought, concentrating on Jovaar's slip. "Could *Mizar* be the final destination? He had said we were to travel to the line of four but..."

"Your crew should be settled and resting comfortably," Iaco continued, prompting the entrance to the wing of guest quarters, gesturing Jovaar and Phydin toward the first door. "I dare say by the look of you it is time you joined them."

***

"An update!" the King shouted, trusting his weight to two rangers, entering as a trio into the massive air ship Command.

"Aye, Sir," the First Officer said, straightening. "We have been circling Kindawa for some time. There has been no site of the Savius thus far, yet we are confident they could not have left the deep unnoticed. I have ordered the Spotter9's to keep watch at the furthest sector. They will not attempt escape undetected."

"I am displeased that they have not been found, Terdoni," the King began, shooing the rangers from him to pace the aisle between stations, his strength slowly returning. "Yet I agree that the Spotters were necessary. Have you sent for the refueler?"

"I was just about to order it, Sir," he answered, crossing his hands at his waist.

"Very well," the King continued, pivoting to face him. "Where is the closest refueling station?"

"We have just performed a search of the neighboring planets and I am sorry to say that the closest tanker is docked at Yani, the small sub-station beyond Booderban in the dastardly lower line," Terdoni answered, stiffening. "Shall I send word of hire?"

"Yes," the King answered, turning to stare out the glass. "Spare nothing and secure continuous refueling. We will not retreat for any reason. Do you understand?"

"Aye, Sir," he answered, turning to the CO who sat waiting at his station. "Send the request to the ordering dock. Accept whatever is offered and instruct them that the funds will be made available in intervals of shipments. Return information must include ship title, fee and holding quantity. Accept no ship below our fueling standard."

"Aye, Sir," the CO answered, entering the data into his panel, Terdoni standing over his shoulder to ensure his orders were followed as directed. "We should have a response momentarily," he added, tapping the screen with the last of the requirements. The wait, proved surprisingly short.

257

>Ship Title: Phobis
>Pilot of note: Gidoran Damuni
>Holding Quantity: 5,000
>Fee: 30,000 stron
>Docked and fueled, awaiting response

"Sir," Terdoni continued, turning to face his King. "We have the information you have requested. The fee is quite substantial."

"Confirm the load immediately," Carsian ordered, not turning from the glass. "We will not fail because of trivialities!"

"Aye, Sir," Terdoni answered, turning back to the CO. "Confirm order for 30,000 stron. We will require refueling within the hazon."

Twenty-Three

>Phobis: Cleared.
>Damuni: Unknown origin. File clear.
>Holding quantity request: 4,500
>Fee: Acknowledged
> Clear to PROCEED

"It seems they have bought it," Gidoran said, his grin widening. Pleased, he tapped the acknowledgement at the bottom of his screen. "And I thought I was known throughout the galaxy. Such a crush to my ego! Is Phobis in fact ready?" he asked, turning to his Yandonian Data Officer.

"Momentarily yes, Sir Gidoran," he answered, slowly standing, his tentacles lowering to his waist with the rise. "She is in loading dock E and being fueled as we speak. Shall I order her to proceed, ready for takeoff? What of her crew?"

"Yes, and do not bother," Gidoran answered, gathering his gear. "Have her waiting on stand-by once final prep is complete. I go alone on this flight and must admit I will quite enjoy fueling the enemy. Take down my line and pull up all data on Savius per the information I have given you. I would like to inform him of my whereabouts."

"Sir," he answered, slowly lowering to his station. "I will download the coordinates to Phobis and uplink the communications with Savius upon location. Everything should be in order once you have arrived onboard. I will maintain all links in an up status so I can make any necessary adjustments as needed. I have informed the crew to debark as requested. Phobis is however, equipped with two transoids and I have ordered them to remain."

"Well done," Gidoran said, holstering his weapon and grabbing his tote, shaking his head at his monotone servant. "Be ready for systems check. I am heading to Dock E now."

"Good luck, Sir," the Yan-do said, pivoting to face his Commander. "I know quite well that you enjoy these adventures, yet please keep in mind the seriousness of the situation."

"You worry too much, my friend," Gidoran answered, patting the being's shoulder and staring at the open panel. "I have spent far too long cooped up in this place. It is time I did my part for Savius and the Resistance. Trust me. I know what is at stake. Now be ready for systems check and uplink those communications. I need to speak with Jovaar immediately."

"Yes, Sir," the Yan-do answered, his voice flat despite his fears, pivoting back to his screen. "I wish you luck."

***

Selena awoke as if in a haze uncertain of her surroundings. Lying for a moment longer, waking slowly to take in the wonders of the cabin, her eyes soon focused, her view proving obstructed by white. Sitting abruptly, she withdrew the sheer cloths from the cot.

Someone had been in her room while she slept closing the linen unnoticed, and with the idea of someone being so close to her as she remained unguarded proved unnerving, Selena pulled back the folds and stared out into the cabin realizing that at least all else was as she had left it. Perhaps Jovaar had stopped in to check on her. Sitting on the side of the cot, she dangled her small feet to the cool floor.

"Did I take those off?" she asked, looking down at the floor at her shoes. "I suppose I was more tired than I thought."

Yawning and stretching her limbs, glancing at the near side table, Selena immediately spied the bouquet of orange petals and below them the monitor Agye had given her, causing her to straighten. "Nitaya!" she panicked, reaching for the device. "How does this thing work?" she thought, turning it from side to side. Spying the small green light in the top right corner, she frantically brought it to her mouth.

"Hello?" she asked, nerves dancing beneath her skin. "Can anyone hear me?" Gaining no response, she slapped the device on her knee and attempted to reprompt the voice acceptance.

"Hello?" she pleaded, rapidly pressing the pair of controls, however still gaining no response she wasted no time and immediately lowered to replace her shoes. Sliding the last of the narrow pair onto her feet, Selena headed for the door in search of Nitaya, device in hand. She jumped back as the door opened prior to requesting its prompt.

"I see you are awake," Agye said smiling, calmly entering the small room. "You were completely out when I came to see to you earlier, and therefore I drew the sheers for you and turned your monitor on so I would know when you woke. I hope I have not troubled you."

"No, I thank you," Selena answered hesitantly, catching her breath as she watched Agye tidy the cot. "But where is the child?"

"Nitaya is in with the other babes," Agye answered, smoothing the last of the folds. "I assure you she is quite well. I heard you stir and came at once to take you to her. Are you ready then?"

"I am, yes," Selena answered, anxiously crossing the cabin to the door. "How long have I been resting?"

"Quite some time," Agye answered, floating her hand over the orange petals and slowly following her to the door. "Please, come this way."

Trailing the young girl through a series of outer corridors, Selena could not help but marvel at the dimly lit sea and its array of colors, wringing her hands in an attempt to appear calm. "If only the girl would walk faster," she thought, choosing to keep her feelings to herself. Passing through the next door however, her tension at last eased as she heard the first stirrings of little ones.

"This is our area of play," Agye said, gesturing for Selena to enter, and walking into the busyness of the cabin, Selena could not help but smile at the obviously happy children.

"Over there is the center for reading," Agye continued, gesturing toward several panel stations to their right. "And through that side door is the pool for water recreation. We do arts and crafts to recall our history here," she continued, nodding to a trio of wee ones looking up at the new arrivals, smiling with water-colored faces. "And in the area for gardening over there we teach the children the value of planting and nurturing of greens. The room for education is through those doors and this way leads to the children's quarters where your beautiful Nitaya awaits. Most of the children are there at this time, preparing for the eve's celebration. The few others will follow along momentarily."

"Celebration?" Selena asked, immediately claiming of Agye's arm.

"Of course," Agye answered, patting Selena's trembling hand. "It is not often we have guests, or rather guests of your status. Prince Iaco has made preparations for a glorious evening. I was certain you would not be prepared for such an occasion," Agye added, spying Selena glancing at her tattered attire, her face flushing regardless of having been rid of the burdensome cloak. "And therefore I have had suitable attire placed for you in my cabin. It is just off the children's quarters and you will have the required privacy there to freshen."

"It seems you have indeed thought of everything," Selena said, blushing and nodding her thanks.

"It is my job to do so," Agye said, shrugging and returning her quest's smile. "Now come. Your Nitaya is just through here."

Walking side by side through the large doors, the pair entered the spacious cabin, children of all ages squealing and cheering before them in various stages of preparation for the celebration. Quickly scanning the chaotic area, Selena spied the infant cots off to her left and excused herself, eagerly passing through a group of larger children.

"There are so many," she said, Agye catching up with her elder's stride.

"Very few have quarters with their families," Agye said, knowing Selena did not understand. "Their momars have full access to them here and spend a great amount of time with them however, everyone in Polatus has a purpose, and that purpose requires much of their time. I am thankful that my purpose is to tend to the little ones. Here she is," Agye added, lifting Nitaya from the fifth cradle down. "She is as beautiful as ever."

"Thank you," Selena said, taking Nitaya into her arms. "I have missed you so!" she added, smiling down at her bundled frame, Nitaya familiarly taking hold of her finger.

"I am sorry," Agye interrupted, nodding to a nearby steward as she gathered another small Polatian. "I of course understand that you would like some time with the child, but you too must prepare for the festivities. If you will follow me," she added, gesturing in the opposite direction. "I will take you to my cabin so you may freshen."

"Of course," Selena answered, lifting her gaze from the child. Following the young steward to the rear corridor and its display of several doors, she found all worries had left her, holding firm to Nitaya. She could not contain the smile on her face as she entered Agye's quarters.

    ***

"Are you certain you do not need us to go with you?" the final crew member asked, crossing down the plank.

"Thanks, but no," Gidoran answered, waving him off. "The droids are more than enough."

"I checked the helm-link before I left and your flight path has been uploaded," the man added, folding his arms at his chest. "Communications should be operational momentarily."

"Very well," Gidoran answered, slapping him on the back. "I have been a bit behind schedule and that should help speed things along. If all goes as planned, I will have your ship back for refueling at daybreak. I know you are eager to join the flight and I may take you up on your offer of riding along if I have any trouble the first time around. I doubt I will, but be ready to debark though, just in case."

"Yes, Sir," he answered, stepping reluctantly from the plank and around the trolley, turning to watch Sir Gidoran board. "I wish you luck."

Gidoran paced the short walk to Command, tossing his gear in a side compartment then took his seat at the helm, the droids sitting ready and alert at their stations. "System check," he ordered into his positioned headpiece, clasping his restraints, the disappointed crew member forgotten.

"Flight path is uploaded and communications are online," the CO answered from Yani Command. "You are fully loaded and are on standby for detachment. My link will remain open for the duration of the flight. As you can see both droids are in position, and all skies are clear. Exto-atmos proves the same."

"Thanks," Gidoran answered, lowering his controls. "Closing main hatch, thrusters at fifty. Prepare for full shields," he added, the droid to his right pivoting to follow the order. "Detach in 5, 4, 3, 2, 1, detach."

The ship rose above the platform, circled one hundred and eighty degrees and sped from the dock. "Shields up," Gidoran ordered, eyeing the droid's progress on his side screen. "Direct flight to," he added, pausing to turn his screen back to main.

"So that is where you are," he whispered, his tilted grin returning to his face. "Direct flight to Kindawa," he ordered, the droid transferring the coordinates to his panel. Prompting the hyper drive as the machine confirmed the order, Gidoran sailed the ship quickly from the Yandonian sky.

***

"It is quite lovely," Selena said, gathering the flowing violet gown Agye had chosen for her. "I have not worn something this beautiful in so very long."

"I thought it would suit you," Agye said, crossing the room to again feel the fabric. "I took a guess at your size. And by the looks of it, I think I got it right. I can keep an eye on Nitaya if you would prefer to change in the facilities. I have placed out an array of accessories so you should have everything that you require."

"Thank you," Selena said, holding the gown and looking at Nitaya sleeping quietly on the cot. "If you are certain, I will not be long."

"Take your time," Agye answered, a tinkling chime suddenly filled the room.

"My monitor," Agye continued, holding up her hand reassuringly, prompting the device at her waist.

"It is the doubles again," a caregiver said sighing, her voice somewhat distorted through the device.

"I will be there in just a moment," Agye answered, releasing the open line. "It seems the doubles are once again up to no good. I will take Nitaya with me to see what they have done this time. We should be back before you are ready to go."

"Are you certain she is no trouble?" Selena asked, watching as Agye comfortably gathered the slumbering child.

"I assure you she is no trouble," she answered, repeating Selena's words and smiling in return. "As you can see, I am quite used to more than one task at a time. Just go and enjoy yourself. We will return shortly."

"Thank you," Selena repeated, running her fingers over the smooth pleats of the gown. "I have my monitor as well...if you were to change your mind."

"We will be fine," Agye answered reassuringly, prompting the door. "Just have a good time and try not to worry. We will be back before you know it." Watching the pair return to the outer cabin, Selena could not help but lower her gaze again to the beautiful gown in her arms.

"Jovaar is going to love this," she whispered, giggling and covering her lips with her hand. Turning to glance at her reflection in the glass, she spied the door to the facilities and quickly set out to prepare for the celebration.

Twenty-Four

"Why can I not go?" Hylin whined, Jovaar standing, folding his arms at his chest.

"Because it has not started yet and I do not want you wandering around getting into trouble," he repeated for the third time, feeling his advanced age. "We have been over this, Hylin. You will go once everyone is ready and not before."

"I have been cramped up here forever!" Hylin pouted, folding his arms in mimic of Jovaar. "And I will not get into any trouble! I just want to explore the area a bit as I was able to do on Yani. Sir Gidoran would have allowed me some freedoms. You know I have never seen a place like this before."

"All in good time," Jovaar said, ruffling his lengthy-blonde hair. "Jax, can you not find something to amuse this young man with until it is time?"

"He is not playing Rodaous if that's what you mean," Jax answered, glancing up from the heated game. "I am up one hundred stron and do not have time to waste teaching the boy. Besides, Kroy is going down and I have to make certain I am the one who puts him there."

"Ha!" Kroy grumbled, holding his Intels and slapping Jax's arm with his free hand. "We will see who has the last laugh!"

"See, Jovaar," Hylin continued, stomping his foot. "There is nothing for me to do. They will never take me seriously and they will never let me play."

"It will not be much longer, Hylin," Jovaar said, adjusting his cloak. Staring at his reflection in the glass, he scowled at the appearing age lines about his eyes. "Be patient, little man. They will send for us momentarily."

Knowing there was no way to convince his elder, Hylin grumbled, stomping across the room. Falling to his cot, he could not contain his groan, angry that he had been told 'no' by Sir Gidoran's so-called friend.

"Sir G would have said 'go, have fun, and explore,'" he mumbled, slamming his fist into the down of his cover before tossing it to the floor in disgust. "Oh, how I missed Sir G."

***

"I cannot go in there looking like this," Khyra said, staring at her reflection in the glass, eying the garnet gown she was given to wear. "Maybe I should go back," she continued, standing just inside her cabin door. Turning to retreat then whirling immediately back to the door, she covered her face in frustration with her hands.

"This is nonsense," she mumbled, reaching up to pat her bundled hair. "It is only a gown."

Taking a final deep breath, Khyra lifted her chin and prompting the door, stepped in to the men's ajoining quarters. Spying Jovaar standing with his back to her, she took a steadying breath, watching as he adjusted his cloak in his reflection of the glass. Pleased that no attention was drawn to her, the men continuing their useless game of Rodaous, she quietly stepped to cross the cabin to the corridor, yet Hylin bumbled off the cot to her right, startling her.

Khyra!" he shouted, leaping and claiming her hand. "Could you maybe take me for a walk before we go? Jovaar said I could not leave unescorted, yet certaininly…"

"Hylin," Jovaar interrupted, straightening the last of his cloak. "I said you will have to…

Saying nothing more and instead silently crossing the spacious cabin, Jovaar stepped before Hylin to claim Khyra's hand. "You look wonderful," he said sincerely. He shielded his smile as she wrung her hands uncomfortably at her waist.

"I do not *feel* wonderful," she answered, attempting to flatten her stubborn pleats. "I do not know how women dress like this. It is extremely uncomfortable and makes it difficult to do just about anything."

"Well I think you look amazing," he said, patting her shoulder and turning back to the rest of the group. "Do you not think she looks…"

"No, Jovaar," she pleaded, nervously grabbing his arms. Please do not…."

It was too late. The men stopped bickering round the low table and the room became immensely quiet as they turned. "Wow," Phydin said, slowly standing and dropping his hands to his side. "I did not know you could look like that."

"Yeah, wow," Jax echoed, sarcastically turning back to his Intels. "A true lady stands before us."

"That is enough," Phydin said, glaring at his comrade. He crossed to her as if in a trance. "I fear if you looked like this every day I would get nothing done."

Blushing, Khyra accepted Phydin's compliment graciously, yet straightened as Vankailo reentered the room. "It is time," he said, raising his arms to the group, dressed in his finest attire. "If you will please follow me…"

Rising and quickly forgetting their game, the men paced anxiously to the door with Hylin closing the gap at their backs. Phydin holding out his arm to accept Khyra's hand, Jovaar watched as he smiled with her accepting nod, graciously accepting his gesture. Seeing that the feud was undoubtedly over, his smile broadened. Lowering his head and trailing the pair from the cabin, he looked up just as Selena and the child joined them in the corridor. Jovaar could not contain his breath and bowed to her arrival.

"You amaze me," he said, rising to kiss her hand. Tucking it gently and familiarly beneath his arm, he trailed after the others, never taking his gaze from her beauty. "I am sorry for leaving you earlier," he whispered, patting her hand with their steps.

"It was no trouble," she answered, looking down at the child. "Agye has proven quite helpful."

"That is good news," Jovaar added, secretly kissing her hand. "Yet I will be certain to spend more time with you after the celebration."

"I am counting on your word," she answered, passing through the last of the shoots and their wonderous playful creatures. Turning to face the large entrance of the main hall, Selena nodded, raising her chin proudly. Jovaar, ever the gentleman gestured for both her and the child to enter before him.

***

"We have entered Kindawa airspace, Sir," the droid said, simultaneously stalling the hyper drive and prompting his mapped panel.

"We have made great time," Gidoran answered, adjusting his screen to also search the area. "Get Polatus online.

"Connecting now," the droid answered, unturning.

"Craft Phobis to Polatus, respond," Gidoran said, prompting the helm's com and staring warily at his panel. "Craft Phobis to Polatus, respond," he repeated. He impatiently tapped fingers upon the awaiting screen.

"Polatus to Phobis, state your intentions," the operator at last answered.

"Phobis pilot Damuni. Seeking conference with Jovaar Savius, respond," Gidoran answered, flatly. Silence filled the air as he waited a response, sailing over the great body of the sea. His impatience growing, he repeated his order a third time.

Sternly speaking his demands, his anger proving he was not often told 'no,' Gidoran grit his teeth in frustration as the voice at last answered over the com.

"Status negative," the foreign voice said, flatly. "Pilot name unknown."

"Blasted!" Gidoran answered, slamming his fist into the side panel. "I know he is there. Operator!" he continued, retapping the com. "Inform Jovaar Savius that Sir Gidoran Damuni seeks conference immediately. Prince Iaco knows my name! Send my request directly to him. Respond!"

"Prince Iaco is being sought," the voice answered, unconcerned. "Hold your position or be prepared to be detained."

"Thank you and that will not be necessary," Gidoran answered, balling his fist and pounding it on his thigh, their flight path to the Sugin ship coming full into view. "At last we are getting somewhere."

***

"State your intentions," First Officer Terdoni said, speaking into the CO's com.

"Craft Phobis, refueler per your order," Gidoran answered flatly, eyeing the back of the nearest droid, the being's hand hesitant at his station.

"Craft Phobis," Terdoni continued, crossing his hands at his back. "Follow your current flight path. Prepare for docking and instructions port side."

"Confirmed receipt," Gidoran answered familiar with the likes of the transaction, watching the data appear as expected on his screen. "Preparing for dock port side."

Entering the coordinates, Gidoran placed the ship on manual then sat back watching the Sugin ship appear ever larger in the glass at the bow. His head shook with excitement as the long arm began its retraction at his approaching ship.

"Release extension, attachment in 5, 4, 3, 2, 1, attach," Gidoran ordered, the droids systematically prompting the controls. With the ship careening with the joining of his fueler, Gidoran turned to his companions, unable to contain his grin.

"Systems stalled, begin the transfer," he ordered, monitoring the progress on his screen. Following his word without question, the droid released the fuel. Altering his own panel, Gidoran searched the Kindawan underworld for his friend.

"Blasted Jovi, where are you?" he groaned, tapping his panel to search for a sign of life, the fuel transfer ticking quickly on his side screen. "We are running out of time."

"Fuel transfer confirmed," the droid said, retracting the line to its former position, his superior running his fingers through his hair.

"Fuel transfer confirmed," Gidoran repeated, his frustration evident.

"Fuel is received and funds have been transferred," the voice continued over the com. "Return for roundabout flight

270

immediately. Continuous order until otherwise stated. Order detachment."

"Ordering detachment for return flight," the droid answered, again straightening before his screen. Altering his own to watch the detachment procedures and regardless of not finding Savius, Gidoran smiled wide, staring at the massive ship. "Nice doing business with you."

***

Tilting at the waist, the two pages dressed in identically bright colored tunics of jasmine and coral opened the over-sized pair of doors, the trumpeters to the right of the entrance sounding their arrival with brightly colored stips of cloths dancing below their horns. Polatians, dressed in their finest splendor sat amongst the round tables on the outskirts of the large room, taking drink and obviously enjoying the celebration even before the main festivities began. They quieted at the sounds of their newest arrivals however, and each turned as first Prince Iaco and then his friends entered the great hall.

"Welcome one, welcome all," he shouted for all to hear, arms raised in greeting. His awkward grandiose cloak flowed beneath his arms as he walked to claim his station. "This night is yet a joyous occasion and I am pleased that all of you are here to enjoy it with me for we have very special guests this evening, who have traveled a great distance and have overcome many obstacles to grace us with their presence. Please give them the welcoming only Polatus is capable of!"

The large hall immediately roared with welcoming cheers and Jovaar glanced at Selena and smiled, uncomfortably patting her hand at the teeming reception. Gesturing for his guests to follow to the main table, Iaco beamed with pride of his accomplishments, the trumpeters sounding their tune and streamers of gold and silver cascading down from the ceiling above over the revelers.

"A little overboard do you not you think?" Jovaar asked, at last regaining the Prince's attention and seeing Selena to her given seat.

"Overboard, no," Iaco answered, obviously enjoying himself. "It is all for you! No one is more deserving, yet I must admit I would do this every night if I were able. Come, my friend," he added, chuckling and patting Jovaar's back, gesturing toward the approaching stewards and their overly-abundant trays of greens. "It is time we nourished."

***

The evening proved even more lavish than Prince Iaco had promised, and every new member was not only well attended, but admired. With the festivities continuing in the tiered hall centered completely about them, Jovaar and Selena sat at the main table just to the left of the Prince, Nitaya laying in yet another cradle between them.

Resting comfortably and nourishing from her bedside arm as she had earlier in the small dining cabin, Selena found that with Nitaya well tended she could relax, able to enjoy the moment and the unending attention of their host. Settling back within her chair, already sated with the Prince's offered abundance, Selena shook her head with the continuous display. Many servants, dressed in lavish costume carrying large trays of meats, cheeses and greens once again entered the great hall while others toting delicate urns of wine, continuously replenished the awaiting mugs.

All the while the group relished in the joyous event, for the moment forgetting the wear and importance of their journey. Dancers in costume paraded by their table and music filled the air from the lutes off to the side of the room. As time appeared to stand still and at last all seemed at ease, relaxing with the glorious occasion, Selena too reveled in the moment, wishing it would never end.

The crew sat off to their side at one of the many round tables amongst the sea of Prince Iaco's bidding, and Selena could not help but smile as they easily joined with the Polatians, relishing the feast and chatting and laughing. Ever the performer, Hylin stood before them to perform yet another of his *amazing* tricks with his utensils.

"Everything is as it should be," Selena thought, turning to look at Jovaar laugh at the newest of Prince Iaco's memories. Enjoying the festivities and calmed by Nitaya's obvious comfort despite the odds she knew they faced, Selena paused, her guard immediately returning as she spied the young dancer approach the table to speak with the Prince.

"Shall we begin, Sir?" she asked, dressed in her thin costume of lavender.

"But of course," the Prince answered, reclaiming his mug from the table, flailing his arms. "Ring them in!"

Bowing low to her master's word, the girl ran off to their left. Instantaneously the lights dimmed with the quieting room and Hylin reclaimed his seat regardless of his obvious unfinished tale. Lutes ceasing their current tune, they began another slower rhythm on cue. Resettling her nerves, Selena sat back to enjoy the performers.

As the dancers, six in all, entered from the side door, each claimed their given places on the tiled floor, beginning their dance with the flow of thin material and olden tinkling bells at their feet and wrists. Turning to spy the men's reaction, Selena shielded her grin with her hand as both the Prince and Jovaar straightened, apparently transfixed by their dance.

"You are enjoying this?" she whispered, chuckling and leaning closer to Jovaar. His composure lost, he attempted to blink from his trance.

"It *is* quite lovely," he answered gulping, leaning toward her yet refusing to move his eyes. Tugging annoyingly at his arm, Selena chuckled at him shaking his head, at last turning his face to her with guilt clear on his face.

"Selena, it is just that..."

"We have word of an incoming ship," the page interrupted, crouching low at Prince Iaco's side. "The pilot says you would know him but thus far we have discouraged his presence. I beg your forgiveness for the intrusion, but he pressed the matter."

"As you should," Iaco answered, lowering his mug to the table. A steward quickly approached to replenish without prompting. "And the name of its pilot?" he questioned, not turning from the beautiful display.

"Our stationed officer says his name is Damuni, Sir," the page answered, standing. "What order shall I give him?"

Having overheard the name of his friend, Iaco instantly forgot the dancers at the center court and Jovaar released Selena's hand, pivoting in his seat to Iaco.

"Gidoran," he said, slamming his mug on the table, abruptly standing.

"Command," the Prince said, rising and gesturing for Jovaar to follow. Helplessly watching the two men scurry from the hall, Selena's eyes darted to the side table where the others sat oblivious to all but the dancing six.

"Can you tend to her?" Selena asked, turning to Agye at her right.

"But of course," Agye answered, laying her hand on the child. "Please. Go as you must."

"Something is wrong," Selena added, dropping her cloth on the table, rising. Running her hand over Nitaya's cheek, she turned and gathered her violet pleats, hurrying toward the large doors, fear filling her being. "Something is most definitely wrong."

***

"Well?" the King asked, annoyed with the delay of pursuit, pivoting to face his first officer.

"Fueling confirmed," Terdoni answered, straightening. "A roundabout has been ordered and we will be continuously refueled as ordered."

"Continuous refueling does nothing when there are no results, Terdoni!" Carisan bellowed, standing to pace the central aisle. "Where is that blasted ship?"

"I am sorry, my King, but there has been no sign thus far," he answered, tipping his head. "We may need to consider submersibles for they may remain below for onars, however I must warn you we have not been able to gather any further data of the deep below. If you send the craft in, you send it blind. You may run into another beast or perhaps something even more dreadful. My strongest opinion is that..."

"I grow tired of your opinions, Terdoni," the King interrupted, ceasing his pacing and abruptly turning. "Do you not see my eyes? Do you not understand what they have done? I will wait no longer! Send all submersibles into the deep immediately. *I* am your King and I will finish this now!"

***

"What is taking so blasted long?" Gidoran fumed, wiping his hands over his face. "We are running out of time. You!" he shouted, pointing to the droid on his right. "How much longer do we have until we leave Kindawan airspace?"

"Sir, we..."

"Craft Phobis," the operator interrupted, startling the DO to silence. "Prince Iaco has been interrupted and informed. He is on his way to Command as we speak. Stand by."

"Well it is about blasted time!" Gidoran answered, releasing the com so his words would not transmit.

"Sir," the droid pressed. "We are...."

"G!" the com rang, interrupting the droid once again. "G, is that you?" the Prince shouted.

"Iaco, I do not have time to explain," Gidoran answered, at once recognizing the familiar voice. "Is Jovi with you?"

"I am here," Jovaar chimed, his breathing labored. "Gidoran, what is wrong?"

"It is about blasted time you rang," Gidoran continued, staring out the glass at the blanket of blue. "I do not have much time to explain so just listen. The Sugin King has ordered a ship off Yani to continuously refuel until your position is located. I have just finished a refueling with Phobis and am heading back for the roundabout as we speak."

"You did what?" Jovaar screamed, his voice booming through the com. "You are feeding them? What were you thinking, Gidoran? We have waited onars for the presentation of the possibles and as we near the final moments you have ruined our..."

"I have made the first pass in good faith, Jovi," Gidoran interrupted, shaking his head at the oblivious pair of droids. "Just relax and listen. I am on roundabout now and should be returning just after dawn. I wanted to inform you of their coordinates so you could use it to your advantage. Set sequence for download," he added, hearing the Prince give the order to his crew.

"Open all channels and tell him to begin," the Prince shouted, darting for a panel to watch the progress.

"Begin the download, G," Jovaar said, his tone only slightly tempered. "I cannot believe you have risked this. Do they not know who you are? Do they not understand..."

"No Jovi, they do not know," Gidoran interrupted, eyeing the mapped route on his screen. "And I do not have time to go into this further as we are about to leave Kindawan airspace. Beginning the download, respond."

"It is uploading, Jovi," Iaco shouted from the helm. "We are almost at half."

"Gidoran," Jovaar continued, the program in process. His crew hurried about their stations, eager to sort the incoming data. "Give me something. What are your coordinates? What is your..."

"Jov..." G interrupted, his voice cracking with the static of the com. "We are...you should...download...Jovaar!"

"We are losing him, Iaco!" Jovaar shouted over his shoulder. "What is your readout?"

"We have almost got it," he answered, eyeing the slow process on his screen.

"G?" Jovaar shouted, slamming his fist on the side panel. "Gidoran?" Nothing but static returned. "Iaco, what have you got?" he asked, breathlessly lowering the device. "Tell me you received it all."

"Not enough," he answered, drained from the excitement, wiping his hands over his face. "Not enough for completion, Jovi. He said he was on roundabout therefore we should be able to retrieve the rest of the download on the next pass." Looking to his subordinate who offered a mere shrug, Iaco nodded, hoping his words would prove true.

"What if we do not have time to wait for the next pass?" Jovaar asked disheartened, falling into a rear seat.

"We have no choice but to wait," the Prince answered, shaking his head. "I will inform my men to watch for his next entrance. Until then, waiting his all we can do."

"The Sugins are still out there, Iaco," Jovaar said flatly, running his fingers through his har. "And it seems they are waiting as well…only now they are fully fueled."

Twenty-Five

"What is happening?" Selena asked, wringing her hands as she entered Command.

"It was our friend," Iaco answered, pivoting to face her. "He has refueled the Sugin ship and we are waiting his roundabout."

"What?" she wailed, turning from Iaco to Jovaar. "I do not understand. Why is your friend helping them?" Jovaar rose, taking her arm and walking her to a rear corner to explain.

"I am not exactly certain what is happening but Gidoran would die before he put us in danger," Jovaar began, claiming her shaking hands within his own. "Calm, Selena, please," he urged, kissing the tips of her fingers. "We attempted to download Gidoran's coordinates of the Sugin ship, but we were interrupted before the sequence could complete. I am not certain if he has left Kindawan airspace or if he was intercepted. All we know is that they are still out there and for now all we can do is wait."

"Wait?" Selena asked anxiously, tears welling in her eyes. All thoughts at once returned to the child. "Wait for what?" she asked. "Wait for them to come after us? There is no time, Jovi. You said yourself that you were uncertain of Gidoran's whereabouts. What if he was captured? What...I am sorry, but what if your friend was killed? We cannot wait, Jovaar. We must act now!"

"Calm yourself, Lena," Jovaar continued, reaching for her flailing arms. Attempting to pull her close, he raised his hands in defense as she pushed him away, wiping her eyes with the sleeve of her violet gown.

"I will not calm!" she shouted, several of the crew peering at her over their shoulders. "Nitaya is at risk as long as we sit here doing nothing. I for one will not let that happen!

They lie in wait as we celebrate? Celebrate what? We have accomplished nothing! We have merely escaped them for the present. I will send for transport! I will..."

"You are safest here, Selena," Iaco interrupted, pacing to the rear corner and waving off his nosy crew. "Jovaar is right. All we can do is wait. The Sugins know nothing of Polatus or any of the outposts, no one knows unless I have chosen for them to know. Gidoran may have made contact, but even he does not know of its exact location."

"Now he said he was on roundabout," he continued, resuming his long-strided steps. "What that means is that he has refueled the ship and is returning to port for more fuel. He informed us that he is to return after dawn and as I have said to Jovaar, it is best for us to wait him out for further data. Selena, you must understand it is best that we wait."

"Wait, wait wait...I cannot do as you ask," she answered, wiping her hands down the length of her gown. "There is so much yet to do. We must..."

"I know of your instincts, Lena," Jovaar interrupted, attempting to reclaim her hands. "But Iaco is right. Gidoran said he refueled in good faith and what that means is that he made the first pass to earn their trust, but more importantly to inform us of what is transpiring. He will not let us down, Lena. We will know more just after the rise of the first day circle."

"Let us go back to the celebration and try to enjoy what time we have," Iaco said, interrupting the pair. Iaco's ill-placed words allowed Jovaar the moment to at last draw Selena into his arms.

"Are you mad?" she shouted, pushing Jovaar away and turning to face Iaco, her finger pointed firm at his chest. "How can you think of drink at a time like this?"

"Well," he shrugged, the expected grin returning to his face. "I was actually thinking of my stewards."

Jovaar did not allow Selena her tirade. Jabbing the Prince with his own fist, he stood back to enjoy him wincing from the pain, rubbing his arm.

"Geez, Jovi," he said, punching him back. "You are really no fun anymore." Glaring, Selena merely huffed, turning to strmp from the room.

279

"What is up with you two anyway?" Iaco pressed, crossing to prompt the rear door.

"You will never grow up, will you?" Jovaar asked, answering his friend's question with his own. Not waiting for another of Iaco's fumbled answers, he turned at the door's prompting and hurried after the title giver.

***

"Selena wait...wait!" Jovaar shouted, attempting to catch up with her quickened strides. She halted at the double doors of the hall, brow tipped to muffled noise beyond. "Iaco did not mean it," he whispered. "Selena, please look at me."

"He did not mean it?" she shouted, brushing his arm away and turning to face him. "Then tell me what he did mean, Jovaar Savius. Am I to go back to that table and smile? Am I to act as if nothing is happening about us while I watch the *beautiful stewards* as they dance? Are we to laugh and nourish knowing that Nitaya is in danger? That we are *all* in danger? I am tired, Jovi! I am tired of wondering if there is going to be another rising of the circles. I am tired of wondering of...of...I am just so simply tired."

"It has been long enough!" she screamed, ignoring the silent pages eyeing one another. "We need to get to where we are going and be done with this. Nitaya has a chance for the throne. It should be given to her without all of this...without all of this chaos! She is an Elitian possible! She is barely a few days old and she has no idea what is happening about her, or *to* her, for that matter. I am tired of it all, Jovaar. I just want things to be peaceful, to wake up knowing there will be another day circle rise filled with promises of the day for the child. She should have that. We all should have that!"

"I promise you, Lena, I will give you all that you have asked for and more," Jovaar said, reaching in an attempt to pull her close.

"You can promise me nothing!" she answered, pushing away from his offered embrace. "They are still out there! Do you not understand, Jovi? I am the one who has sacrificed my life for Nitaya, toiling over text and giving up the only true friend that I have ever loved as I followed the strict orders of my palle without question. I am the one who has been Nitaya's assigned momar while Wynin was...is..." she stammered, catching her breath in an attempt to settle her nerves.

"It is I and I alone who has been her momar, the only momar she has ever truly known," Selena continued, glaring into Jovaar's eyes. "One who understands what is happening about her and what could possibly happen *to* her! Prince Iaco jests without care regardless of his knowledge of our struggles and who knows what your Sir Gidoran is truly up to. He could be captured. He could be dead! And yet I am to go back and nourish and watch the dance of the Prince's stewards? Are you mad? Are you all mad?"

Selena fell silent, struggling to catch her breath. Motioning for the pages to open the door, Jovaar waved them aside however, quickly grabbing her arms and spinning her close. "We have all sacrificed and we are all tired," he said, guiding her away from the door and the prying ears of Iaco's men. "I know you have bonded with the child unlike any of the others ever could, but we can do nothing but wait. My friends have gotten us this far, and without knowing if the Savius family is even out there to help us, I *do* know and trust that *our* friends will see us to the end. I am not asking you to sit idly back and do nothing, Lena. I am asking you to trust me. I am asking you to wait and see what Gidoran has planned. He would not have contacted us if it was not of the utmost importance. Gidoran and Iaco have never once let me down in the past, and I promise you, they will not let *us* down now. You must trust this, Lena. I need you to trust me."

"I am afraid, Jovi," she whispered, balling her fists and ramming them against his chest. "They are still out there! They may not know where we are, but they are still there! We do not know what has happened to your Gidoran. You ask me to wait, but how can I? How can we? There are dangers everywhere and we sit here and do nothing. How can we stand here and do nothing, Jovi?"

"We are not doing nothing," Jovaar continued, reaching again for her arms. "For the moment, Nitaya is safe. We all are. Go to her. Take her to your quarters and try to get some rest. I will wait at Polatus Command with Iaco for Gidoran's return, and I promise as soon as we receive word I will come for you. Please trust me, Lena. I have never let you down and I do not plan on starting now."

"I just worry so, Jovi," she answered, at last giving in and laying her head on his chest.

"I know," he answered, running his fingers through her hair. "I wish you would not, but I know you will continue to do so and that is a quality I so love about you."

"Now go," he added, lifting her chin to look into her eyes. "It will be some time before we hear from him and I will feel better knowing that you are resting with Nitaya. See that she stays with you in your cabin. I know they have steward services, but I like my girls together."

"Your girls?" she asked, a trace of a grin appearing through her fallen tears.

"My girls," he answered, gently kissing her brow. "And as I promised, I will call on you both as soon as I receive word."

***

"Blasted!" Gidoran shouted adjusting the stick, the droids sitting silent at their stations. "We have left airspace communication capabilities then?"

"Yes, Sir Gidoran," one answered, not looking from his screen. "Setting course for hyper drive and informing Yani of our current location."

"How long will it take to refuel?" he asked, already assuming the answer. Prompting is own panel for the impending thrust, Gidoran tightened his restraints.

"Just shy of two hazon, Sir," the droid answered, tapping his screen. The requested route mapped before him.

"There must be some other way," Gidoran groaned, slinking back in his seat.

"Refueling is a process that allows no deviation, Sir," the droid answered methodically. "If you would like I could give you the specifications on the required processes and their specified…"

"No" Gidoran answered, closing his eyes.

"Well then, Sir," the droid continued, his tone flat as he at last turned to face his commander. "There is no way to…"

"I am not talking about the blasted refueling!" Gidoran shouted, wishing he had requested the crew. Instead he glared over his shoulder at the unfeeling being. "I meant that there must be some other way to inform Jovaar Savius of what is happening!"

"We could send an amphibian, Sir," the droid said, offering one of his programmed suggestions. "I can have Yani live on screen in mere moments. We could then order the ship for immediate detachment and thus they would be able to inform Savius of our status prior to our return."

"No," Gidoran sighed, toying with the map on his screen. "It is too risky. A spotting of the Sugins could only set off alarms. We do not need them wondering. Set hyper drive for home. Jovaar will just have to wait. I just pray he does nothing foolish…which is of course not like him, but everything like Iaco."

"Yes, Sir," the droid answered, pivoting back to his panel. "Hyper drive confirmed."

***

Selena crossed back to the head table shaken from Jovaar's words. The dancers finished their melodic display before her, oblivious to the importance of the happenings about them. As a sheer of cloth from one of the many pale costumes glided by, startling her from her trance as she reclaimed her seat, Selena eyed the small cot and instantly panicked at the absence of Nitaya.

Immediately rising, she raced down the length of the slab to the adjacent table. With the crew sitting around its oval undoubtedly enjoying themselves Selena ignored their revelry and reached out to the nearest member.

"Phydin?" she asked, grasping his arm and startling him. Jumping from his trance-like state, he rose to face her as the next set of stewards made their exit.

"What is wrong?" he asked, torn between Selena and the retreating dancers.

"Where is Agye?" she pressed. Frightened, she glanced over her shoulder and back to Jovaar's trusted pilot. "I gave Nitaya to Agye!"

"I did not see her leave," he said, at last focusing on the head table and the girl's vacant seat. "Is something wrong, Selena?"

"Sir Gidoran has attempted to contact Jovaar," she said, attempting to catch her breath. "He was..."

"What are you saying?" he pleaded, the others at last turning to the commotion. "Where is he?"

"Gidoran's status is unknown," she continued, lowering to her knees to steady her breathing. "Jovaar is certain his ship will return and he and Prince Iaco are awaiting his so-called roundabout at Command. I need to know which direction Agye went," she cried, Phydin lowering to one knee. "Phydin, please tell me you know something!"

"I am sorry but I do not," he answered, claiming her hands. "I am fairly confident that they just returned to the children's ward. Ask the others then look for them there. I will go to Polatus Command to see if I can assist Jovaar."

"Khyra," he added, turning to his right. "Nitaya is missing although I am certain she is well. To calm Selena however, ask the others and have them aid you in the search if necessary. I am heading to Command."

Seemingly more at ease in her borrowed attire, Khyra instantly gathered the folds of her gown and stood, turning to Selena. Dismissing Phydin's exit, she tossed a leftover shard of colorful cloth and lowered to Selena's side. "When was the last time you saw her?"

"Quite some time ago," Selena answered, wringing her hands and rising, turning to face the large room. "Khyra, I cannot breathe. I do not..."

"We will find her," Khyra said, rising to claim her shaking hands and turning to address the crew. "Hylin, Jax," she began, sternly ordering their attention. "We have to go now!"

"What is it? What is wrong?" Jax asked, tumbling his mug to the floor and abruptly standing, the last of the stewards having finished their display.

"Just leave it where it lies," she answered, motioning to the dark liquid on the floor. "Nitaya was given to Agye, Prince Iaco's servant," Khyra continued, gritting her teeth. "They were last known to be at the head table but as you can now see," she added, gesturing. "They are no longer there. I am certain there is nothing amiss but we must search them out."

"Selena," she continued, turning to the shaken girl. "Do you know the way to the children's ward?"

"I believe I can find it from here," she answered, attempting to compose her shaking hands. "I believe it should be through those doors."

"Very well," Khyra answered, turning back to the others. "We will start there where I am certain the child is resting. If we do not locate her though, we will spread out and search the entire compound. Now, let us go."

"What is happening?" Fidaldi asked, having been previously engrossed in the end of the display. Taking hold of Jax's arm at the standing of the others, he tossed yet another colorful cloth from the gunner's shoulder.

"I am not certain," Jax answered, glancing about the room. "But it does not sound good. We must get going." Setting down their cloths and prompting the release of their weapons, neither questioned the haste of the others. Despite the lingering of a few oblivious beautiful stewards, their focus at once returned. Abruptly they set off after Khyra.

***

"It is this way," Hylin said, passing through the great doors and turning right.

"How would you know the way to the children's ward?" Khyra asked, trailing after his confident, small steps.

"Er, right. I know I was told not to wander," he continued, head tipped. Hurriedly he paced the corridor, keeping his guilty eyes from his elder. "Yet I was able to steal away for a bit while those girls were dancing."

"Not my taste," he added, shrugging with a sly grin. "But I did not go far," he said, spying Khyra's stern stare. "It is just through here then down a bit more."

285

"Don't look at me," Jax added, eyes wide at Khyra's darting glare in his direction. "You were seated at the table too." Shaking her head, Khyra merely turned and followed Hylin through the next door.

Seemingly endless, she did her best to calm Selena who at the moment was anything but calm. Passing through the lengthy corridors, it appeared the titlegiver's own anxiousness brought about the same amongst the other members. "I should never have left her alone," Selena said, leaning on Khyra's arm. Her welling tears now spilled over her cheeks.

"You did not leave her alone," Khyra said reassuringly, wrapping her arm around Selena's shoulder. "You left her with Agye. It is her job to see to the wee ones. Prince Iaco would never have placed her in our service if she was not trustworthy. I am certain Nitaya just needed changing, or lying down, or something of that nature. I am confident we will find her well and then all of this worrying will have proven to be for nothing."

With the muffled sounds of the children echoing in the corridor beyond, Hylin quickened his pace, racing ahead before the members. Leading Selena at the rear, the pair reached the door just as the boy prompted its opening.

"It is in here," Hylin said, Selena nodding with recent memory. The room opened before them filled once again with the boisterous children. Not wanting to frighten the small innocents, the men at once shielded their weapons.

Crossing through the older children laughing in play, a steward prompted a story on the large-screened station not knowing of the seriousness of what happened about them. Darting to the familiar infant cots filled with the smaller Polatians, Selena continued to the fifth that had been Nitaya's.

"She is not here!" Selena sobbed, reaching within to take hold of the small blanket. Holding it to her face and inhaling deeply, Selena took in the scents of the child and wept. "I should not have left her alone," she sobbed, dropping to her knees.

"I for one remain confident that she is well," Khyra said, attempting reassurance. Lowering to Selena's side, she glanced upward with unease at the others. "We will begin by asking the servants. I am certain they will know where they are."

"Hylin, Jax," she ordered, snapping her fingers. Rising, she struggled with her cumbersome gown. "Ask the servants if they have seen them. Fidaldi, take the others and begin the search of the surrounding areas spanning from here. I will update Jovaar myself. Now go!"

"Selena," she added, turning back and hovering over the younger's quivering shoulders. "You are shaking and you need to sit down in a proper seat. We will find her. I promise you we will find her."

"You," she continued, a servant reaching in to tend to a nearby infant. "Have you seen the girl known as Agye?"

"No, ma'am, I am sorry," she answered, turning back to the wailing child. "She has not returned to the children's quarters since before the celebration."

"Come, Selena," Khyra continued, holding her steady to her feet, the woman turning back to the child without worry. "We will get you to your cabin and inform Jovaar from there. Come, we must hurry."

"I should not have left her," Selena wailed. Folding and refolding the small blanket in her hands, Khyra gently urged her forward. "I should never have left her."

***

"What is happening?" Phydin asked, breathlessly racing into the Polatian Command. Huddled before the helm's station, Jovaar and Prince Iaco looked up at the sound of his words.

"It is Gidoran," Jovaar answered, nodding to Iaco and crossing to his faithful friend. "He uplinked our communications and was able to inform us that the Sugins are hovering above the planet, waiting for our aerial departure. He has refueled their ship once and we assume is on roundabout now."

"He has done what?" Phydin instantly shouted, angrily balling his fists. "I told you we should never have trusted..."

"Calm, Phydin," Jovaar continued, familiarly patting his friend's arm. "We have been over his loyalty many times before. Gidoran refueled in good faith, my friend, allowing himself the opportunity to inform us. I had hoped that the Sugins would have left Kindawan airspace when they could no longer detect

287

our whereabouts, yet I should have known better. Iaco and I have been searching the skies through radar regardless of our limitations due to the density of Iaco's chosen home, and we have come up with nothing thus far...which obviously proves in our favor."

"G was in the process of uploading the Sugin's coordinates, but we lost his connection," Jovaar continued, claiming the open station at the rear of Command. "We have to assume he is still in roundabout and has left Kindawan airspace. We will maintain our monitoring of the skies and will simply have to wait out his return. How are the others?" he asked, attempting to lighten the mood.

"There is a possible situation, Sir," Phydin answered, eyebrow raised. His mind awhirl with doubts of Sir Gidoran and the possibility of a lost child, Phydin folded his arms at his chest.

"What is it?" Jovaar asked, abruptly returning to his feet. "What is wrong? Is it Selena?"

"I am not positive there *is* anything wrong," Phydin answered, shrugging. "Selena returned to the celebration and found Agye and Nitaya not there. She at once began to panic and questioned us if we had seen them leave. I am sorry, Jovaar but the dance had begun and I had not kept a close watch over the child. I assumed the girl was tending to her."

"Where is Selena now?" Jovaar asked, glancing nervously in Iaco's direction across the room.

"She is with Khyra and the others," Phydin answered, following his gaze. "I left them to search the facilities and came here at once."

"I need you, Iaco," Jovaar shouted, turning and crossing to his friend.

"What is wrong now, Jovi?" he asked, nodding to Phydin. "There has been no further sign of..."

"It is Nitaya," Jovaar interrupted, grasping Iaco's arm. "Selena left her with Agye when she came to Command, yet when she returned to the festivities she found both had gone. No one had seen them leave and based on the time Selena spent here, they could have a lead of almost a half hazon. Do you know where Agye could have taken her?"

"More likely than not the children's quarters, or possibly her own cabin, which is just off of the main room," Iaco answered, unconcerned. He mimicked Phydin's gesture, crossing his arms. "Agye is quite capable, Jovi. I am certain nothing is amiss."

"Well I am not so certain," Jovaar added, shaking his head. "Keep watch for the ship and inform me if you find anything. Phydin and I will begin our own search of the facility. We will require clearance and a layout of Polatus."

"Of course," Iaco answered, pulling the ring off his right middle finger and handing it to Jovaar. "This will get you in anywhere you seek. And this," he added, picking up and handing him a portal unit off the rear shelving. "This will show you all ship data and seconds as a communicator. There is nothing to hide."

"Very well," Jovaar said, placing the ring on his finger and securing the unit to his wrist. "We will begin in Agye's cabin and will spread out from there. Keep me updated, Iaco."

"I will send word as soon as..." he answered, stopping to watch his friend race from the cabin. "Typical, Jovaar," he whispered, shaking his head at his retreating friend. "Typical."

***

Docking proved smooth yet refueling seemed to be taking an eternity, and as the men busily reloaded the craft with supplies, Gidoran stood at the bottom of the boarding plank, monitoring their progress. "Can you not speed this up?" he shouted. The workers eyed one another, yet remained silent. Hefting the large UPS up the plank, they could not contain their low grumbles, Gdioran scowling relentlessly at their backs.

Following the next pair of loaders up the plank, Gidoran ran his fingers through his hair, pacing to the helm to get an update on the fueling. "What percentage are we?" he asked the lone droid who had remained at his station.

"Seventy-two, Sir," he answered, staring at his screen at the slowly growing glowing label.

"Blasted, we need to get back out there!" Gidoran said, pounding the back of the droid's seat with his fist. "We should have circled. We should have...we should have done something."

"I am certain you did all you could," the Captain said, Gidoran looking up at the sound of his voice."

"I know, I know," he moaned, covering his face with his hands.

"My men are fully prepared to board and assist in any way, Sir," the Captain continued, eyeing the droid. "Under the circumstances, we were hoping you had reconsidered."

"I do not see the point, Captain," Gidoran answered, at last facing him, leaning on a side panel. "Fueling was uneventful as was the roundabout, setting aside communications of course. The droids proved more than adequate."

"I understand, Sir," the Captain answered, bowing in disappointment, turning to leave.

"However," Gidoran continued, straightening. "I see no harm in having a few of you aboard."

"Sir?" the Captain asked, turning back.

"Yes," Gidoran continued, ruffling the scruff of his chin and nodding. "Have two of your men join us. Although it is precautionary only, it is better to be prepared. You were right. Send for them immediately. We will leave as soon as refueling is confirmed."

"Of course, Sir," he said, an eager gleam filling his eyes, exiting Command. It had been quite some time since he had seen battle, and although this was sure to be another boring flight, he secretly hoped for some action.

"One hundred percent fueled, Sir," the droid said, pivoting his head to face his commander.

"At last!" Gidoran shouted, returning to the helm. "Prepare the ship for detachment. We will be on our way as soon as the others are aboard.

"Yes, Sir," the droid answered, tapping his screen in preparation.

As the final processes were completed, the Captain promptly returned with two of his men, each quickly claiming the last remaining seats in the cabin. "Order detachment," Gidoran said, the anxious captain making the last of the required processes.

"Detaching in 5, 4, 3, 2, 1, detach," he ordered, the ship once again hovering, performing the one hundred eighty degree turn. Gidoran's restlessness proved to be subsiding.

"At last," he whispered, guiding the stick forward. "At last we are getting somewhere."

Twenty-Six

"Now think," Khyra said, brushing the folds of her gown and sitting down on the cot at Selena's side. "Can you think of any other places that Agye might have taken the child?"

"I do not know," Selena answered, rocking herself and clutching Nitaya's blanket to her chest. "I just do not know. I should not have left her."

Khyra patted Selena's knee and rose, crossing to those who stood waiting at the door. "She is no good to us now," she whispered, peering over her shoulder at Selena slowly rocking on the cot, mumbling incoherently into the child's blanket.

"Hylin," she continued, turning back to the group. "You said you were able to sneak away for a spell. Although I do not approve of that and we will certainly deal with it later, is there anywhere you visited that you think Agye might have taken her?"

"I cannot be certain," he answered, shrugging his shoulders. "I was not away for that long. I stumbled upon the children's quarters only because I heard the noise of them down the corridor. There were several small cabins off that main wing though," he added, ruffling his chin regardless of its lack of grown. "I suppose no one took notice of me because of my size."

"Alright then," Khyra said, nodding and looking to the others. "They must be servant quarters. We can start there. Hylin, can you add anything else?"

"I was only able to peek into two other places, a lab of some kind and another loading dock. I know the way to them but certainly a child would not have been brought to either of..."

"We will spread out then," Khrya interrupted, squeezing the boy's shoulder. "Jax, take Hylin and have him guide you to the other rooms. Fidaldi, take the others and head back to the children's quarters and make certain to check out those servant's cabins. I will stay here with Selena and update Jovaar on the com. Report back here if you find anything. And if you do not, spread your search and keep looking. As you all know, everything depends on the child."

"Let's go," Jax said, pushing Hylin and the others through the door. "You heard her. There's no time to waste."

Once all had left to begin their search, Khyra turned slowly to Selena. Shaking her head, she crossed to the com station. "Jovaar," she said, prompting the unit. "Jovaar, it is Khyra. Can you hear me?"

"Has the child been found?" the voice abruptly answered.

"Jovaar, is that you?" Khyra asked, uncertain.

"No, it is Iaco," he answered. "Have you found Nitaya?"

"No," she answered, nervously biting her lip. "I need to speak to Jovaar immediately."

"He should be just about there," Iaco continued. "He raced off with Phydin as soon as he got word of your situation. Inform him there has been no sign of Gidoran's ship. I will update him on his portal once G is within range."

"I will," she answered, startled at Jovaar and Phydin darting into the cabin.

"Lena!" he shouted, running to her side and kneeling next the cot.

"I could not find her," she sobbed, Jovaar claiming her hands. "I should not have left her."

"We will find her, Lena," he said, stroking her hair reassuringly. "You did nothing wrong."

"I did, Jovi," she said, wringing Nitaya's blanket in her hands. "I should have done more. It is my job to protect her. I should have...I should have...I should not have left her!"

Jovaar stood and looked to Khyra who remained at the door at Phydin's side. "How long has she been like this?"

"As soon as she reached the celebration and could not find the child," Khyra answered, eyeing Phydin. "I have done everything I could to calm her, but I assume she is handling this as any momar would. There is really nothing more I can do."

"Is the crew on search?" he asked, prompting the portal's map screen.

"They are just." Khyra answered, nodding. "They left mere moments before you arrived."

"Which way did you send them?" he asked, crossing to the pair.

"Hylin had wandered, although instructed not to," she continued, flippantly waving her hand. "He is guiding Jax to two locations he happened upon while the others search the servant's quarters off the children's wing."

"Show me," Jovaar ordered, pivoting to remove the glare from the overhead lights on his screen.

"I assume the quarters are here," she said, pointing as Jovaar patched the screen to zoon. "Yet Hylin did not say where the two other locations were. However, I am certain he said they were a lab and some sort of dock."

"They should be here and here," Jovaar added, pointing to what appeared to be two plausible locations near the area of quarters. "We will catch up with them here and spread out from there," he added, nodding to Phydin. "Khyra, remain with Selena and do what you can to settle her. I will report back as soon as we have something substantial."

Jovaar sealed his portal and turned to leave, Phydin prompting the door on cue. "I spoke to the Prince when I rang the com looking for you," Khyra said, halting the pair. "He said there has been no sign of Gidoran's ship and that he would update you as soon as he was within range."

"Very well," Jovaar answered, gesturing for Phydin to head out. "But my main concern now is Nitaya."

***

Carsian entered Command annoyed, his dark cloak flowing violently at his ankles. "An update, Terdoni," he ordered, folding his arms across his chest, the First Officer standing swiftly with the demand.

"King Sugin," he said, abruptly. "There has been no change. I was just about to send word for..."

"Enough!" Carsian interrupted, raising his hand to stifle the officer. "I grow tired of this lack of progress from both you and from Sivon, who as I have just been informed, has also not produced his possible. The time has arrived for action, and action we will take, Terdoni! Order all amphibious craft for detachment on my order!"

"And for your lack of progress," the King continued, Terdoni gesturing for his CO to give the order. "I have taken matters into my own hands and have had data officers scouring logs for possible locations and intelligence on the Savius child below. Each amphibious craft will upload the information that I have attained just prior to their detachment."

"You have wasted precious time, Terdoni," he added, grimacing, the remaining crew cowering at their stations. "Pray that this is resolved quickly or it will be you and you alone, who will face the consequences! Now, monitor the craft and crew and see that it is done!"

"Aye, Sir," Terdoni answered, shivering and bowing in respect. Turning to oversee the order, he felt the swish of the King's robe at his ankles as he left the cabin without further word.

"Sir," the subordinate said, shaking Terdoni back to the task. "Four amphibians are being prepped. The fifth is in service. Shall I rush maintenance?"

"Of course, you imbecile," Terdoni answered, taking a deep breath and resuming his pacing of the central aisle. "You heard King Sugin. Have all pilots aboard and awaiting transmission. They will debark on my order."

"Aye, sir," he answered, turning back to his panel to request the fifth ship's services. Terdoni ceased his stride and stood at his officer's back assessing the position of the ships shuttering at the thought of further displeasing the King. "Get updates from the other air craft," he ordered, snapping his fingers at the officer to his left.

"Sir," he answered, pivoting in his seat. "They are due to check in momentarily. Shall we not wait?"

"Order the update now!" Terdoni shouted, slamming his fists into the back of the officer's seat. "Did you not hear your King? The time for waiting is over!"

***

"How much longer must we wait until communications are operational?" Gidoran asked, the Captain prompting the stalling of hyper drive.

"We will be within range momentarily, Sir," he answered, giving him the same answer he had only moments before.

"Blasted," G continued, running his fingers through his hair despite guiding the stick. "This wait will be the death of me."

"Sugin ship attempting connection to the com," the lone droid said, not turning from his station.

"Connection confirmed," Gidoran answered, taking a deep breath.

"Sugan ship connecting to the com," the droid added flatly.

"We have you within range Phobis craft," the officer said from the imposing ship. "Continue your current course."

"Course confirmed," Gidoran answered, the route simultaneously mapping on his side screen as he released the com. "And it is about blasted time!"

"Phobis to Polatus, confirm," Gidoran continued, altering channels.

"We have you on screen," the voice responded. "Gidoran, is that you?"

"Yes," he answered, releasing the breath he had not known he was holding. "Thank the stars I have at last been able to reach you. I need to speak with Jovaar Savius at once."

"Relax, my friend," Iaco answered, stifling a chuckle. "I see you are as impatient as always."

"Iaco, is that you?" Gidoran asked, staring at the blackened face of the com.

"But of course," he answered, his grin apparent over the transmission. "Who were you expecting? It is Polatus you are chiming. You cannot possibly tell me that you had no idea that..."

"I realize it has been a long time, Iaco, but I do not have time for pleasantries," Gidoran interrupted, shaking his head. "Where is Jovi?"

"A situation has developed, G and he is unavailable at the moment," Iaco answered, his tone serious. "Tell me what you know."

"Is this line secure?" he asked, showing caution and glancing warily at the Captain, the lone droid unturning.

"Of course, but hold on," Iaco answered, confirming with his lieutenant commander. "The line is secure, Gidoran, go ahead," he answered the LC giving him the nod.

"We are in route to the Sugin ship, have established communications and should make dock momentarily," he answered, following the mapped route and tapping the stick slowly forward. "Initial fueling was in good faith as I previously stated. I have no choice but to continue with the second process but I believe I have a way for it to fail. As before, I do not have time to go into great detail. Instead, I am prepared to download their coordinates so you can prepare for evasive actions."

"Ordering transmission uplink now," Iaco answered, gesturing to his lieutenant to make the preparations. Crossing to the main panel to request the transmission, he nodded to Iaco with the opening of the line. "Begin download, Gidoran."

"Download in progress," he answered, nodding to the droid on his right to open their end of the line. "We are coming up on Sugin's ship now. Wait, Iaco...I see movement," he added, pausing. "A lower hatch is opening, stand by."

"Gidoran, what is it?" Iaco asked, watching impatiently as the uplink slowly rose on the LT's screen. "What is going on?"

"I do not know yet," he answered, staring out the glass, the massive hatch opening. "I need Jovaar."

"We are trying to locate him now," Iaco answered, rubbing his tired eyes. "G, are you still there?"

"We are attaching to the fuel arm now. Stand by," Gidoran answered, releasing the com.

"I hate all this waiting!" Iaco answered, frustrated as he slunk back into his seat. "Lieutenant, inform me once the uplink is completed and the moment we have located Savius."

***

297

"Amphibious craft standing by, Sir," Terdoni said, hesitantly into the com. "All prescribed data has been downloaded and they are awaiting your order for detachment."

"Very well," the King answered, fastening a fresh cloak in quarters. "Do not order flight. I want to speak to the pilots myself. Inform them I will be arriving on the dock momentarily."

"Aye, Sir," Terdoni answered, releasing the com. "Uplink the data they received to my screen," he ordered, turning back to his officers. "I want to know every detail of their flight and water paths."

"Aye, Sir," the officer answered without question, keying for the transmission.

"There will be no mistakes this time," Terdoni continued, pacing to claim the helm. "We will not fail King Sugin again."

***

Carsian arrived at the dock entrance and waved off his pair of guards, finding the four pilots huddled next to the nearest of the four ships. Dressed in flight gear with their communicators hanging loosely at their necks, they appeared to be deep in discussion, yet turned abruptly, one indicating to the others the presence of their approaching King.

"Your promptness is encouraging," Carsian said, stopping a few paces in front of his pilots. "And now," he continued, folding his arms at his chest. "You will heed my instructions very carefully. All data that we have collected thus far has been uploaded onto your monitors. As you will see once you have taken your assigned ships, there are two separate flight paths and therefore there will be a lead craft with a slider for additional support."

"All communications will be handled through me directly," he continued firmly, walking forward to palm the belly of the nearest amphi. "I admit you may find nothing, but in all probability I believe you will, and thus you may come under enemy fire at any time. I have no specifics on the ships you may encounter, and therefore can not accurately assess your danger. I do, however, have a benefit for your time and bravery."

"Since this flight of yours is pivotal to securing the Sugin reign," Carsisan continued, returning his attention to his men. "I have set documents aside for the crew that finds Jovaar Savius, his support staff and most importantly the child. Those persons will gain immediate and undisputed access to the Elite Members and will be certified as such on my order. This act as you know is rare and gives you and your kin a status they have never known. I trust this will be to your liking."

"Aye, Sir," they answered in unison, each shaking their heads and patting each other's arms at the possibilities before them.

"Very well," the King answered, waving them silent. "Your flight is cleared. Accept your assignment and debark immediately."

"Aye, Sir," they repeated, gathering their gear and heading toward their individual craft.

"Savius, my young friend," the King whispered, gritting his teeth, watching his pilots eagerly board. "As with Mathius, it appears your time has come."

***

Gidoran docked easily with the fuel arm with only a minor tremor, the ship making contact with the extension and fusing as before. "Docking confirmed," he said, releasing the stick and pivoting away from his crew. "Begin the transfer."

Staring out the side glass at the open hatch Gidoran sat silent considering his options. The Sugin ship had not opened its hatch at the last transfer, and uneasiness washed over him as he stared out at the empty eeriness of the massive hull.

"Fuel transfer at 10%," the Captain said, interrupting his thoughts.

"How long until we are are fully depleted?" Gidoran asked, at last turning to face him.

"Not long," the Captain answered, looking up from his screen. "I have set the program at maximum."

"You did what?" Gidoran shouted, frustratedly rising from his seat. "I wanted minimum transfer! Adjust the program immediately!"

"Yes, Sir!" the Captain answered, uncertain as to why his commander would find fault with his actions, prompting to slow with the demand. "May I ask why, Sir?" the Captain hesitantly asked. "I was under the impression you would want to roundabout immediately and..."

"I have my reasons," Gidoran interrupted, his anger subsiding with the slowing of fuel, ignoring the confused look of his captain and pivoting back to the glass. "What the..."

Gidoran was silenced at the sight of four small ships dropping from the Sugin monstrosity, setting course in pairs in opposite directions. "What type of craft are they?" he asked, not taking his eyes from the glass.

"They are amphibious, manned only with a pilot, Sir," the droid answered, flatly.

"Blasted," Gidoran groaned, quickly turning back to his screen. "Iaco!" he shouted, prompting the com. "Are you still there?"

"Well it is about blasted time, G," he answered, his annoyance obvious. "I do oversee Polatus and have other bad things happening at the same time. I do not have time to just sit back and wait for you to..."

"Iaco, *I* do not have time," Gidoran interrupted, slamming his fist into the base of his panel. "Get Jovaar to Command now! We are at approximately twenty-five percent fueling and I just witnessed four amphibious craft detaching from the Sugin ship. Do you have my download of their coordinates?"

"The program just finished uploadng on our end," he answered, his lieutenant nodding in confirmation. "And we are bringing it online now. What can you see is their current flight path?"

"They are flying in pairs, Iaco," Gidoran answered, shaking his head and turning from the glass, the ships no longer in sight. "Two set out completely off your location and the second pair is headed directly toward you. I am going to break off refueling and redirect to Yani. I will somehow find suitable transportation and will get to you as soon as possible. Inform your crew I will be arriving, although it will take quite some time."

"You cannot just break off from Sugin's ship, G," Iaco said, gesturing to his lieutenant to prompt the shields.

"I will find a way," Gidoran answered, confidently. "Just be ready for an attack, Iaco. I will return as soon as I can."

***

"Order detachment," Gidoran shouted, the crew staring at him blankly.

"Sir," the Captain began, lowering his hands to his lap. "We are only at forty percent fueling. I know that you feel a sense of loyalty to your friends below but this does not make sense. I do not understand."

"I know," Gidoran answered, pounding his fist on the panel. "Just do it! I do not have time for discussions!"

"But Sir," the Captain pressed, sweat beading on his brow. "If we detach from the arm they will question our intentions. If they do not like our answers they will undoubtedly attack. We are in fact fully armed, yet if they send out multiple defensive crafts we will undoubtedly be overtaken."

"That is a risk we will have to take," Gidoran answered, pivoting back to the stick. "I allowed you to come along on this mission, now do as I say and detach!"

"Yes, Sir," the Captain answered, gritting his teeth and tapping his screen. "Ordering cease fuel."

"Fuel ceased," the droid answered, unmoved.

"Detachment in 5, 4, 3, 2, 1, detach," the Captain continued, leaning to look out the side glass. "Be on the lookout for enemy craft. They will not sit still for long."

"Ship Phobis!" the officer shouted over the com, Gidoran lowering his ship away from the arm. "Fueling is not complete and you have disengaged. Explain your actions at once!" Gidoran waved off the worried Captain, taking the com himself.

"Malfunction in the transfer line," he said, attempting calm. "Systems were performing at maximum and thinned progressively. Surely this was indicated at your station as well. Returning to base for maintenance and have ordered an additional craft. Transfer is sufficient until one arrives."

"Payment for this annoyance will not be transmitted!" the officer shouted, his anger obvious. "See to it that this does not happen again!"

"Confirmed," Gidoran answered, a sly grin crossing his face as he turned to his companions. "It seems they have bought it."

"Sir?" the Captain questioned, prompting an open route for hyper drive. "You once again confuse me. We have not ordered another craft."

"No, we have not," Gidoran answered, his grin widening. Glncing over his shoulder, he winked at his subordinate. "Yet they do not know that, do they? Hyper drive to Yani at one, Captain. We need roundabout and we need it fast."

"Yes, Sir," the Captain answered, slowly nodding. Turning back to his controls, he at last understood his commander's tactics. Rerouting the ship and confirming the Captain's routed HD, Gidoran raced Phobis through the open sky.

Twenty-Seven

Hylin and Jax reached the corridor just outside the children's quarters, gesturing for the others to continue on ahead to the other areas. "Khyra said for you to take the lab and dock," Fidaldi said, nodding over his shoulder.

"They are just beyond that door and to your right," Hylin answered, waving his hand. "I know you can handle it. We will take the quarters."

Hylin stood firm, watching Fidaldi shrug with indifference before leading his comrades though the adjacent door. Turning to Jax as the pair disappeared from sight, Hylin directed him to the left toward the servant's cabins. "There are six of them," he said nodding, recalling the familiar doors. Jax tapping his temple in a silent confirming response at their numbers, comforted at the recollection of a boy his age. To save time, each darted in opposite directions.

Prompting the first door, Jax found a woman sleeping on her cot, her golden hair flowing atop her pillow. Obviously needing her rest, she did not awake or even stir as Jax glanced about the room. Spying the sparse contents of the cabin, he realized that no one else could possibly be within the cramped confies and slowly crept backwards. Closing the door at his back, he eagerly crossed to search the next cabin to his left.

The next cabin proved deserted, exactly resembling the previous room sans its occupant. Spying the small empty cot with its side table, washbasin, and clothing hook on the wall, Jax found nothing disturbed, yet crept inward to investigate the semi-large right cabinet. Opening it to be certain nothing was left unturned, he sighed when he found it also empty.

"Nothing," he whispered, lowering his weapon and retreating to the next room. Finding nothing but the same in the third, he closed the door, meeting Hylin in the outer corridor.

"I found nothing," he repeated, shaking his head and absentmindedly checking his weapon.

"I found the same," Hylin answered, sounding discouraged. "But we must keep looking. Let us head toward the lab and loading dock where the others are searching. They may have found something and if not they might know of other places to search."

"You're right although it pains me to say so," Jax answered, attempting to sound upbeat, purposely ruffling the boy's hair knowing it displeased him. "Lead the way." Grabbing Jax's hand from his tresses and nodding, Hylin led his elder back through the main cabin and out the double doors, hoping above all hope that Nitaya had been found.

    ***

"There are too many places in this blasted room to hide!" Fidaldi shouted across the lab to the others.

"I know, but we must keep looking," Luvin answered, pushing a free-standing cabinet to the side.

"How many rooms can jut off this place?" Fidaldi asked frustratingly, leaving one room and opening the door of another.

"It is deserted, Fidaldi," Luvin answered, shouting after his friend. "Everyone is attending the festivites. Let us think a moment," he added, Fidaldi joining the rest of the group. "If Agye took Nitaya and meant to do her harm, where would she take her?"

"My first instinct was the lab," Fidaldi answered, stooping to his knees to catch his breath. "I was certain that if she worked for the enemy she would bring death upon the child quickly, and what better place for that than here?" he added, spreading his arms wide about the lab.

"But what if death was not her role, but instead she was ordered to bring the child to them?" Luvin asked, staring out into the empty room. "That would mean the loading dock. Hylin said he had seen it, but which way is it?"

"Which way is what?" Jovaar asked, racing toward the members with Phydin trailing close behind.

"The lab is empty," Fidaldi continued updating the approaching pair. "And we were about to head toward the loading dock. Well, we were about to, but we were not certain which direction to take. Hylin, informed us it was..."

"Khyra has updated us and Iaco has given me the layout of the compound on this portal. If you think the loading dock is where we should begin then that is where we will begin," Jovaar interrupted, opening the small unit and searching for the location. "Here," he added, pointing. "It is this way. Follow me."

Obviously relieved that Jovaar was there to lead them, the members heeded their commander's order. Gladly following him out the lab toward the exterior door, Fidaldi prayed above all that there was still time.

"Do you want me to stay with you?" Phydin asked, reaching the opening of the corridor. "I could possibly..."

"Stay with us," Jovaar answered, reaching about his friend to open the door. "We have no idea of what we are about to face and as always, I need someone I trust at my back."

***

The air flight proved tedious, yet the pilots continued their path unscathed over the Kindawan Sea. "Systems check," one said to the other, glancing to his left out the glass.

"Performing now," the slider pilot answered, prompting his screen. "All data indicates smooth sailing. We are on route to submerge in eighty."

"Confirm that," the first answered, monitoring his panel and agreeing with the results. "Begin preparations for dive."

"Confirm preparations for dive," the slider responded, setting the required controls. "Pressure check, lines check, gauges check. Confirmed dive preparations."

"Copy that," the pilot answered, eyeing the standard processes. "Dive drop fifty-five, fifty, forty-five," he continued, the slider pilot copying his discent. With both ship's panels flapped closed, the anti-shield grew about their main hulls.

"Twenty-five, twenty, fifteen," he continued, his voice calm despite the intenseness of the drop. "I love this part," he added flatly, glancing quickly over his shoulder. "Ten, five, submerge." Water engulfed the craft and instantaneously the pressure shifted within their tight quarters.

"Pressurizing," the pilot said, the slider echoing his command. Several moments passed as the pair adjusted to the weight of the sea and the duo familiarly prompted their systems to adapt to the submersive.

"Contacting Command," the pilot continued, prompting the specified controls to speak directly to his commander. "Air flight complete, King Sugin," he said confidently. "Submerged and in route."

"Well done," the King answered from quarters. "Keep me abreast as often as necessary."

"Aye, Sir," the pilot answered, releasing the com and prompting the stick forward. "We are clear to proceed. Keep your eyes open and stay close. Who knows what we will find down here."

"Copy that," the slider answered, pulling along side of his comrade. As the lead ship darted into the deep, the slider kicked the throttle and raced after him, trailing into the darkness of the unknown.

***

The members made their way to the end of the corridor, rounding the first corner as Jovaar stared at his portal, pointing to Fidaldi the directions to where they were headed. Hylin and Jax veered round the bend in the opposite corner, running directly into him.

"I am sorry," Hylin said, looking up from the floor.

"It was my fault," Jovaar answered, offering his hand to assist. "I was too engrossed in the map. Did you find anything in the children's area?"

"No, nothing," Jax answered for him, leaning against the outer wall. "The children's quarters proved quite quiet despite all the noise from the wee ones. There was no sign of them in Agye's cabin, or the others for that matter. We were on our way to the lab to see what the others may have found. I asume they came up empty also."

"They did, yes," Jovaar answered, straightening the portal on his wrist. "We are heading toward the docks now. Come with us. If we find nothing, we can spread out again from there. It is this way," he added, looking from his portal and pointing.

"I can get us there quicker," Hylin added, glad to prove his worth to Jovaar.

"The portal says…"

"I am certain it is right but I have a better way," Hylin interrupted, glancing in Jax's direction for approval. "You can trust me, Jovaar. If I can outlive my equivalents on Yani, I can certainly maneuver the corridors of Polatus." Knowing that Hylin had secretly visited the docks earlier, Jovaar was inclined to save the time of arguing and let the boy help.

"Lead the way then," he said, closing his portal and looking to the others. With a gleam in his eye, Hylin turned, eagerly motioning for the members to follow.

  ***

"Jovaar?" Khyra asked, Jovaar slowing Hylin and the others. "Jovaar, are you there?"

"I am here," he answered, settling against the side wall. "How is Selena?"

"She is resting now," Khyra answered, staring at her limp frame on the cot. "However, she proved inconsolable and after several attempts to soothe her nerves, I was forced to ring the Med-
Officer. He gave her something I cannot pronounce and she is at last resting comfortably. Have you found Nitaya? As Selena, I have been quite nervous in this cabin with nothing to do."

"No, nothing yet," Jovaar answered, looking anxiously to the others. "Yet we have not been searching that long. We are heading to one of the docks now and we will spread out from there. I will update you as soon as we know something. Have you had any word from Iaco? He has not…wait," he added, spying the side prompt. "He is chiming in now. I will get back to you as soon as I can."

"Iaco, what is it?" he asked, altering to the incoming line.

"I just got offline with Gidoran," he answered, anxiousness filling his words. "He informed me that four amphibious craft have detached from the Sugin ship. They are in pairs, two heading away from us while two are heading directly toward us. I am making preparations for an attack and have ordered the majority of my pilots to the base main dock. Have you found Nitaya?"

"No," Jovaar grumbled, settling the eager search party with his hand. "We are on our way to your alternate dock now."

"It is going to be rather hectic there," Iaco continued, fruitlessly attempting to silence the noise of Command. "Is there anything you want me to do?"

"No, we will manage," Jovaar answered, urging the others forward. "I will report back as soon as we have something. Is G in danger?"

"I would like to say no," Iaco answered, uncertain. "He has disengaged, ceasing the refueling and returning to Yani for roundabout with assistance. He is out of range now and I do not expect his return for some time. I am afraid we are on our own."

"I have changed my mind. Get me a ship, Iaco," Jovaar continued, watching as the others reached the next door. "I will assist with the search then do what I can to protect the compound from the sea."

"Jovaar, I do not think that…"

"There is no time for arguments, Iaco," Jovaar interrupted, resuming his stride. "Just get the blasted ship ready."

"As you wish, my friend, but be careful," he answered, reluctantly.

"I always am," Jovaar said, turning to the others. Crouching before the next opening, they could not help but overhear the transmission.

"Let us go," he added, peering back into the empty corridor. "As we speak the Sugins are on their way and we are wasting time."

***

Continuing down the next series of vacant corridors, the group at last reached the large entrance to the dock. Peering in and spying the Polatian members scurrying about with the pending enemy strike, Jovaar and Phydin counted heads, pilots readying their gear with their droids frantically preparing the ships for battle. As the yellow lights of warning flashed high above, fuel lines were strewn haphazardly on the floor and gear trolleys were dragged next to each craft in preparation for loading.

"Where do we begin," Phydin asked, rising and stepping forward over the first line. "There is so much happening with the impending strike. I cannot see how a child would go unnoticed."

"I agree," Jovaar answered, nodding to the others. "Spread out and search all areas. Search all gear trolleys for smuggling and even if they give you heed, search every blasted craft. Something feels wrong. The timing of this gives me cause for suspicion. She is here. I feel it."

"All right then, you heard him," Phydin said, turning to the others, the whir of ships breathing life at his back. "Spread out and leave nothing unturned."

Racing from the entrance in all directions through the chaotic dock, Jovaar stood back, watching his men and checking his portal for hidden areas, confident with Phyin taking over the search. "Sir," one of the workers said, interrupting his thoughts. "I am sorry to interrupt you, Sir, but Prince Iaco has ordered you a ship which as we speak is being prepped. We need you to check your positioning."

"I am sorry?" Jovaar questioned, shaking his head and looking up from his portal. "What are you asking? My positioning for what?"

"Yes, Sir," the dockhand continued, surprise in his commander's lack of knowledge. "The RZ6's are the latest in technology available to Polatus and each craft is designed to fit a certain body type. We will need you to climb aboard and strap in as if for detachment. The system will make the necessary adjustments about you."

Jovaar was annoyed. He had wanted to spend as much time as he could assisting his crew in the search for the child, yet looking at the oblivious and ignorant man before him, he knew there was no other option. Resigned, he reluctantly nodded in agreement.

"I assure you it will not take long," the worker added, gesturing for Jovaar to follow. Frustrated and although biting his tongue, Jovaar glanced from right to left with each step at the main's back, his eyes searching the anxious workers for any sign of the child.

"She is here," he thought to himself, rubbing the stubble on his chin, the lowly worker gesturing him forward to the RZ6. "The only question is where."

***

"Get out of the way!" the dockhand impatiently shouted, Jax leaning with both hands against one of the moored ships, panting. Extraordinary and nothing like he had ever seen, Jax ignored the lowly laborer and catching his breath, ran his hands over the sleek exterior of the craft. Not pedestal bound as was the norm for an airborne craft these particular ships appeared to be hovering in water, like vessels at a dock on the great sea. The RZ6 ships were slender and did slightly resemble their aircraft counterparts, yet they were painted a dark blue and seated one, with a cramped pit for the pilot to man the lone stick. Leaning against the next and peering within the pilot seat, Jax found nothing but the various controls. Sighing, he knew there was simply no room for anything else, once again noting the tight, expected RZ6 quarters.

Seeing no point in checking the others yet heeding Jovaar's word with his sense of loyal duty, Jax ran down the docks, jumping over the various fuel lines in search of the next craft, the sleek RZ's for the moment forgotten. Again, finding nothing and annoying yet another worker as he busily prepared the ship for detachment, Jax turned, ramming into one of the many trolleys. Grimacing and clutching firm to his throbbing knee, he peered over his left shoulder and spied Kroy questioning one of the workers next to another gear trolley. Chuckling despite his pain at the annoyance his friend was obviously confronting, Jax shook his head, simultaneously noting Luvin to his right, nosily checking another craft.

"This is pointless," he said, discouraged and kicking at the tilted trolley. "She cannot possibly be here." Grumbling and reluctantly continuing down the noisy dock, Jax trotted to the next ship, the pain of his knee subsiding as with his resumed search.

"Nothing," he mumbled, looking away from the empty pit and off to the next. Rising to continue on to the next track however, he spied a pair of ships unlike all others off in the distance.

"*Hello,*" he whispered, noting their grandness. Certain that by their sheer size the two ships must be Prince Iaco's transports, he leaned back against his last search, considering the possibility. "Maybe, just maybe," he thought tapping his chin. Straightening and racing toward the central loading zone between the pair, he noted the numerous gear trolleys just off their main planks, considering it odd that they remained untouched

"Luvin," he shouted in mid-stride, careful to dodge the numerous trolleys and fuel lines. "Follow me. Those are pointless," he added, gesturing and quickening his steps. Turning and at last taking notice of the sister ships, Luvin nodded, quickly trailing after his friend.

"I think you may be right!" Luvin shouted, dodging a pair of workers and struggling to keep pace. "You take that one and I will take the other to save time."

"Good thinking," Jax answered, turning to his right. "No peering in," he shouted over his shoulder. "Get in there and find her!"

"This is it, I know it," Luvin said, climbing the empty plank.

"Get your weapon out and be ready," Jax added, looking over and releasing his own. "Who knows what we are up against."

Mimicking his friend, Luvin slammed his back against the ships's outer shell. Releasing the weapon at his side, he glanced over at the other looming ship and his friend. "Let me know if you find anything."

"You do the same," Jax answered, climbing the long plank. "And Luvin, no matter what, be ready. With everyone scattered throughout Polatus, you must know as well as I do that we are on our own."

***

Jovaar followed the worker to his assigned craft, quickly climbing aboard to begin the sequence. With the interior pit proving surprisingly roomy, he settled into his comfortable seat, peering out the narrow glass shell as the worker made the adjustments to his station from the dock. The panel, tall and slender, stood attached to the craft by a long gray cord. Grumbling as he impatiently waited for the transaction, Jovaar watched as Hylin darted passed to his left, the member calmly keying the transaction, unnerved.

"What could be taking so long?" Jovaar thought, startled with the craft awakening about him. At once the interior controls blinking vibrantly in their various colors. Reaching for the overhead compartment, he abruptly attempted to exit the awakening ship.

"Just sit tight, Sir," the worker said, his voice and the sounds of the dock transmitting through the com as he motioned wildly from his post for Jovaar to reclaim his seat. "I assure you that all is as it should be and the sequence will not take long."

Hesitating, Jovaar reluctantly followed the man's word and reclaiming his seat, sat in awe, the craft's pit forming slowly around him. As the sides narrowed and the seat adjusted to better able him to reach the foot taps, he marveled at the height, also appearing to alter, shrinking to his stature.

"I can make further adjustments if it is not to your liking, Sir," the worker continued into his portal, walking casually toward the ship. "If you would just..."

"No," Jovaar interrupted, tapping the foot controls and toying with the stick, his thoughts for the moment in the present. "I think this will work. Are we done?"

"We are," the man answered, returning to his station. "You may exit the craft to suit up and to wait out the final preparations."

"Very well," Jovaar answered, shifting to climb out. However, as the space proved much tighter than earlier, his exit proved anything but graceful. "My gear?" he questioned, at last reaching the plank. Gritting his teeth he prayed that Phydin was proving his leadership.

"This way," the worker answered, gesturing toward the trolley at the rear. "You should be ready for detachment momentarily."

"Very well," Jovaar repeated, snapping from his thoughts. Opening the top compartment of the trolley, he peered about the dock and finding no sign of his crew. "But the longer it takes the closer Sugin gets."

***

Jax entered the large ship cautiously, his weapon ready at his side. Heading aft in the large mid-ship cabin hugging the inside wall, two workers boarded, glancing him over as they lowered a large crate to the floor. Nodding and lowering his weapon, the pair merely shrugged and returned to the plank, obviously more concerned with their task.

Roomier than he had first anticipated, the ship opened up at its center, revealing transport seats for at least twenty. Rounding the large section for passengers and then the first corner, Jax peered round cautiously, unknowing what lay ahead.

"At least two midship cabins," he thought, peering back over his shoulder toward the bow. Thinking it odd that the two workers had not returned carrying their next load, he felt chills run through his limbs, hurrying to the rear to continue his search.

The gunnery station proved finer than any he had ever seen. Crossing to the midstation and running his hands over the interior controls, Jax forgot his senses and stood in awe at the newest of technology. Claiming a low right seat and prompting the few controls he recognized, he felt the lift beneath him, the seat rising to circle the ship. Quickly retappng the panel, it responded swiftly, again lowing to the floor.

"Adequate," he whispered, grasping the guns. "But you," he added, turning to marvel at the large exterior brute. "You are a thing of beauty."

Daring not to depress the glowing prompt even though he was certain it would not fire while the ship was attached, Jax

313

grazed his hand over the small knob, the senses of his fingers dancing. "But oh how I wish…"

"Sir!" the worker said, startling Jax from his daze, slamming a large crate to the floor. "You should not touch that! You should not even be here! The ships are not fully prepped for detachment. If you were to…"

"I know what I am doing," Jax interrupted, raising his hand to stifle the man. "Have you seen a small child or a young woman boarding this craft?"

"I fail to grasp your reasoning, Sir," the man answered, placing his hands on his hips. "But this ship is piloted by Captain Wozer. He is at the helm and would know of such things."

"But have you seen a child?" Jax pressed, slowly rising from the gunnery station, tipping his head about the overhead contols.

"No," he answered, stowing the small tote from his shoulder in the side cabinet. "I am certain you are mad with what you are asking, but Captain Wozer would know of anyone aboard. You will disengage the gunnery then check with him."

"I will indeed," Jax answered sarcastically, shrugging as he nd crossing to the door. "Is there any other compartments throughout the ship?"

"There is storage to your right on the way to the helm," the man answered, gesturing for the intruder to return to mid-ship. "There are no other quarters as you speak of although there are several cable shoots large enough to pass throughout."

"My thanks," Jax added, peering over his shoulder. "I think it is time I had a chat with this Wozer."

   ***

Luvin was not having much luck with the deserted craft. "Maybe Jax has found something," he thought, glancing round the final bend of the rear before heading to midship. Retracing his steps to the gunnery, he again found it empty, yet opened the various cabinets he had overlooked on his first pass regardless.

"I am certain Jax is enjoying you," he whispered, wiping his hand over the polished station. Knowing he was wasting time however, he quickly turned and continued to mid-ship.

Stepping round the pair of workers loading the transport for sail, Luvin crossed through the numerous passenger seats and spied the small door on his way to the helm. "Surely not," he thought, jarring it open. Eyeing the half empty storage cabinet, relatching it and skirting another worker, he paced quickly to command, finding the door remained firmly locked.

"Open this door immediately," he shouted, banging his weapon on the frame. "I have to search the cabin prior to detachment."

"I am performing systems check and assure you I am the only man aboard," the voice answered, both curtly and firm. "Continue on to the next task on your Polatian checklist."

"I am no Polatian deckhand and I must search this cabin," Luvin pressed, pounding his fist on the barricade. "Release the door for entrance. I will not be but a moment."

"As I have told you," the voice answered, his temper obviously flaring. "I am performing system check and am unable to grant access. Disembark!" Luvin noticed the shift in the man's tone and raised his weapon.

"Sir," he continued, firmly gritting his teeth and eyeing his weapon. "I am ordering you to open this door. I am on orders of Prince Iaco to search all ships! No craft is to leave for battle without viewing. Open the blasted door!"

"As you wish," the voice answered oddly calm. The door rose before him simultaneous with the ringing blast. "Such a pity," the man said bending and dragging the body quickly within. "We were so restricted before and this will only add to the matter."

"You!" he added, gesturing and dropping the lifeless body to the floor without feeling. "Quiet her at once! I assure you, no one will save her now!"

Twenty-Eight

"Phobis to Yani," Gidoran said, prompting the com the moment the brilliant station came into view.

"We have you in sight, Sir Gidoran," the communications officer answered. "Go ahead."

"I need an amphibious craft fueled, fully armed, and on stand by waiting my return," Gidoran ordered, eyeing his Captain.

"Sir," the CO answered uncertain. "I have to search the logs to see if there is a ship of that kind in dock. Those craft are not capable of hyper drive, Sir. May I inquire about your intentions?"

"I need a blasted transport *and* an amphibious craft loaded aboard," he answered, pounding his fist on his side panel. "This is something I should not have to explain to you! Search all logs. There has to be one there!"

"I meant no disrespect, Sir," the CO continued, attempting to hide his nervousness. "But it will take some time. Please maintain your current course and stand by."

"I swear every time I need something...."

Gidoran sailed their current path in silence, staring out the glass with Yani creeping into focus. The station's rises glowed high above the denseness of his home, providing a view he most often cherished.

"Guide us in," he said, gesturing to the Captain over his shoulder.

"Sir?" he questioned, turning from his screen. "You want me to..."

"Transfer the controls and guide us in," he interrupted, repeating the order and reprompting the com. "CO?"

"Yes, Sir, we are still searching, Sir," he answered abruptly.

"I also need another tanker, half loaded and its crew on standby," Gidoran added, eyeing the transfer of the stick to the Captain's station on his screen. "I will give them their orders once we have attached."

"Yes, Sir," he answered, the com again quieted.

"Half loaded, Sir?" the Captain questioned, having overheard Sir Gidoran's order, getting the feel of the lead.

"Yes," Gidoran answered, staring at his prided station out the glass, ruffling the scruff of his chin. "Only half."

***

The screeching of the docks proved deafening as the pilots began boarding, firing their ships in standard yet chaotic order. "Anything?" Jovaar shouted, Fidaldi and Kroy racing toward him and his assigned craft.

"Nothing yet, Sir," Fidaldi answered, leaning down and placing his hands on his knees to catch his breath. "I saw Jax and Luvin headed in that direction," he continued, pointing. "Just around the bend there are two sister ships, larger than the others. We were about to head after them to see if they had found anything. Hylin is off checking the outskirts of the area and Phydin is questioning the dock hands. It does not look like they are here, Sir. It is possible that they..."

"They are here," Jovaar interrupted, securing his flight suit at his neck and scanning the area. "I just know they are. Go after Jax and Luvin and report back immediately. The ships are readying for detachment. I cannot hold out much longer if I am going to be of any use to them."

The pair nodded then turned, racing off through the melee of workers toward the ships, Jovaar trailing after them to get a closer look at the odd pair. Larger than he had expected, he knew their separate Command could potentially hold a crew of more than four.

"Possibly," he said, taking another step forward. Phydin raced to his side however, interrupting his thoughts.

"The dock hands have seen nothing and do not appreciate the interruption," he began sarcastically, shouting above the wailing sirens and thrusters. "I have been informed that all craft

317

need to debark at once so that the shields can be raised. You need to head back into your ship."

"I know," Jovaar answered, setting his headset in place.

"Do you know how to pilot one of those?" Phydin asked, pointing to Jovaar's craft.

"I know enough," he answered, turning to the ship then back to face him. "Here, take the portal. If Nitaya is not found prior to my detachment, I am leaving the search in your hands. Keep Iaco and Khyra fully informed of your status. Iaco will be able to reach me."

"Jovaar," Phydin pressed, taking the portal and placing his hand on Jovaar's shoulder. "What if it is too late?"

"Do not ever say..." he shouted, balling his fists and gritting his teeth, the sounding of another ship firing directly to his left. "Do not ever repeat those words, Phydin," he continued, attempting calm and shaking his head at his friend. "We *will* find her. We must. Now go," he added, patting Phydin's back and turning toward his awaiting ship. "We are wasting time."

***

Jax reached the bow of the ship oddly finding two men making their final preparations for detachment regardless of an empty mid-ship. One was seated at the controls and the other stood at his back impatiently barking orders. "Captain Wozer," he began, stepping to the open door of the cabin.

"What is it?" the man shouted, turning abruptly to face the intruder.

"I am sorry to interrupt Sir, but...

"Then you should not have interrupted!" Wozer roared, flailing his arms. "Why are you not loading the ship? I gave full instructions to..."

"I am no dock hand!" Jax shouted impatiently, glaring over his shoulder in an attempt to calm his anger. "As I was saying, I am sorry that I interrupted, but I am under orders of Prince Iaco to search the entirety of Polatus, which includes this ship, for a missing child and her steward. If you are not capable of sparing a moment of your time than maybe we should get the good Prince on the com to sort this through."

Jax was losing his patience and stood obviously huffing as Wozer rethought his approach. "Forgive me," he said at last, motioning for the man to enter the surprisingly small cabin. "I had no idea that you too were on a mission of sorts. I assure you there is no need to contact Prince Iaco. There is no one aboard this ship but my pilot, myself, and a few dock hands loading essentials. I further assure you that if someone were to happen aboard, I would have known."

"I see," Jax continued, slightly amused, tapping his finger lightly upon his lips. "So when was it that you learned of my boarding?"

"I..." Captain Wozer began, unable to find words. "I..." he added, tipping his head. "I did not know you were aboard, Sir. My apologies, Sir. Please inspect the ship as you see necessary, yet I must insist you do so in haste. We will be detaching momentarily."

"Of course," Jax answered, grinning at the imposing Wozer puddling before him. "But as it is I have already searched the craft and was just checking the Command before debarking. The sister ship?" he added, pointing out the glass to their neighbor. "I will need the name of her Captain."

"Ruvis," Wozer answered, appearing pleased that the intruder would be on his way. "Captain Ruvis is who you seek".

"My thanks," Jax added, turning to leave. "And may your voyage prove safe."

"My thanks as well," Wozer answered, his words lightened, watching the man race from the ship. "Now where is that readout?" he bellowed, regaining his composure. The pilot shook the awe from his face and turned back to his screen.

"I am sorry, Sir," he said, fumbling with the keys for the information. "It is just..."

"Just remember who is in control here," Wozer interrupted, gritting his teeth and staring at his subordinate's back. Shielding his smirk, the pilot merely nodded, prompting Wozer's data.

***

319

Jax reached the ship's hatch and raced down the plank, passing two dock hands with yet another crate of supplies. "How much could they possibly need with noone aboard?" he thought, shaking his head with his discent. Turning and looking up at the sister ship, he slid his arm across its belly, quickening his steps and noting the different labeling to the left of the hatch. Climbing the next plank he paused, glancing over his shoulder.

"Odd," he thought, drawing his weapon to his chest. "Where are the loaders? Luvin?" he shouted, his voice echoing off the walls. Climbing into the empty cabin and staring out into the vacant mid-ship, he turned right, once again dodging the passenger seats to approach the gunnery.

"Luvin?" he repeated, staring at the awaiting station. "Same layout," he whispered, eyeing the brute before turning to race to the helm. Again spying no loaders at mid-ship, Jax paced quickly to Command. Finding the door stubbornly locked, he peered down the vacant corridor before tapping the door.

"Captain Ruvis?" he shouted, keeping his eyes on the corridor. "Luvin?" he shouted, banging louder. "Luvin? Captain Ruvis?" he repeated. "I am under orders of Prince Iaco to inspect this ship! Open the door!"

Gaining no response, Jax turned to the panel but immediately found it useless. The door was firmly locked from the inside. "Jovaar," he whispered, nodding in frustration, turning and running for the plank. "Surely Jovaar will know what to do."

Jax raced back toward Jovaar, leaping over cables and dodging the ever present trolleys and loaders, at last spying his commander firing the ship from the narrow helm. "Blasted," he thought, racing at full stride. "Half the ships have already detached!"

Praying he would reach Jovaar prior to its plunge into the deep, Jax spied Hylin from the corner of his eye in a back alcove. He also caught a glimpse of Phydin speaking to one of the pilots, yet did not stop to see what they had found.

"No Jovaar, wait!" he shouted, running at full speed. Jovaar firing the final boosters in preparation for detachment as expected, Jax rammed a worker to the ground, stumbling forward and screaming at Jovaar's profile in the small pit of the amphi.

"Jovaar!" he shouted, ignoring the angered words of the dock hand, the last ships to his left setting off, their high pitch screeching filling his ears. "Wait! What do I do?" he pleaded, falling to his knees, breathless as Jovaar's amphi sped off into the deep. "I think I found her!"

***

He was gone. Jax knelt on the docks gasping for air, several workers slowly pushing their empty trolleys and loading the scattered lines without stopping to question his cries.

"Jax!" Hylin shouted, racing toward him from the right. "I have searched every corner of this place," he added, panting and kneeling at his side. "I was about to give up until I found a small vent that was partially unlatched in a side wall. You will want to see this," he added, tugging on Jax to follow.

"What is it?" he asked, shaking his head and peering at the looming transports. "I need to get to Phydin. I found a ship and…"

"No," Hylin urged, dragging Jax to his feet. "You must come with me now. I promise you, you will understand once you see. Come on!"

Giving in to the boy's persistence, Jax hurried along at his side, searching with his eyes for the remaining crew throughout the docks. "Quickly then," he added, reluctantly following Hylin to the rear of the empty port. "I think I have found something too."

Twenty-Nine

Blinking against the haziness of the room, Selena raised her arms and turned her head, attempting to recall her surroundings. "Where am I?" she asked, reaching out for someone to take hold.

"I am here," Khyra answered, adjusting the folds of her gown and crossing the cabin, sitting next to her on the cot.

"Where am I? What has happened?" Selena pleaded, struggling to rise.

"Lay back, dear," Khyra continued soothingly, stroking her forehead with a damp coth. "You have been unconscious for some time. I am sorry but I had to request the Med-Officer to give you something to settle your nerves. You were uncontrollable and inconsolable. I am sorry Selena, but I had no other choice."

"Nitaya!" she shouted, instantly sitting upright, her head whirling with the abrupt motion. "Have they found her? Is she alright?"

"Hush, Selena," Khyra answered, attempting to lie her back down. "I am certain she is fine. Jovaar is out there now, heading a search of the entire facility under Prince Iaco's orders. He came to see you just before he left."

"I remember," she whispered, a lone tear trickling from her eye. "At least I think I remember. Please tell me what happened, Khrya."

"Nothing happened that any of us could control," her elder said, attempting to appear positive and giving Selena a small mug of drink. "I am sorry, Selena, but you must know this," she added, sighing. "It is my understanding that Agye still has Nitaya and at any moment Polatus will fall under attack from Sugin crafts."

"Please," she added, raising her free hand in protest and replacing the mug on the side table. "Let me finish. You must understand that I feel your anguish, Selena but I need...no, *we* need you to be strong. I am confident that Nitaya will be found. I do not know how or why I know, but I feel it deep within me."

"On the other matter," she continued shaking her head, again settling the pleats of her cumbersome gown. "There are ships on their way to see not only to Nitaya's death, but death to us all. You must be strong now, Selena. Your medication will soon wear off and once your mind is sound we will head out. We do no good sitting here wallowing in pity."

"So," Khyra added, standing and extending her hands. "Toughen up little one. Use the facilities and splash some cool water on your face. We must leave at once."

Nodding despite the wooze of her belly, Selena did her best to stifle her sobs, standing and relying heavily on the assistance from her friend. "Very well," Khyra said, turning and guiding her to the adjacent room. "Shall I assist you?"

"No," Selena answered, slowly shaking her head. "I can manage. I know Nitaya need us. I will not be long."

"Now that is my girl," Khyra said, turning to give her some privacy. "And once you have finished, we will go find yours."

***

The ship landed with expected ease and Gidoran raced to unclasp his restraints, grumbling as the last refused to open. "Blasted!" he shouted, fumbling with the nuisance. "Does nothing ever go my way?!"

"Do you need some assistance, Sir?" the Captain asked, standing before him, smirking.

"I can manage, thanks," Gidoran grimaced, at last free of the cumbersome binds. "No, wait," he shouted, motioning for his amused subordinate to return. "I could actually use your help. Get the data I requested on the transport and amphi-craft while I go speak with the crew of the fueler. There is too much to do and not enough time for me to do it. We have to roundabout as soon as possible."

"Yes, Sir," the Captain answered, turning to head down the plank. "I will update you as soon as the ships are located."

"Very well," Gidoran answered, setting after him down the plank. "And I will not take no for an answer." Spying the fueling crew on the dock just off to his left, Gidoran raced to them full stride.

"Are you prepared for debarkment?" he asked, eager to detach and return to his friends.

"We are, Sir," the pilot answered, nodding to his comrades. "But I am uncertain as to why we were ordered half full. Never have we been…"

"That is by design, my friend," Gidoran interrupted, slapping the man on the back. "You must refuel the Sugin ship as ordered, but we must hinder the process with a slow transfer. To explain my intentions as to the load, if you were fully fueled we would have no reason to detach. Half fueled and well, you will not be able to give them what they want. No harm, no foul as my GraPalle once said."

"Sir, you are making no sense. I do not understand. Why would we…" he questioned further, shaking his head.

"It is good that you do not, "Gidoran interrupted, once again patting his younger on the back. "Are your coordinates uploaded?"

"They are, Sir," he answered, stepping toward the transport. "And we are prepared to detach on your order."

"Well you have it," Gidoran answered, nodding to the others. "We are on roundabout also and should be just at your tail. We will monitor your progress through to Kindawan airspace then break off at its outer layer. You will then be on your own. I will give further instructions once we are airborne."

"Yes, Sir," the pilot answered, motioning for his crew to board. "Let us go," he added, urging them forward and joining his crew. Gidoran watched with approval as the pilot stood at the base of the plank, patting each of his members on the back with their single file climb up the narrow plank.

"He takes care of his men," he whispered, smiling confidently. "They will be fine." Turning in the opposite direction, the pilot nodding and boarding at the last, Gidoran raced to the opposite end of the dock where he prayed there would be a transport and amphi waiting.

***

"Tell me you have something," Gidoran said, prompting his portal and rounding the loaders on the dock.

"I do, Sir," the lieutenant answered from command. "But I am not so certain she will be to your liking."

"What do you mean?" Gidoran asked, frustrated at yet another dilemma.

"Docking bay B, Sir," the man answered flatly. "Upon your inspection, she is fueled, armed, and ready for detachment."

"Well that does not sound so bad," Gidoran said, closing the line. Jogging the short distance and rounding the corner, he found the transport on standby as ordered, the pilot and two-man crew waiting at the bottom of its plank.

"Sir," the pilot said, stepping forward. "I must inform you that there were no other craft from which to choose in all of the station. This ship had made dock just last evening and her current owners are quite displeased with your order."

"An order is an order and I am in no position for a debate!" Gidoran shouted, facing yet another snag. "Where is this so-displeased owner?"

"Just inside," the pilot continued, gesturing for Gidoran to board. "We will follow you, Sir. She is...how shall I say this, glaring as only a woman can."

***

"Give me a read-out, Iaco," Jovaar said into his headset, attempting to steady the unfamiliar ship.

"Maintain your course just off port side," he answered, running his fingers through his hair.

"And Nitaya?" Jovaar pressed, following the LC's offered lead of testing data on his screen.

"I have no word as of yet, Jovi," he answered, eyeing his own LC. "I was just about to ring for you but then when you chimed in over the ship's com, I assumed you handed the portal off. Whom will I be dealing with?"

"Phydin Heiss," Jovaar answered, sighing. "He is my best man and he will not let me down yet you know as I do I would have preferred to remain behind. Update me as soon as..."

"Of course I will get word to you immediately," Iaco interrupted, staring at the busying room. "Just concentrate on those ships. And speaking of ships, are you certain you know what you are doing?"

"You know I am no idiot, Iaco," Jovaar grumbled, staring angrily at his panel, attempting to decipher the LC's unknown transmission. "I believe I can handle this. Just get me word on Nitaya, and while you are at it check in on Selena for me. Blasted! There is too much happening at once!"

"Calm, my friend," Iaco said, attempting reassurance. "Now that the ships are away, I can concentrate the rest of my men on the search here."

"No," Jovaar answered sternly. "No offense Iaco, but it seems you have less control than you think. Better to leave this to my crew."

"I will not try to understand your motives, but as you wish, Jovi," he answered, taking the snub and motioning for his officer to stand down. "I just hope you know what you are doing."

"Me too, my friend," Jovaar answered, sailing off into the deep, tapping the foreign schematics from his screen. "Me too."

***

"Have the ships reported?" Terdoni asked nervously, crossing his hands at his back and rising from the helm.

"No, Sir," the first officer swiftly answered. "I was just about to order the update."

"Very well," Terdoni answered, staring at the blankness of the large screen. "Send for it at once."

"Aye, Sir," the officer answered, turning back to his panel. "Amphibious craft, report."

Resumming his earlier pacing of the massive central aisle of command, Terdoni maintained his stare out the wide glass with each step, eagerly waiting the response of his searchers. "A1 and slider reporting," the first pair's pilot at last answered. "I am in process of performing the skid and was presently..."

"Any sign A1?" the officer interrupted, sitting straight and peering at Terdoni, the pair eyeing one another, awaiting the response.

"Negative," the pilot answered. "There is nothing out here. The area is completely void of anything other than sea creatures. Shall we continue?"

"Stand by A1," the officer continued, altering his panel. "We are receiving a report from G5."

"Copy that, standing by," A1 answered, silencing his com.

"Sir?" the officer asked, turning to Terdoni.

"Wait until G5 updates," he said, not waiting for the CO to finish, watching his subordinate quickly turn back to his screen.

"G5 and slider reporting," the pilot responded, guiding the stick through the deep.

"Have you found anything G5?" the CO asked hesitantly, eyeing his commander over his shoulder.

"The area is dense with rock, Sir," the pilot continued, his line clear. "Progress has been slow. We have yet to come in contact with any craft and have seen no sign of a population. Wait," he said, pausing, Terdoni abruptly turning.

"What is it?" he shouted, crossing to the CO's station. "What do you see G5?"

"There is movement, up ahead, Sir," he answered, pausing for the briefest of moments. "How shall we respond, Sir?"

"Take evasive actions and do what you can to maintain your secrecy," Terdoni answered, leaning over the CO's station. "If ships have been sent out in defense, we will have confirmation that you are close. Proceed cautiously and use fire only when necessary."

"Aye, Sir," the pilot answered, ending the transmission.

"Get King Sugin on the com," Terdoni ordered, disregarding the King's order of silence, pleased he had good news to report.

"King Carsian," he continued when at last his master had chimed. Terdoni stood erect, confident with the findings of G5. "Sir, I believe we have them."

***

"It is this way!" Hylin said, dragging Jax by the arm.

"Wait, Hylin,'" he said, grabbing the boy's shoulder. "I must let someone know what I have found. Someone has to…no, Hylin, just wait! I will be right back." Hylin stood in place, fuming as Jax raced back toward the the empty tracks.

"What I have found is important!" he thought, crossing his arms over his chest and looking from his find to Jax's retreating back. "What I have found could make a difference!"

Tapping his foot as Jax ran in Phydin's direction, Hylin watched him interrupt an obviously annoyed dock hand attempting to straighten his given line. Regardless of his find, Jax tossed his hands in the air, giving Phydin *his* urgent news.

***

"I am telling you there are two sister ships just beyond that wall," Jax said, pointing to the rear area. Phydin continued his stare at Jovaar's portal unimpressed. Impatient, Hylin gave up and ran after Jax, determined to make him listen.

"I checked out one and Luvin scouted the other," Jax continued, flailing his arms at Hylin's approach. "I found nothing on the first except a vacant shell and an overly robust commander then ran to the second to assist Luvin. I did not find him, Phydin! In fact I found no one! I reached the Command door and it was force-locked from the inside. No one entered and no one left. No one was on any part of that ship that I could reach. No crew, no dock hands, I am telling you something is wrong, Phydin. I believe Nitaya is there."

"You said yourself that it was deserted," Phydin answered. "I am searching Jovaar's portal for other places to hide within the compound."

"You are not listening, Phydin," Jax answered, roughly grabbing his arm. "I think something is wrong. Have you seen Luvin?"

"No," Phydin answered, at last raising his head, his eyes squinting. "I have not now that you mention it. Where did you say these ships were?"

"Just beyond there," Jax answered, pointing again in their direction.

"Alright then," Phydin said, recovering the portal with his cloak, having found no alternatives to search. "I will ask Iaco to ground the ships, both of them just to be certain."

"Kroy!" he shouted, spying his gunner speaking with another worker.

"Yes, Sir," he answered, glad to be doing anything but rummaging through trolleys. "What can I do?"

"Jax may have something just beyond that wall on a transport," Phydin answered, nodding. "Grab Uvis and go check it out. One ship stands deserted with a command door that remains locked. I am requesting Iaco to precautionarily ground them both and I will also request that they review the commander's profiles. Report back as soon as possible."

"Yes, Sir," he answered, turning to head toward the craft. Stopping to grab Uvis who remained wading in the empty submersible tracks, Jax watched him climb out to trail after Kroy.

"Satisfied?" Phydin asked, peering again to his portal. "The dock hand I was speaking to earlier said he had seen a steward that resembles Agye quite well several times recently in the corridors just outside the loading docks. I have been searching the portal for other routes she may have taken and…"

"Phydin," Hylin interrupted, shoving Jax to the side. "I have found something too. I was about to show Jax the…"

"Very well," he interrupted, waving his hand without looking from his portal. "Go check it out Jax and report back immediately. The docks have proven deserted and I believe I may have at last found some alternate locations."

"Yes, Phydin," Jax answered, shaking his head and turning toward Hylin. "Come," he added, patting the boy's back, glancing at the rear wall shielding the sister ships. "Show me what you have found."

***

Kroy and Uvis raced round the corner, Uvis sopping with the wet of the sea from the amphi tracks. They found the sister ships docked per Phydin's instructed.

"Which is the one with the locked Command?" Uvis asked, panting and wringing out his cloak. Kroy merely stood shaking his head.

"I am not certain," he answered, hands on hips. 'Take that one and I wil check this one out. Get your weapon out and be prepared for anything."

"I am one step ahead of you," Uvis answered, releasing his sopping cloak and bringing his weapon to his side. Nodding to one another reassuringly each set out to search their chosen craft.

Kroy raced to the left ship, finding it deserted as Phydin had indicated and immediately felt the eeriness of the hull, certain he had found the right craft. Quickly retracing his steps down the plank to shout for Uvis, he shook his head and reclimbed the plank spying the sister ship's plank was empty. Turning right and crossing through the passenger area, Kroy found the gleaming gunnery station fully armed and awaiting man support.

Surprised Jax had left in untouched, he could not help but run his hand down the sleek track of the uptake. His thoughts quickly returning to the task at hand, Kroy opened the rear door, finding it empty as he surveyed the cramped surroundings with the shaft of his weapon. Confident he was aboard the questionable ship, he turned back and raced through the seated section toward the bow, gritting his teeth and finding the command door locked as expected.

"Open up," he shouted, eyeing the door prompt. "I said open up!" he repeated, again gaining no response.

Looking to the ordinary panel to the right of the door, his nerves dancing with the emptiness of the corridor, Kroy removed the small blade from his ankle holster and quickly began removing the outer cover. "Standard," he whispered, grinning as he set out to dislodge the round lid. "You should not take long."

With the cover quickly removed, Kroy began stripping the wires and soon had the door open, albeit only slightly. Dropping to his hands and knees and peering inward, he sat still as his eyes adjusted to the darkened space.

"Movement," he thought, blinking against the darkness. "This has to be it." Standing, he eagerly set out to finish the rewiring, anticipating the opening of the door and his glory of confronting the girl and saving the child.

"I know you are in there!" he shouted, wiping the sweat from his brow and fumbling with the small strands. "Just open the blasted door!"

"As you wish," the low voice answered, Kroy dropping his blade in surprise. Stepping back and butting against the side wall with the door abruptly opening, Kroy stood frozen as the weapon pointed directly at his face.

From the corner of his eye, Kroy spied Agye sitting off to his right desperately cradling the whimpering child. Although appearing unharmed, he could not be certain if the girl could be trusted and therefore kept the recognition from his enemy. Noting a man on the floor at her feet, head turned obscurely toward the panels, Kroy could not make out his face yet assumed it must be one of Prince Iaco's workers.

Turning back to the weapon pointed confidently between his eyes, Kroy caught a glimpse of something small and white on the floor. Adjusting his focus in the darkened command, he recognized an item that sent chills through his body. An Intel card lay slightly out of the dead man's side pocket, and at once fury filled him. Turning with rage, Kroy balled his fists at his enemy.

"What have you done?" he shouted, his full attention at once on the strange man. Stepping forward without fear, Kroy raised his weapon. The man merely shook his head and smiled.

"Do you think that is wise?" he asked, confidence filling his low words. "I suggest you drop what you aim so that we may have a little chat. I said drop it!" he roared, his anger emitting from the veins in his neck as Kroy took another step forward.

"We have no time for debate. You drop the weapon or…" he added, tilting his head as if considering. "Or I will kill the child," he said flatly, pointing death directly at the babe.

"Alright, alright," Kroy answered, kneeling and tossing his weapon to the floor. With the man foreign to him, Kroy knew that he could take few chances.

"Very well," the man continued, returning his gaze to his intruder. "Make final preparations!" he added, shouting to the apparently willing pilot, his eyes never leaving his enemy's. "I will be in the gunnery *discussing* some important matters with our guest. Be prepared for detachment upon my return!"

"Aye, Sir," the pilot answered, requesting the data without turning.

"Now you," the commander continued, his words firm yet calm as he rammed the butt of his weapon into Kroy's shoulder. "Please, lead the way!"

      ***

"What do I do?" Kroy thought, pacing through the corridor and passenger area. Weapon ready at his back, he looked about the void cabin for something to use against his captor. Finding nothing as the man prompted the gunnery door, the pair entered and Kroy at once turned to face the enemy unarmed.

"You will never get off of Polatus alive!" he began, stalling for time and praying for Uvis to board. "Give yourself up now and the Royal Committee could possibly grant you leniency."

"Ha!" the man answered, annoyed with the man's pleas, gesturing with his weapon for Kroy to step away from the door. "You have no notion of what you speak of, little man," he continued, his rage emerging, slamming the side cabinet with his fist. "And I have no time for this nonsense. Kneel before me!" Kroy stood his ground, refusing the enemy's demands.

"I said kneel!" he repeated, gesturing to pummel him with his weapon.

"Never!" Kroy answered, courageously refusing to lower himself against an enemy.

"Never say never," the man continued, lowering both his weapon and his tone. "Maybe this will help you off your feet," he added, firing a single blast at Kroy's leg. Screeching in pain and grasping his wound, Kroy reluctantly gave in and knelt as the man gestured a possible second blow.

"Very well," the man continued, a tilted grin appearing on the side of his face. "Now then," he continued, crossing to a small cabinet in the exterior wall. "This will make you quite useful."

Turning back to his captive, the man paced the narrow gunnery with an evil look in his eye and a small gray device in his hand. Making a slight alteration with his approach, the commander reached down placing the control neatly around his captive's left ear, sliding the last to the front snuggly over his eye, Kroy's struggles ceasing with the final motion.

"Now rise!" he ordered, pleased that all was easily in place and standing back to admire his work. Immobile except for the man's commands, Kroy rose, following the order with apparent ease despite his injury.

"Dress your wound and take your position," the commander continued, returning to the door. "We leave at once!"

"Aye, Sir!" Kroy answered, turning to claim a med kit from within the now familiar side cabinet. Settling himself at the gunnery post, he quickly wrapped his leg.

"And now," the man added, his tilted grin ever present. Prompting the door, he folded his hands defenselessly at his back. "It appears we conveniently have our gunner."

***

Uvis raced up the plank and into the sister ship finding everything in order for a routine detachment. Supplies were loaded and secured and with the present fuel lines at the dock, the craft appeared properly prepared. Turning right to search the rear, he reached the gunnery and found a man at his station, busily making final preparations.

"Have you seen a small child with her steward," he asked, the gunner quickly shaking his head, lowering to the base of the track.

"This is no nursery," he huffed, rebounding upward to test the shaft.

Uvis left the man to his work. Racing back to midship, he dodged the numerous passenger stations then paced the narrow corridor to Command. Finding what he assumed was the Captain he paused at the open door, listening to the man confidently barking his orders.

"Pardon my intrusion," Uvis began at last. The main glared and turned, his annoyance evident.

"Another one!" he grumbled, folding his arms at his chest. "What is it now?"

"Sir, I have been ordered to…"

"I know, I know," Wozer interrupted, shaking his head. "The Prince has ordered a search for a child. We have been over this. I was quite accommodating earlier, but as you can see we are in a bit of a hurry. Is there anything else you require?"

"No," Uvis answered, nervously running his fingers through his hair damp, short hair. "I pray you have a safe sail."

"Yes, yes, and I thank you," Wozer answered, gritting his teeth and turning back to his pilot. "Now go pester someone else."

Tuning away from Command and the obvious snub of its Captain, Uvis raced toward the plank confident Kroy had boarded the ship in question just as the grounding order rang over the ship's com. Filled with relief of the order to remain, he reached the dock and pivoted his feet toward the sister ship, watching the dwindling workers. Stepping carefully amongst the lines, anxiousness filled him as he stared at the eerie craft. Knowing he had no other choice but to search for his friend, he walked to the ship's side, climbing the identical plank, the hatch closing abruptly before him.

"Stop at once!" he shouted, pounding his fists on the door, its thrusters warming with the impending push. Although knowing his pleas were useless against the noise of the firing engines, Uvis pounded all the same until the detachment sequence retracted the plank. Jumping to the dock and gasping for air, the ship vibrating with full force before him, Kroy watched helplessly as the final lines broke free. Thrusters bursting to main, the craft sailed swiftly down the track and into the deep.

Thirty

"It is just a bit further," Hylin said eagerly, dragging Jax by the arm through the empty docks.

"Hylin, there is really no time," he pleaded fruitlessly, the child leading him even further to the corner.

"Here," Hylin said, pointing toward the large vent positioned low in the nook behind another trolley. "I almost missed it myself."

Reluctantly skirting the barren trolley and taking hold of the monsterous panel, Jax stood in dismay as the boy heft it to the side, its large outer area tricking the mind against its inner shaft. The passage allowed for a mere person rather than the girth of a trolley to enter through its surprisingly narrow pass.

"I cannot possibly fit through that," Jax said, crossing his arms at his chest.

"Use this," Hylin continued excitedly, grabbing a tool off the nearby trolley. Shaking his head, Jax took the tool from Hylin and reluctantly set out to removing the final cover. With the slight of his hand, the contraption slammed loudly to the floor.

"It could be anything," Jax began, running his fingers through his hair. "Perhaps it is merely a…"

"I will go first," Hylin interrupted, climbing eagerly within and waving for Jax to follow. Looking side to side and seeing he had no other immediate options as Phydin had ordered Kroy and Uvis to search the sister ships, Jax took a deep breath and trailed after the boy through the hidden passage.

"Look," Hylin said, standing in the small opening. "Can you believe it?" Finishing his crawl and climbing out just at Hylin's back, Jax stood, staring in awe at the litered space, chills dancing over his skin.

"Unbelievable," he whispered, circling the cramped room, small enough to cause him to stoop at its outer walls. In complete disarray, Jax stared at the makeshift cot in the corner on the floor, kicking at the scattered debris at his feet. Garments littered the floor amongst remnants of nourishment and actual written drawings covered the shortened walls. Images of Nitaya, the Prince, and the entire compound of Polatus stared back at him. Drawn to them, Jax crossed to claim the nearest.

"This has been planned," he whispered, snatching the next image from the wall. "This has been planned for some time."

"I told you," Hylin said, proud of his find and returning to the small shoot. "We should inform Jovaar at once."

"We can't," Jax answered, transfixed by the recent image of Nitaya in his hand. "He has set out to deal with the incoming ships. We must inform Phydin. He has taken over the search. We will have him bring in Iaco. He will certainly know what to do."

"Come," he added, dropping the tattered parchment to the floor. "We must inform them at once."

"You have done well, Hylin," Jax added, ruffling the boy's hair, gesturing for him to begin his climb to the main dock. "Now come. We must inform them while there is still time."

***

"Do you think you are now able?" Khyra asked as Selena entered the main cabin, tucking the last of loose tendrils behind her ear.

"I feel much better, yes," she answered, hesitantly crossing to the small cot. Sitting and doing all she could to hold back the tears that had filled her eyes in the facilities, Selena looked up to Khyra, bringing Nitaya's small blanket. Gratefully accepting, she took a deep breath to inhale its famiar scent.

"We are not helping by just sitting here," she began, stooping to claim her shoes. "Have you had word from Jovaar?"

"No," Khyra answered, crossing to sit at her side. "And that is what worries me. We should have heard at least something by now."

"Then we must find him," Selena answered, standing albeit wobbly. "I am fine," she added, holding up a hand in protest at Khyra's assistance with her rise, crossing the cabin. "Please do not baby me now, Khyra for I am no child. I am however the steward of a very precious child who is at this moment lost. We must use all of our strength to see to it that she is found. We will start with command. Polatus is quite large but that is one place we know how to find. We will check in with Prince Iaco and if there is no word, we will search each and every cabin spanning out from there. There will be no more tears, Khyra. I believe I have shed enough for us all."

"I am proud of you," Khyra answered, pacing to Selena at the entrance. "And together we will find her."

Nodding, Selena claimed her elder's hand, patting it warmly and smiling with newfound strength into her friend's eyes. Prompting the cabin door, they stepped into the corridor as one, chins held high to eagerly begin their search for the child.

***

"We have an unidentified craft entering Polatus seaspace, Sir," the lieutenant said, interrupting Iaco's thoughts. "How shall I respond?"

"Order confirmation," the Prince answered, abruptly rising from his roost on the side panel. "It should be Gidoran and I must say it is about time."

"Identify and state your intentions," the lieutenant continued, prompting the com.

"Nothing, Sir," he added, turning for further orders.

"Request again," Iaco said, growing ever frustrated, fumbling with the scruff of his chin.

"Unknown craft," the lieutenant repeated, pivoting back to his station. "Identify and sate your intentions." Nothing but silence filled the com.

"Sir," the lieutenant continued, peering over his shoulder. "If it is in fact Sir Gidoran, he would have responded. They have requested communications with Polatus and their uplink has been verified. They can hear us," he added, shaking his head. "But they are refusing acknowledgement."

"Understood," Iaco answered, standing to pace the floor. "You know what this means," he added, performing an abrupt aboutface. "This means there are more of them out there."

***

Jovaar teetered through the deep, struggling with the intricacies of the controls. "Blasted!" he shouted in the empty pit, the craft shifting right when he meant for it to shift left. Jovaar barely missed slamming bow-first into a large landmass. Performing a slight adjustment to his panel and tapping back on his stick in hopes of aligning the troublesome craft, he prompted the com to request conference with Iaco.

"Any sign of Nitaya?" he asked, frustration evident at having left things undone.

"No, Jovi," Iaco answered, shaking his head. "There has been no word. I was just about to chime Phydin for another update."

"He would have gotten word to you if there was good news," Jovaar said, dipping high over a large mound, the stick settling within his palm. "What about Gidoran? Have you received any word from him?"

"Again no, my friend," Iaco answered even more frustrated, staring at the back of his lieutenant. "Two ships entered our airspace mere moments ago. I thought it was Gidoran and instructed identification. I got no response, Jovi. I fear you are facing more than you anticipated."

"Copy that," Jovaar answered, averting yet another land mass. "Chime me as soon as G is within range. I need to know what his plans are for Carsian."

"Of course," Iaco answered, wishing desperately he could do more. "Time-wise it should not be long."

"That is the point is it not, my friend?" Jovaar asked, pushing the stick forward to dip down over the next mass, the ship at last agreeing with his movements. "Time is something we do not have."

"Wait Iaco," he added, searching the rapidly altering readout on his screen. "I think I may have found them. I believe two ships just entered my radar, port side. I cannot be certain,

Iaco. As soon as I saw them, I lost them. Upload Sector Six and patch it through to Gidoran as soon as he is within range."

"Copy that," Iaco answered, gesturing to his lieutenant. "And Jovi...be careful."

***

Phydin was getting nowhere. There were plenty of opportune locations on his readout for someone to hide if that were their intention, but it would take hazons to search them all. The men on the loading docks were thinning and the screeching of the engines was beginning to die down, yet regardless of the lessening distractions, he could not search the entirety of Polatus on his own. Jax and Hylin had not returned and for that matter either had Kroy and Uvis. If he did not remain to await their word, they would undoubtedly begin to worry about even his safety.

"And where is Luvin?" he mumbled, staring throughout the almost hollow docks. Setting out in the direction of the sister ships, he turned at the sound of his name, spying Hylin racing toward him quickly trailed by Jax.

"It is about blasted time," he said, the pair breathlessly stopping before him. "Have you seen the others?"

"Not for some time, Phydin," Jax answered, lowering to his knees to catch his breath. "But Hylin has shown me something you need to see. I believe Agye has been planning the possibility of a chosen child's arrival for quite some time. She set up quarters in..." he continued, stopping as Uvis ran up from the opposite direction.

"Phydin," he interrupted, his boots sloshing with each step. "It is Kroy!" he added, attempting desperately to catch his breath, unclasping his cloak and tossing it to the floor.

"What is it?" Phydin questioned, placing his hand on Uvis' shoulder.

"I cannot be certain," he said, inhaling deeply. "I was attempting to board. I shouted but...I am sorry, Phdyin. The ship detached before I could..."

"What are you saying?" Phydin interrupted, gripping Uvis' shoulder.

"I cannot be certain," he repeated, slowly rising. "But I think Kroy was aboard the sister ship when it detached *after* the order to remain was given. I heard the order and searched the other finding nothing. I ran to the next to assist Kroy and as I reached the hatch it closed and sped down the track. Phydin, something is wrong. I know it."

"Breathe, Uvis," he said, turning to the others. "Just breathe. Jax, is this the same ship where you found the door to command locked?"

"It sounds like it," he answered, nodding to Uvis. "And if it is, it is the same one that Luvin was searching. I have not seen him since."

"Then maybe they are both aboard," Phydin said, nodding and looking to his portal. "I will send word to Iaco to chime Jovaar. Jax, what is it you found?"

"You will not believe it, Phydin," he answered, gesturing toward the direction of the vent. "Chime Iaco then follow me."

"Prince Iaco," Phydin began, having already opened the line.

"Go ahead, Phydin," Iaco answered.

"Inform Jovaar that there is still no sign of the child or her steward though we may possibly have a lead on their direction," Phydin answered, nodding to Hylin. "Then add that a ship may have taken off with two of my men. Our numbers are depleting and I am seeking guidance."

"He is a bit preoccupied, Phydin," Iaco answered, frustratedly. "Follow your lead and report back immediately. Jovaar would not have left you in control of the search if he did not hold your confidence. I will inform him of your status as soon as I am able."

"Copy that," Phydin answered, closing the line and turning to Jax. "There is nothing more I can do. Show me what you have found. It might..." he added, pausing to consider his thoughts. "Just show me, Jax."

***

Khyra led Selena steadily by the arm through the glass-lined walls and their wonderous views of the deep to Command.

341

Reaching to prompt the door, she gestured for Selena to enter first, each glancing at to other as they arrived seemingly unnoticed in the bustling room.

"Prince Iaco," Khyra shouted above the sounds of the paneled stations.

"Khyra," he answered, waving and crossing to the pair. "Why are you not in your cabin? I had just attempted to reach you on the com and when you did not answer, I began an order for someone to set out to your quarters."

"I am sorry for your trouble," she said, patting his hand. "Selena arose some time ago and I could not convince her to stay put. Again, forgive me but we insist on doing something to help."

Waving off the searching droid, Iaco looked down at Selena's hunkered shoulders, her hands clutching the child's blanket to her breast. He oddly found a fragile determination in her eyes however, and found himself pleased she had come around.

"I know you are frightened," he said, reassuringly placing his hand on her shoulder. "And as I wish you would not be, I am afraid we have found nothing thus far. Gidoran chimed in some time ago to inform us of some ships headed this way, and so it seems we now have two situations instead of one," he continued, turning from Selena's welling eyes and looking to her stronger elder. "Jovaar is at sea attempting to track the incoming ships and Phydin is overseeing the search for Nitaya. Last word was from docking. If you insist on helping in the search, you could start there although my opinion is firm that you should remain in quarters."

"We appreciate your concern, Prince Iaco," Khyra began, straightening and tightening her grip on Selena's hand. "But I believe we will do what we can to help. If you would just give us the directions to the dock, we will let you get back to your men."

Iaco let out a breath and shook his head. "Women," he thought, choosing to refrain from speaking his opinion. "I will do you one better," he said instead, appearing complacent as he removed a portal from a side cabinet hook up. "Take this. Jovaar gave his own to Phydin prior to detachment. It will give

342

you the entire layout of the compound and if you press here," he added, pointing to the side control. "You will be able to communicate to either him or myself."

"Thank you, Prince Iaco," Khyra answered, strapping the small device to her arm.

"Please," he continued, once the portal was secured. "I believe Iaco will do."

"Then thank you, Iaco," Khyra said, a slight smile crossing her face. "And if you need us, you will know how to reach us."

"Come, Selena," she added, turning to look at her saddened face. "We will have better luck...I promise." Nodding to Iaco leaning against the portal cabinet, Khyra placed her arm around Selena's shoulder and led her slowly from Command.

***

Hylin led Jax, Phydin and Uvis to the far corner of the docks, Fidaldi and Orvi joining them just as they reached the vent opening. "We found nothing," Fidaldi said, panting and lowering to his knees to catch his breath, spying the narrow shoot. "Where are we going?"

"Hylin found something unbelievable," Jax answered, gesturing. "It is just through there." Exchanging uncertain glances at the rather small hole in the wall, Fidaldi crossed to Phydin concentrating on his portal.

"What could possibly be in there?" he asked, shaking his head and looking up from Phydin's map.

"Just crawl through and I will show you," Hylin answered, looking to Jax for help. Huffing as noone appeared to take him seriously, he climbed in first, waving the others in at his back.

Waiting in the small room as one by one the others joined him Hylin felt great pride in watching the expressions on their faces alter. With Jax bringing up the rear, he let them have a moment to take in the cramped surroundings.

"Watch it," Jax shouted, Uvis stepping backward, almost tripping him.

"Forgive me," he answered, grabbing Fidaldi's arm to steady his feet amongst the clutter.

"Wait!" Phdyin shouted, attempting to pass by Fidaldi to face his men. "This is insane. As important as you may believe this to be, there is no reason for all of us to be here. Orvi, Uvis, follow me back out the passage and to command. I need an update on Jovaar and those blasted ships."

"Jax," he continued, gesturing for the other two to head out. "You stay here with Hylin and Fidaldi. Use the com in docking to inform me of anything vital. My gut says there is nothing here but maybe, just maybe you will get lucky."

***

"What exactly are we looking for in this mess of a hole?" Fidaldi asked, uncertain where to begin. The small room slightly opened with the retreat of the others. Staring blankly at the tattered contents, he kicked at the random remnants on the floor.

"We don't know," Jax answered, watching Hylin sour through the drawer of a side cabinet. "This has to be where Agye was hiding and gathering her information. Look for anything that may tell us where she is headed."

Although the quarters remained tight, each spread out in different directions. Fidaldi began his search of the various parchment drawings on the walls while Hylin continued his search on the floor near the low cot and cabinet. Seeing the others occupied, Jax crossed over to the small makeshift table, dumping its contents onto the floor. Kneeling he began sorting the debris.

"There is nothing here," Jax said flatly, lastly sifting through the decayed remnants of nourishment. "Even if Agye *did* use this as a place of recluse which is something we cannot prove, we could not possibly gather anything useful in the time we have. We should return to Command with Phydin and ask Iaco what he knows. As valuable as this may seem to be, we are wasting time."

"Wasting time doing what?" Khyra asked, reaching the edge of the passage and standing.

344

"Khyra!" Hylin shouted, tripping over the clutter and crossing to her. "Where is Selena?"

"I am here," she answered, at last reaching the cramped quarters. "What is this place?" Hylin eagerly filled the women in on his find.

"And so far we have found nothing useful," Jax interrupted with the last of the boy's words. Leaning against the rear wall he was clearly annoyed.

"Well I disagree," Khyra said, circling about the room, careful to clear the low ceiling. "Just look at this place. There has to be something here."

"Jax," she continued, snapping her fingers. "Why do you not take this portal and start searching other areas. Selena and I can stay behind here and give this a woman's perspective."

"That's a great idea," he answered, itching to move on and claiming the portal from her hands. "The dock com is just out the passage and to your left. If you find anything, you can chime us from there."

"Then it is settled," Khyra said, placing her hands on her hips and shaking her head. Jax and Fidaldi quickly darted to the shaft, Hylyin reluctantly followed to its opening.

"Are you certain you do not need me?" he asked, using both his eyes and tone in hopes of persuading Khyra to allow him to stay with his find.

"They will need you more," she answered reassuringly, patting Selena's back. The boy nodded in understanding, crawling with a loud sigh toward the dock.

"Now," she added, claiming Selena's hands in hers and turning her in a circle about the littered room. "Let us see what this Agye has been up to."

345

Thirty-One

"They were there a moment ago!" Jovaar shouted angrily into the com.

"What coordinates?" the pilot asked, searching his screen.

"120 lat, 80 long, quadrant six," Jovaar grumbled, staring amazed at his blank screen. "But the area shows clear now. It is the same as before but I still do not understand it. Send four of your ships to that area, send another four out as searchers in the opposite direction, keep the larger ships closer to Polatus, and you pull along as my slider."

"Copy that," the pilot answered. Jovaar listened as he repeated the orders, the ships immediately rerouting at his command. At the last, the pilot slid in on Jovaar's right.

"We will continue this path," Jovaar stated, getting confirmation from the slider. Adjusting his stick slightly forward, the craft at last smooth against the order of his hand. "I need to speak with Iaco privately. The com will go black for a moment."

"Copy that," the slider repeated. Jovaar immediately altered channels.

"Iaco," he began, settling back within his seat. "Has Nitaya been located and has there been any word from Gidoran?"

"No, and no," Iaco answered, frustration clear in his voice. "I am doing everything that I possibly can. I am sorry, Jovi, but the others have..." he continued, the com suddenly filling with static.

"Jovaar!" he shouted, leaning over his LC's station. "Can you hear me? Jovaar! Leuitenant," he added, grabbing the man's shoulder. "I have lost communications with Savius. Are you able to reach the others or have they too gone black?"

"No, sir," he answered, unable to turn from the panel. His commander's grip tapped furiously at his screen. "All communications are down. Radar is showing black and I have lost visual on all craft. It is crashing, Sir!"

Crossing to the bank of screens at the center of Command, Iaco watched as one by one each phased to haze, replaced with nothing but blackness. All systems were down. Communications were lost. Jovaar and his other pilots were on their own.

***

"Iaco!" Jovaar shouted, tapping the side of his headset. "Iaco!" he repeated. "Can you hear me?" Attempting to adjust his panel, he slammed his hand in frustration into the exterior wall of the ship, knowing the com was dead.

"Slider, attempt communications with Command," he ordered.

"Copy that," the pilot answered, Jovaar waiting impatiently, rounding another mass. "I am getting nothing, Sir," the man answered. "What do you want..." Silence filled the com a mere moment before Jovaar felt the enormous blast.

Turning to look out the port glass, he watched in horror as the slider craft was hit, richochetting off the land mass they had just passed. Almost blinding, Jovaar lifted his right hand to shield his eyes, carefully balancing out the craft with his left. The enemy was upon them.

"Enemy ships in south Sector Five," he shouted, prompting the com and dipping low into a deep canyon. "All small craft report to location. I need back up now!"

"We are sailing up on your rear now," one of Iaco's pilots said, responding to the call. "Enemy craft on your tail and closing in. We are right behind him."

"I know where he is!" Jovaar shouted, rocking the ship upward. "Just get him off me!"

"Veer up and over the next mass on your left," the pilot, continued startlingly calm. "Then sharp right into the cavern, Sir. That should give us enough time."

"Copy that," Jovaar answered, adjusting the stick and dodging the lower obstacles, yet as before his instincts proved wrong and the ship skimmed off the ridged mass.

"Sir!" the pilot shouted, swiftly sailing by. "You just missed the..."

"I know, I know," Jovaar answered, his frustration growing as he fumbled with the stick. "I am taking another pass. Prepare for roundabout."

"Copy that," the pilot answered, circling wide. "I will do what I can to divert his attention.

The landmasses proved to be growing in numbers causing him to divert erratically. Jovaar banked hard round and over a smaller of the heavily approaching three, his arms aching with the forceful push as yet another enemy's blast just missed his right flank.

"Now!" the pilot shouted, the pair repeating the previous path. At his word Jovaar veered sharp right, the pilot claiming the easily duped enemy with a single blast.

"Well done," Jovaar said, feeling the tremble from the blow at his rear.

"Your flight is now clear, Sir," the pilot answered, his tone unwavering. "I am coming about. Word has it there is another craft on the outskirts of the northern sector. I am in route."

"I am right behind you," Jovaar answered, sweat beading on his brow. Wiping the obvious fear from his face, Jovaar pulled hard left on the stick and spying his comrade through the glass port side, straightened his craft. Sailing off in pursuit of the next enemy, he prayed that he was buying his friends enough time.

***

"Radar is showing a craft entering from the east, Sir," the officer said, turning to Terdoni.

"Identify the craft," he answered, not turning from the glass. "It should be the refueler but be wary. Savius could very well know of our presence."

The officer, sensing the frustration of his commander, turned back to his screen, prompting the com. "Unidentified craft," he began, tapping his screen to scan the unknown ship. "You are to state your intentions."

"Replacement tanker ordered from Yani," the voice answered abruptly. "Requesting authorization for our approach."

"Continue with transmission of specifications," the officer answered, glancing over his shoulder at Terdoni. "Awaiting transmission."

>Ship Title: Plina
>Pilot of note: Captain Rutolie
>Holding Quantity: 4,500
>Fee: 30,000 stron
>Awaiting response

"Their specs check out, Sir," the officer said, reading aloud the Plina data. "Shall we continue?"

"Aye," Terdoni answered, his gaze firm on the glass. "Yet we better not repeat the result of Phobis. Order refueling."

"Aye, Sir," the officer said, turning to key the acceptance.

>Ship: Plina Cleared
>Pilot: Captain Rutolie unknown origin
>Holding Quantity requested: 4,500
>Fee: Acknowledged
>PROCEED

"We have clearance," Rutolie said, glancing over his shoulder at his crew. "Continue our current flightpath. Slowing sail."

"Yes, Captain," the navigator answered, honing in on the schematics of the enormous ship. "There," he added, pointing out at the glass. "The arm is extending." Taking a deep breath, Rutolie took a firm hold on the stick, tapping it slightly backward to slow the approach.

"Guiding in," he said flatly, the massive arm stretching out before them. "Let us hope this works."

***

"I have Plina on radar above, Sir," the transport pilot said over the com. "Per my readout, it is hovering just below the

349

Sugin ship as ordered. We have gone clearly unnoticed, Sir. Plina is in route to fueling as I speak. Opening rear hatch. Prepare for drop."

"Confirmed," Gidoran answered overseeing the pilot's path from the helm of the amphibious craft. "Sugin ship in process of refueling and all personnel accounted for and awaiting drop. Standing by." Anxiously awaiting the impending fall, Gidoran peered over his shoulder at his wide-eyed co-pilot.

"Have you ever done this before?" he asked, turning back to his panel and holding firm to the clasps of his restraints.

"No, Sir," he answered, a great fear obvious in his tone.

"Well it is a wild ride," Gidoran added, a wide smile crossing his face. "And something I am certain you will never forget. My first..."

"Sir," the transport pilot interrupted. "All systems go. Ordering the release for drop. Confirmed?"

"Confirmed," Gidoran answered, peering back over his shoulder. "Hold on, my friend. Here we go!"

"Release in 5, 4, 3, 2, 1, release," the transport pilot said, prompting the airborn detachment. The young co-pilot's screams were lost with the massive weight of descent.

Thrust against the backs of their seats with only their restraints keeping them from certain death, Gidoran marveled at the awesome force of the drop even as he struggled with tipping the nose. "Not...much...longer," he said, the weight of the descent making his speech difficult. Forcing the stick forward regardless of the ship's auto assistance, he pushed with all his strength, concentrating on the impending plunge.

The co-pilot did not respond to Gidoran's assurances, yet rather sat with his back melding with his seat, ignoring his monitor and hoping above all hope that he would not lose the meal he had nourished prior to his flight orders. "Oh how I wished the orders had arrived prior," he thought, closing his eyes in concentration.

"Nose...down," Gidoran continued, the words now flowing only slightly easier. "Preparing for plunge. You still with me back there?"

"Yes...Sir..." the co-pilot answered, not opening his eyes.

Gidoran could not help but internally smile at the boy's reaction of his maiden fall, even if his physical self would not allow it. "In 3, 2, 1," he said, waiting as the cabin began to pressurize about them.

"There," he added chuckling, at last comfortable and adjusting the stick with ease. "That was not so bad was it?"

The co-pilot, pale and clamy said not a word regardless of the seemingly nonexistent impact with the water, and instead rather quickly unlatched his restraints and leaned forward, letting go of his meal on the floor of the craft. "Now that..." Gidoran said, his tone of amusement immediately replaced by the emanating stench at the rear. "Now that is not funny."

***

"Prince Iaco," Phydin said, halting his men at the door and crossing command.

"Have you found her?" Iaco asked clearly distraught, rising from the helm.

"No," Phydin answered, holding up his hands in defeat. "Khyra and Selena are scouring a site that I found hidden in the loading docks. I believe Agye had been using it as her own command to store information on Polatus. By the looks of it, she has been doing so for quite some time, although I must admit that I do not believe anything critical will come from it. Regardless, I have been looking over the portal and have some other sites of interest, but we wanted to check in with you first to see what you had learned. Has there been any sign of Sir Gidoran?"

"No," Iaco answered, running his fingers through his hair, looking to the awaiting men cross the room. "But we were expecting him any time with an update, however all communications are down. I have my men working on it but so far they have been unable to uplink."

"Jax is quite capable, Prince Iaco," Phydin said, straightening and gesturing over his shoulder to the men hovering at the door. "Perhaps he might take a look."

"Can you spare him, Phydin?" Iaco asked, nodding. "What about the child?"

"We will manage," he answered, gesturing for Jax to come forward. "Jax," Phydin continued as he neared. "Prince Iaco has a situation with communications and I recommended you to oversee the repairs."

"Just lead the way," he said, thankful to have a more suited task. "I will have you operational in no time."

"Alright then," Iaco said, thankful for the assistance. "Phydin, you and the others get going. I will have one of my men take Jax to Data. Let me know as soon as you find anything. When we have uplink, I would like to be able to give Jovaar some good news."

Phydin nodded and turned, motioning to the others to lead the way back into the corridor. Watching them leave, Iaco turned shaking his head at Jax. "I hope you are as good as you say you are," he said, only slightly encouraged.

"I assure you I am," he answered, confident as always regardless of the task. "These hands can perform miracles."

"That we need," Iaco said, running his fingers through his hair and watching Jax trail off after his men toward Data. "That we most certainly need."

***

"I am beginning to agree with Jax," Khyra said, sorting through a haphazard pile of documents on the floor. "Sure, there are aged drawings and maps of the compound, there are even photos of the various cabins, but there is nothing here that gives us a clue as to where she has taken the child. We do not even know that it was Agye who used this hidden hovel. I think perhaps we should move on."

"There has to be something here," Selena answered, staring at the covered walls and holding firm to Nitaya's blanket. "I can feel it. Can you not? Maybe what we are looking for is not a piece of parchment," she continued, circling the small room, careful to duck the low ceilings.

"Perhaps there is a…oh what do you call it, something that monitors movements."

"You mean a tracking device," Khyra said, kicking at a shard of old nourishment on the covered floor. "The others would have found something like that right away. I believe I should head back to the docks and get Iaco on the com. Maybe he has some news of his own. We could be searching this awful place and Nitaya could be resting comfortably in quarters."

Selena nodded yet said nothing and Khyra shook her head at her endless supply of stubbornness. Standing from the filth of the cot, Khyra wiped the dust off her once beautiful gown. With one last look at Selena's back, she stooped and crawled through the tiny opening.

At last disappearing from sight, Selena turned, spying an oddly placed image fastened to the right of the opening, two sides of it loosened from the wall. Crossing the small space and kneeling to get a closer look, she found the olden image of two familiar young men.

"Jovaar and Prince Iaco," she whispered, pulling the image free and finding a small, hidden opening in the wall. "Khyra!" she shouted, leaning her face close to the wall. "I found it!"

"What?" Khyra answered, having just reached the docks, Pivoting, she raced back to the opening.

"Come quickly, Khyra!" Selena shouted, her eyes welling with hopeful tears. "No wait! Get Iaco on the com and tell him to come immediately!"

"What is it, Selena?" she asked, her voice echoing in the narrow shoot.

"There is no time to explain!" Selena answered, smiling down on the tattered image then looking back through the opening to her find. "Just get Iaco here now!"

***

At Selena's excited cries, Khyra raced to the com on the outer wall, finding it where Phydin said it would be. She could not help her fumbling with the controls. "Prince Iaco!" she shouted, breathlessly turning back to the empty docks.

"Prince Iaco is detained," the strange, female voice answered, flaring Khyra's temper.

"I need to speak with him at once!" she roared, hand on hip as she turned back to the com. "Get him online now! We have found something!"

"Yes ma'am," the woman answered. Impatiently waiting, Khyra stared at the empty shoot across the corner of the dock while the Prince was located.

"This is Iaco," he began, questioningly. "Identify yourself."

"Iaco," she answered, thankful to hear his familiar voice. "It is Khyra. Selena and I are in the main loading dock area and she has found something! I do not know what it is but she is shouting for you to get down here as soon as you can."

"Please Iaco," she added, breathless. "You must hurry! If what she has found leads to finding…"

"Stay where you are," Iaco interrupted, gesturing for his lieutenant to take over Command. "I am on my way. I will request Phydin and the others to meet us there."

"Just hurry," Khyra answered, silencing the com and returning to the narrow shoot. "They are on their way, Selena!" she shouted, her voice echoing in the small opening. "What have you found?"

"You will not believe it," she answered, adding nothing further as she stared at the foreign device. Knowing she should wait for the Prince to arrive so she could guide him to the opening, Khyra leaned against the exterior wall, asking nothing more of Selena despite her eagerness. Instead, impatient and wishing she had had time to change from the cumbersome gown she waited in the hollow dock amongst the remnants of the ships for the Prince's arrival.

***

Prince Iaco grabbed the last remaining portal off the side cabinet hook-up and raced from Command, chiming Phydin and the others on his way through the familiar corridors. "Phydin," he said, fumbling to strap the device in place on his wrist. "It is Iaco. Selena found something at the loading docks. I am on my way there now."

"What is it?" he asked, gesturing to Fidaldi and Orvi to stop in the corridor.

"I do not know," Iaco answered, breathlessly on the run. "They just said for us to come. Gather your crew and I will meet you there."

"We are on our way," Phydin answered, turning to the others who stood waiting.

"The search will have to wait," he said, snapping his fingers for the men to follow. "Khyra and Selena found something in that blasted hole in the wall and Prince Iaco has requested our presence. We must hurry."

***

Khyra spied Iaco racing through the large entrance into the loading area and waved him forward as he looked in her direction. "We are over here!" she shouted, waiting for him to come closer.

"Phydin and the others are on their way," he said, bending forward to catch his breath. "What did you find?"

"In there," she answered, pointing to the small opening. "Selena is waiting."

Iaco lowered his tall frame to a crouch, climbing in the narrow space. Khyra hefted her cumbersome gown to follow, yet paused as she heard the footsteps of the others approaching.

"What did we miss?" Phydin asked panting, the others catching up to his side.

"Iaco is in with Selena now and…"

"I am sending Selena out," Iaco interrupted, Khyra and the others turning to the opening. "Then I want all of you to get back as far as you can. Phydin, are you there?"

"I am," he answered, stepping forward despite the order.

"Very well," the Prince said, his voice echoing in the narrow opening. "I need you in here."

As Selena reached the outer opening, Fidaldi held his hand out to assist her to her feet. "Do what he said and get back," Phydin ordered, watching the group recede to the wall near the dock's com. Once confident all were sufficiently out of harm's way for whatever reason he could not possibly fathom,

Phydin nodded and climbed within the narrow passage to find Iaco.

Thirty-Two

"They must somehow be jamming radar," Jovaar said frustratedly into his headset, rounding the large mass to his left. "I get a glimpse of him one moment and then the next he is gone. Are you seeing only one?"

"I have yet to see anything in this sector," the pilot answered, continuing his search of the northern area. "Are you certain they are still out here?"

"No, I am not certain," Jovaar answered exasperated, slamming his fist into his side panel. "But I know I saw something. Wait," he continued, eyeing movement in his lower left screen. "Two more ships entering from sector six. Did you see that?"

"I think I might have seen something, Sir, but my screen is now showing clear," the pilot answered, jarring the viewer with the backside of his hand.

"As is mine," Jovaar said, making adjustments to the small controls in hope of somehow proving his eyes correct despite the screen. "I just cannot explain it. They were there and now they are gone. If they were jamming our radar they would never have shown up on our screens at all. Any ideas on what is causing the interference?"

"None, Sir," the pilot answered, steadying his sail along Jovaar's left and backhanding his screen a final time. "Perhaps what we saw was…"

The sudden blast was silencing-blind, shaking Jovaar's craft without warning from behind. Careening him to the right, he held firm to the stick, just missing another large landmass.

"Report!" he shouted, gaining control of the craft, knowing his order was most likely useless. "Report!" he repeated, steadying the ship and flanking hard left.

Spying the debris from yet another slider lost, Jovaar shook his head in sadness, staring out the glass still unable to see the enemy that caused the fatal blow. Dodging the underworld obstacles, the tentacles of life clinging to their outer shells, he circled about, trying desperately to pivot his position as much as possible for fear of being truck himself.

"Where are you?" he mumbled, seeing nothing but the open sea on his screen, forced to leave the thoughts of the man lost to do what he must to protect the child most undoubtedly by now found. "I know you are out there."

***

The stench proved unbearable. "Clear the cockpit, boy," Gidoran ordered in a nasal tone, holding his breath and waiting for the systems to air out. Time seemed to stand still as the vents purified the air. Gidoran sailed passed the first landmass of the sector taking intermittent breaths and sighed loudly when he could once again inhale comfortably.

"I told you you should not have nourished prior to detachment," he said, rolling his eyes at the boy's expense.

"I know, Sir," the co-pilot answered, fumbling to reclasp his restraints. "And for that I am truly sorry. Had I known…"

"I know, I know," Gidoran interrupted, shaking his head and knowing quite well what it was once like to be young. "You think you are invincible. Set course for Sector One and get Plina on the com. I want an update on their progress." Although queezy and uncomfortable, the co-pilot took Sir Gidoran's order without question. Soon Captain Rutolie's voice filled the com.

"Fueling now, Sir," Rutolie answered, his tone filled with confidence. "We are at twenty percent and climbing. No problems encountered thus far, Sir Gidoran, but certainly they will send out fighters as we detach at fifty per your instructions. Please advise."

Gidoran had known this moment would come when Rutolie would question his motives of half fueling the enemy, and sailing swiftly through the wonders of the deep in his surprisingly abled craft, he banked hard left round another mass before laying out his instructions. Unbeknowst to Jovaar,

Gidoran had been kept fully informed of the situation with the possibles, and having taken steps within his own community on Yani to be of assistance if called, he now sailed through the deep of Kindawa confidently. Not having trained exactly for this terrain, he was prepared nonetheless through simulation.

Gidoran had always known that Mathius had favored him as a child, and he had used that to his advantage to be kept in his tight circle of information. No, he had not been an intricate part of the plan of escape of the newborns, but he had known that due to the circumstances he might be able to provide his services if called. Gidoran had taken great pride in knowing that although he was not a member of the elite he was far from its central core, and now, this was his chance to prove his worth.

"Minimum output to buy us some time, Rutolie," he answered at last, dodging yet another obstacle. "At forty-five percent give an excuse of system failure. Order detachment using hyper drive past Yani and get your ship to Adoni. You will find such in your data plan that should be uploading as we speak. We do not want those ships circling Yani and causing a commotion amongst all we have worked for. I have pre-ordered an evasive craft to assist you in your escape, however minimal. You must know that you are ultimately on your own."

"I understand," Rutolie answered, glancing confidently at his crew, the data plan appearing on his screen. "We are prepared to give our lives to the Resistance, Sir Gidoran."

"In a time like this, there is no reason for pleasantries," Gidoran answered, shaking his head and dipping low into a crevice. "You are a good man, Rutolie," he added, knowing full well it could be the last time he spoke with his loyal Captain. "I wish you well."

Swiftly sailing passed the first of a series of sea cliffs Gidoran silenced the com and glanced over his shoulder at the shock-stricken youth at his back. "Polatus," Gidoran said flatly, turning back to his panel. "And hurry, boy. No more lives should be lost."

***

"What do you want to do?" Phydin began, wiping the sweat from his brow, staring at the countdown within the wall.

"We must order evacuation at once," Iaco answered, mimicking his gesture. "It will not be made easy with nearly half the craft engrossed with the exterior dangers, but we have to do what we can. Do not, I repeat do not touch the device for any reason, Phydin. I need to inform the others. Let me save as many lives as I can."

Standing, Iaco climbed into the opening, leaving Phydin to stare transfixed at the decreasing numbers. "Just over three hazon," he whispered, motionless as Iaco glanced over his shoulder.

"I know," he answered at last, shaking his head. Quickly passing through the corridor despite his size, Iaco straightened to face the members. "I need all of you listen to me," Iaco began, running his fingers through his hair. "We are on a countdown with the device Selena found and need to evacuate as soon as possible We have just over three hazon to get as many Polatians as we can free of the zone."

"Fidaldi," he continued, his voice calm yet firm. "Chime Command and have them order the evacuation. There should be just enough transports at port for every Polatian but time is of the essence. Have the LC order all dock hands to confirm the status of those transports and make all necessary provisions. There is no time to waste."

"Yes, Sir," Fidaldi answered, turning to the com and repeating the order.

"And what of us?" Selena asked, wringing the child's blanket and stepping forward. "What of Nitaya? What are we to do about Nitaya? She has not been found!"

"I am certain she is no longer amongst us," Iaco answered, flatly, motioning for the approaching hands to prepare the docks. "It is our only hope to see that as many lives are saved as possible, Selena. We will uplink with Jovaar as soon as we can and await further instructions on how he wishes us to proceed regarding the matter. As of now, we must concentrate on saving lives."

"The matter?" Selena roared, slamming her hands into Iaco's chest. "Nitaya is no matter! Her life means everything to the Resistance, to *all* the lives you are trying to save. How could you say such a thing?"

"Khyra, please," Iaco said, nodding for the woman to claim Selena's flailing arms, a pynar nearing for guidance. "I understand her concern but I must do what I can to see to the safety of all."

"I understand," Khyra answered, attempting to grasp Selena's hands as he turned to his pilot.

"I do not understand!" Selena bellowed, dropping her head on Khyra's shoulder, her elder leading her away from the dock. "We must find her! I should never have left her!"

We must hurry," Iaco said, turning from both the women and his pilot, crossing to Fidaldi as he released the com.

"Command is prompting your evacuation order," he said, turning to Iaco.

"Very well," he answered, nodding to the members at his back. "Prepare for boarding. My Polatians leave at once."

***

Loading Dock A was in chaos. Women still clad in their celebration garb poured into the wide area carrying small totes of possessions they could not bear to leave behind as others carried younglings, their stewards close behind. The men busily prepped the large ships, fueling and loading valuables as the pilots made haste with flight prep. The noise proved deafening, even now before the ships were fired and standing back, leaning against the side wall near the entrance, Selena hoped above all hope that she would spy Nitaya passing, although she knew deep within her heart that she was already gone.

"Come, Selena," Khyra said, crossing to her and patting her hands. "Our transport is now loading and Iaco has ordered us to board. We have to believe she is well," she added, placing her hand on Selena's face, reading the fear in her eyes. "And we will do no good for her just standing here. Come, Selena. We must go now."

"I should never have left her," she whispered, all energy drained from within. Khyra did not hear her words with the surrounding confusion but knew for certain her younger's pleas.

361

"I promise we will find her," Khyra said, gently prodding her arm. Peering over her shoulder at the masses that still flooded the entrance, Selena knew she had no other choice. Staring at the multitude of frightened momars and their young as Khyra pulled her free from the rear wall leading her to the awaiting transport, Selena's arms ached with emptiness.

***

"I want the best three security personnel to do what they can to stifle that explosive device!" Iaco shouted, bellowing over the screeches of the first firing ship. "All others spread out amongst the transports and assist with the evacuation. I will board the last transport out of Polatus."

"But, Sir," a guard said in protest. "If we have as little time as you say, you should board now. There is nothing more you can do."

"I am not leaving until all others are safe," Iaco answered, gesturing for an incoming crew to head toward the ships. "Just get in there and do what you can."

The grand transport entrance blurred with the endless arrival of evacuees and the chaos at the many planks sent chills through Iaco. Standing as if frozen in place, the weight of the impending explosion filling him with sorrow. Polatus would soon be no more. Watching as the young raced to their assigned ships, dodging the elders who hobbled the best they could, Iaco spied some difficulty at the craft third on his left and dismissing the evil thoughts from his mind, raced to the hatch to assist the lone loader.

"What is your situation here?" he asked, reaching out to assist the next heavily adorned Polatian aboard.

"We are loading as fast as we can, Sir," the man answered, turning round to locate the next boarder. "We are doing all we can but..."

"I will be right back," Iaco interrupted, following the last woman and child up the plank.

"Everything will be alright," he added, kneeling to the small boy on his momar's lap. "You," he continued, pointing to the loader. "There is not much more room in here. There are just enough ships to house everyone. Why are they forced to sit on the blasted floor?"

"I am sorry, Sir," the man answered, wiping his brow and leading another elderly woman aboard. "I was told that two transports set off with the fighters. We are making due the best we can with what we have."

"I did not authorize transports for detachment!" Iaco shouted, calming the boy with his hand as he rose. "What are you talking about?"

"I did not prep them, Sir," the loader answered, claiming the arm of an elderly man. "I was enjoying the celebration with the others. You will have to check with the Load Master, but if you are leaving with this ship you need to take your seat."

"No, I am not leaving," Iaco answered, looking over the crowded cabin as he dodged a youth skirting aboard. "Use the room for someone else. I will do everything that I can to get the transports to retern to port."

"Yes, Sir," the loader answered, turning back to yet another elderly couple.

"Now," Iaco continued, sharing the down plank with the two scampering above, grasping firm to eachother's arms. "Where is that blasted Load Master?"

***

"Coming up on Sector One," the young co-pilot said, at last feeling back to his old self.

"Very well," Gidoran answered, pivoting the stick. "We are almost there. Uplink communications with Polatus and inform them of our impending arrival."

"Copy that," he answered, prompting the com. Gidoran sailed through the open sea, veering left and then sharp right through the endless caverns, scanning the surrounding areas for any sign of the enemy. With impatience he awaited good news from his friends.

"All systems are reading uplink failure," the co-pilot stated, rekeying the request. "I do not understand. I have run the request twice yet gain the same response, Sir. What do you want me to do? I have never had this problem before."

"Erase the uplink and connect me to the fighters," Gidoran answered, uncomfortable with what he was hearing. "Iaco would have ordered them at the onset of any trouble and therefore they should be in the area. Something is wrong, I feel it. Just do what you can to get Savius on the com. If I am right, he is in the water."

"Copy that," the boy answered, again keying the request. "Polatus fighter craft respond," he said, attempting authority and deepening his voice over the com.

"I have you on radar," the voice swiftly answered. "And was about to do away with you! Identify yourself immediately."

"Gidoran Damuni," Gidoran answered, prompting the com to the bow. "I need to speak with Jovaar Savius at once!"

"Well it is about blasted time, G!" Jovaar answered, relieved to have someone he trusted along side in the deep waters. "The Sugins have somehow jammed our radar. Obviously we are able to communicate with eachother but we are not able to keep their fighers on our screens and I cannot get word from Polatus. The enemy is out there, Gidoran. The worst is that they could be right behind us and we would not know it. Last glimpse had them in the northern area of this sector. We have taken one of them out but since then have been doing nothing but circling. Any ideas?"

"Just maintain your current speed and give me a moment, Jovi," Gidoran answered, tapping his chin. "I need to get a better readout of the seascape."

"That should be hard for you in a one man craft," Jovaar answered, wondering how he could possibly maneuver the controls and run a thorough search at the same time.

"Oh, ye of little faith," Gidoran answered, smugness filling his voice. "Apparently, unlike you I have an upgraded model. It is a two man craft and I just so happen to have a co-pilot," he added, glancing over his shoulder at the boy. "Order the search and give me readouts of all plantlife in the area. I have an idea."

"Plantlife?" Jovaar asked, overhearing the conversation. "You are searching for plantlife? Gidoran, what the…"

"Your faith in me stings, Jovi," he interrupted, his grin widening as he thought back to the wonders of his Yanian simulator. "It really stings. However, I will overlook it once again. Just keep your current path and keep this channel open. I should have something for you soon."

"Copy that," Jovaar answered, releasing the com. "Plantlife," he mumbled, shaking his head and looking out the side glass to his friend sailing by. Veering his stick left, he made a pass around yet another landmass then dipped low into a moderate cavern, keeping watch of Gidoran's path to the right on his screen. "I hope it is made of solid rock."

***

"Hand me the small solder," he said with frustration over his shoulder. "No, I need that one," he grunted, half pointing and turning back to the panel. "Do you not even know your own tools?"

Sweat poured from Jax's brow and his annoyance with the oafs at his back was making his blood boil. He should have had communications up and running by now and he was disgusted with himself for the delay, yet he was even angrier at the two so-called experts Iaco had assigned him on data controls. Useless in their high-tech garb, their advanced tools and their suggestions proved laughable.

"Anything?" he asked hoping for a miracle, wiping the endless sweat from his brow.

"Nothing," the tech answered, attempting to once again power up the system.

"Alright then, just let me think," Jax continued, grumbling and squeezing out from under a cabinet. "We need to try something else. Is there any other location on Polatus where data lines are joined?" The two *specialists* merely looked at each other and then back to Jax, shrugging as one unhelpfully shook his head.

"Alright, just let me think," Jax repeated, huffing at their ignorance, rubbing the base of the solder under his chin. "Maybe we are looking for the wrong kind of problem. Maybe it's not being blocked from their ship but it is actually jammed from within, like a small device attached to the line."

"Impossible," the tech who did all the talking answered, confidently shaking his head. "Anyone who enters this location must go through a series of security measures. There is no way someone without authority could access this cabin, let alone most of the surrounding areas."

"Well, I am telling you the lines are intact," Jax continued, slamming the solder back within the tool pouch. "There must be something internally blocking them, and whether you agree with me or not, I think we should concentrate on finding the device. It would be small and in a position not easily accessed, like tucked neatly behind a cabinet or below a feeder shoot."

"I am telling you it is a waste of time," the oral tech continued rolling his eyes, at last showing a small form of emotion. "Did you see how many check points we had to pass to get here? There is no way someone without clearance passed unnoticed!"

"I hate being doubted," Jax answered, raising his hand to halt the man's attempt at protest. "But I love proving someone wrong. If you are not going to help me search then get out of my way. I have a date with a jammer and I hate keeping my dates waiting. So shall we get started?" he added, the female tech looking questionably to the other.

"Alright then," Jax continued, rubbing his hands together, the pair once again silent. "Let us hurry and find the little nuisance."

"I know the space is small, but spread out the best you can," Jax ordered, pivoting in the cramped space, searching for the best place to begin. "It will not be anywhere obvious. Like I said earlier, reach and feel behind the cabinets or under and behind the feeder shoots. I will take off the panel covers," he decided at the last, lowering to the nearest. "Let's see what I can find inside."

"What exactly does a jamming device look like?" the oral tech asked, peering behind a small cabinet on the floor. Jax merely shook his head. This was going to take a while.

"They are never the same but it would be smaller than your hand," he answered, eyeing the first panel. "I have seen some shaped like a box that adheres to an outer wall of a unit while I have dissolved others that are a gel-like substance that are actually attached to a line, neutralizing the voltage. Just look for something small and out of place."

Nodding yet maintaining their act of silence, the duo quickly began their search of the lower areas as Jax took off the panel he had been studying. Confident it was secure after a thorough scan, he crouched to the next anticipating a find. Again uncovering nothing, he slid to the floor exhausted, yet spied a small cabinet off in the far corner. Standing and wiping the sweat from his brow with his already moistened sleeve, he scooted around his silent friends in the small space and knelt before it, the pair continuing their fruitless search at his back.

"It could not be this easy," he whispered, shaking his head as he removed the panel. Appearing the same as the others, he reached within the panel regardless, moving his hand from side to side, around and behind the deep cavern of wiring. Finding nothing, he began withdrawing his arm, yet paused as he felt something strangely out of place graze the back of his hand.

"Hold up," he said, motioning to the others. "I think I may have found it. I think..." he continued, moving his hand back to the location, the pair turning, kneeling silently at his feet. "I think...yes, there you are! My friends, we have her. Get me the long pair of tongs out of the pouch."

As the silent one reached in, handing him the tool, the pair sat in amazement, watching the newcomer pull the device free from the cabinet, careful not to make connection with the melee of wires. "Ugly little thing isn't she," he said, a large smile crossing his face. As if routine, he placed the gel-like substance in a small metal box on the floor.

"Get the panel cover back in place and power up," he added, standing and crossing to the com.

"Get me Prince Iaco," he ordered, quite pleased with himself, shaking his head at the backs of the scurrying pair. "What do you mean you cannot reach him? Get him on the com now! I have some exciting news."

"Sir, Prince Iaco has ordered an evacuation," the man answered, anxiously. "Surely you have heard of this over the com system."

"We are in the blasted data cabin!" Jax answered, pounding his fist on the wall. "We have not heard anything for a hazon! You must tell me what is wrong at once!"

"A device was found," the man continued, obviously distracted by the noise at his back. "That is all I know. We are preparing to head to loading at this very moment."

"Well then," Jax answered, shaking his head at his silent, awaiting crew. "If we are departing this seems rather useless now. Nonetheless, find Prince Iaco and get him on the com."

"Yes, Sir," the man answered, nervously. "I will do my best, Sir."

Waiting impatiently as the silent tech duo uselessly finished tiding the cabin, settling the panel covers back in place, Jax leaned against the rear wall, shaking his head, certain the above chaos was for not. "This is Iaco," the Prince said at last.

"Prince, this is Jax," he answered, slightly annoyed as he turned back to the com, the silent pair quickly far from his thoughts. "We have communications online beyond Polatus."

"You have done well," Iaco answered hurriedly, his breath obviously labored. "Now get to loading and board your transport. I do not have time to go into detail, Jax, but we have found an explosive and I need all personnel to leave at once. Thanks to you I will be able to speak with Savius and update him on our situation. For that I am grateful."

"It seems we are underappreciated and it is time to leave," Jax added. Shaking his head at the nodding pair, he released the com with Iaco's obvious graciously parting words. Kneeling to gather the tool pouch, he could not contain a slight chuckle at their high-tech garb and gestures. Although he wished he had time to question them on the specifics of their actual capabilities, he knew time was short and instead, motioned the odd pair to lead the way to loading.

Thirty-Three

One by one Iaco watched the transports set out for the deep on the length of their given tracks. "Three to go," he thought, turning toward the large opening in the rear wall. "There is not much time."

"Yes, Sir," the lieutenant answered, uncertain if he was expected to respond. His commander prompted the nearest dock com, eyes hazy with uncertainty. "We were leaving just this moment, Sir."

"Very well," Iaco answered, turning from the almost vacant port. "But before you head this way, patch me through to Savius. Jax has communications back online and as you know it has been some time since I have been able to reach Jovaar. I fear something may be terribly wrong."

"Yes, Sir," the lieutenant answered. "As you have stated, communications are indeed now active. He is online now, Sir," he continued, nodding to his fellow officers. "If there is nothing further, we will get ourselves to loading. Only a handful of us remain."

"You have done all that you can do," Iaco answered, running his fingers through his hair. "Get to your transport and I will meet with you at the rendezvous."

"Yes, Sir," he answered, disengaging the com's line.

"This is Savius," the voice said, his tone filled with annoyance for having been forced to break his line with Gidoran. Iaco had never been more pleased to hear the angered voice of his friend.

"Jovaar," he began, unable to contain a sigh of relief. "Thank the stars you are still with us. We had lost communications but Jax just now got them back online. Have you isolated the Sugin fighters?"

"We are working on that, Iaco," Jovaar answered grimly. "Gidoran has at last meandered his way to the fight. We have found a snag in the radar system though and he is as we speak attempting to break through it. I will keep you informed."

"Very well, my friend," Iaco answered, looking out into the eerily quiet dock. "And I will do what I can on this end. It seems we have our own fight here. I have my best men working on it but I have ordered an evacuation. Three transports are waiting departure and should be leaving momentarily. I will be on the last. Coordinates for the Polatian rendezvous have been downloaded to your system."

"Jovaar," he continued, shaking his head and turning his gaze to the grand entrance. "I have worked my whole life for Polatus, yet I am afraid she will not be with us much longer. Please. Please make them pay for what they have done."

"What are you talking about?" he asked oblivious to Iaco's situation, eyeing Gidoran's frustrated path on his side screen. "Has the child been found? Is Selena alright?" Jovaar listened without interruption as Iaco updated him on his grim situation. When finished, Jovaar could do nothing but shake his head and glare out at the sea before him.

"Even without your own difficulties, you know it will be my pleasure to see to the end of the Sugins," he said at last, tapping the stick back to slow his speed, mirroring Gidoran. "Forgive me for bringing this wrath upon you, my friend. I never meant for it to…"

"I know you meant no harm," Iaco interrupted, running his fingers through his hair. "Yet we have a history, Jovi…one that I have faith in. All things happen for a reason. It is just that…"

"Hold on, Iaco," Jovaar interrupted, torn for having stopped the offered turmoil of his friend. "Gidoran is chiming and we have a situation of our own. I am going to trust that Nitaya is safe and therefore I want you to get yourself to the location we spoke of regardless of the rendezvous you have indicated. I promise we will meet you there," he added, thrusting the stick hard left to avoid another landmass. "Savius out."

Iaco stood motionless as the com quieted, watching his security personnel run toward him trailed by Phydin, grim looks filling their tired faces. "I am sorry, Prince Iaco," Phydin said, halting the others. "We have been unable to disassemble the device. I have never seen technology of its kind. I am certain it is hardwired in and I fear any attempt to dislodge it would be catastrophic. We are down to less than two hazon."

Iaco bowed his head, closing his eyes. Polatus would soon be gone and there was nothing he could do to stop it. "Alright then," he answered, raising his head to their anxious faces. "Get to your transports and see that every last Polatian is secured. There is no time to waste whimpering over what we are about to lose. Life," he added, nodding at the men. "Life is all that is important now."

***

"How can we just sit here?" Selena asked, raising the small blanket to her cheek, glaring at Khyra. "Nitaya is out there and we continue to do nothing!"

"I have told you, Selena," the elder answered, billowing her gown against the stifling heat. "Jovaar and Iaco are doing all that they can."

Khyra had tried everything she could think of to soothe Selena, yet as they sat in the last remaining seats on the increasingly crowded transport, she turned from the woman's sobs and looked to the frightened faces of both young and old. Apparently Iaco was short on ships. Glancing out at those who were forced to sit on the floor against the outer walls, Khyra fidgeted in her seat with guilt filling her, quickly returning her gaze to Selena.

"As I was saying," she continued, diverting her eyes from those seated uncomfortably at her back, doing her best to concentrate solely on Selena. "I am quite certain that at any moment we will receive word that Nitaya has been found and that she is aboard another...Hylin!" she shouted, waving as she spied the lad cram through the crowded hatch.. "We are over here!"

"I am alright," he answered, waving. Calming her eyes as he excused himself for bumping an elder Polatian, he stooped to kneel, scooting to get near. "The others are close behind.

This way!" he added, peering over his shoulder at Fidaldi's approach, trailed by Orvi and Uvis.

"And what of Jax?" Khyra asked, looking up to Fidaldi. "What of Phydin?"

Fidaldi struggled with his answer, having had no word from either in quite some time. "I am sorry, Khyra," he began, shaking his head. "But I..."

"Phydin!" she interrupted, attempting to rise as he entered the hatch. "You are alright! We were so worried. Have you seen Jax?"

"He is right behind me," he answered, gesturing over his shoulder. "He was able to at last get communications online, although with all that is happening, they seem useless now. There he is. Jax!" he shouted, waving over the crowd. "We are over here!"

"So much for my expertise," he said, kneeling at Hylin's side. "It was a jamming device just like I thought. The two so-called techs they assigned to me were useless, so it took a little longer than expected. I am thankful though that they chose another transport so I would not be forced to endure them a moment longer. I can not even imagine being holed up in this thing for onars on end, attempting to play a game of Rodaous with that pair. Do you know where we are going?"

"No," Phydin answered, grumbling in the claustrophobic space, lowering to one knee. "Iaco was rather evasive with the flight plan and only the pilots know the destination. I have to admit that I for one do not like his tactics. The other ships have already left and now we are just waiting for Iaco and the last of his men."

"But how will they fit in here?" Khyra asked, looking about the already crowded cabin, sighing as more were forced to claim seats on the floor.

"Iaco is on the com now attempting to secure two ships that left without authority," Phydin answered, scooting forward to allow room for another boarder. "He is ordering their roundabout now. The problem is, is there is not much time. By my calculations, we have just over one hazon until the device is set off."

"Do not worry though," he added. Altering his annoyed tone, he placed his hand on Khyra's knee, spying the fear welling in her eyes. "Iaco is a smart man. I am certain he will find a way for this to work."

***

Iaco stood against the rear wall, watching as two of the last three remaining transports fired and detached, shooting down the descending tracks and into the deep. As they sped from sight and the docks quieted, he turned his gaze to the one ship that remained, spying the small crowd that had formed at its plank.

"Blasted, I almost forgot," he mumbled, reaching again for the com on the wall. "Leuitenant?" he said abruptly. "Are you still in Command?"

"I am, Sir," the man answered, breathless. "I have sent the others your way but there were some last minute problems that forced me to remain behind. I am certain that..."

"I do not have time to hear the details," Iaco interrupted, annoyed as he stared at the bunching crowd. "I need you to get the two transports that left with the fighters on the com. I am certain we will all not be able to fit in the last transport in port. Order their roundabout at once."

"Connecting now, Sir," the LC answered, Iaco gritting his teeth awaiting word.

"This is Captain Wozer," the voice chimed, low static filling the background. Not recognizing the name, Iaco chose under the circumstances not to take the time to question.

"Captain Wozer, this is Prince Iaco," he began, his voice echoing against the vacant shell of the docks. "You are piloting without authority and I am ordering you to roundabout at once. We are under evacuation and there are not enough transports for all Polatians. Inform you sister ship as well and return to port immediately!"

"Sir," he answered flatly. "We are in the most northern corner of Sector Nine. A roundabout will take some time."

"And we are wasting time discussing this!" Iaco shouted, running his fingers through his hair, knowing the outer sector quite well. "Captain Wozer," he continued, shaking his head in an attempt to calm his tone. "I will get as many Polatians as I can on the final transport, but I need you to attempt roundabout regardless. You have just over one hazon to reach the docks. Attempt a return, Wozer. If you do not make it back with time to spare, about face and immediately head to the rendezvous."

"Yes, Sir," Wozer answered. "But I am uncertain as to what you mean 'with time to spare.'"

"You must arrive within the next hazon or roundabout as ordered," Iaco answered curtly. Angered, he signed off without further explanation.

***

Wozer's grin widened as soon as Iaco silenced the line. "Captain Ruvis," he began, his voice low and confident, chuckling at his subordinate's back. "It seems your clever device has been found as expected. We have been ordered for roundabout as expected as well."

"And so it begins," Ruvis answered, staring out into the darkness of the sea. "Prince Iaco is as foolish as I had predicted. Preparing for roundabout," he continued, snapping his fingers for his pilot to prompt the stick. Turning his attention to the child whimpereing softly in the girl's arms at his feet, Ruvis' grin widened, his confidence growing as he leaned over the edge of the helm.

"We should reach Polatus just as the timer ceases," he began, bearing his aged teeth and glaring at his captives. "Everything is happening according to plan."

***

Iaco raced to the last transport, shouting for the dockhand attempting to complacent the final boarders. "I need you to get as many of them aboard as possible," he began, glancing through the hatch's opening. "I have two ships on roundabout but I am not certain there is enough time to wait for them."

"We are at capacity now, Sir," the man said, peering into the cabin before turning back to the anxiously awaiting final Polatians. "But I will do what I can."

Jax spied the conversation at the exit and crossing through the crowded cabin, reached the edge of the hatch. He shook his head at the Prince motioning for more to enter.

"What is wrong?" he asked, kneeling to hear Iaco above the din of the expectant riders. Motioning for Phydin once Iaco proved spent, Jax knew what must be done.

"Phydin, there is obviously not enough room," he began, gesturing to those that waited to board. "I am requesting to be left behind with Iaco until the other transports make roundabout."

"No," Phydin answered, standing abruptly. "I will stay behind. It is my duty to…"

"This argument is pointless," Iaco interrupted, halting the boarders. "Phydin, I need you to take command at the rendezvous incase I do not make it. And Jax, as dire as this is, I need you to go as well."

Having spied the heated conversation at the hatch, Khyra assured Selena she would return momentarily before crossing to the others. She listened in without notice. "I am staying," she said, startling the men. They turned to her interruption, yet as Iaco began to protest, she held up her hand to stifle his argument.

"I cannot sit idly by while others may lose their lives," Khyra stated flatly, attempting a smile at an awaiting couple. "I am staying, Iaco."

"Fine," he answered, knowing he was defeated. Ramming his fists on his hips he turned back to the men. "Khyra and I will wait for the roundabout, but I insist the rest of you return to your seats. You will be detaching on my order."

***

"You will be alright, Selena," Khyra began, motioning for the elderly woman to take her seat. Knealing before Selena, she explained the conversation on the docks.

"Phydin and Jax will be with you and they will undoubtedly see that you are safe. You must think of the other possibles."

"I am not going without you," Selena protested, rising in anger. Looking to the worried eyes about her, she wiped her tear-stained face with the sleeve of her gown.

"I do not deserve this seat over another and I will not accept it while others are left to suffer!" Khyra shook her head, knowing the debate was pointless.

"Let us go then," she said, claiming Selena's hand. "There is not much time."

"I want to stay too," Hylin said, grabbing the tails of Khyra's cloak, skirting a younger child.

"No, Hylin, you must remain here," she answered, turning in the cramped space to face him. "It is your only chance."

"She is right," Phydin added, reaching for Khyra's hand to assist her down the plank. "And I will need your help will the placement of the Polatians once we reach the rendezvous."

Angered at having again been put in his youthful place, Hylin stomped his foot and crossed his arms, watching Phydin lead Khyra and Selena down the plank. Silently watching Fidaldi trail after them, his anger grew as Phydin shook his hand and gestured farewell, watching him shadow the women. Standing firm as the last of the Polatians boarded, Hylin waited for Phydin to ascend then crossed to him, attempting indifference.

"I am going to sit over there to make room for the others," he said. Phydin merely nodded, turning to speak with Orvi claiming the final space on the floor. Knowing the elder distracted, the *boy* obviously furthest from his thoughts, Hylin slowly made his way for the hatch.

***

With the weight of the decision heavy on their minds, those that chose to remain stepped away from the ship, allowing the last of the Polatians to board. Hearing the shouts of the leuitenant racing toward the transport, hands waving in desperation, Iaco returned to the hatch, the plank beginning its slow ascent.

"Wait!" he shouted, halting the rise with the outer prompt. "There is one more."

"I am sorry I was detained, Sir," he said breathless, the loader extending his hand to assist him climb the tilted plank. "Why are you not leaving with the transport?"

"There is no time to explain," Iaco answered, patting his faithful servant on the back. "You must get onboard at once."

"It has been an honor, Sir," the leuitenant said, extending his hand. At once he understood the grim look on his commander's face.

"The honor has been mine," Iaco answered, the push of the thrusters forcing the others back from the ship. "Get the new Command operational, Leuitenant. Phydin Heiss will lead until I arrive."

"Yes, Sir," he answered, turning to accept the awaiting hand. Knowing full well that he may never see his Prince Iaco again, he turned and saluted as the loader climbed aboard, reprompting the hatch.

***

Watching the dockhand secure the hatch, Iaco took a step back once the ship at last fired. With all Polatians secured and accounted for, he sighed as the final transport sped down the track into the depths of the sea. Taking a deep breath in the eeriness of the quiet docks, he turned and walked slowly back toward the few that remained. Motionless and not knowing what to do, they shared both fear and empathy with the Prince, silently awaiting his next order.

"Fidaldi and I will take one last look at the device," he began, his voice firm, yet wary. "Khyra, take Selena to Command and we will meet you there. It is not the furthest location from the blast but I see no point in waiting this out elsewhere."

"I will stay with you!" Hylin shouted, dashing from behind an empty gear trolley.

"I told you to stay on that ship!" Khyra shouted, holding firm to Selena's arm and gritting her teeth at the approaching boy.

377

"I am sorry," he answered, secretly pleased his venture off the ship had gone unnoticed. "But as you both said, the Polatians deserved the room more than I did."

"There is no time to argue his foolishness," Iaco answered solemnly, shaking his head and turning back to Khyra. "Get Selena to Command at once. Hylin, Fidaldi, let us go."

***

"I have it," Gidoran said prompting the com, the young co-pilot uploading the search results to his station. "The fighters are not jamming our radar, Jovi, they are cammoflaged."

"What are you talking about?" Jovaar asked, his temper flaring as he dodged another landmass. "That is impossible and you know it, G."

"It sounds unbelievable but the data is right here," Gidoran continued, tapping his screen to bring up the plant's composition. "And the good news is that I have had my boy here running some probables. He has found a way to get around their cover."

"I am listening," Jovaar answered, his tone calming despite the eerie darkness beyond his glass.

"Glymop," Gidoran said confidently, sailing at a distance to widen their targets from the enemy. "Glymop is the answer."

"Glymop is what?" Jovaar asked attempting to stifle his anger, waiting for Gidoran's gloating to temper.

"It is a weed, Jovaar," Gidoran continued, smiling widely and tipping the stick low into another crevice. "A weed that is abundant in these areas. We have done research on it in our labs on Yani, Jovi. That is how truly amazing this weed is. It reached even a dry metropolis as my substation. It is a disintegrating agent of the most fascinating kind. All we have to do is steer our ships toward sector two. It is most populous there. Iaco's home was well chosen, nestled in between its protectiveness. What a wonderful species it is."

"You have to be joking," Jovaar answered, prompting his side screen, certain of the sector's location. "As I expected," he continued, shaking his head. "Sector Two is just beyond Polatus,

G. We will be leading them directly to Iaco, and furthermore, you are telling me that a simple weed is supposed to…"

"Jovi?" Gidoran shouted, the com crackling in his ears. "What was that? Repeat your last."

"I am taking fire!" Jovaar answered, banking right on the stick. "I need backup, G! I am dodging hits from either side!"

"We are on our way," Gidoran answered, mere clicks from his location. "We will somehow divert their attention and get them to follow. Do what you can to hold them off and alter your course to sector two. We will lead them right to it."

"Copy that," Jovaar shouted, dodging yet another blast, eager to be rid of the nuisance despite his wariness of Gidoran's plan. "They are firing more frequently, G. You must hurry!"

"Hold tight, my friend!" Gidoran answered. Nodding as he sailed through the deep, the youthful co-pilot whistled his newfound confidence at his his back. "We are on the way."

   ***

Piloting the craft at full throttle, Jovaar rotated the ship lateral, squeezing through the oncoming narrow crevice. Sailing head tipped, he relied solely on the data provided by the craft. Anxiously awaiting the approach of the other side of the looming rock walls, its welcoming image growing increasingly on his screen, he sighed in relief and straightened as he cleared the opening successfully.

Fortunate to have dodged the blasts thus far, Jovaar now faced the falling debris as the ancient rock exploded from its berth. Ricocheting off his ship, it made the stick difficult to maneuver. As the firing appeared to slow and the sailing steadied, the deep opened before him. Shaking his head, Jovaar spied the scattered lights that remained, regardless of Iaco's shield surrounding Polatus.

"At least you are still there," he whispered, circling wide to his left to sector two. "Gidoran is mad," he continued, prompting the area's layout. "They will divert to us alright. They will divert straight to the docks and open fire!"

With no time to reconsider, Jovaar made his ship as assessable as possible, hoping above all hope that the enemy would trail him at a distance, buying him enough time before engaging. With the blasts ebbing, he was certain he had lost them and the tension in his hands at last waned, however Gidoran sailed directly into view, violently careening Jovaar's craft. Gritting his teeth and grabbing the stick with both hands, he struggled to settle its jarring from Gidoran's wake.

"Forgive me, Jovi," he said, chuckling from his slightly larger craft, obviously enjoying the fight. "I did not mean to get quite that close. Circle about once then follow me. I am obviously bigger and more noticeable."

"I know what you are thinking, Jovaar," he added, glancing over his shoulder to his young subordinate, who smiled, reassuringly. "As I told the boy who is attempting to hide his nerves at my back, they will follow. I know it is difficult, but just trust me."

"I see I have no other choice," Jovaar answered, performing the requested circling maneuver. As the roundabout proved smooth and the enemy fire had in fact subsidden for the moment, Jovaar's fears grew as the few lights of Polatus disappeared into the darkness at his back.

"I see no sign of them, Gidoran," he said, handedly pulling up the rear.

"They have no idea what is about to happen, Jovaar," he answered, confidently despite the negative tone of his friend. "We will sail straight through the glymop and you should pick them up almost instantly."

"We just hand delivered Polatus, G," Jovaar pressed, shaking his head and settling the stick, the sea shuttering the craft in Gidoran's wake. "If you are wrong and the others are forced to suffer for your..."

"When have I ever been wrong, old friend?" he asked, his grin ever evident over the com. "You cannot possibly think I would..."

"I can name several times you have been wrong," Jovaar interrupted, monitoring the large mass of oncoming greens on his side screen. "And this better not be one of them."

Thirty-Four

"King Sugin," Terdoni began, turning to the sound of the rear door and the approach of his imposing commander. "A1, G5 and sliders have acknowledged enemy fighters. We have lost one slider thus far, yet I have just been informed of the hidden location of the eluded Polatus. How do you wish to proceed?"

Carsian's acknowledgement was a stern nod at the long awaited find, his evil grin crossing his face as he turned to face Terdoni. "Get Captain Wozer on the com at once," he answered, leaning his hands on the outer rail of Command. "It seems everything is at last falling into place. I have just received word that Sivon is within moments of capturing his own possible and I am pleased that our first is within our grasp as well."

"Aye, Sir," Terdoni answered, oblivious to the King's thoughts. Nodding, he turned to order the request.

"This is Captain Wozer," the voice stated confidently, his voice booming throughout Command for all to hear. All eyes rose booming voice

"Captain Wozer," the King answered, speaking loud for all to hear. "It has been some time."

"Aye it has, Sir," the man answered, his voice both low and confident. "And it is my honor to once again speak with your Magesty and to fulfill your purpose of..."

"All pleasantries aside, Wozer," Carsian interrupted, flitting his hand in the air. "Update me on your progress."

"Of course," he began, briefing the King and all who listened in on the last several onars. "We are in roundabout to Polatus as we speak, and as I anticipated, I am in possession of the child, Sir," he added at the last. "Everything is how you predicted. It is my honor to bring you this joyous news."

"Well done, Wozer," the King answered, grimacing with disgust at Terdoni. "I only wish all served with your obedience.

Continue forth with your route and keep me abreast of your progress."

"Of course, King Sugin," the Captain answered, silencing the com.

"Continue our current flight path to Polatus and stifle that blasted child!" he shouted, his anger returning in the absence of his King's ear. "At last the beginning of the end has come."

***

"Glymop up ahead, just off to the left," Gidoran said, eyeing the glare of light from Jovaar's ship out the glass. "Do you see it, Jovi?"

"All I see is your blasted rear!" he shouted, nodding as the large mass grew on his side screen. "Just get on with it!"

"Such vulgarity," Gidoran chuckled, his grin evident over the com. "We are about to enter...full throttle! This is amazing!" he continued, for a brief moment forgetting the enemy craft as the bluish-brown denseness engulfed the ship. Instinctively he switched from sight to screen.

"Climbing high to emerge," he added, unable to contain his grin. "Do you have them, Jovi?"

"Not yet," Jovaar answered monitoring his panel, the thickness forcing his eyes from the glass. "Wait! I cannot believe this. You were right, Gidoran, three fighters in sight. Preparing for engagement!"

"Do your dirty work," Gidoran answered, at last pulling out of the weed and sailing high in roundabout. "And now my friend, the fun begins."

With the enemy fighters in plain sight on his screen, Jovaar circled round to get a better angle. Ignorantly they sailed at his back, oblivious to their lack of cammoflage.

"Preparing to fire," Jovaar said, the first ship sailing into range. As the blast of contact gloriously everberated against his ship, he could not contain his laugh, eager to begin the chase after the others.

"Circle around, G," he continued, at last confident they could successfully clear the remaining pair. "I will take the one on the left. You get the one on the right."

"Copy that, Jovaar," he answered, turning to adjust his angle. As the enemy fired in a haphazard panic at last realizing they were no longer shielded, their shots proved fruitless against the onslaught of the duo.

"Mine is Polatian fodder," Gidoran said, laughing grandly. The explosion brought minimal jarring to his ship, his co-pilot giggling at his back. "I am coming up hard on your left."

"I have almost got him," Jovaar answered, his target fruitlessly attempting to out maneuver his target. "Almost there," he added, Gidoran abruptly sailing forward and in front, demolishing the pesky craft.

"I am sorry, but I could not wait, Jovi," he said, his tail a brilliant glow before Jovaar's eyes.

"The center of attention as always, Damuni," Jovaar answered, shaking his head and redirecting his craft in roundabout.

"Just enjoying the game," Gidoran answered, eyeing the excited boy at his back. "And it seems once again you have been outscored!"

"Not funny," Jovaar answered, slowing his craft, two ships coming into view from his right. "Do you see that?" he asked, his tone once again serious.

"Yeah, I saw it," Gidoran answered, still reeling from battle. "I flew in front of you and…"

"No," Jovaar interrupted, his tone firm. "Off to your right, Gidoran."

"Copy that," G answered, stiffening in his seat. "Two transports preparing to dock, instead of diverting. What do you want to do?"

"We follow the escaping transports as planned," Jovaar answered, eyeing the large ships on his screen. "All personnel should be away from Polatus, Iaco reassured me as such. Patch the rendezvous I am uploading into you database and pray we are not wrong."

"Copy that," Gidoran answered, stretching his back within his seat. "We are doing the right thing, Jovaar," he said. With the route appearing on his screen via the youth's hand at his back, all laughs at once escaped him. "Iaco would surely have ordered roundabout if we were needed."

"I pray you are right, my friend," Jovaar answered, racing after the mapped transports heading away from Polatus. "I pray you are right."

***

"Hylin," Iaco began, staring at the evil device in the wall of the cramped lair, dusting away the tattered remains near his feet. "See if you can find something on one of the trolleys to dislodge this. It is risky but if I can remove it, I might be able to load it into the waste shoot."

"There is not much of a chance," he added, wiping the sweat from his brow. "But it is our only one. There is not much time left. If it doesn't work, we will head to Command with the others."

"I will find something," Hylin eagerly answered, quickly scooting out the opening. Racing toward the nearest trolley to scour through its hefty lower tool drawers however, his confidence soon waned.

"Nothing," he grumbled, racing round the corner to the amphi loading area, yet spying several trolleys standing scattered amongst the rear fuel lines, he heard a strange noise and paused, turning back to the wall.

"What was that?" he whispered, stepping silently toward the rumbling. As two large ships rolled into view on alternate tracks, a newfound eagerness washed over him. "The transports!" he shouted, his words muffled against the screeching of the engines as they sailed up the parallel tracks. "If I can find something to dislodge the device, Iaco can put it aboard one of them!"

Quickly turning back to the carts at the far corner, Hylin delved into the drawers, finding nothing on the first or the second. With a new excitement filling his veins however, he eagerly pressed on, the whir of the arrival thrusters waning. Reaching the third and then the fourth, Hylin at last found what he was looking for and extracted the largest of the fuel line repair presses.

"This will work," he said, throwing the remaining useless tools to the floor. "For the sake of us all, this has to work!"

***

Captain Wozer stood at his pilot's back as the ship glided in smoothly on the track. The eeriness of Polatus' docks stood before them.

"All systems stalled," the pilot said, prompting final procedures. "Captain Wozer," he continued, lifting the overhead panel. "Docking confirmed, lowering the hatch."

"Very well," Wozer said raising his weapon, the man obliviously turning at his station. "King Sugin would like to thank you for your obedience," he added flatly, the blast ringing out in the narrow space. The babe, having been hushed the last half hazon, wailed out as Agye shielded her with her arms.

The pilot did not see the blast, nor did he feel it. His life was simply cut short when he proved no longer useful, and his death obviously meant nothing to Captain Wozer. "Now," the man said, replacing his weapon beneath his cloak, turning to Agye with menacing eyes. "Stifle that child and wait here."

Pacing the small corridor through the vacant passenger cabin then at last to the gunnery, Wozer found his most recent captive sitting obediently awaiting orders. "You!" he began, snapping his fingers for the man to rise. "Get outside, shoot any and all stragglers and await further instructions!"

"Aye, Sir," Kroy answered, releasing his restraints and withdrawing his weapon as he rose. As his new gunner raced unfeelingly through the rear cabin door, Wozer could not contain his grin at his most fortunate find. "This is has been all too easy."

***

"Did you hear that, Fidaldi?" Iaco asked, kneeling in front of the timer. "It must be the transports Iaco told us about! Hurry, there is not much time. Chime command from the com beyond the passage and get Khyra and Selena back her now!"

385

Clearing the opening and crossing to the com, Fidaldi glanced over his shoulder at the transports and paused, not believing his eyes. "Kroy?" he questioned, widening his arms in welcome. "You are alive! We have to get the others and leave Polatus before the detonation. Help me! Prince Iaco will..."

"Kroy!" he shouted nervously, his friend standing firm pointing his weapon steady at his head. "What are you doing?"

"Disposing of stragglers," Kroy answered, calmly prompting the fire. Eyes filled with disbelief, Fidaldi fell lifeless to the floor.

Hylin stood at Kroy's back in shock. He had been just about to shout out that he had found the press that could possibly dislodge the device when Kroy raised his weapon and fired at Fidaldi point blank.

"No!" he screamed, quickly dropping the rod and reaching for the weapon at his side. Kroy at once turned at his words and Hylin froze in place, the weapon now directed at his heart.

"Another straggler," Kroy said, aiming steadily and tilting his head.

"Please," Hylin begged, closing his eyes. "Kroy, please no!"

Thirty-Five

"This feels wrong," Jovaar said, sailing steadily behind the last of the large ships.

"What does?" Gidoran asked, jaunting aimlessly to the right of the craft and toying with the controls.

"I need to go back," Jovaar answered flatly.

"Are you mad?" Gidoran shouted, straightening his line and looking over to Jovaar's ship through the glass. "There is not enough time, Jovi. You heard what Iaco said. You will not make it out of there alive!"

"I have to try," Jovaar said, prompting his controls for roundabout. "Head to the rendezvous, G, Phydin will need you. They all will need you. I have to know for certain that Lena and the child are safe."

"But…"

"I am not debating this, G," Jovaar interrupted, slowing his stick to allow Gidoran a clear pass. "This is something I have to do. Knowing me you undertand this to be so. Preparing for roundabout. Stay your course, my friend. I will see you again soon."

Gidoran sat in silence as his closest friend circled wide toward Polatus. "I pray you are right," he whispered, shaking his head. Punching the stick as another ship careened in to fill Jovaar's vacancy, Gidoran sailed reluctantly onward after the transports.

    ***

Hylin flinched at the close-ranged shot then slowly opened his eyes in confusion, his arms limp at his side in defeat. "How?" he asked in a mere whisper. Tears streamed down his youthful face. Iaco, having emerged from the small opening at the sounding of the transports, now stood before the shoot, weapon raised.

"Are you alright?" he asked, racing to the boy. Frozen in place however, Hylin did not answer. He could not take his eyes from the injured Kroy, blood oozing from the corner of his mouth. Following his gaze, Iaco crossed and knelt next to Kroy, spying the small, familiar controlling device tucked neatly behind his ear. Wrapping his fingers tightly around it, he yanked the evil controller and tossed it aide, setting the man free.

Wincing at the additional pain of the dislodging, Kroy rocked his head despite the whooziness to face Iaco, confusion obvious in his eyes. "It was not your fault," Iaco said gently, placing his hand on the man's shoulder.

Appearing to understand, Kroy gasped in an attempt to speak, a single tear trickling down the side of his face, his body releasing the last of its breath. "He is gone," Iaco said, closing Kroy's eyes and standing to face the boy. "There was nothing we could do."

"Iaco!" Selena shouted. Clutching Nitaya's blanket, she raced to his side. "We saw the ships on the large screens of Command. They were heading toward the docks and we got here as soon as we could.'

"Oh no!" she cried, spying the lifeless bodies on the floor. "Fidaldi! Kroy! What happened, Iaco? What about the…"

"I will explain once we are in the deep," Iaco interrupted, taking Selena by the arm. "Now hurry. We must get to the transports at once."

"Come Hylin," Khyra said taking control and shaking the boy to his senses. "You heard Iaco. There is nothing more we can do. We must hurry!"

"Hurry to go where?" the dark voice asked at their backs. The four members turned in awed silence to the unfamiliar tone, yet Selena could not contain her shout of utter joy.

"Nitaya!" she screamed, racing toward the child in Agye's arms.

"Not so fast," the man said, raising his weapon and stopping her firm. "It seems my choice in gunners was ill-made," he added, a second man joining him from the sister ship.

"No bother," he continued, shrugging with no regard for the fallen man. "I believe we will all join him soon enough."

"Who are you and what do you want?" Iaco asked, shielding the remaining members. With an air of confident, he walked toward the strange pair.

"Do not come closer," the man answered flatly, gritting his teeth as if contemplating his next words. "It seems pointless now, but alas because you cannot alter fate, I will allow you the truth...that we are in fact loyal servants of our great King Sugin."

"Oh, how foolish you have been," he added, pointing his weapon directly at Iaco. "We have been right under your nose for nearly two onars, taking your orders and doing your bidding and *never once* were our intentions questioned once we landed at your sacred Polatus. We were mere peasants looking for work, or so you were led to believe, and *never once* were our intel-scanners checked. And so it was that your best men trained us in flight, we feasted on your nourishment, and we gathered data on your weaknesses. I must admit there are many," he added, chuckling confidently to his comrade.

"And now," the man continued, straightening as Iaco attempted to once again advance. "According to my calculations, we have little time and I am now through with explanations. If you will lead the way, Prince Iaco," he added, gesturing to the grandly arched entrance. "I believe we will end this fittingly in your great hall."

***

Oddly, the lights of Polatus twinkled in the nearing distance, its welcoming glow eerily filling the surrounding area. Dismissing the thoughts as to why the shield was not in place Jovaar piloted his ship at maximum speed.

"At least you are still in one piece," he thought, maneuvering through the familiar narrow pass, around the last of the large landmasses. Racing through the open deep, steering left around the main compound, Jovaar veered slightly right to make his entrance into the docks. With newfound expertise he glided up the second available track.

Leaving the ship in idle, Jovaar unclasped his restraints and opened the hatch. Rising, he stared out into the deserted port of scattered about trolleys and cables strewn on the floors. A sense of eeriness filled the vacant shell. Leaping from the sopping ship, Jovaar sped through the echoing fighter docks, rounding the wall to transport. Racing for the awaiting com at the back of the port, his step slowed, spying the two bodies on the floor.

His feet at last halting beneath him, Jovaar instantly reached for his weapon, turning back to scan the room. "I knew it," he thought, wiping the sweat from his brow. "Fidaldi, Kroy," he whispered, checking for any signs of life. "Forgive me for leaving you behind. But now," he thought, inhaling deeply and standing to take in his surroundings. "Where are you hiding?"

***

"Keep going!" Wozer ordered, his weapon pointed firm at their backs. "And keep her quiet!" he added, the child continuing her incessant wails. Selena flinched at the man's sharp words and turned to see Agye's feeble attempts of soothing Nitaya. Tear flowing steadily down her face, her arms ached to hold and comfort the babe.

"I need to do something," she whispered, slowing her pace to lean close to Iaco. "She must be so afraid."

"Just stay in front of me," he answered, peering over his shoulder. "If I can make a diversion in the great hall, we may still have a chance to escape."

"No talking!" Ruvis shouted at Wozer's side, the troop reaching the large double doors. "Through there and to the main table," he added, gesturing violently with his weapon.

Iaco nodded reassuringly to Selena then gestured for her to lead the way as the members were guided to their seats. Purposfully sitting next to Agye, her heart ached to reach out and reclaim Nitaya yet as she attempted to extend her arms for the child, Wozer shouted out, startling her at her back.

"No!" he roared, pressing his weapon to her shoulder. "Stay as your were!" Slinking back within her seat and burying

390

her face in her hands, Selena instantly realized that she still clung to Nitaya's blanket.

"Here," she said, bolding handing the wrinkled folds to Agye. "At least let her have this."

"Ha!" Wozer bellowed, his hearty laugh echoing in the large hall. "Go ahead and take it, Agye. Nothing will protect her now."

***

Scanning the docks, now assured that they were in fact deserted Jovaar lowered his weapon and raced to the rear wall. Choosing his words carefully, he prompted the com.

"Maintenace check in sectors I, V, O, & J, report," he said, releasing the device. Iaco, seated at the main table, instantly raised his head in shock, turning to Hylin.

"What was that?" Wozer shouted, ramming the back of his weapon into the edge of the table, just missing Hylin's hand. "How many are still out there?" he screamed, his face reddening as he turned to Iaco.

"I do not know!" Iaco answered, his mind awhirl at the possibilities. "I, V, O & J?" he whispered, squinting his eyes and shaking his head. "There are no sectors that…wait," he thought, freezing as it came to him.

"I, V, O, J., Hylin," he whispered, leaning toward the boy. "It is Jovaar. There is still a chance we can make it."

"What are you saying?" Ruvis asked, forcefully yanking on Iaco's hair. "Who is out there?"

"I said I do not know!" Iaco grimaced, eyeing Hylin at his side.

"I will check it out," Ruvis added, releasing Iaco and turning to Wozer. "Can you manage?"

"It seems futile," Wozer answered, his grin returning as he folded his weapon at his chcest. "It will all be over soon anyway. But go," he added, waving his comrade off with his free hand. "Enjoy your little game. I am quite certain I can handle these fools for what little time there is left."

Nodding, Ruvis returned to the large doors, exiting the room to return to the docks, Wozer roaring with laughter, obviously enjoying the last of their game. "And such little time there is."

＊

Hoping above all hope that whoever remained in the outskirts of Polatus understood his secret message, Jovaar prompted the com to repeat his code, yet released it at the sound of approaching footsteps. Not knowing if the obvious lone tread was friend or foe, he butted up to the side wall and crouched behind a half empty trolley, weapon raised at his cheek as he wiped the sweat from his brow.

The footsteps stopped just beyond his view outside the large arches that adorned the entrance. Squatting closer to the floor behind the trolley for a better angle, Jovaar's eyes tightened as he aimed his weapon. The man that entered the loading docks was no friend.

Shorter than he, robust and graying, the man raised his own weapon with his slowed approached. His brown cloak flowing unhampered at his ankles proved no additional weapon was harbored at his calves. Foolishly crossing the vacant docks into the open, Jovaar was certain that he could easily take him. Hastily checking his own weapon load, he rose slowly to his knees at the rear of the trolley.

"This is my chance," he thought, staring at the man's back. Slowly rising to stand, he took the lone shot, hitting him purposely in the shoulder. As the man fell with a bellowing roar, grabbing his wounded right arm, Jovaar raced over to question his intentions before it was too late.

"What do you want with us?" Jovaar asked, stamping his foot firmly on the man's injured limb.

"You fool," Ruvis began, laughing confidently despite his shallow breathing, wiping with little care the thin streaming blood from his mouth. "I already have what I want. You were just sport for the taking."

"Where are the others?" Jovaar pressed, thrusting harder into the depths of the man's wound.

392

"There is no time," Ruvis answered, choking with his feeble attempt to shrug. "So I lost this round. I guarantee I will win the next."

"I promise you I will find them," Jovaar said, gritting his teeth and digging deeper with his heel. Witnessing the man breathed his last breath, leaving only his blood-stained grin upon his face, Jovaar turned quickly from the body, racing from the docks eager to prove his words true.

***

Stopping at the end of the passage to consider his options, Jovaar leaned against the bend in the corner, staring from the left path that would lead him to the great hall to the right path that led to command. "Which way?" he questioned, shaking his head. Angry with himself for having given his portal to Phydin, Jovaar knew there was no time for second guessing. Since he was certain the distance to the great hall was shorter, he turned left knowing the large doors would be round the next bend. Finding them slightly ajar, he paused to listen and was soon confident he had made the right choice.

"I told you to keep that child quiet!" the man shouted, pounding a hard object on what he assumed was a table. "And you," he continued, pausing between labored rants. "Keep your hands on the slab!"

"Nitaya is here?" Jovaar whispered, anxiously peering into the tiny opening to see clear to the core of the forgotten festivities. There filling him instantly with both hope and dread sat Iaco, Hylin, and Selena.

The steward and Nitaya were with them as well, seated at the head table to Selena's right, with death pointed directly at the girl's small backs. With no time for hesitation, Jovaar took a final deep breath and raised his weapon. As the evil man turned to shout another insult at Iaco, he snuck quietly into the great hall using his friend's overly adorned cloths that streamed down from the ceiling as cover.

Several tables stood between Jovaar and the captor and he hurriedly but quietly crawled from one to the next, doing his best to remain unseen. At last reaching the third, he heard Iaco losing control of his temper and knew he was out of time.

"I will not sit here any longer," he roared, attempting to stand. "We are all about to die anyway! What difference does it make whether I do so by your blasted weapon or by the extermination of my entire world? Either way, we are all finished."

"Ah, yes," the man answered, his grin widening as he stood face to face with the Prince. "But my way would be ever so painful. You see, I could take out your leg," he said, lowering his weapon. "Or perhaps your hand, or her heart!" he added, pointing directly at Selena's head. "This can be ugly if you so choose. I suggest you choose wisely."

"I suggest we end this now!" Jovaar shouted, suddenly standing and taking aim, firing off two quick shots. Now at close range, the blasts proved devastating and all screamed as Wozer stumbled back into another pair of hanging folds.

"No!" he shouted, grasping his chest and falling to the floor. "This is not how it was meant to be! My plans," he added, struggling to catch his breath, blood oozing from his lips.

"It appears your plans have changed," Iaco added, kneeling to claim Wozer's weapon.

"Jovaar," he added, watching the man give his last breath before turning thankfully to his friend. "I knew you would come but surely you know we must evacuate at once."

"I know," Jovaar answered, nodding and turning to the others. "We have to move. Phydin, be certain he is not carrying a detonation device then get to the docks as soon as possible. We will not be able to wait long."

"What about her?" Selena asked, glaring at Agye as she gently, but quickly snatched Nitaya from her arms.

"We will take her with us," Jovaar answered, reaching out and claiming Selena's hand. "She may still be of some use. Now come," he added, leading them round the main table to the large doors. "There is not much time!"

***

"I took care of one of them at the docks," Jovaar said to Iaco, keeping Selena and the child at his back, racing carefully down the corridor. "Are there any more?"

"We only encountered two," Iaco answered, peering over his shoulder. Khyra struggled to keep up with the heft of her gown at his back. "But I cannot be certain."

"There were only two," Agye added, stumbling alongside Jovaar. Selena turned her head sharply, refusing to look at the girl. "Captain Wozer shot his pilot once we landed and I can only assume Captain Ruvis did the same."

"Then we cannot be certain," Jovaar said, nodding as Phydin approached from the rear. "Keep your eyes out, Phydin," he added, checking his weapon and assuming the lead. "There may be one more."

***

Deserted, as Jovaar had left them, the docks eerily hummed with the cast aside machines. Skirting to the right of the bodies, Selena huddling against Khyra, shielding the babe from the gruesome site as the men spread out searching the area. "This way," Iaco said, gesturing to the opposite end of the docks. Racing after him, the weary group dodged both forgotten trolleys and fuel lines all the while the Prince shouted for them to find flight in their steps.

Struggling with Nitaya in her arms, the members rounding the bend toward the transports, Selena stumbled over one of the strewn cables, falling to her knees with the babe. "I have got you, Lena," Jovaar said, turning back and stooping to assist her, swiftly holstering his weapon. "Do you need me to take her?"

"No," Selena answered, running her hand over Nitaya's face to soothe her cries. She refused to give her up after passing so much time without her. "We are alright," she added, Khyra assisting in helping her stand.

"Lead on, Jovaar," Khyra said, motioning toward the ships. "Iaco needs you more."

Jovaar nodded to Khyra's foresight and raced toward the open hatch, quickly following Hylin and Iaco up the plank.

"Close the hatch and restrain yourselves," Iaco ordered, the women boarding trailed quickly by Phydin.

"Jovaar," he said, assisting Khyra with her restraints. "I have your answer on the forth. Agye was right. We should be all clear."

Iaco methodically fired the ship as Jovaar hurriedly assisted Selena with the child in the roomy passenger cabin. "Do you know what you are doing?" Jovaar asked, claiming the mid-ship oversight station as Phydin secured Agye's restraints, adding additional supports to her wrists and ankles. "I cannot imagine how long it has been since you have operated one of these transports yourself."

"Trust me, Jovi," Iaco answered, confidently lowering the overhead controls. "Detaching," he added, tense with the fear of implosion, prompting the ship's release.

"Will we make it?" Selena asked, turning frightened to Jovaar. Nitaya whimpered in her arms.

"We will know soon enough," Jovaar answered, as Phydin and Hylin at last claimed their seats. Saying a quick prayer and clasping the last of his own restraints, his head fell back with the thrust of the boosters, the ship at last sailing them down the track and into the darkness.

***

"How long has it been since we have had contact from Wozer?" Carsian asked, reentering Command.

"Quite some time, Sir," Terdoni answered, stiffening and turning to face his commander. "And I regret to inform you that after repeated attempts we have also had no contact from A1, G5 or our sliders. I have the last amphibious craft through maintenance and on standby, Sir. They are awaiting their clearance for drop. Of course, I was about to seek you for approval."

"You are telling me that we have more than likely lost both fighters *and* both transports?" Carsian roared, waving his fist at his First Officer. "Your incompetence astounds me, Terdoni!" he continued, resuming his familiar pace of the central aisle. "Can you at least confirm that the transports were destroyed?"

"I regret that I cannot," Terdoni answered, tipping his head to await his Commander's wrath. "That is why I was ordering the other..."

"You fool!" Carsian screamed, thrashing the navigational panel to the floor. Turning to Terdoni, his face was filled with rage. "We have lost all ships and you have no status on the Savius possible. This is totally unexceptable! Order the final craft immediately for drop then join me in my quarters!" he added, turning to storm from the cabin.

"Sir," Terdoni added, hesitantly waiting for the King to turn. "Sir," he repeated, Carsian's back stiffening. "We only received half from the last tanker and Yani will not transmit. We only have enough fuel for one final hazon then we must return to port."

Carsian stood silent, grimacing and shaking his head. "Order the drop, Terdoni," he repeated, gritting his teeth and balling his fists. "Then join me quarters so we may *discuss* your incompetence!" Trembling, Terdoni stood frozen as King Sugin stormed from the cabin.

"Order the..." Terdoni began, stopping to clear his throat. "Send the order to the amphi that they are clear for drop. Take over, Plarro," he added, his hands shaking. Staring at the three officers scurrying to gather the irreparable panel, he skirted the remains and walked unsteadily through the door.

***

Speeding through the deep in the transport's midship cabin, Jovaar reached over to steady Selena's hand as she bundled the babe in the small blanket. "We have cleared the initial area," Iaco said, prompting the com from the helm. "We have only to reach the..." Polatus lit up at their backs.

The sense of being suctioned backward preceded the sounds of the blast, the ship whirring with its struggle to push onward. As the light of the destruction proved more powerful then any had imagined, it filled the cabin, blinding the members as they attempted to shield their eyes.

"Hold on!" Iaco screamed from Command. Gripping the stick with both hands, he sailed them through the open deep repeating his shouts, yet the intenseness of the wave while quiet proved deafening and no one was able to hear over thundering violence rolling toward them. In mere moments, the blast engulfed the ship.

Shards of Polatus screeched about the hull as Iaco struggled with the controls through the brightest of lights. Fighting the weight, he rammed his arms into the sides of the overhead panel for balance. Struggling with the mere gesture of realigning the bow, both gravity and rear pressure urged him otherwise.

The ship grew expediently hot with the intense heat of the blast, and water droplets formed out of thin air, raining upon their skin at both the helm and midship. Unable to shield themselves from the drops, the member's bodies remained thrust into the backs of their seats. Jovaar's hand flying backward from where only moments before he had attempted to settle Selena's nerves, made him grimaced from the excruciating pain. Fruitlessly he attempted to pull his aching limb forward.

"Hold on!" Iaco shouted once again, completely engulfed in light and debris, the ship careening with the seemingly ceaseless blast. Pulling back ever slightly on the controls to raise the nose, the thrusters at last responded to his movements.

"Al...most...there!" he shouted, bursting forth from the lightened tomb. Sailing forward and away from all that remained of his dear Polatus, Iaco prompted his side screen with his free hand, shaking his head in relief as all proved operational.

Sighing as the ship appeared to steady about them regardless of the continuing speed, Jovaar pulled his strained left arm forward then used his right to prompt the com. "Ease up," he said, watching Phydin and Hylin attempt to settle. Selena and Khyra remained uncertain however, refusing to relinquish their firm grips. "Iaco," Jovaar pressed, stretching his worn shoulder. "I said ease up."

Hearing Jovaar's words, Iaco at last looked down and at once realized his grasp remained firm on the stick. "I have it," he answered, easing the stick forward and relaxing his fingers. "We made it Jovaar!" he shouted in triumph, turning his attention back to the open sea, Polatus turning to darkness at his rear. "We made it!" he repeated, easily diverting around another mass, oddly chuckling to noone in particular.

"Is everyone alright?" Jovaar asked, releasing the com as it appeared Iaco was too overwhelmed to worry about the others.

"I am good," Hylin answered, turning to Khyra who remained uncertain, refusing to ease her restraints. "That was the iciest ride I have ever had! We made it!" he shouted, echoing the Prince's enthusiasm, slinking back within his seat. "Unbelievable!"

Thirty-Six

"Selena!" Jovaar shouted, struggling to release his restraints with his injured arm, the child wailing out in fear. Fumbling with the last of the clasps and grunting as it at last gave, he reached her side and knelt, Khyra doing the same despite her cumbersome gown. Checking her vitals, Khyra calmly reassured Jovaar with a pat of her hand upon his shoulder.

"She is unconscious but appears stable," she said, reaching to gather the child. "It seems the little one is strong though," she added, rewrapping her in the small blanket and rising to return to her seat. "No signs of trauma. It appears you are indeed destined for greater things," she whispered, touching her finger to the tip of Nitaya's nose. Shooing Phydin away, she smiled as Jovaar continued to coax the slumbering Selena.

"Lena," he urged, gently pulling the loose tendrils from her face. "Lena, can you hear me?" Slightly stirring, Selena's eyes flickered and her breathing deepened at the sound of his voice.

"Nitaya," she whispered, not opening her eyes.

"Nitaya is alright," Jovaar answered, running the back of his hand over her cheek. "We are all alright, Lena."

"Hylin, Phydin," he continued, peering over his shoulder. "Help Khyra with Selena and the child and keep an eye on Agye. Iaco," he continued, rising to prompt the com. "We need an alternative route. Plans had been in place for us to board an amphibious craft from Polatus to reach our final destination. Obviously that is now impossible and I am sorry that we have caused your loss. I am uncertain of the waters in these particular outer sectors and do not know how to proceed. Surely you must know where we can receive shelter until we can acquire another craft."

Feeling remorse for what was lost Iaco took a moment to clear his thoughts, robotically reaching the outskirts of the adjoining sector. "I may know of a place," he began, taking a deep breath and adjusting his screen to maps. "It is primitive, Jovi. I feel I must warn you of that ahead of time and therefore due to our circumstances our layover should be kept brief. I am however quite certain I will be able to obtain a suitable craft."

"If it is safe and we can secure an appropriate ride we will follow your lead," Jovaar answered, disengaging the com. Nodding confidently to Phydin and Hylin, he paced quickly to the helm. Leaning over Iaco's shoulder, he waited patiently for his friend who had lost much, to alter his side screen. "

Show me where," he said, Iaco gesturing to the lower image with his free hand.

"It is quite a distance," Iaco said, leaning over to his right to check his monitors. "We have adequate fuel and the terrain is minimal. It is just a long sail."

"Just get us there, my friend," Jovaar said, turning and dropping into the seat at his side. Hylin entered Command, quietly doing the same. "We are delayed as it is. If you are up to manning this thing for a spell, I would love some time to close my eyes."

"No problem," Iaco answered, peering over his shoulder. "You really are getting old, *Sir Savius*," he added. His grin soon widened as thoughts of Polatus drifted off with the shards of its remains.

"I have no energy to argue with you, *Prince*," he answered sarcastically, glancing over at Hylin and the boy's chuckles. "But I must admit, what you did back there was incredible and incredibly unselfish."

"Men of my youth please others easily," Iaco retorted, winking at Hylin as Jovaar rose, exiting Command. Smiling as the boy claimed Jovaar's vacant seat, securing his own restraints tight against what had been Jovaar's larger frame Iaco settled his eyes back to the deep.

Sighing with the regret of the loss of Polatus, he quickly pushed the thoughts of what had been from his mind and instead chose to look toward the future. With a growing confidence of their task outweighing his grief, Iaco sailed them quickly toward their newest destination.

***

"All known locations have been uploaded to your monitors and you are clear for drop," Plarro said, updating the final amphi over the command com. "You are to be unseen at all costs. What matters most is the intelligence on Savius' exact location. Sail cammoflaged at all times and report immediately upon arrival of the sectors where A1 and G5 were last seen."

"Aye, Sir," the first pilot answered, firing his ship. "Preparing for detachment and drop in 5, 4, 3, 2, 1, detach, drop confirmed."

"Copy that," Plarro answered, overseeing their progress at the helm. "No mistakes, G2. Everything depends on what you find."

No response was given and none was expected as G2 was currently in freefall. Glancing from his screen and the impending plunge without worry, Plarro turned confidently to his Navigations Officer.

"Tracking?" he asked simply, all eyes remaining on the fall.

"As ordered, Sir," the NO answered flatly. Prompting the main screen for all to witness the last of the dip, Plarro smiled. All proved uneventful though grand.

***

"Reporting as ordered, Sir," Terdoni said, hesitantly entering the King's cabin. All others had been ordered from Carsian's quarters. His steps slow, the darkened quietness unnerved him as he approached his Commander's rear station, the door swiftly closing at his back.

The King did not rise, nor did he turn to face Terdoni, yet rather continued sitting with his back to him. Facing his favored monitors, Terdoni's breathing became labored, small droplets of sweat beading on his brow in anticipation. About to speak,

Terdoni bit down on his words as at last Carsian slowly turned to face him.

"I have considered this for some time, Terdoni, and have found I have no other alternative for your lack of progress," he began, his voice deep yet calm with anger. Carsian slowly rose, ruffling his chin.

"I have spent nearly half my life and the entire duration of my reign preparing for this moment in time, preparing for the arrival of the possibles, and although my plans have been flawless, you have somehow *flawed them*. I will grant you a moment to explain, although I must forewarn you that anything you may add is fruitless. Your failures have multiplied with recent events and my patience has proven depleted. I am however, prepared to listen to your drivel if you so choose to add an explanation."

Terdoni had in fact prepared several hindering details on his long walk to his Commander's quarters, yet at this moment, knees quivering, he stood facing his King and knew his justifications were useless.

"I have nothing of substance to offer and I am humbly at your mercy," he said flatly. The King shifted the weight of his cloak to his back in angered response.

"As I expected," Carsian answered, returning his gaze to his monitors. "Proceed," he ordered, prompting the com and peering over his shoulder at his failed subordinate. "Sit there, Terdoni."

Following the King's motion, Terdoni spied the fateful seat emerging from within the wall to his left and instinctively stepped back, raising his hands in defense. "Sir!" he began, trembling with fear, his back butting up against the door. "I assure you Sir, I am quite…"

"Sit!" Carsian ordered gritting his teeth, his dark cloak whirling with the pivoting of his feet. "Time for explanations is over. You may have well cost the Sugin's our rightful reign and it is time you paid for your incompetence!"

Accepting defeat and understanding the cost he would pay for his incompetence, Terdoni merely lowered his head, paced the few steps and sat…waiting for his end to come. As his back met the cool wall of the ship's exterior, Terdoni shook his head at the two transoids entering the cabin, guiding in the familiar metal dislodger. Spying the several compartments lined at its front, his eyes froze upon the top shelf that held the required tools to bring about his demise. Terdoni knew this machine all too well and sat motionless as it glided in before him.

"At least it will be quick," he thought, glancing over at his Commander whirling from his prided station.

"You may leave us," Carsian said flatly, claiming hold of the top of the machine. "I will take care of this myself." Bowing, the transoids turned and left quickly without word, their king returning his gaze to Terdoni.

"The time has come," Carsian said, slowly running his hands over the tools. "Such an easy thing it is really, although I know I do not need to remind you. How many times have you performed this task at my order?" Terdoni did not answer.

"Too many to mention, I suppose," the King continued, pacing toward him and opening the small compartment above Terdoni's head to enter the familiar required code. As the restraints burst forth from within the wall, Carsian glanced down with disgust at his soon to be retired first officer.

"If you will," he said, watching Terdoni reluctantly place his arms within. As the clasp mechanisms closed securely in place at his prompting, Carsian crossed back to the dislodger, guiding it snug up against Terdoni's legs. Terdoni knew this process all too well.

The neck restraint would be next, and indeed as the memorized task filled his thoughts, the King returned to the compartment above his head, entering the additional codes to prompt the device. "Terdoni," the King said simply, and closing his eyes, moving his head within the restraints, Terdoni waited for them to repeat as the arm and leg clamps had, securing around him without feeling. When all was at last in place, Carsian returned to the machine lifting the the first of the two necessary tools.

"Open," Carsian ordered, the dislodger springing to life in his large hand. "It is a pity your life will be taken so quickly," he continued, looking the device over, tipping it from side to side. "How I so wished to see you suffer for all you have caused."

As the black arm of the machine rose slowly upward, stopping at an angle before inching forward, Terdoni sat lips parted and motionless, the prongs reaching within his mouth, opening to secure him in place so that the dislodger could begin its work. Firmly grasping the slender devise, Carsian nodded and transferred the controls, preferring to perfom the act himself rather than allowing the machine to do so manually.

"It will be my hand," he said, firmly staring into Terdoni's eyes. "And I promise you I will enjoy it. No one in my service has disgraced me as you have. No one has been such a disappointment! I entrusted my future reign, the entire Sugin reign in your hands, Terdoni! You have proven yourself unworthy of your title, your command, and my time. Pray now that if there is in fact an afterworld and if your soul still exists in that so-called body, you will receive mercy there for you will not receive it here!"

Carsian, not wasting time further, placed the dislodger tongs through the open hole provided by the prong device. Using the panel on the cart to guide him, he passed it through the opening of Terdoni's mouth, reaching deep within its crevice. Easily spying the strip of sporni, he tapped the top of the tongs to open them, grasping the sporna firmly.

"So easy," he said, Terdoni's legs writhing within his restraints. Abruptly tugging, which was not the standard procedure, Terdoni gasped as the chord was forcefully dragged from within his being. Pulled forward passed the mouth opening and through the prongs, the sporna danced amongst the tongs, rage filling the King's eyes.

"Enough!" he shouted, releasing the tool and grasping the sporna in his hands. Viciously yanking the violent lifeform, its milky white chord connected to the heart of the life vessel spewing forth from within, Carsian watched joyously as Terdoni gasped his last breath.

"I give this word that no droid under my reign will ever possess as much power as you had!" he shouted, tossing the twitching sporna to the floor. Leaving the lifeless body strapped within the multiple restraints, Carsian wiped the mucus covering

405

his hands on his former first officer's cloak and stomped confidently through the cabin door.

Thirty-Seven

"G2 reporting from Sector Four," the pilot began, sailing swiftly through the open deep. "No sign of the enemy craft, Sir. Debris is minimal, but rising."

"Copy that," Plarro responded from above. "Continue on passed the remains to Sector Eight. We have run several pattern alternatives and have found three concrete destinations that span off from there. We are uploading them to your panel now."

"Copy that," the pilot answered, prompting his side screen. "Standing by for upload."

"Confirmed," Plarro added, turning to his fellow officers. "We need this narrowed down. They may very well land at any of these locations but I need the specs on the operations of these sites. They will be searching for an alternate amphibious craft. Run data on all locations and confirm ships that they may have in port. We do not have enough time to physically search them all."

As the officer quickly motioned for his subordinate to run the data, he quickly tapped at his panel, Plarro pacing the floor just beyond their stations. Hands at his back, the others stood patiently awaiting orders.

"Sir," the DO began, having first gathered the data. "The first location has the capabilities to board such craft with minimal security."

"Continue on," Carsian ordered entering Command, his dark robe flowing at his ankles. "You have other options?" he asked, turning to Plarro.

"We are gathering specifications as we speak, Sir," he answered, gesturing to his panel.

"Then continue," the King answered, turning to face the operator.

"As I was saying, Sir," the officer continued, directing his attention to Carsian. "The first location has the boarding capabilities. Searches have proven that two amphibious craft are in dock at present. The second location is larger than the first and they too have the capabilities, yet on a much larger scale. Their present system shows six of the craft docked, or being docked within the next onar. The third is much more primitive. Although they have the ability to sustain the amphi, I am not showing any registered at port."

"I say we run with the largest of plausible ports," Plarro said, nodding and turning to his king. "That would allow them several options for escape. I am prepared to order all..."

"Slow down, Plarro," Carsian interrupted, halting his newly appointed first officer with his hand. "They are not sailing in that direction."

"But Sir, how can you be certain?" Plarro pressed, pointing at the images on his screen.

"It is too obvious and if you are to be in control of this operation you should be aware of that!" the King roared back, glaring at Plarro. "Upload the third destination's quardinates to G2. There may still be time to reach the transport before they make their arrival."

Plarro was incredulous. "Certainly Sir you must agree," he pleaded, wringing his hands. His Commander glared him into silence.

"I do not agree," Carsian answered, sharply. "Last I knew I was the King of this galaxy and did not have to. Order the blasted ship!"

"Aye, Sir," Plarro answered, turning to the others who were staring busily at their panels, avoiding eye contact with the debating pair. "Upload the third destination to G2 and get him on the com," he continued, turning to the CO.

"Aye, Sir," he answered, eagerly prompting his screen.

"Plarro!" the King added, turning to leave. "If you plan on continuing to breathe, I suggest that you do not question me again!"

***

408

Surviving the war-strewn underground corridors of Manine, Adoni, through the substation of Gidoran's Yani, his Palle's Kindawan Neptune and at last through the deep of Iaco's Polatus, Jovaar found himself resting surprisingly comfortable in his seat in the rear cabin. With Selena at his side, performing joyfully-filled lilts for the child, Khyra looked on from her corner seat however Hylin grew ever restless, having been ordered to return to the rear for the duration of flight.

"Jovaar," he said, interrupting the fifth song of Selena's play. "How much longer must we endure until we arrive?"

"The Prince said it will be quite some time," he answered, not opening his eyes, instead purposely hunkering back against the stiff seat. "Surely you need the rest. Try closing your eyes for a while."

"But I am not tired," Hylin restlessly whined, eyeing Selena nestling Nitaya within her small blanket. "Is there not anything I can do?"

"Hylin, I understand your frustration," Khyra interrupted, nodding at Jovaar who refused to acknowledge the boy with sight. "But you must leave Sir Savius to his rest. We are all anxious as are you, but you must understand that you can not be entertained at all times. Close your eyes as Jovaar suggested. I am certain there will be much to do once we arrive."

"If only there were something to do now," he complained further, slumping back within his seat, obviously displeased with the answers he received.

"I will tell you what," Iaco answered, hearing the conversation over the com and knowing full well what it felt like to be a young man and bored. "I could use a spotter if you are up to returning to the helm. Get out of your restraints and get up here," he added. With an exhausted nod from Jovaar, Hylin sprang from his seat without further prompting, quickly racing toward Command.

***

"What can I do?" Hylin asked, entering the cabin at Iaco's back.

"Sit where you left her," he answered, gesturing to Jovaar's vacant seat. "And grab that headset above you."

"What is it for?" Hylin asked, following the order and placing the headpiece in his ear. "I can hear you just fine. I do not need this for communications."

"You are wise beyond your onars," Iaco answered, sensing the boy's need to be treated with respect. "That headset is so you can listen to the ship's exterior sensors. There are often times that another ship will produce a sound wave prior to being sighted on radar and that little earpiece has saved many a Resistance fighter."

"I'm ready then," Hylin said, readjusting the familiar straps. "Now what?"

"Well," Iaco continued, not looking from the deep beyond the glass, concentrating fully on another landmass. "The system is much like a simulator or a childhood game, although all kidding aside your position is quite serious." Hylin, sitting straighter, heeded the details of Iaco's speech for he knew that what he was about to do was important but most of all, he wanted to once again prove his worth to Jovaar.

"The panel before you gives you the readout to our location and what lays both in front and behind us," Iaco continued, prompting the images on Hylin's screen from his own. "As you can see the sea is clear and we are sailing through quite easily. Occasionally though, you will notice, like there…" he added, leaning and pointing at the screen. "There is a large landmass to our right that will cause us to divert our route. It is really an easy maneuver but important to know for obvious reasons. We would not want to hit that head on, now would we?"

"And here," he continued, motioning for Hylin to follow his lead. "There is a large group of sea life. You can tell by the color of them on the screen their location and their aggressiveness. We should sail on through without difficulty."

"I assure you, Prince Iaco that this is extremely fascinating, but where is all the action?" Hylin asked, eager to do more, loosening his restraints.

"Let us just hope that action we do not find," Iaco answered grinning, turning back to the panel above the stick. "But just in case, Hylin, keep both you eyes and ears open."

***

Plarro was anxious. He had to inform the King that their fuel load was significantly low and that due to the odd lack of adequate reload from Yani, they could not remain in their current hover much longer. G2 had just reported in only moments ago and was making steady headway below, yet they would not be able to assist him any longer from above, for their roundabout was imminent. Wringing his hands, Plarro eyed the com to his right, knowing it must be done.

"Sir," he began, attempting to steady his shaking hand.

"What is it Plarro?" the King answered abruptly, his impatience evident.

"Sir," he answered, rubbing his tired eyes. "I am sorry to disturb you but our fuel is at a minimum and we must begin roundabout to port."

"What of G2?" the King asked, obviously less concerned with their current fuel issues. "Has there been word?"

"Aye, Sir," Plarro answered, pleased to give the King at least minimal results. "G2 has just reported in. He has had no difficulty thus far and is within moments of the last sighting of A1 and G5. There has been no sign however of the enemy transport and barring any difficulties, he should be arriving at the specified location within the onar."

"Very well," the King answered, his tone oddly calming. "Prepare the ship for roundabout. G2 will be able to make port and refuel without our assistance. Maintain communications as often as possible. We will be just as attainable from port as we are from this location. Is there anything else?"

"No, Sir," Plarro answered, relieved that the King had handled his update so well. "We will roundabout momentarily per your order, Sir. Shall you remain in quarters, or shall we prepare for…"

"I see no need to intrude on your command," the King interrupted flatly. "Continue onward and inform me of any and

411

all situations as they occur and update me as soon as we are preparing to make dock. I will remain here and I will also maintain contact with G2. Just get us to port, Plarro."

"Aye, Sir," he answered, exhaling loudly, releasing the com and eyeing his subordinates. "Prepare for roundabout at once!" he ordered, confidence once again filling him. Raising his chin with his words, the crew immediately responded to his assertive directive. Reclining in his seat, Plarro confidently watched the roundabout preparations. His peace of mind however, would prove temporary.

***

"There is a small landmass coming up on our right," Hylin said, anxiously watching the shades of color alter on the panel. "And there is another one just beyond that."

"Well done," Iaco answered, making the slight adjustments to the stick. "Keep your eyes on your screen, Hylin," he continued, nodding and rounding the second mound. "Trudor should be in our sights momentarily."

"Trudor?" he asked, straining against his restraints to glance out the high glass. "Is that where we are headed?"

"Yes," Iaco answered, not turning from his station. "It will appear as a rather large landmass on your screen and should be just up ahead and to our left."

"Jovaar," he continued, seriousness returning to his tone as he prompted the com. "Wake up old man. We will soon be making our approach."

***

Jovaar awoke with a stir, uncertain where he was. Scanning the dimly-lit cabin, he rubbed at his eyes to gather his bearings. At last glancing down, he smiled at Selena and the child resting comfortably at his side, Nitaya wrapped tightly in her small blanket in the crook of Selena's arm. Khyra as expected was awake, anxiously staring out the glass. Jovaar adjusted his restraints to peer out from his side as well.

412

"How much longer?" he asked, prompting the com and craning his neck for a better look.

"Not long now," Iaco answered, rounding another bend.

"I think I see it," Hylin said, bobbing eagerly in his seat. "Over there!"

"Right you are," Iaco answered, smiling at the boy's enthusiasm, adjusting the stick with the current. "And see there?" he asked, gesturing to the left of his screen. "It seems the port is somewhat active."

"I cannot see much of anything," Hylin said, squinting at the glass to his right.

"You will shortly," Iaco continued, shaking his head. "The view is merely on our panels at the moment. Just wait. You will see the welcoming lights appearing to our left soon."

   ***

What began as twinkling specks of dancing lights off in the distance grew as Iaco sailed the transport to the rear of the many arriving ships. "See there," Iaco said, pointing out the glass and down the center of the pair of incoming rows. "It appears as though the ships are sailing directly into that large rock, yet as we get closer you will at last spy the hidden opening. It is quite amazing how this place was formed. Remind me to tell you about it some time."

"Three ships off to our right are making their approach," Hylin said, excitement growing in his tone as he watched the newest arrivals through the glass.

"There is also one advancing at our rear," he added, staring nervously at the oncoming vessel on his screen. "It is off in the distance, but headed this way from the same direction as our own path. Could it be trouble, Iaco?"

"I am confident they are just doing as we are, making port to refuel or docking to get some rest from a long sail. Do not fear, Hylin," Iaco added, reaching over and ruffling the boy's hair. "Our journey has been uneventful, we are surrounded by many, and we are about to arrive safely as promised."

"Rerouting for entry," he added, smiling at Hylin before turning back to the stick, guiding it slowly forward with the advancing ships.

"Copy that," the boy answered, his uneasiness slowly waning with Iaco's confidence, he too turning back to the glass. Resting his head in the palm of his hand, Hylin settled against the side wall of the ship to enjoy the bright lights in the hidden cavern of the deep.

***

Jovaar woke Selena softly, gently stroking her cheek with the back of his hand. Smiling, he paused to watch her yawn, stretching her tired arms beneath the light weight of the child. "Let me take her a moment," he said, reaching for the babe.

"How long have we been resting?" she asked, handing Nitaya to him freely.

"Quite a spell," he answered, settling the child in his lap. Adjusting her blanket he looked over to Agye, her eyes remaining closed with the effects of the long sail. "We are about to arrive and I thought you might enjoy the view."

"It is amazing," she said, yawning and craning her head to get a better look. "But I must admit it is not nearly as breathtaking as Polatus." Sensing she may have offended the Prince, spying the bright light of the open com, Selena leaned closer to Jovaar, shaking her head.

"I am sorry, Jovi," she whispered, wringing her hands and peering at Khyra across the cabin for help. "I did not mean to bring up bad memories for Iaco."

"On the contrary," Jovaar said, softly patting her hand. "Our friend the Prince may have one bad memory, but the rest I am certain are quite remarkable."

***

The hidden entrance at last came into view with the ship before them claiming berth, and Iaco hovered comfortably at its rear, chiming the port. "Ship Bevo requesting permission to dock," he said, waiting for a response and nodding confidently to Hylin.

"Ship Bevo report previous port and cargo," the female voice answered, routinely.

"Passenger ship Bevo sailing from Mytov-suk," he answered, nodding again at the boy. "Cargo does not exceed standards."

"Ship Bevo proceed to dock four," the voice answered abruptly. Although Iaco had previously appeared confident that they would be allowed clear passage, he could not contain a sigh of relief. Hylin echoed his response at their acceptance.

"That was wise, Iaco," Jovaar began, entering the com and claiming a rear seat. Nodding, Iaco sailed the transport into the face of the rock. "Mentioning Polatus would undoubtedly have caused suspicions to rise. Surely other pilots in port have heard of the blast by now. Better to state a passage from Pop Sozze's outpost."

"I have told you to trust me, old man," Iaco said, grinning over his shoulder, Jovaar wiping the peaceful rest from his eyes.

"And now," he added, turning back to the controls, the rock walls filling the surrounding glass. "Let us at long last dock this thing."

***

"G2 reporting," the pilot said prompting the com and settling into the seemingly endless line of ships.

"This is Carsian," the King answered, seated at his station in quarters. "What is your location?"

"I have requested and have confirmation for docking at Trudor," the pilot answered, tapping his stick slightly forward. "Yet several ships are in line and are causing somewhat of a delay in my reaching port. There are two crafts up ahead that could possibly be our transport. I have clearance for docking bay two. How would you like me to proceed on arrival, Sir?"

Carsian rubbed his chin, considering G2's approach. "Sir?" the pilot asked, uncertain of the transmission in the rock-filled terrain.

"Make your dock and search the area unseen, G2," the King answered, rubbing the stubble on his chin. "If it is in fact Savius, he will take some time unloading all passengers. Do not make your presence known, but inform me at once once you have confirmation that it is Savius. Plarro currently has us in a required roundabout and you will have no reinforcements."

"Copy that, Sir," the pilot answered, hovering in position. "And now," he added, releasing the com and inching the ship forward with the approaching line. "May the hunt begin."

***

"It is amazing how this apparent hole in the rock is actually a port of life," Khyra said, staring out the glass in the rear of command. "It is like it appears from no where. I would never have located it myself."

"That is the idea," Iaco answered, gliding on the track passed the first row of ships to dock four, a crew member guiding the way.

"What about the others?" Hylin chimed, peeling his headset off and releasing his restraints. "Are they here waiting for our arrival? Will we all be together again?"

"No, Hylin," Jovaar answered, releasing the restraints from his rear seat. "They have continued on to the rendezvous, which at this point I am sorry but for obvious reasons I remain unwilling to divulge. If all goes well, we will secure a ship and leave Trudor as soon as possible. I will then give Iaco the coordinates after our detachment. We will then dock with them and continue on to the final destination."

"Before you ask," he added, pointing a finger at his younger. "I am not willing to divulge that either. You must trust me on this. My silence is for your own protection."

"But what if something happens to you?" Hylin asked, pivoting in his seat, palms turned upward. "What will happen to us then?" Hearing this argument before, Jovaar could not help but consider the boy's words as he rose.

"That is a valid point, Hylin," he said, sighing. Kneeling next to his station in the narrow aisle, he ran his fingers through his hair, sighing. "And as I have agreed for the others to know the bulk of the path we must cross, I will make yet another concession. After you debark with Selena and Khyra, I will spend a moment with Iaco and give him the information. That way two of us will be prepared in the event something unexpected should happen. Satisfied?"

"Very well," Jovaar continued, all nodding in agreement about him. "Now that that is settled, I would certainly like to get off this blasted thing and stretch my legs."

"I agree with that," Khyra said, eagerly pacing to the rear of the cabin. Her gown bouncing off the seats, she grabbed at its pleats, huffing.

"Iaco," she added, prompting the door and turning. "I would have had us docked and debarked by now. Why so slow?"

"Ah, so your patience grows thin unlike that gown," he answered, his grin widening with the ship's slowing in its track. "But alas, dearest Khyra, in your own words, you would not have found it in the first place."

"Preparing for attachment," he added with a slight chuckle, confidently releasing the overhead controls. "Gather at midship if you are able to reach it. We will be unloading shortly."

Thirty-Eight

The port proved abuzz with the overwhelming arrivals and Iaco watched enamored as the ground crew assigned to his ship handily made their final motions, gliding the craft perfectly into port. With only a slight jolt, Ship Bevo made dock.

"Attached and stalled," he said, at last releasing his lap restraints. Rubbing his hands over his hair, he paused only for a moment. The weight of his beloved Polatus hung on him, yet his friends needed him now. "I should debark immediately and begin the search for a ship."

"Not so fast," Jovaar said, standing and leaning over the back of his seat, Hylin returning to midship to leave them alone. "I need to give you the coordinates."

"Right," Iaco answered, reclining in his seat. "What is it you are blessing me with to know?"

"First let me speak to the dock hand," Jovaar answered, ignoring the snub. "There should be some sort of holding area or refreshment galley for new arrivals. We will have the others debark and head there. We can then follow shortly after."

"That sounds good to me," Selena said, standing with the child, startling the pair at having returned to Command. "My joints are aching, Nitaya could use a new napping and honestly, I could stand a change of scenery. Hylin, why do you not lead the way?" she added, attempting to make him feel important as he hovered in the narrow corridor."

"I can find my way around anything," he added, eager for the go-ahead nod to head out. "I knew every inch of Sir Gidoran's Yani. If only we had had more time there. There is so much I could have shown all of you. Jovaar, I could speak to the dock hand if you would like."

"I am sorry, Hylin, but no," he answered, gesturing for them to return to midship, following the trio to release the hatch.

"For your safety, I must know of your whereabouts at all times. I will speak to the worker myself." With the damp air of the underworld Trudor filling his breath with the opening of the hatch, Jovaar had to admit that it was a wonderful change from the cramped space of the ship.

"Hylin, keep an eye on Agye," he said, gesturing for him to release the girl's restraints, Selena and Khyra standing impatiently at the top of the plank, eager to debark. "I will be back in a moment."

***

Spying the dock hand off to his left guiding in the next of the arrivals, Jovaar quickly made his way through the growing crowd, dodging a rather strange crew from another craft to his right. "Who are they?" he asked reaching the worker, unable to contain his curiosity.

"Just some low lifes," he answered. Shaking his head, he motioned for the newest ship to attach. "We get all kinds here. What can I do for ye?

"We have several aboard that are in need of freshening," Jovaar answered, nodding at the ship over his shoulder. "Is there a site where women are welcomed to rest a spell? By the looks of things, I am a bit wary of leaving them unattended."

"And so ye should be," the dock hand answered, walking toward the adjacent vacant track to prepare for the next ship. "Trudor is not known for its civilities. We are only a mere stop-off, if ye will, and mostly get men and their droids piloting transports. Little pents, lots of alone time. Things can get a little rowdy if ye take me meaning."

"I understand," Jovaar answered nodding, warily scanning the area. "But is there a place that they would be welcome if chaperoned?"

"Ye have two choices," the dock hand answered, waving his arms wildly at the next inboarding craft. "Dornal's or Trudor's Pass and both are just through that opening there," he added, gesturing with his head. "Neither is tasteful but one can get nourishment and drink if that is what ye are in need of. If ye need rest I would not head toward Pardoor's. The place is intolerable."

"You sound quite familiar with the area," Jovaar said, motioning for Hylin to wait aboard ship. "Have you been in port long?"

"Too long," the dock hand answered, shouting at another worker. "I'ma comin'!" he roared, securing the last ship before turning back to Jovaar. "Ye are on yer own, my friend," he added, patting him on the back as he turned to leave. "Welcome to Trudor."

Pacing back through the busy port to the transport to gather the others, Jovaar felt uneasy with the descriptions of their options. Climbing the plank however, his wary thoughts were replaced by the ever impatient Khyra at the top of the plank.

"I spoke with a dock hand and I have decided that leaving you unattended is not an option," Jovaar began, leaning against the opening to steady his breathing. "I need you to sit a moment longer so I can give Iaco the information and then we will head to get nourished together."

"This is nonsense," Khyra answered, looking over Jovaar's shoulder and beyond the ship's door. "I can tolerate this cramped space no longer. We will not be but a moment before you, Jovaar. Certainly you must understand that the child needs attended to, and further more we have been enclosed in this heap for far too long."

"Come, Selena," she continued, motioning for her to follow, her dark gown flowing violently with her firm strides. "Let them do what they must."

"Now, Jovaar," she added, turning back to face him, Selena standing wide-eyed at the top of the plank. "Please point the way."

"Khyra, I do not think it is wise," he pressed, attempting to convince her otherwise. Crossing her arms at her chest, she tapped her foot with impatience so noticeably that her hefty gown shook with anger.

"I know, I know," she said, patting his shoulder. "But we are well grown as you can plainly see. Hylin will be with us and as I said, you and Iaco will be close behind. We simply must escape the confines of this thing...and hopefully at some point this gown." Sighing, Jovaar knew he could not convince her otherwise.

"Alright then," he said, hands extended in surrender. "You must take Agye with you and I insist you not speak to anyone. I have been informed that women are scarce in these parts and I am certain the mere sight of you will raise eyes."

"Rubbish," Khyra said haughtily, running her hands over her face. "Now which way is it?"

"Through those doors there are two choices, Dornal's or Trudor's Pass," Jovaar answered, pointing through the hatch. "If it pleases you, ma'am" he added, sarcastically. "I would like to know your choice before you debark."

"Trudor's Pass?" she asked mockingly, Selena shrugging her shoulders with indifference. "Yes," Khyra continued, raising her chin and turning back to Jovaar. "It sounds delightful. You should speak your secrets then find us there," she added, snapping her fingers for Hylin to move ahead with Agye.

"I will have Iaco scout the ship then I will be right behind you," Jovaar shouted, shaking his head and watching them walk down the plank. "Iaco," he said, not taking his eyes from Selena's back. "Did you hear all that nonsense?"

"I did," he answered, a grin filling his face with what he thought to be a silent approach, placing his arm over his friend's shoulder. "Funny, I thought you said that you were in charge."

***

"G2 reporting, Sir," he said, prompting the com and testing the line against the confines of the surrounding rock.

"This is Carsian," the King answered, abruptly from quarters. "What is your status?"

"I was uncertain of the connection, Sir, yet I am pleased to inform you that I am at port and am stalling the controls as we speak," he answered, raising the overhead controls. "I was given berth two docks away from the location of the transports and will make my way there as soon as I am given clearance."

"Very well," Carsian answered, his tone sounding almost pleased. "There is a release on your com that converts to a portal. This serves as communications, yet also removes the

421

cloaking device so that you may use it on your person. This may appear extreme, but I assure you it gives you only minimal coverage. The shield, without the power of the craft will give you use once, and only once and will last mere moments, yet could be handy if you are on the verge of detection. Now, unlatch its clasp, strap it to your arm and keep this lone line open. Head toward the transports and be my eyes. Do nothing that will give any indication that you are a member of the Sugin army."

"Copy that, Sir," G2 answered, releasing the com and finding the clasp at its rear. Unlatching the compact black unit, he quickly strapped it to his wrist then released his restraints, climbing swiftly from the cramped ship.

"I am on ground level and headed toward loading dock four," he continued, prompting the portal beneath his sleeve upon reaching the dock. "Stand by, Sir."

Traversing his way passed numerous crew members, weary pilots and dock hands, G2 did what he could to go unnoticed, which took little effort for no one appeared to care what was happening beyond their given tasks. Finding a small niche in the side half-wall of dampened rock just beyond the transports, he knelt as if fixing the clasps of his boots, his eyes never away from the imposing ships.

"Neither hatch has been released, Sir," he said, shielding the device from the sight of others. "I am in position to see...wait, Sir," he added, stopping as the hatch of the nearest opened.

"What is it?" Carsian asked, anxious to hear if Savius had been found and his prediction to be proven correct.

"One hatch has opened and there are several men debarking," G2 continued, lowering his gaze. "I see no sight of Savius. Shall I search the craft or trail after them?"

"No," Carsian grumbled, rising to pace the cabin. "Wait to see who exits the next ship."

"Copy that, Sir," G2 whispered, lowering to his heels to rest against the low wall. "Stand by."

"May I be of assistance to you, Sir?" a dock hand asked, his approach missed by G2 as he scurried to cover the portal.

"Yes," he answered, standing awkwardly to face the intruder. "I was hoping you could tell me where I might find a place to settle for the night," he said, his eyes never leaving the closed hatch.

"Ah, yes," he answered, pleased to be helpful and away from the busy port. "Through those doors then right you will find Pardoor's. I am certain it will suit you quite well."

"Thank you, my good man," G2 answered, his attention diverted as the hatch slowly opened to the left of the worker's back.

"If you will require anything further..."

"No, you have done enough," G2 answered sharply, lowering quickly to tidy his boot, the conversation obviously over. Watching from the corner of his eye as the dock hand left shrugging his shoulders with indifference G2 stared intently, spying two women with a bundle that could possibly be a child, trailing the lead of a young lad.

"My King," he said, his heart pounding with anticipation, prompting the portal at his wrist. "I believe we have them."

***

Khyra stoically resumed the lead once away from the ship, scooting Hylin's too eager steps to her back. Glancing left and right with each step as any protector would, she eyed both arrivals and workers on the docks, wary of all. "This way," she said, motioning toward the entrance, reaching back to urge the others to keep pace.

"I am fine," Hylin said, struggling against her ordered stare, eager to be free of her clutches. "If I can survive in Yani, I can survive anywhere!"

"Be that as it may," Khyra continued, tsking and firmly claiming Selena's arm. "We are not to dawdle but we are also not to run ahead leaving the others behind. I do not like the looks of these so called *men* and I certainly do not like subjecting the child to all this filth."

"Agye come!" she ordered, snapping her fingers. "Be a good steward for once, stay close to Hylin and keep your eyes open. You never know if someone is watching."

"We know, we know," Hylin mumbled, rolling his eyes at Agye as he claimed her wrist. Despite his eagerness to explore however, he heeded Khyra's words and kept close, he too surveying the dank surroundings.

At last traversing the lengths of track and reaching the large set of doors at the rear of the musty port, Hylin turned to glance back a final time at the ship, wondering how long Jovaar and Iaco would be at their backs. Keeping his eyes wide to his new surroundings, he spied a man kneeling just paces away from the craft within an alcove.

"Khyra," he said, tugging on her soiled gown. "I think I saw someone near the ship."

"The child is what they are after, not some hovel," she said, gesturing for the sentry to open the hefty door, motioning for the group to enter. "We will be safe once we are inside. Now come, Hylin. Nitaya needs tending."

Hylin turned back to get another look at the man, but found he was gone, the alcove empty. Shrugging and assuming the man was nothing more than a lowly worker, he nodded to Khyra, waited for Selena to pass. Tugging on Agye, the odd pair trailed after them for without doubt, the groans of Hylin's belly proved a higher calling.

***

"You know of this location then?" Jovaar asked, standing over the map readouts at the midship station.

"As you know all too well I have not been there myself," Iaco answered, straightening and leaning on the back of the nearest seat. "But yes, I am fully aware of the site, Jovi. If there is nothing further, you really should join the others."

"You are right," Jovaar said, closing the line and crossing to gather his tote. "How long til you can secure a ship?"

"Not long I imagine," Iaco answered, retrieving the data token and tucking it within his cloak. "Knowing this place as I do, any ship can be bought for the right price. And how, might I add, are we to do that?" he questioned, rising to face Jovaar. "I must admit I was not financially prepared for this little endeavor considering our hasty departure."

"Again, I am truly sorry Iaco. Use this code to transfer the funds once the purchcase is confirmed," he answered grimly, handing his friend the information on a shred of tattered parchment. "Chime the portal as soon as you have acquired something adequate."

"No worries, Jovi," Iaco said, taking the crumpled piece of codes and placing it within his cloak with the data token. "I have told you many times to trust me. As required, you will have your ship within the hazon."

"That is good news," Jovaar said, reaching the hatch and glancing selfishly over his shoulder at his friend who had lost so much. "Everything depends on it."

     ***

"What?" the burly man asked, sweat beading on his large brow as he hovered over their table. The stench of his being, circling the air about them, proved equal to his abrasive tone.

"Excuse me?" Khyra asked, turning away from cooing Nitaya in Selena's arms to face the boorish intruder.

"What, ma'am?" he continued, shifting his weight annoyingly, holding his ancient pad and stilo. "Trudor's my hole and you are jammin' my air sittin' in that seat. If you want somethin', you have to tell me, what?"

"Rudeness will get you no where, Sir," she answered, huffing in the man's claimed 'seat' and turning straight to look up into his filthy face. "But alas I will overlook your drivel since we are in such dire need of nourishment. Since you are so obviously engaged, we will each take drink and something fresh from the block. I am certain you will make do." Grumbling, the robust man turned and shouted the order over his shoulder, rubbing his exposed backside as he paced to the next table.

"I swear," Khyra continued, eagerly turning back to the wee one. "That ogre's stench remains in *my* air. Nitaya, I am so sorry to bring your grace to such a place. I pray you will forgive me one day."

"Jovaar!" she shouted, eyeing his entrance and waving. "We are over here!"

Nodding at her shouts, Jovaar hurried through the crowd toward them, claiming the vacant seat between Selena and Hylin. "Khyra," he whispered, leaning across the slab. "I must warn you not to use my name so openly. We do not need to bring attention to ourselves."

"Oh," she said, covering her mouth with her hand. "I am so sorry, Jovaar. It will not happen again."

"Very well," he answered, the large man approaching, slapping the teeming mugs and nourishment onto the table.

"What?" he asked, turning to Jovaar. Looking perplexed as the man huffed in his place before him, rolling his eyes at the newest arrival, Khyra held up her hand and nodded confidently.

"He will have the same," she said, waving him off. Repeating his incessant grumbling, scratching his lower back and walking away, Khyra shook her head, stroking Nitaya's small frame.

"A brute I tell you," she groaned to Jovaar, Hylin ignoring their conversation and claiming his mug. "But I must admit," she added, wiping her hands on her tattered gown, following Hylin's lead. "This does not look half bad."

***

The conversation over the surprisingly large-portioned meal consisted of pleasantries and the degree of exhaustion that all felt, everyone that is but Hylin. Ready for action or so he claimed, he fidgeted in his seat as the last bits of nourishment were devoured.

"Hylin," Jovaar began, wiping his mouth with the cloth from his lap. "Even your *impatience* is exhausting. I informed Iaco that we would remain here until he got word of a ship," he added, turning to the others. "He was heading toward a dock hand when I left him. He is certain it will not be long. I will ask Trudor's owner if there is a place for you to freshen if you are in need, yet otherwise we shall all remain here."

"Nitaya of course needs tending," Selena said, rearranging the child's blanket.

"I will take her," he answered, claiming the playful child from her arms. "I would feel much more comfortable if you were to remain in the open with the others. Hylin," he added, nodding to the lad. "Do *not*, under any circumstances, leave that seat."

"He is quite good with her," Khyra whispered, Jovaar striding confidently to the back of the facilities, Selena and Agye following her eyes and looking on.

"Hylin!" she added, turning to see his attempt to rise. "You heard Jovaar. You are to remain with us!" Groaning and slumping with a loud thump back into his seat, Hylin glared at his elder, crossing his arms in defiance.

"Boys!" Khyra continued, turning back to Selena and their table to tidy the remains of their meal. "Pray all you ever bear are girls."

***

Although less than helpful and reeking with most certainly hazon upon hazon of sweat, the dock worker did however correctly direct Iaco to the port operator. Finding him seated at his central station, he impatiently waited for him to finish speaking with an arriving pilot before approaching.

"What is it you are looking for?" the elderly man asked, annoyance obvious in his tone, refusing to look from his monitor.

"I need an amphibious craft that seats five, fully fueled and on standby within the hazon," Iaco answered firmly, folding his arms across his chest.

"What is the rush, young man?" the operator asked, again not turning from his screen. Assuming the age of the requester in the tone of the man's voice from his onars of experience in port, the man spat his annoyance upon the dock floor.

"I do not believe that is the issue," Iaco answered shifting his foot from the man's angle, frustratedly shaking his head. "Can it be done or am I wasting my time?"

"Anything can be done for the right price," the man answered, grinning as he at last pivoted in his seat to face Iaco. "You said an amphi that seats five? Are you in need of a pilot/charter, or are you looking for a complete buyout?

"I need the buyout," Iaco answered, anxiously eyeing the outer layers of rock. "Price is no object." Immediately standing, hearing the final words of his newest *guest*, the operator's tone quickened. The elder, eager for the rare sale, patted Iaco's hands in most appreciated welcome, this time holding back his spittle.

"Business we will do then," he continued, nodding in excited agreement. "Would you like to freshen while I request the transaction or would you prefer to watch me work my magic?"

"I believe I will remain here," Iaco answered, stepping behind the operator's bench, wary regardless of his open enthusiasm. "I would prefer to witness first hand my available options."

"Then let us begin," the operator said, his aged bones obviously stiffened, slowing reclaiming his seat. "I relish any day that I am able to make a sale."

***

Astounded at the vast number of ships at port from the charts of even lower-depthed coves the operator provided on his screen, Iaco scanned the visible docks right to left and counting, could not nearly reach the total that the man was offering. Obviously the bulk of options were moored from view.

"I sense your questioning at my back," the operator said, tapping his panel to prompt the numbers of his guest's specifics. "But I assure you all ships listed *are* on site. I will just hone the search for your requirements and should have several to choose from once the order is complete."

"There," he continued, habitually spitting upon the floor. Disregarding the disgusting act, Iaco leaned over the back of his seat, staring at the few that remained.

"I have four ships in port that are compatable with your wishes, Sir," he said, nodding. "Are there further requirements to scale this down or would you like me to choose what I feel may best suit you?"

"No," Iaco answered, leaning closer to read the data. "I have no further requirements if one can be fueled and standing by within the hazon."

"Forgive me, I forgot that part," the operator added, pointing his finger upward in hesitation before keying in the further data. Iaco most certainly doubted the man's lack in memory, the shyster that he assumed him to be however, and waited another moment without word to see what the station would produce.

"Three then," the man said at last, spitting and reclining back in his seat. "We have two at the opposite end of port and one in storage below. I am assuming by your impatience that you would like to choose from one already docked.

"You assume correctly," Iaco answered, reviewing the data the man produced, glancing side to side at his options. "We will take this one," he added, pointing over the man's shoulder. "How do we proceed?"

"First, I will inform the current owner, eh…a Pilot Juno, of your request," the operator answered, spitting and narrowing the images to the lone, final choice. "It is listed for available purchase so that should not pose a problem. Price however, is in fact listed as negotiable."

"Whatever it takes," Iaco said, the operator's grin reflecting wider in the screen as he straightened. His teeth proved sparen and grossly unkept.

"Of course," the man answered, turning to eagerly key upon his panel. Waving off an approaching worker, the task at hand proved obviously the most prosperous.

"Please prepare your crew, Sir," he added. "Your ship will be available at dock seven, block four within the hazon as requested. There is however, the matter of payment," he added, peering ever slightly over his shoulder.

"But of course," Iaco answered, retrieving Jovaar's coded parchment from within his cloak. Leaning to the panel to key the information, the machine instantly accepted the data. Impatience assumed by all, the pair watched as it whirred to life as eager as its operator, producing a small chip in confirmation of the completed transaction.

"It has been my pleasure," the man said, handing the acceptance token to Iaco. Tipping his head, the newest guest of port tucked both acknowledgement and parchment within his cloak.

"I am certain it has," Iaco answered, tipping his head in response. Seeing the needed ship was secured, the now profitable operator returned to his station to finalize the transaction, obviously pleased his newest arrival had paid a handsome price. Knowing the demanded hazon would quickly pass, Iaco disregarded the cost of the ship and headed through the large doors toward Trudor's Pass, the fear of a sighting also easing from his thoughts as he set out to join his awaiting friends.

***

"Where is Jovaar?" Iaco asked, warily scanning the crowd. Claiming the vacant seat at the table, he rubbed his hands against the chill of the outer docks shell.

"Iaco!" Selena shouted, jumping in her seat and turning to face him. "You startled me. Jovi went off with Nitaya to…no wait. Here they come now."

"Iaco, were you able to secure a ship?" Jovaar asked, reaching the table and handing the sleeping child gently to Selena.

"I was," he answered scowling, lowering the empty mug to the table. "And at a hefty price I am afraid. It should however, be prepped within the hazon."

"What?" the burly man asked, interrupting their conversation as he returned to the slab, startling the group.

"I will have what the others had, my good man," Iaco answered unbothered, turning back to Jovaar.

"Iaco," Khyra interrupted, yanking on the sleeve of his cloak. "How did you know what he was asking?"

"You did not?" he asked smugly, shrugging and turning back to Jovaar. "The ship is moored in dock seven, block four. I requested five seats but it in fact holds seven. It is larger and we should be much more comfortable."

"Wonderful!" Khyra and Iaco said in unison, both for different reasons…Khyra for the roominess of the new craft and Iaco for the refreshment that was placed before him. Quickly grabbing his own offered my, Iaco downed the contents in one lengthy swallow.

"More, my good man," he shouted, wiping his sopping mouth with the sleeve of his cloak before delving into the plentiful nourishment. Ignoring the staring eyes of the others as

430

the man merely grunted his reply, walking away and once again scratching his incessant backside, Iaco relished his abundant plate. Khyra simply sat silent, dumbfounded and shaking her head.

***

As the transaction occurred at the port's central station, G2 hovered back mingling amongst the unending crowd of arrivals. Confident the unknown port man had requested an amphi ship, the operator handing over the standard chipped receipt, G2 smiled, his instincts having been proven correct. Dodging a young group of pilots and spying the prompted craft on the elderly man's screen, G2 noted that both purchaser and provider proved confident as they parted ways. At last, when he was certain the entire crew of Savius' ship was now away from the docks, G2 approached the old man seated at the panel.

"I believe you to be a man who relishes a good profit," he began, the operator grinning widely yet remaining silent, instead keying the last of his transaction without turning. "I also believe that you have served your King unwisely."

"No," G2 continued, placing his hand firmly on the man's shoulder as he attempted to rise. "I believe you had no intentions of displeasing King Sugin and I am also confident that there is a way to resolve what you have done to made amends."

Aghast that he had been caught in an illegal transaction knowing the hideous outcome it could bring, the operator licked his lips at the threatening tone of the strange man. With the grasp remaining firm on his shoulder, he did not turn, yet spat on the floor, just missing the stranger's foot.

"Who are you?" he whispered, his words barely audible amongst his quivering lips. G2 could not contain his smile.

"I am a servant who will quite enjoy disposing of any traitor of the Sugin reign which is what I am prepared to do unless you give me what I want," he answered, tightening his grip.

"Surely I have done nothing so dishonorable," the operator whispered, nervously keying to alter his screen blank.

"But please, ask what you will and it will be yours." G2's smile widened.

"Very well," he said, releasing the man's shoulder, the operator at last free to turn and face the imposing voice. "Let us begin with the request you just processed." Pivoting back to his station once immediately prompted by the stranger's twirling hand, the operator tapped the prompt with his shaking fingers, the image quicky reemerging on his screen.

"I was just headed to speak with the pilot to confirm the transaction," he began, wiping the sweat from his brow.

"No," G2 answered, jovially patting his back. "Where is the ship moored?"

"Block four of dock seven," he answered anxiously, his words trembling worse than his hands.

"Very well," G2 answered, straightening to scan the ships. "You will speak of our *discussion* to no one," he added sternly, turning to head down the dock. "You may keep your profits for your return to allegiance," he added, patting the weapon at his side, obvious only to the operator. "I will confirm your transaction myself."

Thirty-Nine

G2 found the small transport amphi as expected, moored at dock seven in the process of being fueled and prepped for purchase. Several men scurried about straightening the lines as expected, unloading cargo.

"Where can I find the owner?" he asked the young loader assisting his mate with a heavy load. Saying nothing, he simply pointed to the plank of the craft, wiping the sweat from his brow with his sleeve despite his burden. The owner, standing at the entrance was not what G2 had expected, yet in a foul place such as Trudor, he should have known better.

"You!" he shouted, the man raising his head from his schedule, looking toward the intrusion. "I must speak with you at once."

The owner nodded, standing just outside the hatch of the ship, tapping his portal screen as inventory was withdrawn. He handed the device to the dock hand with the completed load. Once finished, he motioned for what he assumed was the buyer to climb aboard.

"Inside," he said, turning to enter the ship. Scanning the immediate, empty surroundings, G2 hesitated before ducking his head and entering the hatch.

"What is it I can do for you? I only now received word of the transaction. I am afraid the ship is yet to be..." he said, lifting two small totes from the floor, turning to face the stranger.

"You have done quite enough," G2 answered, raising his weapon and firing. The shot proved clean yet loud, and after checking that the man was in fact dead, G2 stood, leaning out the hatch to make certain no one had heard the blast over the chaotic order of the port. If they had, there was no indication, and smiling at his fate as the loaders appeared to be finished with their task, striding away in droves, he quickly sealed the hatch, leaving the plank in tact, turning back to dispose of the body.

***

"We should check on the progress of the ship," Iaco whispered, leaning toward Jovaar as he chewed his last morsel, bypassing the normal sleeve of his cloak and wiping his mouth with a cloth.

"I agree," Jovaar answered, eyeing Selena speaking quietly with Khyra. "But I do not want them out of my sight for a moment. I have a very uneasy feeling about this place."

"I can understand your apprehensions, Jovi, but they are really quite harmless," Iaco continued, scanning the room at the weary crowd. "They are rough but they have their own troubles. Surely they will not bring us harm."

"I do not share your confidence," Jovaar continued, shaking his head and glancing at Agye seated slightly away from the others. Her hands folded neatly in her lap, she only looked up, eyes timied. "And even though we have come this far, I have my doubts that the rest of the journey will be any less complicated. Iaco, perhaps you should go. I should stay here with the others."

"I will go!" Hylin chimed, eavesdropping on their conversation and startling the women, proving all too eager to leave the dull establishment to see some real action.

"You will do no such thing," Jovaar answered, annoyed that they had been overheard. Running his hands frustratingly through his hair and glaring firmly at the boy to remain seated, he sighed before turning back to Iaco.

"We should wait and go together," he continued, now speaking opening to the group. "The risk is just too great. Everything we have fought for depends on Nitaya's safety. There is still time," he added, patting Selena's knee and glaring once again at the young boy. "We are so long over due that a few more moments will not make a difference despite our eagerness to move on."

"Then we will wait and go together, Jovi," Iaco answered, placing his hand on his friend's knee reassuringly,

434

Jovaar shaking his head at his boyish tag. "And while we are at it," Iaco continued, slapping his palm on the slab and smiling at the others. "Let us have another drink."

***

"What do we do with Agye?" Iaco asked openly, glaring at the girl as he set down his latest mug, smacking the thick foam from his lips.

"I have not come to a conclusion," Jovaar answered, leaning close to speak privately. "She has done nothing to give us heed, Iaco, and therefore we cannot disclaim her words that she was forced into Ruvis and Wozer's hands. I see no reason not to bring her along. She may still prove useful."

"But she was in cohorts with Sugin under my order," Iaco slurred, toppling the empty mug from the table to the floor. "How can you trust that she will not attempt another theft of the child?"

"I cannot," Jovaar answered, eyeing the girl questionably. "Agye," he continued, his tone soft yet firm, ignoring his friend's current lack of tact, folding his fingers together across his chin. "You must certainly understand how we feel. What would you have us do?"

"I am at your mercy," she answered, nibbling on the tip of her nail before wringing her hands nervously in her lap. "I understand why Prince Iaco feels as he does, yet I must make fully known why I acted as I had. Please, if you will allow me to continue."

"Go ahead," Jovaar answered, leaning back into his seat to listen, Iaco glaring yet remaining silent, the women eager to learn all they could. "We obviously have time to spare."

"I was but a mere child when the King's army entered the airspace of the Fourth Planet," she began, sniffing the looming tears away, Selena hushing Khyra's groans so they could hear. "Their taxing upon our people quickly brought despair throughout the land, and my momar and palle were amongst the majority that suffered from their wealth and destruction. Seeing no other options, I was reluctantly given to the army as a *tool* for the payment of my family's freedom. I was given to be of use in

435

any way that the King saw fit, and when given my assignment, I was relieved for it seemed the simpliest."

"As I told you," Iaco grumbled, crossing his arms, mimicking Jovaar and reclining in his seat.

"That is enough, Iaco," Jovaar said, annoyed at the interruption, silencing his further protests with a simple glare. "Agye, please continue."

"I was to be sent to the underworld of Polatus, assigned to Prince Iaco," Agye persisted, lowering her gaze away from her commander's stare. "I was to appear as a mere peasant seeking work, although my true task was to seek information. I gathered it as told despite my minor task in the laundering facilities, yet soon was found to be an asset with the children and was thus placed in their ward. I knew not why I was gathering the intelligence, yet knowing my momar and palle's life lie in the balance on the Fourth, I continued to do as ordered with my newfound position, the information more readily available, as you may imagine."

"I meant no harm to you then and continue to mean no harm to you now," she pressed, leaning forward and placing her hands on the slab. "I have waited my entire aged life for someone to come to save me. I realize that we may not survive through to your final destination, or so you refer to it, yet if it means the end of the Sugin reign, I will follow you to that end. If you do not believe me though through all the pain that I have caused, please believe that I will understand."

Jovaar eyed Iaco's shrugging, appearing to consider her argument. Seeking agreement, his stature proving resigned as he pushed the latest emptied mug from within his reach, he gave his friend the heaviest of nods.

"We believe you," Jovaar answered, claiming her small hands in his. "I have seen the destruction to the icy Fourth Planet as well as many others, and I am sorry for your pain and the pain of your kin. I must however, ask one last time to be certain that your words are true. What are your intentions with regards to King Sugin?"

"To see the reign end," she answered, straightening in her chair and raising her chin. "And to do my part in its demise."

"That is what I needed to hear," he answered. Nodding for Iaco to reclaim the now teeming mug replaced quietly from the burly tender, Iaco clanged with his friend, each confidently taking drink as the women looked on.

"But what of the explosive?" Iaco asked, gulping his drink and wiping his mouth, his thoughts brought back to his fated Polatus.

"What are you speaking of?" she questioned, startled as she turned to face him. "I had no explosive. I told you it was my task to seek information. Are you referring to the final blast? Just what are you accusing me of?"

"So you do not know?" Jovaar asked, halting Iaco's protest with his hand.

"Know of what?" she pressed, shaking her head. "Just what are you saying?"

"We are saying that yes, the explosion that took place at my *home* was set previously by someone meaning to do me harm, to do the entirety of my people harm," Iaco interjected, slamming his fist on the table, the slur of his tongue no longer present. "We found a nest, as you will, easily placed out of sight within my docks. The explosion was planned and surrounded in a small alcove that held all sorts of information regarding Jovaar, myself, and data on the entire compound. You were sent to gather data. Are you saying you knew nothing of this?"

"I knew nothing until now," she answered, fighting his glare with her own. "The evil you describe was not by my hand. It must have been Captain Wozer or Ruvis. I knew not of their plans until they took me and the child. I assure you, I was merely fulfilling my duty to save my momar and palle!"

Iaco considered Agye's words as he eyed those nearest their slab, appearing both startled and annoyed by their raised voices. Gulping his drink, his gaze looking to Jovaar for input, he motioned for the others to return to their own devices.

"I believe her," he said at last, replacing his mug on the slab, her heart-felt strength stinging his ears. "With no disrespect, the system that was set was rather intense and above your onars of experience. Jovaar," he continued, slowly nodding. "She could not have possibly done this...at least not on her own."

"I agree," he answered, wiping his chin with his cloth. "My first instinct was disbelief and this now confirms it. Obviously Wozer and Ruvis planned this for some time, and although we cannot discount any small involvement by the girl, she is utterly shaking with your accusations."

Agye sighed in relief at the words the men spoke and was soon interrupted by the coos of the child at her side. Claiming her wee hand in her own, Agye accepted the kind nod of Selena and settled back within her seat, Jovaar nodding to Iaco and the women in understanding. As the burly man approached, Jovaar ordered another round for each. Obviously, they all could use it.

***

G2 found a suitable empty compartment at the rear of the transport. Hefting the burdened weight of the ship's previous owner, he quickly disposed of the body. Tedious work as it was, it had to be done swiftly for he had more pressing matters.

Before placing the owner within the small space, he had efficiently removed the man's clothes then replaced his own with the new. Returning to the site of the slaying, he quickly wiped away any traces of the deceased man. Standing confidently erect, G2 at once became Pilot Juno.

Looking about the roomy empty cabin, he knelt to wipe the last trace of blood from the floor. Spying a small compartment in the side wall that would suffice quite well, its door slightly ajar he climbed within. The transformed Juno then sealed the door, prepared to patiently await the arrival of the others.

***

"It is time," Jovaar said, eyeing the slab and the remnants of their nourishment, turning his gaze to Iaco. "We cannot delay any longer."

"I agree," he answered, slowly rising, Selena dropping her head to Jovaar's shoulder.

"So soon?" she asked, rocking the slumbering child.

"So soon?" Hylin chimed, echoing her words as he abruptly stood. "I have been waiting forever!"

Not raising her head from the scent of Jovaar's cloak, Selena chuckled at Hylin's impatience. "Trudor's is in fact awful," she said, shaking her head and running her slender fingers over the child's face. "But at the moment, I could stay here forever."

"To the end," Jovaar said simply, kissing her brow. "Come Lena, it is time. Mathius has laid Nitaya's path out before us. It is time we saw it though."

Iaco crossed the room and settled the tab with the burly man, Khyra both watching the transaction and claiming the child's tote from Selena. "I think Iaco is being had," she said, standing to gather the last of their belongings.

"Do not be so sure," Jovaar said, smiling confidently as Iaco crossed back to the group. "Any problems?" he asked, folding his arms over his chest.

"None," he answered, tucking the last of the pents within his cloak. "The man straightened when he heard my title. It is a wonder what a name will do."

"You used your name?" Jovaar asked shaking his head, watching Iaco's face alter, his friend slapping his own forehead with the realization of his mistake.

"Blasted," he said, grabbing the last of the totes. "I am sorry, Jovaar. This hiding is so new to me."

"I know," Jovaar said, eyeing Selena tightening Nitaya's blanket. "But did anyone else hear?"

"I do not believe so," he answered, shaking his head. "But if the Resistance suffers in any way because of my…"

"Do not worry over it, my friend," Jovaar interrupted reassuringly, rising from his seat. "Let us just get to the ship." Without need for further words, the members walked as one to the docks, Jovaar placing his arm about Iaco's shoulder. Agye, the newest member, trailed silently yet eagerly at the rear.

***

Pacing through the familiar din of the docks, the moisture of the sea puddling in various stages of their path, Iaco led the

439

anxious members to their newly purchased craft, moored at dock seven as expected. Relieved that they reached the ship without incident, Jovaar nodded to Iaco then crossed the path of the others making their way aboard to speak with the fueler, who appeared to be finishing the last of his tasks.

"Has there been a sign of anything unusual?" he asked, the refueler turning to face the new arrival with an odd look about his face.

"Sir?" he questioned, obviously annoyed with the disturbance. "I do not take your meaning. The ship is in order, you are fully fueled and the previous owner is reported aboard. If you are in need of further information, you must seek him. I have other ships to tend."

"My thanks," Jovaar said, disregarding the snub. "Is the pilot aboard then?"

"I have not seen him for some time," the man answered, huffing with the unending interruption, coiling the last of the line. "I got word that the craft had been sold. Maybe he took his newfound wealth and headed to Trudor's."

"I will try the ship, thank you for your assistance," Jovaar added with sarcasm, the dock hand turning back to his duties, obviously pleased to be rid of the nuisance. Shrugging, Jovaar faced the craft spying the others boarding, Agye in tow at the last. Turning, he quickly entered the side hatch.

"Is everything in order?" he asked, rejoining the group at midship. As Selena busily made herself and the child comfortable in the roomy cabin, Khyra, ever the doter, barked her orders. Typical of Agye, she stood quietly nearby awaiting to claim an unwanted seat.

"This will have to do," Khyra said, tsking and shooing Agye to the rear. "Did you find the pilot, Jovaar?"

"I was told he would either be here or at Trudor's," Jovaar answered, unable to contain his smile. His elder turned annoyingly to face him, hands firmly placed on her gowned hips. "After briefly looking about and getting a feel for the ship, I am assuming he is at Trudor's enjoying his newfound riches. Is Iaco in place at the helm?"

"He is, yes," Khyra answered, huffing a final time before turning back to settle Selena. "He felt it necessary to pilot himself, felt I was not capable," she continued, rambling as she shifted the weight of her gown. "Said I should tend to Selena and the child, which I am doing quite well, I might add. Hylin however was told to remain. I find it quite distasteful that a child should assist when a fully capable woman could do better. I am not certain what your particular history with the Prince has been, Sir Savius, but I quite assure you that you would do better with my assistance in command."

"I will keep that as a consideration," he answered, chuckling and turning to Selena. "If you are well situated, I will look in on Iaco to be certain the former owner is in fact away."

"We will be fine," Selena said reassuringly, handing Nitaya to Khyra so she could strap herself in. "Just get us moving," she added, clasping her final restraint. "I was completely peaceful at Trudor's, but I must admit that I once again sense our urgency."

"I will look in on you as soon as we are away," Jovaar added, smiling. Turning at Khyra's grunting displeasure, Jovaar chuckled and paced the corridor to Command.

***

"How long until departure?" Jovaar anxiously asked, reaching the helm to find his friend busy at the stick.

"I am making the configurations now," Iaco answered, not looking from his panel. "We should be in full sail momentarily. Hylin here has proven quite useful."

"So I can see," Jovaar added, nodding at the boy. "Although Khyra felt she would be better suited."

"I realize that," Iaco answered, shaking his head at the thought of her tirade. "But there was really no need. This system is quite comparable with our previous craft, and I felt her services would be more useful with Selena and the child. I meant no slight nor harm."

"I knew as much," Jovaar said, eyeing the last of the vacant seats. "You have just not spent as many onars with Ma'am Khyra as we have to fully appreciate her position. Have you searched the rest of the craft? Selena has become uneasy and frankly I must agree. Hylin, why don't you head back and

441

search the area?" he asked, the boy jumping at the chance to prove useful, eagerly loosening his restraints. "Iaco, how much time do we have?"

"Not long," he answered, adjusting the panel to his left. "Hylin, do not take long," he added, the boy pausing as he reached the door. "You will need to be fully restrained upon detachment."

"It will not take long," Hylin said, turning to leave hesitating in the jam of the door. "And I will look in on the women while I am gone."

"Good man," Jovaar added, crossing to pat his back before watching him go. "He has been a larger asset than I would ever have imagined, Iaco. You have always found a way to surround yourself with good people. Remind me to thank Gidoran. "

"You speak high of yourself then, old man," he answered, adjusting yet another of his controls. "I have kept you around much longer than the boy."

"Stop referring to me as 'old man,'" Jovaar ordered, standing at Iaco's back. "Why is it that you do that by the way? We have merely an onar between us."

"Ah, but I age so much better than you," he answered, his grin widening as he settled the last configuration of their detachment. "So much better."

***

"Sir," G2 whispered, prompting his portal in the darkened cabinet.

"What is it?" the King asked, eager for an update. "What is your situation?"

"I have concealed myself within a small compartment at the rear of the Savius amphi craft," he answered, shifting his weight in the cramped space. "I am chiming for further instructions."

"You have gone undetected then?" the King continued, pleased as he brought up the schematics of the downloaded ship on his screen. "Well done. Stay where you are," he continued, rubbing the scruff of his chin. "You have a much better chance

442

of taking them by surprise once you are in full sail. I will get back to you momentarily with further instructions."

"Aye, Sir," G2 answered, squirming to get more comfortable, the com quieting simultaneously with a muffled noise sounding from beyond his door. Pulling his weapon slowly and quietly from within its holster, aiming it straight forward, he hunkered down to await the impending arrival of the enemy.

***

"Jovaar ordered me to search the craft prior to detachment," Hylin said proudly, entering midship with chin held high. "I told him I would look in on you as well. Are you comfortable then?"

"We are Hylin, yes," Selena answered, eyeing both Khyra and Agye, Nitaya laying peaceful in her arms. "I could however use my tote that was placed in the rear cabin. There is a small toy inside to entertain Nitaya during the journey. If you would not mind after your search, would you bring it to me?"

"Of course," he answered, searching the small compartments of the cabin as she spoke. "And you Khyra, do you need anything?"

"All I need is to apparently just sit here and be a woman," she answered, her tone rude with jealous annoyance. "Forgive me Hylin, it is not your fault," she added, shaking her head. "Come here. Let me give you some useful advice."

"Never, ever take a female for granted," she pressed, firmly grasping his arms. "Women are beautiful yes, but also wise and useful. We are not just momars. We can infact be warriors, advisors. Remember that when you are older."

"Yes ma'am," he said nodding, anxious to escape his elder's grip. "I will just search the rest of the ship and retrieve your tote, Selena. Iaco said we would be detaching shortly."

"We thank you," Selena answered, looking down at the playful child, Khyra refusing to relinquish her anger, instead huffing loudly in the seat at her side. "She will quite enjoy it…the toy *and* the end of this journey."

Hylin nodded then left silently through the rear door. There was not much to search, but he raised his head high at the task and was ever anxious to once again make Jovaar proud.

***

The rear cabin proved eerily quiet yet Hylin entered enthusiastically, noting several small cabinets off to his right near the gunnery, larger ones to his left. The ship soon vibrated about him with the impending firing.

"No one could possibly fit in those," he thought, yet just to be certain, he opened them quickly, one by one. Finding nothing but random supplies left by the previous owner, he reached the last door then turned.

"What was that?" he whispered, turning to the empty space. Quietly closing the last latch at his back, he crept toward the large cabinet doors, stooping to listen. Pausing, he heard nothing but his own anxious panting.

Opening the first of the larger compartments ready to leap at the foreign noise, Hylin sighed, finding nothing but two sets of flight gear. Closing the door and shaking his head, he reached for the next as the roar of the ship's firing shook the floor beneath his feet.

"Hylin, get up here," Iaco ordered over the com from command.

"Just a moment longer," he answered, reaching for the second door. Yanking it open, Hylin was relieved to once again find nothing but supplies. Securing the door, he reached for the third and final cabinet. Hand on the handle, Iaco's voice rang again through the cabin.

"Hylin, we must leave now! We are cleared for detachment."

"Copy that," he answered, heaving the last door open, thankful to find supplies once again. Seeing nothing more was to be searched, Hylin grabbed Selena's tote at the base of the rear door and heeding the Prince's order, hurriedly raced to command.

***

G2's hand was on the trigger, weapon pointed and at the ready as he felt the opening of the door, bracing himself for the change in plans. Knowing not who he faced yet praying it was Savius himself, he was fully prepared to take him down when he heard the order from the helm.

The jostle of the latch had him aiming, but the door merely cracked light in before opening to full view. Hearing the boy speak, he prompted the cloaking device on his portal as the light from above filled the compartment. G2 prepared for the onslaught to come, uncaring if he faced man or youngling.

The boy however, stood nervously in front of him but did not see. Quickly scanning the contents of the unit as his order rang throughout the cabin, he just as quickly slammed the door.

"Another time, young man," G2 whispered, his evil grin widening, the faithful cloak holding its guise. "But soon...I promise you, soon."

***

"What took so long?" Jovaar asked, seated at the helm and turning as Hylin entered command.

"I searched as quickly as I could," he answered, reclaiming the seat next to Iaco. "Selena asked for her tote which held a trinket for Nitaya, and Khrya, well, she had a few words to share. I searched the rear of the ship as requested. I searched all cabinets and compartments and found nothing alarming," he added, secure the last of his restraints.

"Very well," Iaco interrupted, not looking up from his controls. "I am glad she took her wrath out on you and not me," he added, making the last of the preparations. "Detaching in 5, 4, 3, 2, 1, detach." The tremor of the release filled the cabin as expected and the men vibrated in their seats, the ship breaking free of its own restraints.

"Here we go," Iaco said, guiding them smoothly along the track through the docks. With another brisk jolt, the path fading from view, he had them racing through the deep and at last away from the dangers of Trudor.

Forty

One hazon had passed and Selena nestled the restless child at midship, intermittently staring out the glass into the darkness. Nitaya proved she would not rest even though the jostling had ceased. With the ship appearing to level off to a calm steady sail, Selena resigned herself and at last released her restraints to pace the cabin.

"We need to sleep," she whispered, endlessly rocking the babe. "Oh, how we need to sleep. Selena needs her rest, wee one. See Khyra and Agye?" she asked, glancing over at the pair resting uncomfortably in the cluster of seats to her right. "They are dreaming wonderful dreams."

"Oh, I know, I know," she added, the child wrapping her wee hand about Selena's finger. "You see no need for rest do you? I beg you though, Nitaya, please find that rest. Please, let us both find it."

"Oh, this is useless," Selena said giving up hope, yet could not help but tiredly smile at Nitaya's small face. "You weary me little one, you weary me so. Let us walk then," she added, reaching to prompt the door. "We will look in on the men and then maybe you will close your eyes. I certainly wish I could close mine."

Selena paced the short corridor and prompted the door unsuccessfully appeasing the child, finding the men far from wary to their tasks in Command. "What is wrong, Selena?" Jovaar asked, hearing Nitaya's wails at her nearing.

"Nothing is wrong, Jovaar," she answered, assuming propriety at the ears of the others. "I am simply attempting to walk the child to sleep. So far it does not appear to be working. How is our progress from your point of view?"

"So far we have had no indication that we are being followed," Iaco answered, overhearing their whispers.

"Although any blasted ship could have cammofladge capabilities and could be right on our tail for all we know. Radar has thus far picked up no sign. I for one remain timidly hopeful."

"Just get us out of the deep of the sea, Iaco," Jovaar continued, shaking his head and toying with Nitaya's blanket. "I am praying that if there happens to be a cloak shielding them, that it is a sea-type and not air. If they are in fact close behind, radar should pick them up once we are airborne."

"This is nothing to concern yourself over though," he added, rising and turning to Selena's side. "Why do you not head to the rear so the babe can rest?" he whispered, nodding to the door. "I will look in on you as soon as I can."

Selena peered into Jovaar's eyes and saw his worry yet said nothing, his gesture of seeing to their needs sincere as always despite his eagerness to return to his duties. Smiling with a nod, she simply wrapped the child tighter in her blanket and touching Jovaar's face, left him to the wonderous world of Kindawa's deep...and the possible enemy that could be lurking around every wonderous mass.

***

The corridor remained quiet with the normal hum of the craft as Selena sang her familiar lilt softly to Nitaya. Slightly boucing the child with her steps and prompting the door as she reached the midship cabin, she found Khyra and Agye resting comfortably. Appearing to not have even moved from their earlier postions, she chose not to disturb their slumber.

"Oh, the pain Agye has suffered," she thought, spying the girl resting her head on Khyra's shoulder. "It is so good to see her sleeping well."

Softly creeping by and rounding the pair, Selena took the babe's small trinket that lay in her seat and made her way toward the rear of the craft. "Nitaya, how I wish you would sleep," she whispered, gently rocking the cooing child. "You may not need rest, little one, but I do so deeply. Just a little longer then we will head back."

Reaching the rear cabin door, Selena extended her free arm to prompt its opening, dropping the babe's trinket unnoticed.

Peering in unconcerned, she found the cabin empty and continued her lilt to the restless child as they entered.

The gunnery had forever amazed Selena with the way the seated station would just vanish in its arc up the side of the craft, reappearing smoothly on the opposite side. Jovaar had once, onars ago explained to her how the gunnery system operated, telling her tales of how efficient the newer models proved to be and how mere onars before one would sit stationary, blinded in their position. Selena now crossed to the empty station remembering his words, continuing her quiet song to Nitaya.

Knealing, she leaned forward in an attempt to see up the arc. The track did indeed disappear into the darkness above as expected and for a moment she was tempted to climb into the seat to give the manly tool a try.

"Foolish," she thought, attempting to turn. Nestling the babe to her chest, a hand violently grabbed at her mouth, another holding firm to her waist.

"It was so nice of you to come eagerly to me," the evil voice whispered into her ear. Her limbs trembled, fear filling her eyes, as Nitaya at last attempted sleep in her arms. "You have made this all too easy."

***

"Make preparations for air flight," Iaco ordered. Hylin followed his word without questions, prompting the ever-altering screen at his station.

"I am sorry?" Jovaar asked, questioning his friend from the helm.

"No, I am sorry, Jovi," Iaco answered, quickly adjusting the last of the overhead controls. "I forget you had not piloted an amphi. I am assuming by your eyes that that did not change during our time apart.'

"There," he added, pointing to Hylin's right. "Those need switched over to level two. Hylin, the three large levers to your right control the pressure, the fuel levels and the release. You will need to slowly pull them down toward you in the order that I have said. We will be airborne in mere moments so begin the transfer now."

"I have it," Hylin answered, straining high to his right to reach the controls.

"That is it," Iaco continued, eyeing the progress on his screen. "I do not think they made these with boys...um forgive me, Hylin I mean young men, in mind. You are doing well," he added, looking back to Jovaar and nodding. "That is it, quickly now."

"I got it!" Hylin answered, the last lever shifting with trembling hand into place.

"Very well," Iaco answered, making the last of the air control swap. "Jovaar, keep your eyes on the glass, I will cover radar. If we are being followed, we should get a glimpse as their camo adjusts from sea to air. You were wrong earlier, but I did not want to say so in front of Selena. If they have camo capabilities, they will switch them over as we have done, yet we might just get a glimpse of them during the transaction to the above. I will watch the radar. You keep your eyes on the glass."

"Copy that," Jovaar answered, feeling foolish as Hylin, the mere boy, sat with confidence in his forward seat. "I should have known that," he thought, Iaco interrupting his thoughts.

"Here we go!" he announced, obviously enjoying the ride. Pulling back on the stick as Jovaar stared out the glass for the glimpse of camo, Iaco sailed them swiftly and easily into the air.

"Did you see anything?" Jovaar shouted, shielding his eyes from the brightness of the sky.

"No, not once," Iaco answered, staring at his panel. "Jovi, this seems all too easy. Why would King Sugin allow us to continue? I understand that an amphi is a less common craft in any fleet, but surely he would have ordered several fighters in the surrounding area of our last location."

"What about the camo?" Hylin chimed, attempting to be useful, peering over his shoulder at Jovaar. "Could their systems have upgraded beyond our own? Could they not have made the adjustments so the camos were never disengaged?"

"I suppose anything is possible," Iaco continued, not looking at the pair, instead flying the ship swiftly through the open sky. "Yet I was praying for them to appear during the

449

transition. If they are in fact still behind us, Jovi, we could be leading them directly to our destination."

"I have considered that but we have no other choice," Jovaar said, his eyes at last adjusting to the view of bright blue. "We must head to the rendezvous and reconnect with the others. They will be both waiting and worrying and we need them with us if Nitaya is to survive this. We will dip back down as planned and hope that if the enemy is out there it will catch them off guard, giving up a sign. Continue your flight until my word, Iaco then we will drop back down into the sea. With no other options, you know as I do that it is our only chance."

***

"We have open skies before us," Iaco said, having sailed uneventful for the last half hazon. "The cloak on this craft is not as current as I would have hoped meaning it is minimal at best. If they have infact acquired an updated system as Hylin suggested, ours would prove useless. They could undoubtedly be right behind us."

"I understand," Jovaar answered, turning from his station. "Just do what you can. How long do we have until we dip back down? I was hoping to look in on the child."

"Not long," Iaco answered, flying smoothly just above the sea. "You should be restrained when we do though. As you noticed before, a dip is not a smooth transition."

"I will remain then and reach the others on the com," Jovaar said, tapping his screen for the maintenance readouts. "I want to make certain all is stable at the rear."

"Selena," he continued, prompting the com. "Selena," he repeated, his tone sharp with worry. "Iaco, she is not responding. Dip or not, I must head to the rear," he added, releasing his restraints.

"Use the com and let me know once you are ready," Iaco said, glancing over his shoulder.

"I will not be long," Jovaar said, reaching the door.

"Can I go with you?" Hylin asked, ever eager for excitement.

"No," Jovaar answered, shaking his head. The door swooshed open at his back. "You saw how we jostled coming out of the sea. You are safer here."

"Jovaar, I am coming up on the drop, you do not have time," Iaco argued, spying the opening on his screen.

"I will be fine, Iaco," he continued, spanning the jam. "Just do what you have to do."

***

The corridor proved eerily empty. Jovaar raced to midship sensing Iaco's change in pressure with his prompting of the door, and lunged as it opened, thrust into the exterior wall with the ship's plunge into the sea. The jolt bounced him off the wall to his left, slamming his head and knocking him unconscious. Jovaar fell violently to the floor with the shift. His last view was of Khyra, eyes wide in fear.

***

"That was amazing!" Hylin shouted to Iaco, excitedly dancing his feet beneath his seat. "Sir Gidoran's Yani was boring compared to this!"

"What was Yani like for you, Hylin?" Iaco asked, settling the boy. Diverting around another large landmass, he sailed the ship swiftly through the deep. "What of your momar and your palle? You have never spoken of them."

Hylin's excitement quickly withered as he struggled to find the words to answer Iaco, his elder who had proven a trusted friend. "I never knew my palle or momar," he answered at last, lowering his head. "As far back as I can remember I was scouring the lanes of the station on my own."

"I did alright though," he continued, raising his chin in an attempt to prove confident. "I stole some to get by. I am not proud of that fact, but I did. The nights were best. So many travelers came in and out of Yani from far off places, and sometimes one would hire me for minor tasks. I would clean out a ship, or play servant to their needs. It was not easy, and it paid

451

little, but it helped me survive. I did quite well I might add...much better than others."

"But where did you live, who looked after you?" Iaco pressed, unable to turn from his screens. "It must have been very difficult for you."

"I slept where I could at first, feeding off the older children," Hylin answered, surprised yet filling with ease at the Prince's questioning. "But then I got smarter and learned that they were actually taking more from me than they were giving. I found myself a spot just under the salvage dump, had a small room and everything," he continued, smiling at Iaco's nod, recalling the filthy hovel of the salvage of Yani. He would remind Gidoran of his dreadful task of cleansing as soon as he was able.

"I would *come up*, or so I would say, to the streets during the light," Hylin continued, slinking back within his seat. His eyes gazed without care out the glass. "I would take something here and something there to eat from the vendors then wait for the nights when the older visitors would be too busy to notice a small boy reaching into their pockets," he added, pausing to consider his transgressions.

"I suppose I took more than I initially let on," he continued, eyeing the Prince from the corner of his eye before turning back to the glass, his fingers now toying with his hair. "But one night, oh things changed. I was out like always, looking to find my prey or so I called them, and stumbled upon a group I thought as non-locals. I sat for hazon upon hazon watching them in the shadows of the lane crates. They seemed to be handing pents over like it was no concern, and I somehow knew it would be a night that would make a difference in my life. I could not have been more right, Prince Iaco, although it did not quite play out like I had planned."

"What happened?" Iaco asked, making a small adjustment to one of the controls before glancing over his shoulder.

"I met Sir Gidoran," Hylin answered nodding, his lips curling in confidence. "Sir Gidoran changed everything."

"As I was saying, I was watching this group for quite some time," Hylin continued, for the first time truly eager to

452

share his story. "The loudest of them all was the man that turned out to be Sir Gidoran, yet they were all having a wonderful time. They went from one vendor to another, and were making all sorts of purchases until the sky grew dark above. I followed them and thought I had gone unnoticed, but well, that part comes later."

"I crept behind them, watching Sir Gidoran purchase one thing after another for the women that were with him, giving no thought to the cost of the twinkling tokens. They laughed without care, they embraced, and were quite enjoying themselves as I shivered with hunger. It soon grew dark however and after they took their group inside Globo's I waited outside, watching from the glass."

"Sir Gidoran and his friends remained inside for quite some time and I was about to give up on them when suddenly they came back out into the lane," Hylin continued, forgetting his surroundings and the brightness of the glass as he replayed the tale. "I thought all were stumbling from drink, which is always useful for someone in my position, and I approached them from the rear as they stood just outside the door."

"And then?" Iaco asked, turning to look at the boy. "What happened then?" Hylin paused his story, deep in thought, considering his words for Prince Iaco. "What happened next?" the Prince pressed, he too forgetting the bright blue before him, waiting for the next line of the boy's tale.

"Next," Hylin answered at last, shaking his mind from his daze. "Next, Sir Gidoran changed everything.'

"Sir Gidoran was with his group and exited the facility as I approached Globo's," Hylin continued, returning back to that fateful memory. "And as I reached the painted women, holding out my hand for a token, they appeared too caught up within themselves to initially notice a needy boy. They did eventually hand over a few pents just the same. I believe I gathered three," he added, shifting in his seat.

"While the women were scouring their bags for the pents," he continued, looking out the glass before turning back to Iaco. "I was busily reaching my other hand into their cloak pockets, and I must admit that the finds were more amazing than anything I had anticipated! You see, I would reach in and take quickly, then place the items in the inner pockets of my cloak. I could not examine the finds by sight, but by the feel of them I knew I was doing quite well."

"One would give me their pents then I would work my way to the next. It was a typical ploy amongst the other laners I had learned from and the intake that night appeared to prove enormous for me. I was feeling quite proud of myself as I left them to head back to my home at the salvage dump, yet I was too excited with my intake, and I did not take notice that I had been followed. It was foolish, but in the end I was thankful."

"So what happened?" Iaco asked, sailing the ship upward into the sky, smoothly making his preparations for the next dip. "You keep stopping Hylin," he added, shrugging. "What happened then?"

"Then," Hylin continued, grinning and shaking his, toying with his loosened restraints. "Then Sir Gidoran cornered me. You see, I had reached the salvage dump, passing through the shadows of the night and was making my way down to my room when Sir Gidoran grabbed me by the arm," Hylin continued, absently eyeing the colorful hues on his screen. "I was frightened but turned to face him with all the fierceness I could muster.

"'What do you want?' I had asked him, flailing my arm free. 'Leave me alone,' I shouted, and yet he stood there with this look on his face. It was not anger, although I am not quite certain what it was. He asked me what I had taken and I reluctantly showed him the three pents the women had given me. He then laughed and asked what I had tucked inside my cloak."

"Although I tried to appear stung from his insinuations, I could see that he clearly knew what I had done," Hylin said, noting Iaco's nod for the shift. Thrusting the required levers upward, Iaco returned to the stick for the next dip.

"Yet I reluctantly reached within and pulled out the other pents, the jewels and the trinkets and he merely smiled, shaking his head," Hylin said, shaking his own. "I stood there frightened and the man was smiling at me!" he said exasperated, reclasping his restraints.

"Can you not imagine, Prince Iaco? I stood firm and looked into his eyes as he spoke, and I swear I will never forget his words. 'You are young, you are brave and you are useful,' he had said, his smile never wavering. 'If you have no one to look after you and you are tired of this foolishness, I could use you. Meet me at the door of Globo's at daybreak. I will soon make an honest man of you.'"

"I said nothing as he walked away and was surprised that he did not take back the trinkets I had taken, yet making my way through the narrow corridors to my room, I thought of the words he had said and lay restless through the darkness, recounting all that had happened in the lane. I woke and knew my decision, Prince Iaco. I went to Globo's at daybreak as the man had instructed, and I have been a servant of Sir Gidoran's ever since."

"Amazing," Iaco said, shaking his head and guidng the stick through the deep. "That is simply an amazing tale of fortune, Hylin. If you are not finished, forgive me for the interruption, but I need you to push the levers down once again. We are in route for the next to the last climb and we are at depths that require a further thrust. Furthermore unless you want me to forever refer to you as 'boy,' you will at once drop the title of Prince."

"Copy that," Hylin answered, loosening his restraints to reach the controls. "Yet are we not to wait for Jovaar, Iaco?"

"No," he answered, nodding as Hylin adjusted the first of the controls. "I am quite certain he is with Selena. The man is undoubtedly smitten."

"What do you mean?" Hylin asked, thrusting the last lever into place and reclaiming his seat.

"That is something else you must learn," Iaco answered, smiling and preparing the stick for climb. "Rather than learning from my friend G, although I am certain he would say otherwise, I believe I hold the higher hand for your teachings. And once the child is safely brought to her final destination, I will gladly prove my words true."

Forty-One

All sounds were muffled. Somewhere in the distance a man was speaking, yet his words were indiscernible. Jovaar attempted to lift his legs but they felt as if they were weighed down. Something he could not describe appeared to be hampering their rise. A mere movement radiated pain throughout his entire body and yet the man muffled on somewhere close by without care. Unable to open his eyes, Jovaar could not see who or what else was about him.

"Where were the others? What has happened to Lena and the child?" he thought, struggling with the guilt of being unable to help them. There was no time for answers. As the words of the man muffled on in the distance, unconsciousness prevailed once again.

***

"Do not hurt her!" Selena shouted, restrained in her seat. Glaring at the enemy, she struggled fruitlessly with the clasps that held her firmly in place. Unswayed, she roared her endless pleas at their captor.

"I beg you to leave her be!" she implored, eyeing both Khyra and Agye helpless to her left. "I know I am of no consequence to King Sugin, but I will take the child away! We could leave the galaxy! No one has to know! I will pay whatever you may demand. Do you hear me? You could want for nothing! I beg of you...please spare the child's life!"

"Pitiful woman," G2 began, gritting his teeth. Turning to her strained face, bearing the innocence of Juno's clothing, he snarled his rage.

"Do you not know what the death of this child means to me? Do you truly not understand? I not only will reap the rewards of a lifetime for me and my kin, but most importantly I will win the good graces of our King!"

"I will undoubtedly want for nothing...as you so well pointed out, yet not because of you, you pitiful woman," he repeated, enjoying the glory of the moment. "I will secure my place amongst royalty through the King himself which I have worked my entire life to attain. Your meager requests of pity have fallen on deaf ears, and you will waste my time no further!"

"Please," Khyra interrupted, bound to her seat at Selena's far left, the eyes of her friend imploring her to do more. "Do you not understand the despair King Sugin has caused? Do you not see how if you became one with the Resistance how better off you and your kin would be? Do you really think the King will give you all that he has promised? Think you foolish man! You will return with honor, but you will never receive what you have earned! The King is an evil man. Once he has what he wishes you will be dispensable along with those you call your family. You are nothing to him nor are they. You are merely a pawn in his game of superiority. Surely you must know this! I beg you to please not harm the child!"

G2 had his back to the women, listening to the elder's insight yet refused to even consider the endless rambling of words. "She is wrong!" he thought, slamming his fists on the low cabinet, turning to face the incessant defiant, eyes glaring.

"You know not what you speak of," he shouted at last, his temper flaring with the woman's unfounded predictions. "I have orders that state the intent of my appointment and the futures of my kin. You will be silent now while I end yours."

Khyra knew nothing, not her words or her protest would stop the drive of the man pacing the cabin and she exchanged frightened glances with both Selena and Agye. With Jovaar laying helpless on the floor at their feet, the man turning back to face Nitaya with glaring eyes, each sat breathless as the cooing babe lay unaware on the eerily lone bench at their side. Khyra prayed, spying Selena dip her head slowly in defeat that the end would prove pitifully swift.

***

Rebounding from the dip, the sky proved both bright and welcoming as Iaco sailed them swiftly through the low-lying clouds, away from any sightings of the enemy. "We are making excellent time," he said, peering over his shoulder to Hylin, shifting uncomfortably in his seat.

"Jovaar has been gone for some time, Prince Iaco," he said, glancing at the sealed door at his back, his tale of Yani and the dropping of his elder's title both long forgotten. "Should I not go look for him?"

"He *has* been gone for quite some time," Iaco answered, tapping the stick backward to gain altitude. "Head to the rear and inform him that we are on schedule but that I need him for the exact quardinents of the rendezvous."

"That should get his attention," he added, smiling flippantly over his shoulder. "He has given me the exact information, Hylin, yet will be mumbling that I am irresponsible with such an important task when in fact it is a ploy to lure him from the graps of Selena. He will come forward, my boy, no doubt in my mind. He will just be angry with me. I assure you, I am quite used to it."

"Is this what I have to look forward to in my old age, bickering amongst friends?" Hylin asked, hurriedly releasing his restraints. Iaco looked to him, a smirk crossing his face as he reached the rear door.

"My boy," Iaco answered, unable to contain his grin, searching Hylin's eyes over his shoulder. "You can only hope."

***

Consciousness returning, murky images filled Jovaar's view with the surprising struggle of merely opening eyes. Silently stirring upon the cool floor, he found the pain of his arm had returned, radiating now through the depth of his chest. Regardless of the intenseness of the forgotten long-ago puncture, the sounds of the women reassured him that at least for now, those he promised to protect remained safe. His purpose somehow thankfully remained.

"Nitaya!" Jovaar attempted to shout, her name emitting nothing more than a mere whisper. Jovaar grit his teeth with his fruitless efforts. Struggling to pull the weight of his body into a seated position, all labors proved futile, his chin meeting firmly with the cold, unforgiving floor.

"You are back from the deep," the man said at his back, Jovaar unable to respond. "You have made this all too easy," the stranger continued, tugging on Jovaar's cloak and dragging his body upward to face him, the women sitting helpless at his back. "Per orders, I have been patiently awaiting your arousal, and it appears the waiting is at last now over. I will quite enjoy seeing your eyes as you watch your so called *possible* future destroyed."

"I assure you, although I am a loyal servant of our King, I am also not oblivious to pain. Be that as it may, I will make this quick for the child. You however," G2 added, pausing to ruffle the scruff of his chin, kneeling closer to Jovaar's face. "I must admit that I will quite enjoy witnessing your anguish."

Carefully laid out with the long awaited promise of what was to come, his movements proved holy predicted although G2 could not have imagined their ease. The child laying helpless and unaware to his left, the enemy Savius lying defenseless on the floor, the women sat securely strapped into place at his right. Kneeling beside the side cabinet admiring his prey, G2 confidently prompted his portal.

"It is time, King Sugin," he said, awaiting his master's response. Selena whimpered her chin into her chest.

"This is Carsian," the King answered from his station in quarters aboard the air ship. "Key the code and lay the portal where I will be able to witness the destruction."

"Aye, my King, as you wish," G2 answered, tapping in the number sequence. As ordered, he laid the portal on the side table to his left.

"Ah, so at last the time has come," the King began, sitting upward and gloating at the glorious view. "It is so good to see you again, young Savius."

***

Hylin jogged down the corridor finding it unsurprisingly empty, yet continuing to and prompting the door of midship, he stood in dismay as it remained firmly in place. Attempting to prompt its opening a second time, his frustration grew. Certain there was a mere simple malfunction, he banged his fists annoyingly upon the door.

"Something must be wrong," he whispered, gaining no response with his fourth try. Turning to race to the alternate emergency entrance, he found the narrow door eerily sealed. His fear immediately grew with the possibilities. Pausing to consider the potential outcomes, he leaned back against the solid door to weigh his options.

"Neither will budge and there are no signs of the others," he thought, racing back to the first in attempt to pry it open a final time. Receiving the same result, panic immediately set in. Hylin's eyes wandered rapidly with fear at the glowing light above the door. Instincts urging him forward he turned, all senses alert to the eerieness about him. Seeing no other option, he raced directly to command to inform Prince Iaco.

***

"Iaco!" Hylin shouted, the Command door closing swiftly at his back.

"Hylin, what is wrong?" he asked, glancing over his shoulder. "Where is Jovaar?"

"The doors are locked," he answered, ignoring the question and bending forward to catch his breath. "Both doors are locked. There is no sign of Jovaar or the others and when I tried beating on the door, they would not answer. Something is wrong, Iaco! I do not know what, but something is wrong. I feel it!"

"You checked the entrire ship prior to detachment?" Iaco asked, looking back and forth from his station to Hylin's frightened face. "Are you certain you did precisely as asked?"

"I did!" Hylin answered, pacing to grasp the back of Iaco's seat. "I searched each and every cabin, compartment, I searched it all. Even when you told me I had to restrain with our detachment I turned and searched the last cabinet. I did not miss anything, Iaco. There was no one there!"

"Calm yourself, Hylin," Iaco continued, prompting the manual override. "Perhaps it is merely an electrical malfunction.

Just let me...wait," he added, pausing to stare at his side screen, the search of the ship's layout at last keyed to his station.

"We have a forced lock in both cabins," he whispered, shaking his head. "I will just override the system. Odd as this is, I am certain it is nothing to concern ourselves over."

Prompting the controls and awaiting the results of the function, Hylin ran his fingeres through his hair. The forced locks stubbornly remained in place.

"This cannot be right," Iaco said, performing the override again. "Hylin, are you certain you checked everything?"

"Absolutely certain, Iaco," he answered, anxiously wringing his hands. "I swear on my life, but the light above the door confirms its lock."

"Well something is definitely wrong and I willl need to head back there myself to check it out. Listen to me," he added, releasing his restraints and raising the overhead controls. Rising from his seat and facing Hylin, he reassuringly grasped the boy's shoulder. "I will need you to man the helm."

"You need me to do what?" he asked, taking a step back. He could not take his eyes from the massive controls.

"There is no time for a debate, Hylin," Iaco pressed, hunkering to maneuver away from the pilot seat. "Climb in and strap down. There is nothing to it. The course is preset in the system so all you will be required to do is hold the stick and follow the course, which is outlined before you on the main panel. Hylin, I know you are afraid but we have no time for it. If something is wrong, I need to get back there now. Sit down and take the blasted controls."

Hesistantly, Hylin did as told. Skirting around Iaco, he clasped his restraints and settled into the massive seat. Attempting calm, Iaco reviewed the procedures. Showing Hylin how to gently hold the stick and how to scan the readout on the screen, Iaco stood once he was certain the boy could manage then paced the few steps to the rear door.

"Chime the portal if you run into anything suspicious," he said, not waiting for an answer. Turning, he prompted the door's slide then quickened his steps toward mid-ship and whatever lay there waiting as Hylin manned the craft on his own.

461

***

"After his feeble attempts to break through, the boy ran toward Command as anticipated, Sir. At this moment, Prince Iaco should be learning of the forced locks and should be heading this way as expected," G2 said, the image of his imposing master on the screen for all to see.

"It seems all is as planned," the King answered, crossing his arms and straightening in his seat. "You have done well, G2. I should have set you out from the start. Terdoni could very well have ruined everything I have worked onars for. Now, take care of the girl Agye."

"As you wish, Sir," he answered, turning from the screen and rounding to his prey he stiffened with confidence. "The King has told me of your orders and informed me that you have disobeyed him, young one," G2 began, swiping Juno's nuisance of a cloak to his back. "He had such high hopes for you...and your kin, but alas, you will not see the end...nor will they. You, little one, have failed them all."

Raising his weapon to his face without thought, G2 admired its beauty, surprising all with the sudden swiftness of his hand. The blast rang through the center of Agye's belly and all gasped in fear, the girl writhing in pain from the lethal blow.

"No!" she cried, her screams a mere whisper as she looked down to the narrow stream of blood. "Selena," she said, a stray tear cascading down her cheek, rolling her head to face her only friend. "You must see Nitaya to the end. She is our only hope."

As if responding to Agye's pleas, Nitaya immediately cried out, her wails filling the cabin. Jovaar sat helpless on the floor just beyond her reach, his limbs numb from movement yet filled with sheering pain. Death thankfully came quickly for the girl titled Agye and as all sat helpless about her, G2 stepped forward, wrenching her hair upward before shrugging without feeling, dropping her head in disgust.

"Another waste," he said, turning to face those that for the moment remained breathing. "Be reassured, my King," he continued, turning to lean before the small screen. "This will all

462

be over soon then you may concentrate on finishing off the other possibles."

"You have pleased me and shall be greatly rewarded," King Sugin answered flatly. "Release the forced lock and allow Prince Iaco to enter. Restrain him and repeat the *infection* as you have done with Savius."

"Aye, Sir," he answered, eagerly crossing to the door's prompt. Releasing the blockage, he spanned the entrance's width. Settling himself against the low cabinet, G2 raised his weapon to await the arrival of the Prince.

"Iaco no!" Khyra pleaded, looking away from what was left of Agye and shouting in an attempt to forewarn the Prince. "Do not open the door!"

It was too late. As the door sprang abruptly open, Iaco stood at its entrance eyeing the frightened women, attempting to raise his own defense.

"Lower your weapon," G2 began, aiming straight between Iaco's eyes, shifting to face the height of his adversary's frame. "Ah, how would you say it?" he asked, a smirk crossing his face, Iaco following his order and setting his weapon on the floor. "Ah yes, *Sir* Iaco...welcome to our little celebration!"

***

Iaco could not believe his eyes. Selena and Khyra sat bound, Agye lay lifeless with a fatal wound to her chest, Jovaar was seated seemingly unrestrained on the floor, and the child lay helpless, wailing on a side cabinet. "Who are you?" he shouted, nostrils flaring as he attempted to step forward. "What do you want?"

"I think the answers you seek are obvioius, Prince Iaco," G2 answered, shoving his weapon into the newest arrival's midsection. "Now kneel!"

"I will not!" he roared, the enemy twirling his weapon to point it directly into his enemy's face.

"I said kneel! You will bow at your future royalty. If you want this to remain painless for them," G2 added, gesturing toward the women and child with a nod. "Then you will do as ordered!"

Turning his gaze to Selena, Iaco noted the defeat in her eyes as she stared wantonly at the child. Turning to his friend for strength...for hope, he at last understood why Jovaar had not lashed out to defend them. Something was terribly wrong.

His eyes shone green and appeared glazed over, and despite both eye movement and facial expressions, his body sat motionless, reclined against the outer wall. Attempting to speak, Jovaar's lips moved but no words could be heard, and at last knowing he had no other choice, Iaco stared into his friend's cloudy, defeated eyes and knelt before the evil man.

"Now," G2 bellowed, reaching within his cloak and pulling out the evil vial. "Let our celebration begin."

***

"Stay calm," Hylin mumbled, attempting to follow his own words and steer the ship on the preset flight path. The process appeared almost as easy as Iaco had said, yet every so often he would make an adjustment on the stick and then would overcorrect it in an attempt to get the craft back on course. Minor flinches in the wrong direction would cause the ship to shift from the path, and each time it occurred Hylin would panic, unconsciously holding his breath until he at last got them back in line.

"What is taking so long?" he thought, sweat pouring from his brow as he swatted at it with his free hand. "I am too young for this," he groaned, speaking as if he was not alone. "Something is wrong. Prince Iaco should be back by now."

Glancing to his left next to the side screen, Hylin attempted to discern the various controls and smiled with an idea as one greatly resembled a portal com. "We are almost to the outskirts of our path," he whispered, knowing from Iaco's words that they would need to perform a final dip prior to the rendezvous. Having surmised the next destination by the laid out route on the Prince's screen, his smile quickly widened.

"If we are close enough to the straight line of Booderban, I could reach Phydin and the others," he whispered, hesitantly reaching out for the control.

"What if it is not what it seems?" he thought, quickly withdrawing his finger. "What if I cannot reach them and send a signal to the Sugins instead, alerting them to our location? What do I do?"

Hylin continued his firming grasp on the stick, looking over his shoulder every so often, praying to see his new friend's return. "It is useless to wait," he said, at last making the decision and reaching for the control.

"Hold on, Jovaar," he added with newfound confidence, knowing what must be done. "If I am right, help will soon be on the way."

***

"This is…" he said, hesitating and withdrawing his finger as he prompted what he hoped was both the portal com and the correct line. "I cannot say who we are," he whispered, staring out into the open sky in hopes of finding an answer. "If the Sugins can hear my words, they will lead them right to us! How foolish! Think Hylin…think!"

Running his fingers through his long, curling locks, Hylin made yet another adjustment to the stick then sat still, considering his options. "I cannot simply do nothing. Perhaps if I could…wait! What was it that Jovaar said?" Hylin thought, releasing his breath with a widened smile, his thoughts returning to fated Polatus.

"Yes," he said at last, prompting the com with newfound confidence. "This is Craft Nilyh, requesting assistance to anyone who can hear," he began, staring out into the cloudless sky, his eyes once again filled with hope. "I repeat, Craft Nilyh, N, I, L, Y, H in need of assistance."

Hylin released the com and prayed that he was close enough to Booderban for Phydin to hear and more importantly to understand his plea for help. The first voice that rang through the com, however, stifled his eagerness for it was most certainly not Phydin.

"Burto pana lito," the voice answered, Hylin's right eyebrow lifting as he looked strangely at the com.

465

"I am sorry," Hylin said, keying his end of the line. "I do not understand."

"Burto pana lito," the voice repeated, Hylin trying desperately to steer the craft and tap the locater for another channel.

"Definitely not Phydin," he grumbled, choosing another line. "This is Craft Nilyh. I am requesting assistance to anyone who can hear. Craft Nilyh, N, I, L, Y, H needing assistance," he repeated, releasing the com.

"Phydin, Jax, please," he whispered, glancing over his shoulder and staring into the empty cabin. "Please," he continued, rotating again in his seat and grasping firm on the stick, the impending dip looming before him. "I need you both now more than ever."

Forty-Two

Phydin had remained at Command from the moment the transport had landed at Booderban. His flight had proven surprisingly quiet through the star-filled darkness despite the ship's overcrowding, and once the transport had docked, he assisted the Polatians safely from the ship and to a ward standing by then sent his crew off for some much needed rest. The station's first officer however, proved quite accommodating at Command and did not seem to mind Phydin's constant presence, the newest arrival pacing the aisles between her and her fellow officers.

"Any sign?" he would ask periodically, stopping to stare at the large screen before him. He asked despite already knowing the answer.

"I am afraid it is as before, Sir Phydin," the woman answered, shaking her head and turning from her station. "There has been no indication of the craft you have specified, although several ships have docked since your arrival. Are you certain that Savius and your friends are not aboard one of those?"

"I am certain," he answered, sighing and folding his arms across his chest. "There are too many of our members aboard. The ships are too small and have an incoming heading from the wrong direction."

"Keep looking," he added, crossing his hands to his back to resume his pacing. "I beg of you."

"Of course," the first officer answered, nodding for her subordinate to continue overseeing the inbound. "But are you certain this is the rendezvous that you speak of? We have several hidden Resistance bases throughout the planet. Your friends could have easily diverted to another. Regardless of my questions, you should go off with your commrades and get some rest, Sir."

467

"No," Phydin answered, abruptly turning. "They will come here. If I only knew they survived Polatus I could possibly rest. Since I am not certain, I will remain...unless I have proven a burden to you."

"Of course not, Sir, you may remain as long as you wish," the first officer answered. Another stiffly-suited member approached from over her shoulder.

"Ma'am," the man began, straightening with respect. "I have been ordered to inform you that another Resistance ship has reached port. Its Captain is headed this way."

"Jovaar!" Phydin said, anxiously turning and grasping the man's shoulders. "Have you seen how many are amongst them?"

"I was not given specifics, Sir," he answered, stepping from Phydin's grip and respectfully tipping his head. "Yet the ship that gave the order holds only two,"

Phydin turned back to the first officer's screen to watch the endless line of arriving ships, leaning against the back of her seat to await the arrival of the strange member. Moments later the Command door sprang open and Phydin nodded but did not smile as Sir Gidoran raced toward him, trailed by his young co-pilot.

"Phydin," he began, clasping hands with his new friend. "It is so good to see you."

"Jovaar?" Phydin questioned, looking about the cabin at Gidoran's back. "Is he with you? Perhaps on another ship at you tail?"

"I am sorry Phydin, but no," Gidoran answered, shaking his head. "I followed the last of the transports out of Polatus and he turned back to try and save anyone that may have been left behind. I was hoping you had word."

"We have heard nothing," Phydin answered, turning impatiently back to the screens. "I have sent the remaining crew off for rest. I suggest you and your co-pilot do the same."

"I prefer to remain," Gidoran answered, setting his flight equipment down and claiming an open seat to the left of the data commander.

"Go get some rest," he added to his co-pilot. Without further prompting, the boy nodded and left in search of the facilites. "Are the women secure then?" Gidoran asked.

Phydin turned to him exasperated. "No," he said, shaking his head and rubbing his tired eyes. "They remained with Iaco when there was not enough room aboard the transport."

Gidoran sat in disbelief at what he was hearing as Phydin again turned back to the screens for how could Jovaar allow his words to be true? "Any word on the child?" he asked at last, fearing the answer he would receive.

"No, nothing," Phydin added, raising his head to stare out the massive expanse of glass into the open sky. Seeing his friend in pain, Gidoran rose, placing his hand on Phydin's shoulder.

"Jovaar will make it, Phydin," he said, patting his back and looking up into the bright blue. "They all will. And I will remain with you until they do."

***

The pair waited impatiently together, exchanging their seats to pace the aisle, time creeping slowly by without word. The Command however, remained busy with the docking and detaching of various ships, yet tensions grew with each new arrival as none contained their friends.

"Anything?" Phydin asked, his patience growing thin. He ceased his pacing to question the first officer.

"Again, no," the woman answered, saddened to deliver the repeated news. With the last of her words, the messenger that had approached them earlier returned.

"Ma'am," he began, straightening to face his commander. "A distress signal has been spotted from the direction Sir Phydin indicated and we do not recognize the craft's name."

"As you know, that is typical," the first officer answered, shrugging her shoulders. "We do not recognize most."

"I understand, Ma'am," the man pressed. "But under the circumstances, I patched the transmission to your station for you to hear. It may be nothing, but it could be the craft you have been searching for."

"Upload the link then," the officer answered, certain it was nothing, snapping her fingers at her subordinant to open the line. "Sir Phydin, Sir Gidoran," she continued, turning to face the exhausted, withering pair. "You may want to hear this."

***

Head down and hands to his back, Iaco peered to the side at his friend, eyebrows furrowed with worry. "What is wrong?" he whispered. Seeing Jovaar strain to speak, his answering words proved too soft for him to hear.

"Iaco no!" Selena shouted, startling him anew, turning as the enemy crossed to his side. "Close your eyes!" Selena screamed. "Get away! Do something! You must save Nitaya!"

Iaco raised his head. Spying the dark cloak to his left then straining to peer upward into their captor's eyes, he gnarled his teeth as the enemy held his weapon in one hand and the evil vial in the other. Iaco now fully understood what had brought his friend down to his muted state.

"So easy," G2 said, ramming the weapon into Iaco's forehead. "Look upward! You can do nothing for them now. Do this and I promise you they will receive a painless death. Act out and I will end them most cruelly!"

Iaco glanced over to Selena and swallowed hard, his resolve fim despite her pleading, tear-stained eyes. "It is not over," he said simply, raising his head and giving in to the evil man.

"Not yet," G2 answered, laughing as he opened the vial. "But alas, Prince Iaco, it will be soon."

***

The enemy placed the vial in a small opening within the cabinet then produced a slender metal syringe from within his cloak. Extending it down within the tube of liquid all the while carefully monitoring Iaco's gestures, he extracted only a small amount of the colorless solution.

Iaco did not know specifically what the concoction contained, but he was certain by the look of Jovaar seated at his

470

side that it was deadly, albeit slow. He struggled within himself not to resist.

"He is only one man," he thought, eyeing Carsian's silent grin on the screen. Glancing over to the softly whimpering child however, Iaco knew his own death may stall time and save hers. Turning to see a single tear roll down Selena's cheek, he looked back to his captor as he closed in, the syringe mere moments from his eye.

"I beg you, no!" Selena cried, the syringe penetrating Iaco's left eye. Doing his best to stifle his own aching screams, gritting his teeth in an attempt to withstand the pain, Iaco's writhing, fists clenched at his sides made his suffering obvious to all. Iaco was hurting and there was nothing Selena could do to help him.

She slunk back exhausted, and although she had thought she could shed no more, tears streamed down her face. It was unthinkable that she now watched the same process she had witnessed earlier when Jovaar had received his own injection.

She had cried then too, but at least Jovaar was unconscious and was unable to feel the torture that was being performed on him. She remembered sitting bound and helpless as he had awoken frightened and she could see it again now in his pale green eyes as he watched his friend struggling with pain.

Searching for Selena and struggling to speak, lips moving yet unable to form words, Jovaar attempted to move to defend Iaco yet knew he was unable. His legs remained numb before him, his arm and chest searing in pain from the long ago puncture. Selena could do nothing but watch his suffering. Again crying out for them both, wishing it was her in their place, the evil man quieted her with his threats, and so she sat numb, watching the pair suffer on the floor.

Iaco's injection proved much worse than Jovaar's. Selena knew he had submitted to the torture for the mere hope of extending their lives…however long that may be, and she looked from him to Agye's lifeless body at her side, shivering with guilt at another life she could not save. Turning back to Iaco and watching him at last succumb to the inevitable, screaming violently with the pain, she squirmed as the needle's penetration was forced deeper into his eye.

471

The change came quickly as the enemy at last withdrew the syringe, and placing it back neatly within his cloak, Selena watched Iaco's eyes glaze over. His legs grew lifeless as expected and his body slid sideways, landing him face first on the floor.

"They are both incapacitated, my King," the man said, filled with honor as he beamed at his captives.

"Well done, G2," Carsian answered, leaning closer to the screen to better see the results.

"Shall I continue with the child?" G2 asked, eager to continue on and earn his fated reward.

"No," the King answered, abruptly rising to pace his quarters. "First, take care of the women. Saving the child for the last, I want Savius to witness all of their suffering."

***

"This is Craft Nilyh requesting assistance to anyone who can hear," the voice rang over the com, recomposed at the first officer's station. "I repeat, Craft Nilyh, N, I, L, Y, H, in need of assistance."

"What do you make of it?" the first officer asked, turning to Sirs Phydin and Gidoran.

"I make nothing of it," Phydin answered, shaking his head and turning to Gidoran for agreement. "It is a simple distress signal. Surely you have protocol for such issues. Send out your team or do whatever it is that you do. I need information on a blasted transport from Polatus. Have one of your men see to this drivel and resume your search for my craft!"

"Copy that," the first officer answered, snapping her fingers at her subordinant. "I am certain it is a mechanical malfunction or something of that nature," she continued, turning back to the messenger. "Order a tech to your station to guide the pilot as necessary."

"Yes, Ma'am," the man answered, leaving them as the order rang anew through the station.

"Craft Nilyh requesting assistance to anyone who can hear," the voice repeated, his words obviously strained. "Craft Nilyh, N, I, L, Y, H, needing assistance!"

472

Phydin, arms crossed and irritated by the interruption, returned to his pacing, his back to the screen when the voice once again echoed his plea. "Wait!" Gidoran shouted, grabbing Phydin's arm and yanking him toward the FO's screen. "Replay that message!"

Leaning eagerly on the back of the first officer's seat, Gidoran nodded anxiously as the officer prompted the message for a third time. "That is him!" Gidoran shouted, leaning forward and pounding his fist on the panel. "N, I, L, Y, H! It is Hylin! Concentrate your entire division on that communication, get intel on its location and get us a current line! He would only send a distress order if absolutely necessary. Fuel a ship with hyper capabilities and order our men to stand by. We need confirmation of Hylin's location then we are going out after them!"

"You cannot!" the first officer shouted, abruptly rising. "If the Sugin army knows of your heading..."

"I do not give a damn about the Sugin army!" Gidoran roared, pushing his way through two passing officers, racing toward the door. "Get me that line and order that blasted ship. Phydin!" he added, wildly motioning for the unmoving man to follow. "We are leaving now!"

***

"This is useless!" Hylin said, releasing the com and rubbing the ache in the back of his neck. "They are never going to answer. Surely I am close enough to the direct line to Booderban by now. Why do they not hear me?"

Frustrated and exhausted, his limbs aching with tension, Hylin looked back to the main screen to once again realign his path. "No!" he grumbled, eyeing the impending dip on the mapped course. "How am I supposed to..." he stopped, turning to stare at the large levers to his right.

"There should be two of us," he grumbled gritting his teeth. Anxiety growing he looked from the levers to the screen then back to the levers. "What do I do, Iaco?" he asked the empty cabin, his eyes returning to the growing dip indication on his panel. "What do I do?"

Resolved to the fact that the others would not be returning, Hylin knew he had no other option but to release the stick and transfer the levers on his own. "It is all in the timing," he thought, glancing over his shoulder at the narrow path between seats, thoughts of Booderban for the moment forgotten. "We will shift, but I have no choice I have to do this."

Releasing his restraints, lifting the overhead controls he slowly freed his arms. Careful not to jar the stick, Hylin began to climb up and over when another thought washed over him. Easing back into the large seat and reaching over to the far side panel, he searched feverishly for the screen that overran the locks. On his fifth try he found it. Smiling, he secured the Command door.

"Just to be certain," he thought, glancing back at the narrow path. Eyeing the impending dip that he had patched to the main screen, he took a final deep breath. Releasing the stick he dove at last for the trio of levers.

***

The man crept closer to Khyra leaving Selena for the last. Pushing her head back into the seat and struggling against her restraints, Selena watched as the newly-filled syringe grew closer. Once again filled with guilt, she sobbed as yet another life was about to be taken.

"If only I had not placed the child with Agye," she thought, turning to Jovaar and seeing rage in his misty green eyes. "If I had stayed in my seat at the celebration as the others had done, none of this would be happening."

"Khyra!" she shouted, turning back as the needle was a breath away from penetrating the outer layer of Khyra's eye. "I am so sorry!"

The man lost his footing with the shift. The ship careened violently and Selena's eyes grew wide as she steadied herself with her right leg against the outer wall. The men rolled helplessly upon the floor.

"Hylin!" she thought, the craft's pressure dropping. "No Nitaya!" she shouted, the child falling the short distance to the ground, her blanket freeing as she landed just within Jovaar's reach. Watching as the ship plummeted, Jovaar attempting to soothe the babe with words that would not form, Nitaya wailed out from the fall.

"My King!" the man shouted at the portal, regaining his balance and securing the unit on the cabinet. "The ship is giving way. How shall I respond?"

"The women are bound and the men are useless, you imbecile!" Carsian roared, his eyes glaring upon the screen. "This is not what I had planned. Head to Command and take care of that boy at once! I have just received word from Sivon and he too is close with another Savius contained within the confines of a hanger facility. If you foul this, G2, I swear it will be the end of you!"

"Aye, Sir!" the man shouted. Attempting to balance, he placed the syringe back within his cloak. "We will be on auto soon," he added, spittle splashing her face as he leaned in, gritting his teeth at Khyra. "Then we will finish this!"

Turning and jarring from yet another shift, the man kicked Iaco in the midsection. Securing his weapon and aiming forward, he left his enemies helpless and raced to Command.

***

The corridor seemed longer than before. Its bow tipped he bounced left and right off the walls with the endless shifts. At last reaching the door, G2 placed his hand over the side prompt. The door stood firm.

"That is impossible!" he shouted repeating the motion, the ship dipping violently low beneath his feet. "No!" he screamed, banging on the door and demanding entrance. Somehow he knew it was pointless. Glancing over his shoulder to the empty corridor, he balanced himself by wedging his feet then gave a final pound on the forced barricade.

"Your attempts are useless!" he shouted, quickly regaining composure. "Do what you will, boy! I will finish them off as planned. In the end I may die, but my legacy will remain in royalty for all eternity."

Leaving the boy to do as he pleased, G2 smiled broadly. Gritting his teeth, he quickly made his way back to midship.

"This is Booderban," the voice said, his voice ringing throughout the cabin. "Report your distress."

"Yes!" Hylin shouted, pulling the last lever and reclaiming his seat, the ship careening violently without his guiding hand. "This is ship Nilyh!" he answered, prompting the com. "Preparing for dip, needing further instructions!" he added, struggling to realign the stick with Iaco's map.

"Hylin!" another voice shouted, joy filling his tone. "Is that you? What happened at Polatus? Is the child safe? Where is Jovaar?"

"Sir G!" Hylin shouted, thankful to hear his commander's familiar voice. "I do not have time to explain! I am piloting the ship on my own and need to maneuver the final dip before leaving Kindawan airspace. Prince Iaco went back to the rear to search for Jovaar but has not returned. Selena, Khyra, Nitaya and Agye are there as well but I was unable to reach them. I searched every bit of this ship, Sir Gidoran. I searched all of it! Iaco has not returned."

"We are...wait!" he shouted, pausing as the ship crossed over the mapped indication. "We need to dip now!"

"Steady, Hylin, steady," Gidoran answered, having stalled the hyper drive at the coordinates the first officer had provided. "We have you in sight. I do not see another craft. What is wrong?"

"I told you what is wrong!" Hylin answered, frustration filling in his words. "I searched the ship as ordered, G. Jovaar did not answer and Iaco went after him. The others are in rear and I don't know their status. We are in freefall! I have not done this before, G. We are dipping!"

"Hylin, do you hear me?" Gidoran shouted, eyeing the sharp angle of the ship out the glass. "Hylin?" The com was silent.

***

The ship shook as Hylin tried desperately to hold on to the stick. With the jarring growing more violent, he searched the screen desperately for a reason.

"Sir Gidoran," he began, tapping the com. "This is not right. I can barely hold on!"

"Your trajectory is off, but only slightly," Gidoran answered, thankful that Hylin was still with them as he monitored the dip. "Look at your overall station. There should be a small light on the flat panel just to your right indicating if any of the steps were missed. It should be blinking, Hylin. Is anything blinking?"

Looking down and to his right, Hylin saw a light but with the ship instability, he could not read the label below it. "It is blinking, Sir G," he answered, holding the stick with both hands. "But with the shaking I cannot tell what it is!"

"Look at your levers," Gidoran continued, attempting to calm the boy. "You may have not released one entirely."

"I am running out of time!" Hylin shouted, turning to see the levers on the side wall. The last one remained slightly ajar. "It is the last lever, G!"

"Just release it, Hylin and the shaking with ease!" he answered, eyeing the haphazard dip through his glass.

"I cannot reach it, Sir Gidoran!" he answered, frightened as the sea raced ever closer. "It is across the cabin! The sea is coming! We are almost there! Sir G!"

Forty-Three

Selena screamed with the jarring of the ship, yet Khyra was too busy working on her restraints to calm her. "Selena listen to me!" she began, shifting backward to give her arms more room behind the seat. "I am almost free. We can do nothing for them strapped in. Do what you can to break loose."

"Selena!" she shouted, gritting her teeth in frustration. "Do what I say!"

At Khyra's stern words Selena attempted to focus, yet struggling against the weight of the downforce, the straps at her back remained firmly in place. "I cannot do it!" she shouted, staring across the room. "Just look at them! I have failed them all!"

Having no control over his limbs, Iaco's large frame slid back and forth about the cabin. With the newest jolt he hit the side wall, moaning from the newest pain. More fortunate, Jovaar was somehow wedged between the bench Nitaya had been lying on and the seat at his side and was holding firm although how Selena could not fathom.

Nitaya lay next to him crying out, and Selena watched as Jovaar used his head and shoulders to hold the child in place. Sitting frozen and forgetting her own restrains, she listened to the child wail, her body rhythmically swaying with the diving ship.

"Selena!" Khyra shouted, her tone sharp with anger. "Nitaya needs you! Get that blasted strap loose!" Selena did not hear her. Selena could hear nothing but the helpless child.

"I have..." Khyra shouted, pausing with the evil man's return.

"You have what?" he questioned, using the walls of the cabin for balance. "You think that you have won? Are you mad?" he roared, bracing the seats one by one as he neared. "If we die from the eratic dip I still win you foolish woman!"

478

Glaring at Khyra half way to her seat, G2 turned to look for the child, finding her sheltered by Jovaar on the floor. Releasing the back of the seat, he shifted across the cabin to reclaim her.

"King Sugin!" he shouted, gathering the wailing child in his arms and turning to hold her high across the cabin for his master. "I have her! I have the possible! Shall I continue?" Receiving no response, he lowered the child to his chest.

"King Sugin!" he repeated, balancing toward the portal. "Can you hear me, Sir?" Again there was no answer. Shifting his weight and the screaming child into the crook of his arm, G2 reached the cabinet that held the small screen, stooping before it. "King Sugin!" he shouted, leaning close. "I have..."

"Never turn your back on a woman!" Khyra shouted, striking the back of his head with a stray piece from the bench, rendered free during the dip. Slinking forward and slamming into his King's image, G2 groaned in pain as Khyra reached for the child. Despite her strained efforts, the man's grip remained firm.

Slowly straightening and turning to face the wretched woman, the hatred emanated from G2's eyes as the dark liquid drizzled from the crown of his head. "So it seems," he said, grabbing the metal and pointing it firmly at her chest. "Our little celebration continues."

***

"Gunnery is secured and there has been no sign of the enemy," Jax said, prompting the com and circling the ship's outer track. "Did you see Hylin's radical dive, G?" he added, having overheard the conversation over the com. "That boy has guts. To pull a dip at that angle and..."

"I did, Jax, thanks," Gidoran answered, sighing. "Just concentrate on the open skies."

"Sir Gidoran," the first officer interrupted over the additional line to Booderban. "If you are in need of additional support, I could send two transports yet as I am certain you will agree, I am hestant for they would undoubtedly raise notice to your presence."

"I have considered that," Gidoran said, nodding to Phydin across Command. "But at this time we are better served on our own. Just keep the line open," he added, circling the ship above the dip's impact. "It is our only link to the Resistance."

"Phydin," he added, turning to his friend and releasing the com. "Prepare us to tail the boy's dip."

***

Hylin held firm to the stick, the transport plunging violently into the deep, appearing almost grateful for the sea as the jarring at last subsided. "Sir Gidoran!" he shouted, knowing his friends would maintain sail above. "I need to release the stick and straighten the levers. Sir G!" he repeated, gaining no response.

"He is on his way, Hylin," the strange voice answered. Hylin froze, startled by the words from the unknown woman.

"Who am I speaking with?" he asked, hesitantly.

"Relax Hylin," the woman answered, grinning from her station. "This is First Officer Zinu of the Resistance, Viao Station Booderban. I spoke briefly with you earlier. Release the stick quickly and set your levers for the deep. Sir Gidoran and your friends are preparing to follow your lead."

***

Gidoran ordered Orvi to assist Phydin with the final sequence of the dip to speed the timing as he heard Zinu easing Hylin below. "All systems are operational and preparing for dip," Phyin said, Orvi releasing the final lever at his back.

"Ordering dip then," Gidoran said, nodding to Phydin before turning to stare out the glass. "Dip in 5, 4, 3, 2, 1, we are in fall."

"Hylin," he added, his voice strained with the pressure of the ship's descent. "Hang on," he said, Jax's joyous shouts filling the background of the com. "We are on our way!"

***

The ship at last calmed and the man spoke to his frightened captives, his pacing resuming the length of the roomy cabin. Relishing the anguish of the Resistance members, G2 dabbed at the blood from his wound, scowling at the elder woman across the cabin.

"It seems the boy survived the plunge," he said, hands once again folded at his back. Stepping over Jovaar, he circled the room. "We should celebrate his feat, do you not agree?"

"I suggest you sit," he added, gesturing to the woman with a nod. Glaring at her enemy yet stepping backward toward the lifeless Agye, Khyra knew she had no other choice. Never leaving his gaze, she slowly sat, her cumbersome gown bunching at her back as the intruder continued to point the metal rod at her chest.

With the elder woman once again in place, G2 leaned down, placing the wailing child on the cold floor. "All in good time, little one," he said, turning from her cries back to Khrya. Crossing to the elder's back and restraining her, he yanked tightly, securing the straps and openly enjoyed her wincing.

"You will not break free again," he said, his voice confident as he gave the restraints a final tug. "And now," he continued, rounding the row of benches and raising the metal rod to her face. "Let us see what this was destined to do."

***

"Hylin, this is Gidoran," he said prompting the com, sailing the ship swiftly through the deep. "Can you hear me?"

"I am here," he answered, staring intently at the laid out path. "I spoke with First Officer Zinu. She said you were on your way. We survived the dip and I am continuing on Prince Iaco's mapped course."

"I have your readout and are closing in at your back," Gidoran continued, nodding to Phydin over his shoulder. "I need you to make some minor adjustments to your course though."

"I do not understand," Hylin answered his frustration returning, his body aching with the weight of his task. "It is mapped out clearly before me. I am to follow the trail then sail upward, directly to Jovaar's final destination."

481

"Just listen to G," Phydin interrupted, impatient despite Gidoran's annoyed glare. "If you fly steadily and someone is in fact aboard, you are giving them a smooth sail."

"I want you to jar intentially," Gidoran continued. Phydin merely shrugged at his back, returning his eyes to his own screen. "It may buy us some time."

"I still do not understand," Hylin pressed, shaking his head. "Iaco never showed me how."

"I know, Hylin, I know," Gidoran continued. Nodding, he watched the boy's progress on his readout. "I will walk you through it. I promise it is easier than you think."

"Just tell me what to do," Hylin answered, gritting his teeth at the thought of another jarring and wiping the sweat from his brow.

"Alright, Hylin," Gidoan continued, prompting the intel of the ship to his side screen. "Follow everything exactly as I say."

***

Hylin listened without interruption, his brow beading with sweat as Sir Gidoran gave the detailed instructions. "You can do this," he said, reassuringly. "Trust me as always, Hylin. The shift is a minor transaction but takes precision and strength to properly work. Just move the stick in a quick motion to the rear, then forward. Make sure that it is aft then bow, in that order," he pressed.

"Dropping down then upward will cause the nose to sink and will disrupt your pressure among other terrible things that I assure you we do not need to discuss. I am certain that you do not want to know what those other things are. Just know that if you do it in reverse, you may not be able to correct it."

"You will prompt the small button on the right of your stick to begin then will hold on firmly for the leveling," he added, pausing. "Do you understand?"

"Yes," Hylin answered, fluttering the button that until this moment was unknown to him, beneath his fingers. "Back then forward, holding firm," he repeated, wiping his brow with his free hand. "Do it now, Sir G?"

"Do it now, Hylin," Gidoran answered, running his fingers through his hair. "I will monitor your shift on my screen. Just follow my instructions and hang on tight."

Taking a deep breath Hylin looked down. Eyeing his fingers dancing lightly upon the stick, he prepared himself for both the procedure and its outcome.

"Here we go," he said, hesitantly tightening his grip. Looking back to his screen and trusting Sir Gidoran's words, Hylin prompted the button and jerked the controls.

***

"What the..." the man shouted, the ship careening about his, causing him to lose balance and fall back against the row of seats. "The boy is shifting intentially?" he roared, catching himself at the last moment on a side cabinet, just missing the child. "He could not possibly know how to perform a shift."

"Tell me now!" he ordered. Screaming at Khyra he waved the metal rod before her face. "I could not have miscalculated your numbers! Is the boy in fact alone in Command?"

Khyra sat frozen in her place with only the swaying of the ship to rock her, staring to her side at Selena and refusing to answer. "I order you to tell me now!" G2 roared, haphazardly crossing the rocking cabin. With a slight grin crossing her face as the man paced to her however, Khyra winked at Selena then at last turned, looking with firm resolve into his dark black eyes.

"Do what you will to me," she said, her grin defiantly widening. "You will have to learn the rest on your own."

Wretching back with the plunge, the metal rod searing violently into her chest, Khyra wailed out in pain. Refusing to acknowledge the man's darkened chuckle, she attempted to hold back her tears. Selena at once darted upright with the act, startled that the man followed through with his evil word, performing the most gruesome of tasks without care for life.

Glancing slowly downward to face the inevitable, the level of agony had oddly waned and Khyra spied Jovaar on the floor before her, his eyes wide in fear. Looking deeper, her breathing labored, she at once found understanding.

He would not be able to help her. No one would be able to help her. As the cabin appeared to calm, her vision blurred and her breathing shallowed.

"Selena," Khyra whispered, gasping. Facing the tear-stained eyes of her newest, most-dearest friend, Khyra swallowed hard to release the last of her words. "Selena, your time has come to lead." Dropping her head, Khyra fell silent.

***

"You are still in sight," Gidoran said, eyeing Hylin's craft just ahead and to his left. "Rest assured, Hylin, we monitored your shift for the duration and you have done well, as I most confidently expected."

"Now," he continued, zooming round the large land mass to bring the boy's ship full into view. "I will need you to divert from your flight path. You must listen to me carefully, Hylin. You must divert and slow, causing the ship to begin stalling. You must not let the stall occur however, for it will give whoever aboard the knowledge that you have assistance attempting to board. All you need to do is slow enough for us to make the connection then speed will no longer be a factor. Hylin, you must be brave. If we are to save the others, you must do exactly as I say."

Hylin paused a moment staring at his screen, watching the shortening flight path clearly lined out by Jovaar. Taking a deep breath at having already survived both the plunge and the shift, he looked back to the glass and the open sea, confidently answering at last.

"I am ready, Sir G," he said, stretching his limbs in his seat in the empty cabin. "You were there for me on Yani, you were there for me with the dip and I know you are again with me now. I will follow you anywhere, Sir Gidoran. Just tell me what I have to do."

Forty-Four

Hylin listened carefully as Gidoran rang out the next series of orders, following each step carefully as given. Working well together regardless of their distance, every so often Phydin's voice would come over the com, surprising them both to add additional instruction. Regardless of the giver however, Hylin performed each task as instructed.

"You do this, Hylin, and I promise that you will be one of the men playing the next game of Rodaous," Jax added, attempting to ease the tension from the gunnery. "You will sit at my side and I will teach you all the tricks of the game from a true master of menace."

"So you do cheat!" Uvis shouted, seated across from Jax in his mirrored station.

"That is enough!" Phydin roared, interrupting his so-called men. Shaking his head, he nodded for Gidoran to continue.

"Hylin," Gidoran said, wringing his hands with the quieting of his gunners. "Orvi has uploaded your new flight path. Tap your main screen and it should appear before you."

"Hold on," Hylin answered, following Gidoran's instructions, sighing with relief as the screen altered without difficulty. "I have it," he said, nodding. "Sir, G, are you truly certain I can do this?"

"I am, Hylin, and stop referring to me as Sir," he answered, shaking his head at Orvi. "I believe you have earned dropping my title. Now, take this slow, Hylin. Re-route and initiate stalling in 5, 4, 3, 2, 1, perform re-route."

Hylin shifted the stick slightly to his right, slowing the transport and watching as the incoming ship came into view round the bend at his back. "I see you, G!" he shouted, feeling triumphant, the transport maneuvering with ease at his hand.

"Well done, Hylin," he answered, nodding in relief as Phydin prompted the main screen to zoom in on the craft. "All is on schedule, yet we are not yet done. Hold firm to the stick and prepare for connection."

***

"This is not happening as planned!" the man shouted, reaching down and grabbing Jovaar's hair. "But do not you worry," he continued, spitting on his face. "You will lay helpless as I finish off the others, for I am saving you for last!"

Dropping Jovaar's head back to the floor, G2 crossed the small space to the cabinet that held the portal. "King Sugin!" he shouted, picking it up to shake the intermittently responding monitor. "King Sugin, can you hear me?"

The screen showed only static with oddly random glimpses of the King, and although his commanding voice sparingly escaped the device, G2 struggled to understand the meaning of what his master was demanding. Titling the unit to the side, G2 did what he could to adjust the mechanics, yet as the the picture cleared the audio simultaneously vanished.

"King Sugin!" G2 bellowed, his face mere inches from the screen. "If you can hear me, please signal!" The King nodded at his subordinate's prompting, yet sighing with disgust at the lack of consistant communication, G2's shouts proved louder yet fruitless with his growing frustration.

"I have secured the rear of the ship, Sir! Both men are incapacitated and two females, both young and old are confirmed dead! The other, more significant will be next and then I will deal with the child possible! As ordered, her death will be in plain view for you to witness!"

G2 watched as the King gestured wildly, yet he was unable to understand his words with the surprising inconsistency of the link. "I am sorry, my King, but I cannot hear you," he continued, turning the portal again in his hands in attempt to correct the malfunction. Finding a control he had missed earlier, G2 turned the knob, yet despite his efforts, heard only remnants of his King's words.

"G2!" Static.

"Shift to…" More static.

"Enemy Resistance…" again static.

"Others…" the portal proved resolved to silence.

G2 stared at the screen, uncertain how to proceed. "Others?" he questioned, sensing the ship slow about him. "Not if I can help it," he added, rising. Turning to scan the cabin, his enemies cowering on the floor, he lowered the monitor to the cabinet knowing that most certainly with both the shift and the slow, enemy resistance were on their way.

Jumping over the helpless survivors on the floor, G2 quickly raced out the midship door for Command, hopes of his kin gaining their rightful status filling his thoughts. Knowing most assuredly that anyone in his path would meet their untimely fate, he checked his weapon and rounded the next bend to face whatever was to come.

***

"You have it, Hylin," Gidoran said, encouraging the boy and the forward movement of his ship, slowly doing his part to shorten the span between the pair. Easy now, easy."

Hylin continued the required slow on his end, carefully dodging the looming mass to his right and watching anxiously as Gidoran's ship appeared dauntingly from above. "Coming up on connection," Jax added, feeling the waters stir about the hull and nodding to Uvis as he lowered to the base of the arc.

"Almost there," Phydin whispered, concentrating on the hatch upon his screen intermittently eyeing Gidoran steering them in.

"That's it, that's it, just another moment, connection," Jax added, laughing and shaking his head at Uvis. "Hylin, we are hooked. I never thought that you would…"

"You did it, Hylin, you did it," Gidoran interrupted, openly sighing with relief. "Hold tight. I am sending Jax to you now. Simply keep your current path and I will raise your speed from my end. We will sail through the deep as one ship."

"Copy that," Hylin answered, breathing easier for the first time in onars. "How long until Jax is aboard?" he asked, settling the ship. He could not contain his smile knowing Gidoran assumed the helm from above. Turning to face the rear of Command, Hylin sighed with relief knowing his friends were near.

"Rest easy, Hylin," Gidoran answered, nodding the order to Phydin. "Help is now on the way."

***

Jax had his restraints released just moments before connection and found himself giddy with laughter, his feet carrying him eagerly toward the main hatch. "Uvis!" he shouted, glancing over his shoulder. "Let's go already!"

"I am coming," he answered seeing Jax's impatience, freeing his last restraint. "You have your weapon?" he asked, reaching his closest friend in the corridor.

"When do I not?" he answered unable to contain his grin. Turning, Jax waved Uvis' typical worry aside and knelt to open the manhole transportal. Eager to shake hands with their youngest member, he smiled at Uvis and prompted the opening below.

***

Breathless, G2 waited at the MT station, listening to what he was now certain was the joining of ships. Confirming the slow of the craft as he had sensed upon leaving his captives, he raced quickly to the transportal to await the arrival of the enemy. G2 was confident that someone was coming. The only questions that remained were who and how many.

"How many?" he wondered, raising his weapon above his face. Using the side wall as leverage, G2 knew he had mere moments to lay out his plan.

"My last breath for King Sugin," he whispered, lowering to his knees for balance against the weighted joining of the pair. Both anxious to confront the arrivals yet nervous to face their

488

possible numbers, he awaited the arrival of the enemy and his ultimate fate.

***

"Jax," Uvis said, grasping his friend's shoulder in the narrow corridor. "Let me go in first. We don't know what we are about to face. You may be handier at the gunnery but in hand to hand, you know I outdo you."

"Do not argue," he added, halting Jax's argument with his hand. "This is not open for debate."

Jax paused facing his friend. Clasping the back of Uvis' hair, their foreheads met with common understanding. "For the Resistance," he said, swallowing his pride and releasing his friend, Uvis standing confident upon the outlined MT.

"Arms in, eyes open," he added, winking and reaching for the lever.

"I know, I know," Uvis answered, eagerly standing at the ready, and speaking with their eyes, each nodding confidently, Jax took a deep breath and pulled the lever. Sighing with both excitement and worry, Jax stood by watching his friend fly quickly beneath the craft toward the unknown.

***

G2 heard the hum of the now operational MT, his ears alert to both the out of range mid-ship and transport's inner command door. Silently changing his awkward position, he crouched round the bend closer to midship for cover.

"At least they will arrive one by one," he whispered knowing the limitations of the MT and glancing over his shoulder, he steadied his body against the outer wall to await the first of the arrivals. "This should prove all too easy." Listening impatiently to the growing hum of the machine, G2 knew that the time had come.

Rising, G2 stood firm yet out of view as the first man shot down to his level, his frame slighty skewed with the narrow slats of the system. Weapon raised, he watched the man peer about the area, appearing frieightened as he looked for any sign of a struggle. He found none.

Unbeknownst to the newest arrival, the struggle was deep within the ship and G2 stood quietly round the corner as the man openly questioned which way to turn. Right would lead him to command, left directly to him.

"What to do, what to do," G2 thought, tsking with man's steps to the right. "Your choice is in error," he whispered, shaking his head in the eerie silence. "At least turning left would have you facing head on."

Stepping quietly at the man's rear just as he reached the Command door, G2 fired a lone blast, hitting him square in the back. "One down," he said triumphantly, caring not who fell slain, his hushed words unheard against the hum of the ship.

"And now," he continued, pivoting back to the MT, the whir of the machine startling him from his darkened thoughts. "Who will we be meeting next?"

***

Selena had listened to the words of her dying friend and sat motionless trying desperately to think of a way to help the others. "It is useless," she whispered looking down to the men on the floor and wringing her hands at her back. "What could I possibly do to help?" Nitaya instantly wailed out in answer.

"Yes," she said, strength beginning to flow within her as she struggled against her restraints. "I am coming, child," she continued, thrashing wildly at the slowly loosening straps, her gaze never leaving the door. "I am coming."

***

Dragging the lifeless body to the Command door, G2 dropped the hefty weight at his feet then turned to await his next victim. "One by one," he whispered, checking his weapon for ammo despite confident there was more than sufficient. Eyeing the gauge at almost full capacity, he slammed the shaft of the meter back into place and hunkered low, wiping the sweat from his brow.

Awaiting the arrival of whoever proved unfortunate enough for the Resistance to come next, G2 smiled with confidence. The enemy was near and once again, his thorough preparations had proven well beyond adequate.

***

Jax stepped onto the platform the moment it returned, prompting the remote device for the quick repeat shot downward. Weapon at the ready as he landed, he found the corridor eerily quiet. "Uvis!" he whispered, eyeing the corridor and awaiting a response. "Uvis!"

With no sign of his friend, Jax quickly shifted, pointing his weapon down the right corridor then the left. Stepping from the platform, he leaned against the inner wall, spying no sign of either enemy or struggle.

"Jax, have you reached Hylin?" Gidoran asked, the portal providing its loud echo against the silent walls from the command above.

"I'm on my way now," he whispered, his words muffled behind the folds of his sleeve. Knowing the boy anxiously awaited his arrival, Jax grit his teeth at Uvis' heroics for straying from the corridor and quickly raced to command.

The weapon was pointed square at his chest as he turned and Jax froze his steps, slowly raising his arms. "You are too late!" the man shouted, teasing the trigger. Raising the weapon to point directly at Jax's eyes however, the man's expression suddenly changed with the ringing out of the lone blast. Surprise, then fear crossed his face in a mere moment before he fell forward.

"Jax," Uvis gasped behind the man, dropping his weakened arm to the floor. "You must get to Command!"

He had no choice. Leaping over the dead intruder then kneeling, Jax grasped hands with his dying friend. "Hang on!" he said, looking from the door to Uvis.

"Hylin needs you. The Resitance needs you," Uvis sputtered, his words broken and soft as he released his friend, clenching his chest. "Jax, you must go now."

Jax stared into his friend's eyes and nodded, knowing he must leave him to breathe his last breath alone. Standing and placing his hand over the prompt, Jax reluctantly opened the door. Unable to turn back, he instead looked forward and with a weary grin, found the now grown man pacing the helm.

***

Selena struggled against her restraints. Thankful to feel them slowly subside, she stared with newfound determination at Nitaya across the cabin. Yanking with all her strength, she pulled furiously at the straps at last feeling them give.

"I am coming, Nitaya," she said, uncaring if the man returned, the clasps falling to the floor behind her seat. Reaching down to release the restraints at her ankles, she disregarded the bleeding lashes at her wrists and at last rose, racing across the cabin to cradle the frightened child.

"I have you," she said, tears of relief streaming down her face as she circled the cabin, the babe safely tucked into the crook of her arm.

"Jovaar," she cried, crossing to kneel at his side. "What can I do?" she pleaded, stroking his damp hair. Nitaya's cries fell to a low whimper, yet as the man she loved struggled to form words that produced no sound, Selena found herself unable to contain her own, Jovaar's eyes having grown ever greener with the passing of time.

"Iaco," she thought, wiping away her tears with the sleeve of her gown. Rising, she hurried to Jovaar's friend across the cabin. "Blink if you can hear me, Iaco," she pleaded, her fingers leaving Nitaya's wee face to caress his cheek. Lying motionless, his head askew on the floor, Selena sighed with relief watching his lids slowly flicker.

"Thank the stars you are still with us," she whispered, her hand shaking, her fingers sliding a loose tendril from his face. "I will chime Command, Iaco. If I can reach Hylin, maybe he will know what to do."

Standing, Selena paced with purpose to the com at the rear of the cabin, holding firm to the precious child knowing that she and the others were relying on her to see them through.

492

"Hylin, it is Selena," she began, trying desperately to steady her breathing, hoping above all hope that he was safe. "Hylin are you there? Has the man found you?"

Jax tilted his head at the newest Resistance pilot, a grin growing wide across his face as he eyed the com. "Shall I?" he asked seeking approval, one brow coyly tilted. Hylin nodded, pride filling him as he watched Jax chime the rear com.

"Selena, this is Jax," he said, joy clear in his voice. "Help has at last arrived."

***

Grasping the com firm in her hands, Selena rejoiced with the news of Jax's arrival. Smiling, she looked down at the child in her arms, noting that although she could not explain the sense of acknowledgement from the small child, Selena knew that somehowNitaya understood.

"Nitaya, they are truly coming," she whispered, replacing the com and trailing her finger down the babe's cheek. "We have made it!"

"Hold on, Selena continued, crossing back through the cabin toward the others. "Jax is on his way, Jovaar! Iaco, did you hear? Sir Gidoran and the others have come to save us!" Pausing half way through the cabin, Selena spied the small portal that sat slightly ajar on the side cabinet, and turned, the image of King Sugin glaring before her.

"You are just a man," she said, lifting the lightweight device to stare directly into his eyes. "And an evil man who sends others to do his bidding. Well, I say this to you now as a citizen under the soon-to-end Sugin reign. You have done nothing but cause despair to the people of our worlds, yet that will be no more! I hold in my hands one of our fated possibles. You may find the others. You may do harm to the others, but this one," she added, hands shaking as she spoke, cradling the child in the crook of her arm. "This one guarantees your reign will end.

Selena watched the image of the King shouting before her, yet for reasons she did not understand, his words remained thankfully unheard. Shaking her head, her smile widening as she

493

refused even the King's glare to whither her strength, Selena prompted the break in signal, closing the evil image from her eyes.

"We are saved, little one, for his powers can no longer hurt us," Selena said, touching her finger to the tip of Nitaya's nose. "Yet now, let us use our own to help save the others."

Forty-Five

Jax arrived at the midship cabin, having left Hylin to confirm their progress with Gidoran, moments after giving Selena the good news of their arrival. "Hang on," he said, straining with the heft of lifting Jovaar from the floor. Once seated, he quickly strapped his commander within the seated restraints to the left of the center aisle and turning, repeated the steps for Iaco to the right.

"We will get them back to Booderban and get them tended to right away," he continued, gesturing to the others with a slight nod. "But what of Agye and Khyra?"

"It is too late," Selena answered, tears rising anew despite the comfort of knowing the babe was safe within her arms. "The man fired at Agye but did not repeat his blast or inject Khyra like the others. The beast simply stabbed at her with a metal rod."

Jax placed his hand on Selena's shoulder sympathetically then turned to head back to Command. Pausing however, he sensed a small trace of movement at his back.

"Selena," he said, crossing to Khyra to reach around the folds of her worn gown, kneeling to better feel the base of her neck. A tense moment passed as Selena watched him lift her seemingly lifeless head.

"Selena," he repeated, newfound hope filling him as he grasped Khyra's face with both hands. "Thank the stars she is still with us."

***

Orvi entered the mid-ship cabin weapon raised the moment Jax closed the med supply tote at Khyra's feet. "I saw the body," he began, gesturing to the main door. "Are there more?"

"No, Selena has informed me there was only one," Jax answered, focusing his attention to Khyra. "She is alive, but we need to return to Booderban as soon as possible. Jovaar and Iaco have been injected with a virus and simple as that would normally prove, I have not seen this particular strain before and have been unable to help them thus far. Selena, although she witnessed the enemy's process could not determine its type. What I do know is that it has numbed their limbs and their eyes are murky and shaded a hazy green. Get back to our ship and order Gidoran to detach then ask Phydin to run a search on the criteria I have given you."

"I will inspect and dispose of the enemy's body along with Agye's," Jax added, his tone serious as he turned to face the body of the young girl. "Then I will sail into port with Hylin. We will not be long at your back."

"Copy that," Orvi answered, scanning the cabin before turning to leave. "Is there enough time?" he asked, pivoting back as he reached the door. Jax merely looked to him, exhaustion evident as he tossed the med tote into a side cabinet amongst some gear.

"We can only hope."

***

Gidoran remained at the helm of his ship, anxiously awaiting a report from Jax below. Ceaselessly watching his monitors, he noted the prompting of the manhole springing to life then nodded thankfully as Orvi returned.

"Jax, Uvis?" he asked, grasping the controls and sailing slowly forward with the added weight, awaiting confirmation.

"I am sorry, Sir," Orvi answered, awkwardly straightening. "Jax is safe with the others and has ordered the detachment. He has requested to remain behind with the boy."

"And Uvis," Gidoran pressed, turning from his station to look directly into Orvi's welling eyes. "He was a good man," he added somberly, recognizing his subordinate's grief. "I did not know him as well as you, but I did know that he was a strong member, eager to serve for our good."

496

"That he was," Orvi answered. Reclaiming his seat at Phydin's rear, he strapped in without returning Gidoran's gaze. "That he most definitely was."

***

The ship detached at the steady hands of Sir Gidoran as Phydin's gaze remained captivated with the image upon his screen, the other craft receding at their backs into the darkness of the Kindawan Sea.

"We will see you at port," he said to Hylin, Gidoran looking on from the helm.

"Copy that," Hylin answered, Jax stomping confidently into Command.

"Stall the ship," he said, placing his hands on hips. The swish of the door closed at his back. "I need to scan and dispose of the bodies."

"Is there time?" Hylin asked, eyeing him questionably over his shoulder. "Orvi said that..."

"I know, but I also know what must be done," Jax continued, sighing and running his hands over his face. "Stall the ship, Hylin. I will return shortly and then we can be on our way."

Not waiting for further comment, Jax turned and paced from Command, wishing it was not his responsibility to deal with the unwanted task. Stepping into the corridor and spying the bodies of both enemy and friend however, he felt the slow of the ship as Hylin followed his order, and knew the time had come to do what must be done. Only then, with the task complete could they truly feel safe.

***

Kneeling next to the lifeless body of the enemy, Jax ran his hands quickly over the man's waist and found nothing but a standard harness. Concentrating on his arms however, he found the small device strapped as expected to his wrist.

"There you are," he whispered, yanking the apparatus free.   "Tracking," he said, nodding as he recognized the common mechanics. "Now this," he added, pausing to peer closer. "What exactly are you?"

Hesitantly depressing the small device, Jax watched the man fizzle, although only sightly before him. "Cloaking," he whispered, shaking his head. "It explains why Hylin missed him."

Quickly restrapping the device to the man's arm, Jax nodded when he found no other anomalies then with everything returned to its place, he dragged the lifeless body to disposal.

Placing both him and his gadgets in position in the cramped hull and prompting the pair of controls, Jax watched as the enemy quickly shot into the deep. His final task however, Jax lowering his head to the cool frame of the ship as he considered what must be done, would prove more than difficult.

With the remains of the enemy washed away into the deep of the sea, Jax returned to the mid-ship cabin to gather Agye. Although he moved quickly for Hylin awaited him at Command, he stepped unneasily as he at last reached the girl, her last burden proving weighty, both physically and mentally filling him with dread.

With Selena busily tending to both the child and the men, silently but guiltily ignoring the lifeless Agye lying restrained in her seat, Jax turned from her penetrating eyes and quickly crossed to Agye's small frame, unclasping her straps. "She only acted as she did out of the safety of her kin," Selena whispered, coddling the child at his back yet refusing to look as he gathered her body. "She proved both loyal and brave until the very end."

Attempting to ignore Jax's task, instead crossing to assist Jovaar, Selena knelt at his side as Jax raised Agye's body to carry her from the cabin. Upon reaching the door however, he paused with Selena's final plea.

"Jax," she said, causing him to turn, his movements filled with surprising ease despite the added weight of her frame. "She should have this." Jax stood motionless as Selena rose, crossing to him.

"Jovaar is unable to truly speak but I was able to make out what he was attempting to say," she continued, raising the wee token before him. "I know that Jovi has worn this his entire life, but he feels that this day Agye has earned it."

Slowly placing Jovaar's medallion about the small girl's neck, Selena nodded to Jax when it was at last in place then stood back as he turned without word. Rebundling the babe and settling her within the crook of her arm, Selena merely stood silent as he carried the girl from the room. The last sight of Agye before her disposal was of her wearing one of Jovaar's most prized possessions.

***

When at last both bodies were set to sea Jax turned and paced to Command, rubbing the aches from his neck as he slumped through the door. "Fire up," he ordered, entering and reclaiming his rear seat.

"Copy that," Hylin answered, turning back to the pilot's station.

"You took care of him?" he questioned, the ship's engines roaring to life, once again free of the joined craft. "But how? How could I have been so careless? I should have found him during my search of the rear. He was here all along!"

"Well now he is sea fodder," Jax groaned, clasping his final restraint into place. Faling silent for a moment, considering what he had said knowing full well that the small girl had now joined the evil man just beyond their walls, he turned to Hylin at last, shaking his head.

"It was a cloaking device, Hylin," he continued, tapping his screen to routinely pull up their route. "I would have missed it, any one of us would have. I promise you though there was nothing you could have done differently. I found the device on the man just before sending him to sea. He must have used it while you searched the rear cabin."

Hylin steered the ship with his newfound ease through the deep and prepared for the upward thrust, at last breathing easier knowing that there was for certain nothing he had overlooked.

"Now," Jax added, sensing Hylin's dissipating tension with the shortening of their depth, the pressure easing as he pushed all thoughts of the young girl wearing Jovaar's medallion from his thoughts. "I believe it is time we joined our friends on Booderban."

***

Selena remained torn as she reclaimed her seat at Jax's warning regardless of the impending thrust into the blue sky she knew awaited them. Nitaya was safe from all harm it was true, yet the others remained in doubt, silent in their own seats across the cabin.

In the end, Selena had been unable to assist poor Agye in her final moments of life, and now she wished for nothing more than to see Jovaar and Iaco's pain ease. A small joy however, did ring through her body knowing that the child would most certainly reach the Royal Committee, although so did a slight fear as she undoubtedly worried about reaching that final destination...wherever it may be.

"Selena," Jax said, prompting the com from the helm. "We are preparing for port. Do not fret," he continued, his voice uncharacteristically sincere. "We are almost there."

"Almost there," she whispered, snuggling Nitaya to her breast. Turning from the child's precious face, she looked out the glass at the approaching lights of Booderban.

"Almost there."

Forty-Six

Phydin stood anxious at the Command entrance to the Central Booderban dock, its aerial loft safely mounted high above the moored ships. Its large mouth of port just off to his right, he watched with uneasy fingers tapping on the single rail to his right as the ship at last sailed into port. Stepping upon the platform and descending to ground level, he quickened his steps to the pre-positioned station to await the arrival of the members.

Knowing the procedures of debarkment yet waiting impatiently despite them, Phydin watched as the firing of the engines at last ceased. As the lone dock hand prompted the lowering of the plank, he folded his arms across his chest, grumbling with the tedious length of the processes. With the hatch at last opening however, his scowl turned to smile, his friend's eager faces emerging into the awakening port. It seemed to be eons since he had glimpsed his commander and although he was anxious to hear the tales of his friend's journey, Phydin nervously awaited his debriefing with Jovaar.

Gidoran was first to descend from his ship, nodding toward his newest friend's uneasy wave. Joining Phydin at the dock and patting his shoulder, each stook watching the hatch slowly open eager to see the members debark.

"Did I miss anything?" he asked, eager to regroup with the arrivals.

"No," Phydin answered, shaking his head without turning. "They should begin their exit any moment now."

Standing side by side yet stepping back with the arrival of the medmen upon the narrow slip, each stood eagerly watching as the group ascended the plank, hurriedly entering through the ship's central hatch. Phydin held up a hand, halting Gidoran's impulsive intrusion.

"Let them do what must be done," he said holding firm, eyeing the trio's entrance. With time passing slowly however, both Phydin and Gidoran's impatience grew. Despite his own eagerness, Phydin once again stopped his friend, the portalcot simultaneously exiting the ship, quickly passing them by.

"Khyra!" Phydin shouted, his stiff demeanor instinctively waning. Gritting his teeth with the sight of her unresponsiveness, this time Gidoran grasped Phydin's shoulder, urging his friend to remain calm.

"She is far from well," the medman said flatly, turning back to tend to his patient's wound.

"No," Phydin thought, his breathing surprisingly labored. Startled by Gidoran's hand returning to his arm, his eyes quickly darted to the emergence of the next portalcot.

"Iaco!" Gidoran shouted, forgetting Phydin's fears as he raced from Khyra to his friend's side. "What did he do to you, Iaco?" Unable to gain a response, Gidoran looked up with annoyance when Hylin and Jax exited the craft full of life, walking briskly down the plank. With the lifting of his hands, the med workers resumed guiding Iaco's cot toward medbay.

"We have been told they will whole-heartedly survive," Jax began, eyeing the fear in Gidoran's eyes. "It will take some time," he added, Phydin motioning for the med crew to move on as he approached the plank. "But they assure us they will be around to order us for onars. Please trust me in this Gidoran. I would be as worried as you if I had not heard so from the medofficer himself." Phydin grasped Jax's hand, unable to control his obvious relief at the news.

"Follow them," he said at last, motioning to the rear door. "We will wait for Jovaar."

Jax nodded and placed his free hand on Gidoran's shoulder. "Hylin did it," he said beaming, shaking his head in disbelief. "You should be amazingly proud."

"I am," Gidoran answered, nodding to Hylin and patting the boy's shoulder. "And I am forever grateful for his role in your return."

Pivoting as one at the sound of the med-officer at long-last descending the plank, each member stood silent as Jovaar emerged on the final portalcot. "I will see you in medbay,"

Phydin whispered, nodding to both Hylin and Jax to continue on. Once alone, he turned to his commander, raised his chin and walked confidently toward the bustling medcrew.

"It is so good to see you, Sir," Phydin began, nervously clearing his throat. "I know you cannot speak, but forgive me for I must say this."

"Hear me," he added gulping, his hands shaking against the hovering cot. "I will follow you anywhere, Jovaar Savius and...I am sorry. My life is now yours. You must be strong. You must for the sake of the child see this through."

Gidoran approached silently yet said nothing as Phydin spoke his peace and instead waited patiently for his turn with his old friend. "You will recover," he began, doing his best to appear confident when they were at last alone. Chuckling, he lowered to whisper so that only Jovaar could hear. "Old men die hard."

Gidoran thought he spied a glimpse of a smile, yet knew in Jovaar's current state that it was too good to be true. Instead, laying his hand briefly on his sholder, Gidoran straightened, nodding for the medcrew to lead his oldest friend from the docks and to the bay.

***

Medbay was alive with the newest arrivals and Selena stood off to the side unnoticed as the attendants scanned Nitaya for any damage to her fragile system. Khyra's cot had been placed at the opposite end of the room and several others were seeing to her wounds, so many so that Selena could not see beyond their backs. The elder had yet to awaken and although Selena had been reassured by a steward of her stability, she remained fearful that Khyra would never fully recover.

Jovaar and Iaco had been brought to a special sealed off room across the corridor from where she now stood. The separate facility would not allow visitors of any kind, yet the med-officer had sworn to her that they would in fact be able to heal them in time. Even with his confidence however, Selena remained anxious and seeing she had no other options, she did what she could to concentrate on the small child rather than the worry she held for the others.

"She is doing well," the attendant began as Selena neared, running the machine slowly over Nitaya's small body. "The scan should be completed momentarily."

"Thank you," Selena answered, the first sign of ease appearing on her face.

"There," the attendant added, prompting for the device to recede into the ceiling above. "We will of course keep the child for observatory purposes and you are more than welcome to look in on her at any time, but I pray that you understand that the med-officer will want to monitor her for quite some time."

"That I do understand," Selena answered nodding, inwardly struggling with the rear, closed door. "And I thank you. However, will I be able to visit the others soon?"

"The med-officer should be with you momentarily to answer any questions," the attendant answered, turning back to the child. Nodding and trickling her finger down the cheek of the now resting babe, Selena knew there was nothing more she could do for her, that she was in the best of hands. Spying the other stewards busily attending to Khyra with no hope of gaining access passed their seemingly joined shoulders, Selena turned anxiously to the sealed outer door. Crossing through the crowded cabin she set out in search of news of the others.

***

The door remained closed. Looking both left and right for someone to appear in the empty corridor to give her news of Jovaar and Iaco, Selena grumbled, attempting to release the controls on her own. The door stood stubbornly firm in its place. Resigned and closing her eyes, she touched the brow of her head to its cold frame saying a heartfelt prayer for the safety of the one she loved and her newest friend. Deep in thought, she did not hear the arrival of the others.

"Selena," Gidoran began, approaching hesitantly, Phydin, Jax, Orvi and Hylin trailing at his back. "I spoke with the med-officer just moments ago. All is going well but it will be some time before we are able to see them."

"Khyra's condition has stabilized," he added, attempting to draw her near with good news. "We must rest, Lena," he whispered, using the name that only Jovaar usually spoke. "Jax has been given instructions to where we can rest for the night. Come. There is nothing more we can do."

Selena knew Gidoran's words to be true yet leaving even the corridor beyond their individual struggles seemed so hard. Giving in reluctantly despite the yearning of her heart however, she raised her head and looked into the tired eyes of her mere four friends that remained.

"If you insist," she agreed, dipping her head into Gidoran's chest. "But they will send word if anything changes?"

"Of course, Selena," he answered, placing his hands on her shoulders, the others standing hushed at his back, heads tipped. "We have all waited a long time to get to this point in our journey. Surely we can wait a while longer."

Following his lead, Selena slowly made her way down the corridor, glancing back a final time at the closed door. "Just a while longer," she whispered, reassuring her own fears and turning, smiled at Gidoran's tired face. Nodding to the others who had done so much, Selena walked with her friends to quarters.

***

Although small, their cabins proved comfortable and the Resistance members required little effort as all were set at ease with the hospitality of their newest host base. All knew that their journey was not yet over and that a quiet rest is what they sorely needed. With each member settling into their cots in their respective quarters, Selena sat, watching her nursemaid busy herself, pulling her down cover back and placing her few things in a small cabinet off to the side. Her robe of pale blue flowed swiftly at her ankles.

"Rest well, ma'am," she whispered, bearing obvious sympathy for the beautiful, tired girl. "I will come for you once there is word of Sir Savius and his friend."

"I thank you," Selena answered rubbing her arms. At last giving into her aches, she laid down upon her cot. "I thank you for all that you have done."

Nodding, the woman merely closed the door, leaving Selena alone in her cabin. Folding the warm coverlet over her body and slowly closing her eyes, the images of all she had experienced danced wildly against her heavy lids. The images however, proved brief, their fight unable to withstand the onars of ache on her limbs as sleep quickly claimed her.

***

The men shared a cabin across the corridor from Selena and quickly claimed their cots, their nursemaid stowing their belongings in the far cabinet. Holding true to his word, Jax sat down and pulled the Intels from his tote for the promised Rodaous game with the new man of their group.

"Hylin," he said his grin widening, welcomingly patting his cot. "I believe I owe you a game."

"Yes!" Hylin answered, youthful excitement easily returning to his tone. Rising he crossed to Jax with wide eyes.

"Let it sit," Phydin interrupted, removing his boots and laying down on his own bunk. "The morrow brings the last leg of this journey and I need you both well rested. Without the assistance of Jovaar and Iaco, we will rely heavily on you both."

"Rest now," he stressed, rising up on his elbows. "You can play your game once we reach Mizar."

"Mizar?" Hylin questioned, regathering the Intels and handing them to Jax.

"Yes," Phydin answered, reclining his head to stare at the beautiful view of colors upon the ceiling. "I believe you all have earned the right to know of the final destination. Now I insist you rest. We will gather the others and leave at the break of day."

Gidoran smiled, pleased his friend was at last confident giving orders. "Phydin," he said, rolling his head to the right, kicking the bundle of covers at his feet to the floor. "Jovaar would be proud."

Phydin nodded gratefully at Gidoran's confidence. Prompting the darkness yet saying nothing, he lay wide awake pondering his fate. The others however, fell quickly to sleep about him.

***

Selena awoke startled in the darkness, the ringing of the chime resounding throughout the cabin. "Yes?" she asked, uncertain of her surroundings, the lights about her slowly returning with her words.

"Selena," the familiar voice began. "I am sorry if I frightened you. We are waiting for you at medbay and are prepared to leave within the hazon."

"I thank you, Phydin," she answered recognizing his serious tone, the colorful images of flora dancing above her head

"Ma'am," the nursemaid said softly, entering and crossing the cabin. "I just received word of your imminent departure. We will need to ready you at once."

"I know and I thank you," Selena answered, openly stretching. Standing from the cot, she quickly disregarded both the offered tray of nourishment and the ceaseless wonders of the ceiling. "The others are waiting and I must be on my way."

***

The men stood impatient at the entrance to medbay, the door standing open to the sealed section of the room as Selena hastily approached. "Can we see them?" she asked, breathlessly claiming Gidoran's hands.

"They have transported Khyra and Jovaar to the ship," he answered, nodding to the others who had already heard the latest update of the wounded. "We are now waiting for Iaco to be transported and then we will be off."

Selena's disappointment was evident. "They are all stable, Lena," Gidoran said reassuringly, sensing her worry and placing his hands on her shoulders. "You must however prepare yourself for their slow recovery. Jovaar and Iaco are awake but their speech is shallow and any movement has yet to occur." He paused with the arrival of Iaco's cot in the corridor.

"Iaco," Selena whispered, crossing to him and grasping his hand. Although his eyes were less green and more their true blue, the evil pale color remained.

"Hold on," she added, glancing over her shoulder to Gidoran, the medcrew leading the cot toward the docks. "You knew of his tone of eyes, did you not? You did not seem as startled as I."

"We did yes, Selena, but forgive me, it is time," Phydin interrupted, gesturing over her shoulder to Gidoran.

"Jax, take Hylin and Orvi and ready the ship for detachment." Nodding without further prompting, the pair silently trailed Jax's lead, pacing slowly down the corridor.

"At last," Selena said, turning to face Gidoran, Iaco's cot at last from view leaving the pair alone in the corridor. "I do believe that although we have many hazon...perhaps onars of struggles ahead, I also believe that the time has come for us to see Nitaya safely home."

***

Gidoran and Phydin gave their thanks to the Resistance members at dock, saving the last for First Officer Zinu. "I wish there was something we could do to repay you for your kindness," Phydin said, claiming her hand. Officer Zinu accepted his gesture and merely smiled, nodding to Gidoran.

Raising a hand in farewell one final time, each of the men said their good-byes to Booderban before turning to walk the plank side by side, climbing aboard their newest ship. With those of Booderban behind them, Gidoran nodded briefly to his comrades as the entered Command before turning and claiming the helm. Strict with formalities, Phydin crossed the cabin to see to the final needs of the crew. When confident they were properly in place, he settled into his station, prompting his panel.

"An update," he said, waiting for Jax's reply. Strapping in the last of the restraints, he looked up to his comrades, eyes furrowed as he awaited a response.

"All systems online," Hylin answered, causing all in the cabin to smile.

"It is nice to have you with us, Hylin," Gidoran added, turning to face the boy.

"All systems online," he repeated, pivoting back to the stick. "Hylin, fire the ship. Ordering detachment in 5, 4, 3, 2, 1, detach

The crew sat silent with the small ship's swift retreat, Booderban becoming yet another blur in the distance. Its infamous gravitational pull had not affected their sail and Selena could not have been happier, her eyes filling with familiar tears. Despite the boisterous lights and sounds of yet another craft acquired for their journey, she thankfully snuggled the child at the rear of Command.

"It is foolish," Jax began reluctantly, staring out the side glass at the diminishing planet. "But I wish we could have remained longer. There was so much left to see, so much left to learn. They proved the most hospitable of all of our stays, don't you agree?"

"Perhaps another time," Phydin answered, Gidoran rerouting their outlined path. "Just thank the stars that they were there when we needed them...and that thanks to them soon both Jovaar and Iaco will be well."

With their ship now in route, all settled in for the next leg of their journey, both weary and eager for it to be their last. With the next request given by his elder, Hylin punched the hyperdrive as ordered, all about him smiling with his newfound ease of the controls.

Gidoran, unturning but most proud of them all, relished the moment silently, proud of the one he had brought from the lanes of Yani to the midst of providing a possible. Racing with his younger's guiding hand, he knew he did not need to question Hylin's coordinates and instead grasping frim to the stick, raced his surviving friends with confidence through the open skies.

Forty-Seven

Darkness had fallen over Mizar, its fated Day Circles having completed yet another trilogy cycle, completing the next steps in their endless dance across the sky. Arriving safely within the black, shielding cover, the ship sailed onward with Gidoran's confident hand toward Oasis Nyllo. Soaring high above the dunes of sand, the scattered lights of those below shaped a creative welcome upon the darkened scape for those above. The member's ship, at last reaching the tree lined port sailed over their inviting glow. Overwhelming yet quaintly subtle, Gidoran maneuvered a smooth, uneventful landing.

"At last," he sighed, gratefully stalling the craft. Thankful that the final trek had proven smooth, his responsibility for the safety of the possible now somewhat waned. Finalizing the routine steps of the landing procedures, Gidor saved the release of his restraints for the last. His arms surprisingly ached.

Rubbing the now obvious tensely, strained muscles, he pivoted slowly in his seat. Admittingly, he was not surprised to find his friends sitting motionless, appearing both tired from the long journey and sad with the exact moment of realization that their time together would soon be over. Phydin, sensing he should say something in Jovaar's absence, released his own restraints and turned from his forward station.

"We have accomplished the impossible," he began uncharacteristically nervous, loosening the cloak at his neck and clearing his throat. "Each of us has faced joys and regretfully losses, yet that is what we have come to expect if all members are to ultimately overcome the Sugin reign. You have all made me proud to be a member of the Resistance, yet as one we must face the realities of what now lays ahead. We cannot all remain upon Mizar that is something we all regret yet know to be certain. It was inevitable, the ultimate of our sacrifice, the connection growing with the one yet knowing there to be more. Accepting our fate does not make it easy, yet remember that Selena holds a precious possible in her arms, and that Nitaya would not be alive without the courage displayed by each and every one of you."

"Please come, my friends," he added, slowly rising and crossing to the hatch, turning to offer his hand. "Most certainly they are waiting."

Motioning for Jax to come first to the opened hatch, Phydin patted his friend's shoulder in time with his steps. Jax turned in welcome to face the cool air of the night. Pausing however, he looked from the hopeful lights and smiled, wanting to share his moment with Hylin across the cabin. His joy somewhat fading, Jax empathized with the boy who for the first time appeared less eager to rise, his eyes unable to contain their sadness as he too toyed with the last strap of his restraints.

"Hylin, you must see this," he said, extending his hand to his newest friend. Eyes instantly brightening with the gesture, he rose and crossed to his comrade at the hatch. At once feeling the cool breeze upon his face, Hylin looked out with awe into the twinkling lights, thankful to be sharing this moment with his friend. Before them, the landing strip was filled with the Mizan people, each holding lightrods and ringing cheers for the arrival of one.

"Now do you see?" Jax asked, clasping tightly to Hylin's shoulder. "Do you see the importance of what we have done? We have brought the possible! The galaxy will surely feel what we have done."

"All is right, Hylin," he added, jostling the boy's hair. "All is right!"

Gidoran joined Phydin at their backs, beaming with both pride in their accomplishments and awe of what was to come, his eyes alight with the glowing gifts of the awaiting Mizans. As one, sensing the hope in their welcome, the members huddled at the hatch knowing they had infact altered the future.

"Hold your heads high, my friends," Gidoran said, interrupting their somber silence within the exit, the Mizan cheers ringing out below. "The time has come for us all to rejoice."

***

Trailing Gidoran's steps to the midship cabin, Selena and Nitaya were the last to step from the craft. As prepared as she had believed herself to be for the joyous crowd, those too who had waited onars for this moment, she could not help but be startled by their cheers.

Gripping the narrow opening of the hatch with her left hand, she clutched firm to the folds of Nitaya's blanket with her right. Pain immediately filling her stiffened fingers however, she looked down to the babe and eased her grip, only then smiling at the untroubled child in her hands. With the dancing flickers of light emitted from the hundreds of high rods throughout the oasis, the roars of joy growing with her descending the plank, Selena paused to relish the moment, only resuming her steps with the calls from her friends below urging her forward.

"What of Jovaar, Iaco and Khyra?" she shouted over the din, accepting Gidoran's offered hand.

"Look," he answered, pointing to additional medhands skirting the Mizan's toward the rear hatch. "The three will be well tended, Selena, and so we must relinquish their care and make our way through the crowd, at long last crossing over the Falen Bridge in their honor."

"Yes," he added, smiling at the dazed look of her eyes, his palm opening to claim her mall hand. "Even *I* know of the path the child must take. Come, Selena. The members of the Royal Committee are waiting."

"The Royal Committee?" Selena asked, nervously running her free hand over her hair. "I could not face them now," she shouted above the din, shaking her head and stepping back within the crowd, uncertain. "I am not ready! I could not possibly face the Royal Committee in this state. Just look at the condition of my gown! Perhaps if we were to…"

"You are more ready than you know," Gidoran interrupted, reclaiming her hand and parting the tear-filled crowd, urging her toward the fated bridge. "Lena," he whispered, leaning close so that only she could hear. The twinkling lights of Mizar danced vibrantly above their heads.

"You understand as I do that the possible must rightfully claim her place?"

"But of course I do," Selena answered, looking down to the child, all other eyes upon the pair. "It is just that we have searched so long, we have traveled so long, I prayed that this moment would come but I..."

"We are here with you," Hylin interrupted, nodding confidently to Gidoran, Phydin and the others close at their backs. "If you will allow me, Selena, I would be honored to lead you."

Selena's nerves left her. Looking into Hylin's eyes, then Gidoran's, she knew at once the moment had truly arrived. Turning to accept the welcoming embrace of the nearest Mizan, Selena smiled, tears welling in her eyes as she shared the moment with the woman and the cooing babe for nothing could compare to the joy the strangers shared...knowing a possible had indeed arrived.

Looking forward to the boisterous patting of hands upon Hylin's back however, Selena knew they must move forward for many still awaited their arrival. Unable to contain her smile as the aging boy's led the way, Selena welcomingly reclaimed Gidoran's arm. Raising her chin and taking a deep breath, knowing that they were at last truly safe, Selena walked confidently at his side toward the first fated passage of Nitaya's Acceptance.

***

The newest arrivals crossed the Falen Bridge one by one, Gidoran releasing Selena's hand at the last for she had been destined to bring forth the child on her own. With respect, the crowd at their backs had slowed as Gidoran led Selena to the edge of the bridge, watching in awe as she took her first steps with the child onto the once thriving tree.

At last ceremoniously claiming their places within the aligned row, Selena and the child at its center, the seven members of the Royal Committee sat stoically opposite the lane, the makeshift hall erected for the historic event amongst the sydadis and umperti. Although joy certainly filled their hearts, they would not ever, out of the importance of the occasion, let it be shown, and instead remained patient until the last of the members arrived.

"It is alright," Gidoran whispered, urging her forward into the row's center as she glanced back at the smiling faces. "They know as we all do that this is a sacred occasion. We all know that it is saved for her. We are only present because Martus and Wynin could not be. Head high as you were taught, Lena. This is a moment never to forget."

Opposite the bridge and standing aligned in the center of the lane, Gidoran claimed his own position in line once Selena was in place then paused, awaiting the approving acknowledgement from the Committeee. When the last of the crowd's cheering ceased and the sounds of the night once again danced softly amongst the air, the prominent Sir Gowdar stood.

"We have patiently remained here for some time," he began, his voice confident and low, raising his hands high before the proud members and Mizans. "Yet as we all know, there is no time too great for what we are about to witness."

"Please," he gestured, requesting Selena to bring the child forth. "It will not be this eve for us to determine if the babe you hold will rule the throne, yet as custom, she will be annointed as a possible. It is on our order that she will live amongst the Mizans, a child not unlike the others in the dwellings. She will not know of her greater purpose, or more importantly of her newfound royal status. She will instead live free, free yet protected as a child of an Elitian so deserves."

"You have brought her here to her home and your losses have not gone unnoticed," Sir Gowdar continued, passing his gaze over each individual member in line. "And your courage in flight gives status to your name which I now bring forth for all to hear. Let it be known from this moment forward that your names hold title and therefore so will you heritage. We give a moment for those you have lost, yet rejoice in the knowledge that their passing has cause for great joy. Please, step forth with the child."

"Her name?" Sir Gowdar questioned, claiming the slumbering babe from Selena's arms. Softly speaking her answer, Selena stood back in awe. Releasing the child so that Sir

Gowdar could raise her for all to see, she at last ceased the wringing of her hands, confidently lowering them to her side.

"She is knows as Nitayatinus Savius!" he said, his tenor words booming loud with joy for all to hear. "Rejoice, my friends, for I now hold your first possible!"

**

The crowd continued their celebration below the darkened sky, waving and congratulating the weary, yet awakening members when they were at last offered to clear the sacred bridge. It was indeed an evening to remember.

Small lights littered the shrouded area amongst the greens, in entrances of the Oasis homes and in the hands of its revelers. Music, filling their ears from a berth tucked off in the distance amongst the fauna brought lightened steps to them all as a lilt of hand made instruments played its tune of hope by joyous lips. Drink was passed, nourishment proved plenty, and the Mizan's danced in the open lane, their worries ceased with the arrival of one.

Having remained in their seats, the Royal Committee at last received the eager Mizans in line, their first possible lying snug in the crook of Sir Gowdar's arm. Selena, standing behind the arced row of Royals, eyes never straying far from her dear Nitaya, wished that she could enjoy the festivities with the other members however the earlier result of her leaving the babe's side and Jovaar's current condition lingered amongst her thoughts. She had been informed that the medhands had taken him along with Iaco and Khyra to a hidden location beneath the ground on which she now stood. She was not certain of its exact point of entrance, yet with Sir Gowdar's assurances, did entrust their care in the hands of her newest friends.

"If only I could speak to him," she thought, crossing round the row to address Sir Gowdar. "Your highness," she said, politely crossing before the next Mizan in line, slowly lowering before her elder. "I beg for you to excuse my absence but I feel I must see to the condition of the others. Only in your hands do I feel safe to leave the child."

"You are an honorable woman," he answered, laying his hand upon Selena's shoulder. "Nitayatinus is blessed with your presence both in physical and in mind, as am I. Go, dear girl," he added, slowly waving his hand. "As we know, she will never be far from your heart."

"I am humbled," she answered, tipping her head to her hands in custom with leaving the presence of royalty. Returning the smile of her most respected elder, Selena rose, freeing her hands with his nod of aproval. Reaching out and touching Nitaya's face, Selena whispered her thanks to Sir Gowdar and returning his nod, quickly ran off in search of Jovaar.

***

"It is amazing," Hylin said, Selena having found him near the source of the lilting music, quickly dismissing the festivities to question him on the secret location below. "Not many are allowed to enter, yet since I was one to help bring Nitaya to Mizar, I was granted entrance with only a wee bit of persuasion."

"This way!" he shouted over the beginning notes of the next tune, gesturing for her to follow with a giant wave. "It is not far."

Racing as quickly as possible through the dense crowd, the revelers at last thinned as the pair reached the outskirts of the lane. Pacing down a narrow dim-lit path through the greens, the lilt left behind a mere whisper at their backs, they at last arrived at what Selena assumed must be the entrance.

"They call it the Crossing Door," Hylin said, proud of his newfound knowledge. Beaming with energy and prompting the release to the side of the cave-like structure, he gestured for Selena to wait as the hidden door slowly opened before them.

"Life floor, sublevel two," he told her, his words echoing against the hardened walls as they descended the bright, cool staircase. "I have not been there yet myself, but I was told exactly where Jovaar and the others would be." Claiming the steps in pairs and reaching the first level side by side, Hylin chuckled at Selena's ability to keep up and prompted the next door, allowing his eler to peer out so he could watch her reaction,

516

her face contorting as expected with the view of an odd series of the same.

"Which way?" she asked, grimacing with the number of barricades. "You said Sublevel Two. Why are we stopping now?"

"This is the amazing part," Hylin answered, racing ahead down the corridor, only stopping to place his face oddly against the wall. "I only have to…"

"Hylin, I do not understand and my patience is running thin," Selena interrupted, catching both her breath and the boy. "I left Nitaya to the care of Sir Gowdar and the Royal Committee only to briefly visit with Jovaar. Now, please stop this foolishness at once!"

"Just wait," Hylin said, unturning. Staring straight into a narrow slit in the wall that Selena could not have found without the boy's prior knowledge, Hylin held his breath, Selena standing in awe, eager to see what he appeared to find so interesting. Unable to contain her curiousity a moment longer, she reached out to touch the walled obstacle, only to quickly grasp firm to Hylin's shoulder as the floor beneath her trembled to life.

"I got clearance not long ago!" Hylin shouted, raising his arms wide at the newly-formed entrance. "Of course bringing forth a Possible has its advantages. Selena, welcome to Sublevel Two!"

Selena stood in awe at the expanse that had opened at her feet. Shaking her head and turning to Hylin, she accepted his extended hand and descended the next staircase at his side, at last reaching the lower level. Left with only one option, albeit its entrance firmly closed, Selena smiled warmly at the boy.

"This is it," Hylin said, placing his face against the lone door. Immediately jumping to the side and clinging desperately to the wall, fearing the floor would once again give, Selena sighed with relief, her cheeks blushing as the door merely opened in approval. Racing before Hylin through the entrance of the large room, its center shrouded in an odd, opaque cloth, Selena searched over the brightly-lit space, her eyes at last falling upon Jovaar, Iaco, and Khyra. Completely surrounded by androids, Selena's fear instantly returned for her friends.

"What is happening?" she asked, approaching the center of the room. Reaching high to push the opaque cloth from her view, Selena immediately stepped back as an imposing android appeared from her left, grimacing.

"Clearance number," he said flatly, his rather large arms folding at his chest. Selena did not know how to respond. "Clearance number," it repeated, taking a large step forward.

"Clearance number J0728," Hylin said, proudly reaching her side. The android, remaining firm in its close-quartered space openly scanned its database. Accepting the information, he turned his head slightly right and down to answer Selena, its tone remaining flat and unfeeling.

"The woman is recovering as expected, the first male is gaining movement and the other is showing no clear sign of emergence," he said, pivoting back to his duties.

"What did you say?" Selena asked, yanking on the being's arm. "Which male? Exactly who are you referring to?" Selena's anger grew, her eyes flitting about the room as the android simply repeated the bland information.

"I must see them!" she shouted, grabbing the droid's shoulders, its frame unmoving against her small hands. "I demand to see them now!"

"The time has yet to arrive," the droid answered, turning back to his panel at the center of the room. Proving finished with the intruding pair, Selena's eyes welled at the being's back. Shaken, she looked to Hylin for an answer.

"I do not know," he said, reading the worry in her eyes and shaking his head. "Let us just watch for a sign. Surely we will see who moves and then we will know."
Struggling with hope for Jovaar and guilt for Prince Iaco, Selena looked helplessly away from Hylin. Wringing her hands against the worn folds of her gown, only stopping when he claimed her hand, the pair stood silent together, staring through the clear cloth for a sign.

***

Iaco moved. It was slow but clear for all to see. Iaco raised his arm at the approaching android carrying nourishment.

Selena now knew that it was Jovaar who was not improving and tears immediately flooded her eyes with worry. Hylin released her hand, instinctively placing his arm about her shoulders. Torn, Selena was thankful that Prince Iaco would heal, but what of her Jovi? Guilt filled her for her thoughts, and shame crept into her heart.

"I truly am thankful, Iaco," she whispered, hoping that Hylin had not heard, wiping the trickling drop from her cheek. "But what of Jovaar?"

Not waiting for approval, Selena quickly stepped toward the clear cloth. Yanking it aside, she ignored the central droid and crossing the small space, skirting a pair of medhands to stand next to the man she secretly loved.

"I am here," she whispered, gently claiming Jovaar's hand. "No, I am not leaving," she said sternly, waving the medhands and android aside. Watching her frustration at the droid's angered insistence Hylin stepped between the pair, ordering the droid to leave them.

"I will take care of the others," he added, turning from Selena to face the newest approaching pair. "Just take your time."

"Jovi, can you hear me?" she asked, her tears cascading from her reddened cheeks to his hand. "Blink Jovi, please tell me that you can hear me!" Waiting, she saw the slow motion of his eyes.

"I need you!" she pressed, urging her beloved for more. "We all need you. Please Jovaar, you must be strong!"

Rising from his cot yet not releasing his hand, Selena stood shaking as a single tear fell from the corner of his eye. She could not contain her laugh. "It seems we are both crying," she whispered, wiping the tiny droplet from his face with the back of her hand. "But there is no time for tears, my love. I promise I will not leave your side until you are well."

"What is it?" Selena asked, peering over her shoulder at the approaching woman, surprised one was able to escape Hylin's reach. "Why is he not improving as the others?"

"The injection remained in his system much longer," the woman answered, placing her hand on Selena's shoulder. "We are uncertain as to how much damage it has caused. All we can do now is wait. We are ever hopeful, yet you must be prepared for the worst. His speech will surely return in time, but we are not as certain of his movement."

Selena gathered her strength then looked back to Jovaar, the woman patting her shoulder before leaving them to their privacy. "We will do this together," she began, swallowing back the tears that threatened to return. Reclaiming Jovaar's hand, Selena leaned down to his face, looking deep into his opening, pale eyes.

"Together," she whispered, smiling bravely for them both. "Together, Jovaar Savius, you and I can do anything."

　　　***

Time passed slowly. Selena kept her promise and visited with Jovaar as often as she could, but there was much excitement astir above ground and her presence was often required elsewhere throughout Nyllo. The Royal Committee was meeting the next eve to discuss Nitaya's future prior to their departure and the oasis was abuzz with the news for it was rare in anyone's lifetime to bear witness to such an event.

Khyra was recovering well considering the degree of her injury and looking over at her now, Selena could not help but smile. Her elder was quite rude to the androids, ordering them about and frazzling their systems. Obviously Khyra enjoyed outwitting the multitude and therefore all were pleased that she would be able to leave the sublevels soon.

Iaco too had greatly improved. Every hazon would bring greater movement to his limbs and it brought joy to Selena's heart. Ebbing her earlier guilt-filled thoughts, she was truly thankful that he was now sitting and taking nourishment on his own. He smiled over to her now, raising his hand to her as if understanding.

"I will be just a moment, Jovi," she whispered, gently kissing his cheek. Rising from her familiar post, she crossed the large sterile room to Iaco's side. "You are doing so well," she said, sitting on the edge of his cot.

"I feel almost whole again," he answered, seeing the pain behind her attempted smile.

"He will come through, Selena," he continued, placing his hand upon hers. "It just takes time. Has the Committee met then?" he asked, attempting to change both the subject and her somber mood.

"Next eve," she answered, glancing over to Jovaar. "I so wanted him to be there."

"I know that you did," Iaco answered, wiping the stray morsels from his chest. "But if you would not mind a stand-in, albeit a temporary one of course, it would be my honor to escort you to the proceedings."

"But, Iaco," she questioned, rising and stepping back to look him over. "Are you certain you would be strong enough?"

"At this rate I should be walking with the rising of the first day circle," he answered, raising his arms in triumph. "Shall I go with you then?"

"Of course," Selena answered, beaming. "I would be greatly honored." The machines chimed loud across the room. Startled, Iaco and Selena quickly turned to the noise, their smiles fading.

"Medofficer," the android shouted, rising from his central post. "We need you!"

Leaving Iaco, Selena hurried to Jovaar's cot, the angered droid attempting to block her from his side. "Let me through!" she shouted, struggling against the strength of the being.

"Let her pass," the medofficer said firmly, passing the scan over Jovaar's frame.

"Ma'am," he continued somberly, eyeing her skirt the last of the masses. "The time has come." Fear soared through Selena as she searched Jovaar's eyes.

"Time for what?" she screamed, fearfully looking to the man, her entire being shaking with fear. "What did the scan tell you? What is wrong with him? What are you saying?"

"I can speak, Lena," Jovaar said, hoarsely but clear.

"Oh Jovi!" she cried, forgetting the others and leaning in for an embrace.

"The worst is over," the medofficer interrupted the reunion, clearing his throat at her back. "Movement will follow soon." Selena raised her head from Jovaar's chest, thanking him with her eyes.

"You did it, Jovi," she whispered, tears of joy cascading to her smile, her fingers dancing over his cheek, over his lips, uncaring who witnessed her love. "I always knew you would!"

***

Khyra was cleared to leave the sublevels soon after the excitement of Jovaar's newfound recovery, and Selena joyously accepted her hand, assisting her friend slowly to Jovaar's cot. "Stay strong," Khyra said, nodding confidently at Jovaar. "And do not worry. I will see to the others above…with the help of this little man, of course," she added, ruffling Hylin's hair.

"Thank you, Ma'am," Jovaar answered, grinning thankfully with his words.

"Khyra will do now, Jovaar," she answered, shaking her head. "Khyra will most certainly do. How often must I need to remind you?"

Selena and Jovaar watched Hylin assist Khyra through the now open medbay, its clear cloths long forgotten, hidden somewhere in the recesses above. Turning back at its entrance, all smiled and waved as the pair passed through the main door toward the ground above.

"She is back to her old self," Selena said, turning back to Jovaar, her eyes glowing with joy.

"And soon I will be," he answered, reaching out slowly and touching her arm.

"Jovi!" she shouted, jumping back from his cot. "Your hand!"

"It will not be long now, Lena," he answered, thankful that her love was his. "I could not have done this without you."

Iaco stood back, smiling and secretly listening to their love-filled words. With the impending festivities above however, he at last stepped forward to intervene. "It seems my time has come as well," he said, laying his hand upon Jovaar's shoulder. "We must head up to the Committee. I promise to take good care of her, Jovi."

"Just not too good, Prince Iaco," Jovaar answered, sneering in jest at his trusted friend.

"Go, Lena," he continued, urging her from his cot. "I have good people tending and my movements will only increase more rapidly now." Selena knew she must leave, but felt torn that Jovaar could not go with them.

"Go," he pressed, smiling proudly. "It is Nitaya's time."

Leaning down, Selena pressed her lips softly to Jovaar's then smiled warmly before rising to leave. Iaco nodded to his friend before trailing after her.

"Your time has come, little one," Jovaar whispered, thinking of the beautiful child of Martus he had helped save and the future she would rightfully hold, perhaps saving them all. "Your time has most certainly come."

Forty-Eight

Having reclaimed their stance across the Falen Bridge, the Mizan's stood anxiously hushed as the Royal Committee patiently awaited in their given seats against the backdrop of pinus and riolus. The ceremonial arrival of Selena and the child was at last upon them. Sir Gowdar, dressed in his finest splendor, took notice of the lowered words of the people and waved his hand to bring silence to the oasis as Selena approached, his arms open wide in greeting.

Passing slowly by the wonderous falls with Iaco's guided hand, Selena tipped her head in thanks to the people of the oasis, only then releasing her friend's now fully-healthy lead. Turning, she bowed with tradition to the additional members, gently patting Nitaya's small frame before standing full before Sir Gowdar. Shaking her head at the formalities however, no longer able to contain her joy, Selena reached out to embrace her elder, looking from Sir Gowdar to Nitaya who remained peaceful in the safety of her arms. Unable to hide her smile, Selena straightened and stepped back, gently handing Nitaya to the awaiting female royal.

"This way," Sir Gowdar said, seriousness filling his tone despite Selena's display of affection. Gesturing curtly for her to follow, Selena bit her cheek in an attempt to shield her display of joy.

The remaining committee members rose formally as one, waiting respectfully before their seats as Selena and Sir Gowdar passed, tipping their heads at their equal member carrying Nitaya close at their backs. Walking slowly across the Falen Bridge, the Mizans respectfully retreated with their approaching steps, eagerly allowing the royal's passage.

Nearing the staircase encased in the low mist and ascending without words, Selena noted the door to the home above the falls stood invitingly open. Watching Sir Gowdar enter, she smiled, folding her hands as her elder greeted a man she did not know.

"Please come," the man said, motioning for the others to enter. Standing back, he nodded warmly, his home soon overflowing with royalty.

"Selena, if you will reclaim the child," Sir Gowdar said, nodding to the female royal. Turning yet remaining silent, Selena reclaimed the child from the woman's arms.

"At last," Sir Gowdar continued, appearing to shield a wisp of a smile. "At long last we shall begin."

Nodding her thanks and claiming the offered seat in the center of the home's main room, Selena wrapped Nitaya tightly in her small blanket. Smiling, she slowly turned to face the others.

"The time has come for the order of the Royal Committee to be carried out," Sir Gowdar began, intertwining his fingers at his chest, the remaining six royals standing confidently at his back. "Nitayatinus is indeed a strong child and I have foreseen that she will prosper in this glorious place of peace beneath the Quito Falls. It has been determined that Jovan and Lydra Riolle will rear her as their own in their home here, above the misting falls. Nitayatinus has infact been given the gift of caretakers as well as a sibling in Norelle Riolle. She will grow with the graces of the stars as other possibles are located and brought forward throughout the galaxy. It has been determined that fifteen onars, passing by with the day circles above, will be the limit to this quest for the possibles that remain lost. At that time, Nitayatinus will be brought forth, as will the others, to be filled with the knowledge of her legacy."

Selena could not find comfort in her seat, struggling with the words Sir Gowdar had spoken. She had known all along that this time would come, yet she could not contain the welling in her eyes with the realization of parting with the child. Peering down into her wee, smiling eyes, Selena's heart wrenched knowing their time together would soon be over.

"Shall I not remain, Sir Gowdar?" she asked, pleading with him with her eyes. Although she knew the question to be foolish, she could not help but plead the words.

"The search goes on, dear Selena," he answered flatly, his tone firm yet familiar. "As does your task for the Resistance. This you know, as I do, to be true."

"But Palle!" she wailed, Nitaya joining her cries with a slight whimper of her own, Selena straightening defiantly upon her seat. "I simply cannot do as you ask."

"You shall, Selena," he answered, containing his own anguish as he watched his child suffer. "You must continue on in search of the others. The Royal Committee has chosen a select few who will stay to assist in Nitaya's rearing. Jovaar Savius will remain, with the boy Hylin and the woman they call Khyra."

"My child," he said, softening his words. "You must fulfill your destiny. You must take your part in all remaining quests if you are to claim your title."

"I know your words to be true," Selena said, her face reddening against burning tears. Adding nothing to the pair's sadness, the Royals remained sympathetically in their places, knowing the task of Selena, of them all to be difficult if the Sugin Reign was to truly come to its end.

"But it is so hard to say goodbye, Palle," she said at last. "I never believed it would be this hard."

"Goodbye is not forever," Sir Gowdar said, kneeling uncustomarily to embrace his child. "Please Selena, hand over the possible so that this chapter may end and others begin." Selena knew it was indeed time to move on to the next chosen child, yet looking down to the once again sleeping babe in her arms, she felt the tug in her heart, unable to cease the faint trace of her finger upon Nitaya's face.

"May the graces of the stars look favorably upon you, little one," she whispered, the royals at last returning to the mist-covered staircase. "I make this promise to you, Nitayatinus that this goodbye is not forever." Leaning down, Selena placed a small kiss on the child's nose then rose, turning to face the woman Sir Gowdar called Lydra.

"Please do well in caring for her," she said, hastily giving Nitaya to the woman. Remaining close to carefully wrap the last fold of her small blanket about her, Selena's eyes openly revealed her sadness when she at last turned to face her palle.

"There is something else I must do, Sir Gowdar and then I will return to the docks for departure."

"I know what it is you seek, my child, and it is there that I too must go," the Royal said, placing his hand reassuringly on her shoulder. "I will walk below with you for there is one more task that I must also do."

Nodding, Selena followed her Palle to the door of the home above the greens, glancing back a final time at the beautiful child that rested peacefully in the arms of her new momar. Knowing as she looked to Jovan, Lydra and Norelle that Nitaya would be reared with the love of family, not only from within the home but throughout the wonderous greens of the oasis and the many that thrived beneath its falls, she nodded, wiping the final stray tear from her cheek. Turning and holding her chin high to prove her confidence, Selena descended the mist-covered staircase at her palle's back.

***

Jovaar sat with his back against the tilted cot, Gidoran toying with the med-officer's array of tools at his side as the regal pair entered medbay. Sir Gowdar dressed in garnet splendor, entered the lower cabin with his ever-present air of authority, his child at last appearing more at ease with the oasis underworld at his back. Startled from his trance of their arrival, Jovaar grunted with Gidoran's sudden elbow to his shoulder and rolling of eyes. His thoughts immediately returning to his current state, Jovaar attempted to sit upright, adjusting the cloths of his cot as the pair neared.

"Please rest, Sir Savius," Sir Gowdar began, smiling with Jovaar's feeble attempts to tidy, instead urging him to lay back and rest. "I must begin by thanking you both for all that you have done. It has been ordered, Jovaar that you will remain here to see that Jovan and Lydra Riolle tend well to the possible, yet despite the weight of your newest task, there is other news that the Royal Committee has decided that you now deserve to hear."

"Martus and Wynin Savius did in fact give this galaxy the hope the people needed with young Nitayatinus," Sir Gowdar continued, nodding warmly to Selena as she reached for Jovaar's hand. "Their courage in doing so and your bravery in succeeding to see the child safely to us, gives me great pleasure in giving you this glorious news. Martus and Wynin did not produce one possible, but three. The search for them has already begun."

Jovaar was silent as absorbing what he had heard. "Three?" he asked shaking his head, turning to search Selena's eyes. "But how? I was there. We knew of the chance of a second that Drider was to see to safety if it were indeed so, but three? We had not prepared for three," he added attempting to rise, his mind awhirl with questions. "How could they possibly escape with..."

"You were there for the first," Sir Gowdar interrupted, hushing Jovaar's fears with a hand upon his shoulder. "And as your siblings awaited the arrival of the most possible second, Martus was fully aware of, and had informed the Royal Committee of the fact that a third would be born...that we would be graced with another possible. Take joy, Jovaar Savius that another may have survived."

"But if there was to be another, why would Martus not have informed us?" Jovaar pressed, unable to process the news. "Preparations had been made for onars to bring to safety one, possibly two. But three? This does not make sense Sir Gowdar. Surely you are mistaken. My brother would not have risked a possible life without the safe cover of his kin."

"It seems he was to provide his own safe cover," Sir Gowdar continued, folding his hands calmly before his waist. "Perhaps it was he who felt he knew best. Perhaps he believed hiding the knowledge of a third would provide a better shield than even kin. It is not for us to know, Jovaar Savius...at least for the moment. Perhaps once they arrival safely before us, perhaps then your Martus will entrust in you why."

"Yet now, I must go," he added sighing, turning his eyes to his child. "I shall leave you to say goodbye, Selena, yet do not keep us long. The remaining searches are depending on you."

"Again," he added, turning back to the men. "I thank you, Jovaar, Sir Gidoran. Your accomplishments will forever remain with us."

The trio watched in silence as Sir Gowdar turned, walking briskly from the room, his ornately adorned cloak brisking softly at his ankles. "Lena, I do not understand," Jovaar said, searching her eyes for an answer.

"I will leave you also," Gidoran said, sensing his presence was most definitely awkward. Nodding to the pair who could not take their eyes from one another, Gidoran patted Jovaar's shoulder then quickly crossed the room so they could spend their last moments alone.

"Goodbye?" Jovaar asked, releasing her hands. "Tell me, Lena. Tell me why."

"I am sorry, Jovaar, but the time has come to move on in search of the next," she began, tears once again welling in her eyes. "I have been instructed by the Committee that Khyra and Hylin are to remain with you, but for me it is not to be. My heart aches, Jovi, for I know not when I will see you again. You must understand though, that my duty to the Resistance is firm. I wanted so desperately to remain, to help oversee Nitaya's rearing, but I knew and have struggled all along with the knowledge that it would not be possible."

"Stay with me, Lena," Jovaar pleaded, claiming her arms and pulling her close. "There are others that are prepared to serve. I need you."

"The lost possibles need me as well," she answered, straightening her gaze to face him. "You will never be far from my heart, Jovi," she added, rising from the cot. Leaning down and softly pressing her lips to his, Selena quickly turned to walk away. Two steps forward however, she hesitated and turned to look into his eyes one final time.

"I love you, Jovaar Savius," she whispered, wringing her hands, her feet refusing to continue.

Pleading with her eyes that he knew her heart true only to him, Selena took a final deep breath and at last willed her body to move. Jovaar's returning to full health proving evident by his extended arms, she nodded to Gidoran across the cabin, knowing that he would be safe with his friend at his side. Looking from one strong man to the other, Selena prayed for a deeper strength for herself then at last turning from their stare, she raced for the door before her heart won over her knowledge of what must be done.

***

The Royal Committee members stood at the bottom of the plank to the massive ship thanking the Mizans, their hosts wishing them a safe journey in the quest to find the others. Sir Gowdar, standing at the front, took notice of Selena's arrival to the docks and waved for her to come forward as the royals slowly climbed aboard.

"Is it done then?" he asked, his child approaching, accepting his offered hands.

"It is done," she answered, her face reddened from brushed away tears. "Are Nitaya and her new family not coming to our departure?"

"That would only have made this more difficult, Selena," he answered, gesturing for her to walk aboard at his side.

"Of course," she answered, lowering her head in anguish, shouts of joy ringing out at her back.

"Surely you would not leave without saying goodbye, now would you?" Khyra roared above the crowd, Hylin leading her still fragile frame to the plank. Turning to her elder's words and beaming at the sight of her new, dear friends, Selena returned to the dock, embracing them, her sadness for a brief moment escaping her.

"I so wish there was more time," she began, nodding at her Palle's warm smile as he entered the ship to leave her to her own goodbyes.

"And Hylin, I am counting on you to look after Jovaar," she added, ruffling his golden hair. "He will be depending on you...now more than ever."

"You can count on me," he answered, embracing her tightly. "I promise I will not let the Resistance down."

The trio turned at the sound of their remaining friend's arrival and Selena smiled genuinely as all five...Sir Gidoran, Phydin, Jax, Prince Iaco and Orvi passed through the crowd to join their huddle. Filled with the deepest love for her newfound friends, Selena stood back watching as one by one each embraced the other with tears of both joy and sadness.

At the sounding of the ship's firing however, Selena knew the moment for detachment had arrived, and extending her hand for Iaco to claim, they waited as the others walked up the plank, at last together following hand in hand at their backs. Reaching the entrance, the thrusters strengthening at the rear, Selena turned and glanced over her shoulder at the two who had been chosen to remain.

"We will find them," she said confidently, smiling at Khyra and Hylin below, Iaco holding firm to her hand.

"It is time, Selena," he whispered, his wave of goodbye falling to his side. "It is time to begin the next of your chosen journey."

"I know, Prince Iaco," she answered lifting her chin and wiping the tear from her cheek, at last turning to face her gaze to his. "It is time to find the other possibles."

Nitaya

Nitaya lay motionless, gathering her feelings to the newfound knowledge of her past, the viewscreen blackening abruptly before her. She had just witnessed a life that was in fact hers, yet one she had never known. Questions undoubtedly raced through her mind as the screen lifted from her face, receding into the wall at her back.

At last free to rise, she did so slowly, dangling her legs over the side of the cot. Opening her eyes once again to Selena, she sat silently staring at the woman who stood wringing her anxious hands, obviously eager to begin.

"I have so much to ask," Nitaya whispered, clearing her nervous throat. "And so many things to be thankful for, that I do not know where to begin. Where are my Momar Lydra, Palle Jovan and Norell? Were they hurt in the raid of Nyllo? Where are Martus and Wynin Savius? Did my siblings that Sir Gowdar spoke of survive? What of Jovaar? What of Prince Iaco, Sir Gidoran and Hylin? What has happened to them and the others?"

"So it seems you do know where to begin," Selena chuckled, crossing to claim the child's hands. "I know you have questions, Nitaya and it is my duty and privilege to tell you all that you seek. We have some time before the celebration begins, and until then I will answer all that you ask."

"Let us sit together," she added, gesturing for Nitaya to follow to the white benches in the center of the room. "I have provided nourishment and drink if you so require, yet as I am certain you are, I too am eager to discuss your viewing."

Selena glided over the floor, her long white robes flowing softly at her ankles. Once the now familiar pair were seated at the low benches, she poured them drink, her movements purposeful yet soft. Eyeing her task, yet shielding her impatience, Nitaya instead focused on the orange flower that had reappeared from her quarters. Task complete and sitting forward, both drink and nourishment left untouched, Selena reached again for her hands.

"My dearest Nitaya," she said, tucking a stray tendril behind her younger's ear, beaming at the child's gloriously grown face. "Please allow me to start at the beginning."

***

Although anxious to learn all that she could in the short time they had been given, Nitaya had grown tired and had asked to be excused to her cabin. Selena had answered her questions without falter, never holding back on her version of Nitaya's life, and although she knew there was more to learn, Nitaya felt at ease with the knowledge of the necessary intrusion of her home on Mizar in a ruse to outsmart King Sugin's army and the assured safety of her family. She merely now needed to lie down and close her eyes.

At the end, Selena had said there would be a celebration in her honor and that a gown, one that had been carefully chosen for her, awaited in her private quarters. Entering the small adjacent cabin with a slight prompt to the door, Nitaya found her nursemaid eager to be of assistance, and although spying the cot in the far corner, she shrugged her shoulders and smiled tiredly at the woman's energy.

"There will be time, Ma'am," the nursemaid said, nodding in understanding. "And although I have been informed of the length of your journey and your desire of rest, we must dress you at once if we are to arrive when called."

Nitaya sighed knowing she had no other choice. Slowly following the nursemaid to the side cabinet, the woman opened its door foor and stood back eager to witness Nitaya's reaction. Nitaya's weariness immediately escaped her. Lips parting in amazement, she stared at the most amazing view, astonished that what she was seeing truly belonged to her.

Made of the most glorious materials of various shades of orange, like that of the delicate flower somehow reappearing in her quarters, the hues vibrantly danced down its length. Hesitantly, Nitaya reached out to feel its lushness.

"Let me," the woman whispered, gently lifting the gown from its hook. Releasing the last of its folds, she crossed the room, laying it gently on the cot for Nitaya's close inspection.

"She knew it to be your color," the nursemaid continued, admiringly pressing down the numerous pleats. "Selena said she just knew."

"She had been right," Nitaya whispered, running the textured cloths through her fingers, her eyes lost in its wonder. Eager to climb within to feel its grandness against her skin, the thoughts of rest far from her mind, Nitaya at once began removing her old clothes to step into the new.

***

The nursemaid continued with confidence, expertly closing the clasps and straightening the pleats as Nitaya stood silent within the surprising comfort of Selena's chosen gown. Only when satisfied that all was as it should be, did she gently pat Nitaya's cheeks, leading her to a side chair so that she could begin dressing her hair.

"Such beauty," she murmured, setting it into a tailored coif, little tendrils purposely left to dance beneath her chin. "You have such natural beauty."

Selena entered the cabin moments later as Nitaya stood admiring herself in the glass, turning only from her view with the sounding whoosh of the door. Slowly shaking her head, Nitaya watched Selena's eyes well with tears.

"You are as beautiful as the moment I first saw you," Selena said claiming Nitaya's open arms, relishing the deep embrace.

"Please do not cry," Nitaya said, feeling calmly at home in her arms. "For it will make me cry also, and the steward has worked so hard to prepare me for the celebration."

Selena took a deep breath, inhaling the wonderous scents of the child she had held so long ago. At last sighing, she released her slender arms, stepping back to get a better look at the precious young girl.

"You have grown into a beautiful woman," she began, shaking her head at Nitaya's trimmed image. "I am so honored to know you."

"No, Selena," Nitaya answered, reclaiming her elder's hands. "If it was not for you I would not even be standing here. The honor is indeed all mine."

"Well, we may debate this for eternity but it will have to wait for now," Selena answered, taking a deep breath and smiling proudly, the nursemaid quietly leaving the cabin before them. "You have been called, my dearest Nitayatinus. It is time for you to seek your title."

***

Walking hand in hand down the vacant rounded corridor, Nitaya's gown flowing both elegantly and honorably at her ankles, Selena stopped, squeezing the child's hand as they reached the entrance to the Hall Grand.

"It is for you to do alone," she said, firmly urging Nitaya forward. "But I promise I will be close behind. Hold your head high and be brave, my sweet child. Your life is about to change forever."

Kissing her gently on the cheek, Selena gestured for the pair of appearing sentrys to open the large doors, nodding for Nitaya to pass through on her own. Patting her hands reassuringly she stood back and watched proudly as the now beautiful woman, dressed in the finest of gowns, made her way toward her new world. Once again holding back tears, Selena sighed, thankful that her task of bringing forth the first possible was soon to be complete.

***

Nitaya entered the Hall Grand through the parted doors before her, anxious nerves filling her as cheers roared out from the levels below. Crossing across the small space to the boxed ledge, her knees threatened to give way as she grasped the railing and stared out into the teeming pit of the room.

As if atop a high cliff looking down amongst a sea of revelers, Nitaya's anxiousness soon turned to joy as she spied many of her friends from the viewscreen down and to her left. Their platform proved raised high above many others with what she assumed was their importance to her arrival. Grasping at each other with her recognition of twinkling fingers in their direction, they shouted her name in pride.

Larger than any room she had ever entered, having lived all of her onars amongst the Mizan's in her home within the Nyllo trees, the Hall Grand stood stoic and regal, intricately detailed with moldings honoring those that had come before, topped with five other balconies along its arced wall, spread out amongst the high circle. As Selena had told her, representatives from all the planets and substations of the galaxy had arrived for this occasion, and Nitaya stood proud, head held high as instructed to accept the offered greeting. Eyeing the familiar royal seated at the center of the high floating pad encompassed by the endless sea of waving cheers, she nodded in a comforting sign of respect.

With all appearing gathered, Nitaya knew that as Selena had foretold, soon the time would come for the one possible to be chosen. Although she was uncertain as to exactly how, she stood firm in her place to be deemed. Glancing slightly over her shoulder, she watched as Selena at last entered the rear of the balcony and her eyes grew wide with joy at the trio surprisingly entering at her back.

"Jovaar, Hylin and Khyra," she whispered, a single tear trickling down her cheek. Nitaya could not contain her smile of joy as Jovaar entered at the last, nodded reassuringly as he placed his arm about Selena's shoulders.

"All is as it should be," Nitaya thought, turning with newfound strength to face the crowd, another cheer simultaneously ringing out from below. Standing anxiously in place and glancing to the next door atop the adjacent balcony, she firmly grasped the rail at her waist as the second possible stepped out before the crowd, Sir Gowdar turning to offer his proper approval.

Smiling graciously as the beautiful girl emerged, dressed in a similar gown of her own yet in glorious shades of blue,

Nitaya's confidence waned at the apparent surety of her competition. As her smile began to fade however, she spied two familiar men stepping out behind the young girl. Chills at once danced over her skin.

"Sir Gidoran and Prince Iaco!" she thought, at once recognizing their faces from the view screen. Beaming over at her and the trio at her back, all exchanged quick glances and tears of joy, lovingly embracing those near.

"Sir Gidoran and Prince Iaco were sent to find my siblings," she whispered, her mind awhirl with questions. "Could it be?" she thought, turning back to Selena for any sign of recognition. "Could it possibly be?" Yet before she could question the ones who had risked so much for her life, the next set of doors opened into the Hall Grand. Filled with excited hope, the crowd rang out anew from below.

Anxious to set her eyes upon the newest arrival, Nitaya glanced back and forth from the woman dressed in blue to the young man that emerged atop the balcony, the third of the six galactic possibles.

"Can it be?" Nitaya thought, wringing her hands in an attempt to remain calm, endless cheers of joy filling her ears from below. "Can it possibly be?"

To find the truth, Nitaya would have to wait.

Made in the USA
Lexington, KY
17 October 2013